Marching With Caesar – Revolt of the Legions

By R.W. Peake

R.W. Peake

Also by R.W Peake

Marching With Caesar® – Birth of the 10th

Marching With Caesar – Conquest of Gaul

Marching With Caesar – Civil War

Marching With Caesar – Antony and Cleopatra, Parts I & II

Marching With Caesar – Rise of Augustus

Marching With Caesar – Last Campaign

Marching With Caesar – Rebellion

Marching With Caesar – A New Era

Marching With Caesar – Pax Romana

Marching With Caesar – Fraternitas

Marching With Caesar – Vengeance

Marching With Caesar – Rise of Germanicus

Caesar Triumphant

Caesar Ascending – Invasion of Parthia

Caesar Ascending – Conquest of Parthia

Critical praise for the Marching with Caesar series:

Marching With Caesar-Antony and Cleopatra: Part I-Antony

"Peake has become a master of depicting Roman military life and action, and in this latest novel he proves adept at evoking the subtleties of his characters, often with an understated humour and surprising pathos. Very highly recommended."

Marching With Caesar-Civil War

"Fans of the author will be delighted that Peake's writing has gone from strength to strength in this, the second volume...Peake manages to portray Pullus and all his fellow soldiers with a marvelous feeling of reality quite apart from the star historical name... There's history here, and character, and action enough for three novels, and all of it can be enjoyed even if readers haven't seen the first volume yet. Very highly recommended."

~The Historical Novel Society

"The hinge of history pivoted on the career of Julius Caesar, as Rome's Republic became an Empire, but the muscle to swing that gateway came from soldiers like Titus Pullus. What an amazing story from a student now become the master of historical fiction at its best."

~Professor Frank Holt, University of Houston

For Gregarius Titus

The Newest Legionary of the Peake Legion

Table of Contents

Historical Notes

Although there are certainly ancient sources that spend a fair amount of time on the tumultuous events that began with the Varus disaster, when it comes to providing a level of detail that would satisfy someone like myself, the record is frustratingly vague, particularly about locations. Therefore, there is a certain level of supposition in Marching With Caesar®-Revolt of the Legions that is over and above what is normally in my work. And, for that, I ask the readers' indulgence, and I will explain where I am making somewhat educated guesses.

That supposition begins when, in the immediate aftermath of the Varus disaster, Tiberius arrives from Pannonia with several Cohorts, which in the book I identify as the 13th and 15th Legions, simply because they have been part of the Army of Pannonia in my previous books, and we do know that Tiberius had just finished putting down the Batonian Revolt.

What has proven even more difficult, at least for me, and to a level where I feel confident, is the placement of the Legions after the Varus disaster, especially the 2nd and 14th Legions, which were sent to the Rhine after the loss of the three Legions. Since I have seen sources claim the 2nd in particular being located in both Mogontiacum and Vetera, and the 2nd and 14th appear to be the two Legions that did not participate in the revolt of 14 CE, I decided to place them in Vetera, for a number of reasons. For those readers who are of the school that have these two Legions in Mogontiacum, I beg your indulgence in this matter, and recognize that placing them in Vetera may be in error. However, since they do not figure prominently in either the real event, or in my story, hopefully this will not prove to be ruinous to the enjoyment of the tale.

Another supposition on my part, but one I feel a bit more confident in making, is in my characterization of the quality of the men salted into the ranks of the Legions by Augustus, in the emergency *dilectus* conducted in Rome immediately after the Varus disaster. Both Tacitus and Dio make comments that would lead one to believe that these men were the dregs of Rome, if only because there had already been a draft of able-bodied men a couple years earlier, as a result of the Batonian Revolt. What I could not find anywhere from the available ancient sources is any information about the fate of these men, at least as far as how long they were expected to serve. Given the level of hysteria that infected Roman citizens, even in the city itself, it makes sense to me that Augustus would have attempted to figuratively kill two birds with one stone; send reinforcements to the Legions on the Rhine, and remove a troublesome element from the streets of Rome. However, Augustus' decision-making in the last years of his life was not the best; naming Varus as Legate is one glaring example, and I am of the opinion that his handling of the aftermath serves as another. Whether or not Percennius was a man of this second *dilectus* is unknown, but for the purposes of this story, I have made him one of them.

Also, Titus reflects his creator's thoughts in the level of coordination that he believes is behind the uprising of both the Rhine and Pannonian Legions. While it is in the realm of possibility that these twin mutinies occurred spontaneously, at the same time, several hundred miles apart, and it was merely a coincidence, triggered by the death of the Princeps, I am of the school that does not believe in coincidences, especially when it concerns such momentous events. Which, of course, means that Titus does not believe in them, either.

My use of the town of Gelduba is based on its importance as a trading center, and because it was a fordable spot across the Rhine, which is presumably why in the First Century CE the Romans built a fort at that location, which is now modern-day Krefeld-Gellep, Germany. A bit more than twenty miles to the west was another important trading post, Blariacum, which was on the left bank of the

Meuse River, and is now Blerick, Venlo, Netherlands, which I also use in the story.

Finally, when Titus returns to his childhood home of Arelate and observes the Julian aqueduct, this is the modern Barbegal, which features one of the best preserved Roman mills of the ancient world.

Chapter One

"Uncle Titus! Have you heard?"

The fact that Alex burst into my office told me that something either important or momentous had occurred; that he addressed me by my given name was another indication of his agitation, if only because he had learned the hard way that I did not tolerate the use of familial titles when we were functioning in our respective official capacities. I was in my private quarters, behind the outer room that serves as the Century office, seated at my desk, preferring the privacy as I struggled with the arcane but never-ending requirements that are now part and parcel of a Centurion in the Legions commanded by the Princeps.

Despite sensing this was, indeed, something important, I was irritated at the interruption because I had been in the process of adding up sums, which I do not have a great affinity for, so I snapped, "Obviously not! I've been sitting here for the last watch, trying to get these totals to come out right!"

Although it was not my intent, this served to distract Alex, his brow furrowing as he came to stand behind me and peer down at the wax tablet.

Suddenly, his finger thrust down as he pointed at a figure in one column and said, "Here's the problem. You didn't carry over the figure from the first column."

Honestly, I remember this moment not just because of what I was about to learn, but at the sudden, unexpected memory of another time, when I had been younger than Alex, and his father Diocles standing where his son now stood, correcting another Pullus, his family serving mine for more years than I could remember. Then, following on the heels of that was yet another memory, when a much younger Alex had shown up in my quarters when I had been Optio, bearing the news that my

10

brother had been killed, although I suspect that it was because of his demeanor, which was informative in itself.

Ignoring how he seemed to shimmer a bit in my vision, instead, I replied gruffly, "Ah. Yes. You're right. Now," I changed the subject, "what has you barging in here and forgetting everything you've learned?"

I cannot deny that I was pleased that my words made him flush, but that thought was almost instantly swept away when he said excitedly, "There was an ambush of Legate Varus!"

"Ambush?" Naturally, this caught my attention, but when he said nothing else, I demanded, "And? What happened?"

Suddenly, my nephew looked, if not confused, then uncertain, but I understood why when he answered, "His entire command was wiped out." He paused, then added quietly, "To a man."

I heard a gasp, which I assume was mine, but honestly, I was physically dizzy, so I have no idea whether it was me or Alex reacting from my clear distress, and so disturbing was the news that I temporarily forgot which Legions had been under the command of Varus, and I asked Alex about their identity.

"The 17th, 18th, and 19th," he replied.

Then, for a long moment, there was nothing said as we stared at each other, both of us trying to absorb the larger implications.

Finally, I asked him in a voice that sounded as if I had only recently recovered my ability to speak so that it sounded to my ears like a rusty hinge, "How do you know this?"

"One of Gaesorix's men came in when I was at the *Praetorium*," he answered without hesitation.

If he said anything else, I did not hear it, grabbing my *vitus* and hurrying past him and out the door. My hope that we could learn more about this before the rankers did lasted the time it took me to reach the end of my Cohort street, when I ran into a small knot of Legionaries, who immediately tried to appear as if they were not talking in hushed tones that I could nevertheless hear were tinged with alarm. I thought about stopping and remonstrating with them for spreading rumors, then decided against it until I knew more. Walking into the *Praetorium*, I instantly saw that, if anything, the news was every bit as dire as what Alex had heard, made evident just by the way the place was akin to a beehive that has been knocked over. Clerks were literally running across the room, one of them with a wax tablet, another carrying a scroll, while others conferred with each other, and despite them speaking in whispers or hushed tones, so many of them were talking that if one wanted to be heard, they would have had to raise their voice well above a conversational level. The door that led to the Legate's office was closed, and I was not surprised to see it that way; once my initial scan of the room did not find Crescens, I assumed my Primus Pilus was closeted with the Legate, who at that time was none other than Lucius Arruntius, who had been Gaius Atticus' defender at his Tribunal. Scanning the room, I saw small groups of men attired as I was, almost all of them holding a *vitus*, and it did not surprise me to see that men naturally congregated towards those others with whom they served in the same Cohort. This made finding Macer, Vespillo and Cornutus easier, and I approached them first, joining my fellow Centurions.

"What have you heard, Pullus?" Macer asked me in a low tone, but when I told him I had only heard what turned out to be the same news he had, although I did not know why, he seemed disappointed.

"So," he muttered, "all we know is that it's bad."

"Bad?" Vespillo raised an eyebrow. "If three Legions were wiped out, I'd say that's more than bad!"

"If," Macer countered calmly, "that's the case. But, you know how these things are. How often do they turn out to be as bad as you first hear?"

12

"True," Vespillo granted, then added, "But this just feels...different."

While Macer did not reply verbally, I saw by his expression that he essentially agreed with Vespillo. And, if I had been asked, I would have concurred with that assessment. Additionally, perhaps I can be excused for thinking that, of all the men standing there at this moment, I had by far the most experience in dealing with rumors and gossip, stretching back to my earliest days as a child of the Legions, acting as a *de facto* spy for my father, who had once held the same post as Marcus Macer, albeit it in the 8th Legion. We were just debating whether to return to our area when the door to the Legate's office opened, and our Primus Pilus strode out, but while I knew it was him, it was a version I had never seen before. Quintus Valerius Crescens was now the third Primus Pilus under which I had served, and like Publius Canidius, or Urso, and Gaius Sempronius Atticus, who was now the Camp Prefect of the Army of Pannonia, he was a hard man, seemingly made of iron, even now at his advanced age of around fifty. The man who staggered out into the large room of the *Praetorium* looked as if he had aged ten years, his normally swarthy, weathered complexion now ashen. In that instant, Macer and I exchanged a glance, sharing our understanding that our worst fears were confirmed.

Crescens stood there for a moment, and I noticed that the entire large room, now full with perhaps fifty men, had fallen as quiet as I am sure that it ever had before, which turned out to be a good thing because his voice was barely more than a hoarse whisper when he said, "We need to summon the Legion to the forum. I'll have the call sounded." For the first time, he actually seemed to look around him, and it was with some surprise that he saw how many of his Centurions were already present. "Right, well then." The effort he made to regain his composure was, in some ways, more troubling than his initial appearance, if only because it was clear it required a massive effort. "Centurions," finally, he sounded somewhat like himself, "assemble your men."

Then, without saying anything else, he abruptly turned about and reentered Arruntius' office. Just before he closed the door, I caught a glimpse of the Legate, who, at least in his demeanor and pallor, could have been Crescens' twin. We filed out, but I do not even remember having any kind of conversation.

About a sixth part of a watch later, the 1st Legion was assembled in the forum, while the men attached to the *Praetorium* had dragged out the small, wooden rostra that was designed to be broken down into smaller pieces, an innovation that had arrived with the Praetor, who, we had learned less than a full watch before, was now dead. What we were still unsure about was the fate of three Legions, the six Cohorts of auxiliaries, and the three *alae* of cavalry that had been stationed out of the recently enlarged encampment at Vetera. The reason for our uncertainty was based in something that, in these heartbeats of time before we learned what had occurred with Varus, we all would have insisted was an incontrovertible truth; there was no force in the known world that could not only defeat, but wipe out three Roman Legions. However, we were about to learn very, very differently.

Both Arruntius and Crescens emerged from the *Praetorium*, their faces suitably grim as they strode towards the rostra, and one sign of the difference in the air was how, without being told, the men of the Legion instantly stopped their muttered conversations, drawing themselves to *intente* without any order being given. The only moment of, if not levity, then confusion came when the Legate and Crescens reached the rostra, whereupon it became clear that they had not actually discussed who would make the announcement. As we stood there, there was a whispered exchange, and judging from appearances, Arruntius used his rank to be the man who stepped up onto the rostra. If my eyes were any judge, however, the instant that he did so, he regretted it, and the haughty patrician that I had first met in Rome was nowhere to be seen in this man.

He stood for a moment, surveying the Legion, before he began speaking. "The reason you have been summoned is because I must convey to you, the men of the 1st Legion, some truly grievous news."

When he paused for a moment, I cursed, silently of course, recognizing that this was an example of how men of his status felt a pressing need to be considered orators on a level commensurate with Cicero, thereby forcing us to stand there as he dramatically scanned the Legion, with one arm extended in the orator's pose, before he resumed speaking.

"We have received reports," Arruntius began, and while he spoke in a ringing tone, I had heard the man often enough to know that he was shaken, "that we believe are reliable, that the Praetor, Quintus Varus, and his army," I could see him swallow hard as he paused for an instant, "have been destroyed."

It had been quiet before; if I did not witness it myself, I would have sworn it would have been impossible for it to go even quieter, and I believe it was because every man in the 1st Legion, for a brief moment, stopped breathing. That silence probably only lasted the span of a heartbeat, then the air exploded in a sound unlike anything I had ever heard, a sort of collective moan rising from the throats of thousands of men before the shouting began.

"No! That's impossible!"

"How?"

"When?"

"How do you know?"

These things and many more exploded from the ranks, yet despite not giving the men leave to move from their position,

15

when rankers began shifting about, turning to their friends next to them, waving their arms about, and generally behaving in a manner unworthy of a Legion of Rome, no Centurion stopped them, and I included myself. Despite having just a bit more warning and knowing what was coming, I suppose hearing it again and seeing the reaction of the men under my command still caught me off guard to the point I stood there dumbly, doing nothing more than watch as my Century degenerated into little better than a mob of angry, scared men. I did glance over to Macer, but he was as nonplussed as I was, although he must have sensed my eyes on him, because he turned to meet my eyes, giving only a shrug as he used his head to indicate Crescens, who was standing next to the rostra as the Legate held his hands out in a plea for silence. So uproarious was it that I saw our Primus Pilus' mouth open, and it was clear that he was bellowing something at the top of his lungs, but being in the Fourth Cohort, I could not hear a word he was saying from where we were standing. The pair exchanged a look, then I saw the Legate jabbing his finger at the men who, I must admit, were near to rioting, but it was Crescens' reaction that was most telling, as he raised his hands in a helpless gesture that spoke more eloquently than whatever came out of his mouth, I am sure. Then, the Legate wheeled about, turning his back on the recalcitrant Legion, hopped off the rostrum and stalked away, and I was suddenly reminded of another moment, back when I was still a *Gregarius* and the Legate then had accused Urso of a number of crimes that turned out to be nothing more than an extortion attempt, albeit a successful one. The one difference, besides the identity of the Legate, was that the Legion Arruntius was leaving behind was not angry, as the men of the 8th had been, but, frankly, scared out of their collective wits. And, I must admit, that while I had never before given much thought to the fact that Ubiorum was a one Legion camp at the time, with the bulk of the Army of the Rhenus stationed at Mogontiacum during the winter, that thought was foremost in my mind then. This was also the first moment I also recall being struck by the realization; did the Army of the Rhenus still exist if it just consisted of us? Before I could go down this path in my mind, Crescens hopped up on the rostrum, beckoning to his *Cornicen* as he did so. Carrying his heavy horn, the man trotted over, listened to the Primus Pilus, nodded since he could not render a salute, then began blowing the notes that, under normal circumstances, would have been sufficient to instantly stop the commotion of the men. While I did not keep exact count, I know that it took more than three blasts of the horn, so that by the time the men finally calmed down, the *Cornicen*'s face was the color of a plum.

Finally, it was quiet enough for Crescens to be heard, and he at least sounded somewhat like himself as he ordered, "Pili Priores, report to me in my quarters immediately! Centurions, march your Centuries back to your area, then dismiss them." He paused a moment, then added, "And all but those with duties are restricted to their section huts until further notice!"

He did not bother finishing the normal ritual with an exchange of salutes, hopping down and stalking away, except to his quarters and not the *Praetorium*. Turning about, I began shouting our orders, my voice mixed with all of the other Centurions doing the same thing, and in the final mark of what had been an unprecedented assembly, we officers quickly realized that there was a practical problem with Crescens' orders to dismiss the men. The normal procedure for an assembly then dismissal of a Legion is that some men are dismissed in the forum, then are allowed to move to wherever they are ordered to go on their own, while some Centurions march their men back in formation. Commanding all Centurions to conduct the Centuries back to their respective areas, as a unit, meant that it took a certain amount of space to maneuver, and very quickly, the forum became a jumble of Centuries being marched into each other, since no instructions had been given about the manner in which we were to accomplish this. Under any other circumstances, I would have found it amusing, even as I marched my own Century into the flank of the Second Century, but I recall this as just another example of how shaken an entire Legion had become. Perhaps the only positive thing that can be said for this debacle was that no Centurions came to blows as they argued about who had the right of way on passage to their area. Otherwise, what should have taken no more than a count of five hundred to dismiss the men to return to their areas and have them do so took perhaps a sixth part of a watch before I returned to my own quarters to wait. Alex was there, waiting with a cup of wine, but when he handed it to me, I took a sniff, then shook my head.

"It's watered, just like always," he assured me, and I realized he had misunderstood why I had demurred.

Thrusting the cup back at him, I ordered, "Pour it out. Then refill it. No water."

Naturally, he did as I told him, then I also realized that I did not feel like drinking alone, so I waited until he filled his own cup before I took the first sip, which quickly turned into a swallow, ending in a drained cup. Without saying anything, Alex stood and walked over to me, bringing the amphora with him, refilling it.

Returning to his own seat, only then did he speak, asking quietly, "That bad, Uncle Titus?"

"That bad, *Nepos*," I assured him. "That bad."

Before I go into what happened with the 1st Legion in the aftermath of what is the worst military disaster in our recent history, and one of the worst going all the way back to Cannae, although I am certain that those who read this will know about what is called the Varus Disaster, I think there may be some value in relaying what was known immediately after the actual event, and more importantly, how we reacted. Despite what we had been told, that all three Legions – the 17th, 18th, and 19th, along with the six Cohorts of auxiliaries and two *alae* of cavalry – were lost, this simply was so unbelievable that I do not know many men who accepted this, at least right away. And, it must be said, I was among those who simply refused to believe that this was even within the realm of possibility. There was no nation capable of destroying an army consisting of a bit less than eighteen thousand men, of which some fourteen thousand of them were men of the Legions, even the German tribes, if only for the reason that they hated each other almost as much as they hated Rome, and no single tribe was strong enough to inflict such damage. As we would all learn, that word "almost" was an important distinction, but that would not become evident until several days after the disaster. What we knew on the day Arruntius announced the news was that it had been an extremely busy campaign season for everyone but us in the 1st, where it was more or less the same mundanity that, to this point at least, made me somewhat contemptuous about how hazardous duty on the Rhenus supposedly was. Certainly, I had been involved with Tiberius' campaign during my first year with the Legion, and there had been numerous skirmishes and even a few battles over the previous time, but considering that this was the fourth and final year of the revolt in Pannonia, almost exactly a year after I had returned from my time with the *Legio Germanicus*, as it was now called, I did not view Germania and the Germans with much trepidation. But then, Publius Quinctilis Varus had been named Praetor, and in a somewhat unusual move for men of that rank, had insisted on taking military command.

As we quickly heard, Varus was no Saturninus, his predecessor as Praetor, but not only because he was unduly harsh in his treatment of the tribes that inhabit the area east of the Rhenus and north of Ubiorum. The Tencteri, Sugambri, Tubantes, Bructeri, and even the Marsi – all of these tribes

19

experienced the iron and lash – but as bad as that was, it was his repetition of essentially the same mistake that had been made in Pannonia that was partially responsible for the rebellion there, the levying of a tax that amounted to double the previous sum demanded by Rome. At the beginning of the season, we in Ubiorum quickly heard that Varus had been sending detachments out, and while the official version was that he was doing so to provide security for smaller villages that could not defend themselves from roving warbands coming from the east, near or even across the Visurgis, word of what was really happening inevitably reached our ears. Initially, I will confess that none of us put much credence in what one or two itinerant traders were saying in the wineshops outside camp, but after a month or so, when these rumors persisted, and more importantly, became more detailed, we started paying attention.

"Varus is letting his men run wild," was how I heard it on one of the relatively rare occasions Macer and I went out into town for a cup of wine, some gambling, and other fleshly pursuits. We were seated at a table, just beginning our evening, when we heard this blurted out, and we both turned to examine the man who had said it. He was bearded, and his tunic, cut in the longer, German style, had seen better days, but it was his Latin that informed us he was either born in Italia, Umbria if I was any judge, or had lived there from childhood, making it likely he was a Roman citizen. That he was attired as a barbarian and was wearing a full beard, and not the neatly trimmed version that was only beginning to become popular among the fashionable set, was not surprising; any Roman who ventured on the eastern side of the Rhenus either had to be marching with comrades, and well-armed ones at that, or if they were alone, their best chances lay in blending in with the natives and drawing as little attention to themselves as possible.

"What do you mean by that?" Macer asked the man, his tone cold, but if the trader, for that was my assumption, was intimidated, he did not show it.

"What I mean," he countered, calmly but firmly, "is that the Praetor is trying to impose his will on a half-dozen tribes, and in the process, has given his men license to rape, flog, and kill anyone who resists."

Macer gave me a troubled glance, and it was right that he should look to me, since I had spent the previous season essentially doing that same thing in Pannonia, except it was at the height of the Batonian Revolt, and it was common knowledge to every tribe and province under Rome's rule that this was how rebels were treated. The German tribes, however, were not in revolt, at least at that point.

Whether the trader divined our thoughts, or it was a natural conclusion to make, I have no way of knowing, but he voiced what was inside my head when he added, "He's treating those tribes as if they're a settled Senatorial province and have been under Roman rule for years." Shaking his head, he concluded, "They're not taking it well."

"I should think not," Macer replied dryly, but now he addressed me, asking, "What do you think, Titus?"

I considered for a moment; this was perhaps only the third or fourth time that we had even discussed Varus, the first shortly after my return when Macer had informed me he was the new Praetor. All we had known about him at the time was that he had been posted to Syria previously, and most importantly to anyone familiar with Roman politics, was a close and trusted friend of the Princeps. Despite what little we knew, nothing I had heard to this point indicated he was made of the kind of stuff that would make him such an oppressive governor. And, while it was technically true that Rome had annexed the lands east of the Rhenus and west of the Visurgis, making Varus the lawful governor of that territory, one did not have to be a veteran of the

Rhenus to know that what was true in theory back in Rome bore very little resemblance to the reality.

Feeling the eyes of not just Macer but the trader and now the half-dozen or so men within earshot, instead of answering, I asked the trader, "Do you have any idea who's advising him to do this?" When he looked confused, I clarified, "I mean, did he get these orders from Rome? Or is someone giving him the idea that this is the best way to handle the Germans?"

The man's face cleared, and he nodded as he answered, "Actually, I've heard he's being advised by someone who knows the tribes better than any Roman, because he's a German." His face creased into a frown as he tried to think of the name, then came up with, "He's a Cherusci, at least I think he is." He had no way of knowing, but with the mention of that tribe, I already knew the answer as he supplied the name for everyone else to hear. "His name is Arminius."

From this initial conversation, over the ensuing weeks, more information of this sort made its way back to Ubiorum, and there was such consistency in these bits and pieces of news that we soon accepted that, at the very least, Varus was laying an extraordinarily heavy hand on the Germanic tribes. One difficulty in this account is trying not to color this description with all that we learned later, particularly concerning Arminius and his role in what was taking place. I had seen him once, shortly after my assignment with the 1st, and all I really remembered at the time was hearing that he was going back to Rome to learn our ways, particularly in the area of military matters. Since then, I might have heard his name mentioned once or twice, but only in the context of how he was acting as a Tribune; honestly, I did not even know his Germanic name until much later, and I suppose it is sufficient to say that we all thought he had become thoroughly Romanized. Not until relatively late in the campaign season did we start experiencing any effects of Varus' actions to the north, when a delegation of Usipetes appeared at the floating bridge at Ubiorum. When they were ushered into Arruntius' presence, they made both a complaint and a request for aid, something that, if I had known about, I would have urged them not to do in the same meeting, waiting to present one, then the other at a later time. They told Arruntius that their villages in the northern portion of their territory, which abutted the Sugambri lands, had become overrun with fleeing Sugambri who were trying to escape the depredations of Varus and his Legions. Perhaps if they had taken a different approach and not combined this complaint, which was essentially a demand that Arruntius do something to stop a man who was his superior, maybe the Legate would have at the very least roused the 1st to go and investigate. And, if we had, perhaps some or all of us would have noticed something when visiting these Usipetes villages that were now unwilling hosts to a different tribe, one that under normal circumstances they would never have had anything to do with, at least in peaceful terms. Not until later did we find out that, while what the Usipetes told Arruntius was true, there had been an influx of Sugambri, it was the fact that they were exclusively composed of terrified women, children, and the elderly that might have alerted us that something larger was afoot. However, since Arruntius heard them out, then refused to do anything more than offer a curt dismissal, not only of their persons in his presence, but their pleas for Roman intervention, none of us had the opportunity to notice that there were no Sugambri fighting men present in these Usipetes villages. Again, when one is looking back, after some sort of cataclysmic event has occurred, only then are the signs so easily seen that would have warned us all of what was to come, which means that the other aspect of that season, how relatively quiet it was for the 1st, only became significant after the proverbial dust was settled.

The other puzzling aspect in the immediate aftermath was exactly how the catastrophe had occurred, but with this, at least, we would not be in the dark for long. Four days after Arruntius' announcement, I happened to be near the Porta Praetoria and heard the *bucina* sounding the call that tells us of a party approaching the camp. Any other time, this would have been routine, but nerves were so on edge, and there was such an air of anxiety enveloping the entire Legion, I found myself walking quickly towards the gate. I was more than curious, and I could tell just by the body posture of the men standing on the rampart standing watch that this was not a routine matter. Stopping, I waited for the Centurion on duty to determine the identity of the unseen party, which happened quickly, and he gave the order to open the gates. Because of where I was standing, I did not actually see the group until they passed through and into the camp, and while my eyes took in the dozen men on foot, it was the sight of one of the mounted men escorting them that gladdened my heart, to the point I completely forgot myself and the dignity of my rank.

Before I had any conscious thought, while I was not quite running across the open ground, I was moving rapidly, and I thought my smile would split my face as I called out to Gaesorix, "You look like *cac*!"

For one of the few times in our association, now going back a few years, the Batavian Decurion did not return my smile with one of his own, instead only saying wearily, "I feel like it."

At first, I thought he would pass by, but then he pulled aside, calling over his shoulder to the troopers with him to continue on towards the *Praetorium*, and as they did so, it gave me the chance to examine the men on foot. My initial impression had been that they were prisoners, despite the fact that none of them were bound in any way, and I had been so focused on seeing my friend that I had not really given them more than a glance. The pleased surprise I had experienced a moment before when seeing Gaesorix turned into a combination of shock, and I confess, a shiver of fear at the sight of the dozen men, each of them still covered in what appeared to be a mixture of grime and blood. As we learned later, one reason I had not immediately identified them as Legionaries was because, whether they did so on their own or as part of a group decision, they had covered their red Legionary's tunics with mud in order to blend in with their background, along with applying it to their exposed skin. However, it was their manner that had misled me, as not one man among them glanced in either direction, simply plodding straight ahead, following the horsemen leading the way, and I recognized these were men simply at the end of their collective tethers, their minds long before surrendering and allowing whatever it is inside a man that drives him forward in an attempt to survive take control of them.

"We found them about ten miles upriver from here." Gaesorix's voice jerked me from my fixation on what I had now deduced were some survivors from Varus' column. When I turned to look up at him, I saw how drawn his face was, and he was weaving in the saddle as he continued, "I've got detachments out still searching for more survivors."

"Who are these men from?" I asked, and such was his fatigue, he only gave me a blank stare, and I added, "Which Legion?"

"Oh," he frowned, "they're from all three, but I don't remember which ones are which."

The procession had continued past us, and Gaesorix turned his horse to catch up with them, prompting me to call out as he trotted away, "Come round to my quarters when you're done. I'll have Alex cook something up and we can have a cup. Or two."

He gave a weary wave of his hand, and I headed for my quarters to let Alex know we would be having company.

25

"Honestly, none of them talked much."

Gaesorix was seated next to my stove, legs stretched out, holding a cup of wine after consuming two bowls of the soldier's porridge that Alex had hurriedly prepared. I could see my Batavian friend was struggling to stay awake, and I told myself to hold back on my questioning of him, but I believe I can be forgiven that I did not, since this was more than just a matter of idle curiosity.

"What," I asked with a patience I did not feel, "*did* they say?"

He answered immediately, "That it was a trap from the outset. That that bastard Arminius planned the whole thing, and Varus was a fucking fool."

This was the first I had heard personally of Arminius' role, and it actually took me a moment for my mind to make the association.

"Arminius?" I repeated the name. "I thought he was..."

"He's a Cherusci." Gaesorix suddenly became animated, and when he leaned forward to spit on the floor, I suppose my warning glare caused him to change his aim, aiming instead for the stove, where the phlegm hit and sizzled for an instant. "Which means he's a faithless, gutless, cocksucking *cunnus*!" Honestly, there were several other epithets used, but since they were in his native tongue, I do not know the specific terms, and I finally had to raise a hand to cut him off.

"Yes," I chided wryly. "I think I get the sense of what you're trying to say."

He looked chagrined, then gave me a grin that was more familiar than his previous countenance, but it vanished as he continued, "Anyway, from what little bit I got from them, they had just left Vetera, heading here to take ship down to Mogontiacum. Two of those survivors were part of the vanguard that first day, and they said that some of the German scouts that

Varus used came from the east and said that there was an uprising in Tubantes territory."

"German scouts?" This did not make sense to me, but I assumed that Gaesorix was only passing on mistaken information. "You mean that were part of one of the *alae*?"

To my surprise, he shook his head. "No. I know because that's what I thought, and I asked them." He turned to give me a direct look, which was explained by his words. "Arminius convinced Varus to use some of his fellow tribesmen as a separate scouting arm for the army. He persuaded Varus that using native troops on their own would be better than having them attached to our cavalry, because they would be able to move about more freely and wouldn't draw suspicion." Giving a bitter laugh, Gaesorix raised his cup in a mock salute. "Well, Arminius was right about that part, just not about who should have been suspicious." He paused to take a swallow, then continued, "Anyway, apparently, Varus took the bait, because that's what it was. There was no uprising by the Tubantes, at least not quite yet. From some of the other survivors, what I pieced together is that when they marched into the Tubantes' land, the village that was supposed to be where the uprising started was deserted, and the scouts told Varus they had fled farther east."

It did not take long for me to summon the mental map of the area in my head, and only an instant longer for me to remember what lay east of the Tubantes territory.

"They lured him towards the Teutoberg." I breathed the name, to which Gaesorix gave a grim nod.

"That's not the worst part," the Batavian assured me. "The one thing every one of those men said was that the route the scouts led Varus on was prepared beforehand."

I did not understand the meaning of this, so I asked him what he meant.

27

Gaesorix looked slightly uncomfortable, and his frown deepened as he admitted, "Actually, I'm not sure. I mean," he added, "I know what they told me, but it just doesn't make sense." When it was clear he still was not eager to talk, I actually had to reach out with my foot to nudge him, prompting a sigh. "All right! I'll tell you, but I just don't see how it's possible. They said that the Germans had prepared a position that they drove Varus and his army towards, where they were penned up like pigs and slaughtered."

At the time, this was hard to believe, but even in the moment, I recall thinking that I, and most of my comrades, had found it impossible to believe that three Legions could be exterminated, yet it was becoming increasingly clear that this was the case. And, as we all would learn, it would only get worse.

Starting that day, four days after the announcement of the disaster, over the course of the next week, survivors trickled in to Ubiorum, almost always in groups of at least four and usually under escort by the cavalry patrols that worked nonstop, although sometimes just one or two men would show up at the gate, unaccompanied. And, as more survivors showed up, a more complete story of what had taken place began to take shape; if anything, it was worse than the initial reports. It was not until two weeks after we received word before we went two straight days without some survivors showing up, then there was a stretch of three more days where a lone man arrived on the first day, and pairs of men the next two. After that, no man from Varus' Legions ever showed up, and when the final tally was made, far less than five hundred men from the entire force actually made it to Ubiorum. This is not to say that more men did not survive the initial onslaught, but from what we could determine, most of those who managed to make their escape at some point in what we learned was a multi-day battle almost to a man slipped away in either the first day or the next. If they had not managed to slip through the ring of iron, wood, and flesh by what turned out to be the last day of the slaughter, as far as I know, not one man still alive on the final day ever made it to safety. It should come as no surprise that things were tense, and Arruntius was undoubtedly correct to order the Legion on half alert, starting the day the news arrived. Regardless of it being the right decision, having half a Legion standing guard at all times means that in a matter of two or three days, it suffers from the combination of sleep deprivation and the toll constant vigilance takes on men.

Speaking of the Legate, as I recall, it was no more than two days after this that he received a summons from the senior Legate remaining on the Rhenus frontier, Lucius Asprenas, who was not only with the 21st in Mogontiacum, but was also the nephew of the slain Praetor. While Gaesorix was the ranking Decurion, he was still out searching for survivors, so the Legate took the remaining *ala* of cavalry as an escort, along with a Cohort of auxiliaries that had been ordered down from their camp a day's march north of Ubiorum, at a place called Novaesium. It had been constructed more than twenty years before but had fallen into disrepair until Varus' aggressive expansion of the forts along the Rhenus. Instead of splitting one or two Cohorts off from the 1st, five Cohorts of auxiliaries had been holding it, most of them from Gaul. With the reduction of that force by one Cohort, there was a strong feeling among the officers that Novaesium was the most likely to be attacked next, simply because it was an easier target. If there was any bright side whatsoever, it was in the knowledge that, when Varus began his movement to Mogontiacum, he had ordered the ditches filled in and the towers burned at Vetera, so when it was time to take the offensive, we would not be forced to storm a Roman camp. That this would not be happening before the next season was in some ways also comforting, but at the same time, we all understood that the Germans knew this as well, which contributed to the conviction that we would be under attack before we were reinforced. Working parties were tasked with strengthening the defenses of the camp, while the male occupants of the town outside our walls did one of two things; they either attached themselves to the column led by Arruntius back to Mogontiacum, which consisted of a large proportion of Legionaries' women and children, or they did what they could to create a makeshift barrier that could be manned by the townspeople who remained. Before he departed, the Legate gave strict orders that none of the civilians be allowed inside our camp, one which was destined to last only as long as it took for us to be sure he was well on his way. Simply put, the population who chose to stay in Ubiorum was composed of a large proportion of women and children who were tied to the Legion that, even if it was not recognized by Rome, was by a bond that is stronger than allegiance to the city in whose name we march, fight, and die. This did not mean that two of the Tribunes who had been left behind did not attempt to stop this from happening; Crescens, however, understanding how raw men's nerves were already, convinced them that the men with families were under enough pressure without having to worry that, once the expected hordes of Germans arrived at our walls, their women and children would be slaughtered. If the rumors were true, his argument also composed of pointing out that, should the Germans behave as we expected, and we managed to repel them but at the expense of the families of those men who had them, the likelihood of the man who forbade us from sheltering them was probably not long for this world.

Between standing watch, then being turned to some sort of physical labor as we tried to make the camp as impregnable as we could, it did not take long before men were exhausted to the point that, even if the Germans had shown up across the Rhenus, we would have been unable to put up much of a fight. With every passing day, the tensions rose and our readiness declined, as first a week, then another passed without any sign of what we had learned was a confederation of tribes that we were all sure were heading our way. During that time, the information provided by the survivors, a handful of whom had made it to safety only to die a day or so later, continued to fill in the picture of what had taken place. Perhaps the best thing that can be said is that Publius Quinctilis Varus dying with his men was a better fate than he deserved, because once we knew enough to get a relatively clear idea of what had taken place, the man would have been scourged and crucified, his friendship with the Princeps notwithstanding. Nothing could have saved the man, if only for his blatant stupidity in ignoring the signs that every survivor whose account I heard claimed were so obvious a blind man should have read them. More than one of his senior officers, including at least one of Legate rank, one Numonius Vala, tried to convince him that he was being falsely played by Arminius, but it was when we heard that none other than Segestes, the brother of Arminius' father Segimerus, made multiple attempts to persuade Varus that his nephew was not to be trusted that men stopped having any sympathy or tender feelings for Varus. Not only had he refused to heed the warnings from Segestes, we also learned that he had not even deigned to send out scouts, although when I heard this, I confess I wondered if it would have mattered, since he seemed to have put all of his faith in the Germans Arminius had convinced him to use. However it happened, once we heard the survivors' description of the terrain, not a man among those of us who had marched with Tiberius just a few years before needed to be told where Arminius had lured Varus and his army.

"That cunning bastard Arminius managed to draw the entire army into the Teutoberg." Crescens relayed this information at a meeting of the Centurions and Optios, held in the *Praetorium* in an attempt to have some sort of control over the word spreading before we were ready to deal with the inevitable backlash. "And," he continued grimly, "to a specific part of it." Pausing, he added, "I'll let you work out where that would be on your own. What's important is that the ground was clearly prepared beforehand." Glancing down at a wax tablet for reference, he went on, "The Germans created a line of entrenchments, and as hard as it may be to believe, there was a stretch of wooden wall as well. The only dry ground was the narrow strip Varus and his men were on, and it was too narrow for them to open their formation. They didn't bother fortifying the opposite side of the track because it's all bog."

Stopping then, the Primus Pilus seemed content to allow us to whisper amongst ourselves for the next few moments, and the exchange Macer and I had was typical.

"There's only one place like that," Macer mused, then allowed, "At least, from what I've heard. What about you?"

I was reasonably certain we were thinking of the same place, but I did consider for a moment as I searched my memory for any other place in that dense, practically impenetrable tract of land for another spot that would provide the same conditions that Crescens had just described.

Finally, I shook my head and agreed, "No, I think you're right." Just to make sure, I added, "You're thinking of that strip on the northern edge of the forest?"

Macer nodded, and was about to add something when Crescens, apparently deciding that he had allowed us to speculate long enough, cleared his throat and said irritably, "Yes, all right. I can see most of you know exactly where I'm talking about. Now, let's talk about what this means."

Not surprisingly, the last of the whispered conversations instantly ceased, since this would be the preface to the discussion of our immediate future. However, for a moment, it seemed as if our Primus Pilus had either lost his train of thought or he had not actually thought matters through, and he sat there staring down at the tablet in front of him, the silence becoming so oppressive that I imagined I could feel it palpably lying across my shoulders.

Finally, he resumed, but it was to ask a question. "Can anyone here recall a time when these barbarian tribes ever carried out something as complex a plan as this had to be?" Before any of us could answer, he added another question. "And actually built something like a wooden wall and rampart?"

I almost raised my hand, because my first thought was about my time just the year before in Pannonia, with the *Legio Germanicus*, and how the rebelling tribes not only adopted our tactics, but had begun copying our techniques for siege warfare and the like.

Fortunately, I stopped myself, so that it was actually the Quintus Pilus Posterior, Vibius Licinius, who offered, "Don't those tribes in Pannonia steal our ways?"

Crescens' reply was openly scornful. "That's true, Licinius, but the last I checked, none of those tribes have managed to escape from Tiberius to invade Germania and make mischief. I don't care about what some barbarians are doing somewhere else. I'm talking about the tribes up here."

I did not know Licinius that well, but I certainly bore him no grudge; however, the primary emotion I was feeling at that moment was gratitude that he was the one who exposed himself to Crescens' ire and not me. I also recall very clearly admonishing myself, Titus, you dodged the bolt on that one. Make sure you don't go and ruin it by opening your mouth.

Whereupon, before I could stop myself, I blurted out, "Primus Pilus, do we know which tribes are part of...whatever this is?"

I suppose the gods were looking at me kindly that day, because this not only did not seem to irritate Crescens, he actually nodded his head in approval.

Then he ruined the moment by pointing at me, but while addressing Licinius, "Now *that* is the right question to ask,

Licinius! Pullus asked the most important question, so try to keep that in mind next time you want to open your mouth."

I managed to contain my groan inside my body, but it was no less real because it was silent, as I thought, Thank you so much, Primus Pilus. Now I have someone else who hates me. For a brief instant, I did harbor the hope that Licinius would not focus his ire on me, but while I kept my eyes on Crescens, I felt the eyes of the Pilus Posterior boring into me.

It did not help matters when Macer murmured loudly enough for only me to hear, "Good job, Titus. If looks could kill, you'd be dead on the floor."

Fortunately, Crescens either did not hear or chose to ignore this, running his finger down the wax tablet as he said, "Obviously, the Cherusci, since Arminius is the man behind all of this, and the Marsi, Chatti, Chauci, Sicambri." He stopped then, and I thought he was finished, but I understood why he paused when he added a final name. "And the Bructeri."

If someone unfamiliar with Germania beyond the Rhenus had been present, I suspect they would have been surprised at the collective sudden intake of breath, muttered curses, and whispered exchanges at the mention of the Bructeri. However, to all of us who served in this province, the mention of the Bructeri when combined in a statement about the Cherusci, and with no mention of how they were fighting each other, was so singularly unusual that it made our reaction not only understandable, but the proper one.

"So," the Primus Pilus Posterior Tiberius Sacrovir spoke up, "if this Arminius was able to bring the Bructeri to his standard, and given what we know of how carefully they prepared this whole trap…we're fucked."

That certainly seemed to sum matters up nicely, and I would offer this as an example that proves the gravity of the situation that Crescens did not even bother to reprimand Sacrovir for this gloomy assessment. What was not known to any of us at the time was that our Primus Pilus had other matters on his mind that made this seemingly desperate situation not quite as dire for him; indeed, he had just been handed a promotion.

It is so difficult to recall the exact sequence of these smaller moments when compared to the backdrop of the larger situation. Therefore, I cannot say with any confidence when Macer summoned me to his quarters, other than to say it was after we learned of the confederation that Arminius had managed to put together. When I got to his quarters, he waved me to a seat, and without a word offered me a cup that I saw was already full. This was not all that unusual; that it was unwatered at this time of day and given all that was taking place most certainly was, and as I sat down and took a sip, I studied his face intently.

He seemed to consider how to begin, then asked, "Have you noticed anything...unusual about the Primus Pilus?"

I did not take his meaning immediately, so I thought about it, then finally shook my head, saying, "Not really."

"Well, I have," he replied. "It just seemed to me that he wasn't quite as...worried about the avalanche of *cac* that's heading our way."

He paused then, and I suspect he did so to allow me to catch up, because when put this way, it suddenly seemed very clear, and I recalled that feeling I had had when he held the meeting about what we had learned about the composition of the force that we were certain would be arriving on the opposite bank of the Rhenus.

"That," I agreed slowly, "is true, now that you mention it."

I looked at him sharply, studying his face for a clue, before I realized he was deliberately tormenting me, something that he did with a frequency that was, frankly, annoying.

Finally, he took pity on me at least partially, asking, "Did you hear about Prefect Caedicius?"

Obviously, I had not, since all I could think to say was, "Only that he's down at Mogontiacum. Why?"

"Because he wasn't at Mogontiacum," Macer answered. "Varus summoned him about a month before they broke camp at Vetera."

Suddenly, it all made more sense to me, although I still was not quite convinced that I was understanding completely. Part of this was due to the fact that any man who attains the post of Camp Prefect, beginning with my Avus and the other men who were the first in the post that had been formally adopted by the Princeps, are already legends in the Legions. And, while I would not put Lucius Caedicius in the same class as Titus Pullus, his reputation was formidable.

"So he was slaughtered with Varus?"

I gasped, sitting back in my chair, my shock such that the cup almost slipped from my grasp, but my confusion returned when Macer shook his head.

"No," my Pilus Prior answered, then went on, "he didn't fall with Varus. We just got word of this, but apparently, Caedicius managed to gather some men together, and they cut their way out of the trap. They headed for Aliso. Do you remember hearing about that place?"

It took me a heartbeat, then I recalled, or thought I did. "That was a temporary camp Varus built earlier this summer, right?"

"That's the one." Macer nodded. "But while we don't know for sure exactly why, Varus had ordered it left intact."

"Probably they planned on using it when they came back this way," I mused, but Macer was not convinced.

"Remember when they built it," he pointed out. "This was at the beginning of the summer, before they started chasing those rebels."

"That didn't exist," I retorted, then added, "although they didn't know that."

We sat in silence for a moment, I think each of us trying to come up with a reason why Varus would have created a camp, then ignored the standard practice of destroying that one, but Macer was the one who correctly pointed out, "Actually, it doesn't matter why. What does is that Caedicius and some men managed to make it to Aliso. Which is one reason why the Germans haven't shown up. They've been trying to take that camp so they wouldn't have Romans in their rear when they headed for us. They're holding out now but are completely surrounded."

This was not altogether surprising, but I did ask, "Then how did we find out?"

"Gaesorix and his *turma* captured a scout for Arminius," Macer answered. "I just happened to be at the *Praetorium* when I heard about it."

I was certainly interested in hearing more about Caedicius and whoever was with him, but I interrupted, "Wait. There are scouts on this side of the Rhenus?"

Macer shook his head.

"No, he took his men across the Rhenus to try and find other survivors, but they found a scouting party instead."

While I was not particularly happy that a man who had become a good friend was venturing across the one barrier to what we now knew was a huge army, that he was now safely back with us allowed me to return my attention to the other news.

"So, if Caedicius and his bunch aren't dead by now, they probably will be in the not too distant future," I mused, to which Macer shrugged and said, "I'd assume so. I can't imagine him surrendering, especially knowing what happened to the men who did."

I considered for a moment, then asked, "So, are you thinking that Crescens is going to be promoted to Camp Prefect should things happen the way we think and Caedicius is killed?" A thought occurred to me. "Have you heard something already?"

"No." Macer shook his head. "I haven't heard anything. But he was expecting to get the post for the Army of Pannonia that your old Primus Pilus got instead, and it's not much secret that he was next on the list of all the candidates in either our army or the one in Pannonia."

All I could really think to say was, "I suppose he might get the posting after all. Just not until after all this is over."

More days passed, turning into another week, then two, as everyone attached to the 1st Legion in any fashion waited for the inevitable. By the time a month passed, we had learned about the stand of Caedicius, and there was some talk of trying to mount a relief force, but orders came from Mogontiacum that we were to do no such thing, as word was relayed that Tiberius was hurrying from Pannonia. It became evident that Caedicius and his men were proving to be a serious threat to Arminius' plans, and their stalwart defense bought us enough time for Tiberius to arrive, bringing with him a mixed force, composed of some Cohorts from the 13th and 15th, along with a few Cohorts of auxiliaries. Very quickly, he took command from Asprenas, who, it must be said, had behaved in a prudent manner, keeping a cool head at a time I can only imagine he was being urged to all manner of rash actions. Naturally, it is impossible to separate rumor from fact, but we heard that leading citizens of Mogontiacum demanded that he alternately either cross the Rhenus to "teach the barbarian scum a lesson," with one Legion against a foe that had destroyed an army of three Legions, since they would never stand for sending both the 5th and 21st and leaving Mogontiacum completely undefended, or more believably to me, that he evacuate Mogontiacum and provide the 5th Alaudae as little more than security for the convoy loaded down with the combined wealth and portable property of the merchants fleeing to safety. Fortunately for all of us, Asprenas did neither, so that when Tiberius arrived, he was able to turn over essentially whole and untested defenses. Confluentes, which had grown from a trading post to a small fort normally manned by no more than a

Century of auxiliaries, was reinforced with a Cohort, as was Rigomagus, while the auxiliary camp at Bonna was reinforced as well, but with a Cohort from the 15th.

No more than a full week after Tiberius' arrival, every post between Mogontiacum to where we were up in Ubiorum had been reinforced with fresh men; fresh, at least, in the sense of being new to the province and the situation. Tiberius had been forced to bring men who, just weeks before, had finally quelled the last sparks of the rebellion in Pannonia that had started almost four years before. During the period of time Tiberius spent at Mogontiacum, we began hearing about the panic that had infected the citizens of the city of Rome and how they were demanding that Augustus do something to prevent the Germans from suddenly appearing in the Forum. Frankly, this was silly in the extreme, but apparently, the feeling was quite real, and it prompted Augustus to call another *dilectus*, similar to the one that had created the *Legio Germanicus*. There was only one problem: nobody answered the call, or at least not in sufficient numbers to fill out more than a Cohort or two. Only later would the consequences of the Princeps' decision to essentially force citizens who had no interest or desire to serve in the Legions to do so come back to haunt all of us. Not that this was of more than passing interest at the time, especially once we were summoned to the *Praetorium*, where Crescens was waiting for us, having taken the place of Arruntius as the senior commander, who never came back to Ubiorum.

"We've received orders from Tiberius," he informed us, for the first time since this all began looking and behaving like the Primus Pilus we all knew. "Three Cohorts from the 13th are marching here, while the Second, Third, Fourth, and Fifth Cohorts are going to be marching north."

While I would not characterize it as an outburst, there was certainly a reaction, and Macer leaned towards me to whisper,

"By the gods, I hope he's not expecting us to go all the way up to Vetera."

This was my fear as well, but fortunately, this was not to be the case, at least for us in the Fourth.

"You're going to Novaesium and relieve the auxiliary Cohorts there." Crescens paused for just a moment, then he continued, "They will be marching north to Vetera and rebuild the camp there. Once that's done, the Fifth Cohort will join them there."

Not surprisingly, all eyes turned to Gnaeus Clepsina, but only those of us who knew him well could see beneath his normal, stolid exterior to where the dismay was expressed in the set of his jaw.

"How much time do we have to prepare our boys?"

This came from the Secundus Pilus Prior, Lucius Sentius, who would be serving as the senior Centurion in command of the detachment, though we all naturally were interested.

"Unfortunately," Crescens took a quick glance at the tablet in his hand, "not as long as you'd like. Tiberius orders that you have to be ready to march at dawn, day after tomorrow."

The chorus of groans and soft curses was by no means universal, confined only to those of us who would be leaving Ubiorum, but this was far from the only concern, which was instantly brought up by Clepsina.

"Primus Pilus," to my eyes, Clepsina actually appeared as if he had not already heard all the bad news, which I understood when he asked, "where are the Cohorts from the 13th going to be quartered?"

Crescens appeared surprised, answering immediately, "Why, they'll stay in your area and those of the other Cohorts going with you."

I know this would seem to be an obvious matter, but when the chorus of groans erupted, my voice was among them. Since Sentius would be our *de facto* commander, naturally we looked directly to him, and while he certainly looked unhappy, it was impossible to know whether it was because he was being put on the spot or he shared our concern.

Either way, he did reward our confidence by raising his hand, but Crescens held up his own, anticipating the objection by saying, "You're just going to have to have your men put the valuables they're not taking into your Century strongboxes and leave them here. We'll put them in the *Quaestorium*."

"Primus Pilus," Sentius started to object, but the Primus Pilus' eyebrows, which were now as iron gray as the hair on his head, plunged down towards each other, a sign every one of his Centurions knew portended an eruption of his temper, which, while not often seen, was sufficiently intimidating that none of us wanted to rouse it.

"Sentius, do you really want to waste valuable time trying to make sure your men don't lose some of their trinkets and plunder? If we can't put enough men in place to at least spot when Arminius and his bunch come for us, will it really matter?"

That Crescens did not raise his voice actually had a more sobering effect than if he had bellowed at the top of his lungs, and speaking for myself, it reminded me just how grave the overall situation was, and that in the grand scheme of things, having some of our light-fingered comrades from another Legion relieve men of those possessions that would not easily fit into their packs was low in terms of priorities. With this matter settled, even if it was not to our collective satisfaction, we were dismissed to tend to our Centuries.

"This," Macer commented to the five of us, his Centurions, "isn't going to be fun, but let's at least beat Sentius and those other bastards to the punch. If we do," he promised, "we'll give the men tomorrow night off so they can get some drinking and whoring in."

This prompted a barking laugh from Macula, the Hastatus Posterior, who pointed out, "There's only a dozen whores left in

41

town, Pilus Prior. And they aren't the pick of the litter, if you get my meaning."

"That's true," Macer admitted, while the rest of us chuckled, then he grinned at us and said, "So the boys will just have to learn not to be so picky. Besides," his smile vanished, and his words had the same effect as he reminded us, "considering where we're going and what's ahead, they're going to want some good memories to keep them warm."

Even as he said this, snowflakes began drifting down in the first snow of the coming winter.

Although the turn in weather made matters more difficult in many ways, it was one of the only times I ever saw men, of every rank, thankful for it. This is not to say it was not always easy to keep in mind that this was a blessing from the gods; as is usual for first snowfalls, the temperature did not stay low enough to keep it from melting, which meant that when we left Ubiorum, before the first watch, our feet and lower legs were covered in mud. This was certainly an inconvenience, but the practical problem it caused was in the slowing of our progress, with more stops than normal because one of the wagons would bog down. Fairly quickly, Sentius ordered the rotation of Centuries marching drag behind the baggage, since these are the unfortunates who are responsible for freeing those wagons from their sticky bondage. And, of course, it was not long before my Century found ourselves at the rear, but apart from the inevitability of men slipping and falling as they heaved or pushed one or more wagons out of the mud, which was always met with laughter from their comrades, it was being motionless and vulnerable that was the most trying. Since my Third Century was not rotated to the rear until we were more than ten miles from Ubiorum, it was not far from our minds that, while it would have been difficult, it was not inconceivable that a force from Arminius' confederation could have crossed the Rhenus in the stretch in between Ubiorum and Novaesium to our rear. And, as Varus and his Legions had discovered, a Roman army is at its most vulnerable on the march, especially when surrounded by the kind of thick forest that is a feature of both sides of the Rhenus. While it was true that, by this point in time, towards the end of the year where the suffect Consuls were Marcus Pupilius Mutilus and Quintus Poppaeus Secundus, much of the western bank along the Rhenus had been cleared and was now populated by small homesteads, there were still stretches of land where our side looked exactly like the eastern bank. Essentially, Rome had transformed the landscape in a swathe around each settlement of just a couple miles, which in turn surrounded an armed camp like Ubiorum, or a fort like Novaesium was at that time. By the time my Century took its turn, we were in the area between civilized patches, which meant that, whenever we stopped and a section of men were involved in extricating a wagon, the other nine sections were standing, with grounded packs and shields unlashed, although I allowed them to remain covered.

"Pullus, if I didn't know better, I'd think you don't trust me and my men."

It was perhaps our fourth or fifth time to stop when Gaesorix, who had been splitting his time between his advance guard and the other half of his command at the rear, said this to me, grinning down at me from horseback.

"I know how drunk you got last night," I countered, "so is it any wonder?"

My Batavian friend just laughed, shaking his head as he went trotting back to the front, but the sight of him reminded me to take advantage of this unscheduled stop. Telling Structus to take over, I turned and went in the same direction as Gaesorix, heading up the column to where Alex was standing, next to his horse Lightning, but I was not there to check on him. Latobius had clearly smelled me coming, because even as I stepped around the lead wagon to where the Century and Cohort slaves and mules were located, he had his head turned and his ears pricked forward.

"I never could sneak up on you," I complained.

"Not as long as you're carrying an apple," Alex scoffed, and almost as if this was his cue, Latobius thrust his neck out as his nostrils flared, unerringly locating the fruit in the bag I carried slung across my shoulder.

Knowing from experience that if I did not produce his treat, my horse would take it upon himself to retrieve it on his own, I laughed as I pushed his head aside to pull it out, and as always, I experienced a small, quiet thrill at the feel of his soft nose against my palm as he snatched up the apple, evoking memories of another horse and another time.

While my animal munched contentedly, I asked Alex how he was faring, and he shrugged, saying simply, "I'm bored, but otherwise, I'm fine."

"You know that being bored is a good thing, right?"

"Yes," he sighed, "I know. But," he lowered his voice, "you don't have to sit and listen to those two squabbling."

He indicated with his head to where Lucco, the Cohort clerk and Alex's best friend, was riding next to the clerk for the Second Century, Demas, and even in the brief time I paid attention, I heard what was the continuation of their long-running debate about which chariot racing team was superior, the Whites or the Greens.

Grinning at my nephew, I just said, "Better you than me."

After giving Latobius another pat, but not another apple, despite his insistent tugging at my bag, I walked back just in time to see Trigeminus and Centho, the latter man the one who had gotten his arm broken by my former Centurion Macer, from my Fifth Section, fall face-first into the muck when the wagon suddenly lurched free. Naturally, this was met with much mirth from their comrades, and equally understandably, neither man appreciated it, but when Trigeminus launched a kick at the

44

nearest man, I had to step in, although I was careful to use my *vitus* to keep my distance, having learned it is a ranker's trick in such moments to try and spatter their Centurion with the filth covering them.

"You two get cleaned up as best you can, but you better not take too long doing it," I said with a straight face, "because Arminius himself might be out there somewhere, and he'll be quick to snatch up a couple of laggards."

I knew that of the two, Centho would actually take this seriously, glancing nervously into the dense foliage just a dozen paces away, while Trigeminus simply spat the mud that had gotten into his mouth and growled, "Let that dog-fucker come and I'll end this nonsense right now!"

Shoving Centho, Trigeminus stepped to the side, both of them grabbing their spare neckerchiefs out of their pack to begin rubbing themselves relatively clean, while the column resumed its progress. Such was the nature of this march; the only difference being the identity of the Century in the rear, since ours was rotated out soon after this. Of course, once we were back ahead of the baggage train, that did not mean the complaining about the ordeal stopped; all it did mean was that it was a normal day on the march.

We knew, at least in a general sense, that the camp at Novaesium would not be comparable to ours, but when we emerged into the cleared swathe of land to get our first glimpse of what would be our new home for the foreseeable future, there were simply not enough *viti* among the Centurions to beat the dismay and bitter curses out of the men. Although it was true that the auxiliaries were not living under canvas, that is perhaps the kindest thing that can be said about matters. The only building of any substance was the *Praetorium*, which reminded me of the one at Ubiorum back when I first arrived to take my post with the 1st, and from a distance at least, it looked to be the standard size and configuration. Otherwise, what greeted our eyes in terms of the housing for not just the rankers, but the Centurions and Optios, resembled the hovels and shacks that were outside the gates of Ubiorum; indeed, just from appearance, it was as if some god had managed to pick up that miserable collection, transport it here to Novaesium, and the only difference was they were neatly arranged in the normal grid pattern of a Roman army camp, although this was where the similarity to Ubiorum ended. Regardless of the appearance, I will say that the Centurion in command of the auxiliary Cohorts was thoroughly professional, although Sentius did not appreciate it very much, requiring our commander to stand outside the gate while the orders he had brought with him were examined. Frankly, I cannot say any of us took it well, but I ascribe that more to the natural disdain for auxiliaries we in the Legions hold for them.

"What do they think we are?" Structus grumbled. "A bunch of Germans wearing…"

He did not finish, picking up on the obvious before I could point out that what might have been considered outlandish just a matter of a few weeks before was now not only in the realm of possibility, but could be considered a very real threat.

Nevertheless, I could not resist rubbing it in a bit. "Yes, Structus, exactly that. We *could* be Germans dressed up as Romans."

"I figured that out already, Centurion," he grumbled, but he was nothing if not a bit stubborn, and he pointed out, "but hardly any of us are wearing beards or have hair in braids! And you know much those German *cunni* love those things!"

"That's true," I agreed, or seemed to, until I pointed out, "but somehow, I think that Arminius would be able to convince them to shave and cut their hair, considering he managed to get all those tribes to stop killing each other and focus on us instead."

Structus did not reply to this, although it was likely that it had more to do with the fact I was his Centurion than because he recognized he had been outmaneuvered, but it did not matter, since we finally resumed moving immediately after this, entering the camp. Once inside, the process of settling into the huts that had been vacated just watches before when the auxiliary Cohorts had departed for their new posting began, which quickly degenerated into a situation that prompted an emergency meeting.

"These fucking auxiliaries live like pigs," the Tertius Pilus Prior Servius Maluginensis informed Sentius, who had been summoned from his meeting in the *Praetorium*. "My boys refuse to go inside those fucking hovels, let alone spend a night in them."

"Same with ours," Macer offered, which was certainly the truth with my Third, and I saw the other Centurions of the Fourth were nodding their heads.

Honestly, I had not yet had the opportunity to inspect any of the huts assigned to my Century, but since every section had done so, and the opinion was unanimous that these were the filthiest quarters they had ever encountered, I believed they were telling the truth. Even if they were not, it did not really matter all that much, because this was one of those occasions where the mood of the men was what mattered. Sentius, understandably in my eyes, seemed completely nonplussed, while the Centurion commanding the auxiliaries, a man of perhaps forty years who might have once had a muscular build but was now running to fat, stood there looking very much as if he was praying that the ground swallow him up.

"My boys," he finally spoke up, speaking with an accent that was familiar to my ears, having heard my Avus and some of the other veterans from Hispania, "aren't the best at keeping their areas tidy…"

47

If he was going to continue, he did not have a chance, when Maluginensis cut him off with a barking, incredulous laugh that was lacerating, then repeated scornfully, "'Tidy'? Your men are fucking filthy animals! I wouldn't put my dog inside one of these shacks!"

This stirred the Centurion to anger, and he jabbed a finger back at Maluginensis as he shot back, "Oy! Centurion! We aren't the same as the Legions, but we do the best we can with what little we're given! Besides which," to my surprise, and to the others, the auxiliary commander actually took a step towards the Pilus Prior as he hammered back, "we've been standing continuous fucking watch since we got our orders and heard about the Praetor! So I made the decision that things like hut inspections could wait until later, until after we had a fucking idea if we were going to live through the winter!"

"And," Sentius took this opportunity to step in, and I must say I was impressed with how smoothly he handled what was growing into a confrontation, "we are thankful that you did your duty. We're just happy that those German bastards didn't come swarming down on our heads from your direction. Now," he spun and pointed at Maluginensis, "while I understand your concerns," his voice hardened, "frankly, I don't give a brass *obol* if things aren't up to your men's standards of cleanliness. Tell them if they want spotless accommodations, they're welcome to apply to the fucking Praetorians. But until then," he finished by pointing his *vitus* in the general direction of the Cohort areas, "you and your men are going to get settled in and I don't want to hear any more whining about it. Is that clear, Pilus Prior Maluginensis?"

Now, I must make mention of the fact that there was already no love lost between Sentius and Maluginensis, and this certainly did not help matters, but the lower ranking Pilus Prior knew an order when he heard one, stiffening to *intente* and replying in a monotone, "I understand, Pilus Prior, and I will obey."

Without waiting to be dismissed, he spun about and stalked away, leaving Sentius to turn to where Macer and I were standing, but my Pilus Prior was by no means a stupid man, so when Sentius snapped, "Well, Macer? You have something to say?" he merely saluted and replied cheerfully, "Not a word, Pilus Prior."

As the six of us went back to the section of the camp that had been assigned to us, there was not much talk, but while I do not remember who said it, they summed matters up perfectly.

"I have a feeling that this winter is going to be fucking miserable."

If anything, this was an understatement.

We passed an uneasy night all crammed into the camp, but Clepsina's Fifth and the auxiliaries were gone at dawn the next morning, whereupon the men began the task of making our habitations, if not satisfactory, at least habitable. In my case, it meant that Alex performed the manual labor, but in this respect, we were both lucky, since the Centurion's quarters I had been assigned were not in the same condition as the rankers' huts. Unfortunately, that was where our good fortune ended, because while it was essentially clean, the construction of the building was so slipshod that, despite Alex's best efforts, there were simply too many cracks and gaps to effectively plug them all. Very quickly, one thing became clear to all of us, officers and men alike: the amount of firewood, and more importantly, charcoal we would need was significantly higher than we had anticipated. Thus began one of the predominant features of this winter that men of the Second, Third, and our Fourth would be talking about for months afterward, the almost daily battle to march out of the camp and gather enough wood for both the purposes of the open fires that we kept blazing around the perimeter of the camp, and to make charcoal. Thankfully, Sentius had the foresight to send men farther out in the beginning of what would be a months-long ordeal, then work our way back to the camp, although those of us who were among the first to provide the labor for this critical task were not all that appreciative. Such was our state of mind that there were never less than three Centuries sent out to perform the actual gathering of the wood; one Century did the work, while the other two stood watch in a protective ring around the laborers. So important was this task that, while our slaves certainly participated, in much the same way only Legionaries are allowed to construct a camp, they just performed the more mundane tasks of loading, then driving the wagons that carried the wood back. A semi-permanent addition was made to the western end of the camp, with the dirt wall partially torn down, then an enlarged space was created where the huge clay amphorae that are an integral part to making charcoal were placed. Before a full week had passed, two things had occurred: the first was a heavy snowfall that did not melt and which marked the true beginning of our winter, and the realization that aside from worrying about the Germans appearing, we would have to put considerable effort into simply surviving.

"The huts are finally clean, but they're as bad as sleeping under canvas!"

While I do not recall who said it, this statement was a troublingly accurate one, and as soon as I heard it, I realized that the same thought had crossed my mind, as I tried to compare the memory of the winter campaign with Tiberius shortly after I was transferred to the 1st a few years before, and the sensation of what it was like to wake up inside a building, yet still have to break ice out of the wash basin sitting on the chest in my room. And, when I speak of sensation, I am actually speaking of the lack thereof, particularly in my extremities; honestly, I spent an inordinate amount of my time staring down at my feet as I wiggled my toes, needing the visual reassurance of seeing the movement, since I could not feel a thing in them most of the time, and that was wearing fur-lined socks. So dire was the situation that there was actual, serious discussion about whether or not the men would be better served to return to living in their tents, for the simple belief that, while the walls and roof might be made of fabric, they were at least whole in their construction, with waterproofed seams that helped insulate from the cold somewhat. Although this was seriously considered, Sentius decided that the only way this would work was either by enlarging the camp, tearing down the existing huts, or pitching the tents in the streets, none of which was feasible. Ultimately, all of us, regardless of rank, did what they could to chink the cracks, with men trying a variety of materials, none of which proved to be successful for anything but a short time. Mud from the river was favored, until, of course, the riverbank froze, but even this proved to be a temporary fix, lasting for at most three or four days before it dried out, and the constant force of the wind made it crumble and fall out. Some men tried using bits of cloth, but they quickly learned that not only was it not particularly effective, there were gaps in most of the huts that were of such a size that it would have required men to use more than just a spare neckerchief, meaning that they would have had to sacrifice a tunic. Not surprisingly, since most men were now wearing both tunics, and no man in a section was willing to make this sacrifice, this did not work either. The most successful material turned out to be leather, from the sheets that are part of the supply the leatherworking *immunes* keep on hand, but it quickly became apparent that there was not enough leather to both allow men to make their huts more livable and for the *immunes* to keep our leather gear, particularly our *caligae,* in good repair.

"I'm not going to let the men use the leather then have them walking around barefoot before the winter's out," Sentius told us flatly, and while we knew this would not be viewed with any favor by our men, it was also the correct decision.

It was Maluginensis who suggested, "What about letting the Centurions have a sheet of leather for our own huts?"

There was no way for me to be certain, but I sensed that this was more an attempt by Maluginensis to force Sentius to make a decision that might ruffle the feathers of his fellow Centurions, since I saw more than one head bobbing up and down at this idea. Glancing over at Macer, I was happy to see that he was not one of them, and I suspected our thoughts were aligned on this; while I cannot lie and say I was not tempted by the idea of doing something that would make my quarters more livable, given the overall situation, I felt certain it would cause more trouble than it was worth. The mental condition of the rankers, which was exacerbated by their shared physical misery, was a dangerous mix of disgruntlement and, if I am being honest, fear, making for a situation that I had certainly never encountered before, nor had I ever heard of anything like this. Thanks to my Avus' account, however, I was perhaps a bit better prepared, because when I looked around at my men and listened to their conversations, I was reminded of the part of his account that described the campaign in Parthia under Marcus Antonius. Without having been there personally, this is something of a guess, but what I was witnessing firsthand were men who had been shaken to their very core, much like the men of Antonius' army as they marched across the wastes of Parthia, having suffered horrible losses, most crucially the entire baggage train. The one difference was also the most important reason for the mental state of the men, and that was, while Antonius' army suffered heavy losses, relatively few came from a Parthian arrow, lance, or *gladius*. Most of those who never made it out of Parthia fell because of illness, exposure, or a combination of both, but the same cannot be said about the Legions slaughtered by the Germans. Knowing that three Legions had been wiped out by an army that, if I am being honest, we had always sneered at as being nothing but a collection of barbarians who, while individually brave, were unable to behave as a cohesive entity like the Legions of Rome, was perhaps the largest contributing factor to the state of collective shock, dismay, and fear that infected every man. Somewhat paradoxically, as days turned to weeks, with not even a sign of activity on the opposite riverbank, rather than beginning to relax the men and officers, the tension increased on an almost daily basis. This was exacerbated by the lack of information coming from Ubiorum, although later we learned it was not because Germans were intercepting couriers, but matters were in such a state of uproar and panic that, once Tiberius returned to Rome, the men he left in command simply either forgot or did not think it important to keep us informed of developments. Not surprisingly, there were men, not just in the ranks but in the Optionate and Centurionate, whose natural tendency to view such matters in the direst light exacerbated matters, declaiming at every opportunity that there was only one possible reason why we were not receiving any couriers. All of these things contributed to the tension remaining at a level that, while I cannot prove it, I believe had as much to do with the inordinately high number of men who did not survive the winter.

It is inevitable that men under the standard are at least as susceptible to falling ill as any other citizen; indeed, as my Avus observed, and my own experience supports, it is more likely for a Legionary to be stricken by the type of malady that seems to arise when we are in enforced closeness. While I do not fault Sentius, what I will say is that his standards for cleanliness for the men was inferior to that imposed by Crescens, but I also believe that the combination of an extraordinarily harsh winter and the aforementioned tensions had at least as much to do with the plague that struck the camp around the Ides of December. That it happened during the coldest part of the year is why I believe there was more involved than just the latrines overflowing because the channel that had been cut to run water from the river froze solid. When I discussed it with older veterans, none of us could recall experiencing or even hearing about the plague striking this late in the year, yet we could all recall the camp sewer freezing several times over the past winters. The first man to die was in the Fifth of the Third, but he had been struggling the previous week with a cold, which weakened him to the point that, frankly, it was not a surprise. And, if I am being honest, the next half-dozen deaths were of a similar nature; men who had already been on the sick and injured list for some reason succumbed first, but this is not unusual, although over previous winters, it had been men who were wounded during the campaign season. It was when the deaths did not stop with those already weakened that we all began to grow alarmed, despite the fact that it was not until the new year began before any man of the Fourth Cohort fell ill. That we had managed to last that long without suffering our first loss I attribute to the work of the gods, and, perhaps, my relating to Macer my Avus' conviction that frequent bathing, despite the frigid cold, had something to do with it as well. Unfortunately, when it became clear that the Fourth Cohort was consuming more charcoal than the others, Sentius put a stop to our practice of heating water for purposes other than cooking alone. Macer unsuccessfully argued with Sentius that, if anything, the other Cohorts would be better served to follow our practice, since even by this point in Januarius, we still had had less men stricken at all, let alone succumb. But in this, Macer was thwarted by the simple but powerful fact that it is impossible to prove that making the men do more than just a scraping with oil was the reason for our better condition compared to the others.

"Maybe Febris just likes your offerings better than ours," was how Macer told me Maluginensis put it at the meeting of Pili Priores.

"Well, if Macer is right, then we're sacrificing to the wrong god to begin with, and it should be Valetudo." Macer recounted that this came from Sentius, and while it was odd that the Secundus and Tertius Pilus Prior were in accord, ultimately the reason they were of a like mind did not matter.

And, within a week after ceasing the practice, our sick and injured list was roughly comparable to those of the other Cohorts, then not long after that, I lost a member of my Eighth Section. Before the end of Januarius, well more than a tenth of our force was incapacitated on any given day, which may not sound like much, but it is the same as a Legion losing an entire Cohort. Work parties became more difficult to fill, although Sentius' foresight in having us range farther afield when we first arrived helped relieve the burden on the healthy men who were now going out on a daily basis. The river froze out to a point where there was a gap of perhaps a dozen feet between the ice on our side and the opposite bank, which created even more tension, since the ice was thick enough to support an armed party out most of the way.

"All they would need is a couple of boats to bridge that gap, and we'd be fucked," Philus said gloomily, when his Century was relieving mine from guard post one day.

We were standing on the rampart, looking out across the river as our Optios went through the ritual of exchanging sentries, yet while I could not really argue that this was a possibility, I was not as concerned as Philus.

"I think that if they were going to cross, they would have done it by now," I countered, albeit somewhat cautiously.

Philus, however, was a gloomy sort and always tended to view things in a more pessimistic manner, and he waved a dismissive hand, scoffing, "Or they're just waiting to see if the river completely freezes over. Or maybe," he persisted, "they're just watching for the moment we have half the men sick from this fucking plague, and our guard is down."

Again, this was something with which it was hard to argue, although I was struck by something, and I asked Philus, "You've been on the Rhenus longer than I have. Has the river ever frozen solid enough to let anyone come across?"

He shook his head, seemingly reluctantly to my eyes, which was supported when he agreed, "No, I haven't. But," Philus turned and began scanning the rampart around us, which was confusing until he spotted someone, "Nerva has." Before I could say anything, Philus bellowed, "Nerva! Come over here and attend to your Centurion!"

The Gregarius did as he was bid, of course, and I recognized the man immediately; while I had not known his name, he had been pointed out to me as the oldest serving member of not just his Century, but our entire Cohort. Like most men of the Legions, he was not much to look at, no more than three or four inches over five feet, and even with the bulk of his *sagum*, *bracae,* and the woolen scarf he had wrapped around his throat, it was easy to see that he was as stringy and lean as dried beef. But, as I also knew, both from my own service and growing up among men like this, any man who survived three or more decades under the standard would be tough and hard to overcome. As he saluted us, Nerva's expression was one that every man of the Legions has worn at one time or another, no matter what their current rank may be; his seamed features were a study in a mixture of suspicion, wariness, and a little apprehension.

"Nerva, didn't you tell me once that you've seen the river frozen over?"

Seeing that he was not in some sort of trouble, the old veteran's face cleared, and he actually grinned, exposing a mouth where there were only three or four teeth left.

"Yes, Centurion," he answered cheerfully, I suppose happy now that he was no longer subject to a thrashing for something. "It was in my second year under the standard." His face screwed up as he tried to think what year that might have been, but Philus waved a hand. "I don't need to know exactly what year it was, Nerva. But you *did* see this river frozen all the way over?"

The veteran nodded, his expression now becoming apprehensive as he seemed to actually examine the surface of the river for the first time, seeing the brown ribbon of water that, if the ice was thick enough on both sides, looked almost narrow enough for a man to leap across.

"Actually, Centurion," Nerva's voice changed now, matching his expression, "I've seen the Rhenus freeze twice, but only once was it thick enough for those German savages to come across."

"And," I interjected, "did they?"

"Oh, yes, Centurion Pullus," he nodded emphatically now, "they did. It was a band of Marsi, as I recall. That," he explained, "was back before the Princeps had Tiberius shift them all around. This," he lifted his javelin to indicate the opposite bank, "was all Marsi lands back then, not Sugambri."

"How much damage did they do?" Philus asked, but to this, Nerva could only shrug and offer, "Oh, the usual. Burned some farms, killed some settlers, stole some livestock. Then," he made a whistling sound, "they were back across the river, quick as Pan."

"See?" Philus turned to me, happy to be vindicated in his gloomy assessment, but I was watching Nerva's expression as his Centurion crowed, "I told you! And this time it's not just a band of Marsi. It's a fucking army that wiped out three Legions! So," he turned and pointed at the river, "if that freezes the rest of the way, you can bet every *sestertius* to your name they'll be coming across."

And, I thought, why are you saying that loud enough for every one of your men, and mine, to hear? To my ears, it sounded very much like Philus would have rather been proven right and see us wiped out in the process than that gap in the water not freezing over.

However, despite my technically outranking Philus, there is an unwritten rule that Centurions, at least those belonging to the same Cohort, do not contradict each other or argue in front of the men. Unless, of course, it is on a subject like the best chariot racing team, most imaginative whore, or something of that nature.

Consequently, all I said was, "Well, Philus, I'm going to go give an offering to Mars and their goddess Danu to make sure that doesn't happen."

Although I am naturally something of a skeptic when it comes to the gods, I confess that I have sometimes wondered if that sacrifice, which was in the form of most of my evening meal, might have had something to do with the fact that we made it through that winter without the river freezing over. More importantly, we were not attacked, nor was there any incursion by any Germans, at least of those tribes now united under Arminius. It would not be until much later before we learned that, as unprepared for defeat as Rome was, the Germanic tribes commanded by Arminius were at least as unready for a victory of such epic proportions.

In the larger world outside of Novaesium and our own travails, in terms of substantive action, nothing much happened. As the winter progressed, Tiberius returned to Rome, as did Germanicus from his posting in Pannonia, and the uproar in the city died down once it became apparent that there would not be any Germanic hordes sweeping down the Via Tiburtina. On a day in March, in the year of the Consulships of Publius Cornelius Dolabella and Gaius Junius Silanus, a courier arrived from Ubiorum, recalling us back home. That the Consul Silanus was none other than the older brother of the man who served as the prosecution in the Tribunal of my former Primus Pilus, and in essence tried to destroy the career of Gaius Sempronius Atticus did give me some pause, wondering if this was an ill omen. Regardless, since Atticus was now the Camp Prefect of the Army of Pannonia, this was an example of how truly inept Quintus Silanus had been in presenting his case, and I had to wonder just how alike the two brothers Silanus might have been. Not, I must add, that it mattered all that much; the office of Consul has been ceremonial in nature for quite some time, and although the Princeps was in his last years, nothing led any of us to believe that he was still not the complete and total master of Rome, and by extension, all of us. Our return to Ubiorum only took place once the auxiliary Cohorts arrived from Vetera, along with Clepsina's Fifth Cohort, meaning that once more, we spent a tense two days with both Legionaries and auxiliaries sharing a camp designed for a much smaller force. However, somewhat to our surprise, while it could not be said that our men suddenly viewed their auxiliary counterparts as anything remotely resembling equals, now that we had experienced a taste of the auxiliary life and how much harder it is in comparison to those of us in the Legions, after an initial period where every officer of both forces walked around with their *viti* or other implement, waiting for trouble, it became clear that there would be none.

"As much as I hate to admit it," Structus remarked as we stood, watching our men begin, tentatively at first, to interact with the auxiliaries, "those bastards have it a lot worse than we do."

This was nothing more than the truth, and while I had gotten a glimpse of their rougher existence during my time serving under Germanicus as part of the *Legio Germanicus*, I suppose it was a good reminder of this reality. At the time, frankly, all I cared about was that none of my men tried to bash the skull of an auxiliary, nor did the opposite happen. Marching away from Novaesium the next morning, we had one wagon filled with the urns of men who had died over the winter, all of whom we

burned in one mass cremation, the final toll now well over a
tenth part of the three Cohorts who had been at Novaesium. We
had been forced to store their frozen bodies in a tent erected
specifically to hold their corpses in a corner of the camp, and
sacrificing the final reserves of our firewood, whereupon we
apportioned an amount of ash to each urn inscribed with each
man's name, far from an ideal situation, but one that could not
be helped. The Fourth had done slightly better, but not much,
with all but three sections now missing at least a man and with
one section losing three, forcing me to shift men around. This is
a common enough practice, but usually losses like this are a
result of battle, yet in that regard, that entire year had been
extraordinarily quiet for the 1st, and the winter had passed with
only a handful of sightings of Germans, all of them on the
eastern side of the Rhenus, consisting of scouting parties
watching us as we watched them. The march went without
incident, aided by the fact the track was still frozen, enabling the
wagons to pass without men being forced to heave them out of
ruts. When we reached Ubiorum, it became clear that, while not
completely back to normal, the inhabitants of the shantytown
had begun drifting back, with the camp itself appearing
unchanged. And, although none of us, and I include myself,
would have ever considered Ubiorum as a model of what a
permanent camp should look like, since it was still somewhat
ramshackle, with the rankers' huts still being constructed of
wood, given our experience at Novaesium, the men, and
officers, raised a spontaneous and heartfelt cheer at the sight of
home.

"I'm going to love being able to sleep in just my tunic and
not wrapped up in every fucking piece of clothing I own," Macer
commented.

"I just want to take a bath, a *real* bath," I offered, the very
thought making my face itch as I added, "and get rid of this
fucking beard."

"I'm going to go see if any of my favorite whores are back yet," was Vespillo's contribution.

Conversations identical to this one were taking place all up and down the column, as by unspoken yet common consent, the officers allowed the men to chatter and begin to relax, even before we dismissed them. Arriving at the gate, we were allowed in without delay, unlike our approach to Novaesium, and it reminded me that not only would whoever was commanding the guard recognize us, the collective nerves of the 1st were calmer than they had been five months earlier. Pausing in the forum only long enough for the men to stop in formation and come to *intente*, Sentius wasted no time dismissing us, our ordeal ending in one final spontaneous cheer as the men actually ran towards their respective areas, eager to get back to what we all thought of as home, where the section slaves had already gone to unload the mules. The Secundus Pilus Prior turned and walked to the *Praetorium*, while Macer and the rest of the Centurions of the Fourth, including me, followed behind our men. I had sent Alex ahead of me as well, telling him to make sure that the slaves who were assigned to the bath were already stoking the fires since it was still early, and they did not normally start readying the bath until a watch before the end of our day. I could hardly keep my mind on the conversation, thinking ahead to the feeling of the hot steam softening what felt like the accumulated grime of a hard winter, while I scratched my chin, relishing the knowledge that the beard that had protected my face would be a thing of the past in the very near future. Parting ways at our Cohort street, each of us made our way to our quarters, and I found Alex waiting, whereupon he informed me that he had accomplished his mission, then we began the small ritual of shedding my armor. Alex had barely settled it on the wooden rack when our idle conversation was interrupted by the blast of a *cornu*, but coming from the direction of the Cohort office and not the

Praetorium, sounding the call for all officers to attend to our Pilus Prior.

"Pluto's balls," I grumbled. "Can't a man get a moment to himself?"

"Not if they're a Centurion," Alex said in what sounded to my ears like an obscenely cheerful tone, and when I glared at him, he just grinned as he handed me my *sagum*.

After I took it and draped it over my shoulders, I took a small revenge by snatching up my *vitus* and brandished it in his direction, growling, "I'll deal with you later."

He knew me too well to be intimidated, laughing as he said, "Maybe the Pilus Prior's news is good. Maybe we're getting a bonus from the Princeps!"

I shot him a sour look, then left my quarters, just in time to meet Cornutus, Philus, and Macula, all of whom were in a similar mood.

"This better be good," Macula muttered. "I was just about to head into town."

"Without taking a bath first?" I shook my head in disgust. "How can you stand the itching?"

"Oh, I've got an itch," he countered, giving me a leer, "just not one that a bath will fix."

We were at the Cohort office then, and we entered, where Vespillo was already waiting, but when Lucco indicated that we should go into Macer's quarters, the Pilus Prior actually came out, stopping him.

"This won't take long," he said, but while he did not appear alarmed, or angry for that matter, there was something in his manner that informed me that something important was happening.

We waited just long enough for the Optios, all of whom had been busy making sure the men were settled in and taking note of any complaints about the condition of the huts that had been occupied by strangers.

Once we were all together, Macer said, "I'm going to keep this short. It's not an emergency or anything like that, but I suspect that you all will want to hear what I just learned." As he paused just a moment, I saw his chest rise as he took a breath, then announced, "We have a new Primus Pilus."

Chapter Two

Quintus Valerius Crescens' patience had finally been rewarded by the Princeps, because what we learned from Macer was that he had finally achieved the post he had been coveting for so long, the office of Camp Prefect of the Army of the Rhenus, replacing the fallen Caedicius. Although this was certainly momentous news, as Macer understood, while we all were happy, albeit to varying degrees, to hear that our Primus Pilus had been promoted, of more immediate concern was who had replaced him. In this, at least, for the first time in recent memory, the Princeps, or perhaps Tiberius had been empowered to make the decision, the longstanding tradition of elevating the second in command had been followed, meaning that Tiberius Sacrovir was now our Primus Pilus. Although there was no way to know with any certainty, my opinion at the time was that, given the extraordinary circumstances of the previous months, either Augustus or Tiberius had decided to forego what had become the more common practice of selecting a Primus Pilus from outside of a Legion. More importantly, with the elevation of Sacrovir, it seemed that less attention was paid to the man's political reliability in the eyes of the Princeps than his familiarity with the Legion, and his competence as a Centurion worthy of leading an entire Legion. And, I must stress, Tiberius Sacrovir's reputation alone marked him as worthy of promotion, yet even with this being the case, there was also a fair amount of trepidation with all of us, of every rank. Adjusting to a new Centurion is always something rankers worry about, and when it is either a new Pilus Prior or the Primus Pilus, that worry is extended to any Centurion or Optio who will be under that new man in the chain of command. Not surprisingly, the men of the Second Century of the First Cohort became some of the most popular men in Ubiorum as they were plied with drink, their debauching with whores paid for, or were offered a substitute for some unpleasant duties, whereas for the officers, Sacrovir's former Optio was the only source of information we had. I doubt he passed one off-duty watch sober, nor did he have to touch his coin purse to pay for anything, but while I would have happily been one of those plying him for any scrap of information, Alex actually stopped me.

"You know you don't have to do that," he pointed out when I mentioned I was going out into Ubiorum to the spot where the officers of the First Cohort congregated. "There are going to be plenty of others who are willing to spend their money trying to find out something about Sacrovir. If you're patient, you'll hear it all."

Which was exactly what happened, and it served as another reminder that, as young as he was, Alex was the son of Diocles in every respect. What we learned was that, while Sacrovir could not be characterized as a striper, he was a stern, tough disciplinarian and was especially hard on repeat offenders. He also had a family, consisting of his woman who, not coincidentally, ran the wineshop favored by the First Cohort, three daughters, and a son, who was now an Optio in the Second of the Eighth. His physical appearance was not particularly imposing, being of an average height and a build that was slightly reminiscent of my father's, being more lean than muscular. Whereas Crescens' only visible scar was the missing top of one ear, Sacrovir's right arm bore a puckered scar in the forearm, where it had been pierced by an arrow, and he was missing the tips of the last two fingers of his left hand. The actual promotion had taken place at the beginning of Januarius, but again, since we had been cut off from communication, it was news to the four Cohorts who had spent the winter away from Ubiorum, so rather than repeating the formal ceremony, the day after we returned, our four Cohorts were assembled on the forum and formally introduced to Sacrovir. Honestly, the one notable thing he said only became so after the fact, when he mentioned that he was working on a plan to replace our losses from the plague; this was not considered unusual in the slightest way. Ever since the Princeps had begun the reform of the Legions after Actium, we had become accustomed to being plumped up, usually during the winter months, with *probationes* brought to us by the men who had bid to take on the role that was once filled by the *conquisitores* during my Avus and father's time. The only slight difference was in the timing, although our concern was compounded by the belief that, despite a quiet winter, Arminius and his Germans would be certain to at least try and finish what they started with the slaughter of Varus and his Legions. None of us wanted to be tasked with training *tiros* while conducting an active campaign, and while I understand why Sacrovir came up with this as a solution, it cannot be denied that it was a decision that would create a massive amount of trouble, for all of us.

"He's planning on asking Tiberius for permission to draft from the *dilectus* that Tiberius brought back with him from Rome," Macer informed us.

Looking back, perhaps if we had been back longer and had more time to ask around, we would have heard enough to warn Macer and the other Pili Priores who had been at Novaesium and Vetera that we should resist this alternative. Unfortunately, I was like my fellow Centurions in that I was more worried about being saddled with completely raw *tirones* before going into what we felt certain would be the campaign to avenge Varus and his men, and we knew that these men had at least undergone training. Now, I also will not deny that, even in the relatively short period of time we were back in Ubiorum, we had heard grumbling about the relative quality of these men who had been part of the second *dilectus* the Princeps had called in Rome, but honestly, none of us took that seriously. To our ears, it sounded like the same kind of complaining that Centurions and Optios made about every new batch of recruits who showed up, and it would not be until quite a bit later that we would experience the true consequences of what happens when the dregs of our society are impressed into service. And, by this I mean that, as we would learn to our detriment, the men of what became known as the second emergency *dilectus* were truly at the bottom of the heap of the Head Count, or for a few, equestrians who had run afoul of Augustus in some way. Whereas, with the first complement called for by the Princeps in response to the Batonian revolt, his call for volunteers in response to the Varus disaster had been a total failure, requiring sterner measures. Those measures included essentially cleaning out the slums of the Subura, snatching up men who, up until that moment, had not passed a sober watch in years, ignoring men with obvious deformities who would not normally have been considered, and even worse, enrolling men whose character was so base that they were considered unfit for the Legions. And, as anyone with experience of the men of the Legions can attest, that particular barrier is already very low, which should support my comment about them being the bottom of an amphora that was already drained almost dry. However, as problematic as the men of the Batonian *dilectus* would prove to be in many ways, they were a shade compared to the rotten core of these replacements, and I will cross the river still convinced that they were the real source of the problems that would be confronting us in a matter of a handful of years.

At the time, however, our immediate concern about the qualities of our new replacements were focused on the obvious things our eyes could see.

"Is he really a hunchback?" Structus asked me, his tone expressing the same kind of doubt I felt as he pointed to one of the ten new men I required to fill out my Century. "Surely he's trying to play a joke on us. Isn't he?"

Honestly, I felt torn, because I understood Structus' disbelief, yet I could not summon a reason why a ranker would think that his first meeting with his Centurion and Optio would be the right time for some sort of prank. Also, while this man's affliction was certainly the most noticeable at first glance, I had been examining the others, and he was not the only one who concerned me. There was one man who, while appearing sound in body and was, in fact, almost my size, stood with his mouth hanging open in a slack manner that, coupled with a gaze that appeared as if he was daydreaming of something, concerned me almost as much as the man with the hump. Frankly, there were only two men out of this group who, from outward appearances, gave me no qualms about their ability to carry out their duties as rankers in the Century; I have often thought of this moment, reminding myself of the danger of judging a man based on what the eye can see.

"Somehow," I finally answered Structus with a sigh, "I don't think he is."

These men had been assigned to my Century by Macer, but while I was not happy, I also knew that they had been drawn by lot, and I trusted my Pilus Prior to not do anything underhanded, like trying to select the best men for his own Century, then leave the rest of us to scramble for ourselves. As I quickly learned, this belief was not shared by my fellow Centurions, each of whom were certain that they had been given the worst of the bunch of men who had been sent from Mogontiacum, which was where they were stationed by Tiberius once they had been enrolled back in Rome. That my fellow Centurions all seemed to be equally disgruntled was what I used as proof that Macer had done everything aboveboard and fair in the distribution of these new replacements, and while it did not stop the grumbling, once I pointed this out, it did quell the accusations of Macer playing favorites. Almost as troubling as their physical appearance were their records, a copy of which had been recorded on a wax tablet and sent along with them, under escort of a Century from the 5th Alaudae. On its face, this was understandable; the Varus disaster was barely six months before, the expected attack from Arminius had not come, and while not at the same level, there was still an air of anxiety that permeated every day. Perhaps if one of the Centurions of our Cohorts had been present and watched long enough when our new men arrived, they might have noticed that the Century from the Larks was less about protection than it was about escorting men who, if left to their own devices, would have vanished long before arriving in Mogontiacum. Unfortunately, we were unaware of this reality, although the first hint came when, once the men were assigned to each Century, we Centurions and Optios began the process of integrating these men into our Centuries. And, thanks to the Princeps and his insistence on proper documentation, this starts with studying each man's record. It was Alex who noticed it first as he sat at his desk in the Legion office with a double stack of tablets in front of him.

"How many men did you say we're getting?"

"I already told you," I confess I was a bit irritable from my cursory examination of the new arrivals, "we get ten men, which brings us back up to strength."

Alex did not reply immediately, causing me to turn away from watching Structus inform each man of his new section and where it was located, and when I did, he simply pointed to the twin stacks.

"Then," he said quietly, "why are there fifteen tablets here?"

I should note that, for a man who has served a substantial period of time under the standard, the fact that his record might require more than one tablet is not only not unusual, it is expected. But, as both Alex and I understood, these men had

69

been in the army a matter of months, and I distinctly recall a slight fluttering in my stomach as I walked slowly over to the tablets. Apparently, I stood there for a fair amount of time, staring down at them, and I suppose I was just trying to delay what, in the span of a couple of heartbeats, I was sure would be an unpleasant task.

When Alex cleared his throat, I started, which he cleverly ignored, and he asked, "What do you want me to do, Centurion?"

Sighing, I said, "Start with matching which of those tablets belong to which man. Once you do that, we'll know where to begin as far as knowing which one of these *mentulae* have already managed to fill up more than one tablet."

It did not take long, but while Alex was busy organizing them, I went back to the window to see that Structus was with the last two men to receive their new section assignment, and I thought for a moment of having the Optio stop, then recall those who had already taken their packs in the direction of their new quarters. I discarded that fairly rapidly; convinced as I was that Macer had been scrupulously fair in his allocations, and knowing that the likelihood that the other new men were just as bad was almost a certainty, I realized there was no point.

"Uncle Titus?"

We were alone, so I did not reprimand him for his use of my familial title, walking over to his desk, where I eyed the tablets, now arranged in multiple stacks.

"The good news," Alex informed me, "is that there are actually only four men who have already filled up more than one tablet." He did not need to point those out, since there were indeed four tablets on the desk, upon which another one rested, but it was the stack of three that caught my eye, which Alex noticed. Since he had opened each one and scanned their contents, he handed me the top tablet on this stack, saying, "This is the standard information for Gregarius Publius Atilius Pusio." As I opened it and read its contents, my nephew did the same with the second tablet, informing me, "And this is the list of punishments that have been levied on Gregarius Pusio since he enlisted." Naturally, this got my attention, and when I glanced at him, Alex turned the tablet so that I could see that while it did, in fact, have several lines inscribed in the wax, it was not even close to full, which prompted me to point to the third tablet and ask, "So, what's in that one?"

Alex opened it, and I saw the blood drain from his face, his jaw dropping as he gazed down at the incised lines, which naturally prompted me to lean over and try to get a glimpse of what was written there. But, while I did not see the actual words, the sight of the style of the letters incised in the wax, with their peculiar forward slant, caused my heart to start hammering against my ribs, realizing that the likelihood of two men writing in the same manner was almost nonexistent.

"Dolabella wrote this?" I gasped aloud, and Alex's reaction to my words matched the pallor that had come over his face, telling me that he was no less aware of the author of whatever was in this tablet.

"Do you want me to read it?" Alex asked, but I shook my head, and I am afraid that I may have been a bit abrupt in the manner in which I snatched it from his hand, though my motive was pure; I did not want him possibly tainted by whatever the spymaster who worked for either Augustus, Tiberius, or more to my way of thinking, both of them, had attached to this man Pusio's record.

"No." I tried to keep my voice level. "There's no need. I'm going to take this into my quarters to read. You," I pointed back to the stacks that contained more than one tablet, "look at those and let me know if there's anything I need to be worried about." As I turned and headed to my room, I could not stop myself from adding, "Besides this."

As such things went, the information contained in Pusio's record as compiled by Dolabella was more or less the same kind of thing that he compiled on a number of men that I had seen during the years I had been one of Tiberius' men. What made it unusual was that I had never seen this amount or type of information attached to the record of a Gregarius, particularly one who was barely more than a *Tirone* and had only been under the standard for a matter of months. And, while I was not surprised, I was somewhat dismayed to see that Dolabella had not included the reason why this Pusio had earned the scrutiny of Tiberius' spymaster. I read the account twice, trying to find some sort of underlying message that might give me an idea of why he was worthy of such suspicion, before I realized that perhaps the answer was not as much in Pusio's actions but who he was, or more likely, to whom he was connected. Before I made that determination, I summoned Alex, telling him to bring me the other tablets for Pusio, and it was with some chagrin I realized that if I had read the entries into Pusio's record first, Dolabella's observations would have made more sense. Reading the report quickly, which is an arcane skill in itself given our practice of abbreviating most commonly used words, once I did, matters made more sense.

"It seems," was how I put it to Alex, "we have a budding demagogue in our Century."

Since Alex had already read Pusio's record, his response was in the form of a grim nod, and despite his youth, I felt a sense of gratification that his assessment matched mine. As far as Pusio was concerned, the reason why he had come to the attention of Dolabella was now clear to me; on no less than four occasions, he had been disciplined not for any kind of normal infraction, like reporting late for a duty or losing a piece of gear, but for urging his comrades to be more vocal about claiming their rights as Roman citizens. Specifically, he insisted that, because he and his other comrades had been part of an emergency *dilectus*, there was no requirement for them to spend sixteen years under the standard. Even as I read this, I confess I felt a grim smile tugging at my lips as I wondered how Pusio would react if he knew that, because of the Varus disaster, one of Augustus' measures had been to extend enlistments to twenty years, something that had been rumored to be coming for many years. Varus' demise had given the Princeps the pretext for doing so, yet I had already heard that this was a compromise measure that, according to Dolabella, Tiberius had managed to persuade him to take, rather than the twenty-five years Augustus now wanted. If I am being honest, I cannot say that I was not at least somewhat sympathetic to Pusio's complaint; it did strike me as unjust that men who had been essentially forced into service would then be required to serve a full enlistment. However, I had heard nothing to suggest that these men were not aware of this, and even if they were, by this time, they had been in long enough to know that things like justice and fairness of treatment are in short supply for men like us.

"All right," I thought for a moment, then decided, "we're putting this Pusio character in Pictor's section."

That Alex did not seem surprised told me he had assumed as much, and he gave me a grin as he offered, "Pictor's not going to love you for that."

This was certainly true, but I also knew that I could count on Pictor to keep this Pusio on a short tether, and if the man did display the kind of behavior listed in his record, I could think of no better man than Pictor to take care of it in a manner that, frankly, saved my *vitus* the wear and tear, if one takes my meaning. With Pusio's immediate fate decided, we went through the rest of the troublemakers' records, and ironically, I was actually relieved to see that these men were more in the nature of shirkers, malingerers, and one of them was clearly a man who loved his wine to the point it had gotten him into trouble. Even without matching names to records, I was certain I knew which man this was, just from his appearance when they were standing in front of the Century office, which was why when, after my visual inspection, I had ordered Structus to put him in the Tenth Section. My reasoning was straightforward, since the Sergeant of this section was known as a man who despised those who worshiped Bacchus a little too fervently, having something to do with the Sergeant's father being one of those from what I had heard, although I never asked. Otherwise, only Pusio was not going to the section Structus had designated for him, and I sent Alex to inform my Optio while I finished familiarizing myself with the rest of the records belonging to the new men of the Third Century. Like every other officer in the Legion, I felt a sense of urgency in getting these replacements settled in as quickly as possible, certain that we would be marching out of Ubiorum in a matter of weeks. When Alex returned, it was with Structus, whose normally saturnine expression was gone, replaced with a look of, if I was judging correctly, satisfaction. I also noticed he was out of breath, which meant that Alex, after glancing at the Optio, who gave him a curt nod as he regained his wind, was only too happy to tell me what had transpired.

With a grin, my nephew informed me, "Apparently, Gregarius Pusio was…unhappy at being moved from the Second Section to the Fifth."

Structus had caught his breath by this time, because he interjected with a sour laugh, "Unhappy? That's a nice way of putting it. The bastard had just emptied his pack on his bunk when Alex found me and told me he was going to Pictor's section." Shaking his head with what I took to be mild disbelief, he continued, "And he refused to repack his things. He said he had been assigned to the Second Section, and that was where he planned on staying."

This was so unusual that I was suspicious that my nephew and Optio had decided to make this into some sort of joke, although when I thought about it immediately afterward, I could not only not think of a good reason why they would do so, I could not fathom how this could be turned into a source of amusement.

But, when I looked over at Alex, he assured me, "He's telling the truth. I was standing there when Pusio said it. And then he…"

"This is my story, boy, let me tell it," Structus growled, though not with any rancor. In his own way, Structus was as fond of Alex as I was, which was why my nephew rolled his eyes as he made a gesture that Structus continue this tale that was at least something to break the monotony of life in garrison. "Then," the Optio continued, "the bastard sat down on his bunk and said he wasn't going anywhere!"

Before I could stop myself, I laughed, more at the indignation of Structus than the idea that I countenanced this kind of blatant defiance.

"So?" I asked.

"So," Structus tapped his turfcutter handle dangling from his *baltea*, "I thrashed the *cunnus*, and I thrashed him good."

Glancing at Alex, I saw that this time he was not smiling, just giving me a grim nod; even when a man deserves it, there is nothing pleasant about seeing him getting beaten. At least, not to most men.

I was struck by a thought. "Please don't tell me that he's…"

"No," Structus cut me off, somewhat indignant. "I didn't do anything that will give him an excuse to report on the sick and injured list."

Honestly, I was not overly concerned about this, but given this Pusio's actions in the brief period of time he had been in my Century, I wanted to make sure.

"Where is he now?" I asked, and this made Structus grin.

"Where do you think? He's with Pictor. Now," he allowed, "he might be moving a bit slower than you might like, Centurion. But he's where he belongs."

Despite this good news, I suspected that, while this would be the first, it would not be the last conversation about Publius Pusio we would be having.

The one consolation I can take in how wrong I was about our prospects for a busy campaign season is that so was everyone else. Days, then weeks passed, yet despite being kept on a high alert, with the word from the *Praetorium* that we were simply awaiting orders to march, that word never came. Indeed, the entire year passed without any Roman Legion, or subunit for that matter, crossing the Rhenus, and our activities were devoted solely to construction projects, although we also maintained our normal training schedule. As part of the latter, in my role as weapons trainer for not just the Century but the Fourth Cohort, every one of the replacements faced me with a *rudis*; most of them only had to do so once, because it had become something of an initiation into the Fourth that they face me. And, at the request of their Centurions, a half-dozen of them were forced into the square, the boundaries of which were formed by their comrades, two times, while one recalcitrant in Macer's Century suffered at my hands on three separate occasions. However, the record holder was one Publius Pusio, who achieved the dubious honor of facing me on a total of five occasions, but what made this even more unusual was that two of those times was at his "request," in the sense that he challenged me to face him. Why he did so is still a mystery, because, frankly, he was not very good with a *rudis*, although he was not the worst man in my Century. Even so, after our first bout, which I confess I prolonged a bit because of the trouble he had been causing for Pictor, and by extension Structus and me, it was clear he was not ever going to be a threat to defeat me. Nevertheless, on two separate occasions, at the end of our time at the stakes, Pusio stepped forward with a *rudis* in his hand, the normal procedure for letting me know someone wanted to face me. That there was

76

now a purse of three hundred *sesterces* that would go to the man who defeated me had proven to be a temptation to other men in the past, but they were all vastly more skilled than Pusio, and I had not heard that he had a gambling habit that had put him in debt. It would not be until much later that I learned what Pusio was up to, and given all that transpired, as much as I despise the man to this day, I must salute him for his cunning. At the time, while I was slightly mystified why he put himself through this torment, given the amount of trouble he was causing Pictor, I was more than happy to oblige him in whatever he was seeking. On more than one occasion, I considered moving Pusio yet again, because the type of trouble he was causing was not the usual sort; it turned out that Pusio was a very, very clever man and, from somewhere, he had gotten hold of a copy of all the various regulations that have steadily grown since the time of my Avus. And, worst of all, he had studied them carefully, particularly the parts where certain rights that are accorded all Roman citizens have been subordinated for the good of the Legions, but are still technically in place. Specifically, even rankers are afforded the right to appeal every punishment that is substantial enough to be recorded in the Century diary, which is turned in to the Cohort, whereupon from there, that list is combined with the other Centuries, then sent to the Legion office. One reason that the Primus Pilus has no less than five clerks is because of this requirement, since there are three copies made of what becomes the daily report; one is kept with the Legion, another goes to the *Praetorium* of the camp where the Legion is stationed, and one is sent to Rome, although this only occurs on a monthly basis. Such is the Princeps' belief in proper record keeping, but as any man who has spent more than a few months under the standard knows, the Legion that is represented in the official record and the actual, real workings of it are vastly different, and one of the largest discrepancies concern the supposed rights a Legionary has to appeal any official punishment. As men learn very quickly, not only does this serve to antagonize their Optio or Centurion even further, because it requires more tablet work, but the chances are next to nothing that an Optio or Centurion's decision will be overturned by his superior. Unfortunately, another reform by Augustus also gives a man the right to appeal that decision all the way up the chain of command to the Princeps himself, which means that it is either a supremely desperate or stupid man who is willing to endure the consequences if the Princeps denies his appeal. Put in its simplest terms, if matters reached this point, the flogging that the ranker was facing will almost certainly become so much more severe that their chance of living through the punishment is nonexistent. Which is why, to my memory, I never recall any ranker being that mulishly persistent, but Pusio certainly came close.

We learned very quickly that Pusio was not only literate, he was extraordinarily well educated for a man of the ranks, although he was not quite up to my standard, but I had learned very early on that, if any man did have a tutor like Diocles, as Sextus and I, they were wise enough never to mention it. Neither did either my brother or I, for that matter, but our family name practically guaranteed that there was no way for us to keep that secret. In the case of Publius Pusio, I had learned from Dolabella's report that Pusio was connected to one Lucius Seius Strabo, Pusio's father being a client and trusted friend. He was an equestrian, which explained much about the man, both in his attitude and his level of education, but what was something of a mystery was how he had run afoul of the Princeps and ended up being essentially forced into the ranks instead of being allowed to at least be an Optio. While this was never confirmed, I do think that Dolabella guessed correctly, that Pusio was one of the men who Augustus decided to make an example of, when there was such a paltry response to the second *dilectus*. If the rumors were true, despite appearances to the contrary, and I am sure how

Pusio felt about it, he had been luckier than some of the men the Princeps had executed as an example to the recalcitrant citizens who did not answer the call. The problem was that, since Pusio could not lash out at Augustus, he fought back in a manner that was at least unique, using and twisting the written regulations to make us, his officers, starting with Pictor and ending with Sacrovir, miserable. Within the span of two months after his arrival, I found myself having my first private meeting with Tiberius Sacrovir to discuss Gregarius Pusio, and it was illuminating and disturbing in equal measure.

"It appears," the new Primus Pilus began our meeting, "that we have a problem, Pullus."

"Yes, Primus Pilus," I heartily agreed, and I confess I was hoping to hear from him that he had a solution, "we do."

The meeting began routinely enough, despite the unusual subject, with me reporting to him as he was seated behind his desk, but once salutes were exchanged, he had gotten up from his desk and waved me to a seat at a table where I presumed he took his meals. Now we were seated across from each other, each holding a cup of wine that I asked to be watered more than usual, which he clearly noticed with a slight smile, but made no comment as the slave did as I requested. Sacrovir had brought what I assumed was Pusio's latest appeal, this one complaining about the monetary fine he had been assessed by me for the loss of a *baltea* strap. Sacrovir sipped from his cup as he perused the tablet containing Pusio's appeal, which Macer had, of course, denied, deeming that the three *sesterces* I had assessed was a fair and just punishment.

"What Gregarius Pusio is claiming is that he had lent the strap to another Gregarius in his section, which his comrade confirmed when this Pictor conducted a routine inspection?"

While I was unsure why Sacrovir posed this as a question, since I was sure he knew the reason, I affirmed that this was the bare bones of the matter.

79

"So," Sacrovir asked mildly, "why did you fine him?"

"Because, Primus Pilus," I answered frankly, "Pusio has turned into a disruptive element in my Century, and he's begun to encourage other men to follow his example."

Sacrovir seemed unsurprised at this, since he nodded his head thoughtfully, but I was completely unprepared for what came out of his mouth next.

"Given that the strap wasn't actually lost, don't you think that the fine is...excessive?"

Honestly, I was too shocked to answer immediately; it had never occurred to me that the Primus Pilus would be anything but completely supportive of one of his Centurions, but I did manage to point out, "Primus Pilus, I actually checked the regulations, because that's what that *cun*...Gregarius Pusio has been using against us, and what it says is that," I recited from memory, "'any item that has been issued to a Gregarius from the *Quaestorium* that cannot be produced on inspection is to be considered as lost, and the Gregarius punished accordingly for this loss.'"

"I'm aware of what the regulation says, Princeps Prior," Sacrovir replied icily, and he sat back as his lips compressed tightly enough that the blood seemed to disappear. He glared at me for a moment, then he relaxed, his expression returning to what it had been a moment before, sighing as he said, "Pullus, I understand what you're doing. You're proving to Pusio that the regulations can work two ways, and that he's in a position where, no matter what he tries, he'll always lose if he tries to buck the system." Sensing that he wanted something from me, I only nodded, which prompted him to continue, "And, under normal circumstances, I would agree with your approach." He paused for a moment, but when he resumed, I heard a caution in his tone that I was not sure whether it was meant for me or he was choosing his words carefully for some other reason. "But these aren't normal circumstances. Would you agree with that, Pullus?"

"I would," I answered no less cautiously, wondering what we were speaking of exactly; I assumed it was because we had yet to respond to Arminius, but I also recognized there could be something else at play.

"Given that you agree," Sacrovir continued, "then you shouldn't be that surprised when I tell you that I'm granting Pusio's appeal. Not," he held up a hand, clearly seeing my mouth open, "because I think he's right, Pullus. I don't. But there are several factors to consider here. What," Sacrovir suddenly seemingly switched subjects, "have you heard from your friends in Pannonia?"

I confess I was somewhat proud of myself because, while he caught me by surprise, I quickly determined why he had brought it up, or thought I did, so I answered, "That there's a lot of discontent about the extension of enlistments."

"And," Sacrovir asked, "is that any different than it is here?"

"No," I admitted reluctantly, "not really."

"And that's why I've decided that appeasing this Pusio is in the best interests of the Legion."

"But, Primus Pilus," I protested, "isn't that actually going to make matters worse?"

"Yes," he agreed, or seemed to, but then he added, "for you. It will. But I also know who you are, Pullus. And," with this, he rose and walked back to his desk, then pointed to a double stack of tablets that I had barely noticed before, "Pusio is just one of many problems that we're facing right now. And, frankly, he's the least of my concerns when it comes to discipline. There are men throughout the Legion; good, solid veterans, every one of them, who are becoming angrier by the day, and I have to think of a way to keep that anger contained until we can go out on campaign, because you know as well as I do that nothing will take the edge off of all that anger like a good, hard fight."

I sat there, considering his words, yet, while I did see his overall point, I could not agree with it. Regardless of this, I elected not to say anything, mainly because I did not know Sacrovir well enough, other than by his reputation and what I had observed in the months since he had been made Primus Pilus. At the moment, I was actually quite happy with myself for deciding to accept this loss with as much grace as I could, although it did leave a bitter taste in my mouth at the thought of having to refund Pusio his five *sesterces*. And, I confess, there was an element of calculation in my acquiescence, thinking that it might put me in Sacrovir's good graces in the future.

"I understand, Primus Pilus," was what came out of my mouth, "and I'll do whatever you need me to do."

"Thank you, Pullus." Sacrovir actually seemed relieved, and it gave me a glimpse into the strain he must have been feeling, trying to keep a lid on the boiling pot that was our Legion. "I appreciate this, and when the moment's right, I promise, I will back you on whatever you deem necessary with this Gregarius. Now is just not the right time."

With that, I was dismissed, and as I walked back to my quarters, I decided that this was one time I was going to delegate a task and have Structus hand the money back to Pusio; I was afraid that if the man smirked or in some way expressed any kind of satisfaction, I would be unable to control myself. The reason I bring this episode up is that, first, as I had learned from Sacrovir, Pusio was just one of many men in the Legion causing trouble, and in hindsight, while many faulted not just Sacrovir but the Primi Pili of every Legion involved in what was to come, I now honestly believe that if they had cracked down earlier, it would have only accelerated events.

Despite the simmering discontent, that entire year passed without any bloodshed, either against an enemy or within our own ranks, although there were more than the usual number of brawls out in the town. Speaking of the town, the original populace had returned, but in yet another example of how quickly people forget, by the end of the next year after the Varus disaster, the town had grown even larger. Perhaps even more tellingly, the construction of more permanent brick structures had begun taking place, almost exclusively by the merchants who supplied the army, it must be said, but it was a stark contrast to the mood in the months after Varus. More than likely, it had less to do with a lifting of spirits than it did the reassignment of the 20th Legion from Dalmatia to our camp in Ubiorum. Not surprisingly, the Varus disaster had forced there to be some shuffling of the Legions from one army to another, as the14th was sent from Pannonia and now was stationed in Vetera, along with the 21st Legion, which had been sent to Mogontiacum early on to serve with the 5th, that reassignment being made permanent.

It was not until the year of the consulship of Marcus Aemilius and Statilius Taurus that, finally, Tiberius arrived in Mogontiacum with the express purpose of waging a campaign against the Germans. He did not come alone; Germanicus came with him, but in the status of a *Proconsul*. This was unusual, although not unprecedented, but usually *Proconsular* status is only conferred on those who have served as Consul at least once. While I certainly welcomed having my former commander from my time with the *Legio Germanicus* now three years earlier attached to the army, of more immediate concern to me, and to every other man, was how large our force was going to be. Before Varus, an army composed of three Legions marching on campaign would have been considered more than sufficient to handle anything any barbarians could have thrown at us; now, with four Legions slated to march, men were still decidedly

83

nervous, and I include many of the officers. Despite this, our preparations went smoothly enough, including the 1st being sent north to Vetera, which was going to be our launching point for the campaign. Starting on the Kalends of March, elements of the Army of the Rhenus began migrating from their normal stations, and we marched for Vetera while there was still a fair amount of snow on the ground. This time, however, we did not have to struggle along a rutted, muddy track; this had been one of our construction projects the previous year, and while it was not a truly Roman road like the Via Appia, it had been graded all the way to Novaesium, with adequate drainage and partially paved with gravel that had been hauled from somewhere. Not only did this mean that men were not forced to heave our wagons, of which we had an even larger complement since we were hauling the supplies for the entire campaign, out of ruts, our progress was much faster than the previous time. Reaching Novaesium, we were greeted by the same size force of auxiliaries, although from a different levy than the last time we had been there, but what was not lost on any of us was that there had been virtually no improvements made to the living conditions of the men in the intervening time, something that Sentius told us he brought up in his report back from our winter spent there. The only visible change was that there was now a wooden wall, with towers and reinforced gate; otherwise, their situation remained unchanged, and I believe that, for the men of the Cohorts who had been forced to winter there, there was a feeling of sympathy, and somewhat to my surprise, a little anger.

"I know they're not citizens, but you can be sure that Tiberius' horse has it better than those poor bastards."

This comment had come from Structus, and while I did not reply, I agreed, albeit silently. Because it was the entire Legion, we made camp outside the walls, then moved on the next day, which also meant that we reached the end of our road improvements and were back to the same rutted track.

Fortunately, the temperatures had held enough that the melt happened gradually, so while the track was soggy, it certainly was not as bad as it could have been. Not that one could tell from the complaining of the men marching rearguard, and when we made camp that night, I will say that they were every bit as filthy from the time spent behind an even larger baggage train than normal. Of course, this meant that the last day's march would find the men of the Fourth Cohort slogging behind the last wagon, reaching Vetera covered in muck. It was the first time for all but the Fifth Cohort to come to Vetera, which had been the base of operations for Varus and the vanquished Legions, but was now occupied by another five Cohorts of auxiliaries. The difference between Novaesium and Vetera, however, could not have been more dramatic, and served as a reminder that, when a man of Legate rank has the favor and trust of the Princeps, no expense will be spared in ensuring that not only the fortifications but the accommodations will be exemplary, although the former had deteriorated somewhat, which had been beyond the capabilities of the auxiliaries to repair on their own. Most importantly, the camp was even larger than Ubiorum, because from the beginning, it had been constructed for a three Legion army, and as Sacrovir pointed out, since we were the first there, we naturally had the choice of where to settle in to wait for the rest of the army. This meant expelling the auxiliaries from the street nearest the *Praetorium*, which was done with a bit of squabbling from their commanding Centurion, but by the end of the day, the 1st was quartered, and smoke was rising from the chimneys of the huts as the evening meal was prepared. While our Optios took care of these details, Sacrovir summoned the Centurions to discuss our orders.

"I'm sure most of you noticed that there need to be some repairs made to the camp," he had begun, "and we're going to make them while we're waiting. That should keep the men busy enough to stay out of trouble."

Like every Centurion, I was all for anything that kept men occupied, especially when they are vibrating with tension from the thought that they would likely be in battle in the near future, but the one thing that Vetera was missing was a town outside its walls, at least of a size that could come close to accommodating an entire Legion, so I was not altogether sure this was the real reason. In my mind, it was more likely that Sacrovir was trying to show some initiative that Tiberius would recognize, appreciate, and I am sure, reward in some manner. Since this would benefit the Legion by extension, I certainly did not begrudge the idea that the men would be kept busy, although I did not think it would occupy an entire Legion, but Sacrovir had thought of this as well.

"The odd-numbered Cohorts are going to be working on repairing the camp, and the even-numbered Cohorts are going to either repair or replace the bridge boats and the cables holding them together."

Now, I was not quite so happy, and I saw that Macer and the other Pili Priores of this second group shared my feeling. The task we had been assigned was straightforward enough, but the complication was twofold; the first was that there was still ice in the river, and men would inevitably be getting wet and muddy. The second, and most concerning, was that the riverbank was within bow shot of the opposite side. Across from Ubiorum, we had long since cleared the opposite bank of any vegetation that could provide cover, and our forays for gathering wood meant that there was no cover of any sort for more than a mile. Here, however, Varus had only seen fit to have his pioneers clear a swathe of perhaps three hundred paces in an arc, the center of which being where the pilings that moored the other end of the boat bridge when it was extended across the river were located. The trees had been felled in a wider semicircle, but the undergrowth had not been cleared for more than a year, and small vegetation in that part of the world grows so quickly that it was impossible to tell if it had ever been cleared in the first place. What this meant in a practical sense was that we would have to have at least one Century standing ready with their shields, prepared to provide cover in the event some Germans could not resist the temptation of a Roman working party. Complicating matters even further was that, after discussing it amongst the Pili Priores, it was decided that the men who would be forced to work near the river could not afford to wear their armor. Between the slippery bank and the current that was running even more swiftly than at Ubiorum as the Rhenus neared the sea, any man who lost his footing and went in would be swept away so quickly, dragged under by their armor, or both, and would be lost before any of his comrades could help. Nevertheless, we had been given our orders, and we began work the next morning, preparing for the rest of the army to arrive.

While our work did not go unobserved, we were not beset by a shower of missiles as we had feared, but almost from the first watch, we saw Germans, who were making no attempt to hide themselves as they watched us work. That was all they did, however, watch us, although we never let our guard down. Judging from the colors of their tunics and style of their hair, they were of more than one tribe; at least the Tencteri and Sugambri were identified, although several men claimed they saw other warriors wearing the Marsi colors. All that mattered to us as Centurions was that they did not attempt to make any mischief, but neither was it lost on us that those tribes not only occupied the lands immediately across from where we were working, they were part of Arminius' confederation of tribes. Speaking of the German chieftain, during this period of quiet, we had learned more about why Arminius and his hordes had not crossed the Rhenus and swept us aside, or even attempted to do so. Much in the manner my Avus had faced when marching for Divus Julius, the most potent aid to Rome's cause were the barbarians themselves, and over the previous eighteen months after the disaster, Arminius had been forced to consolidate his position of leadership over the tribes. To someone like me, who had read not just my Avus' account, but that of Divus Julius, it was eerily reminiscent of the challenges faced by Vercingetorix, who, before Arminius, almost conquered us and was regarded with a level of respect for a barbarian who had proven to be Rome's most dangerous foe since Hannibal. Like his Gallic predecessor, Arminius had been beset by tribal jealousies and rivalries that ran back for countless generations, particularly by a faction led by Segestes, who we had learned after the fact had tried to warn Varus that Arminius was plotting against him. And, to the ultimate dishonor of Rome, Varus had not listened to him, supposedly because he fancied that, since Arminius had spent time as a hostage and had been well treated, he was the true friend of Rome and not Segestes. Now, if the rumors were true, Arminius had faced a challenge from Segestes, the former arguing to finish the job he had started, and the latter that continuing to war against Rome would lead to their ultimate destruction. I took it as a sign that there were cooler heads among the chieftains of the other tribes that at least made it difficult for Arminius to carry the question, or, more likely in my mind, those chieftains were jealous at the idea of a Cherusci commanding them. Whatever the true cause, I know I was not alone in being thankful that their internal troubles had given the Princeps and Tiberius the opportunity to shift Legions to the Rhenus. The immediate danger was now past us, but I know that I was not alone in the feeling that the state of near panic that had been so pervasive with all of us, of every rank, was still fresh in our collective memories. No man, at least no man who claims to be a warrior, likes being scared almost out of their wits, and the memory of those days following word of the disaster served as a powerful goad to all of us, making our jobs as Centurions to ensure the men remained alert an easy task.

We managed to finish the repairs on the boats without losing anyone, but several men, including two from my Century, did slip and fall into the river. They were fished out quickly enough, but the water was still frigidly cold, while the temperature of the air was only slightly above freezing, and almost every one of the unfortunates caught cold and had to be put on the sick and injured list. A few days later, I heard that at least two men had died as a result, but since they were not from my Century, it was only a matter of passing interest. Three weeks after we arrived at Vetera, the *Bucinator* on duty sounded the call that there was a force approaching. As it happened, I had my Century at the stakes outside the camp, but they were on the northern side, so it was not until we were finished and returned to our area that we saw the rest of the army arriving. Since the 1st had chosen the best spot, putting us closest to the forum, I was marching the Century down the edge to our area when I heard someone call my name from the direction of the *Praetorium*. Turning, I saw none other than Germanicus, who was still mounted but had turned his horse and come trotting towards me, a grin on his handsome features that I returned. Ordering Structus to take over, I strode in his direction, meeting him just as he slid from his horse, offering a salute, which he returned, but with a laugh, then thrust out his arm, which I took.

"Well, Pullus, it's been a while," he said, then with a mock frown, he made a show of examining me, then added, "but you've clearly been loafing."

While I was certain he was jesting, I was puzzled enough to ask, "What makes you say that, sir?"

"Because you don't have any more scars than the last time I saw you!" As I am sure he intended, this did make me laugh, somewhat ruefully, then he pointed down to my knees, commenting, "Those are some ugly knees, Pullus." Glancing up, I saw he was actually serious, and he asked with some concern,

"Are those scars as painful as they look? It must hurt to bend your knees."

"Sometimes," I admitted, "but it's not that bad."

There followed a brief silence, and I am sure our thoughts were aligned, remembering the night assault we had made on Splonum, when I had been knocked to my knees, directly on top of smoldering coals from the fire we had used to affect a breach in the wooden wall. It had been an excruciating span of several heartbeats, and standing there with Germanicus, I could distinctly recall not only the agony of the moment, but the smell of roasting flesh as Germanicus saved my life by forcing me to stay kneeling long enough for him to dispatch the barbarians trying to put an end to me.

"Yes," he broke the silence, "well, now we're about to start on another adventure, neh?"

"'Adventure'?" I gave him an amused look, and given our relationship, I felt it was appropriate for me to tease him back a bit. "I see you still have all that boyish enthusiasm."

As I had hoped, now it was his turn to laugh, admitting cheerfully, "What can I say? I developed a taste for it."

"You certainly did," I agreed. I was slightly concerned I was about to sour the pleasant mood, but I felt compelled to ask, "I take it you've forgiven me for abandoning you before the job was done?"

To my relief, Germanicus seemed genuinely surprised at my concern, assuring me, "There was nothing to forgive, Pullus. I completely understood. And," his still boyish features turned grim as he added, "if I had been smart, I would have figured out a way to get out of Pannonia myself." As he shook his head, his mouth twisted into a grimace. "It was ugly, Pullus. Very, very ugly. Those Pannonian tribes just didn't know when they were beaten, and we had to do some...things that I know we'll have to answer for in the future." Although I had heard as much from Domitius, in one of his rare letters, I decided to remain silent, and he said something that I had cause to remember later, even if in the moment, he said it as more of an afterthought. "It was especially hard on the Legions down there, and I don't know that they'll ever get over it. And," he finished with a sad smile, "I know they blame me and my father for making them do the things they did."

Realizing that this was heading into dangerous waters, I decided to change the subject, albeit awkwardly, saying, "Well, now we have to teach these Germans a lesson, neh?"

"Yes," he answered with a firm nod of his head, "we do. And we will."

Suddenly, another voice called out, this one for Germanicus, and we both turned to see one of the clerks standing on the porch of the *Praetorium*.

Sighing, Germanicus said ruefully, "I suspect I know what that's about. My father is chomping at the bit to get across the river, and we have more plans to make." Clasping arms once more, Germanicus led his horse away, then called over his shoulder, "I'm sure we'll run into each other across the river." Then, with a laugh, he added, "I'll try to stay out of trouble, but if I need you, I'll be calling for you!"

"And," I assured him, "I'll be there."

We ended up spending another week at Vetera, waiting for the final train of supplies that would be left at the camp, guarded by the auxiliaries, waiting to be sent to wherever the army was located across the Rhenus. Then, the auspices were taken, the augurs pronouncing the omens favorable, as we all knew they would, and the process of crossing the Rhenus began. Two boats were rowed across the river first, trailing smaller ropes that were attached to the larger cables, while the Batavians, led by my friend Gaesorix, swam their horses across to provide security. Once across, large wooden pulleys were attached to the pilings, the smaller ropes threaded through them, then the team of men

91

assigned to the task began heaving the cables across. When this was done, the mounts of a half-dozen troopers were used to haul on the cables, taking out the slack before the line of boats began moving across the river. This had to be done slowly, and it was hard work even for the horses, especially cavalry mounts that were not accustomed to being used as draft animals. Because the current is so strong at Vetera, care had to be taken not to pull the boats so quickly that the end facing upriver dipped down enough to swamp even one of the twelve boats since that extra resistance would likely be enough to snap one or both ropes that are as big around as my wrist. Then, once the boats were safely pulled across, the cables pulled taut and secured to the pilings, the *immunes* attached to the *Praefectus Fabrorum* and woodworkers, along with a few dozen slaves, laid the planks that would serve as the surface of the bridge atop the boats, lashing them securely to the series of spikes that had been driven into the gunwales and sides of each boat. It is a process I had seen several times, but every time, I found myself watching with a combination of interest and pride, knowing that there is no nation, let alone barbarian tribe, that can operate with such efficiency.

A full watch after it began, the bridge was deemed safe enough to cross, and once more, we had to deal with the somewhat treacherous footing caused by the rippling movement of the boats from the men crossing before us. Fortunately, this time, the entire army made it across without one man pitching into the water, something that was instantly pronounced as a good omen by the more pious, or superstitious, among us. The 14th was leading the way on this day, while we were second in the column, directly behind the officers and all their attendants and bodyguards, with the 20th behind us and the 2nd with the unpleasant duty of marching behind the baggage train. Our normal practice when crossing the Rhenus was that the first day on the march was spent with the men allowed to wear just their tunics and *bracae*, which had become standard issue for the entire year for the Legions of Germania. When we were down in Ubiorum, this might be extended to even the next day, simply because our control of the eastern bank extended more than twenty miles, mainly because it was the Usipetes now occupying that strip of land. This, however, was not a normal day, not just because of the reason for the campaign and the aforementioned issue with the amount of cover, but the tribe to whom this land belonged was part of the confederation of Arminius, meaning we were in armor from the first day. Since it takes so long for an army of four Legions and all its baggage to cross on a bridge made of boats that is only wide enough for one wagon at a time, we made it only ten miles deep into Sugambri territory. Because of the size, our camp was not finished until shortly after dark, which was exacerbated by the days ending earlier in spring, and because Tiberius deemed it prudent to put an entire Legion on guard while the other three worked. In what would become a pattern, the Legion who had marched drag, the 2nd, got to stand watch, and it was no longer cold enough that their lack of movement did not equate to shivering and numbed extremities. Honestly, it was one of those ideas that, when Tiberius introduced it, I know that I was not alone in wondering why this had not been thought of earlier, if only for relative peace and quiet from the complaining that inevitably came from both marching drag and then having to construct camp. Also, two Centuries were sent out to chop the necessary wood for the towers instead of one, while the same held for the party gathering wood for fires. Nobody was surprised when those Centuries came back and reported they had spotted movement around them that was not that of animals, although it was no more than a fleeting glimpse. The Fourth was assigned watch once camp was finished, and as I had experienced in my first campaign across the Rhenus, it had only been dark for perhaps two parts of a watch when the wolves began to howl. This was something to which I had grown, if not accustomed, then inured to somewhat, but it was the crashing in the undergrowth that I knew from experience was meant to be heard by our sentries. Thankfully, my men, along with the rest of the Fourth, were mostly veterans, and the new replacements were always paired with a man who knew not to waste javelins; more importantly, they knew not to sound the alarm, since this was what the Germans intended. We all knew that it was not their intent to attack a fortified camp; say what one will about Varus and his incompetence, but they had been ambushed on the march, and when Camp Prefect Caedicius managed to gather enough men to escape the site of the battle and make it to the abandoned camp, they held out for a few weeks. All these Germans outside the camp hoped to accomplish was to rattle us, perhaps force a panicked sentry to sound the alarm that would then rouse the entire army. Thankfully, that did not happen when we were standing watch, and the night passed peacefully.

Within a matter of a week, it became clear that, rather than stand and fight us, Arminius had decided the time was not right for another offensive action. However, what became equally clear, and was a bit disconcerting, was that neither did Tiberius seem anxious to hunt down and close with Arminius and his army. Instead, he appeared content with what was essentially nothing more than a show of force that took us from one village to the next, where we put everything to the torch. Adding to the unusual atmosphere was that, since it is impossible to move an army of four Legions with stealth, none of the villages were occupied when we arrived. On a couple of occasions, there was still smoke rising through the holes in the roof of some of the huts, but there was no sign of people, or animals for that matter, all of them retreating into the surrounding forest. For a short time, there was a rumor going around that Tiberius was waiting to send us out to hunt the villagers down, although nobody could come up with a reason why he would do so. Naturally, this did not mean that men did not try, and this became the predominant topic of conversation, both around section fires and among the officers.

"I think when we get to the Marsi lands, he's going to set us loose," Vespillo offered one night when we were meeting in Macer's tent. "We all know they were part of Arminius' bunch."

"But so were the Sugambri," Philus objected, which was true enough. "So why are we not doing anything now?"

"We aren't 'not doing anything'," Macer said. "We're torching their villages."

"Yes, but you know what I mean," Philus persisted. "These *cunni* owe a blood debt, and it's almost been two years since Varus."

Frankly, I had nothing much to contribute, except my fellow Centurions did not think so, all of them assuming that, since I had served with Germanicus, I possessed some sort of inside information, but aside from that conversation on the day of his arrival, we had exchanged hardly a word. If these men had known that, while I served under Germanicus, I actually worked for Tiberius, I can only imagine what their reaction would have been.

Of course, this meant that Cornutus turned to me with a raised eyebrow, which I had learned meant he was about to ask a question, but hoped whoever it was aimed at would divine his meaning just from that expression, he being a man who hated any kind of controversy or awkward situation.

When I refused to acknowledge his silent plea, he heaved a sigh, then asked, "Well, Pullus? What does Germanicus say?"

"Say?" I replied. "About what?"

"Pluto's balls." Vespillo was the one who growled this, snapping irritably, "You know what! What's Tiberius waiting for? Surely he said something to you. You were his Primus Pilus for, what, a year?"

"Close enough," I admitted, yet even if I had actually talked to Germanicus, I would not have divulged whatever he might have told me, not as much because I did not want to betray his confidence, although that was certainly a consideration, but if I did so, the questions would never stop. "But he hasn't told me anything, because we haven't talked since the day he arrived."

"Then," Cornutus said hopefully, "maybe you could go to the *praetorium* on some errand, and while you're there…"

"I'm not doing that," I cut him off, and I used the same tone I did with rankers when I added, "and don't ask me again."

This, also not surprisingly, created an awkward silence, then Macer said mildly, "It doesn't really matter, does it? We're going to do whatever we're ordered to do, one way or another."

This was certainly the truth, and nobody argued with this, which I am sure had more to do with it being our Pilus Prior who spoke than Cornutus or Vespillo actually being satisfied. Over the course of the next few days, we continued our slow movement, stopping at every village whose location was known to us beforehand, or that was found by our cavalry, burning the buildings, fouling the wells, and searching for their stores of grain. Because of this, our progress eastward was minimal, as we moved along a more northerly/southerly axis, scouring Tencteri, then Sugambri lands as we inched eastward. The only casualties we inflicted were tribespeople too elderly or infirm to flee, and while we put them to the *gladius*, I will say there was some bickering about whether we were inadvertently doing the barbarians a favor by ridding them of a burden. Nevertheless, we carried out our orders, while tension began to mount as we all waited for what we felt sure was inevitable, none of us believing that tribes that were part of Arminius' confederation, as these two were, would not prevail upon him to at least attempt to stop us from our depredations. Given our meandering progress, it was not until the end of April when, one night in camp, Alex came to inform me that I had a visitor, whereupon he led Gaesorix into my private quarters. It had been weeks since we had spoken in more than a passing manner, but the first few moments after he dropped into the chair I offered were silent as he – moodily, from my observation – sipped from the watered wine I offered.

Finally, I felt compelled to observe, "You look tired."

This prompted a weary smile, and I cannot say why, but this was the first time I thought of Gaesorix as being older than I was, despite knowing that he was, by perhaps a decade. Normally, he did not look his age, but to my eyes, if anything, he looked even older than his forty-odd years.

"I *am* tired," he admitted. "We've been in the saddle nonstop since we crossed the river, and I've worn out two of my best horses. They're going to need at least another four or five days before they're sound again." The Batavian chuckled tiredly as he added, "Too bad there's not a way for their riders to do the same thing. But that's not why I came to see you."

Something in his tone caught my attention and signaled this being more than just a friendly chat, so I was somewhat cautious as I replied, "Oh? If it wasn't for the wine and the joy of my company, that might hurt my feelings."

"While I normally applaud you for your taste in wine, this," he held up the cup and made an exaggerated grimace, "isn't your finest offering. As far as your company," for the first time, he flashed the grin that was more what I was accustomed to, "let's just say it's better than talking to myself." Becoming serious, he paused for a moment, and I had the sense he was considering how to proceed, which only made me more alert that I was not likely to like what was coming. Finally, he said, "We found something today, and when I reported to Tiberius, he said that's where we're headed tomorrow."

While my first reaction was to think Gaesorix and his Batavians had come across the first village belonging to the Tubantes, since we were close to the boundary between their tribe and the Tencteri, I knew how unlikely it was that my friend would be warning me about what was a routine matter.

"So? What did you find?"

"Caedicius' camp," he replied quietly, then said nothing more.

Suddenly, I understood why Gaesorix had come to see me, and I confess it warmed me that he would do so, particularly given how our friendship had started, and at that moment, I recalled how I had taken an instant disliking to the man when he had teased me about my perceived lack of horsemanship. It still ranks as one of the worst misjudgments about a man I have made, but this was neither the time nor the place for any kind of mawkish confession on my part; at least, this was what I told myself. Besides, most of my mind was grappling with the momentous news that Gaesorix had just imparted to me, and more importantly, the ramifications from it.

I broke the silence, asking, "How bad is it?"

"Worse," Gaesorix answered, still in the same quiet tone, "than you can imagine, Titus. Worse than you can imagine."

My Batavian friend was not exaggerating, and I know this because, as the Fates decreed, the Fourth of the 1st was the vanguard of that day's march, meaning that we were the first to arrive at the camp occupied by the survivors of the initial ambush led by Camp Prefect Caedicius. Even worse, from a personal leadership standpoint, it was my Century's turn as the advance Century, although I did get a bit of warning when Gaesorix sent Cassicos back to warn me that we were less than a mile from the spot. Gaesorix's Optio was one of the toughest men I have ever met; any man who can survive a partial flaying must have some real iron in his soul, and while he was not a friend the same way Gaesorix was, we had a warm relationship and a bond formed by the fact that I was one of the men who had rescued him from the Varciani, who were in the process of finishing the job they were doing on him. Like Gaesorix, Cassicos was normally cheerful, but when he came trotting up, his face looked as if it had been carved from stone, and I was struck by the thought that this was the second time he had viewed whatever was waiting for us, yet he was still shaken by it. He drew me aside several paces to issue his warning.

"It's just on the other side of these trees," he told me in a low voice, then echoed his Decurion as he warned me, "and it is bad, Pullus. Very bad. I would say you need to prepare your men, but," he shook his head, "I do not know how you would do it."

With a wave, he turned his horse and went trotting back up the track we were following, yet while I did not doubt that trying to warn the men about what was coming would be close to futile, I decided that I should do something. Ordering Centumalus to sound the halt, I silently began counting as I waited for the inevitable Tribune, sent galloping ahead by Tiberius to determine the cause, while I went walking back towards Macer, who was behind us, as I did.

Reaching my Pilus Prior, I indicated that we should step away from the column, then told him in a low voice, "We're about to reach Caedicius' camp. Gaesorix sent Cassicos back to warn us."

Macer listened, then regarded me with a frown, asking, "All right. But why did you order us to stop? You know that…"

He did not finish, because his warning was not needed, the sound of drumming hooves cutting him off as we both turned to see one of the Tribunes, his straight back and haughty expression perfectly in place, come cantering up to us, and I believe the way he curbed his horse so that we were sprayed with dirt clods as the animal skidded to a halt was no accident.

"The Legate wants to know what the delay is about," he demanded peremptorily.

Although I was the one who ordered it, it was Macer who spoke, informing the Tribune, "I called the halt because we've been informed we're very close to the site of Caedicius' camp."

My hope that the Tribune would grasp the significance of what this meant vanished when he shrugged and answered, "So? Why does that warrant stopping the entire army?"

Since we never spoke of it, I can only assume that, despite Macer not immediately grasping the significance of my command, in the intervening moments, he had realized that what awaited us was something that warranted some sort of warning to the men, given that he replied calmly, "Because we're about to see the handiwork of Arminius and his warriors, and I doubt any of us are going to like it, Tribune."

Now the Tribune did not look quite as arrogant, and he shifted in his saddle as he considered Macer's words.

Then, to my surprise, he suddenly nodded, and said, "I'll inform the Legate that this was a necessary halt and explain why."

We thought to salute, but he had already turned and gone to the canter, leaving us standing, slightly mystified, prompting Macer to comment, "Maybe this Tribune isn't one of the useless ones." Before I could answer, he returned his attention to me and said quietly, "Go talk to your Century, and I'll have the rest talk to theirs. Let me know when you're ready to resume."

Walking back to my men, all of whom had grounded their packs and were looking back at me expectantly, I tried to come up with the right way to warn them, but then Structus stopped me, his face twisted into a scowl that I knew meant he was angry about something.

"They already know that it's Caedicius' camp up ahead," he informed me shortly.

I cannot say I was altogether surprised, but I had thought I was careful with Cassicos, walking several paces away from the column to converse with him, so I asked my Optio, "Did they overhear me?"

Structus shrugged, saying, "Honestly, I don't know how they figured it out. But," he glowered in the direction of the middle of the Century, "I can tell you who the clever bastard was who let everyone know."

Sighing, I said, "Pusio."

My Optio nodded in confirmation, but I had neither the time nor the inclination to devote any energy in dealing with the ranker who had become the rock in my *caliga*, other than to begin, "So, thanks to Gregarius Pusio and his big mouth, I'm guessing you already know what we're about to see. The camp where Camp Prefect Caedicius and the boys who survived the ambush is just up ahead, and Decurion Batavius has warned me that what we're about to see won't be pretty." I stopped then, realizing that there was really no way to know how bad it would be until we saw it with our own eyes, so I finished somewhat lamely, "So pick up your packs and make yourselves ready for whatever it is that's waiting for us."

I nodded to Centumalus, who hefted his *cornu*, then blew the notes to resume the march.

I believe it was within a matter of a dozen heartbeats that I realized there was absolutely nothing that could have prepared us for what we saw when we reached the camp that had not been demolished by Varus, and Caedicius had selected for what would turn out to be the last stand of the remnants of three Legions. The camp itself was relatively intact, although once we were able to inspect all four sides, we saw three places where the dirt wall had been breached. The palisade stakes were missing, but that was hardly surprising, and I doubted whether they had ever been there in the first place; given all that we knew about the panic and confusion that accompanied the slaughter of three Legions and their Legate, the fact that Caedicius managed to

101

rally men and make it to this spot was an impressive feat in itself. Not until a few months afterward did we hear that Caedicius and no more than three or four Cohorts worth of survivors managed to stave off Arminius' warriors until sometime in November, before a combination of casualties, weakness brought on by starvation and consistent pressure finally made the Prefect and his command succumb. Not until the next summer did we learn that, in fact, there were survivors of this last battle of the Varus disaster, and we knew this because word came from Rome that German nobles had sent emissaries to the families of some of these men, demanding a ransom. As far as I know, there were only a handful of families with the means to pay the Germans' demands, but just like those men who survived the initial onslaught and made it back to safety, they were banned from ever returning to Italia by the Princeps. Those who fell with Caedicius we "met," after a fashion, in the form of a triple row of skulls that had once been severed heads impaled on spears that were embedded in the ground, the first thing we saw when we entered the clearing surrounding the camp, arrayed a distance of perhaps fifty paces across. The only mercy, albeit a small one, was that the carrion birds and scavenging animals had picked the flesh from the skulls, although there were some with leathery scalps and tufts of hair remaining. However, it was Macer who noticed something when, without me giving the command, my Century came crashing to a halt, which Macer either anticipated or reacted to very quickly, because he had his Century move to our flank and align with us, followed by the Second on the other side.

When I walked over to him, he pointed at the skulls and said quietly, "Pullus, those fucking savages made sure that those skulls were back where they started, and they probably did it within the last day or so." Puzzled, I asked him how he drew that conclusion. "Because over the last eighteen months, once all the flesh either rotted or was eaten away, there's no way every one of those skulls stayed in place on those spear shafts."

The instant he said it, I not only knew he was right, but I experienced a sudden stab of alarm, and while I kept my voice down, I could hear the urgency as I said to Macer, "You know, we can't see inside that camp. It's possible that they're waiting for us."

Macer considered this, though not for very long, quickly giving me a curt nod, then, turning to Centumalus, the closest *Cornicen*, ordered him to sound the call for the nearest senior officer to come to our position. Understandably, this command is not used very often, which means that Macer was taking a bit of a risk; it also meant that within a matter of a handful of heartbeats, we were alerted that an officer was approaching. Looking back in the direction of the column, I spotted the white crest of Sacrovir, coming at the trot, but he was barely out of the trees when, from behind him, Tiberius, Germanicus, and what seemed to be both of their contingent of bodyguards came thundering past our Primus Pilus on their mounts. Very quickly, we were surrounded by horsemen, their animals dancing about in response to the nervous energy exuding from the men, both those of us on foot and those on their backs, but it was Tiberius who mattered, and it was to him Macer offered his salute.

Tiberius returned it, but before Macer could say anything, the Legate demanded, "What is it, Pilus Prior Macer?" Then, for the first time, he seemed to notice what had ostensibly caused us to stop, and for one of the few times I was in his presence, Tiberius visibly blanched, his normally thin lips almost disappearing at the sight of the rows of skulls. When he spoke again, his voice had suddenly turned hoarse, and he swore in a manner that would have done any ranker proud. Tearing his attention away, he stared down at Macer. "Is this why you summoned me? So I could see this?"

"No, sir," Macer answered immediately, "that's not why. Princeps Prior Pullus noticed that someone must have been here recently to make sure that all of the skulls were still set on top of those spear shafts." I opened my mouth to argue, but before I could say anything, he continued, "Then he pointed out that it's possible that they're inside Caedicius' camp, waiting for us. I'm asking if you want us to go ahead and enter the camp now, or if we should wait to bring the rest of the Legion up to surround it."

Tiberius did not hesitate in answering, "The latter, of course!" Turning to where Sacrovir had just come up at the trot, he ordered our Primus Pilus, "I want the 1st shaken out to surround this camp on all four sides before anyone goes in it." Returning his attention to the dirt walls, he frowned, saying, "I honestly don't think they're in there, but it's exactly the kind of thing that cunning bastard Arminius would at least consider trying."

It was left to Centumalus to send an entire Legion into motion, while we in the Fourth were consigned to standing there, staring at the grinning, empty-eyed skulls of men that, even if we had not known them, wore our uniform, making them our comrades. Tiberius, Germanicus, and the gaggle of junior officers went on a scouting tour around the perimeter of the camp, and when they began moving away, Germanicus caught my eye and threw me a wink.

"Good job, Pullus," he muttered as he went past me, which did not have the effect I suspect he was aiming for, because I turned to confront Macer.

"Why did you give me credit for picking up that the Germans had just been here arranging this?" I gestured towards the skulls. "That was you!"

Shrugging, he said, "What matters is the possibility that there's an ambush in the offing, and you're the one who figured it out. Trying to explain to Tiberius which of us did what and said what; I just decided it would be a waste of time."

When he put it in this way, it made sense, but I was still suspicious, certain that this was not the only reason my Pilus Prior and friend had for doing as he had done, although before I could make more of an issue of it, there came the sound of several *cornu*, as each Cohort signaled they were in position surrounding the camp. Also, by this point, Tiberius and his party had made their circuit around the camp, and came trotting up to where we were still standing.

"Since this camp only has two gates, I think it's best if you and your first three Centuries go," he pointed to the southern side of the camp – we had approached from the western side – and ordered, "through the breach the Germans made on the southern side of the camp. It's just around the corner there. Enter the camp, and have your *Cornicen* sound the call if it's all clear."

There was nothing for Macer to do but salute, then give the command for his Century to begin marching, while I followed him since the Second Century was on our left. When we marched away, the last three Centuries simply moved forward so that the ring around the camp was unbroken. As Tiberius had said, the place where the Germans had managed to breach the wall, pulling it down and filling in the ditch, was just about thirty paces from the corner of the western and southern walls. The men of the Ninth Cohort were standing directly across from the breach, but this was a time when there was none of the usual jeering banter back and forth between men of different Cohorts, and I suspect it was because, just like there was a display on the western wall, for the first time we saw that the Germans had completely encompassed all four sides of the camp with the grisly display of their victory. And, I immediately noticed, just like the rows with which we had been confronted, whoever had preceded us had ensured that every skull was perched atop the shafts buried in the dirt. Later, we learned that the Germans had done this on all four sides of the camp, arranging the shafts with a precision that, although I never heard confirmation, I am certain was no accident but was a mockery of the Roman love of order and regularity. It was when we entered the camp, however, when we realized that the skulls were just a hint of the horrors to come. Confined within the dirt walls of the camp were piles of bones, the remains of men who had been stripped down to their tunics, all of which had been reduced to rags by the elements that weakly fluttered in the slight breeze. It quickly became apparent that the heads had been removed and were those on display around the camp, since there were relatively few skulls lying in the dirt. Naturally, the Germans had stripped the dead of anything useful, leaving behind the detritus and debris of what had once been several hundred Legionaries, and none of the Centurions had to issue any orders for the men to remain quiet as we examined the site of Caedicius' last stand. I did hold out a faint hope that, perhaps, Caedicius' remains would be distinguishable from the piles of moldering bones, but we never found anything that would positively prove that the Camp Prefect had been singled out in death for any kind of special treatment. Arranged in neat rows that bespoke of the manner in which Caedicius had managed to enforce at least a semblance of order, were squares of black, scorched earth and small piles of charred wood and ash, the remnants of the tents that were part of the reason the defenders managed to hold out for so long, somewhat sheltered from the elements. As I mentioned, we already had learned from survivors that Varus had constructed this camp on the march to his doom as he pressed eastward, but instead of destroying it, had left it not only intact, leaving behind some men who had been struck by a bloody flux and a Century to guard them, the remains of these men I assume were mixed in with those brought to this place by the Camp Prefect. Strewn about everywhere were scraps of leather from the *baltea* of the slain, snapped javelin shafts, although every piece of iron had been salvaged by the victors, but it was the sight in what had been the forum of the camp that was most unsettling. In a grisly imitation of the neatness shown in the skulls, the forum contained what had once been four rows of headless skeletons, although it was difficult to tell because animals had scattered them as they feasted on the flesh that had encased the bones.

"They must have brought the survivors here and beheaded them, one after another." Macer's voice was a combination of tightly controlled anger, and if I was any judge, sadness, which was explained when he said, "I can't even imagine what it must have been like, waiting for your turn."

While I could not argue this, I also felt the need to point to the row of six crosses that had been sunk into the ground where the *praetorium* had once been, underneath each of which were piles of bones, and significantly, had skulls near each one of them.

"At least these weren't crucified like those poor bastards," I told Macer. Struck by a thought, I mused, "I wonder if the Prefect is one of them?"

"Maybe," Macer shrugged, "but only the gods know now."

Later, that night when we made camp a short distance away, there was quite a bit of argument about one aspect of the camp, and that was the smell in the air. Some men insisted that the camp stank of death, while others scoffed at this, saying that the parts of a man that corrupt and provide the stench had long since either been consumed or rotted away. Personally, I was in the former school of thought; I was certain I could smell that distinctive odor of human remains that every soldier who has seen battle knows. It was certainly faint, and I suppose it is possible that, just as with eyesight, some men have keener senses of smell than others, but I did not ask any of my fellow Centurions whether they had caught the scent of mortality like I had. One fortunate thing occurred to the Fourth; since we had been the first ones into the camp, we were excused from the grisly task of collecting the remains of the defenders, standing guard instead as the others worked. In what I considered to be both a shrewd and impactful decision, Tiberius ordered that, before the cleanup began, every man from all four Legions be marched into the camp so that they could see for themselves this evidence of what is certainly the worst military defeat in our collective lifetimes. And, I will say that, at the time, I was certain that we would never see anything this horrible and sobering again.

Regarding the remains, it was decided that, rather than taking the time and making the effort to cremate the bones in our manner, they were to be interred in the ground. And, while I do not fault Tiberius for making the expedient decision to use the ditch surrounding the camp as a mass grave, I also can understand why there were a fair number of men who grumbled at this. Not, I would add, to the point where it consisted of anything more than muttered conversations around the fire, but given all that was to transpire with the Legions, I have wondered from time to time whether or not this was just one more small perceived insult added to the list of issues that created what was to come. At the time, however, it was simply another thing about which soldiers like to complain, and it was overshadowed by another, more potent concern, the lack of any kind of resistance by the Germans. From Caedicius' camp, we marched east, along the Lupia (Lippe) River, but only for a day, torching one village, which as with the others, was deserted. This put us on the western edge of Bructeri lands, and we all expected that we would be visiting the same destructive punishment on them as we had on the Tubantes, which was why when Macer summoned us to his quarters after a meeting of the Pili Priores, we were in for a huge surprise.

"We're crossing the Lupia, and heading south," Macer informed us. "But," he hesitated, and we understood why when he finished, "we're heading back home."

There was a brief silence, then we all burst out, although we were essentially asking the same question: why?

"The Legate has decided that it's pretty clear that Arminius has no intention of trying to stop us," Macer explained, while I studied his demeanor carefully, trying to determine where his sentiments lay in this matter, "and while we've made it a hard winter for the Tubantes and the Marsi, we haven't managed to inflict the kind of casualties we were hoping for."

This was certainly true, as far as it went, particularly where it concerned our inability to capture or kill any able-bodied tribespeople; personally, I was I shared the sentiment of those men who had been complaining that we were inadvertently doing the Germans a favor because those few people we did put to the *gladius* were uniformly old and incapacitated in some way, and had been left behind by their own people when they fled into the forest. Still, this did not sit well, and I was not alone, but we also all understood that, ultimately, our feelings did not matter. We would be expected to relay the orders as if we wholeheartedly agreed with them, so aside from some muttered comments, which Macer ignored, we were dismissed to return to our Centuries to alert them about the coming day. In itself, this was not a particularly important moment, but I do believe that, in the same way as Tiberius' decision concerning the remains of Caedicius' men, this was another incident that was added to the list of grievances that the rankers were accruing against the Legate, the Princeps, and Rome.

We crossed the pontoon bridge back to Ubiorum, and while I did not speak with Centurions from the other three Legions, just judging from the demeanor of the rankers, the entire army was of a like mind, that we had not come close to avenging Varus' Legions. The disgruntlement was not only plain to see, it was quite disconcerting, but not because the men were being vocal or physically demonstrating their displeasure. Instead, it was in the form of an almost total silence, one so pervasive that the only sounds were the rhythmic thudding of hobnails on the hard-packed surface of the unpaved road, the jingle of metal, and the creaking of leather. There was no buzzing of conversation, yet beyond that, there was not even an occasional comment or a cough; frankly, it was a bit unnerving, but it was the manner in which the men were staring straight ahead, not even glancing in my direction as I made my usual occasional circuit around the Century as we marched, and when we stopped for the rest period, the men obediently grounded their packs and sat on the ground, yet still remained silent, although I could overhear an occasional whisper. I joined Macer and the other Centurions and Optios, walking a safe distance away to discuss matters.

It was a sign that Macer was as disturbed as I, and judging by the others' expressions, our counterparts, when he blurted out, "You've all been in longer than I have. Have any of you seen them act like this?"

Under normal circumstances, our Pilus Prior, who had purchased his posting, was loath to mention his relative lack of experience, although by this point, he had more than proved himself, and with only one exception, had been accepted by the rest of us as being worthy of the post of leading a first line Cohort. That he led with his inexperience was almost as telling as the question itself, and we all were quick to assure him that, no, none of us had ever seen them behaving in this manner.

"I've seen men angry, and I've seen them disappointed, but nothing like this," Vespillo said, and I took this as yet another sign of how unusual this situation was, because the Pilus Posterior rarely missed an opportunity to needle Macer about his lack of experience, so when the Pilus Prior himself brought it up, the fact that Vespillo ignored the opening was telling in itself. Shaking his head, he finished, "I don't even know how I would describe this."

The rest of us more or less agreed with Vespillo's assessment, but it was Cornutus who offered what would turn out to be a futile hope, although at the time we shared it. "I think that once we get back to where the whores and wine are, they'll get over whatever this is."

The *cornu* sounded the call to resume the march, and we returned to our posts. As I moved to my spot next to Gemellus, my *Signifer* was completely absorbed in tying the thong to his headdress, which was not unusual, but when he made sure to turn his body in such a way that there was no way our eyes would meet, I knew this was no accident. A *Signifer* is one of the most important men in a Century, for one obvious reason, but also because he serves an important function for his Centurion, acting as something like a weather vane that tells him which way the proverbial wind is blowing in his command. That Gemellus was going out of his way to avoid being put in a position where I might actually demand to know what was happening with the rankers in my Century was just one more troubling sign, and I spent the remainder of the march trying to think of what could be behind this sullen silence. Thankfully, once we were across the Rhenus, Tiberius dismissed the men and gave them the liberty of the town, and at the time I wondered if this was because of his recognition that the army was in a state of mind that meant further demands could lead to some sort of trouble. Whatever his reasoning, I was not alone in welcoming this tiny gesture, and while it did not return the men to their normal behavior, I think that ultimately, it was impossible for the men to remain in this sullen state when the prospect for drunken debauchery was beckoning. Unfortunately, this did not extend to the officers, simply because of the problem that Ubiorum did not normally house four Legions, although we had expanded to accommodate three. More crucially, the supply of whores and wine was not sufficient to handle the excess either, resulting in inevitable brawls when a dispute broke out. Truly, I do not think

111

any of us got much sleep the next two nights, summoned to mediate some disagreement, or more commonly, break up a fight. I am afraid that I took out my resultant foul mood on Alex, which was especially problematic since I was relying on him to act as my eyes and ears among the rankers, trying to get a better idea of exactly what was going on. By the time Tiberius ordered the town closed to the army, I had an even dozen men on the punishment list, which was not that much higher than normal, but three of them had been deemed worthy of being flogged, though thankfully, not with the scourge. A ranker in Vespillo's Century, however, had been involved in a brawl where a man from the 14th was killed by a dagger thrust into his eye, but since he had not been the man wielding the dagger, he escaped with his life, barely, being given fifty lashes, of which the last ten were with the scourge. The murderer was from the Fifth of the Third Cohort, and both the 1st and the 14th were paraded to watch the man's comrades beat him to death, something that, even for those who have witnessed it before, is still hard to watch. Then, a day short of two weeks after we returned, Tiberius and Germanicus departed for Rome. For most of the men, it would be almost two more years before they would see either of them again. That, however, was not to be my own fate.

With the end of what can only be charitably called a campaign, the other two Legions actually returned to what from that point forward would be their normal home of Vetera, while the 1st and 20th resumed life in garrison, and fairly quickly, things seemed to return to normal. It is only with the clarity that comes after an event that I, and my fellow Centurions, now know was simply a lull before the impending storm that would descend upon us. In the larger world, word came that Arminius still had his hands full trying to remain as the effective ruler of the confederation of German tribes, and I know I was not alone in being thankful for the other tribal leaders keeping him occupied.

It was not that I no longer wanted to avenge the lost Legions, but like with all such things, time tends to cool the ardor. And, as I was forced to acknowledge, only to myself, I was not getting any younger. Gone were the days when I arose every morning after a day's march without feeling any lingering effects, and I had begun to notice that my knees in particular seemed to bother me, to which I ascribe the restriction caused by the scar tissue from the burns I suffered when I marched for Germanicus. If I am being honest, as I have sworn to do in the same way as my Avus in his own account, I tend to wake in a foul mood now, and the best thing I can say is that I do try very hard not to take out my sour disposition on Alex. He had grown into his full manhood, and while he was taller than his father Diocles, he was still much shorter than I was, with the same kind of slender build as his father, but in one of those quirks of fate that I have given up trying to understand, while he has hair as black as a crow's wing, like Diocles did, he inherited his mother's startling blue eyes, which, as he learned, were quite an attraction to the ladies. In fact, he was carrying on what he thought was a secret affair with a young maiden, and not just any average ranker's child either. His love, for that is what she was, was the daughter of an equestrian merchant, one Lucius Salvius Poppaeus, though he went by Salvius, the man who supplied us with both grain and olive oil. Poppaea, the young woman, was quite lovely, and it would be a lie if I said I did not notice her beauty, but more than anything, seeing them together proved to be quite painful, reminding me of a young Gregarius who fell in love with the only daughter of a merchant in Siscia. Perhaps I can be forgiven, but I was less than encouraging when Alex broached the subject of pursuing something more than a brief liaison with Poppaea, which I did under the guise of the inherent problems in our society of any kind of lasting attachment between people of different classes. That was certainly a consideration, but it was not the main reason I discouraged it; I am afraid that my own

113

past clouded my view of this young couple's prospects for happiness. Unfortunately, Alex actually heeded my advice, though I was happy about it at the time.

Young love notwithstanding, the business of the Legions continued, where we resumed our occasional forays across the river, but we never went more than ten miles deep. Thus passed the year, a time where it seemed as if things had returned to at least a semblance of normality. Meanwhile, in Rome, Tiberius was finally given a triumph for the Batonian Revolt; that it was a full three years after the revolt was officially crushed is perhaps the best example of just how much turmoil and upheaval the Varus disaster had caused Rome and her Legions. This was certainly well-earned by Tiberius, and I confess that up until the moment when it would not be physically possible to do so, I had held out hope that my time as the Primus Pilus of the *Legio Germanicus* would be recognized, and I would be summoned to take part. However, my wounded pride was actually soothed by a balm, in the form of a letter from young Germanicus himself, written in his own hand, which I still have in my possession. It was not long, but he conveyed to me that there was no slight intended by my exclusion, that it was simply a matter of time and expense, and he swore to me that my name was included in the rolls for individual honors, which is read to the crowd, usually at the traditional feast that is held after the event. Probably not surprisingly, this was extremely flattering, but it was actually another piece of news, which he imparted to me, that I took as a sign that I was still viewed with favor by Germanicus. I brought it up the night I received the letter, when I was seated in Macer's private quarters, which had become a nightly routine, since neither of us particularly liked going out into town when we had no intention of availing ourselves of the whores or drinking ourselves senseless.

"I got some news from Rome," I began, but this was no surprise to Macer, since all missives are routed through the Pilus Prior's office first, nor was the identity of the author a secret.

"So?" he teased. "What great state secrets did your patron give you?" Laughingly, he added, "Any hint about our future?"

"No," I admitted, "at least about our future. But," I paused then, deliberately, and as I expected, Macer's expression changed, reminding me once more of how much of a political creature we Romans are, "I do know who our consuls for the coming year are."

His smile faded as he asked, puzzledly, "How so? They haven't held the election yet. They're not for, what," he paused as he recalled the date, "almost another month? How can you know before that?"

"Because," I replied smugly, "my *patron* trusts me enough to confide that he's going to be named Senior Consul for the coming year, along with," I confess that this time I was the one pausing, trying to recall the name, coming up with, "Gaius Fonteius Capito."

I shot him a grin then, but Macer was as quick a thinker as he was on his feet, and he also knew how to deflate my pride, which was what prompted him to shoot back, "So, Germanicus trusts you…and you can't wait to come running to tell me about it?" Fortunately, he was unable to contain his own mirth, bursting out laughing as he pointed at my face, hooting, "You look like you just swallowed a rat turd with your chickpeas!"

"You're just lucky you outrank me," I grumbled, but that only made him laugh harder.

By the time he was done gloating over my gloating, I could not help seeing the humor in it, and I knew that he would never betray me by telling others what I had told him, and the rest of the evening passed in its normal comfortable, affable manner. And, when the announcement was made several weeks later, during the morning formation, we exchanged a secret smile and wink. That Germanicus was only twenty-seven was notable; if this had been sixty years before, it would have been unthinkable, but it was none other than the Princeps himself who shattered centuries of tradition when he assumed the Consulship when he was only nineteen. Honestly, it had very little impact on our daily lives or routine; I suppose that it just gave me a sense of pride that someone from the patrician class with whom I had a relatively close relationship had reached the highest step available to a Roman as long as the Princeps still lived. This is not to say that we did not hear of his accomplishments, such as the games that he held, and it quickly became known that, between the two of them, it was on Germanicus' shoulders that the bulk of the work fell, given to him by the Princeps. This served as yet another sign that Germanicus was being groomed for bigger things, but in this I was more troubled than pleased; I served Tiberius, after all, not Germanicus, and I could not help wondering how the older man viewed this mark of favor by Augustus, particularly since it was not his son by blood, but by adoption. I suppose the best way to characterize it is that my heart was with Germanicus, but the rest of me was owned by Tiberius, which was reinforced in the spring of Germanicus' Consulship, when one evening, Alex knocked on my door.

When he entered, I had learned by this time to interpret his expressions, so I was not altogether surprised when he announced, "Tiberius Dolabella is here."

Fighting the urge to simply refuse him entry, instead I gave Alex a weary wave, understanding that there was no point in trying to avoid talking to Tiberius' spymaster, which was what I had deduced he had become by this point, more of a manager of those whose job it was to listen in on conversations, purloin indiscreet letters written by members of the Senate, and if necessary, make their authors disappear. While I had not been called on by Tiberius, through Dolabella, of course, to perform any of those tasks of which I will not speak for some time, when the man entered my private quarters, I felt certain that this spell was about to end. Why else, I thought sourly, would he be here? Outwardly, I waved him to a seat, and even managed to avoid sounding grudging when I ordered Alex to fill two cups of wine, although I did know that, without being told to do so, Alex would not pour from the amphora containing one of the good vintages, like Falernian or Chian.

"*Salve,* Pullus," he said as he dropped onto the chair across from my desk, and while I was not disposed to care all that much, I took notice that he looked weary.

I did experience a flicker of surprise, however, at the sight of the silver strands in his black hair, and I tried to remember if they had been there the last time we were in each other's company.

Oddly enough, I took some satisfaction in the grimace he made after taking a sip of the wine, then he plunged straight in. "I won't waste our time together engaging in pleasantries, if that's all right with you."

Of course, this was perfectly acceptable, though I merely nodded in agreement, whereupon he said, "I am guessing you've heard that Germanicus is now the senior Consul for this year."

"I have," I answered, albeit cautiously. "The Legate made the announcement to all of us."

Dolabella nodded his understanding but then went on, "I doubt that he told you all of it, though." Pausing a beat, he said, "Germanicus intends to serve the full year."

The spymaster was correct; the Legate had made no mention of this at all, and as I write these words, without knowing what the future will hold for those who come after me and bear the Pullus name, I realize that my reaction to this seemingly straightforward statement may come as a surprise, because I sat back and I believe I muttered, "*Gerrae!*" I thought for a moment, then offered the verbal form of the kind of test shot we make with a *ballista*. "I can't imagine Tiberius is very happy."

This elicited a snort that was Dolabella's version of a laugh, and he shot back caustically, "Oh? Really?" Shaking his head, he stared down in his cup, then said moodily, "That's a bit of an understatement. It's because," he sighed, "Germanicus has some…ambitious plans."

"Plans?" I asked cautiously, yet I was intrigued at the same time. "What kind of plans?"

"Well, he's already held games, although those were to honor Tiberius' triumph," he allowed, "but he also has this idea that our justice system needs some…" he frowned for a moment before coming up with "…reforms. He's decided that he's going to actually sit as judge for the civil courts, and for certain criminal trials. Although," Dolabella added hastily, "only the common sort; murder, theft, that sort of thing."

I considered for a long moment, because despite appearances, a Roman noble who was elected Consul serving a full year, while at one time was completely normal, was no longer the custom, and had not been for many years under the rule of the Princeps. The office of Consulship was usually passed around in a given year to at least one other candidate, although it was usually more, so Germanicus, who as the senior Consul held the most sway, insisting on serving the entire year of his Consulship was, to put it mildly, highly unusual. Most importantly, to me anyway, was trying to determine how Tiberius would react to Germanicus' program, and almost as crucial to those of us who were the most immediately impacted by the actions within the family of the Princeps, whether this was done with the tacit approval of Augustus. And, finally, what it all meant. As Dolabella and I sat there, neither of us speaking and seemingly absorbed in our own thoughts, I recall thinking with a rueful amusement, at least this will make the long winter nights pass more quickly. As it would turn out, it was much longer than just a winter, and I know I was not alone at the time as I began to relax and think that, perhaps, the loss of Varus' Legions would go largely unavenged.

This is not to say that the ensuing period was completely uneventful as far as the fortunes of the Fourth Cohort were concerned. It was in the month named for Divus Julius that, as often happened when we were in camp for an extended period of time, a plague swept through our ranks once more, and, as happens from time to time, the mortality that is inevitable when sickness hits struck the Centurionate. Specifically, Decimus Macula succumbed to the bloody flux, leaving a post unfilled. During the time of my father and my Avus before him, replacing a Hastatus Posterior, even in a first-line Cohort would most commonly be handled as a matter of Legion business, although there were certainly occasions when the Legate in command would make his wishes known about who should replace the departed Centurion. Since we were not on campaign, there was not the same urgency to fill the post, but on the first full day after Macula succumbed and crossed the river, Macer was summoned to the Primus Pilus' quarters and informed by Sacrovir that the decision had been taken out of his hands. I learned of this when Macer summoned me to his quarters, whereupon, once my cup was filled and settled in my normal seat in his private quarters, he launched into a diatribe that, surprisingly to me, was not aimed at Sacrovir.

"The Primus Pilus informed me that he has been instructed that we're going to fill this post with a paid man," he began bitterly, using the term we had adopted for this custom, now well more than a decade old, that allowed men of equestrian rank to purchase a posting in the Centurionate. Macer was actually pacing back and forth behind his desk, staring at the floor with a frown, so he did not see the expression on my face when I interjected, "Yes, the gods know those paid men are as useless as tits on a man."

So distracted was he that it took him a moment to grasp the irony, as he began, "I know! And what with this business with Arminius still unsettled..." Suddenly, he stopped in mid-step, turning to regard me with a scowl that dissolved into a sheepish grin as he said, "Useless as tits on a man, eh? Well, I'm glad to know what you *really* think about your Pilus Prior." We shared a laugh at his sudden remembrance that he, Marcus Macer, was, in fact, one of those paid men, and I did not feel I was being false when I offered, "You turned out pretty well, so we can hope for the best, neh?"

Macer did not immediately answer but did choose to drop heavily into his seat, snatch up the cup from his desk, and take a deep swallow of the wine before he said with a grimace, "I forget sometimes how I got started and how green I was. And," he gave me a look that ignited a quietly unsettling twinge in my gut, "I certainly know that it's within the rights of the Princeps and Tiberius, for that matter, to appoint whoever they want to an open posting." To my ears, Macer's tone sounded careful. "It's not that I'm complaining necessarily, it's just that..."

"That you don't like the choice being taken out of not only your control, but without any say in the matter," I finished for him, and I could not miss the expression of relief that flooded his features at my words as he nodded. Deciding to slightly move away from what I could see was a troubling topic, I asked, "Did Sacrovir give you any kind of time for how long the post remains open?"

Instead of easing his mind, this seemed to agitate Macer even more, but I understood why when he replied, "No! He said, 'as long as it takes.'" He actually did a fair job at sounding like our Primus Pilus. "And he also told me that he didn't think it would be filled for at least a month!"

This, I understood, was at least part of Macer's concern, because of all the Optios in our Cohort, Numerius Gillo was the one who I knew Macer worried about the most. Not, it must be said, because of his incompetence, but because of his reputation for petty cruelty and vindictiveness, which, although I have no wish to speak ill of the dead, Macula did not do much to quell. Frankly, I was of the private opinion that Macula was scared of Gillo, although I never shared that with Macer since he never asked. Understanding that this was more about Macer's need to vent his frustration about his powerlessness, I decided to shift the topic, though not before offering, "Well, there's no use in worrying about something you can't control."

"No," he agreed, then grinned and said, "but I still can whine about it."

We moved on to other topics, and this was the last time I heard Macer complain about the unknown new Hastatus Posterior; it would indeed be another month, yet when the newly minted Centurion showed up, I quickly learned that he would prove to be a rock in the *caliga*, not for Macer, but for me.

Chapter Three

His name was Gnaeus Claudius Volusenus, and the first I became aware that we had a new Hastatus Posterior was when Alex informed me that not only had he arrived, he had already made quite the impression.

"Lucco was entering his name in the Cohort roll, and he only put down his *Praenomen* and *Cognomen*." Alex came to find me, and since I was in our Century office, he made no attempt to hide his feelings. "But the new Centurion threatened to thrash Lucco for 'insulting' his family honor."

This elicited a snort from me, since this was simply the standard practice of the army and I had heard of other men complaining about it, but Alex was not finished, and I got a bare hint of warning as his expression changed, subtly, yet in a manner that told me he was worried about how I would react.

Which meant, of course, that I made no attempt to take his feelings into account, demanding, "What? What else is there?" Suddenly, I thought I knew, prompting me to gasp, "He didn't actually touch Lucco, did he?"

While, technically speaking, I suppose this new Centurion had the right to do so, I had never heard of anyone so arrogant and, frankly, simple-minded, that they would show up to their new posting and immediately beat the chief clerk of not just the Century, but Cohort. To my relief, Alex shook his head, yet his manner did not change all that much, but it was his use of my familial title that was somewhat alarming.

"Uncle Titus," he said haltingly, "I don't really know how to put this…"

"Then," I snapped, my patience wearing thin, "just come out with it!"

"He's…big," Alex said, then stopped.

"Big?" I was momentarily puzzled, then asked, "What do you mean? He's big like me?"

Relief flooded my nephew's features, and he nodded with what seemed to be a bit too much enthusiasm, exclaiming, "Yes, Uncle Titus! That's what I mean! He's," he paused as he took a step backward to examine me in a manner that, frankly, I found a bit unsettling, "actually a bit taller than you. But he's also as..." Rather than say it, Alex held his hands out to roughly correspond with the breadth of my body. Unmindful of the consternation he was causing me, he went on to say, "The instant I saw him, he reminded me of you. I mean," for the first time, he seemed to understand why I might not find this good news, "his arms aren't as big as yours, but he is..."

"Big," I supplied, and despite my own feelings, I had to acknowledge that it amused me to see how quickly he nodded.

Sighing, I tried to make light of this moment when, for the first time in my career, I was confronted with the prospect of someone who might match my physical prowess, clapping Alex on the shoulder as I said, "I can't wait to meet this new Hercules."

I got my chance quickly enough, when Macer summoned us to his quarters the next morning, ostensibly to meet the new Centurion. I had no reason for doing so, but I realized when I entered Macer's office, I had been doubting Alex's judgment about the new Hastatus Posterior, having convinced myself how unlikely it was that there could be a Roman who could match me physically. Seeing Gnaeus Claudius Volusenus sitting there, wearing nothing more than a soldier's tunic that was still bright red, cinched by an equally new *baltea*, with a *vitus* standing vertically in between his knees was one of the more startling, viscerally brutal shocks of my life. Even taking into consideration that Volusenus was seated, I instantly saw that, if anything, Alex had been kind. Not surprisingly, the moment I entered, our eyes locked; what I saw reflected in his eyes, a level of disdain that I had long since learned seems to be inherited at birth by those fortunate enough to be born in one of the classes higher than those of the Head Count, only served to inflame me even more. Honestly, I cannot say with any certainty, but I acknowledge that it is highly probable that even if this Volusenus had given me the blandest expression possible, I would have found fault with it. Whatever the truth may be, what is certainly true is that we were destined to clash, and I could see just by Macer's expression as he studied my face that he was intensely interested. However, it was Vespillo who, in his normal manner, made matters even worse.

He had come in behind me, but I had not noticed his presence until he gave a sharp, barking laugh, then exclaimed, "By the gods, Pullus! If I didn't know better, I'd say our new Hastatus Posterior could be your son!"

I spun about, so I missed Volusenus leaping to his feet to cross the distance, so his voice was immediately behind me as he snapped, "I can assure you that the Centurion and I aren't related! I'm the son of Quintus Claudius Volusenus, not this..."

Now I reversed myself, and for the first time, Volusenus and I were face to face, and I confess I did not like what I saw; Alex had been right, this man was a bit taller than I was and his chest was every bit as broad as mine. Being forced to look up, even if it was only a matter of an inch or so, was a distinctly unsettling feeling, but I was also pleased to see that he was clearly uneasy as well; I suppose the scars on my face, arms, and knees might have played a part in that.

"Not this what?" I asked quietly enough, but Macer knew me well enough to understand that my mild tone was deceptive.

"Have a seat, Volusenus. And you, Pullus," Macer did not raise his voice, but it was no less a command, and naturally I complied, though I chose to glare at Vespillo, who tried unsuccessfully to look repentant for his role in the tension.

124

By the time Volusenus and I were seated, the rest of the Centurions had arrived, and the next few moments were occupied with everyone getting settled, while Lucco filled and distributed cups of wine. Once he saw we were taken care of, Macer began speaking.

"This is just an informal meeting now that we are back to our full complement of Centurions. As you can see," Macer indicated Volusenus, who at that moment, was staring at the floor, "Hastatus Posterior Volusenus has purchased the posting." At the sound of his name, the youngster, who I guessed to be around twenty years old, lifted his head, his chin tilted to the proper degree that I always associate with a member of the classes above the Head Count, but I also noticed that he studiously avoided looking in my direction. Macer continued, "Why don't you tell us something about yourself, Volusenus?"

I had not thought it possible, but Volusenus proved me wrong by tilting his nose at an even higher degree as he spoke, with a diction and pacing that, when I do not think about it, is a part of my speech as well, which bespeaks of a private tutor, saying stiffly, "I am the son of Quintus Claudius Volusenus, and I was born in Aquileia, although my family moved to Mediolanum when I was very young. He is a very important man in Mediolanum, and has served there as one of the *duumviri* on two separate occasions."

"What's his business?" Cornutus asked, to which Volusenus replied with obvious pride, "He has several business interests, so it's impossible to say exactly what he does."

The smile he offered was, I supposed, to be somewhat self-deprecating, but if this was his intent, it had the opposite effect, as Philus groaned, "Pluto's balls; another rich boy?"

Volusenus stiffened at this, and before Macer could interject, he shot back, "I can assure you, Centurion, that my father's wealth has nothing to do with my qualifications to be in the Centurionate!"

125

"Oh?" Vespillo's tone was dry, and his eye swept the rest of us as he said, "So the Princeps just heard about this young version of Mars himself and waived the fee?"

The youngster's face reddened, and he admitted, "No, I'm not saying that. Everything was done properly, I can assure you. But," he insisted, and as he did, I noticed that he subtly but unmistakably thrust his chest out, pulling the new tunic tightly across his chest, "I've been performing the exercises on the Campus Martius of Mediolanum starting even earlier than normal, because of my size." For the first time since our initial encounter, he looked directly at me, and his tone turned belligerent as he finished, "And I know that I can acquit myself quite well...against anyone in this Cohort."

I am certain that the mood in the room changed in that instant, but I was barely aware of it, ignoring Macer's warning glare as I stood, and once more, moved closer to Volusenus.

"Anytime," my voice was steady, and I made an effort to imbue my speaking with a cool, almost bored tone, "you think you're ready, Volusenus, I'm easy to find."

"That's enough," Macer snapped. "There will be plenty of time for sparring. First," he turned to Volusenus, and his voice was harsh, "you need to take command of your Century and prove that you know what you're doing." With this said, he returned his attention to the rest of us, his tone every bit as unyielding as he commanded, "And I expect the rest of you to do your part making sure Hastatus Posterior Volusenus is worthy of marching with us in the Fourth Cohort. And," he warned, "if he doesn't, I am holding each of you equally responsible."

That I was the last man he looked in the eye as he finished might have been a coincidence, but I did not believe so.

As loath as I am to admit it, Volusenus did a creditable job assuming command of the Sixth Century, although like every new Centurion, he was a bit lost when it came to the record keeping required by the Princeps, which I learned through Alex, who was friends with the Sixth's clerk Krateros. For the rankers of the Sixth, however, there was another benefit, which I learned from Macer.

"I don't know what the new boy said to Gillo," Macer told me one evening, about a month after Volusenus' appearance, "but the word is that his Optio is minding his manners." As proof, he waved a tablet in the air. "This is the lightest punishment list from the Sixth in months."

While Macer seemed pleased, I was not willing to credit the young Centurion with this development, and I dismissed it by saying, "That's probably because Volusenus is trying to win the favor of his boys by rescinding whatever punishment Gillo is handing out."

"I thought that as well," Macer answered with a shake of his head, "but I asked one of my little birds in the Sixth, and he swears on the black stone that Gillo has suddenly become a model Optio."

"One of your 'little birds'?" I asked dryly, "You mean a 'little bird' who wears a wolf headdress?"

Macer's face reddened slightly, and he sighed. "How did you know?"

"That the *Signifer* is your source for information?" I laughed. "Because I was under the standard before I was under the standard, that's how."

Macer instantly understood my meaning, that I had been around the Legions my entire life, hence I knew that a shrewd Pilus Prior cultivated the man who is considered the steadiest, most reliable man in a Century. A man selected to be *Signifer* has to be made of iron when it comes to nerve and willingness to stand in place, not moving until he is ordered to do so, and while I only knew the Sixth's *Signifer*, Vibius Macerinus by reputation, it was what I would expect of a man in his post.

127

"Anyway," he grumbled, "I don't think it's because Volusenus is cozying up to the men." When I did not make any reply, Macer took the moment to take a swallow from his cup, but I sensed there was something else on his mind. It was when I noticed him seemingly occupied with setting the cup carefully back on his desk while keeping his eyes fixed on it that I had a presentiment this would be something I would not like. "You know, Titus," he said with a casualness that I could hear was forced, "I know Vespillo was just trying to stir things up like always, but I have to say," only then did he raise his head to look at me, "you and Volusenus *do* resemble each other."

"We're both big." Even this acknowledgment seemed to stick in my throat, but Macer shook his head.

"I mean, besides the obvious," he said. "There's just…something in the way he carries himself."

"So," I tried to make a joke of it, "what are you trying to say? That I'm an arrogant bastard like him?"

Macer laughed, but he was unwilling to let it go, insisting, "No, it's more than that." I suppose he read my expression, because, suddenly, he gave a shrug and finished awkwardly, "I don't know. There's just…"

"Yes," I cut him off, trying to keep my growing anger under control, "there's *something* about him. But," I swallowed hard, caught by surprise at how painful it was to say, "while I did have a child, about twenty years ago, he died. And," I finished bitterly, "so did his mother. In childbirth."

"Ah," Macer looked embarrassed, and he admitted, "that's right. I forgot. What was her name again?"

"Giulia," I barely whispered her name. "Her name was Giulia."

I left shortly after that, and Macer never again brought up the topic of this supposed resemblance between me and the new Centurion.

The rest of the year of Germanicus' Consulship passed in a routine manner for us, with regular patrols across the Rhenus, rarely deeper than a day's march east, and always with at least a Cohort and, even more importantly, two *turmae* of cavalry, who formed a protective screen around us to serve as an early warning of any German force. And, despite not suffering any major losses, there were at least a dozen minor skirmishes, usually starting in the form of an ambush, perpetrated by small bands of warriors, and the Fourth and my Century were not immune. The air of tension, dread, and readiness that seemed to permeate the very air we breathed in the aftermath of Varus' defeat had certainly eased, if only because it is so exhausting to try and maintain a state of alertness for such a long period of time. Nevertheless, every one of us in the Centurionate was determined that we would not be caught unaware like our dead counterparts of the three perished Legions, which was what led to the first clash between Volusenus and me. It was the Fourth's turn to march, and we were in Sugambri territory, perhaps twenty miles east of the river, nearing the end of the day's progress, reaching the base of what is gently sloping ground that climbs eastward. Heavily forested, there is a natural track that follows along a small river that feeds into the Rhenus, with the first few miles from the Rhenus having been improved by us over the years, but by the point where the ground noticeably tilts upward, it was back to that narrow, rutted road that is most common in Germania. While it was not Macer's intent to do so, it was the turn of the Sixth to be the advance Century, while my Third was immediately behind them in the column, and I honestly do not recall whether Macer, or any of us for that matter, warned Volusenus that this stretch of ground was particularly dangerous, having been used many times as a good ambush spot by the Germans. At the time, I suppose that I, and the other Centurions, assumed that Gillo would warn Volusenus that this was the case, proving once again how dangerous assumptions can be in the business of the Legions. As was our standard practice, there was a wider gap between the leading rank of my Century and the rear rank of the Sixth, which has been done long before I was ever under the standard and, frankly, was one of the myriad things that none of us ever thought to question. Once I did think about it, I supposed it was some Legate's idea to dangle a lone Century out as bait with the appearance of a larger gap between the leading element and the rest of the column, and like so many things we Romans do, we just kept doing it. Regardless of how it developed, that day the Sixth was leading the way, and following the course of the river, had completely disappeared around a bend when, with nothing more than one warning shout from the ranker in my First Section who marched on the outer file, a gnarled veteran named Gnaeus Clustuminus, who was also the section Sergeant, we were ambushed. He paid for his alertness by taking a javelin in the thigh, part of a hail of missiles that came streaking out from the thick undergrowth just a dozen paces away, but he was luckier than two of my boys. We were in our armor, naturally, and wearing our helmets, but the men had their shields covered and wore them slung on their backs in our normal fashion. Because of the curvature of the shield, it does provide some protection, but in a situation such as the one we were facing then, the only way to bring this protection fully to bear is to either unsling the shield, which takes too long, or literally turn away from the attack in order to present the entire shield to the missiles. Not surprisingly, this latter move was not what most of the men on the outer file did, which was why several of them were struck. Being where I was, I had to rely on Structus, marching at the rear opposite side, and I heard him bellowing over the shouts and cries of pain from Clustuminus and the others struck.

"Close up! Shields out, you bastards!"

While Structus was handling what was now the front rank, as without any orders from me, the rest of the Century not under direct attack dropped their packs, unslung their shields, and pivoted to their left to face this ambush, I ordered Centumalus to sound the alarm for the entire Cohort. Since my view was blocked by the ranks of the Century, I had yet to actually see any attackers, but even before Centumalus began blowing the notes, I was moving at a run to reach the outermost file to the left, which was now the front rank. Clustuminus was down, but his section mate, who an instant before had been to his right and was now the man behind him, had managed to step over his comrade and unsling his shield, while the wounded man had dragged his own protection over his body so that only his lower legs protruded, as he was trying to drag himself backward using just his right arm. Beyond them, I caught a glimpse of movement in the trees, just a flashing sense of a figure in greenish brown, but it was the blurred streaking missile that came slashing out of the underbrush that, thankfully, I saw heading my way. Twisting my body, I felt the disturbed air as it narrowly missed me, while my sudden movement caused my feet to tangle with each other, and I stumbled forward, bent over at the waist as I tried to avoid from falling flat on my face. I sensed more than actually saw the second javelin that went streaking inches over my back, although I somehow managed to recover my balance and pull myself erect. By the time I did, my momentum had brought me next to where Clustuminus was lying, protected by his fellow section member Publius Tetarfenus, who had one short throwing spear stuck in his shield, which he was holding in front of him but slightly lower than normal to give his wounded comrade extra protection. Aside from that first glimpse, all I saw of the attackers were their fleeing backs as they went dashing through the heavy underbrush, quickly vanishing and leaving only the sounds of their retreat as they ran deeper into the forest.

Clustuminus' wound was serious but not life-threatening, the iron head penetrating through the outer part of his thigh without severing a vessel. Quintus Florus, however, was not so lucky, the Sergeant of my Fourth Section taking a javelin through the lung, dying shortly after being struck, while a man in the Eighth Section lived only a matter of a watch longer. Three more men had been struck, but their wounds, confined to their upper extremities, were relatively minor, and they could still march, albeit without their packs. Our casualties were not confined to the Legionaries; two of the section slaves, who naturally were unarmored, were slain, along with a mule. Alex was unhurt, and in fact, he and the three other slaves trained as *medici* were moving forward even as the last javelins were still flying. My natural inclination was to send at least five sections, half the Century, in pursuit, but I had been under the standard too long to give in, knowing this was likely exactly what these attackers wanted. I did set up a defensive line, and first Vespillo, who was following my Century, then Macer, whose First was behind Vespillo, came running up to me, just as, at last, the rear ranks of the Sixth Century reappeared from around the bend up ahead. At least, I assumed it was the rear ranks, but then I spotted their standard, the first indication that partially explained why they were so late arriving.

"Did he make them reverse their formation?" Macer asked, but although this was a valid question, I had other matters on my mind, and without thinking, I headed directly for Volusenus, who was next to his *Signifer*.

I cannot say what my state of mind was when I began walking towards the youngster, but within a matter of a few paces, my rage was growing so rapidly that even if I had been inclined to do so, I doubt I could have kept it under control.

"*How the fuck did this happen?*" I bellowed when I was still a half-dozen paces away. "*How did you miss that many fucking Germans?*"

While Volusenus' face betrayed not only being startled, I was gratified to see what I knew was fear there, although he did stand his ground as he replied stiffly, "I don't know what you mean, Princeps Prior Pullus!"

Pointing in the direction of the woods, I demanded, "How far out did you have your flanking guards?"

The answer was in his expression, but before I could make more of an issue of it, Macer had arrived, and he adroitly placed himself between me and Volusenus, yet doing it in a way that it seemed as if he was only addressing the other Centurion instead of keeping us separated.

"Hastatus Posterior Volusenus," compared to my tone, Macer's voice was gentle, "did you have a flank guard?"

"Yes, Pilus Prior," Volusenus answered immediately, then he hesitated. "At least," he added awkwardly, "I did."

"You did?" I blurted out. "What the fuck does that mean?"

"That's enough, Pullus!" Macer turned and snapped at me, but when he turned back to Volusenus, he essentially repeated my question, though it was done more politely. "What exactly *does* that mean, Volusenus?"

"Well," now there was no way to mistake the discomfort of Volusenus, "I made sure the men out on the flank guard were relieved every third of a watch, just like you commanded." He swallowed hard, then admitted, "And while I brought the last set in during our last rest stop, I must have forgotten…"

"You stupid *cunnus!*" I raged, but even when Macer whirled on me, clearly furious, I was beyond caring as I pointed back to where the comrades of my casualties were performing the tasks that are part of our training when a man falls. "Look at what your forgetfulness cost my Century! I've got one dead Legionary, and another who will probably be dead before the next sunrise! *All because you don't know how to do your fucking job!*"

"*Princeps Prior Pullus!*" I had seen Marcus Macer get truly angry before, but it had never been turned on me; until this moment, at least. "*By the gods, that's enough!*"

133

Without realizing it, I had sidestepped Macer to get closer to Volusenus, who stood there eyeing me with a gratifying level of nervousness, but then Macer reached out and grabbed me…right on the scar tissue of my left arm. Despite the fact that it was more than a decade earlier, during the ambush at The Quarry when Urso had been Primus Pilus of the 8th, my first Legion, and the actual scar had turned white, when it was grabbed as firmly as Macer did it, my reflex reaction was automatic and unthinking, caused in part by the sudden flash of pain.

"Get your fucking hands off me," I snarled at my superior, and even worse, a man I considered a close friend.

To his credit, Marcus Macer was the only one who kept his head, because he did let go, but while he lowered his voice, his tone was as harsh and unyielding as any time I had ever heard it, as he ordered, "Princeps Prior Pullus, attend to your Century…now. I will not tell you again."

Thankfully, either the words or the tone penetrated the red haze of my rage, and I stopped moving towards Volusenus, turning back to my own men, but I was still sufficiently angered to glare at Volusenus and mutter, "You and I will settle this later."

I expected Macer to make an issue of this, yet to my surprise, he did not, choosing instead to pull Volusenus aside to speak to him, while I returned to my Century, ignoring the eyes on me from both the Sixth and my own men. Not much longer after this, we resumed the march, with a makeshift litter fashioned to carry Clustuminus and Plautus, the Gregarius who was clinging to life at the moment, but with the Fifth Century switching with the Sixth. We finished the march for the day, making camp about four miles from the site of the ambush, and by the time the ditch was dug and the tents raised, Plautus had died. I was not surprised when Lucco came to summon me to Macer's quarters, which served as the *praetorium* in our small camp, and I braced myself for some sort of reprimand from my Pilus Prior, wondering yet again if my temper had put me into a predicament that might permanently damage my career. Yet, even as I chastised myself, recognizing that I had acted in a completely untoward manner with Macer, the memory of two dead rankers, and, although not as impactful, two dead slaves, was still fresh in my mind, so that I arrived at Macer's tent prepared to argue my case, such as it was.

And, at first, it seemed as if Macer was intent on setting aside our personal relationship and act as Pilus Prior, his face seemingly chiseled from stone as he watched me enter and march to his desk.

He did return my salute, but his face gave nothing away as he said curtly, "Sit down, Pullus."

His discarding of my *praenomen*, our normal form of addressing each other under different circumstances, gave me another hint that this would probably not be pleasant. Naturally, I did as he commanded, dropping onto the stool that was placed in front of the tiny camp desk, and as always, I felt somewhat foolish, given the relative size between me and the stool; frankly, I was always surprised that it did not collapse, especially when I dropped down as heavily as I did then. I sat there, taking some comfort in how, even when I was seated, I still was able to command the high ground, in a manner of speaking, but Macer regarded me coldly, his face betraying none of his thoughts.

Finally, after a silence lasting several heartbeats, he suddenly heaved a sigh and said, "He made a mistake, Pullus. He's green."

"A mistake that cost me two men," I countered immediately, and his face darkened, although his tone was even as he answered, "I'm aware of that." He paused then, before adding, "And he knows that he bungled the job, I can assure you."

"That doesn't do much for Plautus and Florus."

135

Even as the words came from my mouth, I knew I was being mulishly persistent, yet I could not seem to help myself, and it was plain to see that it stretched Macer's patience.

"Pluto's cock," he snapped, "I just said that Volusenus knows he erred, so there's no need for you to keep flogging that dead horse!"

Somehow, I managed to refrain from responding, and we lapsed back into staring at each other.

Finally, Macer broke the silence by saying in an offhand manner, "You know, I had an Optio once who told me something that I've never forgotten."

Macer had had four Optios by this point, but I was fairly certain that not only did I know the identity of this Optio, I would not like whatever it was that I had said at some point in the past when I served under him.

Nevertheless, I decided to match his demeanor, replying, "Oh? And what knowledge did this wise Optio impart to you?"

For the first time since my entrance, I saw the glimmer of a smile forming on his lips as he answered, "Only that as far as he was concerned, if a Centurion didn't make a mistake that ended up badly, that man was just an empty uniform and not worthy of the rank. But," he went on, and if there had been a smile coming, it vanished, "the truly dangerous men were the ones who made the same mistake twice."

Even as he was speaking, I recalled that, indeed, I had said that very thing to him, not long after I had been transferred from the 8th Legion to ostensibly aid in the development of a paid man who had purchased the posting of the Third Century of the Fourth Cohort of the 1st Legion. When I had said these words, I was trying to imbue Macer with the confidence that a Centurion needs to do his job, and while I had certainly meant them, I confess I did not much care for the taste of them being shoved back down my throat at this moment.

136

"I don't know who that Optio was," I told him, "but he sounds like a fucking idiot to me."

As I hoped, this made Macer laugh, but while the worst was over, he was not quite through.

"Titus," he said seriously, "while I don't know exactly why you hate Volusenus so much, I can guess the reason. And you need to give the man a chance."

"I don't hate him," I protested, yet I felt the need to add, "exactly. I just…" I struggled to articulate what it was about this young Centurion, aside from his obvious carelessness, that disturbed me so much, finally settling on, "…don't trust him, that's all. He's certainly got the same advantages that I do with his size and strength, but he's a spoiled, soft, rich equestrian from everything I've seen. And he thinks his *cac* doesn't stink."

I was being honest; at least, as honest as I was capable of being at this moment, but while I hoped that Macer would at least understand my viewpoint, instead, he said in a lightly mocking tone, "Now, I seem to recall someone telling me that that was exactly what people thought him, that because of who he was, he was soft and spoiled and thought his name would be enough to win him respect."

This conversation, which I had been dreading, had turned out even worse than I feared, just not for the reason I had imagined, and once more I was forced to experience the bitter taste of my own words.

"That was…different," I finally managed, but even I heard how lame this excuse sounded, and was. Thankfully, Macer chose not to answer, but after a moment of him regarding me with the same kind of expression he bore when he had beaten me at a game of tables, I muttered, "All right, maybe not that different."

"If it makes you feel any better," Macer said, "I've ordered him to make a formal apology for his error to your Century."

This was something, at least, and I asked, "When?"

"Tomorrow, before we break camp, at our morning formation."

While this was still not enough to completely satisfy me, I did take some pleasure in the idea of the haughty youngster forced to make a public statement, taking responsibility for what had happened, certain as I was that his pride would take a severe beating because of it.

"And, Titus," Macer broke into my thoughts, and while he spoke in a conversational tone, there was a severity to it that I rarely heard aimed at me, "don't ever show me that kind of disrespect again. Do you understand me?"

In fact, I did, quite well, and I assured him that I would not. And, I have not.

As ordered, Volusenus stood in the small forum of our camp and expressed his regret at the outcome caused by his error in forgetting to send flanking guards out after our rest stop the day before. He spoke clearly enough, and despite my feelings towards him, I could see the remorse was genuine, although I told myself it might be counterfeit. Not once did he look in my direction, choosing to keep his eyes riveted on an imaginary spot just above the heads of the men in the middle of the formation. Once he was finished, he spun about, and marched to resume his spot next to the Sixth, but Macer had nothing to add, other than the command to break camp and begin the day's march.

Our original task had been to make an appearance at two Sugambri villages, part of the program prescribed by Tiberius after our campaign after Varus' defeat, both to remind the natives Rome was still here and to perform a search for supplies of weapons, over and above the bare minimum allowed by the Princeps. We reached the first village less than a watch after resuming the march, where we were met with the same sullen but muted hatred, as the village headman stood in front of his assembled people in their version of a forum, the standard practice Rome demanded. Macer conducted a brief interrogation of the headman, using the freedman interpreter who was more or less permanently assigned to the Fourth Cohort whenever we ventured across the Rhenus, while the rest of us supervised the search. And, as we expected, we found nothing in the way of armor and weapons; the only slight oddity was that their food supplies seemed to be quite a bit more than the number of villagers present would require, something that Macer called the rest of us to discuss.

"They have more grain than they need to feed the number of people they have," the Pilus Prior mused.

"Last winter was fairly easy, and they had a good harvest," Philus observed. "Maybe this is just surplus."

This, we all knew, was true, but while Macer nodded in seeming acceptance, his tone was doubtful as he answered, "That's certainly possible." He looked over at me, asking, "What do you think, Pullus?"

"I think that we need to assume the worst," I answered honestly. "All that being true, it's just as likely that they're missing men."

"The headman did say there was a hunting party out right now," Macer said, but I was not convinced.

"Did he say how many?"

"A dozen," Macer replied.

"The amount of grain we found will feed a lot more than just a dozen more mouths," Vespillo put in, then pointed out, "and we all know that we never find every single cache."

This was nothing more than the truth, and I saw that this scored with Macer, and he slowly nodded, then said, "We need to make sure we report this to the Legate when we get back. Otherwise, there's not much we can do."

"Not much we can do?" To this point, as he should have been, especially given the events of the day before, Volusenus had been silent, but he burst out with this now, and before we could say anything, he continued, "They're clearly lying to us! They should be punished for that!"

This outburst was greeted with mutters from my counterparts, but while they were smart enough to let Macer handle this matter, I could not stop myself from growling, "You've done enough damage for one march, *boy*. You need to keep your mouth shut when your superiors are talking!"

As I hoped, Volusenus did not take this well, stiffening and staring at me with undisguised hostility, which I returned in kind, until Macer's voice cut in, "That's enough, Pullus. But," he turned to Volusenus, "the Princeps Prior is right in that you don't have the experience with these matters that the rest of us do. So you should spend your time listening, not talking." Volusenus clearly did not care for this, though he did not say anything more, while I ignored his glaring at me as Macer continued, "We'll report this to the Legate when we get back. Otherwise, I'll let them know we're done. And," he paused, "I've decided we're not going to go check on the second village. It's another five miles east, and I don't like us being any deeper across the river than we are."

Frankly, I was relieved, and I saw that the others were as well; with one exception, of course, but he kept his mouth shut. Within a few hundred heartbeats, we had formed up and were marching back towards the river, which we reached the next day, crossing back over to Ubiorum with only my Century suffering any casualties.

The night of our return, I was sitting at my desk, writing out the report that is required whenever a Centurion loses men under his command. Naturally, this meant that my mood was not the best to begin with, but it was about to get worse when Alex knocked at my door.

"Centurion," his use of my title alerted me that this was not a routine matter, but it was his expression that was even more telling, "someone is here to see you."

I had been so absorbed in my report that I had not even heard anyone enter the outer office, and I asked him who it was.

"It's Hastatus Posterior Volusenus," Alex said carefully, although the flat inflection he used was one with which I was familiar. "He requests a moment of your time."

I signaled him to close the door, and when he did, I asked quietly, "Did he really request it? Or did he demand it?"

The shrug he gave I considered eloquent proof that Alex was being judicious, and in his way, trying to watch out for me, and I confess that, despite the flare of anger I felt at this display of arrogant disrespect, in my own way, I heeded it.

Not commenting further, I said only, "Send him in." Alex turned, but before he opened the door, I added, still speaking quietly, "And send Balio for Structus. Have him wait in the outer office."

My nephew simply nodded, then opened the door and stepped back out, which partially muffled his voice as he told Volusenus, "The Princeps Prior will see you now."

Without a word spoken, I heard Volusenus' heavy tread, but because of the door, I only caught a glimpse of the manner in which he brushed by Alex, not even acknowledging his presence, just like every other haughty bastard who viewed those around them as nothing more than furniture; there only to serve a specific purpose. Regardless of this display of brusque rudeness, I admit that even if Volusenus had been polite to Alex, it would not have altered the outcome of what was about to take place. Volusenus did not walk as much as march the few steps across the room, stopping in front of my desk, and while it caused me to grind my teeth, I gestured to the chair in an unspoken invitation.

"I prefer to stand for this," he said stiffly, his eyes aimed at a spot above my head.

I gave a shrug that I hoped conveyed my air of disinterest, saying, "As you wish. Now," I asked pleasantly, "what can I do for you, Hastatus Posterior Volusenus?"

This was the moment he looked down at me, and when he did, I realized with a jolt of an energy that this was really the first time the two of us had looked each other directly in the eye and reminded me of a time I had almost forgotten. And, while I cannot say with any certainty, I got the sense that Volusenus experienced something similar, because an expression of what I took to be confusion briefly washed away the look of grim determination that he had been wearing less than a heartbeat before. As far as what that sensation was, I can only speak for my own state of mind, which was that there was something queerly familiar in those eyes of his, as if they belonged to someone I knew, or more accurately, had known. How could he possibly remind me of Sextus? I wondered.

Volusenus stood there for what was perhaps two heartbeats of time, then the mask he had been wearing when he entered returned, and he finally spoke, saying, "I have come for an apology from you, Princeps Prior."

My initial reaction was to tell him that, since he had already offered a public apology a couple days before, there was no need for him to do so in private, but then my mind caught up with my ears, and I managed to stop my initial response.

What came out was something of a gasp as I sputtered, "An apology? From me?"

"Yes," he snapped. "You publicly humiliated me the other day, and I will not tolerate that kind of thing, not from anyone." He paused, then added, "Especially not from you."

Honestly, at this moment, I was more bemused than angry, and without thinking how it might be taken, I began, "Son…"

"I. Am. Not. Your. Son!"

So enraged was Volusenus that he actually took a step towards my desk, his empty hand curling into a fist, although he did not raise his *vitus*, which told me that he was at least partially in control of himself, since that could have spelled his doom. I was sufficiently alarmed that I rose to my feet as well, but I was also getting angry too, which a part of me took note of, and I took a breath.

"Volusenus, that is just an expression," I began carefully, "because you're a youngster..."

"My age has nothing to do with this!" he shot back, and while he un-balled his fist, it was to do something even worse, and that was to point a finger directly at me. "You've shown me nothing but disrespect since the day I arrived! I'm in the Centurionate, just like you..."

"You're in the Centurionate," I agreed but matched his harshness, "because your Tata bought you a spot. And," I went on, realizing that, despite my intention to keep it in check, my anger was now loose, "you're an arrogant boy who got my men killed."

"I apologized for that!" He was shouting now and had taken another step closer, so that we were now separated by only the width of my desk. "But you've been insulting me before that even happened, and I won't tolerate it!"

Rather than shout right back, I forced myself to take a breath, then deliberately pitching my voice back to a conversational level, I asked, "And? What do you propose to do about it if I don't stop? Write to Tata? And then what? He'll run and tell the Princeps?"

As I hoped, this scored a blow, his face flushing even more than it already was, which also told me that he had been considering doing that very thing.

"I don't need my father to fight my battles," he finally replied stiffly. "I assure you, Pullus, I can handle myself quite well."

"Oh?" Now that I felt I had the advantage, I was not about to let up, and I gave a laugh that was as mocking as I could manage. "Can you, *boy*? Did your gladiator tutor really teach you enough that you think you can best me?"

"I know all about your reputation," Volusenus retorted, "but that doesn't scare me."

"It should."

This did not come from my mouth, and we both jerked in surprise, Volusenus spinning about while I bent at the waist to look past him to the man standing in the door. Marcus Macer was leaning against the frame, in his tunic without his *baltea*, although he was carrying his *vitus*, which he pointed directly at Volusenus.

"Volusenus, I don't know what this is about, and I don't care. But I heard enough, and consider this a fair warning. If you want to spar with Princeps Prior Pullus, I'm going to be held responsible for the damage he does to you."

"Or I do to him!" Volusenus shot back, having clearly lost his self-control.

I expected Macer to lose his temper then; instead, he stared, long and hard at Volusenus, then he glanced over at me. Correctly interpreting his look, I gave a small shrug, sending him the message that I was more than happy to take this matter to its conclusion, yet rather than looking pleased, he seemed as irritated with me as he was with Volusenus.

"Fine!" he snapped. "We'll convene in the bathhouse a third of a watch after the call to retire. Only the Centurions and Optios of the Fourth will be there. I'll bring the *rudii,* training shields, and the protective gear. Then you two can bash each other's brains out for all I care. But," now he lifted his *vitus* to point it again, first at Volusenus, then at me, "once this is over, if either of you tries to get revenge because you lost, I will bring you both up on charges, and I'll do everything in my power to see that you're busted back to the ranks. Is that understood?"

"Understood," I answered first, which, as I hoped, got under Volusenus' skin, because he shot me a poisonous glare as he answered Macer, also in the affirmative.

"Now, let me go get this arranged so we can get this nonsense out of the way," Macer said as he strode out of my quarters, leaving Volusenus and me to stand there.

I waited until our Pilus Prior was out of earshot, then gave Volusenus a grin that I did not mean as I said, "Well, at least I've been in the ranks before."

Just as I hoped, this seemed to rattle Volusenus even further, but he had the sense to keep his mouth shut and stalk out, following Macer, and leaving me to watch through my open doorway at his retreating broad back. Naturally, he slammed the door on the way out, and after the shouting that had been going on, the sudden quiet after his departure was a bit unsettling. While I had a view out into the outer office, I could not see either Alex or Balio, a Gaul who had been born a slave and now served as Alex's assistant clerk. Despite there being no sign, I was not fooled.

"You might as well get in here," I said loudly enough that there was no way either could claim they did not hear me.

I heard a voice mutter something, then Alex stepped into the doorway, alone, looking understandably cautious.

"I told you to get Structus here," I said severely, "not the Pilus Prior. Or," I thought to add, "was that Balio's bright idea?"

"No," Alex answered readily enough, but I also noticed he seemed content to stand just inside the doorway, "it was mine."

I stared at him, hard, then I grunted, "Good boy. That was the right thing to do."

For an instant, I thought he would faint, but he recovered himself quickly enough that it might have been my imagination, then he came bustling in, moving to the rack to get my armor and make sure it was properly oiled, which I knew it was.

"Uncle Titus," he looked at me with an intensity that he only used when he considered a matter to be of the utmost importance, "I want you to knock that *cunnus* out."

Technically, I should have admonished him for speaking about a fellow Centurion in such a flagrantly disrespectful manner, but I suppose I just was not in the mood to do so.

Gnaeus Volusenus was certainly strong, probably second only to Draxo, the Colapiani chieftain I faced and slew the night Urso died. And, if I am being brutally honest, he was not unskilled, so it took me a bit longer than I would have liked to demonstrate to him, and the other officers of the Fourth who were watching, that I was still the best man with a *gladius*, not only in the Cohort, but in the Legion. Only once did he have me in any real difficulty, after he landed a hard thrust to my ribs that, even with it being a blunted wooden blade, and wearing armor and padded tunic, knocked the wind from my lungs and forced me on the defensive for the length of time it took me to catch my breath. His youth also helped him last longer than I would have liked, as I noticed that, even after catching my wind, his own breathing was always easier than mine. Nevertheless, I found myself standing over him after knocking him flat on his back with a combination of a feinted thrust that forced him to overcommit himself, followed by a shield punch that hit him square in the chest. The sight of the soles of his *caligae*, particularly given his own size, flying up in the air as he landed heavily on his back, a great whooshing sound as the air left his lungs from the impact, was quite gratifying, although the gasps and mutters of surprise from our onlookers was almost as good. Nevertheless, I was also strangely dissatisfied, not because I had not proven my superiority to the extent that I wished, but at myself, because before we began, I had promised myself that, short of shattering his arm, I was going to punish Volusenus the way I had Maxentius, now more than twenty years before.

146

However, when the moment came, rather than prolong the bout so that I could inflict more pain on my opponent, I found I could not do it, choosing instead to end it in the manner I just described. Even more unsettling, at least as far as I was concerned, was that I did not feel nearly the sense of satisfaction I thought I would; indeed, there was a part of me that was disgusted with myself for having participated in this bout at all. Even as the others were pounding me on the back, laughing and joking about how easily I had put this young, haughty paid man in his place, I was struggling with the unexpected sense of worry I was feeling for Volusenus. Not physically; he had gotten to his feet quickly enough, and had even insisted on continuing, but Macer had put a stop to that immediately, and now he was standing in the corner, alone, stripping off the arm padding and untying the wicker faceguard from his helmet.

"That'll teach the young pup!" Vespillo laughed, and without thinking, I shot a glance over at Volusenus, but his back was to us.

Macer, seeing me look over at my vanquished opponent, turned and walked over to Volusenus. The others were still chattering away, reliving the bout, such as it was, and asking me questions about certain moves I had made. I kept my eye, surreptitiously, on the Pilus Prior and Volusenus, and I saw the younger man shake his head at something Macer had said. While he did not raise his voice, I knew the look on Macer's face, so I prepared myself for what I was certain was coming.

"Pullus! Get over here," Macer commanded, then added, "The rest of you as well."

We walked over; only after Macer took Volusenus' arm and physically turned him about did the younger man face me, and I was again assailed by the uncomfortable feeling caused by the stab of sympathy I felt at his flaming cheeks, the shame of his defeat plain to see.

"You two are going to shake hands, just like after every sparring bout," Macer commanded.

I thrust mine out, and while Volusenus hesitated, it was barely noticeable, or perhaps it was my imagination. Still, we clasped arms, and as we did, Macer said loudly enough for the rest to hear, "This is the first and last time we're ever going to speak about this. And this stays in this Cohort. If I hear a whisper about this from anyone outside, I won't stop until I found out who ran their mouths. And," he finished with a grim, harsh smile, "I'll have Pullus here thrash you. And I won't stop the bout. Does everyone understand me?"

Not surprisingly, the nine other men all swore on the black stone that not a word would be heard about this. Somewhat surprisingly, they all proved true to their word; I suppose it is because of my hubris that I like to think that Macer's threat had something to do with it.

When I returned to my quarters, Alex was naturally still up and waiting for me, where he helped me out of my armor and the sweat-soaked tunic, then gave me a quick scraping. I had just changed into a fresh tunic and was looking forward to collapsing on my cot to get some rest when Balio knocked on my door, which Alex opened, since he was about to leave.

"Centurion, you have a visitor." Groaning, I was about to tell Balio to send them away, when he added, "It's the Hastatus Posterior."

Alex and I exchanged a surprised glance, and I told Balio to see him in, while I hurried to sit behind my desk, wondering if this youngster was truly foolhardy enough to continue pursuing this matter. Volusenus entered, but this time, while he did not say anything, he acknowledged Alex with a nod, while my nephew stood there, looking at me questioningly. Waving at him to leave and shut the door, I pretended to have my attention on this, although I was surreptitiously eyeing Volusenus. And, I confess, I was happy to see him moving gingerly. Like the last time, when I motioned to the chair, he shook his head, which seemed to confirm my fear that this hardheaded equestrian rich boy was going to make both our lives more miserable.

Instead, I was shocked when he said ruefully, "If I sit down, Princeps Prior, I don't know if I can get back up again."

Before I could stop myself, this evoked a laugh, which caused his face to darken, then even more surprisingly, he actually chuckled; weakly, but it was unmistakable.

"What can I do for you, Volusenus?"

I tried to keep my tone light, but this seemed to agitate him, and he muttered something under his breath that I could not make out, then he burst out, "It's just that I've never been beaten before! And," I saw the knob of his throat bob, "you did it so easily." As he shook his head for a second time, there was not a hint of the arrogant, haughty youngster who had marched into my office just a matter of a couple watches earlier. "I just...it's...hard."

Before I could think about it, I was standing, and I circled around my desk to put a hand on his shoulder; frankly, I do not know which of us was more surprised at my gesture, but I was cautiously pleased that he did not jerk away. Sitting down on the edge of the desk, I regarded him for a moment, trying to think of the best way to approach this unexpected matter.

Finally, I began, "I'm guessing you know who my grandfather was."

Nodding, he answered, "Of course. Titus Pullus, Primus Pilus of the Equestrians, one of Divus Julius' favorites and one of the first Camp Prefects, named by the Princeps."

"That," I agreed, "is the bare bones of it. But," this time, I was the one who shook my head, mainly because this mention of my Avus stirred up so many memories, "he was more than that to me. He was my first real teacher about what..." I waved one hand around at our surroundings. "...this life is all about."

Pausing again – this time, I was trying to frame my thoughts – I then asked, "How often do you work the stakes?"

"Now?" Volusenus shrugged. "Whenever I have time. Being a Centurion is new to me. Well..." He gave me an embarrassed grin, the first time I had seen him display this kind of emotion, and I experienced another unexpected stab of...something. Which, naturally, he was oblivious to, as he went on. "...you know that. But I suppose I wasn't prepared for all the paperwork involved." This did make me laugh in agreement, and he returned to the original question. "So, now how often am I at the stakes?" Shaking his head, he admitted, "Probably no more than twice a week, if that."

"My grandfather," I told him, "and my father, for that matter, worked for at least a third of a watch a day, every day, working at the stakes on their forms. In fact," I remembered, "my grandfather did that after he retired, up to the day he died. Naturally," I did add, "it's not always possible, like when we're on campaign. But in camp?"

"Do you do that?" Volusenus asked.

"Yes," I assured him. "It's gotten to be such a habit that if I miss a day, I don't feel right."

He nodded thoughtfully and acknowledged, "I can see how that would be the case."

"Your size is a blade that cuts both ways," I continued, deciding on the fly to keep going, "and you've gotten accustomed to using that size to just overpower your opponents. Which will work...most of the time." I paused for a moment, trying to decide how far down this road I could go before I pricked his already battered pride. As usual, I plunged ahead. "Until you run into someone like me." Before he could say anything, I hurried on, "And, trust me on this, Volusenus, while you and I are unusual for Romans, I've seen more Germans than I can count that are at least as big. And," I added, "even larger. And we're not the only ones who train a lot."

I shut up then, watching the other man absorb this, and I saw that he was taking my words seriously, looking thoughtful.

Still, I was not prepared when he asked abruptly, "Will you help me, Princeps Prior? Will you," again, I saw the knot of his throat dip, "train with me so that I can move and fight the way you do?"

This was so unexpected, given our previous interactions, I was at a loss for words, which he interpreted as a rebuff, because his face closed up, the head tilted again, and I realized that I had to speak quickly, or this moment would be gone.

"I'd be happy to help you." The words felt foreign as they left my mouth, but they clearly did not strike a false note, since Volusenus' face expressed his relief. "But," I warned him, "we both need to go to the Pilus Prior and tell him about this, because if he sees us in the square…"

"He'll bust us back to the ranks," Volusenus finished, and again, the grin appeared, which completely changed his entire countenance and demeanor. "And you're right. I've never been a ranker, and I don't want to find out what it's like."

Standing erect, I offered my arm, and this time he took it without any rancor or reluctance, and I told him, "We'll start tomorrow."

His expression changed, slightly, which I understood when he asked, "Could it be the day after tomorrow? I'm a bit sore."

Laughing, I assured him that was fine, and he left me in my quarters, in a thoughtful mood.

Somewhat to my irritation, Macer did not seem a bit surprised that Volusenus and I had reached this agreement, which was only partially explained when he observed, "It makes sense. You're the only other man his size in the Cohort, and one of the only ones in the Legion. And," he added, "you're better with a *gladius* than any of those other giants."

151

This certainly made sense, yet there was something in Macer's manner, a certain air of smug satisfaction that not only told me there was more to his words, but rankled me deeply. Regardless, I made no comment, other than to say that we would be sure that our training would not impact either of our Centuries. As he had requested, we began sparring two days after our bout, and fairly quickly, I realized something that was not only unexpected, but was quite pleasing; I was enjoying myself immensely. Not, I must clarify, for the reason one might think, that it gave me an opportunity to reassert my superiority over Volusenus, but because he was so eager to learn, and, frankly, a quick study. It was perhaps a month after we began, when the frost was becoming a daily occurrence, before I sensed that our relationship had reached a point where I felt I could ask a question that had been nagging at me.

"You know," I began, "you clearly have a natural talent for fighting." This clearly pleased him, so I was encouraged to continue. "Forgive me if I'm wrong, but what I remember is that your father never served under the standard."

"No," Volusenus answered readily enough, "he didn't." Suddenly, he broke his gaze away from me, studying his feet, and he continued, "He wasn't particularly happy that I wanted to serve in the Legions. He expected me to take over his business."

Honestly, I was struck by this, recalling a recent letter from my father, which prompted me to say, "Well, that's not surprising, really. I have," even now, some years later, I had to amend, "actually, I *had* three brothers." At this, he looked up at me as I went on, "And you know about my family history. But not too long ago, I got a letter from my father, who was a Quartus Pilus Prior like Macer until," the bitterness I still felt surprised me, "he lost his leg. Anyway, he was telling me that my two younger brothers, Gaius and Septimus, have made it clear they have no intention of joining the Legions. Not like me. Or," I had to take a breath, "my brother Sextus." Shaking my head, I finished, "The point is that sons don't always follow in their father's footsteps. And that's not a bad thing."

Volusenus seemed to consider this, nodding thoughtfully. Then, he asked, "Where's your brother who's serving? Is he in the 1st?"

Despite knowing he meant nothing personal with his question, nevertheless, I felt a deep, acute stab deep in my gut, which I tried to ignore as I answered flatly, "No. He was in the 8th. And he's dead now."

Volusenus' expression conveyed his embarrassment, and he mumbled, "I'm sorry. I didn't know."

"No reason you should," I answered him, hoping this would be enough.

For a moment, he seemed as if he was going to pursue it, but I suppose he saw my face; instead, he asked, "How did your father take your brothers who don't want to serve in the Legions?"

Shrugging, I answered, "The way he looks at it, he had two sons who served Rome, so he's satisfied."

"I'm an only child," Volusenus said glumly. "So my father had different ideas for my future. But," he shook his head, "as long as I can remember, all I've ever wanted is to serve in the Legions."

"What about your mother?" I asked, only slightly curious, if I am being honest.

The look he gave me was somewhat veiled, which I understood when he admitted, "Actually, it was my mother who gave me the idea about serving in the Legions." He sighed, then gave a shrug similar to the one I had just given. "She's always seemed to know that I'm not cut out for being in business like my father."

We talked no more about it, resuming our sparring session, and very quickly, I forgot the conversation until recently.

The Legions went into their winter routine as Germanicus finished his Consulship, and all we had to show for this campaign season was a bit more than two dozen men dead, spread over the Legion, all of them in ambushes like the one in which I lost three men, a few burned villages, and a frustratingly small number of dead Germans. While I cannot say we had become complacent, we had definitely become accustomed to an atmosphere of almost constant rumors swirling around Ubiorum, whispers of secret pacts between tribes who wanted to unseat Arminius, who still held sway over the confederation of Germans. That his grasp of power was tenuous was no secret; the evidence was the fact that, now a couple months more than three years after Varus' defeat, we still had not been inundated with a Germanic horde, rolling across the Rhenus to slaughter every Roman they found. I can only imagine how foolish the citizens of Rome felt, given the level of panic we heard had infected the populace, to the point where there were barricades thrown up around the Subura and slaves were offered manumission in exchange for serving in a scratch military force. Although this fever had subsided, we in the Rhenus Legions were still dealing with the effects of those days, namely in the rabble we had been forced to fill our depleted ranks with, like Pusio. Over the previous three years, he had learned, albeit the hard way, to at least be circumspect in his seemingly never-ending attempts to incite his comrades into a state of almost constant discontent. If there was one positive thing I could say about Pusio, it would be that he could take a beating; I know this to be the case because, when a thrashing at the hands of his Sergeant, then by Structus did not seem to get across to him his activities would not be tolerated, I took my turn, not once but on three separate occasions. The last time, my frustration got the better of me, and I broke two of his ribs, injuring him enough that he could not perform his duties, although he was wise enough to insist that he had fallen in the bathhouse when he was put on the sick and injured list. And, while it pains me to admit it, I allowed him to lounge on the list for a few days longer than was necessary for him to recover, which made him something of a hero among his comrades. Any man who is able to somehow subvert the regulations, escape regular duties that the men consider onerous or unpleasant, and in myriad other ways cheat the entity known as "the army" is destined to become an admired figure within his Century, and even by the Cohort. This was something I forgot on occasion, so I must take my share of responsibility with creating Pusio as a figure of admiration, one who held a considerable amount of sway over men who had grievances of their own.

Those grievances, it also pains me to say, were legitimate; for three years after the Varus disaster, there were no extended leaves allowed by any of the Legions of the Army of the Rhenus, even in the case where a man's parents died and his presence was required for the disposition of the will. This extended to officers, both in the Optionate and Centurionate, and it had a direct impact on me as well, because I received a letter from my brother Gaius in Arelate, who was now in his mid-twenties, that my father, Gaius Porcinianus Pullus, had finally died, much like my Avus, peacefully, in his sleep. Normally, even when leaves were technically restricted, if a man was willing to pay enough, those rules could be overlooked; these were not normal times, and I did not even attempt to do so, mainly because I had seen both Cornutus, in my own Century, and the Quintus Pilus Prior Clepsina have a similar situation, and they were both denied, despite offering the Legate a hefty sum to go home. Next to my Avus, I can think of no other man who deserved to die in such a manner, at peace and in his bed. I would like to think that, since it happened with the first Titus Pullus, and my father, perhaps I will be lucky enough to make old bones and die in bed. Somehow, while I have never given it much thought, the few times that I have, such as immediately after reading Gaius' letter, I cannot picture this as a likely fate for me, though neither can I say why I feel this way. Nevertheless, knowing that I could not go home to pay my respects to my father sat no better with me than it had with Cornutus, Clepsina, and the men of the ranks who suffered a similar loss. This was one thing; Augustus' decision to extend enlistments to twenty years because of the Varus disaster was the decision that aroused the ire of most of the men, even among the Centurionate. Frankly, it did not matter to me all that much, if only because I had set as my goal long before of spending as much time under the standard as Titus Pullus, but that did not mean I was not sympathetic to the complaints of men who, thinking they were nearing the end of their enlistment, were told that they had four more years. This was bad enough, but as loath as I am to give credence to any complaints by men like Pusio, their plight was even worse, since they had been pressed into service because of the Varus disaster, then only after they were under the standard were they told they were expected to fulfill a complete enlistment. Then, less than two years into their term, they had another four years added to it. Augustus did not make many errors in judgment, but his decision to apply this term of service on every man in the Legions, and not only to new enlistees, who would have at least known what they were signing up for, was one of his worst, and I was far from alone in that opinion. Although none of us ever heard any confirmation, it was also accepted among us that what was behind Augustus' decision as far as the men of the special *dilectus* was to remove some of the more troublesome elements from Rome, more or less permanently. One reason for this belief was the relatively high number of men of the equestrian order; granted, they were not the wealthiest of the class, but in the months after their arrival, Centurions who had been stuck with these men who had connections to someone in the city made discreet inquiries, which was how we learned that every one of these men, including Pusio, had been agitating for any number of reasons. Regardless of the reasons, they were with us, and we had become accustomed to their presence, although a fair number of them had been winnowed from the ranks in a number of ways over the previous three years. Most of this latter category either fell ill, like in the plague that claimed Macula, or were one of the sprinkling of men who were killed in what little action we did see during this time period, and if I was a suspicious man, I might find it peculiar how they seemed to be a disproportionate number of the casualties. Only after Macer pointed this fact out to me, I must add; he was also the one who noticed how many of these men were also involved in the inevitable brawls out in town, and how few of them were the victors in these combats, usually between men in different Cohorts, or since we had been joined by the 20th, a different Legion. Once I gave it some thought, I surmised that, when it came to the events outside camp, this was an example of how the rankers in the Legions handle their own problems, dispensing justice as they see fit, and in a manner that we Centurions and Optios could suspect was more than met the eye, yet we could never prove it. Looking back, I believe that the officers were guilty of becoming complacent; while it was true that there had been this mood of resentment, it always remained just subdued enough that, as the weeks turned into months, and then into years, we learned to turn a blind eye to all but the most egregious examples. There was some good news coming in our future, though, which also helped keep the lid on the boiling pot a bit longer.

On the Kalends of Januarius, the Centurions of both Legions were summoned to the forum, where the Legate made an announcement that, for one Centurion in particular, was welcome news.

"The Princeps has named Germanicus Julius Caesar as the Praetor of all of Germania and Tres Galliae, with *Proconsular* imperium." His tone was flat, giving nothing away in terms of his personal feelings on the matter that he was now outranked. "He will be residing in Colonia Copa Munatius Felix, although I am sure that during his duties, he will be visiting us here in Ubiorum, as well as the Legions in Vetera and Mogontiacum."

Not unexpectedly, this created a ripple of comment through the ranks, while Macer elbowed me in the ribs and said, "I bet you're happy about that. Maybe he'll request you to be his bodyguard. Or something," he added, which caused me to give him a sharp glance, but his face did not give me any hint of his meaning.

It had been quite some time since I had had any communication either with Germanicus or Tiberius, for that matter, through Dolabella, of course, but I was quite thankful for seemingly being forgotten, although I was also aware that Macer had long harbored suspicions that I played some sort of role for Tiberius.

"No more happy than anyone else by the sound of it," was all I said, and he did not pursue the matter.

With this piece of news, we dispersed, back to our areas and the realities of the mundane and constantly restive atmosphere of our men. On our way back, Macer and the rest of his Centurions walked in a group, and after a brief discussion of the news about Germanicus, as we had been doing for months, we ended up on the topic that was foremost in our collective minds and concerns.

"I think that we need to get stuck in to those fucking Germans, once and for all," Vespillo said, as emphatic as he always was when expressing this opinion.

When he had first made this pronouncement, I had dismissed it, although a fair amount of this came from my personal feelings towards the man, who was still rankled that

Macer was Pilus Prior. By this time, it had now been more than six years, and Vespillo still resisted Macer's authority, much like my Avus' old nemesis Celer when he took command of the Second Cohort of the Equestrians, which had done more to alter my original opinion of Vespillo than any other single factor. However, as loath as I was to admit it now, I had begun to believe that, in this, Vespillo had the rights of it.

"Well," this from Philus, "I certainly haven't heard anything that would suggest we're going to be marching. At least," he added, "as an army."

"It would still be at least four months before that could even happen," Cornutus put in glumly, indulging in his natural tendency towards pessimism and viewing matters in the worst light possible.

As he said this, I was reminded of something Macer had said about Cornutus, and I was forced to look in the other direction to avoid him seeing my smirk.

"You could give that man an amphora of honey, and he would empty it out on the ground, certain there was a rat turd in there somewhere."

Still, like Vespillo, he was only speaking the truth, no matter how gloomy it may have been. As odd as it may sound, I agreed with the others that the best thing to quell this growing discontent would be going on campaign, with the entire army, and closing with Arminius' confederation of tribes once and for all. Not only would it give the men an enemy to focus on that was not Rome, in the person of the Princeps, just based on the law of averages, it would perform a further winnowing of those malcontents who spent more time complaining than time at the stakes. Speaking of the stakes, I noticed that, while all of the Fourth Cohort Centurions expressed an opinion, Volusenus seemed content to wait for the rest of us to speak, then when he did open his mouth, it was to essentially proclaim that he was willing to follow the lead of our Pilus Prior. By this point in time,

I had spent a fair amount of time with the younger man, and aside from what I considered a natural tendency towards haughtiness, and the belief that he was superior not just by virtue of his size and strength, but his ancestry, I had come to think that he had the potential to be a good, perhaps great Centurion. Working in his favor was that he had discerned the manner in which Gillo had been running his Century, and had put a stop to it in a way that left us wondering, and Gillo with his fair share of bruises, although the Optio refused to comment on how he came by them.

Although Germanicus did go to Colonia Copa Munatius Felix, he was not there more than three months before moving to Ubiorum. At first, this was met with something close to jubilation, because it was instantly assumed that his reason for doing so was to prepare us for campaign. However, no orders issued from the *Praetorium* to begin the work we knew had to be done in order to make the Legions ready to march. Through Alex, who pumped his friends among the clerks in the headquarters building, we learned that Germanicus had radically different priorities than avenging Varus, at least at this point in time.

"He's busy conducting a census of all the Gallic provinces," I informed Macer within moments of learning this from Alex.

Macer was surprised, commenting, "That doesn't seem like something he'd be involved with directly."

I had thought this as well, which was why I had pressed Alex, so I replied, "Apparently, he's directing the effort personally." As we sat there, sipping our wine, I tried to think of something, finally coming up with, "I *think* the last time a census was conducted of the provinces was by Germanicus' father. But," I shrugged, "I could be wrong."

Macer let out a low whistle.

"That would be, what, twenty years ago?" he ventured.

"More than that," I assured him. "It's at least twenty-five."

Macer considered, then said with a shrug, "Then I suppose it's time. And, given how fast these Gauls and Germans breed, I can only imagine how many more people are there."

"And they all owe the Princeps tribute," I reminded Macer, "which means some of it will come our way."

"You mean they owe Rome a tax for the protection we provide them, and all the other good things we bring to these barbarians, don't you?"

If it had been someone other than Macer, I would have taken this as a warning that I had overstepped and was now treading in dangerous territory.

Instead, I just grinned and replied, "One man's tax is another man's tribute. All I care about is some of that money trickles down to us."

While I was being deliberately lighthearted, Macer was not fooled, understanding the real concern I was feeling about the state of the Legion, which I knew he shared, signaled by his own grin fading, followed by a heavy sigh.

"I'll give an offering to make it so," he said soberly. We sat in silence for a moment, and I could see he was considering something, which he finally articulated by asking, "If we don't march this year, what do you think is going to happen?"

While the question was not unexpected, I did not particularly want to answer, if only because I knew my opinion would distress my Pilus Prior and friend.

"I think," I tried to be careful with my words, "that if we don't march, it's a virtual certainty that there's going to be some sort of trouble with the rankers. I mean," I added hastily, "more than what they're already giving us."

"You mean a mutiny?" Macer's voice was hushed, as it should have been when using this word. "You really think that's a possibility?"

"If you had asked me a few months ago, I would have said it was unlikely," I answered. "But now?" Shaking my head, I finished, "I think it's probably going to happen unless we march."

It was barely more than a week later when it seemed as if our collective prayers were answered, but I was still wrong.

"The Germans have crossed the Rhenus!"

Alex had burst into my quarters, having run all the way from the *Praetorium*, where he had been dropping off the monthly ration request. Looking up from the schedule I was working on for the coming week, I saw he was not only breathless, his eyes were alight with the kind of eagerness that reminded me that not just men under the standard look forward to the idea of going on campaign.

Nevertheless, I was not quite as willing to get excited, simply because this had happened before, which I reminded him, but he dismissed this by saying, "I already heard the Legate's chief clerk talk about what needed to be done to march as quickly as possible."

That brought me to my feet, and taking Alex by the arm, I took him to Macer's quarters, where he repeated what he had heard. Macer knew and trusted Alex, but he was, if not doubtful, at least cautious about whether or not he would rouse the Cohort to make preparations.

"We did that once before," he pointed out, "and we didn't march. And," he reminded me, although there was no need, "it caused us more problems than it was worth."

This was true, certainly; several months before, word had come from one of the northern settlements that a large horde of Germans had swarmed across the river. That time, it had actually been Macer's clerk and Alex's best friend Lucco, who had come hurrying from the *Praetorium* after overhearing an almost identical report. The one difference turned out to be the crucial one, since Lucco had been present when a near-hysterical courier had burst into the building, blurting out this lurid tale of rampant slaughter by what he swore was the entire German host. Thinking to get ahead of the frenzied chaos that is a Legion marching on short notice, and more importantly, placing us at the head of the line at the *Quaestorium*, Macer gave the order to start preparing, and we Centurions worked the men like dogs, through the night. When the morning dawned, and we paraded the men, stumbling with exhaustion but ready to march, only then did we learn that new information had arrived after the first courier, and that the "horde" of Germans turned out to be another warband of perhaps a hundred men. More importantly, they had spent less than a full day on our side of the Rhenus, retreating back across the river shortly before sundown. The only thing that saved the Fourth Cohort from being the object of mockery and ridicule by the rest of the Legion, which is the favorite sport of Legionaries, is that all but two Cohorts had behaved in the same manner. More importantly, it gave the men something to complain about, and the week after this incident saw the Centurions and Optios working even harder than normal, meting out punishment, both official and unofficial, before the men lapsed back into obedience; a sullen, resentful obedience, but this was one of those times we looked the other way. This time, however, was different, which Macer discerned, so that when we began grabbing our Centuries from what they had been doing to start preparing to march, the Fourth Cohort, along with the Second, Third, Sixth, and Eighth were able to report to Sacrovir that they were ready to march whenever Germanicus commanded two days later. More importantly, at least to me, was the identity of the Legate who would be commanding us, the 1st and 20th, in the field, and I learned it from Germanicus himself. We happened to run into each other by chance, as he was exiting the *Praetorium* and I was on the way to the

Quaestorium in the next building, but despite clearly being in a hurry, he stopped and called my name, a broad grin on his face.

He returned my salute, except then he extended his arm, which I clasped, as he said, "You're as large as ever, I see, Pullus!" Then, Germanicus made an exaggerated gesture by pointing to my hair which, while still short, was in desperate need of a trim, hooting, "What's that I see? Gray hair?"

Matching his bantering tone, and counting on our previous relationship, I countered, "It comes from being sent all over the place by Legates who don't know what they're doing."

As I hoped, this made him laugh, and he answered, "Well, I hope I do a better job of it." Suddenly, the humor vanished from his face, and he turned sober as he asked in a quiet tone that only I could hear, "How are the men? Are they ready to march? And," his voice dropped even lower, "will they fight?"

This I felt confident about, assuring him, "When we're formed up and ready to get stuck in against those Germans, I promise you, they'll fight."

"Good!" he exclaimed, then in a manner that indicated he was confiding in me, he almost whispered, "This should be a fairly easy matter, Pullus. True, it's a sizable force, about three thousand infantry and five hundred cavalry, but it shouldn't pose a problem. But," his face set in the same kind of grim lines I had seen when marching with him in Pannonia, "I intend to move faster than they're expecting so that we can trap them on this side of the Rhenus."

This was fine with me, and I said as much. I also asked, "Any information on what tribes are involved?"

Germanicus did not answer immediately, giving me a sidelong glance, the grin returning, "Is that your way of asking if Arminius is leading them?"

I had to laugh, admitting, "You caught me."

"No," Germanicus answered my unspoken question, "it's not Arminius. In fact, there aren't any Cherusci. At least,

164

Batavius hasn't seen any. My guess is that this wasn't authorized by Arminius, because from what our spies tell us, he's still too busy fighting with the other tribes. So far, it seems to be only Tencteri and Sugambri."

This was instructive, not only because of the identity, but it also told me roughly where this incursion was, but to be sure, I queried, "Does that mean they're between us and Vetera?"

"So far." Germanicus nodded. "Although by the time we're ready to march, it's possible they could bypass Vetera and head north."

The manner in which he said this told me that he was actually asking a question, something that I had become accustomed to when I served under him, so I considered for a moment.

"Maybe," I made no attempt to hide my doubt, "except then when they crossed back over the river, they'd either have to come back south to use that spot near Gelduba, where the trading post is located. Otherwise, anyplace north of Vetera, the current is too strong."

Germanicus considered this for a moment, then nodded thoughtfully. "So you think they're just heading west? Deeper into our part of Germania?"

His forehead wrinkled up as, or so I imagined, he tried to envision the map inside his head of what lay to the west, but when he did not come up with the location I was thinking about, I supplied it for him.

"There's that village on the Mosa," I said, "where the bridge is."

His face cleared, and he nodded. "Ah, that's right. What's it called?"

That, I must confess, took me a moment to recall, but it came to me. "The locals named it Blariacum, I believe. And," I added, "the Mosa is the boundary for the Aduatuci."

"Who," Germanicus replied with a dawning recognition, "have been warring with the Sugambri since Rome was a village." I did not feel the need to respond verbally, although he said, "Thank you for reminding me, Pullus. We," he kept his voice low, "are going to head for Blariacum. You can tell your men that you heard it directly from me."

We parted then, both of us returning to our respective business. I was happy that Gaesorix and his *ala* of Batavians would be involved in some manner, gathering from Germanicus' mention of my friend that he was currently out in the countryside, watching this band of Germans. He and his men, all hardened veterans, were much too experienced and wily to allow a warband of this size to slip past them. All we had to do was march out and allow Gaesorix's men to guide us to the Germans. Then, at least some of our problems would be solved with a sharp, bloody action. And, if I was afforded the opportunity, I planned on using the chaos of a battle to remove one of my biggest headaches from the ranks, something that I once swore I would never do again, not just because I did not want to follow the example set by my first Primus Pilus, Urso, when he ridded himself of Philo, but because of my slaying of Caecina and Mela the night Urso was slain. More than anything else I have related, this should serve as the most potent sign of the true state of affairs in the Legions of the Rhenus, because I knew I was not alone.

Chapter Four

The 1st and 20th Legions, each leaving behind the third line Cohorts, marched out of Ubiorum with Germanicus leading us. Normally, as in before the Varus disaster, a warband of thirty-five hundred Germans would have only warranted the dispatch of a single Legion, but none of us were unhappy about the overwhelming force that Germanicus was leading. At that time, the 5th and 21st were still in Mogontiacum, while Vetera had been rebuilt and was now manned by the 2nd Augusta, and five Cohorts of the 14th, while the other half was at Novaesium. Although the 2nd and 14th were closer to the German incursion, Germanicus had ordered that they stay put, the idea being that, being the most likely Legions to respond and hence under observation, their inactivity would lull whoever was leading the warband into thinking that we Romans were still cringing behind the safety of our walls, cowed by the might of the German tribes. And, despite our initial skepticism, Germanicus' gambit worked perfectly, because we clearly caught the warband by surprise. Following the road that leads west from Ubiorum that connects to Atuatuca, we made camp the first night outside the settlement of Iuliacum, which was built on the site of a town that had once belonged to the Eburones, before they had been extirpated by Divus Julius and his Legions, with men like my Avus. As my Century worked on their part of making the camp, I found my mind wandering, wondering if I was perhaps standing on ground that had been trod by the original Titus Pullus. The villagers, numbering perhaps three or four hundred, composed of what appeared to be an equal mixture of Romans and a motley collection of native tribes, viewed our appearance with what, to my eye, looked to be composed of equal parts relief and a fair amount of worry. Men with wives and daughters were, quite

167

rightly, the most obviously concerned, and honestly, it was somewhat amusing to watch them form a sort of picket line between the town, which had no wall, and the two Legions. Germanicus was not blind to this, calling the Centurions together to issue stern instructions to keep an eye on our men and make sure that none of them tried to make a nocturnal visit.

"As of today," he reminded us, "we are on campaign, so make sure your boys know that they'll be punished accordingly if they try to sneak out of camp tonight."

We all assured him that we would be vigilant; the thought that crossed my mind was that Germanicus should have been as worried about his Centurions and Optios as he was the rankers, and while I did not do so, nor as far as I know any other Centurion in the Cohort, I have little doubt that there were men wearing transverse crests prowling about the two muddy streets of the village that night in search of wine, a woman, or more likely, both. Regardless, when we broke camp the next morning, there was no delegation of angry villagers with defiled daughters or missing wives, although there was not much chance of the latter, given the lack of a tail we had on this march. It was another consequence of the Varus disaster; the normal contingent of camp followers that have been a feature of a Roman army on the march for as long as Romans have been marching was missing, and had been since the unfortunate civilians accompanying Varus were either slaughtered along with the Legions, or taken as slaves. Still, it was not inconceivable that an errant wife or a wayward daughter was secreted away in one of the wagons, but this did not appear to be the case, since we left Iuliacum behind without incident.

Heading due north, Germanicus had ordered the 1st to lead the way since we had been second the day before, and with the Third Cohort serving as vanguard, followed by the First, with the Fourth following behind them. Because we were nearing the last known position of the Germans, Germanicus had ordered the baggage trains for both Legions to be combined, with a Cohort of the 20th trailing behind it, including our section mules. This meant Alex, Lucco, the rest of the clerks, and the section slaves were all congregated with the baggage train as well, and while I did not seriously worry that they were in danger, it was conceivable that a party from the main warband might try a hit and run raid on the slower moving wagons and mules. Shortly after the midday break, there was a shout from farther up the column warning us that a small group of riders were approaching. A matter of heartbeats later, they became visible as they negotiated the slight bend in the road, and I instantly recognized that Cassicos was leading another half-dozen of Gaesorix's troopers.

Seeing me, he veered his mount to draw alongside me, wearing a grin on his battered features that was informative by itself, which he confirmed by saying in his accented Latin, "We found them, Pullus." The smile faded somewhat as he continued soberly, "They've made a camp about three miles south of Blariacum, and the Decurion is certain they plan on attacking it." He leaned slightly to peer farther down the column and asked me, "Where is the Legate?"

"He's behind the Sixth, which is just behind us," I informed him, and with a wave, he resumed his progress, followed by the other Batavians, all of whom either gave me a grin or a wave.

Considering how our acquaintance had begun, when my desire to reach Siscia after I had been detached by Tiberius to serve with Germanicus had led us into an ambush that cost several men their lives, I was, and am thankful that these hard-bitten cavalrymen had been as forgiving as they proved to be. Not long after that, the *Cornicen* attached to Germanicus sounded the signal for a halt, followed immediately by the signal for the Centurions of both Legions to attend to the Legate. I waited for Macer and Cornutus, whose Century was leading, and we walked together back to join the other officers. Germanicus stayed mounted, and I could see from his demeanor that he was impatient to begin sharing the news, and presumably what he intended to do about it.

"The cavalry has located the Germans," he began even as I saw there were still Centurions from the 20th coming at the trot from their spots. "And Decurion Batavius thinks that they are about to attack Blariacum, which is about three miles north of where they are camped. He said they appear to be settling in for the rest of the day and aren't making any preparations to attack immediately. His guess is they are going to move in the night and fall on the town at dawn." He paused, waiting long enough for the rest of the tardy Centurions to arrive, whereupon he got to the meat of the matter. "We're going to hit them before they do it. Here's how."

For the span of several moments, he outlined this plan that he had clearly just come up with, and I can say I was probably one of the only, if not the lone man who was not surprised at the audacity and scope of what he had in mind. It would require a level of coordination, although it was not nearly as intricate a plan as the one for Raetinium, or Splonum for that matter, but more crucially, it would mean moving, and doing it quickly, both to cover the distance, then to begin the execution. Once he was finished, to that end, his normal willingness to patiently answer questions from his officers was nowhere in evidence, only entertaining one from the Primus Pilus of the 20th, Lucius Neratius, while ignoring Sacrovir's raised hand. Well within a sixth part of a watch, the first five Cohorts of the 1st had grounded their packs, leaving the Sixth and Seventh, taking only what rations they could squirrel away inside their tunics, a canteen, and of course their javelins. There was a brief discussion about taking entrenching tools, with each man in a section carrying one of them, but Germanicus finally decided against it.

"We're not going to be settling down long enough to need any kind of breastworks or a ditch," he said, "and I don't want the men carrying any extra weight. We," he gave us a smile that was tinged with a hardness that I had only rarely seen from him, "are going to move like Divus Julius' Legions did."

And, as we all quickly learned, he was true to his word.

While Germanicus' plan was audacious, I observed how much he had matured in the years since the Batonian Revolt, as it is now called, when he had been thrust into a position of immense responsibility for a youth of his age. There was no hesitation this time, no sidelong glances towards his subordinate Legate, in rank but not age, one Quintus Poppaeus Secundus, who had also served as Consul in the year of the Varus disaster, although as a Suffect. All we knew about him on his arrival several months before Germanicus had been appointed as governor was he had been a co-sponsor of the Lex Papia Poppaea, which was a source of great amusement to us in the ranks, since it was designed to curb the rampant adultery that was taking place in the upper classes in Rome. This practically guaranteed he would be the object of much snickering and ridicule, behind his back, naturally, so I am compelled to admit that Secundus never really stood a chance of gaining our respect. Militarily speaking, he was a completely unknown quantity since this was the first time a force larger than a Cohort had marched, and now Germanicus was in command. Regardless, it became clear fairly quickly that Germanicus was no longer the wide-eyed youth, but was now a battle-tested commander, one who had finished a term as Consul, at that. For his part, Secundus seemed resigned to playing a minor role, although anyone with eyes could see he was not particularly happy about it. Like the great general he had invoked when giving his orders, Germanicus chose to march on foot, leading his horse, which he occasionally mounted to gallop up and down the column, exhorting us to keep up what was by any measure a crushing pace. Even unencumbered as I was without a shield or javelins, I was sweating freely, and my breathing precluded all but short, usually sharp, words, aimed at the men of the Century, particularly Pusio, who was obviously struggling more than his comrades. And, I took notice, not one of the other men of his section offered him any encouragement, or, as other men in other sections were doing for their struggling comrades, helping by carrying his shield for a short distance to let him catch his breath. This, more than any other thing, was a potent sign that Pusio was neither liked nor respected by the men around him at moments such as this, which fueled my determination to remove him from my Century at the first opportunity. Germanicus did not signal a stop at the normal interval, pushing on for another third of a watch longer before finally allowing us to stop for a brief rest. My tunic under my armor was soaked so thoroughly that as I stood there with Structus and Gemellus, drops of sweat fell from the hem, darkening the ground around my feet. Germanicus' face gleamed with perspiration as we gathered around him for our final instructions, which he was only able to give after catching his own breath, which made me feel quite a bit better about my own plight, given how much older I was than him.

"I'm going to lead the 1st," he began, "while Secundus is going to stay here with the 20th." Again, he did not offer the other nobleman even so much as a glance, but he did turn his head to indicate Neratius, a thickset man from one of the Hispania provinces originally, who had one milky eye like my former nemesis Caecina, with iron gray hair that he wore long and tied behind his head. For his part, Neratius seemed more put out than Secundus, but Germanicus apparently chose to ignore his sour expression as he continued, "According to the scouts, we're less than three miles away from the German camp." Suddenly, he squatted down and began drawing in the dirt to explain his plan, drawing a thin line that he explained was the Mosa, which was a few miles to our west, then marked an "X" immediately next to it, saying, "This is Blariacum. The road we're on gradually curves west," he drew a line that began parallel to the river but curved to meet the first line at the town, "but we're not going to follow it much longer, because it will bring us too close to the German camp, and if they have any scouts of their own out and about, the surprise will be ruined. So," Germanicus announced flatly, "we're going to use a track that splits off and heads due north until we're directly east of Blariacum. Then we're going to march cross country." As he continued, he drew a straight vertical line that branched off his line marking the road, then when it was directly to the right of the "X," made a perpendicular line that he drew so that it was just below the "X." "This is going to add about three extra miles, maybe more," he admitted, "but we have to be in place before it gets dark. Decurion Batavius informed me that there is a thick forest about a mile south of Blariacum that runs almost up to the riverbank. South of that forest the ground is open, and the Germans will have to cross this open area to get to the town." Stopping, he looked up at us, ringed around him, and he caught my eye, offering a quick grin as he spoke directly to me, "I bet that Pullus can tell you what I'm thinking."

Naturally, all eyes turned towards me, but the scrutiny from Neratius was the most pointed, and in that moment, I realized that it was natural for him to do so, given how unlikely it was that he knew about my previous service with our Legate, although this did not stop me from answering quickly, "You're going to use us as the hammer, and the 20th as the anvil."

Clearly pleased, Germanicus nodded enthusiastically, exclaiming, "Exactly right!" Turning to Neratius, for the first time, he demonstrated he had noticed the Primus Pilus' displeasure at seemingly being relegated to a support role. "See, Neratius? Your boys are going to be the anvil, because we'll drive them right into you. In order to do that," he returned his attention to his drawing, sketching the relative disposition he wanted the 20th to take, "you're going to have three Cohorts in a single line perpendicular to the river, and the other two you're going to place parallel to the river, but at the end of your line of three."

Once he was done, Germanicus had essentially sketched a box with four sides, with the river serving as one side and the five Cohorts of the 1st serving as the lid. Provided his basic assumption was correct, that the Germans would wait to attack the town at dawn, they would be walking into a trap. Our break done, we resumed the march at the same pace, then about a third of a watch later, we separated, the 1st continuing north, while Secundus and Neratius took the 20th in a westerly direction, heading for the Mosa. The sun was now on its downward arc, becoming almost as much of an enemy as the Germans, since none of us had any desire to try to move into our final position in the dark. We were met by more of Gaesorix's men, who were waiting to guide us on the track, which was so narrow that we had to reduce the width of our marching column in order to maintain our pace. The thought did cross my mind that, if Germanicus was wrong in his belief that the Germans would only move after it was dark, then before dawn maneuver into position or shortly thereafter, we might be too exhausted to give a good account of ourselves. That, I decided, was something that was beyond my abilities to do anything about, so I shoved it from my mind, instead focusing on what was my main job at that moment, to appear as if I was not fatigued in the slightest, and make sure none of my men did not straggle. Which, of course, meant that this very thing would happen, and that it would be Pusio.

I became aware that something was amiss when I heard Structus snarling, "Get up, you fucking *cunnus*!"

Before I could turn around, I heard Pusio's petulant, whining voice. "Optio, I can't! I swear on the black stone I can't go another step!"

I did turn about in time to see Structus, using the cut down turfcutter handle favored by most Optios, strike Pusio on the meaty part of his thigh at a somewhat awkward angle since Pusio was on his knees, his shield having fallen next to him, although he still managed to clutch his two javelins. Yelping with the pain, Pusio did not rise, even after Structus struck him twice more. Muttering a curse, I snapped at Gemellus to keep marching, which the Century did, flowing around the Optio and kneeling man like water, while I stalked back to the two of them.

"You heard the Optio," I made no attempt to hide the contempt I felt for Pusio. "Get on your feet before I give you a couple of taps with this," I brandished my *vitus*, "and you know by now how much harder I hit than Structus does."

Pusio glared up at me, and likewise, he made no attempt to hide the hatred he felt for me, which I returned in full measure, but just as I drew my arm back, he struggled to his feet, picked up his shield, and with Structus cursing him, began a stumbling trot to catch up to our Century, which I had to do as well, putting me in an even fouler mood and gasping for breath when I resumed my spot.

We made it to the place Gaesorix had picked out before it was fully dark, but it was a close-run thing, and the last mile we moved at double pace until, just ahead through the trees, the setting sun made the water of the Mosa shimmer with a golden hue, signaling the end of the march. Coming to a halt, Germanicus, who looked every bit as fatigued as the rest of us, gave the command to align ourselves in a single line of Centuries in order to provide the longest line possible, except for three Centuries from the Fifth Cohort, who he positioned in a perpendicular line to protect our left flank. The river protected

175

our right, and Germanicus had our First Cohort anchoring the line, with the Second next to them. In a slight variation, the Legate ordered my Cohort to be next to the Second, with the Third to our left and the Fifth on their opposite side. Only then did he give the command that we really wanted to hear, and that was to sit down and rest in place, although saying that the men collapsed right where they were standing would be more accurate.

"If Fortuna is loving our Legate, we'll be able to get at least a couple watches of rest before those German bastards show up," Macer said hopefully.

I wholeheartedly agreed, and while I would not ascribe the respite we got to the gods, I was nonetheless as happy to be a recipient of Germanicus being proven right as the rest of the men. While we had left our baggage behind, every Century brought their contingent of *medici*, including those who acted as stretcher bearers, and if things went really badly, extra hands who could at least apply a bandage. This meant that Alex, Lucco, Balio, Krateros, and several others were with us, but aside from my nephew, most Centurions viewed them as smaller, weaker versions of mules, forcing them to carry extra food along with their normal load of medical supplies, especially the slaves. More than one of them had been tasked by their masters to tote either extra cups, not for drinking but to hold the dice, and the portable version of the tables, which were quickly distributed but ended up going unused for the most part, because all of us, from the lowest *Gregarii* to our Legate, were close to exhaustion. In a practical sense, this meant that the men who were selected to stand the first watch were those men who had either run afoul of their Centurions during this rapid march or were those who more or less stayed on the mental list every Centurion keeps in his head. Which, of course, meant that the man who, by his declaration was the most exhausted of all his comrades, would be standing the first watch. Thankfully, for both of us, my warning to Pusio was still sufficiently fresh that he did not complain, verbally at least, but I did not feel guilty in the slightest when I informed Structus that I expected him to remain awake as well, not only because it was a standard practice, but I was certain that Pusio would fuck it up and fall asleep. Which, I will confess, I hoped for, since falling asleep on watch during a campaign, which this could be defined as, would be all the pretext I needed to rid myself of him for good. Something that he obviously understood, because when Alex roused me a watch later at midnight, Structus had to inform me that Pusio, and the other men who stood first watch, managed to stay awake.

Relieving Structus, I set the next watch, which Germanicus had decreed would be a full quarter of the men from this point forward until shortly before dawn, wondering if we would make it the full watch before the Germans were sighted. I had yet to see Gaesorix himself, although his men were constantly moving back and forth between our position in the forest and where the Batavians were bedded down two miles to the south, in the next expanse of trees. Like any good officer, he was staying with his men, and while I had no way of knowing with any certainty, I was certain that he had spread his command out, probably by *turma*, along a line that essentially mirrored our line to their north. Germanicus was certainly taking some risks with his dispositions of our five Cohorts; arraying us in a single line of Centuries as he did, while he extended our line to almost a mile in width, he was sacrificing depth in the form of our more normal disposition of a double line. Frankly, this worried me, and the rest of the Centurions, the most, given how unlikely it was that when the Germans approached, they would be spread out in a manner where we could bring our entire force to bear on them. Granted, Germanicus had thought of this and had come up with a plan to deal with what was almost a certainty, but as any experienced veteran will tell you, once the fighting starts, the most carefully laid plans tend to evaporate like a drop of water on a hot stove. The only way we would find out if what he had in mind would work would be when it happened; consequently, I spent my time on watch thinking through every situation I could come up with in my mind, something that actually helps me remain calm, as strange as that may sound. Of course, I did this on my feet, walking along the two sections who were standing, or more accurately, leaning on their shields, staring south towards the open ground that began about a dozen paces away. Not that there was much to see, given the quarter moon, but a body of men the size of the German warband, crossing what was essentially a large meadow close to two miles across would be impossible to miss. Behind us, there was a low buzzing sound of men who were whispering to each other, punctuated by the deeper sound of men snoring, mostly those veterans who knew the value of sleep. If I am being honest, this was the one aspect of being a Gregarius that I missed the most, because I have always treasured my sleep, and for any man wearing a transverse crest, this is something in short supply. When my watch ended, I did consider lying back down and trying to catch another third or two of a watch's sleep, then decided against it. Instead, I found Macer, who was also coming off watch, and we went back to where Lucco had prepared a spot that enabled Macer to recline against a small clump of brush, using his *sagum* as a ground cloth. I dropped down next to him, and we passed the time in desultory conversation, watching in some amusement at what, despite the gloom, we knew was Germanicus, striding back and forth along the rear of our line, made identifiable by the three Tribunes following behind him.

"Do they remind you of ducklings?" Macer asked idly at one point, perhaps the fifth or sixth time our Legate had passed by.

Laughing, I admitted, "Only every time I see them doing that."

178

As diverting as it was, we soon lapsed into a silence, and I did not need to look over at Macer to see that he was gazing in the same direction, towards the east, waiting for the sun to begin to lighten the sky.

We heard the drumming hooves before we saw the pair of riders who, taking something of a risk, came galloping towards our lines from the south. Not only were they in danger of an overanxious sentry; as I knew from experience with Latobius, galloping a horse across unknown ground in the dark often ends up badly. Still, these were Batavians, superb horsemen and, as importantly for their health, they knew the correct watchword, which they began shouting as soon as they came within hailing distance.

"We better go see what's going on," Macer remarked, pulling himself to his feet; if he heard my groan as I did the same, he was wise enough to ignore it.

Following behind him, mainly so that he could not see me hobbling from the aches and pains caused by the combination of a hard march and a night spent on the equally hard ground, we made our way towards the commotion that marked the Batavians entering our lines. Germanicus was hurrying from the opposite direction, and very quickly, we were gathered around the pair of cavalrymen, and while I could not make out his face, I recognized the voice of Cassicos.

"The Decurion sent us ahead," he told Germanicus, "but he is withdrawing to the east as you ordered to allow the Germans to pass by. They're about a mile on the south side of our position." Pausing for an instant, he amended, "At least, they were when we left. But they are moving fast. And," Cassicos added, "their cavalry is leading the way, just as you suspected, sir."

This, at least to us Centurions, was news; Germanicus had made no mention of the cavalry or his suspicions that they would

179

be in advance of their infantry, yet clearly, he had thought of it, and I looked over to see him nod.

"Gaesorix knows what to do next," he said, with a confidence that was reassuring, even while at the same time my thought was, I'm glad someone knows what's going on. Oblivious to the thoughts of his former Primus Pilus, he went on, "Once he draws the cavalry away, we'll wait and see how their infantry responds. I doubt they'll stop to wait for their cavalry to come back, since they're trying to hit the town before the inhabitants are up and about. And," Germanicus finished with a grim smile, "they're going to walk right into us."

Macer and I exchanged a glance, but at my silent urging, shook his head, since I knew our thoughts were running in the same direction. Appropriately, it was Sacrovir who spoke up.

"What if they don't?" he asked quietly, but if Germanicus was irritated by our Primus Pilus not addressing him in a manner that many men of his rank demanded, he gave no sign of it.

"Don't what?"

"Well," Sacrovir shrugged, "either the cavalry doesn't take the bait and stays with the infantry. Or, they do take the bait, but the infantry stops to wait for them." Turning, he gestured in the direction of the clearing. "Out there, too far away for us to do anything that wouldn't expose us and spoil the surprise."

This caused a reaction from Germanicus, a thinning of the lips and a sudden bulge of muscle along his jaw that I had seen before that I had learned indicated irritation; whether it was because of Sacrovir's lack of formality, that he thought the questions impertinent, or he was upset with himself because he had not thought about it, I had no way of knowing.

"If that happens, Primus Pilus," the manner in which Germanicus emphasized Sacrovir's rank seemed to me to provide a hint about what had caused Germanicus' reaction, "I'm sure that we'll be able to come up with something."

With that slightly unsatisfactory admonition, we were sent back to our Centuries, and I was thankful that we did not have as far to walk as Clepsina and his Centurions. As we did, while five of us were chatting quietly, I noticed that Volusenus barely said a word, which in turn reminded me that he had been almost completely silent on the entire march. The sky to the east was now unmistakably pink, and our Optios had already roused the men, who were now crouching or kneeling in their spots, their shields leaned against them as we waited for the first sign of the approaching enemy. I occupied myself during this period by walking up and down the ranks, offering a quiet word to one ranker, a shared jest with another, and a few glares at men who were on my mental list, performing what had become a ritual in itself. This, honestly, was something I was unaware of until, one time, I did not do it, and Structus approached me on the behalf of the men to ask if they had displeased me in some way, which was not the case. While seemingly trivial, it was an important reminder to me just how superstitious men under the standard are, myself included, and since that time, I never failed to do this whenever the moment arose just before a possible action. Once that was done, I tried, as casually as I could do so, to make my way to where the Sixth Century was located, at the end of our Cohort, standing next to the First of the Third. Even in the semi-darkness, Volusenus was impossible to miss, and I experienced a queer sensation as I realized for the first time what others must experience when trying to pick me out in the dark. I had long before forgotten about being conscious of my size, but as I thought on it while I approached Volusenus, I realized that his presence had caused me to do so more in the time he had been in his post than I had devoted to it in years. His *Signifer* spotted me coming, prompting Volusenus to turn and face me, so that as I drew closer, I tried to get a sense of his state of mind, hindered by the darkness and my own clumsy attempt to not appear as if I was doing that very thing.

"Princeps Prior," he said conversationally enough, but I thought I detected a note of caution. "What brings you down here?"

"Just stretching my legs, Hastatus Posterior Volusenus," I tried to sound casual, then I offered, in a lower voice now that I was within a pace of him, "and trying to loosen up some after that march. And," I do not know why I felt compelled to add, "lying down on the hard ground is for young men like you. Not," I laughed ruefully, "for someone as ancient as I am."

His chuckle did not seem forced, and indeed, I was sure I caught just a hint of pleasure in it; whether it was simply that of a younger man relishing the fact that he is not as decrepit as an older man, or because it was me, I chose not to think about.

"So," I turned to survey his men, most of whom were in the exact posture as mine, kneeling or squatting as they waited for what came next, "your boys look ready."

"They are," he answered instantly, and there was no mistaking the pride in his voice.

Dropping my voice to almost a whisper, I asked, "And? How about you?"

At first, I was certain that I had erred, that his young pride and the arrogance he still had a fair amount of would make him say something that would cause both of us problems and rupture the still-fragile relationship that had been forming through watches spent on the training field.

Then, he took a breath and answered, in the same tone, "There's only one way to find out, neh?" I nodded, pleased that he had chosen not to bluster, which seemed to encourage him to ask, in a clearly plaintive manner, "But what if I'm not? Ready, I mean?"

"You are," I replied firmly and without hesitation, not just because I believed it, but knowing from observation how the slightest hesitation from a comrade can shatter a man's confidence in himself when it is, frankly, at its most fragile point, just before he goes into battle for the first time and learns one way or another. "I'd tell you if I thought differently. But," while it felt somewhat awkward, perhaps because it was the first time in my life I actually did not have to place my hand on a shoulder lower than mine, "you're ready, Volusenus."

It could have been pitch black and I would have been able to see how much this pleased him, but even in the short time in which we were speaking, his features had become more visible, so I did not miss the flush of pleasure.

"Riders coming!"

The shouted warning broke the moment, and more importantly, reminded us why we were there, but before I returned to my Century, I said, "We have a tradition here in the Fourth of the 1st." Thrusting out my arm, I intoned the words we Centurions always used with each other, although this time, I said the entire thing, "May Mars and Fortuna bless you and your boys."

Without hesitation, he clasped my forearm and repeated the words, and I took heart that there was no tremor in his grasp, although his palm was a bit sweaty. Saying nothing more, I turned and went trotting back towards my Century.

Much to Germanicus' satisfaction, especially given Sacrovir's doubts, and I suspect with some relief, the German cavalry behaved in precisely the manner he had predicted. The first riders our men had spotted were the advance riders, a half-dozen men leading the way, and they had been the ones who, just when the first rays of sun poked over the horizon, spotted movement to their right, or to the east, away from the river. Our vantage point, such as it was, meant that we could not see past the bulk of the Cohorts to our left, though even if they had been out of the way, the trees of the forest in which we were hidden would have obscured what took place. All that mattered were the results, which began when the German scouts galloped back to

183

the main body of cavalry, and shortly thereafter, the whole bunch of them went galloping east, in pursuit of the Batavians. By the time the dust had settled, the German warriors following behind were plainly visible, moving in their shambling, disorganized manner that always reminded me of a wave of dirty brownish-green water. Once the Germans were within a mile of the outer edge of the forest, of their own volition, the men had risen to their feet and begun performing their own small rituals and exhibiting the mannerisms of men about to go into battle. For some, it is fidgeting excessively, shifting from one foot to another; for others, they actually go completely still as their minds go to some place, and for me, it was my habit that I developed even before I was under the standard, in an attempt to emulate my Avus by making those slow, tiny circles with the tip of my *gladius*, which I held loosely in my hand as I watched the Germans coming. Germanicus, on foot, made one more pass behind our lines, reminding us to watch and wait for his command.

"If they stay close to the river as they've been doing, it will be the First and Second who will spring the first part of the trap," he told Macer, "and your Cohort will have to move quickly in order to get lined up correctly to hit them from the flank."

Like any good, or wise, Centurion, Macer simply assured our Legate that he could count on us and not point out this had to be at least the fourth time Germanicus had given these instructions. Then, he was gone, moving at a trot as he hurried to essentially repeat himself to the other Cohorts, or at least as many as he could safely reach and still have time to return to his spot behind the First. Frankly, I was somewhat concerned that, even with the screening underbrush, since the eye, especially a trained one, is attracted to movement, by his own actions, our general would prematurely alert the Germans. And, for a span of perhaps a hundred heartbeats, it appeared as if they might have been warned, because less than a half-mile from the edge of the forest, the mass of warriors suddenly stopped. Fortunately, as we watched, we could see that they were gazing east, which I assumed was due to whatever Gaesorix and his men were doing to the German cavalry. Knowing that the Batavians and Sugambri held no love for each other, I was certain that Gaesorix would ensure that however many of the German cavalry were Sugambri would identify our cavalry as the hated Batavians, which could only help our cause. Before anything could be done, without any overt signal that I could see, the warband resumed their approach, and now that they were closer, we could see they were moving at almost a trot, clearly understanding that the dawning sun was their enemy if they wanted to reach the town early in the coming day. This served our purposes perfectly, not only because it was the best sign our presence had not been detected, but it is difficult to be vigilant when moving so quickly. There was no need to admonish the men to be quiet, as their entire attention was watching, not without some difficulty because of the undergrowth, the advancing Germans, and it was becoming clear that they would run into the area of the First Cohort, to our right, although they were still too far away to tell precisely where along the line it would be. Looking over in the direction of the Pilus Prior, who was not willing to risk a shout, he made a gesture with his hand that mimicked a swinging door or gate, and I saw Vespillo, whose Century was between mine and the First Century, nod, while I raised my hand in acknowledgement.

Turning slightly, I spoke in a low conversational tone, warning the first section, "Be ready to move. It looks like they're going to run right into the First, so we're going to have to move quickly to hit them from the flank. Pass the word back, but," I warned, "keep your voices down."

Manius Caninas was the most veteran man of the First Section, but more importantly, he was the first ranker in the first file, and as I instructed, he relayed my orders, first to his section, then turning and telling the second man of his file, while I resumed watching the Germans, who were now about two hundred paces away. I was certain that they were close enough, and the sun was almost completely over the horizon at this point that they could see deeply enough into the forest to spot us, yet the four warriors, who I assumed were the leaders of the warband, were still moving quickly, their men just behind them carrying the normal motley collection of weapons and shields. When they were perhaps a hundred paces away, with all eyes on them, one of the leading Germans suddenly slowed, and I could see that he was staring straight ahead. This was the last moment of relative calm before our surprise.

As with most such moments, one has to piece things together afterward, both from one's own recollections and from others; this time was no exception. The German who was clearly the first to spot something ahead of his warband stopped so abruptly, and the men behind him were moving so quickly, that the German warrior immediately behind him either did not see him do so or could not react in time because he slammed into his leader from behind, sending the man sprawling. The entire bunch was close enough that his shout of alarm came as a thin cry across the intervening distance, but while this elicited a reaction from his comrades, the man disappeared from sight as the following warriors could not arrest their momentum, so I have no idea if he ever got back to his feet or not or if he was trampled by his comrades. This created a disruption in the center of the mass of oncoming warriors, who, now that they were within a hundred paces of the forest, we could see were spread out to a width that covered all of the First and Second Cohort, so that the Germans on either side of this collision and the resulting confusion continued on for another few paces before anyone else in the larger body spotted our crouching figures in the brush. Within a span of perhaps two or at most three heartbeats, hundreds of Germans' voices shouted the alarm, causing the entire bunch to come to a chaotic, stumbling halt, with the Germans nearest our position and those closest to the river less than fifty paces away from the edge of the forest, while, because of the delay caused by the stumble of the warrior who had raised the first warning, the center was still perhaps seventy paces away.

"First Cohort! Advance!"

Somehow, I heard the command even over the shouting of the Germans, and the excited talk from my Century, followed immediately by the same command by the Secundus Pilus Prior, which prompted me to look over to Macer, waiting for his own command. He was staring to his right, although the men of the Second partially obscured his view of Germanicus, who I assumed had given the first command, but while he was holding his *gladius* aloft, he did not move it.

"Come on," I muttered, "let's go!"

It is moments such as this where the lack of discipline and a clear command structure hinders barbarian tribes, not that I am complaining, since it enabled both Cohorts who were directly across from the warband to march the couple dozen paces forward to place them in javelin range, while the Germans were still milling about in confusion.

"Ready javelins!"

"Fourth Cohort!" Macer bellowed. "Advance!"

"Release!"

"March!"

This was when I realized that Macer was not tardy; he was using the chaos he knew would be coming from a volley of javelins to our advantage. The response was automatic, our start almost as smooth as if we were in the forum, although there was some difficulty in concentrating since the horrendous racket of javelins slamming into shields and bodies was almost in perfect unison with our first step forward, which made it difficult to hear Macer's next command.

"At the double quick!"

"Ready javelins!"

"March!"

"Release!"

I saw the second volley streaking through the sky out of the corner of my eye, while we burst out of the underbrush a heartbeat after it impacted.

"Fourth Cohort! Right Wheel! March!"

Then, from the area of the First and Second, *"Porro!"*

Honestly, I do not think if we rehearsed this maneuver a hundred times we would have ever gotten the timing as perfect as we did that day; afterward, the rankers were quick to ascribe this as further proof of how Germanicus was the gods' favorite. Even as the First and Second Cohorts, having exhausted their supply of javelins, went to the run to close the final distance before slamming into the now thoroughly disorganized, reeling Germans, the Fourth Cohort was wheeling just as Germanicus had demanded, swinging to slam into the right flank of the warband.

"Prepare javelins!" I shouted the command even before the notes of Macer's *cornu* command had finished. As I did so, I realized that if we hurled both javelins, we would be well behind the Second Century to our right, and even more so with the First, so I bellowed the order to release, then almost immediately, I filled my lungs to slightly alter the normal sequence of commands.

"Drop your second, boys!" A fraction of a heartbeat later, *"Porro!"*

If there was a mistake in this part of the battle, it was one of omission; neither Germanicus, nor the Primus Pilus, or even Macer in regard to the Fourth Cohort had accounted for the difficulty in ensuring that a Cohort executing a wheel maneuver such as this had to account for the longer distance needed to be covered the farther down the line one went. This is something that even a Centurion commanding a single Century needs to remember; the men at the far end of the formation have farther to go. In this case, when it is a Cohort, especially in a single line of Centuries, it meant that Volusenus had to move his Century at close to a sprint in order to coordinate an attack so that every Century was hitting their foes at the same time, something that at that point in time, he was too inexperienced to realize, particularly in the heat of his first battle. What it meant in practical terms was a sort of rippling effect, where the First Century slammed into the Germans immediately behind the front ranks of the warband who were now under assault by the First and Second Cohorts, followed perhaps three or four heartbeats later by the Second Century. Honestly, I have no idea how much time elapsed before we went slamming into what I could see was a ragged, uneven line of Germans who had turned to their right, although it appeared to be only three or four men deep, but I suspect that it was about the same amount of time. I assume the Fourth, Fifth, and Sixth Centuries were similarly ragged, but I was already busy, picking out a warrior with bright red hair and a bushy beard that was so strikingly a different color, being a dark, chestnut brown, that in a random corner of my mind, I was certain that either hair or beard was dyed, and I actually wondered why a man would do such a thing. Fortunately, this did not distract me as I suddenly chopped my headlong charge by shortening my stride, hoping that this warrior, who was armed with a spear and shield, would mistime the thrust he had drawn his arm back to make. Unfortunately, he was too experienced to fall for this maneuver, even giving me a smile, noticeable for the missing front teeth. To my left, Caninas slammed into what I saw out of the corner of my eye was a beardless youth, also armed with a spear and shield, but unlike his older comrade, he lacked a chainmail vest. Trusting the veteran, I launched my first real attack, coming in from a high second position, which he blocked easily enough, but as I expected, he immediately countered with a thrust of his spear. I did not have a shield, holding my *vitus* instead, except that even as I was executing my thrust, I was dropping the *vitus* to free my left hand, so that when I leaned to the right to avoid his spear, the point shooting past me, before he could recover it, I grabbed the shaft. Counting on the strength in my hands that came from performing the exercises of my Avus, thrusting my splayed fingers into a bucket of sand, then closing them into a fist, consequently, while I felt him putting his weight into repeatedly yanking the spear, it did not budge in my hand while barely moving my arm, although I felt a twinge of pain from my old wound on my outer forearm. After a few tugs on his part, I mimicked his action, adding to it twisting my hips and torso, and the combined force of this maneuver, my weight, and strength was such that, since he refused to let go, I pulled him towards me, causing him to lurch a step that was violent enough that it caused him to react involuntarily, moving his shield arm out from his body in an instinctive reaction in order to keep his balance. This, of course, was exactly what I wanted, and just that quickly, the point of my *gladius* punched into his eye, perhaps an inch above his shield, and he suddenly relinquished his grasp on the spear as he dropped to his knees. Using my knee, I knocked him out of my way to get at the German who had been immediately behind my first kill.

As usual, the noise was at its peak, both from the tremendous collisions of men slamming into each other, shield to shield, and from the snarling bellows of hatred, fear and rage that are inevitable when men are a matter of no more than three feet from each other, separated only by what is ultimately a thin layer of wood. In a span of perhaps a dozen normal heartbeats of time, my Century had cut its way a few paces into the flank of the warband, roughly equal with the Second Century, who were a matter of three or four paces to my right. Now that we had established ourselves, it was time for me to step back and assume my role not as a Legionary, but as Centurion, and I put the bone whistle in my mouth, watching down the front rank to time my call for the relief. We were pressing the Germans from two sides, but there was another barrier on the side opposite from our Cohort in the form of the river, and it was not long before the Germans recognized that their plan to attack Blariacum, and presumably cross the Mosa into the heart of the fat, soft lands to the west, full of prosperous farms and small settlements ripe for plunder, was ruined. Consequently, we sensed more than saw the shifting movement of the Germans deeper in their formation as they began to retreat to the south, back towards the shelter of the forest from which they had emerged. The Third and Fifth Cohorts had, or so I presumed, marched from their spot out into the open area by this point, and I wondered if their Pili Priores had essentially maneuvered their Cohorts to mimic our own movement and just extended the line running parallel to the river, or if they had possessed the presence of mind to place themselves athwart the German line of retreat. This, naturally, was something about which I, or anyone other than Germanicus could not do anything about, so I concentrated my attention on what was before us. I was pleased to see that, to this point, we had only suffered three casualties, although one of them appeared to be, if not mortal, then serious, given how he was unable to help himself as his comrades grabbed his inert form to drag him back, slowly, through the formation to the rear, where Alex and the *medici* were waiting. Because the man's face was turned the other way, I could not see who it was, but more importantly, I knew who it was not; Pusio was still in his spot, and his rank had yet to go into the rotation, so perhaps I blew my whistle a bit too quickly. Although this prompted some startled glances, neither did any man complain, but I was more concerned with how rapidly the resistance was melting away, as the Germans not immediately in front of us were abandoning their comrades who were engaged with us, the First, and the Second. Essentially, the Germans who were not running lost the security that comes from knowing one's comrades are at your back, as the barbarian formation, such as it was, became hollowed out until there were no more than two men behind the warrior who was currently engaged. Fairly quickly, I realized that any opportunity to rid myself of Pusio would have to wait for another day, causing me to snarl a string of curses in frustration, which Gemellus misinterpreted.

"They're running away too fast for us to finish them, eh, Princeps Prior?"

He shouted this over the noise, which startled me since I had been unaware that I had expressed my anger aloud.

"Right," I mumbled, or something to that effect, but before my *Signifer* could reply in any way, the collective nerve of those last men who had remained stalwart suddenly collapsed, and with a simultaneity that would not have done shame to a Legion, turned about and began fleeing after their already departed comrades, although none of us heard any kind of shouted command.

It was inevitable that the Germans who were the first to be cut down were the men who had been engaged, their flight hampered by the bodies around their feet; I was able to dispatch two such warriors with quick thrusts to the back as, without thinking, I began pursuing the enemy. Seeing me do so, my Century naturally followed my lead, although we were not alone, with the Second Century doing the same to our right, the Third to our left delayed only a matter of heartbeats. A pursuit of a fleeing enemy is never as straightforward as I have just described it, at least in the sense that my Century was with me as I tried to kill as many of the Germans in the easiest manner possible, from behind. While it is true that most of my Century followed, there are always men, in every Century, in every

Cohort, in every Legion who will take advantage of the confusion and disorganization to stop and loot the bodies of the men they or their comrades have just slain rather than follow their comrades in a pursuit. And, of those men in my Century, Pusio was one of them, but thanks to Structus, while I was unable to permanently remove him, it did not mean he escaped unscathed, as my Optio, in his spot at the rear of the formation, saw the handful of men who stopped, and like a good Optio, he knew who his Centurion was most concerned about. I was ignorant of this show of initiative by Structus until later, when Pusio went limping past me, one eye swollen shut and a bruise already forming along the side of his face that just happened to look the exact width of a turfcutter handle. While Structus was doing this, some of my men and I had managed to dispatch perhaps a half-dozen Germans, a couple of whom, sensing they were about to be caught, chose to at least turn and die from a wound to their front, like a true warrior should. Very quickly, any semblance of cohesion was gone, as the Centuries from all three Cohorts became hopelessly intermingled, which was what prompted Germanicus to order the recall, stopping the pursuit, and it was at this moment we learned that the Third and Fifth Cohort had, in fact, not positioned themselves in a blocking position, albeit for a good reason, which we learned fairly quickly.

"The German cavalry came back!"

I do not know who shouted this, but naturally, we all turned to the east to see that this was the case, but they had been met by the Third and Fifth Cohort. Later, we learned that it was Clepsina, the Quintus Pilus Prior who took the initiative to turn eastward instead of facing the German infantry, a decision that Germanicus lauded afterward. It was during the consolidation, as each Cohort arranged itself, this time in the more normal double line of Centuries, but facing south, with the belief that

193

we would be following in pursuit, that we first noticed something.

"Where's the Sixth Century?"

It was Structus who asked this, trotting up from his spot at the rear of the formation, and although I had to move a bit to see, it was not because I doubted him, just that it was so unusual. Before I could comment, Macer came trotting past, and while he did not say to do so, since Vespillo was right behind him, I followed.

Heading straight for Philus and the Fifth Century, Macer did not bother with formalities, snapping, "Where the fuck is Sixth Century?"

Philus' answer was clearly unsatisfactory, shrugging as he said, "I'm not sure, Pilus Prior. I was busy with my own Century."

The answer came from his Optio, Publius Closus, which made sense since he was on the side closest to Volusenus' Century, but what he said was alarming.

"Centurion Volusenus led them after the Germans," he told us, then after a slight hesitation, amended, "Or, maybe I should say that the Centurion went after the Germans, and his Century followed."

Before Macer could reply, we heard the sound of approaching horses, turning to see that Germanicus, followed by his staff, was trotting in our direction, prompting a groan from Macer.

Turning to me, he spoke in a low tone, "What should I tell him?"

Frankly, this surprised me, mainly since I had no more of an idea than he, and I told him as much, which he did not like at all, grumbling, "Why did I bother asking?"

By then, Germanicus had ridden up, and we all offered a salute, but while he returned it, his eyes were on the empty ground where the Sixth should have been; not that it was hard to miss, especially once the Fifth Cohort had assembled next to us, which I would liken to how a row of teeth appears when one is missing.

Germanicus, clearly puzzled, asked Macer mildly, "Pilus Prior Macer. Are you missing something?"

"Er," Macer stammered. "Yes, sir. It seems that Hastatus Posterior Volusenus has gone off in pursuit of the Germans, sir."

Germanicus stiffened, his eyes narrowing as he tried to place our new Centurion, asking, "Volusenus? He's new, isn't he?"

"Yes, sir," Macer replied, then after a hesitation that, if I was not the only one who noticed, was probably the only one who understood why, added, "He's a paid man, sir."

Turning to look south, using the advantage of being on horseback, Germanicus squinted for a moment, then said, "I see them. At least, I see the tail end of them. They're entering those woods." Macer and I exchanged an alarmed glance, but before we could say anything, Germanicus ordered us abruptly, "He's part of your Cohort, Pilus Prior. You need to take the rest of the Fourth and go after him."

Saluting, Macer paused as he thought for a moment before turning to me and saying, "The way we're formed up, it makes sense if your Century leads the way. The Second will follow," he told Vespillo, "then we'll be behind them. The Fourth and Fifth fall in behind us."

He did not even wait for me to acknowledge the order, trotting back to his Century. Thankfully, the men all heard, so they had already hoisted their shields, although I rued that I had not thought to have them retrieve the one javelin they had not thrown, although in a wooded area, they were of limited value. Shouting the orders, rather than perform a wheel maneuver that would place the front rank facing the forest, instead I had the men simply face to the left, which made for a slightly wider formation of ten men, rather than the normal eight. More crucially is that it placed men in a situation with which they were unaccustomed, the man to their right protecting their weak side unfamiliar to them in case there was a fight. Nevertheless, they did not hesitate in stepping off, following me and Gemellus, which was not surprising, knowing that almost every man had a friend in the ranks of the Sixth, a man they had gotten drunk with, whored with, and gambled with, so none of us wanted to lose any of those friends. From the spot where we had formed up, about a half-mile from the forest where we had been hiding, it was perhaps a mile and a half to the edge of the forest to the south, so I did not think it prudent to go to the double quick so early. Germanicus, with his Tribunes and bodyguard, went galloping ahead, but if thickly wooded ground is bad for the Legions, it is worse for cavalry, no matter for whom they march, so I did not expect them to penetrate the dense undergrowth that lay thickly between the trees. Nevertheless, Germanicus led his *ad hoc* force right up to the edge of the woods, but he did not elicit any kind of reaction, either in the form of resistance or by a signal from our missing Century. Finally, when we got to what I judged to be perhaps five hundred paces away, I gave the order to pick up the pace closing the distance to the line of trees, where Germanicus and his cavalry had drawn up, although I saw the Legate actually urge his horse forward into the forest. Despite being occupied with my own job, I winced at this, although several of his bodyguard kicked their mounts to go plunging after him, but as foolhardy as Germanicus was, I suppose it could be argued that I was no less so, because I did not slow the Century down, crashing into the heavy undergrowth. However, within a dozen paces, I called the halt, only because the trees were arranged in such a manner that a neat row of men, especially ten men wide, could not penetrate any farther than that. Cursing, I called a halt, although it was as much to catch my breath as my recognition that it would be impossible to march through this mess.

"Spread out, five sections in a line, the other five behind the first by a half-dozen paces," I ordered, and while the men complied, I was examining the ground.

Germanicus came trotting up, and he pointed me in the right direction, aided by his higher vantage point.

"There's a line of bodies heading that way." He indicated a southeasterly direction, which made sense, given that was away from the river and would give the fleeing Germans more time to maneuver.

Saluting, I led my now-formed men in that direction, finding the first German corpse in a matter of a few paces, although only his feet were visible from under a thicket of tangled vines and plants, reminding me how often dying men resemble animals, spending the last of their energy crawling to some private place to spend their final moments. Between the trampled down vegetation, the blood trails, and the scattering of bodies, we followed the Sixth Century, finding them about a half-mile deep into the forest. It was one of the men at the end farthest from me who spotted them first; my vision was obscured by the vegetation, and we altered our direction slightly. My first thought was to approach cautiously, but I quickly realized that there were no sounds of fighting, which would have carried farther than our line of sight, and within a few paces, I spotted them as well. They were in what could only be charitably called a formation; to my eye, it appeared more like they were clustered around something. Or, I thought with a stab of alarm, someone, and before I had the thought to do so, I broke out into a run. Not a trot, but a full-out run, crashing through the brush with the same force and as much grace as a bear fleeing hunters, a most unseemly display on my part, but in the moment, I did not care. In my mind, there could only be one reason a Century of Legionaries would be standing there, completely disorganized, and when I got closer and saw they were surrounding a large tree, and all looking downward at something at its base, I was

197

certain that I would find Volusenus there; or more accurately, his corpse.

I was right, in a sense, but while he was there, he was not a corpse, although he was literally covered in blood, and he was not supine on the ground, instead sitting upright with his back against the trunk. As arresting as the sight of him may have been, my attention was drawn away by what was surrounding him, what I counted was more than a dozen corpses, spread out in a rough semicircle, with Volusenus and the tree the base.

"We found him like that."

Gillo's voice jerked my attention away from my examination of this scene, and I looked over at the Optio, asking him sharply, "What do you mean you 'found him like that'?"

"I mean they," Gillo pointed to the bodies, "were already there. And the Centurion," his voice lowered, and I heard something in his voice that I was only able to place later, "was sitting there, like he is now."

Turning back to Volusenus, this was the first moment I examined him closely, but he seemed oblivious to our presence, sitting with his knees drawn up, his arms around his knees...and a *gladius* that was literally caked in blood and bits of gore for its entire length, the ichor dripping from it still in his hand. I could see he was conscious, yet to this point, he had not made one move or indicated in any way he was aware of the presence of not just his Century, but me, even after I crouched down next to him. A quick visual examination showed that, aside from a long but superficial cut running down the outside of his left forearm, none of the blood appeared to be his.

"Volusenus?"

I used a low tone, similar to that when I talked to Latobius, but only after I called his name twice more did he respond, turning his head slowly to look at me, his eyes dull and vacant, at least until he seemed to recognize me. This prompted a reaction, his expression changing first, but then he began to try and rise to his feet, except that his legs could not seem to support him, which I probably understood better than anyone else, given our size. Thankfully, my own considerable bulk blocked the view of his failed attempt from his men, and I put a gentle but firm hand on his shoulder to push him back down.

"Not until you're ready," I told him quietly, to which he gave a perfunctory nod. "So," I asked him with what I hoped was a light tone, "what happened?"

I cannot say what I was expecting, but it was not the look of confusion that flashed across his face, then, following my gaze, he turned and seemed to see the strewn bodies arrayed around him for the first time, because he let out a quiet gasp.

Looking at me, I could instantly see that the shock he was showing was unfeigned, and he whispered, "I don't know."

"Princeps Prior Pullus?" The voice of Volusenus' *Signifer* Macerinus caused me to turn about to see that he had moved a bit closer than the rest of the Century. "Is Centurion Volusenus all right? Is he wounded?"

"No," I assured him, and the manner in which not just Macerinus but the rest of his Century reacted told me that Volusenus had at last managed to win the loyalty and affection of his men, despite his haughty ways and inexperience.

Maybe, I thought, there's hope for him yet. Returning my attention to Volusenus, I saw that he had gathered himself, and with some surreptitious help on my part, came to his feet. He took several deep breaths as he collected his wits, then gave me a curt nod, stepped around me, and resumed command of his Century. By this time, most of the Cohort had arrived, so that we were able to march out of the forest, intact, where Germanicus and the other four Cohorts waited, whereupon Germanicus promptly ordered us to turn about and go back into the forest to pursue the Germans.

It was not until the next night before I had the chance to spend more time with Volusenus, inviting him to my quarters back in our now-consolidated camp a few miles from Blariacum. The campaign, such as it was, was over; just as Germanicus had planned, the fleeing remnants of the warband ran directly into the five Cohorts of the 20th, who had moved into position just south of the expanse of woods into which we chased the Germans. Our victory was complete, and although there are always men who manage to escape, if there were more than two or three hundred of those out of the entire combined force, I would have been surprised. Not that we killed all of the rest; there were a bit more than a thousand prisoners, who Germanicus had informed us would be sold into slavery. Because they were warriors, this was still a death sentence, albeit delayed to one extent or another, since the fittest among this lot would be sent to a *ludus* somewhere, destined to use their skills in the sand, for the entertainment of Romans. I must confess that these men elicited a feeling of some sympathy in me, to which I attributed my time in Arelate spent with Vulso, who was as almost important a tutor in fighting as my own father, teaching me in the skills of the arena that, more than once, have kept me alive. Once you get to know someone, even gladiators, as men, it is difficult to view them as little better than animals whose sole purpose is to bleed and die for our entertainment. At least, this is the case for me, although a secondary consideration is that I can understand how bitter a draught it must be for a warrior to suffer defeat and captivity, but kept alive only for the amusement of those who are responsible for your condition. It was the lot of the others, however, that was, in every way imaginable, the worst fate, because these men were destined for places like the silver mines of Hispania, where it was said that a healthy, strong man might survive for a year, before being literally worked to death. Not, I will also confess, that I spent much time thinking about the fate of men who, if they had had the chance, would have slit my throat at the first opportunity. Now that it was over, we were waiting for orders from Germanicus, with the expectation being that we marched back to Ubiorum so that Germanicus could resume his duties as *Praetor* and continue his work on the census he was taking of the entirety of Gaul. Whatever was in our future, the mood in the camp was celebratory, and it was in that spirit I sent Alex to extend an invitation to Volusenus to share the evening meal with me in my private quarters. He accepted readily enough, appearing at the exact time, wearing a freshly laundered tunic that, even now, was still a deeper red that practically shouted its quality, and I congratulated myself for choosing one of equal hue and not one of my faded ones. I had decided beforehand that I would not broach the topic I had in mind during the meal, and we ate companionably enough, chatting about the previous few days, while I assiduously avoided the day before. When we were finished, I waited for Alex to clear everything away, then with my own hand, poured a couple cups of wine after sending Alex on a pre-agreed, non-existent errand, digging into my stock of Falernian, something that Volusenus immediately noticed.

"Princeps Prior," he said this genially enough, but I sensed there was more than a bit of irony in the manner in which he lifted his cup, "I salute you on your choice of wine."

Before I could think better of it, I answered, "Well, I just wanted to offer you something you probably drank every day."

As soon as it was out, I inwardly cringed, worried that this would prick his touchy pride, but to my faint surprise, he actually laughed and raised his cup in salute.

"I'll admit it, I've missed this," he replied, then after a pause, he added, "and yes, we did have this every day. Even for our *posca.*"

Now it was my turn to laugh since it is more common to use the worst quality wine, the spices added to it hiding that fact, and I returned his salute with my own cup. The next moments were silent, then I decided that it was time to broach the subject for which I had invited him to this meal.

"So," I asked abruptly, "what happened yesterday?"

I do not know why, but his lack of surprise actually served to unnerve me more than he was by the question, clearly expecting it by the manner in which he set his cup down, his face betraying nothing. However, he did not speak for a span of some time.

"I don't know," he finally replied, his eyes meeting mine unwaveringly. "Nothing like that has ever happened to me before."

"And," I tried to sound casual, "what do you remember?"

He considered my question, and the manner in which he did so indicated he had given this much thought; I believe this was the first moment where I had the faintest glimmering of recognition.

"Not much," he finally answered soberly. "The last thing I do clearly remember was seeing the Germans running for the woods. And," he shrugged, "I just followed them."

"You did more than 'just follow them,'" I retorted, yet without any rancor or rebuke.

"That," he acknowledged with what I took to be a grimace, "is true." Pausing, he continued, "Honestly, the only thing I really remember is how angry I was."

This caught my attention, and before I could stop myself, I found I was sitting on the edge of my stool, listening intently, something that Volusenus clearly noticed, his brow furrowing at my sudden interest, yet he did not visibly react when I asked him, "Why were you so angry? They," I pointed out, "hadn't actually slaughtered the people of Blariacum, and they only raided some farms and a couple villages." Pausing, I asked, "How many casualties did your Century take?"

"Only a handful," he admitted, "and none of them were killed."

"So?" I pressed, only dimly understanding that this was as important to me as it was to him at this point. "Did one of them get you?" I indicated the bandage on his arm. "Is that when you got that?"

"No." He glanced down at the bandage. "Honestly, I don't remember when that happened." He seemed to be gathering his thoughts, with a furrowed brow that seemed familiar to me, then went on, "I was just…angry, although I can't say exactly why. Oh," he allowed with a slight wave of his hand, "I suppose I was just so excited since this was my first engagement."

Volusenus stopped then, ostensibly to sip from his cup, but I sensed that he was at a loss, which was what prompted my decision to speak.

"Let me tell you about something that happened to me." And I went on to relate the times I had experienced what I had come to believe, and still do, was a divine fit of rage, passed on to me by the first Titus Pullus, starting with when I was a boy and I split the dwarf slave Spartacus' skull, to the time against the Marcomanni when, for the first time, I was actually able to summon this madness on command.

I talked for a fair amount of time as he listened intently, while I included everything I could think of or recall from those moments. His attention on me never wavered, and while I did not look in his direction, I felt his eyes on me as I talked. When I was finished, he said nothing for a span of heartbeats that seemed to stretch out forever.

Finally, he said, "That sounds like what happened to me." Thinking about it more, he added, "And, now that you mention it, I do remember that I had gotten so far ahead of the Century that the Germans we were after must have seen me isolated, so they turned on me. And," he shrugged, "that enraged me for some reason, so I suppose instead of either waiting for the men or running back to them, I went after them." When I did not respond once he finished, he finally asked, "Why do you think that happens to both of us?"

Although I had thought about the cause of these bouts at length, this was the first time I had to contemplate the idea that there was someone else, other than the first Titus Pullus, who experienced anything like this.

Now, I thought for a moment, then offered, "It clearly has something to do with our size. My Av...my grandfather, Titus Pullus, experienced the same thing. Although," I allowed as I added, "he wasn't really my grandfather, he was my uncle. My paternal grandmother's brother. He adopted my father in his will."

Volusenus considered this for a moment, then shook his head, saying only, "If everything I've heard about his size is true, I don't think it matters whether he was your true grandfather or your uncle. Your size obviously came from him. But," his face shadowed, "I have no idea about where mine came from."

"Your father isn't a large man? Or his father?" I asked, to which he shook his head. "What about your mother's side? Have you met her family?"

"My mother's parents are dead," he answered shortly, in such a way that I sensed this was a sensitive subject, so I let it alone.

Returning to the larger topic, I said something that I had never uttered before, not to Alex, not to my dead brother Sextus, not even to Giulia more than twenty years earlier, "I think that, being our size, we've become used to being better at..." I searched for the right word, finally settling on just waving my arm in an encompassing gesture, "...all of this, especially the fighting. And when someone challenges us in some way," I shrugged, then finished, "we get angry."

"'Angry'?" Volusenus commented dryly, one eyebrow lifted in a mannerism that reminded me of the way Sextus would react to something I said. "That's certainly one way to put it, but

I think it's more than that. I mean," he gave a self-conscious laugh, "I don't have the best temper under the best of conditions, so I get angry if my meal is cold, or if one of the men drops one of his javelins when we're on the march. But this?" He paused for a long, long period, and I had just opened my mouth when he resumed talking. "What if it happens again? But not in a fight? What if I just lose control because one of the men has made me so angry I go into this…rage?"

"Honestly," I replied immediately, "I don't think that you have to worry about that. From what you've described, it sounds like the same thing that happens to me, and it only has happened in moments of extreme danger." I gave a laugh, hoping that it did not sound forced. "And I doubt that Publius losing his *baltea* right before inspection can be considered extreme danger."

"No," he agreed readily enough, then gave me a grin. "At least, not for me."

We shared a quiet laugh, two Centurions sharing one of the many small ordeals we must endure, the clumsiness and stupidity of some of the men we are responsible for, but the smile faded from his face, and he peered down into his cup, as if he would find some answers there.

"Am I cursed?" he asked abruptly, his voice almost a whisper, and he looked up to meet my gaze. "By the gods, I mean?"

Honestly, of all the things Gnaeus Volusenus said to me that night, this was the one that pierced my heart, as I was suddenly transported back to a time roughly three decades earlier, when I asked my father this very question, after I had slain Spartacus; I was ten years old.

Perhaps that was why I told him with as much sincerity as I could muster, "No, you're not cursed. In fact, what my father told me, about my grandfather, and me, is that Titus Pullus believed he had been given a gift by Mars and Bellona, but he said that it's a gift that comes with a price. And," I experienced what felt like a lump of lead suddenly threatening to clog my throat, as a rush of memories came flooding into my mind, but I forced myself to continue, "that price can be a heavy one. Trust me when I tell you that I've found this to be more true than even my grandfather might have known. But, if you need it, it will come to you, and it will probably keep your men, and you, alive."

We did not speak much after that, both of us content to sip from our cups, then Volusenus rose, and thanked me for the meal and hospitality, leaving me in a thoughtful mood, recalling moments and events that I had not considered for some time.

As expected, we returned to Ubiorum, whereupon Germanicus resumed his duties as *Praetor* and we settled back into life in garrison. Under normal circumstances, our foray against the Germans would not have been considered worthy of being called a campaign, and our engagement a true battle, but because of who was leading us, both of these conditions were considered met, not that I am complaining since these are entered into the record of every participant. Although he was not awarded a triumph, or even triumphal ornaments, much was made of Germanicus' victory, including coins being struck, and a statue of him was erected in Blariacum in thanks that they had been spared because of our intervention. We had declared him *Imperator* earlier in the day of my talk with Volusenus, but by common consent, we had done this in the camp, before returning to Ubiorum; none of us wanted to be indirectly responsible for Germanicus running afoul of the Princeps. I had even more reason than most, because my interactions with Tiberius and his treatment of Germanicus four years earlier had convinced me that the older man held his adopted son in suspicion that Germanicus coveted Tiberius' spot as presumptive heir to the Princeps. Returning to his task of ordering Gaul, I only caught occasional glimpses of him, usually when he was leaving

Ubiorum to travel west to one of the towns or cities in one of the Gallic provinces. The rest of the year passed in this manner, with no further incursions by Germans across the Rhenus, so that soon enough, the temporary suspension of the state of discontent on the part of the men ceased and the grumbling resumed. I call it "grumbling"; it was much more than that, and it got worse, seemingly by the day. The number of brawls between men of the 1st and 20th out in town almost doubled, and while Germanicus was not one to sentence men to floggings, or worse, executions, lightly, from my viewpoint, he was forced into that position by the actions of the men. Which, not surprisingly, only made matters worse, reminding me of something that I not only read in my Avus' account, specifically during his time in Alexandria with Divus Julius and a situation with which he had to contend, but my father had tried to get across to me when he realized I was determined to live a life under the standard.

"Rankers don't care about fair," he had told me on numerous occasions. "They care about whatever makes their lives easier or puts coins in their purses. The only time they care about fairness is if it benefits them in some way. Otherwise..."

He seldom finished this thought with anything other than a shrug, and I had read as much in Titus Pullus' words to keep this in mind, even before I saw it proven with my own eyes. This was one of those occasions; men knew they were in the wrong by getting into a fight out in town, yet they, and more importantly, their comrades were every bit as angry at receiving punishment for it as if it had been unwarranted. Any action by Centurions and Optios, whether it be on the books or with the *vitus*, was beginning to be viewed as an abuse of our authority, and not just by men like Pusio. One day, I overheard Clustuminus talking to Caninas, and if I had not recognized his voice, I would have sworn that it was Pusio or Trigeminus from the Fifth Section doing the talking. What made it doubly shocking was that I had been preparing for the time when Structus was promoted,

207

because he not only had served long enough as Optio, but he was deserving of it, and Clustuminus was my choice for Optio, although I did not share that with either of them. Hearing such talk from one of my most solid, dependable men shook me to my core, yet when I brought it up with Macer, all he could do was commiserate.

"I've got the same thing going on in my Century," he had told me, "and so does everyone else."

Perhaps the only positive note, at least for me, was that the expression of discontent in my Century was confined to being verbal in nature; the only other Century of the Fourth who could claim the same was the Sixth, and I did not then, nor do I now believe that this was a coincidence, especially after Volusenus' episode in the forest. Speaking of Volusenus, shortly after we returned to Ubiorum, Macer invited me to an evening meal, which was not uncommon; what was unusual was the topic.

"How worried should I be about what happened to Volusenus?" he asked me bluntly, and I remember thinking, at least when I talked to Volusenus, I waited until we had finished eating. "Is he likely to have something like that happen again, but here in camp?"

I did not reply immediately, mainly because I was caught by surprise, not as much by Macer's question, but the anger that it stirred in me, although it took a moment for me to realize why.

Instead of answering him directly, after a silence, I said, "How much have you heard about me? I mean," I saw the look of confusion cross his face, "as far as before I was assigned to the 1st?"

He regarded me curiously, but he replied readily enough, "Just that you had had some sort of trouble when you were with the 8th that had something to do with a rebellion."

"Anything else?" I pressed.

Now his face shadowed, and this time, he clearly hesitated, admitting, "Well, I may have heard some...things. About a couple of fights where you were involved." When I did not say anything, he added reluctantly, "Something about you killing a chieftain of one of the tribes when your Primus Pilus was killed."

"And?"

Shrugging, he looked away as he said, "And not much more, really. Just that there seem to be times when you…lose your head," he finished lamely.

"Did your father ever tell you about my grandfather? Did your father ever see him do anything that sounds like what you're describing?"

"No," Macer answered, then after a pause, he allowed, "but he heard stories about him."

"Well," I told Macer firmly, "without knowing the specific details, what I can tell you is that there's probably a bit of truth in them. I," I amended, "we, as in my grandfather and me, have experienced…moments in a battle where, as you said, we lose our heads. Except, we don't *really* lose our wits. I know what's happening, but it's as if," I searched for the proper description, then remembering what I had come up with for myself, continued, "whoever I'm fighting is suddenly encased in honey and they're moving so slowly that I can see what they're going to do before they do it. And," I added, "it's not that I don't know I'm in great danger; I just don't care." Macer absorbed this, but I was not finished making my point. "Now, how many times have you seen me behave like I've lost my wits?"

"None," Macer agreed, then added with a faint grin, "and I'm not sure I want to."

"Considering that it only happens when I and the men around me are in real danger of losing a fight, neither do I. But," I continued, "I've talked to Volusenus, and it sounds exactly like what I've experienced. So, if I haven't suddenly started chopping Publius," I almost had said Pusio, but caught myself in time, "into bloody bits because he dropped his shield by this point, I think you're safe. From both of us."

This made him laugh, and he said, "Fair enough."

He moved on to another topic, yet while I listened, it was with only half my mind. The other half was worried that, if Volusenus found out about this conversation, he would view it as a betrayal of confidence, although why I cared all that much was beyond me, other than, of course, because it might affect the Cohort in some way. How that might be, I had no idea, and I soon pushed it from my mind.

Over the years since I have begun this account, I recall mentioning how the matter in which time passes is a somewhat unusual, strange thing, where there are days that seem to last forever, and other times when you seemingly blink, and a year has passed. Such was the case with the rest of that year with Germanicus as *Praetor*, as the Legions continued to perform as they always did during a time of relative peace, on the surface, at least. Just like the current of the Rhenus that is constantly flowing past the docks of what has now become a good-sized town, almost a small city here in Ubiorum, with the quelling of this one crossing by the Germans, the days resumed flowing past in a routine fashion. Oh, there were punishments, and promotions; men were broken back to the ranks, and fines were levied. We still made regular forays across the Rhenus, but the defeat we had dealt the Sugambri and Tencteri seemed to have sent a message to the other tribes, and they restricted their activities accordingly. Speaking of Germans, Arminius was still the ostensible leader of a united clan of German tribes, but such was the political intrigue, secret dealing, and betrayal among those tribes that he simply could not seem to bring them together in the manner he had with Varus. Going into the year of the Consulships of Sextus Pompeius and Sextus Appuleius, really the only notable thing was that, not only had the Princeps extended Germanicus' tenure as *Praetor*, he was also awarded *Propraetor authority,* whereupon he left Ubiorum to resume the interrupted census of Gaul he had been conducting. Then, without any warning, our entire world was turned upside down.

Chapter Five

"Augustus is dead!"

Even writing the words, some time after the event, I see my hand shake slightly. How, I wonder, can someone such as myself, a somewhat educated man but no writer by any stretch, accurately describe to you, dear reader, what this cataclysmic event meant and the impact it had? Not just on a grand political and diplomatic scale, since he embodied Rome itself, but on the everyday lives of not just Roman citizens, but anywhere Rome has a presence? Truly, I am sitting here, at my desk, at a loss as to how I could even begin to describe the turmoil and upheaval that began, almost within watches after Gaius Octavianus Caesar Divi Fili Augustus breathed his last. I suppose I will start with the bare bones of it: he had been traveling, Tiberius with him, to Nola, when he took ill. He stopped there, while Tiberius continued to Illyricum, preparing to take command of the Legions there for another campaign. Apparently, he initially recovered from a bilious fever, then took a dramatic turn for the worse; of course, this was guaranteed to engender all manner of speculation that the Princeps had been helped along by Livia, since he had finally officially named Tiberius as his heir. Personally, I did not believe that, though it was not because I did not think Livia capable of such an act, but simply put, the man was seventy-five years old, closing in on seventy-six. Honestly, because of my intimate knowledge of the Princeps, albeit second-hand through the eyes of my Avus, I was astonished that he lived as long as he did, and when I met the man for the first and only time in my life, where he essentially coerced me into serving him in the matter of trapping my former Tribune Claudius in intriguing against Augustus by writing the man letters, the contents of which were dictated to me by the

Princeps, through Dolabella, of course, I thought he would be dead long since. That meeting had been more than a decade before, and I was certain that he could count his time on this side of the river in months once I laid eyes on him.

As far as how and when I learned of this momentous event, it was actually out in town, where Macer and the other Centurions of the Fourth save Vespillo were taking a rare night off, spending it at our customary spot for all men of the Fourth Cohort, a place down by the river named The Dancing Faun. The bearer of the message was, considering the nature of the news, understandably excited, having burst in, flinging the door open and shouting what I have described, wild-eyed and, in a voice tight with the tension and fear that was completely appropriate, given the enormity of what he was relaying. If he said anything after this, I have no way of knowing because of the eruption of noise as men, almost as if the order had been given by our Primus Pilus, came to our feet, knocking over chairs, with cups crashing to the floor, shattering and leaving their contents spread all over the wooden planks, while men shouted their dismay, grief, and if my ears were any judge, fear. A fear which, I would argue, was not only understandable, but was warranted, given that no man currently present had even been alive for a time when the Princeps did not rule all. For some reason, my first thoughts went to my father, who had died just the year before, but honestly, it was my Avus who I missed the most, and while I did not say anything aloud about it, I resolved that, given the first opportunity, I would consult the scrolls that are my most treasured possession. I think my reasoning was and still is sound; the only event that could compare to the death of Augustus was the death of his adoptive father, Divus Julius, and the first Titus Pullus had lived through all that had transpired from this event. At that moment, however, there was no time, as Macer had to practically shout to be heard over the uproar.

"We need to get back to camp and see what the situation is," he told us, but Cornutus was not willing to give up on the night's debauching, complaining, "For what? I say we stay here and offer the Princeps toasts in his memory! I know he'd appreciate that."

Before I could stop myself, I gave a derisive laugh, knowing that of all the men there, there was only one who had even been in the presence of the Princeps, and that was me. Macer shot me an inquisitive look, but I gave a small shake of my head, sending the message that I had no intention of explaining why I had reacted in the manner I did.

"Well, Cornutus," Macer countered, "he very well may, but there will be time for that later. We need to go...now."

We had all learned that Macer had a certain tone in his voice that told us when he was no longer debating or discussing a topic, that he was giving an order, so we all rose to our feet, save Cornutus, who was either already too far in his cups or, for some unfathomable reason, had decided this would be a good time to test our Pilus Prior.

"I don't see what the hurry is." He was actually pouting, reminding me that he could become quite petulant if the mood struck him. "It's not like he's going to come back to life."

"Get on your feet," Macer snapped, and at first, I thought Cornutus would disobey, staying seated for a long span of time, glaring up at our Pilus Prior.

But finally, with a great show, he dragged himself to his feet, grumbling under his breath as we hurried out the door, leaving the turmoil of men trying to understand what was ultimately the inexplicable as far as they were concerned. Leaving them behind, we walked in a group, quickly seeing that, unsurprisingly, the news had already spread throughout the town, as small clusters of men wearing soldier's tunics, most of them carrying *viti*, were hurrying back in the same direction we were heading. Meanwhile, the citizens of the town had come flooding out into the streets, where women were sobbing, and even men were shedding tears, all of them betraying their true concern; what now?

"What do you think's going to happen?" Macer asked me in a low tone, while the rest of the Centurions followed behind us.

"Whatever has happened already has," I pointed out. "I don't know exactly how long ago it was, but Augustus didn't just die. It's been at least a week, so if someone is going to try and take over the title First Man in Rome, it's already happened."

"True," he granted, but then he shot me a sidelong glance, "unless that someone happens to actually be in Gaul right now."

I did not hesitate in reacting, shaking my head and replying without any hesitation, "No. Germanicus wouldn't do that. He'll abide by the Princeps' wishes."

Macer shrugged, saying only, "I suppose you would know," but the manner in which he said it told me he was not convinced.

And, truthfully, he had good reason to feel this way, and I knew he was far from alone. Tiberius was certainly respected by the men of the Legions, but he was not loved, and Germanicus had both from those of us under the standard. If I am being completely honest, I cannot say that I would have been upset all that much if he had made his bid for power, despite the fact that it would have put me in quite the dilemma. Although it had been some time since my last...errand, as far as I knew, I still was considered one of Tiberius' men; at least, Dolabella had never appeared in my quarters and informed me that I was no longer bound to the man. Still, ever since I had been Germanicus' Primus Pilus of the short-lived *Legio Germanicus*, I had recognized in the younger man the kind of essence that I had envisioned Divus Julius possessed, back when he was a little-known Praetor in Hispania, and a sixteen-year-old Titus Pullus, underage but oversized, had enlisted in the *dilectus* for what

215

became known as the 10th Equestris. And, as events later proved, Tiberius was the man who was most suspicious that Germanicus harbored dreams of usurping him in his role as Augustus' heir, and who is only now being referred to as our second *Imperator*. None of this, however, was known to us as we returned to camp, but as put out as Cornutus was by the early end to our evening, fairly soon after our arrival, the provosts were sent out by the Legate left in command by Germanicus, Aulus Caecina Severus, the same man who had been involved in the Batonian Revolt, to recall all the men out in town, ordering them to return to camp immediately.

"He's going to make the announcement that Augustus is dead," Macer surmised, but then added in a whisper, "and who knows what else he might say? What if he declares himself for Germanicus?"

I was beginning to become irritated with my friend now, so certain was I that, if it even occurred to Germanicus to declare himself for the title of *Imperator*, it would not be because he had been pressured into it by our Caecina, which is what we called him. Instead of saying anything, I just sighed, resigned to the fact that Macer would not believe it until he heard it from Germanicus' own mouth, whenever he returned from Gaul. Having our Pilus Prior thinking along those lines was bad enough, but when we split up to return to our respective quarters and wait for the rest of our men to arrive from town, Volusenus followed me, making it obvious he wanted a word with me.

"Pullus," he blurted out within an eyeblink after me shutting the door to my private quarters, "what if the Pilus Prior is right? What if Germanicus declares himself as the rightful heir to the Princeps?"

As frayed as my patience had become, I could see that the younger man was genuinely worried; besides, now that we seemed to have reached a level of, if not friendship, then cordiality, however tenuous it may have been, I did not want to rupture that.

Forcing myself to respond with a patience I did not really feel, I said, "While I don't see that happening, what exactly is your real question? Are you asking if I think the 1st would declare for him? Then march with him to Rome?"

As I hoped, putting it this baldly seemed to bring him up short, and he blinked several times before he answered with a frown, "Well, yes, I suppose that's what I'm asking."

Deciding on the fly to indulge Volusenus, I turned my mind to thinking about something I had refused to consider before this moment, yet despite my opinion not being changed about Germanicus' likely actions, I did feel a stirring of unease. This sense was brought on by the combination of the event that precipitated this conversation, the death of Augustus, and the current mood in the 1st, and 20th as well. Although I had not personally been to Mogontiacum or up to Vetera, there was enough intercourse between these major Roman forts to know that, while it was impossible to determine the degree, the air of disgruntlement was certainly permeating the Legions stationed in those places at least as much as it was present in Ubiorum. Suddenly, what had seemed to me to be about as remote a possibility as pigs sprouting wings was not so outrageous. Indeed, the more I thought about it, the more I recognized that, if Germanicus did in fact harbor ambitions, he would find a receptive audience in the men of the Army of the Rhenus.

Outwardly, only a matter of a heartbeat or two had passed, and I answered Volusenus honestly, "*If* Germanicus did something that mad, then yes, I think it's possible that our Legion would give him our allegiance. The 20th as well, I'm fairly certain. As for the other Legions?"

I ended with a shrug and shake of my head, but Volusenus was not done.

"And?" he asked quietly, his eyes suddenly intently studying my face to a point it was uncomfortable. "What would *you* do?"

Quite abruptly, something inside me seemed to freeze, forming a cold ball somewhere between my chest and stomach, the thought lancing through my mind; why is he asking me this? Is it curiosity? Is he looking for some sort of guidance? Or, is he working for someone? And if so, whom?

Finally, I said, "I don't know, honestly. I think it depends on what Germanicus had to say when he got back here and what reasons he gave for his decision."

"But what if you don't agree with his reasons for doing it, but the men around you do?" he pressed, and I relaxed slightly, understanding that this was probably the real cause for his questioning, that he *was* looking for some sort of guidance. "Would you still refuse to follow him? Or would you go along with everyone else in order to..." His voice trailed off, but I finished for him, with a laugh that sounded harsh in my ears. "...stay alive, you mean? So that you don't have to worry about your own men killing you?" The look of relief on his face was intense and unmistakable, and he nodded vigorously. "Yes. That. I mean," he faltered a bit. "It's just that, with the way the men have been behaving and all. I just think that it's something to think about."

This, I realized, I could not argue, not that I was any more convinced that this was even a remote possibility, but I was actually impressed by Volusenus' questions, because it indicated to me there was a sense of honor and duty to Rome in him that he foresaw might put him in a position where he had to worry about being slain by men under his command by refusing to either go along or be swept up with the rushing tide.

Thinking to assuage his worry, I offered, "Honestly, I don't think it will come to that. Besides," I added, "one other thing I learned from my grandfather and father: you can't spend your time and energy worrying about something that you can't control. And Germanicus is going to make his decision without any input from us."

He still did not seem convinced, but he also clearly saw that I had been as patient as I was willing to be, so he thanked me, then immediately excused himself, leaving me to watch as he left my quarters, his shoulders barely clearing the door, and only then because he twisted his torso. Once more, I was struck by the oddest sensation, thinking, that must be what I look like walking away. Indeed, as I thought about it further, I realized that I did precisely the same thing, turning my body slightly so that I could fit through a standard doorway without touching the doorjamb. Having someone my size around was turning out to be quite the unusual experience, though I quickly dismissed that line of thought, sitting down and waiting for the sound of our men returning and knowing they would be unhappy about it, no matter what the news may have been.

As it turned out, neither Volusenus nor Macer, nor any other man of a like mind, had anything to worry about, at least about Germanicus trying to seize power, and I believe the truth of this started with the speech given by Caecina. Just as I had predicted, the assembly that was called and was held by torchlight by the time both Legions had been assembled was for the purpose of the Legate announcing what every man now knew, and absolutely nothing more. Frankly, I thought it a bit of a waste of time, since everybody had already heard of the demise of our Princeps, but I also knew that the Roman upper class feels obligated to perform certain functions, no matter how useless they might be. Nevertheless, I will say that it was clear that the Legate was deeply affected by this news; there was a quaver to his voice that was normally not there, but more telling was that, given my position in the front rank formed by the front-line Cohorts, I could see the glistening of his tears, caught by the dancing light of the torches. Not lost on me was that there was in all likelihood a fair amount of self-interest, and frankly, worry about the demise of Augustus, if only because Tiberius had made it clear that he placed much of the blame of what occurred during the Batonian Revolt on his shoulders, but thanks to the intervention of the Princeps, he was still in favor.

"We have suffered an enormous loss," I remember this part of his words, mainly because of what happened immediately afterward, "one that will take months, perhaps even years before any of us can fully comprehend its meaning. But," his voice became firmer, "Rome itself will endure! It will endure because our wise and beloved Princeps ensured that there would be an orderly succession of power. And now, it is the turn of Tiberius, who was known as Tiberius Claudius Nero but is now Tiberius Caesar Divi Augusti Filius Augustus, to guide us, to lead us, to inspire us to continue performing our great deeds…for Rome!"

Now, I cannot say there was not cheering for these words of his, but even in the torchlight, I could see that Caecina heard the same thing I did: a distinct lack of enthusiasm. If he, or I for that matter, had known this was as good as it was going to get that evening, I wonder if he would have said anything differently, or perhaps not made his announcement at all. The trouble began almost immediately after he finished, and before he could even give the order for dismissal.

"When is the new *Imperator* going to address our grievances?"

"What's Tiberius going to do about our bonuses?"

"Are you going to speak for us with Tiberius so we can get what's coming to us?"

This is just a sample of the hundreds of shouted questions that I was able to hear before everything became a hopeless jumble of noise that drowned out the combined efforts of Centurions and Optios to get men in hand. Before a span of twenty heartbeats, the completely verbal nature swiftly turned into physical demonstrations as men left their spot in the ranks, raising their fists and shaking them at the Legate and his staff. While the Legate himself did not look frightened, his staff did, although he was clearly disturbed by the vehemence on display, only made worse when some Centurions were unable to stop their men from surging forward, leaving their spots in the formation to approach where Caecina was standing on the rostrum. Fortunately, as far as I was concerned at least, I turned about quickly enough and liberally used my *vitus*, with Structus right beside me swinging his turfcutter handle, so that our Century, while they may not have stayed in place, at least did not get past us and close to the Legate. Being occupied with my own concerns, I could not pay much attention to what was going on around me, but afterward, we all agreed that it was every bit as loud as any battle we ever fought, and chaos reigned for several moments. All but two of the staff of Tribunes fled back to the *Praetorium*, so that only Caecina stood there as if rooted to his spot, refusing to not only move, but even to acknowledge that men were trying to press in on him, although I have no idea what any of them had planned if they did manage to come face to face with him. I do want to stress that, at this point, none of the men wanted to harm the man; this was the consensus among the Centurions and Optios, just that they wanted to present their long-simmering grievances to him personally.

Finally, a semblance of order was restored, just long enough for the Legate to formally announce the end to the formation, and only then did he return to the *Praetorium*, walking in a studiedly unhurried manner, sending the message that he was unafraid of the men under his command. Without being told to do so by him, a couple dozen Centurions, equally divided between the 20th and 1st from what I could see, and including myself, turned and faced the men, forming a curved line around his path back to the headquarters. While we said nothing, I was secretly hoping that someone from the ranks would try to get past us, because I was seething with anger. As far as I was concerned, the men had behaved like rabble, little better than animals, and it was an affront to my sense of what it meant to be a Legionary of Rome that they had comported themselves like this. Nevertheless, while this may sound odd, when it came down to the substance of the complaints on the part of the rankers, I was largely in agreement with them. Despite my intention to serve under the standard for as long as I was able, I did and still do think it was extremely unjust for the Princeps to change the term of enlistment, and do so for all men currently under the standard, and not just for new enlistees. In matters of pay, because of Augustus' odd genius for the minutiae of regulations, coupled with his insistence on a strict obedience to the letter of every one of them, monetary fines that had been overlooked in the past were no longer treated in this manner. This was more of an issue for the longer-serving men, most especially those on their second enlistment. These men, while relatively few in number, who could count their service back to the first decade of what is now called the Empire, were seeing fines being levied for things that, when they began, were not against regulations. Little by little, over the years, the Princeps had seen fit to add more rules where the punishment was monetary in nature; just a handful every year, but over time, it was not uncommon for even the most senior rankers to have almost half of their pay deducted because of a missing lace or a broken javelin shaft that their Centurion had deemed to be damaged because of negligence and not normal wear and tear. The quality of the food had gone down in recent years, and men were now often augmenting their normal rations out of their own purses. This, naturally, was a boon to the merchants in town, and was one large reason why Ubiorum's growth had been so explosive. In fact, many enterprising merchants in the town offered a valuable service, offering various bits of gear for sale, usually at a price just a few *obols* less than what the army would deduct from a man's pay for replacing it officially. And just as naturally, there were always the sharp operators who offered items that may have appeared to be identical to that issued by Rome but were made of shoddier material, something that any semi-competent *Immune* could spot and identify as essentially being counterfeit. And, several years before, Augustus had introduced a regulation strictly forbidding the substitution of pieces of equipment bought from outside merchants that were not approved by Rome, so what often ended up happening was that a ranker, in a bid to save some money, might end up out not only the money he paid for the shoddy piece of gear, but for the official piece…and the fine for violating the regulation. All these things, in and of themselves, were bad enough, but when you also factored in the number of Centurions and Optios who, like my former Primus Pilus Urso, saw their men as a means of income over and above what Rome paid to lead these men, it was easy to see, at least for me, why the men were so unhappy. Regardless of these things, and my personal sympathy for many of their complaints, the manner in which the men behaved that evening was shameful, and once they were in hand and we marched them to our respective areas, I made directly for Macer's quarters. Not surprisingly, I was greeted by the others, and we entered as a group, making our way through the outer office, where Vespillo rapped on the door, then entered without waiting for Macer to respond. Normally, this would have been a breach of custom that would have prompted a sharp rebuke, but our Pilus Prior was clearly expecting us, as was Lucco, who had already poured five cups; I noticed that Macer had obviously drained one because he was already holding his, which he held out for Lucco to refill.

"The Primus Pilus has called a meeting of all Centurions at the end of the watch," he told us without preamble. "So we don't have much time." Pausing for a moment, as if to collect his thoughts, he finally shook his head in exasperation, asking plaintively, "What do we do?"

"We stripe any bastard who behaves the way they did tonight," Vespillo answered immediately. "We're not fucking rabble, we're not the mob in Rome. We're in the fucking Legions!"

When he was finished, he glared around at the rest of us, as if daring anyone to challenge him, and I exchanged a wryly amused glance with Macer, knowing that at least part of this display by Vespillo was calculated. Whether it was because he was guessing that this would be what Macer planned on saying, or words to that effect, or he wanted to stake out an opposing position to what he thought our Pilus Prior would take was impossible to know. What had remained constant was that Vespillo still chafed and fumed, privately of course, about being passed over for a position that he viewed was rightfully his, until Macer showed up as a paid man. And, if I am being brutally honest, at first I was quite sympathetic to Vespillo's plight; he had been second in command of the Fourth Cohort for some time, and like me had worked his way up through the ranks and not purchased his posting. However, Marcus Macer had long before proven himself to be worthy of leading our Cohort, and from my viewpoint, Vespillo was only making himself more miserable by continually harping on the injustice that had been done to him, although I cared less about that than I did about him inflicting his sour disposition on the rest of us.

"Under any other circumstances," Macer answered him, "I'd agree with you, Vespillo. But," he turned his attention to the rest of us, asking, "have any of you seen anything like what happened tonight?"

Truly, it was not as much a question as a statement, since he knew fully well that none of us had. The breakdown we had all witnessed this night, even taking into account the extraordinary circumstances that came with the announcement of the death of Augustus, was unprecedented, but even recognizing this, I confess I felt a bit smug about the fact that, relatively speaking, the Third had been well behaved, resorting to only some fist-shaking and shouting. Thinking of this made me glance over at Volusenus, and he must have been thinking along the same lines since he met my eyes and gave a grin.

"I'm glad you think this is amusing, Volusenus," Macer snapped, but like a guilty schoolboy, before our Pilus Prior could look over at me, I wiped my own smirk from my face so that when he did, I did my best to look as solemn as a Vestal Virgin, "but unless you have a suggestion, I'd caution you against taking this lightly. You," Macer finished, "are the least experienced Centurion in the Cohort. Maybe that's why you don't view this as being as serious as it is."

Chastised, Volusenus wisely said nothing, just dropping his head to stare at his feet as Macer held his glare for a matter of a couple heartbeats before returning his attention to the rest of us. Once he did, I caught Volusenus scowling at me out of the corner of my eye, yet I did not feel the slightest bit guilty, and if I could have gotten away with it, I would have shot him another grin. Nevertheless, despite this moment of levity, I was also as worried as the rest of the Centurions.

"Pullus?" Macer looked at me. "We've heard from the Pilus Posterior. What does the Princeps Prior think? Any ideas?" Then, proving he had been paying attention, he added, "Your Century, and," he nodded his head towards Volusenus, "the Sixth were the only ones who didn't completely fall apart."

"While I agree with Vespillo in spirit," I answered carefully, "I also agree that we can't afford to crack down too hard on the men." As expected, this produced a snort of disgust on Vespillo's part, which I ignored as I continued, "I think a lot depends on the next few days. There's no way either Caecina or Germanicus, once he returns, can ignore what happened, and while it's possible that either one of them could order us to crack some heads and stripe some backs bloody, I don't think they will."

"That's because he's soft," Vespillo sneered. "He always has been. He's more concerned with being loved by these bastards than with being feared!"

While Vespillo could have been referring to the Legate, we all knew he was not, and this did cause me to turn and regard Vespillo, eyeing him coldly as I struggled to maintain my composure, but I finally answered, "Germanicus may be a lot of things, Vespillo, but soft isn't one of them. You weren't there with him at Raetinium, were you?" While posed as a question, it was not, and as I intended, it shut Vespillo's mouth; my point made, I turned back to Macer. "If I'm being completely honest," I continued, "I don't see where Germanicus has much choice but to address the men's grievances, because I'm certain that the Legate won't. Although," I did think to add, "ultimately, it will be the decision of Tiberius, since he's now the man in charge."

I could tell just by the expressions on the faces of the others that it was as strange for them to hear this last statement as it was for me to say it, and I thought, this is going to take some getting used to, referring to Tiberius as Princeps. One by one, Macer asked the others; Cornutus did his best to not express an opinion that could be construed as having one position or another, while Philus was quick to agree with what he thought Macer's position was, which I had noticed he had yet to clearly articulate. Finally, it was Volusenus, who was obviously still smarting from Macer's rebuke, and there was a vestige of the haughty equestrian youth who had first arrived in Ubiorum in his demeanor, causing me to inwardly wince, worried that his temper would get the better of him.

However, his tone was measured and calm, as he replied, "As you pointed out, Pilus Prior, I don't have enough experience to even presume to know how to deal with this situation, but whatever you decide, I swear on the black stone I will obey to the fullest. You'll have no reason to worry about the Sixth."

Macer's smile was faint, but it was plainly visible, and he nodded to Volusenus, saying only, "I didn't have any doubt about that, Hastatus Posterior." There was a brief silence, then Macer said, "Well, let's go find out what wisdom Primus Pilus Sacrovir has to offer, shall we?"

Draining our cups, we all stood, following Macer out of his quarters, and headed for the Legion office; it would be cramped with all sixty of us, and I was not looking forward to that.

The meeting was not only as cramped and close as I had feared, with all sixty men standing shoulder to shoulder in the outer office of the Primus Pilus, but it was as unsatisfying as our own Cohort meeting had been. Ultimately, Sacrovir was as flummoxed as the entire Centurionate of the 1st; the only difference was that he had sent a message to Caecina, asking for some form of guidance, but when we held the meeting, no word had come from the *Praetorium*.

"The Legate's got other things on his mind," Sacrovir had said, in what I thought was the biggest understatement I had heard in some time.

"I still think he's weighing his options about whether to support Germanicus or not," Macer whispered to me, but by this point, I had deduced that he said these things more to needle me than because he believed them, so I did my best to ignore him.

Oblivious to our back and forth, Sacrovir went on talking. "He has decided to send a courier to where Germanicus has picked back up with the task he was given by the Princeps, the census of Gaul, and he had told the Legate he was planning on going to Gallia Belgica." Sacrovir shrugged, adding, "My guess is that the Legate's trying to behave as if this is just a routine matter."

227

I, for one, could certainly see the sense in this; my only equivocation had more to do with the current state of unrest and the need for it to be addressed immediately, but I instantly saw that I was in the minority, as Secundus Pilus Prior Sentius, raised his hand, and while it was posed as a question, there was no way to miss the worry in his voice as he asked, "So we're going to just follow whatever Caecina commands, even if it's to ignore what's happening with our men? Is that what you're saying?"

Sacrovir glared at Sentius, but he admitted, "Yes, that's what I'm saying."

This immediately created an outcry by almost every Centurion present, and I essentially agreed with their concern about Caecina, thinking him to be a nobleman who had proven to be more in the mold of the man I still loathed more than any other, Lucius Aemilius Paullus. Speaking of that toad, as far as I knew, he was still in Rome, although I held out hope he had choked on a fig, or better yet, one of his slaves had slit his throat. Whereas even I will admit that, speaking in strictly military terms, as in actual campaigning, Caecina was not just competent, he was considered a good commander; his problems had all stemmed from his harsh treatment of those lower than him in the social order. He was also known as a striper, which meant that if there was a worse choice for a Legate to command the 1st and 20th at this point in time, I never heard of him.

Sacrovir's mouth twisted into a grimace, and he snarled at us to shut our mouths. "I don't care who our Legate is! He's been duly appointed by Rome, and that means we'll obey his orders as if they came from the mouth of..." Suddenly, he stopped himself, yet another example of how we were all struggling to cope with this enormous change, and he finished, "...Tiberius himself."

Once it became clear that there was nothing more that would be forthcoming from our Primus Pilus, Pilus Prior Sentius, speaking on behalf of the rest of us, asked for Sacrovir's leave, which he quickly granted; honestly, he seemed as happy to get rid of us as we were to escape. After we had made our way back to our own area, I tarried a bit outside each hut; while I did not go so far as to press my ear against the door, I did listen intently. Frustratingly, I could not make out any details, other than an occasional raised voice as one comrade shouted angrily at another, and I soon gave up and returned to my quarters. Neither I nor, I suspect, any man wearing a transverse crest or Optio's stripe got much sleep that night, but to our surprise, it passed uneventfully.

Caecina had chosen to delay sending a courier to Germanicus for two days, erroneously believing that matters would settle down. It was a decision that would come back to haunt him, and for which he drew a fair amount of criticism from the Centurions; or, I should amend, those Centurions who did not participate in what was to come. Personally, I do not believe Germanicus' presence at the moment things went from the smoldering burn they had been for months into the fully blazing conflagration that was in our very near future would have made any difference, but we will never know one way or another. After the departure of the courier, we all spent a tense couple days, pretending they were normal ones, filled with the routine tasks of life in garrison, but despite nothing untoward happening, by the time I would retire for the evening, I would be as exhausted as if we had been on campaign. Regardless of my fatigue, I slept badly, waking up more often than normal to listen to the night sounds, trying to discern any hint of impending trouble, but dawn arose to a seemingly normal camp. Which, of course, meant that Caecina then decided to make matters worse.

"We're leaving Ubiorum," Sacrovir informed us, having summoned the Centurions once more. "The Legate has decided that a," his mouth twisted as he quoted Caecina, "'good, stiff march' is just what we need."

The reaction was immediate, and loud, as we all voiced our protests at what was one of the more stupendously stupid ideas that any of us had heard in some time. Sacrovir clearly agreed, but he was also Primus Pilus, so finally, after allowing us to vent our collective anger, he bellowed at us to shut our mouths, which we did reluctantly.

"The Legate has decided this," he repeated, "and despite my best attempts, along with those of Primus Pilus Neratius, we were unable to change his mind. We're marching day after tomorrow." He paused then, and we understood the reason he was reluctant to continue when he finished, "And we're marching across the Rhenus."

If he said anything after that, there was no way to hear it, but once it became clear he had nothing more to say, we quieted down enough for him to dismiss us, and we left the Legion office, each Cohort's Centurions clustered together as we discussed this latest development.

"It's almost as if Caecina wants the rankers to mutiny," Macer muttered; that even Vespillo agreed with this assessment was a mark of how serious this was.

"But why would he want that?" Philus asked, and while it was a reasonable question, I was the one who answered, "I don't think he does. I just don't think it even occurred to him that this is about the worst time to do something like this. And," I added, "I'm willing to wager that it has to do with the fact that Germanicus is gone now. He's trying to assert his authority over us and remind us that he's still in command of these Legions."

"Then he's truly a fool," Vespillo said sourly. "And we're the ones who are going to have to pay for it."

That, as we all knew, was true, but by then, we had reached our Cohort area, where our Optios had been busy with the men performing their morning routine, and Macer paused in the middle of the street.

Sighing, he said only, "There's no point in delaying this." Looking at each of us, he said simply, "You know what to do."

And we did, each of us suddenly bellowing out the call of our own Century, striding in different directions, heading for the huts of our men. Because of where we started from, I actually worked in opposite order, starting with the Tenth Section instead of the First, but in a slight change of how I normally did things, I actually knocked and announced myself, then waited a couple heartbeats before entering. Any other time, I liked to keep my men on their toes, foregoing this formality, often catching men in some minor crime like lounging on their bunks during the duty hour, which was forbidden, although I very rarely put men on punishment for it. There were exceptions, of course, like Pusio and a couple other men like Trigeminus, but on this day, even Pusio got the gentler version of his Centurion. Not, it must be said, that any of the men seemed appreciative, although their sullen anger was more about the orders I was giving than anything else. I would be remiss if I did not say that this was one of the times where I struggled to maintain my distance as a Centurion, because for one of the few times in my career, I wanted to let the rankers know that I was in complete agreement, at least as far as the needless stupidity of being forced to march, simply because a Legate desired it. Regardless of my personal feelings, I kept them to myself, and only later did I recognize that, in fact, I probably went too far the other way, lashing out at the men in more than a verbal manner, using my *vitus* inside their quarters, something that I had never done before. Although I do not know where it came from, if it was from the time of my Avus or even earlier, it had been an unwritten rule that Centurions did not thrash men inside their quarters unless it was to stop some sort of brawl that broke out between comrades, which was common enough. Otherwise, however, men were brought outside if their Centurion felt the need to apply the *vitus*, but such was my tension and the surliness of the men that at least one man in every section felt the sting of it. Somewhat surprisingly, when I reached the Fifth Section, I did not strike Pusio, who confined his defiance to a glare, although on reflection, I suppose that he had experienced enough of a taste of my "medicine" to know when it was time to keep his mouth shut. More troubling was the man who I did have to apply this discipline to, when for a span of heartbeats, it appeared that Clustuminus would refuse and did not move until I lashed out not once, but three times, striking his legs. Not only was it that he was the Sergeant of the First Section, but I was still considering him for Optio, despite some troubling signs from his behavior. Finally, though, he began moving, and if he did it slower than I would have liked, I chose to ignore it, leaving the men to their preparations to tell Structus and the other men who shared his quarters. Not long afterward, I heard from every Centurion of my Cohort, including Macer, that they had run into the same problem.

"At this point, I'm not sure they'll obey the command to march when Caecina gives it," Macer worried, and while I would have liked to offer some form of encouragement, I could not.

Perhaps the only saving grace was that Caecina had not decided to begin the march the next morning, because we would not have been ready, and neither would the 20th, as we heard their men were acting in the same manner as our own. Even in the watch before the march, I know that there was not a Centurion, nor Optio for that matter, who would have been willing to wager a brass *obol* on whether or not when the *bucina* sounded, the men would respond. When they did so on that second day, falling out of their huts, dragging their packs, their shields strapped to their backs and carrying their javelins and *furcae*, I tried not to show my surprise, and I knew Structus felt the same way from the glance we exchanged. Deciding in the moment that I would behave as if nothing untoward was happening as far as my expression, I also understood that acting as if this was a normal day would mean I used my *vitus* when men were moving too slowly, and I refrained from doing that. From what I observed, neither did any of the Centurions, so that our forming up in the Cohort street was much slower than normal. The Fourth was far from alone, and our assembly as a Legion in the forum was so leisurely that we were certain Caecina would take exception and destroy the fragile calm by insisting on some sort of punishment. Thankfully, while he sat his horse, watching as the 1st and 20th formed up, he did not seem perturbed, which I felt certain was due to the fact that he was at least aware of the tension, which I cautiously took as a good omen. Somehow, when he ordered his *Cornicen* to give the command, the 20th, selected to lead the way, stepped off just as always, and we followed behind, with the baggage train following. The pontoon bridge had already been strung across the river, and he and his staff, along with Gaesorix and his *ala,* led the way across.

While we waited for the 20th to start, Macer and the rest of us stood together, and I saw that we were all still trying to pretend that everything was normal, while Volusenus asked Macer, "Pilus Prior, do you have any idea where we're headed?"

"No," Macer said with a short laugh, "our Legate hasn't seen fit to inform us." Seeing our inquiring looks, he admitted, "I asked Sacrovir if he knew."

"I wonder when he plans on letting us know," Vespillo muttered.

"Hopefully before we walk into some German ambush," Philus offered, which did nothing to settle our nerves.

Then it was time for us to march, and we headed to our respective Centuries, none of us knowing what a catastrophe was waiting for us.

When Caecina turned north, just a couple of miles east of the Rhenus, it raised no comment; when we continued north, by midday, the men were muttering to each other, though they were still more curious than anything. Despite being on the east side of the Rhenus, we were heading in the direction of Novaesium, where part of the 2nd Augusta was stationed, with only the width of the river and a couple miles separating us. It was when this became obvious that the talk started, as men began questioning why, if we were heading this far north, was it not the 2nd and even the 14th in Vetera who was marching? And, not surprisingly, the farther north we marched, the louder and more insistent became the chatter, as men who had been careful to keep their voices down were now no longer bothering. Then, when I was certain matters could not get worse, during a rest interval, I saw Gaesorix come trotting back, obviously going to check on his Batavians who were stuck as the rearguard, along with our Eighth Cohort, who had drawn the short straw and were behind the baggage train. Seeing me wave to him, he turned and came readily enough, but one look at his face, which was missing his customary smile, made me wonder if I had done the wise thing.

"*Salve,* Titus." Only then did he give me a grin, but it was not a happy one. "Enjoying this fine day?"

Returning his greeting, I ignored his nicety, although as far as the weather went, it *was* actually a pleasant day, not too hot, asking, "What has you looking so sour?"

Rather than answer immediately, he jerked his head and led his favorite horse, a black stallion he called Tanarus, which was some Batavian god, away from the men, who were sprawled out on the ground. Even with this precaution, I felt their eyes boring into my back, and I knew that at that moment, they were conducting a furious, whispered debate on how they could overhear the Decurion and me talking.

Once more than twenty paces away, only then did Gaesorix answer, "Do you really want to know? I'll tell you, but," he glanced over my head back at the men, and this time his grin was a bit more like his usual self as he admonished me, "you're not very good at hiding your feelings, and when I tell you what's going on…" he shrugged, but I could not deny what he said, and I promised that I would not react in a manner that alerted the men. Only then did he continue, "I found out where the Legate intends on taking us." He lowered his voice even more. "We're about to turn northeast. We're heading in the direction of Caedicius' camp."

Despite giving my word, before I could stop myself, I let out a string of oaths, earning me a glare from Gaesorix, and I was sufficiently chastened to mumble an apology, and I did manage to lower my voice when I asked the obvious question. "Why? Did he give any kind of reason?" Before he could answer, I added, "Not that there can be a reason."

"Oh, there's a reason all right," Gaesorix answered bitterly. "You're just not going to believe it." When I said nothing, just looked up at him inquiringly, I saw him actually take a breath before he went on, "It seems that our Legate isn't quite as oblivious as he seems. He knows the men are angry, so he thinks that taking us to Caedicius' camp will 'put some fire in their bellies,'" he mimicked Caecina's nasal tone surprisingly well, "and remind the men how fortunate they are."

"Fortunate?" I echoed, shaking my head in disbelief. "What? Fortunate to be alive?"

Gaesorix shrugged, saying, "I suppose so. Honestly, I did not ask him."

"Did you at least try to talk him out of it?"

The look my Batavian friend gave me was bitterly amused, and he retorted, "What do you think? And I wasn't the only one. Neratius tried; even a couple of the Tribunes tried, but he's convinced that this is exactly what the men need."

"Does Sacrovir know?" I asked, but Gaesorix answered he did not know, then said he had to finish attending to his men, and I thanked him, which he acknowledged with a wave as he resumed his progress back to the rear.

I immediately walked to where Macer was standing next to his Century, keeping my gaze averted from my own men, feeling their intense stares, and I cursed my curiosity, thinking it would have been better not to know where we were headed. Gesturing to Macer when he saw me approaching, I drew him aside and relayed what Gaesorix had told me, instantly regretting forgetting to admonish him beforehand about not reacting in a manner that would alert the men.

"Does Sacrovir know?"

I repeated what Gaesorix had told me, then before I could say anything, he said curtly, "Come with me. We need to hurry before…"

His words were cut off by the blaring of the *cornu* from the head of the column, prompting a string of oaths that, frankly, had me staring at him, impressed because my friend and Pilus Prior did not normally display such a rich vocabulary of curses.

"All right," he muttered, "we need to get the men on their feet, but once we get going, you and I are going to have to run up the column to tell Sacrovir."

Frankly, I did not relish the idea of running the length of three Cohorts, and I protested, "What if he already knows?"

Macer did not answer, verbally, instead giving me a scathing look, and I muttered my assent, then turned to go back to the men, who as I expected, were only slowly coming to their feet, while Structus was now prodding some of them with his handle. Not, I noticed, using it as anything more than a goad, which I thought was a wise move. Only slightly slower than normal, thankfully, the men were ready to resume the march, and as soon as we began again, with a muttered curse, I broke into a brisk trot, going to where Macer was waiting for me, and together we headed to find our Primus Pilus at a fast pace.

"He *what?*" Sacrovir's mouth hung open in astonishment, giving us the answer as to whether or not he had been informed of Caecina's ludicrous decision. Turning to me, he demanded, "Who did you hear this from, Pullus?" I told him, and his shoulders sagged as he admitted, "Well, he would know since he's riding up at the front. Pluto's cock," he spat in the dirt, "this is a right fucking mess." Returning his attention back to me, he asked, "And you said that Neratius tried to talk him out of it?"

"As did Batavius and some of the Tribunes," I assured him.

Cursing again, he rubbed his chin, ignoring the men marching by; we had stopped long enough that it was the Sixth of the First by this point who went marching by, all of them making no attempt to hide their interest in our small conference.

"I don't know what the fuck to do," Sacrovir finally said quietly, and he glanced over at Macer, who interpreted the Primus Pilus' look to be that he was looking for suggestions, although Macer could only offer, "I don't think there's anything you can do, Primus Pilus. There's no way to get the word to the rest of the Centurions without the men overhearing." Sacrovir nodded, though he clearly did not like Macer's assessment, then looked to me. All I could offer was, "I think the Pilus Prior's right, Primus Pilus. We're going to have to let the men figure it out for themselves." Once more, Sacrovir nodded, his expression about as grim as if we were about to go into battle, while the thought crossed my mind that we very well may have been, just not with the Germans. "All right," he said finally, "I need to catch up to my boys." Before he left, he said sharply, "And say nothing to anyone. At least," he amended slightly, "don't tell your other Centurions when the men have a chance to overhear."

We both assured him we would take adequate precautions, and he went off at a loping run, heading for the front of our Legion, while we waited for our Cohort to catch up. Once more, I had to keep my eyes on the ground, not wanting to let any of the men even catch my eye. When we took a narrow track that, for the first time, turned from a direction that was paralleling the Rhenus, no more than a count of five heartbeats passed before the men started talking.

"Why the fuck are we going this way?"

"We're heading towards the Teutoberg!"

Perhaps the only positive thing that could be said was that I had gotten a hint of warning of what was coming, as the men ahead of us erupted in a dull roar of questions identical to those I was hearing. Most surprising to me was that our progress did not appreciably slow, telling me that, so far, the 20th was still following along behind Caecina and his command group. The day ended with our halting in a large open area that we had used before, with the edge of the forest and the beginning of the gradual slope that marked the beginning of the Teutoberg to our right. Despite the fact that we were not actually within the confines of the forest, the men were still nervous and upset, and those of us who knew our destination, that we would reach the day after the next one, recognized this was as good as things were going to be for the foreseeable future. At this moment, the men just suspected that they would not care for wherever we were headed; as soon as they understood that it was anywhere near Caedicius' camp, which was considered by men of all ranks to be cursed, inhabited by the *numeni* of the men who had been slain there, despite our interring their bones in the months after the disaster, only the gods knew what would happen. Nothing good; that was the only certainty, and it was awkward because Macer and I were the only ones of the Fourth who knew our destination. That I was the man who asked Gaesorix and became the first one to know did not make me feel any better, yet despite being approached by every one of my fellow Centurions on the remainder of that day's march, I rebuffed them, giving answers that I saw did not convince any of them. I did not even tell Structus, finally snapping at him when he tried for the third time to broach the subject in a manner slightly different than he had tried the time before.

Making matters worse for us, the Fourth was one of the Cohorts assigned to digging, which is considered the most onerous of the tasks in constructing a marching camp, but once again, I did not use the *vitus*. Later, I learned that most of the Centurions, of both Legions, adopted this approach; most, but not all, and that started the first flare-up of tempers. Since it was on the far side of the camp, where the 20th was assigned, we only became aware of it when matters had escalated to the point that first a Century, then a full Cohort was involved. The uproar of hundreds of men shouting at the top of their lungs drew our attention, and when I turned to look at what caused it, I saw men waving their spades and turfcutters as weapons in the direction of a small cluster of Centurions and Optios, I was thankful that my men had already dug the ditch deep enough they could not see what was going on. Naturally, within a span of heartbeats, the men of the Second Century, who had been charged with packing the spoil and creating the rampart, let their comrades down in the ditch know, while Vespillo roared at them, in vain, to return to work, which they deliberately ignored. Hurrying up the partially completed rampart, I stared down to see that, not surprisingly, Pusio was leading the way, heading for the single ladder that we lower into the ditch to enable men to climb out when they are finished, obviously intending on climbing out.

"Don't." I did not shout, but I pitched my voice loudly enough I knew everyone gathered at the base of the ladder could hear, while I stared directly into Pusio's eyes.

He looked up at me with a hatred that was even more virulent than usual, and for a span of heartbeats, I thought he might actually defy me and try to come up the ladder. Whether he would or not I will never know, because Clustuminus, standing just behind Pusio, reached out and grabbed Pusio's elbow, saying something I could not hear, but the Sergeant's face was a mask that did not betray how he felt personally in any way. With this tiny insurrection quelled, I returned my attention back to the larger one, seeing that even in the short span of time, more men from the 20th had appeared, and I guessed that they had done what Pusio and the others tried to do, ascend out of their portion of the ditch. Just bare moments before, I could spot the Centurions, but now they were surrounded and completely obscured from view, which turned my concern into rapidly growing alarm. For the first time since I had been under the standard, I thought it was not only possible, but likely, that the rankers would turn on their Centurions, which as one might imagine, is the stuff of nightmares for any man wearing the transverse crest.

"Get the men back to work."

I turned to see that Sacrovir was striding past where the 1st was working, and I assumed that he had been repeating this message as he passed by, making his way down the line. He seemed to make a point to look each of us in the eye, both Centurions and Optios, but he said nothing more than that, at least in my hearing. This, I thought, was easy for him to say, yet I turned back and looked down into the ditch.

"You heard the Primus Pilus," I snapped. "This camp isn't going to build itself."

Once again, I thought the men would refuse, but finally, they turned back around and began attacking the dirt with their spades, except they did so silently, another unusual aspect of this day. Deciding to set the example, I refused to turn back around, trying to determine what was happening behind me with my ears, telling myself that if there was trouble, I would have some warning, if only by sound. Fortunately, the men of the 20th were brought under control, and what I heard in the immediate aftermath was that, while there were dire threats made by some men, none of the Centurions or Optios were actually physically assaulted. Somehow, though I never really understood how, the camp was finished, the tents erected, and the men settled in, though it was about two parts of a watch later than normal. I made one pass down my Century street, but the hostility radiating from the men around every fire was so unsettling that I elected to go commiserate with Macer, only to learn I was the last one to arrive, the other Centurions already there.

"What do we do?" Cornutus asked plaintively. "Am I going to have to make Demeter stay up all night to make sure my own men don't come into my tent and cut my throat?"

Under any other conditions, I would have mocked Cornutus mercilessly, but it was a valid question, as troubling as it was, and I saw the others were similarly discomfited at the thought that they might have to set a watch to ensure their own security. Personally speaking, I was not very worried, knowing that it would take more than one man from my Century to strike me down, even if they came charging into my tent. I was more worried about Alex, honestly, since he slept in the outer office whenever we were out on the march, sharing the space with Balio, and as we talked, I made the decision that he would be sleeping next to my cot that night, whether he liked it or not. Otherwise, after discussing it, we came to the collective decision that there was not much we could do, other than try to get some sleep. I suppose I must have dozed off but came jerking awake at the slightest sound outside my tent, which naturally brought Alex leaping to his feet every time, and despite the darkness, I could see he was clutching his dagger. The *bucina* call to begin the next day found me wide awake, and after he lit the lamp, I saw how haggard Alex appeared, making him look much older than he was, although I am certain I looked worse. Nevertheless, we began the morning routine of a Legion on the march, and

241

despite our fears, the men behaved in a manner that passed for normal during this time. Today, the 1st led the way, and the Primus Pilus designated the Sixth to be in the vanguard, with the Third behind them, and with the Seventh being pissed on by Fortuna to march drag. Despite the men being convinced we would be heading into the heart of the Teutoberg, when Caecina led us on a course that skirted it, this seemed to calm the men down some, but it was still much quieter than normal. Only the deep, thudding sound of thousands of hobnails striking the ground, the slight creak of leather, and the clinking when metal bits struck each other filled the air, punctuated only occasionally by a muttered comment by someone in the ranks. No banter, no arguments, good-natured or otherwise, and certainly no songs were being sung, making for an extremely gloomy atmosphere, despite the sun shining brightly, with only partial clouds, and it made me realize how I had always taken those signs of good spirits for granted before this moment. Regardless of the mood, the men were moving at the pace set by Caecina, and the day passed slowly, but it passed without any major incident, until we reached the spot where we would camp for the night. Switching tasks as is the practice, it was the turn of the Fourth to set the palisade for the 1st, one of the easiest tasks that can be drawn outside of standing guard, yet even then I suppose I should not have been surprised to hear men complaining about it. And, once more, it was Pusio who was leading the chorus of discontent, but what troubled me was seeing how many heads were nodding or adding their own voice to that chorus. Fortunately for all of us, they were doing so in such a low tone of voice that I could not hear exactly what was said, but one did not need to be an experienced Centurion to know, just by the manner in which the men were conducting themselves, that they were not singing the praises of anyone higher up the ladder than they were. There was another outburst, and to my dismay, it was the 1st this time, though I was not surprised, specifically the Seventh Cohort.

What *was* surprising, indeed quite shocking, was that two of their Centurions and all of their Optios were with the rankers in their protest that, since they had marched drag, they should not have been assigned to digging the ditch. All work ceased this time, and while Sacrovir had not given us any instructions to that effect, there was an unspoken consensus that this was not the time to force the men to return to their respective tasks. Truly, I, and I know I was not alone in this, was just thankful that my men were content to watch the mess rather than take part in it, at least to this point. I wandered over to where Volusenus, Philus, and Cornutus were standing, and we stood there much like our men, an audience to the small drama being played out in front of us.

"Why are they complaining?" Volusenus asked, but while Philus shrugged and said he did not know, I was certain I knew the reason.

"Because they marched drag today, they don't think they should be digging the ditch," I explained.

"But wait," Cornutus interjected, "didn't they do the palisade stakes yesterday?" When I affirmed this, he said indignantly, "Then that's only fair! They shouldn't be getting the easy duty two days in a row!"

While the others agreed, I held my tongue, reminded yet again of how the majority of men in the ranks are only concerned with fairness if it benefitted them. As we watched, I spotted movement from the *praetorium*, which as always was the first tent raised, and when I turned and saw that it was the Legate, trailed by his Tribunes and his bodyguard, I could not stop a groan escaping from my lips, prompting the others to turn to see the cause.

"Oh, fuck me," Philus muttered.

"He's not going to try and do something about this, is he?" Volusenus asked, and there was no missing the anxiety in his voice.

"It looks like it," I answered grimly, watching Caecina striding towards where the Seventh was now clustered together, all semblance of a formation gone, simply a mob of men.

Armed men, I thought miserably, and for a moment, I thought that perhaps Caecina realized this, because when he was about a hundred paces away, he came to a stop, quickly surrounded by his gaggle.

"Maybe one of those Tribunes will convince him what a bad idea that is," Cornutus said hopefully, and in fact, it appeared that way, because Caecina reversed himself, eliciting a collective sigh of relief from us.

Macer and Vespillo, seeing us standing together, made their way to us, so that we were all together to watch as, contrary to our hopes, Caecina had not thought better of inserting himself into this mess with the Seventh. Instead, he mounted his horse, which had been brought to him, which was bad enough, but then he made it even worse.

"Look!" Macer pointed, saying in disbelief, "He ordered his bodyguards to get on their horses too!"

"Pluto's balls," Vespillo gasped. "He's not going to try and have those bastards break this up, is he?"

"It looks like it," I heard my voice, though I barely recognized it since my throat closed up at the sight.

Indeed, once the bodyguards, a mixed lot of Germans, Gauls, and even a couple of gladiators that belonged to the Legate personally, were all mounted, they quickly arranged themselves into a wedge, while Caecina pointed towards where the Seventh was still protesting. Not surprisingly, none of them were paying attention to what was happening behind them, and one glance at the others told me we all were of a like mind; a significant number of our comrades in the Seventh would be cut down. Understanding this, it was Macer who began moving first, heading in that direction, but I was right behind him.

"We've got to do something," I heard him say as he broke into a run.

Before we got a dozen paces, off to our right, I saw the lean figure of the Primus Pilus, running at an all-out sprint, heading directly for Caecina, who had just begun walking his horse towards the Seventh. Sliding to a stop in front of his horse, Sacrovir's appearance obviously surprised the Legate's mount, which reared violently, sending the Legate flying off his saddle. Despite the gravity and danger, I let out a barking laugh as I watched the supposed commander of the Legion flail wildly in mid-air, rather than try to gather himself for what would be a hard landing, and he hit the ground flat on his back.

"Maybe," I heard Vespillo behind me, his breathing harsh, "we got lucky. Maybe he's dead."

He was not dead, nor was he badly injured, just having the wind knocked from him. Most importantly, thankfully, Sacrovir was able to stop the Legate from doing something that would have made matters much, much worse. Normally, such a precipitate action on the part of a Centurion, even a Primus Pilus, would bring immediate repercussions; fortunately for Sacrovir, the events that were literally a matter of watches away from taking place made his "crime" be quickly forgotten. As far as the Seventh, they finally went to work, not because of anything the Centurions did or said, but because their fellow rankers in the other Cohorts who had done their jobs, however leisurely they did them, turned on them and demanded the security of a fully constructed camp. No, we were not in the Teutoberg proper, but we were on the wrong side of the Rhenus, and none of us, Centurions included, wanted to spend a night without a ditch and wall around us. The camp was not completed until after dark, the evening meal consumed in a moody, sullen silence that draped over the entire camp; I do not believe I heard anyone chuckle, let alone a full belly laugh. Just the low buzzing of men

245

muttering to each other, which came to a stop when they heard my footsteps approaching, whereupon they watched me pass with unfriendly eyes, although the few times I met a man's gaze, they quickly looked away. Normally, I made at least three passes around the tents, but this night I only did one, then retired to my tent to sit, moodily sipping from the cup of wine that Alex had set out for me. Before I finished it, there erupted a noise that instantly sent a shiver up my spine, a bellow of what was clearly rage as voiced by many, many men. As I jumped to my feet, Alex was already ready, helping me into my armor, something I would not have thought of doing at any other time before I rushed out of my tent.

"You're coming with me," I ordered Alex, who appeared as if he was going to argue before he saw my face and relented.

Even in the short span of time it took us to emerge onto the Cohort street, the noise had grown, the cause being that one or more men were rushing from one section fire to the next. Before I had gone a half-dozen steps, I heard what had caused the uproar.

"They're marching us to Caedicius' camp!"

"The Legate wants to curse us all!"

"We're not going anywhere near that fucking place!"

Somehow, the men had learned of Caecina's intention, and I spared a moment of thought to what I would do to the man who had let this slip, intentionally or otherwise. What I did not expect was that I would be the object of Sacrovir's suspicions, though I would find that out soon enough. At this moment, I moved as quickly as possible without running in the direction of Macer's tent, with Alex immediately behind me, while every step of the way, I was accosted by angry men, who for the first time did not even pretend to pay me the deference due my rank.

"Is it true?" Centho demanded, stepping directly into my path, and while he was clearly angry, he was also just as nervous,

246

his gaze shifting back and forth from my face to my *vitus*. "Is the Legate really taking us to Caedicius' camp?"

"Yes."

I said this despite not giving any conscious thought to how I would respond; somehow, in the time between the moment I heard the uproar and this confrontation, I must have decided that I did not see the point in lying. More likely, it was because deep down, I agreed with not just the sentiment of the men who were protesting, but perhaps a part of me also thought that Caecina deserved no less than what was happening. Centho was clearly not expecting me to answer him in this manner either, because even in the dim light, I could see that he did not know what to say, and for a long moment we stood there, staring at each other, as his comrades in his Fifth Section came drifting over to stand behind him.

"What did he say?" Trigeminus asked him, which prompted me to snap, "I'm not invisible, idiot. If you want to know, ask me."

Before Trigeminus could, Centho said hoarsely, "The Princeps Prior just told me that that fucking Legate *is* taking us to Caedicius' camp."

I was not surprised that Centho had spoken up before Trigeminus could do so; they were close comrades, and Centho was very protective of Trigeminus because of the two, Trigeminus was the duller, although nobody would ever accuse Centho of being a deep philosopher. In another sign of how things stood, the other men burst into a ragged chorus of curses and exclamations, raging at Caecina, and saying things that, if I was to obey the letter of the regulations, would not only see them on the punishment list, but strapped to the rack for a flogging, or worse. Yet, I just stood there, silently watching them until finally, they ran out of breath.

"Did you get all that out of you?" I asked them, and somewhat sheepishly, most of them mumbled their assent. "Good. Now go back to your fire and calm down."

Most of the men complied, except for Pictor, their Sergeant, who essentially assumed Centho's position blocking my way, but while I could see he was not eager to confront me, he regarded me steadily for a heartbeat before asking in a quiet voice so that the others would not overhear, "Did you know about this, Princeps Prior? Did you know he was taking us to Caedicius' camp?"

For the barest moment, I was about to lie and say no; instead, I admitted, "Yes, I knew."

He did not look surprised, but his mouth twisted into a grimace, and he said bitterly, "Which means the Pilus Prior knew. And," the anger was clear to hear, "the Primus Pilus." Suddenly, he gave me a shrewd look and challenged, "It was yesterday, wasn't it? When you stopped Batavius as he was riding past us? That's when he told you." I only replied with a nod, and there was a note of triumph in his tone as he exclaimed, "I *knew* it! I knew just by the way you reacted that it was something bad."

This exchange served as a powerful reminder to me how, even when they do not appear to be doing so, the men are always carefully observing and listening to any conversation or interaction between their superiors, all in an attempt to get an idea about their immediate future. My first reaction was a flicker of irritation, but not only did I know this was not the moment to indulge my temper, the larger reason was that Pictor was only doing what I would have done in his place, and had done when I was a ranker myself, serving as the representative of his tent section in a contentious matter.

While I was not going to make an issue of it, neither was I willing to be delayed any longer, and I told Pictor, "You need to move out of my way, Pictor, and let me find out what's going on."

He did step aside, but as I passed, he said to me, "What's going on is that we aren't going another foot closer to that place, Princeps Prior."

Ignoring him, I resumed my progress, and while I was assailed by the others, none of them blocked my path, although the streets were now filled with rankers. Once we left the Fourth's area, making our way to Sacrovir's quarters, the men from other Cohorts were not quite as willing to move out of our way, though none of them responded when I shouldered them aside, to which I attributed my size and reputation, especially after I heard about how some of the Centurions were actually jostled and shoved around on that night. Again, going by the letter of the regulations, and how strictly they were interpreted, those offenders who had laid their hands on a Centurion could be executed, but such was the atmosphere that none of the Centurions who had been accosted were willing to write up charges. More importantly, none of the men bothered harassing Alex, who never hesitated following me, despite the fact that I could see that he was scared out of his wits. Finally reaching the Legion office, I saw that it was virtually surrounded by men, all of whom were shouting, shaking their fists, and essentially making it clear that they were very, very angry. This was bad enough, but when the men on the outer fringe turned and saw me approach, this time, they showed no inclination to move, and in fact, more than a dozen turned to face me.

"We're right behind you, Pullus," I heard and recognized the voice of Vespillo, prompting me to glance over my shoulder to see the rest of the Centurions had caught up and joined me, save Macer, who I assumed was already inside the Primus Pilus' tent.

Catching Volusenus' eye, I indicated with my head that he move to my side, which he did readily enough, though he did not look happy doing so, for which I blamed him not a bit.

"This is the first time I'm not happy to be our size," he muttered, to which I laughed, more for the benefit of the men blocking our path than any real humor, showing them that I was not the least bit intimidated.

"It does have its drawbacks sometimes," I agreed, but once my attention had returned to the mob, my eyes never left them.

That was how I saw a hand, holding what appeared to be a turfcutter handle, surreptitiously move to offer it to one of the men standing nearest us, and while it was difficult, I clearly saw the white stripe of an Optio who was trying to lose himself in the crowd. The man directly opposite me took the handle, and before a span of another heartbeats passed, easily a half-dozen men, all of them on the outer edge of the mob were handed similar implements from deeper in the crowd.

"They're not going to try and stop us, are they?" Volusenus gasped.

"It looks that way," I answered, but in doing as they had, these men had just entered into an outright mutiny, and now I was angry, so that before I had any conscious thought of doing so, my *gladius* was in my hand, which I held loosely, point down and making tiny, perfect circles.

Suddenly, the men holding cudgels did not look quite so resolute, glancing at each other, while the men deeper in the mob, alerted to a change of some sort, were turning their attention away from shouting imprecations and threats in the direction of the Primus Pilus' quarters towards this more immediate, and dangerous, threat to their own safety. I was heartened to hear the metallic hissing sound of my fellow Centurions drawing their own weapons, but frankly, I did not care whether they helped or not, as for the first time in a long,

long span, I felt that thing I thought of as the beast that resided deep within me begin to uncoil itself.

"Wait here," I told Volusenus and the others, then without waiting for them to acknowledge me, I walked a few steps closer to the men.

As I did, the noise level was dropping dramatically, with more of the mob, which I estimated to be well over two hundred men, turning their attention towards the large Centurion walking alone towards them. While the men I could see were not in the Fourth, I knew they recognized me, another thing that comes with being one of the largest men in the Legion, and I was also certain that my reputation, particularly as it pertained to the skill with which I handled my *gladius*, was another factor.

"Move out of the way," I said, this time loud enough to be heard by more than just the men immediately facing me.

I suspect the ranker who answered, taller than average but nowhere near my height, with a lean build and missing the top of one ear, was bolstered by the numbers behind him, because he shot back belligerently, "Nobody passes! Not even Centurions!"

"Not until we hear from the Primus Pilus what he plans to do about this!"

This came from deeper in the crowd, but I immediately recognized the voice, confirming my suspicion that at least one Optio was involved. That it was the man belonging to the First of the Fifth, Clepsina's Optio, a man named Marcus Cartufenus, was shocking in itself. It might have shaken me, but my dark beast was already beginning to stretch itself, fueling a burning deep within my gut, which meant that instead of trying to reason with them, I took a step closer, grimly pleased at the manner in which not just the ranker who had spoken first, but the men surrounding him, all of whom were holding a club of some variety, took a step backward. This was evidently not acceptable to their comrades immediately behind them, because the tall ranker suddenly lurched forward to regain the backward step he had taken, clearly shoved from behind.

"It looks like one of your friends wants to get you killed," I said conversationally. "Do you owe him money? Or," I actually grinned, though it was not a nice one, "does he owe you? That would be my guess."

"We can't let you pass," the tall ranker said stubbornly.

"Besides, look how many there are of us, and there's only five of you!"

"And I," I replied calmly, "have this." I lifted my blade slightly, then in what I can only consider a divine inspiration, I lifted it above my head, pointing it towards the night sky, and I raised my voice. "How many of you know who this *gladius* belonged to? How many of you know who I am?" There were only a few mumbles from the men, but I accepted that as enough of a sign of recognition, and I continued, this time allowing my anger to color my voice. "And you think you're going to stop *me? I am Titus Porcinianus Pullus and I will gut any man who tries to stop me!*" I bellowed this so loudly that it made me lightheaded, but I ignored the slightly dizzy feeling, lowering my arm, slowly, until I was pointing my *gladius* directly at the tall ranker, and my voice back to a normal tone, I said calmly, "And you'll be first."

Then, before any of them could react, I sensed a presence to my left, and while my eyes never left the mob, I could tell just by the bulk that it was Volusenus, who sounded astonishingly calm as he said, "I'm no match for Princeps Prior Pullus with a blade…yet, but he's taught me more than enough to handle any of you."

Vespillo came to my right, and just that quickly, the collective nerve of the men facing us failed, and without having to order it, the mob parted, opening a path to allow us to pass. Leading the way, I walked in between the two parts of the now-separated mob, followed by the rest of the Centurions of the

Fourth. As I did, there was a low, growling sound, emanating from the men forming this impromptu gauntlet, but none of them made any kind of move that could be construed as an assault on us, to which I attributed the fact that I was still holding my *gladius*. In a breach of custom, I did not pound on the square of wood that hangs outside the tent of every Centurion and Optio, only pushing the flap aside to enter the outer office. Or, I should say, I tried to do so; in the office proper, there appeared to be at least half of the Legion's Centurions and a good number of Optios, so I had to essentially shove my way inside to make room for Volusenus and the others. I stood next to the flap, but while it might have appeared as if I was ushering the others in, I was making sure that Alex, who was following so closely behind Volusenus, and was the last one in the tent, that despite the tension, I felt a grin form on my face. For his part, my nephew still appeared calm, but the lamplight reflected the sheen of sweat on his brow, and when he passed by and I gave him a pat on the back, I could feel him trembling.

Sentius was closest to the flap, and as he watched me sheathe my blade, he commented dryly, "Well, at least there's no blood on it."

"No," I agreed, trying to hide the tremor in my own hand, which matched the shaking of my legs, "not this time anyway."

Cornutus gave a shaky laugh. "Juno's *cunnus*, Pullus! I thought you were going to kill that bastard."

"So did he," Volusenus said before I could respond, "and his friends. That's what mattered." Turning to me, he gave me a grin as he told me, "Honestly, I don't know what I was thinking stepping up next to you like that."

"I'm glad you did," I told him frankly. "That's what convinced them."

Volusenus looked doubtful, but I was being honest.

"Well, that's all well and good," Sentius interjected sourly, "but now you're just as fucked as we are."

Turning back to the Pilus Prior, I scanned the faces and noticed something.

"Where's the Primus Pilus?" I asked Sentius. "Is he in his quarters?"

"Not here." Sentius shook his head. "We don't know where he is."

"Then why are you all here?" Vespillo asked, and I was as curious as he was, but the answer was simple and obvious.

"We all thought he'd be here," Sentius answered, "but now that we're here, none of us are willing to go out there. Not," he jerked his thumb in the direction of the flap, "with that bunch out there, howling for blood."

"They let us in," Volusenus protested, "and all we had to do was show them our blades."

Sentius shot the young Centurion a bitterly amused look, and he pointed out, "That's because they've got us where they want us. That's why they let you in, you fool."

Volusenus' face flushed, showing another similarity between us, but he did not offer a retort, probably because he realized, as I had the instant Sentius said it, that this was the likely cause. Only then did I think to scan the faces in the office, and I started to worry when I realized there was one in particular who was missing.

"Where's Macer?" I asked, but Sentius could only shake his head in response.

"I haven't seen him. And I haven't seen Clepsina either."

This finally prompted an attempt to take a more accurate count, and once finished, it was determined that the highest ranking Centurion among us was the Primus Hastatus Prior, Gnaeus Varo, who showed absolutely no interest in organizing us or in taking command, meaning that it devolved on to Sentius' shoulders. There were two other Pili Priores missing besides Macer and Clepsina, and while there was some discussion about organizing ourselves and leaving the Legion office to search for them, Sentius was adamant that we do no such thing.

"Listen to them out there," he argued. "They're not calming down; they're getting more worked up. Anyone wearing a crest is going to be a target." He paused then, his face grave as he added, "And if we're being honest with ourselves, some of those bastards are definitely Optios, and," he took a breath, "I know at least one Centurion in my Cohort is probably with them as well."

While neither I nor any of us could dispute that this was highly possible, I was equally certain that Marcus Macer was not one of them, but I also quickly realized that only five of us going to search for him would prove to be dangerous to all of us. After a whispered discussion, the Fourth's Centurions unanimously agreed that we could do nothing unless a good number of the other Centurions and Optios present went with us. One glance around told us none of them were disposed to budge from this spot, choosing what I considered the flimsy protection of a layer of canvas, although it was more the strength in numbers that was the deciding factor for them. One by one, men had dropped to the ground, making themselves as comfortable as possible, trying to hold conversations while, outside, our Legion went mad. Not long after we settled down, the smell of smoke came drifting under the flap.

For the second night running, there was no sleep to be had, and even if I had wanted to, I knew I would have been unable to do so. About a watch before dawn, the noise outside finally subsided, as even men who had been whipped into a frenzy by the discovery of our destination could not maintain their outrage. Still, when Sentius announced that we would leave the Legion office, we did so with our weapons drawn, at least those of us who carried them. About half of the officers had thought to wear their *baltea* and harness, but only a dozen of us were wearing our armor as well, which not surprisingly meant that we led the

255

way. Stepping out into the beginning of a day that none of us had any idea what it would bring, I first braced to be met by the same mob that had been surrounding us most of the night, but they were nowhere to be seen. I had also prepared myself to see the charred remnants of tents; indeed, I was resigned to the idea that those tents belonging to Centurions would be their target. However, I, and judging by the surprised exclamations of the others, was pleasantly relieved to see that the lines of tents were unbroken and intact. More importantly, personally speaking, I sent Alex to check and he quickly returned to report that our quarters had been undisturbed. This did not explain the cause of the smell of smoke, and it was one of the Optios who, as we stood examining our surroundings, noticed and correctly deduced the cause.

"They pulled all the palisade stakes," he called out, and when we turned as a group to see where he was pointing, we saw for ourselves that this was the case.

"That must have been what we smelled burning last night," Sentius concluded.

"Yes, but where?" someone behind me asked. "I don't see any signs of a fire."

I believe we all reached the same conclusion at roughly the same time, but it was Sentius who said aloud, "The forum. They must have brought them to the forum."

"Maybe that's where everyone is now," Varo suggested, but personally, I thought it unlikely, believing that it would be next to impossible for us not to hear them, even from where we were.

Our view, naturally, was blocked by the tents of the Centuries and Cohorts, and which started to disgorge their occupants even as we milled about, trying to decide what to do. Those rankers who were emerging naturally saw us standing there, but while they did not resume their shouting at seeing us, there was the same hostility in their gazes.

"If we're going to do something, we need to do it now," I spoke up, and Sentius grunted in agreement. Turning to address the group, he spoke just loudly enough to be heard, "Right, we're going to head to the forum now. Any of you whose tent is on the way, if it looks possible, you should duck in and at least grab your weapons, but armor as well would be better. But," he warned, "if it looks like any of these bastards are going to try and stop you, don't try. We don't want to start a brawl if we can avoid it."

Waiting only long enough for a mumbled chorus of agreement, Sentius then turned his attention towards arranging us in a semblance of a formation, putting those of us who were armed and armored on the outside of our group, while the others were put in between us.

Turning to me, Sentius gave me a sour grin, saying, "You know where your spot is, right?" Nodding at Volusenus, "And him?"

Sighing, I did not reply, simply stepping into the spot Sentius indicated, while Volusenus did the same, except this time, he was to my right. This did not take long, but even in this short span of time, more men had left their tents to come out into the streets, another unusual sign, since during this time of early morning, rankers can almost always be found in front of their tents, stoking the fire from the night before in preparation for breaking their fast, or heading to the latrines. Although I was leading the way, I did not give any command, just began walking, and while I did not draw my *gladius*, I kept my hand near the hilt by hooking my thumb in my *baltea* as I led the group. I also did not look anywhere but directly ahead, though I kept watch for any sudden movement by any of the men lining the street. In a manner similar to the night before, this time, the rankers seemed content to stand on either side of the street, but while none of them made an overt move, nor even made the kind of threatening gestures they had displayed the night before, they were far from silent.

"We're not marching another step!"

"Go tell the Legate to go fuck himself!"

"We've had enough!"

Such was the nature of the calls and taunts, to which I said not a word, nor did anyone else in the group; I believe we all sensed that, while relatively calm compared to the night before, the margin of error was razor-thin, and an untoward response could ignite another demonstration. Reaching the intersection, I took a left down the street that headed directly to the forum, and once we did, we could see the top of the *praetorium*, prompting a collective sigh of relief.

"That must be where the Pilus Prior is," Volusenus said softly, to which I nodded and added, "And the Primus Pilus."

"I wonder where Neratius is?" Sentius, who was immediately behind me, asked, though I do not think he was looking for an answer from any of us.

"We'll find out soon enough," I replied, but as soon as I said it, I regretted it, because I could see that the street ahead was now completely blocked by men.

Most of them were facing the forum, but one of them hanging at the back of the mob must have sensed us coming, because before we could react in any way, the majority turned about to watch us approach. I slowed down, more to give us time for a quick discussion about how to proceed, but before we were through, someone in the crowd blocking our path must have given an order, because once more, those men stepped aside. For the first time since this had all begun, I suddenly experienced a sensation that had, in the past, warned me of danger, a combination of what I would call an itch in my right hand and a tingling sensation that ran up my spine, resulting in the tiny hairs on the back of my neck to stand erect.

"What are you waiting for?" Sentius demanded. "They're letting us through. We need to get to the *praetorium*, now!"

I have spent much time in reflecting on these moments, wondering if there was anything I could have or should have done differently, but despite my best efforts, I have been unable to come up with an action that would have altered the outcome. Nevertheless, I must bear some responsibility for essentially walking us into an ambush; that it was at the hands of our own men made it no less so.

Piecing matters together after a battle, even one such as this when it is between combatants who normally fight side by side, is always difficult, and as far as I know, nobody ever determined if what took place was planned, or if it was a spontaneous combustion of a combination of rage and frustration that was triggered by the identity of one of the men of our party. Once the rankers stepped aside, after Sentius gave me what I considered an order, I resumed walking, Volusenus still to my right, and without thinking, I muttered so that only he could hear, "I don't like this. Something's wrong. Be ready."

"Ready for what?" He matched my tone, barely above a whisper, but honestly, I could not tell him.

Not that it mattered, because we were less than halfway through the crowd when, above the low murmuring of the men, I heard a man shout something; specifically, a name.

"Look! There! It's that *cunnus* Cinna! I see you, you bastard!"

That was the last intelligible thing we heard, because of an eruption of sound from the lungs of dozens of men, which accompanied a sudden flurry of movement that originated behind me to my left. Before I could stop myself from reacting, I turned to see the cause, just in time to see a half-dozen men lunge at the man behind me, an Optio from the Fourth of the Third, one of those wearing armor. They were not after him, however, only knocking him aside to seize one of the Centurions only wearing their tunic, the Septimus Pilus Prior, Tiberius Cinna. Before the Optio could react, two rankers had grabbed Cinna by each arm and were viciously yanking him back into the mob, although I did not see the ending of this, because one of the men to my immediate front must have seen his own chance. Suddenly, I felt a terrific impact in my midsection, simultaneously turning and looking down to see that a ranker had thought to tackle me, though he only knocked me back perhaps a half-step while he caromed off my mail-covered body, staggering back to land on his ass. Actually, it would have been more humorous than anything, but any amusement I might have felt vanished in the time it took for a ranker next to him to lash out with what I recognized as a spade handle, which he aimed at my head, though he missed by a substantial margin. Despite the fact that I was wearing my helmet, I could tell that if the blow had landed, it would have stunned me, yet even as it was happening, I could see the man's heart was not in it, and I assumed he had been swept up in this instantaneous explosion of anger. Behind me, I heard the alarmed and frightened shout of Cinna, yet despite the efforts of the Optio who had been knocked aside, the men who had grabbed the Septimus Pilus Prior pulled him deeper into the mob. As alarming as this was, we had our own troubles, because there were others among us that the men had decided to seize, one of them being another Centurion who was on Volusenus' side but two men removed, except this Centurion, from the Ninth Cohort, having a heartbeat's more warning, was attempting to draw his *gladius*, except that before he could, he was struck in the head…and he was not wearing a helmet. Meanwhile, the ranker who had attempted to tackle me had scrambled to his feet, but when he lunged again, it was Volusenus who, taking a short step in front of me, felled the man with one punch, made more impressive that it was with his left hand, and he was clutching his *vitus* as he did so. I would have thanked him, but another man launched his own wild swing at me, forcing me to turn my head, and while he missed, it was a much closer miss than the first attempt with the cudgel. Pandemonium reigned, the next span of time just a series of fleeting memories, composed of fragments of what happened, which I consider as the moment when the revolt of the 1st and 20th truly began. Honestly, I have no idea why I did not draw my *gladius* and begin laying into these men, despite them technically being part of the Roman army. All the anger and frustration, the causes of which ranged from the extension of enlistments, the excessive use of monetary fines, and if I am being honest, the drudgery of their lives for the previous four years, when instead of marching and avenging Varus and his Legions, they had been in garrison, which is never a good thing for fighting men – all of it came boiling out at this moment. Nevertheless, I will step into Charon's boat certain that, without the agitation by those men of the emergency *dilectus*, like Publius Atilius Pusio, who were by far the angriest, most bitter, and frankly, the most experienced in agitating large groups of men, this revolt would not have happened. Only in retrospect did the scope of the mistake the Princeps made in the aftermath of the Varus disaster become clear, and it culminated in what was taking place at this moment. In effect, all the Princeps had done was to remove those men who had proven to be the ablest, most persistent troublemakers from the city of Rome...and transplanted them into the ranks of his Legions, where they merely continued their activities, finding a receptive audience in their comrades. None of this mattered in the moment; even if my heart was with the mutineers, we had to try to fight our way to the *praetorium* where, thanks to my height, I could see what I was certain was the entire complement of the Legate's bodyguard, arrayed in full armor, with their weapons drawn, and protecting the headquarters tent.

"Follow me!" I bellowed, then using the combination of my *vitus,* my right fist, and the tricks I had been taught by Vulso in the art of fighting dirty, I pushed and shoved my way forward, with Volusenus protecting my right in the same manner.

There was certainly no way to tell at the time, although I heard later that, whether it was out of respect for my lineage, my size, or as I would like to believe, the reputation I had earned on my own, the men who stood in my path were clearly half-hearted in their attempts to stop me. Volusenus had not built enough of a reputation to be known by men from other Cohorts, or other Legions, but immediately afterward, he acknowledged he had experienced much the same thing. Personally, I think it was not only his size, but the fact that he had knocked a man senseless with one blow and made it look easy that helped him keep up with my progress. The men behind us were not so fortunate; again, it was only putting it together later that we learned that, while nine of those men immediately behind us managed to maintain a tight enough cohesion with Volusenus and me that they made it with us to the tent, there was a separation between the last of these nine and the men immediately behind them. I was only dimly aware that something bad was happening, but I did not dare turn to look. The men in my path may not have been willing to fully commit themselves to attacking me, seeming to be content to make lunging feints, or in a couple of instances, poking the ends of their clubs in the general direction of my face, but there was still no way I was going to risk turning around to see what was happening.

Volusenus, however, did, because he shouted, "They just grabbed Sentius and an Optio!"

For the briefest instant, I considered turning around and attempting to rescue the Secundus Pilus Prior, who to this point was the highest-ranking Centurion detained by the mob, and perhaps something in my demeanor tipped that, because a man I did not recognize, meaning he was from the 20th, apparently decided that felling a man my size, particularly a Centurion, would be a notable achievement. And, perhaps I was distracted by the furor behind us, because I was unable to dodge the blow, aimed directly at my head. From my viewpoint, I had the barest sense of a blur of movement before a terrific impact slammed into the side of my face, where the cheek piece of my helmet protected my skull from being shattered. Not that it felt like it helped much; lights of a thousand colors exploded in my vision, rendering me completely blind for just long enough for my mind to comprehend it, but even worse, my legs buckled. Even as I felt myself dropping to my knees, the thought that flashed through my mind was the despairing one that I would die at the hands of a fellow Roman and not against an enemy. I had seen just enough in the face of my attacker, in the eyeblink before he struck me, to see the madness of battle in his eyes, and I held no illusion that the man would stay his hand because of my identity. Indeed, since he was from another Legion, and I was a hated Centurion, even through the fog in my mind, I was certain I was breathing my last. Fortunately, Volusenus had seen it happen, and I felt more than saw him leap forward to interpose himself, once more saving me from further damage. By the time my vision was restored, as those lights gradually faded away, what I saw was eerily similar to the moment where Germanicus had stood over me, saving my life during the assault on Splonum, a pair of legs positioned directly in front of me. Before I could completely recover my senses, I heard more than saw Volusenus defend me, though it did not sound like the sound of a *vitus*, or even a fist striking my attacker. Then someone grabbed me by the back of my armor, dragging me to my feet, just as we were quickly surrounded by the Legate's bodyguards, who had been a matter of paces away. Half-dragged, I was manhandled into the *praetorium*, then unceremoniously dumped on the floor, which I barely noticed since I was still trying to gather my wits.

Barely conscious of all that was going on around me, I actually pulled my way up to all fours, shaking my head to clear it.

"Are you all right?"

Volusenus' voice cut through the fog somewhat, then after a few steadying breaths, I drew myself to a kneeling position, reaching up to feel the left side of my head, my fingers first brushing the cheek guard. There was a deep indentation in the metal, but I did not feel any wetness, telling me that the skin was unbroken, and I gingerly pulled my helmet off. As I was attending to myself, there was a flurry of activity around the entrance, and while I was certainly absorbed in checking myself out, the furor was such that I did turn to see that a small band of mutineers were trying to force their way into the tent. To this point, there had been no real bloodshed, and it was clear that Caecina' bodyguards had been ordered to keep their weapons sheathed. That changed in an instant when, whether from fear or anger, I saw one of the men standing in the doorway, one of Caecina's gladiators, draw his *gladius,* and in the same motion, thrust it into the chest of one of the rankers, who dropped to his knees in an unintentional mimicry of my own posture at that moment. Just for a heartbeat, everything went quiet, and I clearly saw the looks of shock and disbelief on the fallen man's comrades, first staring down at his body, which fell facedown but still twitching, then looking up at the gladiator. His back was to me, so I could not see his expression, though he took a slight step backward, giving me the impression he realized what he had done. That movement broke the spell, as one of the rankers, his initial expression of shock twisting into a mask of hatred, howled with blind rage and literally threw himself at the gladiator. Fortunately for him, the bodyguard next to him kept his head and used his shield to knock the lunging ranker backward; unfortunately for the first gladiator, a ranker to his left, taking advantage of being somewhat screened by the second bodyguard's shield and body, used the full turfcutter handle he was wielding not as a club, but as a stabbing weapon, thrusting it directly into the face of the slayer of his comrade. Because I was behind the action, I did not see the actual strike, though I saw the results as the bodyguard's head snapped back, and that first backward step he had taken just a couple heartbeats earlier turned into him reeling backward so violently that I had to scramble to my feet to avoid him colliding with me. He managed to execute a half-turn while still on his feet, giving me a view of where the ranker, either through luck or skill, had plunged the end of the handle into the man's eye socket, and judging from appearances, the only reason the end did not burst out the back of the man's skull was because the handle had a blunt end. Truly, it was a grotesque sight; the handle thrusting out from the gladiator's head for its entire length, save that portion that was embedded in the bodyguard's skull. The gladiator took a tottering step back into the tent before his legs finally collapsed, yet before matters turned even bloodier, from somewhere outside, I heard a bellowed command, ordering the mutineers to withdraw. That they obeyed was quite startling, though in the moment, I was still trying to regain my wits and only dimly noted this as unusual.

"Are you all right?" Volusenus asked again, and this time, I could respond and assure him that I was, more or less, recovered. He did not seem convinced, looking at the side of my face critically, commenting, "The way that's swelling up, you should see a *medicus*."

"I'm fine," I insisted, then for the first time took a moment to turn and examine the large room that serves as the outer office of the *praetorium*. "Besides," I observed, assuring myself that the blurred vision I was experiencing would go away, "is there even one here?" Before he could answer, even as unfocused as my sight was, I spotted a familiar face, and I briefly felt a return of the dizziness that had just begun to fade, except this time, it was from relief. Pointing, I told Volusenus, "There's my

265

nephew; he's got some training. And," my scanning the room had been fruitful, because I pointed, "there's the Pilus Prior, and that's the Primus Pilus near him! Let's go see what the situation is." Climbing to my feet, I signaled to Alex that I wanted him at my side, while I started making my way through the crowded room, not even checking to see if Volusenus was following.

Both Primi Pili turned out to be in the *praetorium*, as were a majority of the Pili Priores, though not all of them, and it was left to Varo as the ranking Centurion of our party to inform Sacrovir that Sentius had been seized by the mob outside, who were still making an enormous racket, but had at least retreated from the entrance. The corpse of both the ranker and the gladiator had been unceremoniously dragged away from the flap, and I silently wondered if we would be trapped within this tent long enough for their corpses to start stinking. Caecina' bodyguards moved back outside, just on the other side of the flap, which naturally had been lowered from its normal position serving as an awning above the cut that functioned as a doorway. Becoming more steady on my feet with every step, I made my way to Macer, where the other Centurions were already gathered, along with three Optios, though none of them were mine.

"Where's Structus?" Macer asked me, but all I could offer was a shake of my head, which I instantly regretted because of the pain it caused. He must have noticed me wincing, since he leaned slightly to look at the side of my head, and he let out a hiss. "It looks like you have a hen's egg under your skin, Pullus! Are you sure you're all right?"

Actually, I was not sure, because he, and everyone else, was still slightly out of focus, but given everything that was happening, I did not feel right saying as much, so I assured him I was fine.

Clearly not believing me, he turned to Volusenus and ordered, "Keep an eye on him. You're the only one of us strong enough to haul his fat ass off the ground if he passes out."

Ignoring my protest, and that of Alex, who was behind me, the young Centurion assured Macer he would not let me out of his sight; with this settled, the Pilus Prior told us what he knew, little that it was at the moment.

"Caecina is in his quarters, refusing to come out and face the men," he began, not hiding his disgust. "A delegation of men from both Legions approached Sacrovir and Neratius first, demanding an audience with the Legate to discuss their grievances. And," Macer grimaced, "the Legate didn't refuse, exactly, but when he said that he wouldn't do so until he heard from Germanicus, well," he finished with a bitter wave, "you can see how that was received."

"That's not the only reason," a new voice interrupted, and we all turned to see Sacrovir, who had been talking to Neratius and some of the Tribunes when we first burst into the *praetorium*. "I just heard something from one of the Tribunes, and if it's true," the Primus Pilus paused, then went on, "well, let's just say now our problems are a lot worse."

This prompted a barking laugh from Vespillo, who spoke before Macer could open his mouth, a clear breach of custom, "Worse?" he echoed, shaking his head. "How could things possibly be any worse?"

"Because a rider came in just before dawn," Sacrovir replied, seemingly ignoring Vespillo's discourtesy, which I saw as another indication of just how unsettled the Primus Pilus was, because under normal circumstances, he was adamant about men of subordinate rank paying the proper respect to their superiors. "He'd been riding all night, coming from Mogontiacum. The 5th and 21st have risen up as well."

This was understandably staggering news, and Sacrovir did allow us a moment to express our shock and dismay.

"Wait," Macer spoke up, his eyes narrowed in an expression I had learned meant he was thinking matters through. "Excuse me, Primus Pilus, but you said this rider came in just before dawn?" When Sacrovir nodded, Macer went on, "All this..." he waved a hand in the general direction of the forum, "...whatever it is, started yesterday."

Sacrovir frowned, clearly not taking Macer's meaning, but while I was not completely certain, I thought I had an idea where my Pilus Prior was headed, though it was proving extremely difficult for me to concentrate.

"Yes," Sacrovir replied shortly. "So?"

"So," Macer explained, his tone patient, which was one of the qualities I admired in him, probably because I have none of it, "if the courier rode all night, then it stands to reason that whatever's going on in Mogontiacum started at about the same time as here."

I saw by Sacrovir's expression that he immediately grasped Macer's point, and indeed, he finished for him, "Which means that it's either one of the biggest coincidences that I've ever seen, or this was coordinated somehow." Before any of us could react, the Primus Pilus spun on his heel, searching the room. Then, spotting Neratius, who had moved off a distance to confer with some of his own Centurions, he began striding towards him, but as he did, he called over his shoulder, "Follow me."

Of course, we all complied, but I must have staggered a bit when I turned to follow Sacrovir, and truthfully the move did make me a bit dizzy, but a hard hand clamped on my bicep, then Volusenus was there, grinning, "Easy there, Princeps Prior. Remember, the Pilus Prior told me to watch you."

"I'll talk to him about that later," I growled, but when I assured him I was fine, he let go, and we both hurried to catch up, neither of us wanting to miss anything.

We arrived just as Sacrovir was explaining to the 20th's Primus Pilus what was essentially Macer's deduction, though I was not surprised that he did not mention the Pilus Prior's name, presenting it to Neratius as if it was his own conclusion. I glanced over at Macer, but while his face was composed, he caught my glance and gave me a slight eye roll, which was not noticed by the two Primi Pili. Neratius listened, but while he did not say anything at first, I saw the line of his jaw tighten as Sacrovir made his case that there had to be a level of coordination in this revolt, of which none of us had been aware.

Once Sacrovir finished, Neratius was silent for a moment, then said, "So, this nonsense about not wanting to be near Caedicius' camp was just a pretense all along." Suddenly, his mouth twisted into a snarl, and he smashed one fist into his palm, exclaiming, "I *knew* it! I knew there was something more going on than just their not wanting to march to that camp." Looking at Sacrovir, he said, "Come on, we need to tell the Legate about this."

For a moment, our Primus Pilus looked as if he would refuse, but I suppose that to do so in front of us would have created even more problems. Making his reluctance obvious, which Neratius ignored, Sacrovir nevertheless followed the other Primus Pilus in the direction of the partition that separated the Legate's office and private quarters from the outer office.

"I'm fucking dying of thirst," Philus suddenly said, and as almost always happens, once one man mentions it, the rest of us realized that this was the same for us.

Frankly, since I was finding it difficult to concentrate, and if I am being completely forthcoming, I was finding it hard to summon much interest in what was taking place at the moment as well, I took this as a sign that the blow to my head was more serious than I had thought. However, I did think about Alex, aware at least that once Macer had assigned Volusenus to be my caretaker, he was essentially dismissed, and I scanned the large room, finding him, not surprisingly, in the darkest corner, along with Lucco and Cornutus' clerk Demeter, mixing in with a couple dozen others of the same station. When he saw me as I made my way over to him, his mouth dropped open, and I realized he was staring at the side of my head.

"Uncle...er, Princeps Prior Pullus, that lump has gotten even bigger! Are you sure you're all right?"

Before I could respond, he hurried over to me, the concern in his expression making me feel better, in an odd way, reminding me once again, albeit at a decidedly peculiar moment, the importance of having a family that loves you.

"I think so," I answered him honestly, then once more reached up to touch my head, the first time I had actually done so since the immediate aftermath. I was gentle, but even so, I could not help wincing as my fingers touched what, as Macer had correctly described, was a lump the size of an egg, laid by a good-sized hen. "But," I admitted, "it hurts like Dis."

"Have you been seen by a true *medicus* yet?" Alex asked, and when I shook my head, he actually put his hands on his hips to demand, "And, why not?"

This was a mannerism that he had gotten from his mother, Birgit, and just the sight of it, as unconscious as it may have been, made me smile at the sight, even if doing so made my head hurt.

"Because I haven't had a chance!" I answered. "Besides, I don't think there are any around."

Obviously not satisfied, my otherwise bashful nephew looked around the room, then apparently spotting what he was searching for, marched over and, exchanging a few words with the Optio, appropriated the stool on which he had been seated. I will say that, at first, the Optio, who I vaguely recognized as belonging to the 1st, but that was the extent of my memory of him, looked as if he was about to argue, whereupon Alex merely pointed in my direction. This was clearly enough, because he instantly hopped to his feet and actually reached down to hand the stool to Alex, who returned with it in his hand, but not before stopping to confer with another man of his station. This man – youth is more accurate – I did recognize as the clerk for the Fifth of the First of our Legion, but more importantly, also served as a *medicus* when required, and he immediately turned to accompany Alex, who returned to where I was standing, a bit slack-jawed if I must admit.

Putting the stool down, my nephew pointed and said simply, "Sit."

Now, at any other time, I would probably have bridled at this, especially in front of other officers, yet this time, I found myself obediently dropping onto the stool, to which I attribute my injury.

"Let Parmenion take a look at you," Alex said. "He's practically a full *medicus*, and he's had experience with head wounds."

"It's not a wound," I protested, then amended, "exactly. It's just a bump on the head."

"And quite a bump it is," Parmenion agreed, leaning down to peer at the side of my head. I did appreciate that, before he touched me, he warned, "This might hurt a bit, Centurion, but I need to feel your skull to make sure it's not broken."

I did not answer, merely nodding, mainly because I was girding myself for the pain. Which, I quickly learned, was coming the instant he touched me, and even with my admonition to myself, when his fingers pressed into the side of my skull, I let out a yelp of pain.

"I know, Centurion," Parmenion said soothingly, which I found somewhat odd because he was, at most, five or six years older than Alex, making him much younger than me. "I know it hurts. But…" He stopped speaking then, as his fingers apparently found something, and the dizziness came back with a vengeance as he pressed harder into the side of my head, just above my ear. I was seriously worried that I would pass out, but he suddenly relented with the probing, standing up straight, as he pronounced, "I'm almost positive that your skull isn't broken. Now," he warned, "that doesn't mean there might not be bleeding going on inside your skull." This sounded quite dire to my ears, particularly when he turned to Alex and directed, "Do *not* let him fall asleep for the next three watches. And," he glanced down at me to ask, "have you had anything to eat?" Honestly, I could not remember, which I told him, and he turned back to Alex to explain, "If he throws up, don't be alarmed. That's normal. Otherwise," Parmenion returned his attention to me, shrugged, and said what all physicians and *medici* always say, "it's in the hands of the gods."

While I was being attended to, Sacrovir and Neratius had not only seen the Legate, but had already returned to the larger room. By this time, everyone present had gotten wind that there was information pertaining to our situation, so the instant they emerged from Caecina's office, they were accosted by a crowd of very worried officers. Not everyone scurried over; I was content to remain seated on the stool, which I naturally had not surrendered to the Optio from whom Alex first procured it, ignoring the man's glare at me. I've got a reason to sit on my ass, I thought. You're just lazy. The matter of the stool was quickly forgotten by the Optio, who joined the rest of the officers crowding around the two Primi Pili. My interest was aroused, slightly, by the idea of learning what Caecina had said, but not enough to get up; thankfully, Sacrovir spoke loudly enough for me to hear.

"Some of you may have already heard this," he began, "but we learned that the 5th and 21st have mutinied as well as our Legions." He paused for a moment as the officers reacted, understandably, to this bit of news, and their response told me that not many had heard or deduced this. Sacrovir resumed, "The fact that it happened yesterday, at roughly the same time as our..." he searched for the right word, finally settling on,

"...troubles began, well, neither Primus Pilus Neratius nor I think this is a coincidence. This was planned ahead of time, by whoever the ringleaders of this are, inside each of our Legions."

"What did the Legate say?" A voice shouted the question, yet even before Sacrovir verbally responded, despite my blurred vision, I could see by his expression what the answer was, but before he could respond, someone else asked, "What about the 2nd and 14th? What do you know about them?"

"The Legate," Sacrovir answered, in as close to a neutral tone as I believe he could manage, "is awaiting instructions from Germanicus."

He said something immediately after that, but I could not hear because he was drowned out, nor could I read his lips, the officers reacting in a predictably negative fashion; later, I learned that his information at this point was that neither the 2nd nor 14th had mutinied.

"How does that help us now?"

This is the essence of what men were yelling, which did perk up my attention a bit, since I was every bit as invested in the answer as anyone. The thought of being trapped inside the *praetorium*, which was only serving as a refuge because, to this point, none of the mutineers had worked up the nerve to slice through the canvas walls, was beginning to infuriate me, although it did help cutting through my fog. I was worried about Structus, mainly because it never occurred to me that he would take part in this uprising, along with men like Centumalus, Ambustus, and Gemellus, for the same reason. While I was just as intent on reaching the safety of the *praetorium* as any of the officers from the 1st who departed from the Legion tent, now that I was here, I was beginning to think that all we were doing was cowering in fear of an angry mob of men like Pusio. My line of thought was interrupted by Sacrovir who, only after some difficulty, finally got enough quiet to continue.

273

"Right now," he continued, "the Legate's orders are for us to stay here, in the *prae*..." He got no further than that, many of the officers erupting in protest, which at least told me I was not alone in my disgust at being penned up.

"And let them do what, exactly?"

This, truly, was the crux of the issue. Were we, these Centurions and Optios who clearly were not playing a role in this revolt, nor one of those like Sentius and the others who had been dragged out of our group, supposed to sit idly by and watch as men ran rampant? At this particular moment, I do not think any of us had any really solid idea of what the mutineers were intent on accomplishing, other than the redress of the grievances they had been uttering for more months than I could count. However, and in what I have to believe was one of those cruel moments arranged by the gods, we were about to get our answer. Before either Sacrovir or Neratius could answer the question being asked by what I saw was the majority, although it was far from unanimous, one of the bodyguards shouted to the two Primi Pili. Apparently, he had to repeat himself the gods know how many times before he got the attention of everyone else, but it quieted down enough for him to be heard.

"Primus Pilus Sacrovir, Primus Pilus Neratius," the bodyguard, who did not appear to be a gladiator and spoke with a German accent, "your presence is requested."

Outside the *praetorium*, the men who were the ringleaders of this mutiny had managed to achieve at least a semblance of order among their fellow mutineers. Clearly reluctant, both our Primi Pili nonetheless stepped out of the *praetorium*, although Caecina's bodyguards formed a protective circle around them. On the orders of Sacrovir, two of the bodyguards pushed the heavy flap up and affixed it to the two poles that were driven into the ground, although I was certain that it was not to provide shade, but to allow those of us still inside to see what was taking place. Naturally, a crowd quickly formed around the opening, but it was Volusenus who was the one to use his size to muscle through the small crowd, ignoring the protests of the other officers. Then, much to my surprise, he turned, caught my eye, and beckoned to me, which prompted me to rise from the stool, ignoring the sudden rush of dizziness that assailed me, and I made my way to his side. By the time I got there, the two Primi Pili had walked, very slowly, away from the relative protection of the Legate's bodyguards, to meet with a small group of men who were standing a short distance in front of the mass of mutineers. The mass of men were not in a formation, strictly speaking, but to anyone with a modicum of experience, it was easy to see how they naturally divided themselves into smaller groups that I was certain were arranged along Century, Cohort, and Legion lines. As interesting as that may have been, my attention was naturally drawn to what I had now counted as a half-dozen men who were clearly serving as the representatives of the mutineers. I blame the blow to my head as the cause for the delay in reaction when I examined these men, so that before I could react, Volusenus jabbed me with an elbow in my ribs.

"Isn't that your Optio with them? Structus?"

Even if Volusenus had not driven an elbow into me, I would have gasped, but it would have been from the combination of shock and dismay.

I felt my mouth open, then my mouth worked once, then twice before I managed, "Yes, that's Structus."

Now, I would add that my Optio was not standing in the front of the small group, and I recognized that one of the men was none other than the Quintus Hastatus Posterior of the 1st, Aulus Poplicola, who I knew was a paid man and considered one of the weakest Centurions in the Legion, at least when it came to the job. Standing next to him was a lean, taller man who I only vaguely recognized, but I learned his identity from the man standing on my side opposite Volusenus.

275

"That's Decimus Regillensus," this man whispered. "He's the Nones Pilus Prior of the 20th."

I asked him, "What do you know about him?"

"He used to be the Tertius Pilus Prior," the man explained to me, still whispering, "but Primus Pilus Neratius had him demoted."

This, not surprisingly, tore my attention away from the scene in front of us, and I looked down at the man, asking, "Why?"

Suddenly, the other Roman, who was an Optio, did not seem eager to meet my gaze, but he did answer, "Nobody knows, really. Oh, there are rumors," this prompted him to look up at me, "but that's all they are, just rumors."

"Rumors about what?"

Now the Optio clearly demonstrated that he would have rather been anyplace but where he was, yet I pinned him with a hard stare, until he finally relented.

"Supposedly," the Optio had dropped his tone to just above a whisper, "Regillensus was too close to his men for the Primus Pilus' comfort. He made no secret that he agreed with the rankers about all their grievances. So," he concluded, "the Primus Pilus made an example of him."

Turning my examination towards the men who had become the focal point of our entire attention, only a cursory glance at them confirmed that, in all likelihood, what the Optio had said was true, judging just from the manner in which the Primus Pilus and the Nones Pilus Prior were regarding each other. They did not speak loudly enough for us to hear, but then the man the Optio identified as Regillensus suddenly turned and pointed back to where a sizable knot of men were standing. And, from that group, there emerged a trio of figures, two of whom were clearly grappling with the third man whose identity I could not immediately make out. Then after a brief struggle, the pair dragged the man forth, and I saw then that it was none other than

Sentius, the Secundus Pilus Prior of my own Legion. Because I was so intent on watching this drama, I did not notice the men dragging one of the large wooden frames used for punishments out onto the forum. Until, I should say, they dropped it into place, essentially on the same spot where it normally went for official punishments. Over the years, through the dozens of punishments a month that are part and parcel of life under the standard, where everything from a striping with just the whip to the gruesome and often fatal use of the scourge, the lifeblood of countless men had stained the stones of the forum in that spot in our permanent camps like Ubiorum and Siscia. It had been a custom that, as I learned from my father, back when I was a child in Siscia and had first seen these darker stones, that men crossing the forum always went around it, never stepping on the stones that contained what was essentially the only physical remnant of so many men.

"It's like stepping over a man's grave," my father had explained, and while he was not overly religious, nor that superstitious, I vividly recall the way he shuddered when he talked about it.

None of that mattered much here, since it was a marching camp, and now, watching what was clearly a tense and angry exchange, despite the appearances, I was certain that the mutineers were only putting on a show that they intended to punish Sentius in some way. Then, when the two men dragged the Pilus Prior to the frame, while the Centurion still struggled mightily and everyone around me began shouting in alarm, I still did not believe they would go through with it. The pair had to have help, but when they gestured towards Structus, who was nearest to them, and whether it was an accident or he had spotted me through the opening, our eyes met an instant before the two men called to him. I would like to think that what he read in my expression played no role in him shaking his head, and I saw him mouthing his refusal, although by this moment, it would have

277

been impossible to hear him over the roaring of the men who were lustily cheering at just the idea of seeing a Centurion flogged. When one of Sentius' guards risked taking a hand off the Centurion to jab an accusing finger at my Optio, the Pilus Prior did not hesitate, violently jerking his arm from the man's grasp, then in one motion turning and punching the other ranker in the face. It was an instinctive, and from my viewpoint, completely justifiable reaction, but it was also the worst move he could have made given the circumstances. Even before the ranker went reeling backward, clutching hands to his face, the blood pouring through his fingers, easily a dozen men who had been standing at the front of the rude formation leapt forward, and before Sentius had gone a couple steps in the direction of the *praetorium*, clearly intending to escape, he was tackled and slammed bodily onto the packed dirt of the forum. It was short work for the men to drag him to the frame and strap him down, and now I was no longer so certain that he would not actually be whipped. Sacrovir indicated Sentius, who appeared to be dazed, which was understandable, and now there was no mistaking that he was pleading with Regillensus, but we clearly saw the Centurion, who I at least now accepted as being the ringleader of the mutiny, or one of them, shake his head in a clear refusal.

But it was something that both Volusenus and I noticed, a furtive move of Regillensus' eyes that flickered back in the general direction of the mob that prompted Volusenus to mutter, "I think that bastard's just as scared of the mob as we are."

That was precisely the reaction I had from watching what was taking place, although I seriously doubted that this would save Regillensus from punishment, especially if our new Emperor deemed it so. Once it became clear to Sacrovir that he would be unable to sway the leader of the mutiny, he gave Sentius one glance of apology, then looked away and refused to look in his direction again. Sentius was now strapped to the frame, and he began thrashing his head wildly and shouting incoherently, which was quickly cut off by one of the mutineers thrusting a gag in his mouth. He spit it out once, but after the mutineer punched him in the head several times, the next time it was shoved into his mouth, it stayed there.

"They're not really going to do it, are they?" Volusenus murmured, but while I found it hard to believe, I was beginning to suspect that we were about to find out.

Neratius had allowed Sacrovir to plead his case for Sentius, and I assumed, the other Centurions and Optios who had been grabbed from our group or, as we had learned once we made it to the *praetorium*, had been detained earlier during the night before, but once Sacrovir was finished, he began speaking. Now there was no hiding the outright hatred on the part of the rogue Centurion Regillensus for his former Primus Pilus, since I was certain that no matter what happened in the aftermath of this, Regillensus would never serve another day in the 20th. And, it was easy to see that hatred was returned in full measure by Neratius, matters quickly becoming more heated between them, until with a roar that could be heard even above the shouting of the revolting men, the Primus Pilus raised his *vitus*, clearly intending to strike Regillensus. Thankfully, Sacrovir managed to grab his arm before he could swing it at the Centurion, but just that was enough, because suddenly out of the crowd, a dark, streaking blur issued forth, and Neratius was struck fully in the face by what, only after it bounced to the ground, I could see was a stone that probably had come from the tributary of the Rhenus that flowed just outside the camp. Reeling backward, now it was Neratius' turn to bring a hand to his face to try and stem the flow of blood, while Sacrovir, whose grasp on his counterpart's arm had been wrenched loose when Neratius recoiled from being hit, reached out and reacquired his grip on the other Primus Pilus, and snarling a curse at Regillensus, began half-dragging, half-assisting Neratius away. As he did so, a hail of missiles came flying from the mob, but thankfully this time, it was a mixture of refuse, composed of rotten fruits, what looked like hunks of spoiled meat, and not surprisingly, piles of *cac*.

"Get out there and help them!"

I heard someone roar this, but while the bodyguards did so reluctantly, I grabbed Volusenus by the elbow and said simply, "Come on."

He gave a small shout of what sounded like a protest, though he yielded to my pressure, following only a step behind me as I began crossing the thirty paces still separating the two Primi Pili, while it took the bodyguards, no doubt shamed by being the men ordered to move first, a heartbeat longer. Very quickly, they caught up, and since they had shields, Volusenus and I were content to allow them to form a protective barrier around the two Centurions, Neratius now leaning heavily against Sacrovir, the blood flowing so freely from in between his fingers that his mail glistened red almost down to his *baltea*. Without being asked, I put an arm around Neratius' waist, prompting a gasped thanks from Sacrovir, and we returned to the *praetorium*. Just as we made it inside, there was a huge tumult, over and above what had become a dull roaring of yelling men, and I heard one of the men still standing in the doorway shout something, but I could not make it out. Instead, I helped guide the Primus Pilus of the 20th to a desk that had been hastily cleared, where Sacrovir and I helped him onto, then had him lie back.

"Where's Parmenion?"

It was Alex's voice I heard calling for the clerk, who quickly appeared, but while I was certainly interested to see what injuries Neratius had sustained, which were impossible to see through the blood and the hand he still clasped firmly to his face, I was more interested in what was taking place outside. I stayed long enough to see that only one eye was visible, and I was actually struck by a memory, specifically that perhaps this was how Divus Julius had looked when he celebrated his four triumphs, in which my Avus was the only man from the ranks to march in every one.

"They're doing it! They're flogging him!"

My desire to see how badly Neratius was hurt paled in comparison to this, and I joined the mad rush of men to the opening of the tent, and I freely admit that I used my size to muscle my way to a spot where I could see. And, within a matter of heartbeats, I was sorry that I had done so.

Sentius was the first, but he was far from the last of a number of officers, from both Legions, and including Centurions and Optios, to be given lashes. Perhaps the only positive that can be said was that they did not use the scourge, even on Sentius, who received the worst punishment. Along with the others, we stood and watched helplessly as men took turns applying the lash to Sentius' back, composed mostly of men from his own Century at first; I was certain I recognized well more than a dozen men. I am certain that while it did not seem to be the case, Sentius was actually fortunate that none of the men who took their turn whipping him had any experience in how to use the whip, and if I am being completely honest, the marks they were leaving were markedly similar to what a *vitus* might have left. That one of us observing kept count informed us that Sentius had been given sixty lashes is ironic proof of the inefficiency of the mutineers, since there should have been no remnant of skin left on his back when they were through. Once they were finished, they untied Sentius, who collapsed to his knees, barely conscious, while the mutineers unanimously jeered, laughed, and threw insults at the Secundus Pilus Prior, and the thought flashed through my mind that Sentius, no matter what happened, was through as a Centurion in Rome's Legions, provided he survived; no Legionary would follow him after this. He was unceremoniously dragged off, a man holding each arm and quickly disappearing into the mob, while Sentius' replacement, wearing just a tunic

281

with the white stripe of an Optio was shoved forward. Before I could watch another officer be flogged, I heard someone call my name.

Turning, I scanned the room, which was becoming rank with the smell of fear sweat, crammed with men who, but for the blessing of sweet Fortuna, would be out there waiting to be whipped and beaten half to death. Finally, I saw that it was Sacrovir, except he was no longer at the spot where Parmenion had now helped Neratius to a sitting position, but was standing directly in front of the flap that led to the Legate's office. Making my way through the room, I did give Neratius a cursory examination; one eye and half his face was obscured by a crude bandage that was already blood-soaked, and I wondered if he had lost his eye. Since it was not important in the moment, this was all the thought I gave, reaching Sacrovir and feeling slightly ludicrous for rendering a salute, given everything taking place.

"You're coming in here with me to see the Legate," he said abruptly, catching me completely by surprise.

"Why?" I blurted, but while he did not owe me an explanation, he did not seem all that put out, answering me by saying, "Because you're going to go with one of the Tribunes that the Legate chooses to go to Germanicus with the list of demands."

"Demands? What demands?"

Sacrovir produced a tightly wrapped scroll from his *baltea,* telling me, "That bastard Regillensus gave them to me to give to Germanicus. He's saying that they won't accept anything Caecina offers, even if he gives them everything they want." Shaking his head, he finished, "They won't trust anyone but Germanicus."

"I still don't see why I'm involved," and at this, Sacrovir's patience wore thin, and he snapped, "Because I told you that you're fucking involved, Centurion! Or," he had to look up to do it, but he pinned me with a gaze that was nonetheless chilling, even if I towered over him, "do you want to join those fucking mutineers?"

"No, Primus Pilus," I answered meekly, and perhaps my tone was conciliatory enough that he deigned to explain, "There are two reasons I chose you, actually. The first is," he leaned back a bit as he held out his hand in a gesture that swept up and down, "because you're one of the strongest men in the Legion, and I know that you're the best with the *gladius*." Whether it was his intention or not, this I heard with receptive ears; find a man who says he does not like being praised by a superior in such a manner, and you will find a liar. "The second reason is that you've served with Germanicus in a unique capacity, and I know he trusts your judgment." Lowering his voice, I understood why when he continued, "And I don't trust the Legate to inform Germanicus just how serious this is. He's been in a state of shock since it happened, but when he does speak, he keeps saying that this must be just a..." his mouth twisted with the word, "...misunderstanding." Something in my expression must have triggered the response, which was a harsh chuckle, and he said, "Exactly. Which," his tone turned brisk, "is why you're coming in with me."

Then, without saying anything more or even seeing if I was behind him, Sacrovir pushed through the flap. This was a breach of the normal procedure, but given all that had happened since the night before, it did not seem to be that important. Nonetheless, I was just behind Sacrovir and my view was partially blocked, but I saw enough, as one of Caecina's bodyguards partially drew his *gladius* as he turned to face the flap, only relaxing when he saw that it was the Primus Pilus. This did not disturb me all that much; the terrified and even more undignified yelp of the Legate, who even though he was wearing his full armor, scurried to the far side of his office to place his desk between himself and what I supposed he thought was an attack, now, that did trouble me.

"Oh," Caecina muttered to Sacrovir, "it's you." He at least looked a bit embarrassed about his behavior, which, in the manner of many nobles, he then turned into anger, aimed at a safe target. Pointing a finger at me, he demanded, "Who's this Centurion? And why is he here?" Then, he leaned over slightly to look past Sacrovir and for the first time, he seemed to actually examine me, and I saw a glimmer of recognition. "Ah, yes. That's…" I pretended not to hear the slave whose station was at a smaller desk slightly behind and to the side of his whisper my name. "…Princeps Prior Pullus, of the Fourth Cohort of the 1st." Suddenly, a look of alarm flashed across his face, and he turned to Sacrovir, "You're not bringing him here to protect me, are you?" Cocking a head, he listened to the muffled sounds of the proceedings outside, then turned back to Sacrovir. "Do you think they're going to attack the *praetorium*?"

"No, sir," Sacrovir answered without hesitation, then used this as an opening, producing the scroll. "We have the guarantee of…" my Primus Pilus paused for just the briefest instant, "…the leaders of this mutiny that they will make no moves against us here in the *praetorium*. Provided," he had been crossing the room to the Legate, who still stood behind his desk while he was speaking, and he thrust the scroll out, "we send this list of demands to *Propraetor* Germanicus, and that he come here immediately to listen to the grievances of the Legions."

He had not given me any indication he was going to do so, but I somehow knew the use of Germanicus' rank was no accident; meanwhile, Caecina was staring down at the scroll with an expression that practically screamed he had no intention of touching it.

However, he suddenly frowned, as if something had just occurred to him, and we learned what it was when he said, "Wait, Primus Pilus. What did you say?"

Sacrovir answered, "We have to send for *Propraetor*…"

"No," Caecina cut him off abruptly, "before that. You said this was a mutiny?"

"Why," Sacrovir replied, the surprise clear in his voice, "yes, sir. This is a mutiny."

"It is no such thing!" Caecina snapped. "This is *not* a mutiny or revolt of any kind!" He slammed a hand down on his desk, and I instantly noticed how neatly manicured his hands were. "I will not have you going to Germanicus telling him this nonsense that this is a revolt! It's simply a..."

"...Misunderstanding," Sacrovir cut him off, which angered Caecina, though he did not say anything. "Yes, sir, you've said that before." Since I was still standing behind and a bit to the side, I could not see my Primus Pilus' face, but I recognized the tone when he went on, "Since this is just a misunderstanding, then perhaps you should be the one, in your rank as Legate, to go talk to the...men." I guessed that Sacrovir had almost crippled himself by using a term that would only exacerbate the Legate's agitated state but had recovered in time. "If that's all it is, then I'm sure you'll be able to straighten it out just by talking to them."

Caecina regarded the Primus Pilus with a poisonous glare, but I knew as well as Sacrovir that the Legate, under the best of circumstances, was a serpent with no venom, and these were far from the best of circumstances.

And, as I was certain he would, he quickly broke his gaze, muttering, "Very well. Tell him whatever you want. I don't care," he concluded petulantly. Then, he turned his attention to the more important matter in his mind. "So," he said hopefully, "you're saying that if we send a messenger to Germanicus with these," he still had not taken the scroll, just gave a disgusted wave in its direction, "demands, everyone here in the *praetorium* is safe?"

"Yes, sir," Sacrovir answered, then for the first time, turned to indicate me, "which is why I brought the Princeps Prior with me. I think he's the best man for the job of riding to Germanicus, as far as a man from the ranks is concerned. But you need to select one of the Tribunes to go with him."

Caecina considered this for a moment, then turned and told the bodyguard standing nearest to him, "Go get Asprenas and bring him here."

It took a supreme effort of will for me not to groan aloud when I heard the name. Marcus Nonius Asprenas was the son of Lucius, who had been the Legate at Mogontiacum when Varus marched his three Legions into Arminius' trap. While Asprenas acted prudently, and some said courageously, by leading his two Legions to the rescue of Varus' survivors, during the intervening years, there had been persistent rumors that he had plundered the property of the slain. This did not seem to harm him in the eyes of the Princeps, and honestly, none of us cared much about what he might have done during those days. His son, however, was a different story, demonstrating the same kind of haughtiness and arrogance of the Tribune Paullus back in Siscia during Urso's time as Primus Pilus of the 8th, although the only positive note that could be said was that he had not been given command of anything to this point. Asprenas arrived, and it was easy to see that the youngster was torn between trying to display a complete disregard for the mob outside that was separated from us by nothing but a thin layer of canvas and betraying the same kind of concern that those of us who understood the danger were exhibiting.

"You called for me, sir?"

I do not know how he managed to do it, but Asprenas' tone conveyed his sense of annoyance that he had been pulled from whatever truly important task he was doing, counting the number of chickpeas left, perhaps. His air of indifference about the turmoil outside lasted as long as it took Caecina to inform him of the task he was being assigned.

"Wait…er, excuse me, sir?" Asprenas' reaction led me to believe that he had not really been listening to the Legate; perhaps he was trying to decide what vintage of wine would make the evening meal better. "I'm not sure I understand."

"What's to understand?" Caecina snapped irritably. "I'm entrusting you with carrying this…" he waved a hand at the scroll, which was still in Sacrovir's hand, "…message to the *Propraetor*. It's a matter of great importance and great responsibility. Or," he gave the Tribune a hard stare, "are you acknowledging that you don't possess the necessary qualities to deliver a message under admittedly difficult circumstances?"

I ducked my head and studied my *caligae*, but Asprenas, as I assumed he would, responded stiffly, "Of course not, sir. It would be my honor to deliver any message to the *Propraetor*."

"Good." Caecina gave Asprenas a smile, then turning his attention back to Sacrovir, he indicated that the Primus Pilus hand Asprenas the scroll, which he did. Then, when he said nothing more, Sacrovir cleared his throat, which was apparently enough of a hint, because the Legate went on, "Oh, yes. And," once more, he waved a hand, this time in my direction, "you will be accompanied by Quartus Princeps Prior Pullus of the 1st."

Only then did the Tribune turn and give me a cursory examination, but he did not seem all that pleased by what he saw, and he turned back to the Legate; I learned why when he said stiffly, "I assume that I will be in command between the two of us."

"Of course," Caecina agreed, and only then did Sacrovir speak up.

"Sir," he spoke to Caecina, "with all respect to the Tribune, I would suggest that, should there be trouble of some sort, Tribune Asprenas defer to Princeps Prior Pullus. He's extremely experienced, and…"

"And he's a Centurion," Asprenas cut him off. "I'm a Tribune. And," Asprenas turned to address Sacrovir, "I can assure you that I'm every bit as skilled as your Centurion. I've devoted myself to my exercises on the Campus Martius with a diligence that was complimented by no less than the Princeps himself. Can," he twisted slightly to regard me, his upper lip curled, "this man claim as much?"

I was just opening my mouth to respond when Sacrovir, giving me a warning glance, cut in, "Actually, Tribune, the Princeps Prior was personally decorated by Germanicus' father in his very first campaign as a Gregarius, and he served Germanicus as the Primus Pilus for the *Legio Germanicus* six years ago. I can assure you that the Princeps Prior is more than qualified." Then, he said, "I can also assure you that you're in good hands with Pullus."

Now, I cannot lie and say I did not like hearing this, yet at the same time, I inwardly groaned, knowing how likely it was that Asprenas would take offense at this, which was confirmed when, his face flushing a deep red, he said hotly, "And I can assure *you,* Primus Pilus Sacrovir, that I don't need this man's protection."

"Of course you don't," Caecina interjected, and for one of the few times, I appreciated his politician's touch, "but nevertheless, it can never hurt to have two men who can handle themselves, neh?"

Rather than mollify Asprenas, he seemed unsettled by Caecina's words, and he turned back to the Legate to say, "We're going to have an escort, of course." I was watching Caecina then, but clearly Asprenas was not skilled at reading another man's face, because he would have gotten his answer; instead, he went on, "We shouldn't need more than twenty of your bodyguards, sir."

The silence that followed quickly grew awkward, before Caecina finally responded, "Yes, well. In light of the situation here, I can't spare that many men, Asprenas."

"Then," Asprenas' voice was suddenly tight with tension, "how many can you spare, sir?"

Again, Caecina did not immediately respond, while I exchanged a glance with the Primus Pilus, reading a mixture of amusement and scorn in his expression that I shared as these two noblemen wrangled with each other.

"Frankly," Caecina answered him, "none."

Only then did Asprenas think to glance over at me, seemingly wanting my support, to which I was more than happy to shrug off and say only, "As long as we're allowed out of the camp, I'm not worried about any Germans."

This seemed to remind Sacrovir of something, because he turned back to Caecina, informing him, "About that. The mutineers have agreed to allow a party to leave the camp unmolested."

"I really wish you would not refer to them as such," Caecina grumbled, but he turned to Asprenas and said with a confidence that sounded false to my ears, "See? You have nothing to fear, Asprenas."

"I'm not afraid!" Asprenas shot back, and I had to bite my tongue lest I react in a manner that exacerbated the situation, contenting myself with the thought, Then why are you so worried about a bodyguard?

After some more back and forth, it was decided that we would depart in a third of a watch from the camp, and I was dismissed back into the outer office.

"I'll find you when it's time to leave," I said over my shoulder, again without thinking, which earned me a hard shove from the Primus Pilus, who was following me out.

The only part of this process where Caecina allowed some of his bodyguards to participate was when they escorted Asprenas and me to the stables, where we quickly made preparations. Naturally, the Tribune had his own mount, while I was given the pick of the pool of spares, and we both chose an extra horse as well. The first clash between Asprenas and me came when he wandered over to where the mules were kept, selecting one and leading it out of the pen.

"May I ask, Tribune," I was polite enough, but I had already decided I would be damned if I called this youngster "sir" – he was younger than Volusenus, "why you're selecting a mule?"

He seemed more surprised than offended, answering, "For my baggage, of course!"

"Baggage?" I echoed, not quite believing my ears and eyes. Shaking my head, I said, "Surely you don't think we're going to be stopping long enough anywhere for you to unpack whatever it is you're planning on bringing." Instantly, I could see that I had caught him out, but his pride would not let him admit that this was exactly what he thought, that every evening, we would camp, where I would erect a tent since we were taking no slaves, then he would sip wine in comfort, which led me to ask, "And you weren't planning on bringing any of your slaves, were you?" A silence. "Were you?"

His lips thinned down, and he expelled an exasperated breath, then a bit too roughly, yanked the head of the mule around, then slapped the animal on the rump hard enough to send it galloping back into its enclosure.

"Fine," he finally said sulkily, walking back to the horse, which had been saddled.

I had not had long to talk to Macer, even less time to talk to Alex, but the one thing I promised them, and all within hearing, that we would ride as quickly as humanly possible to where Germanicus was, although we did not know exactly where he was at the moment. Not, I would add, that he would be hard to find; everyone within a fifty-mile radius would know where the governor of the province was staying. Leading our horses and spares, we made our way back to the *praetorium*, and I ignored the hard stares of the men who were loitering around the horse pens, although there were not many; most of them were still congregating around the forum where the floggings of those Centurions and Optios was still taking place, or so I assumed. Handing the reins to some of the bodyguards who had not removed themselves from their spot protecting the *praetorium* entrance, most of them watching the spectacle that I suspected that, deep down, they were enjoying seeing men being whipped who, under normal circumstances, looked down on them as being little better than hired slabs of muscle. Asprenas headed immediately for Caecina's office, while I chose to stay with everyone else, saying my farewells to Macer and Alex.

"Take care of him," I told Alex, pointing to the Pilus Prior, and while he still did not look very happy at being trapped inside this tent, he smiled at me and assured me he would.

"Princeps Prior." I turned to see Volusenus, who solemnly offered his arm as he said, "I'll make a sacrifice to blessed Fortuna that you and the Tribune get to Germanicus quickly." I was strangely moved by this; I suppose that it must have reflected in my face, because he gave me a grin and added, "Because the sooner you do, the sooner I can get out of here. It," he actually made a sniffing noise, "is really beginning to stink in here."

I had to laugh, both because it was funny and he was correct; every passing third of a watch, the stench was getting worse, particularly since by this point, men were now pissing in a corner of the tent. So far, nobody had had to relieve their bowels, but I was thankful that I would be leaving before that happened. Sacrovir had moved to the opening, and although I did not see him disappear, he apparently had slipped out, because once Asprenas exited the Legate's office, with a small bag slung over his shoulder which I assumed contained the precious scroll of demands, the Primus Pilus reappeared at the entrance. Neratius was now on his feet, though he was visibly shaky, and Alex whispered to me that Parmenion had informed him that he had lost an eye. Waving to us at the entrance, we approached Sacrovir, who was holding something, a wax tablet this time.

"This," he said, and I could hear the anger there, "is from Regillensus. He says," Sacrovir's lips curled into a sneer, "it's a safe conduct pass that will be recognized by any of the mutineers."

This did not make sense to me, and I asked him, "But why would we need that just to get out of camp?"

"Because," Sacrovir answered bitterly, "they've sent out patrols out into the surrounding area."

"Patrols?" Asprenas broke in incredulously, and in this I was of a like mind. "For what?"

"To gather supplies," Sacrovir answered. "At least," he added, "that's what Regillensus says they're for, just to find food. But I'm willing to bet a thousand *sesterces* that they'll be coming back with a lot more than just food."

It took a moment for me to realize what he meant, but when I did, I felt my stomach twist.

"Women." I breathed the word, to which he gave a grim nod.

"That's my guess," Sacrovir answered, "although when I pressed Regillensus, he wouldn't admit as much. But he did give me a *cac*-eating grin. And," he added with a touch of outraged indignation, "he *winked* at me. Like we were best fucking comrades! I swear on the black stone," Sacrovir's tone turned savage, "I'm going to gut that cocksucker."

"We should tell the Legate," Asprenas said, but when he turned to go, Sacrovir stopped him by assuring the Tribune that he would do that himself.

From his reaction, I got the strong sense that Asprenas was trying to delay, which was why I took it upon myself to thrust out my arm, just as Volusenus had done to me, saying, "We'll be leaving now, Primus Pilus."

"Mars and…" the Primus Pilus began what was our ritual before battle, then stopped himself with a self-conscious smile, "…actually, I don't think that's the proper blessing for this. Hopefully, neither of you will have to draw your *gladius*." Suddenly, he seemed to realize how this might be taken by the Tribune, so he said hastily, "But, Tribune, if you do, Pullus here is the best man in the 1st with the *gladius*, and one of the best I've ever seen during my time under the standard."

Rather than settle the youngster down, this only served to make him puff up, and he replied stiffly, "I thank you, Primus Pilus, but I can take care of myself, I assure you."

I stifled a sigh, then, there was no more waiting. Before I stepped outside, I turned to see Macer, Alex, and Volusenus, along with the other Centurions of the Fourth, standing there watching us, and I gave them a brief wave, which they returned. Then, I led Asprenas out into the forum.

Chapter Six

While I was somewhat expecting some sort of ordeal exiting the camp, it was not for the reason I thought it would be. I had envisaged that the men would be sure to crowd us, moving out of the way slowly if at all, and otherwise enjoying exercising what had to be a heady feeling, of being the ones in complete control at the moment and doing everything they could to demonstrate their power. Although it did take some doing for Asprenas and me, each of us guiding our spare horse, to make our way from the forum towards the Porta Praetoria, and it was because there were men in the way, it was not because the men were surly. Simply put, it appeared that at least half of both Legions were drunk, and men were staggering about in the Cohort streets, acting more as if it was a festival than a mutiny. Fortunately, at that moment, Asprenas seemed content to allow me to lead the way, so I nudged my horse, a sturdy chestnut that I had chosen because of its size, through the throngs of men who were shouting, singing songs, and cursing anyone and everyone who wore the transverse crest. Honestly, it was somewhat amusing, since most of the time, these men had their backs turned as they boasted to their equally inebriated friends about what they would do if they had the chance to face a Centurion, any Centurion, man to man. Until, at least, the man facing my direction, seeing me coming, either shoved or grabbed his friend to turn him around to see, not only a Centurion, but a mounted one, a very large mounted one at that, and more than once, the comrade who had alerted the boasting man tried to convince the braggart to make good his threat to thrash anyone wearing the transverse crest. I was being careful not to get impatient, and was as gentle as possible guiding my horse through the crowd, not wanting to ignite some sort of incident, because I had absolutely no faith that waving a wax tablet would keep us out of trouble. Just one time did I stop, and that was because I spotted a man I knew, and he had already seen me. Stepping directly into my path was Pusio, holding a wineskin and sneering up at me, full of liquid courage, as insolent as always.

"*Salve,* Centurion!" he cried out with a gaiety that made it clear how much he was enjoying himself, which he confirmed, "It is a truly wonderful day, isn't it?"

"It certainly seems to be for you." I tried to keep my voice level and not betray any real emotion.

"That it is, that it is!" he crowed, then waved his wineskin around him at his fellow mutineers. "A glorious day for true citizens of Rome, when we reclaim our rights!" And, as I expected, the smile and false cheerfulness vanished as if it had never been there, and he pointed up at me as he snarled, "And you just may be one of those who we seek justice from!"

Now I knew that I could not afford to indulge my temper at this moment, but oh, it was difficult. Somehow, I managed, and making an exaggerated show that I was not moving towards him in an aggressive fashion, I walked my horse slowly up to him where he stood, glaring up at me.

"Pusio," I did not raise my voice, nor did I particularly give it any inflection, "you and I are going to talk about this again. But right now, I have somewhere to be."

Then, without waiting for an answer, I urged the horse on, and we continued through the camp. Finally, we made it to the gate, where one mystery was cleared up, albeit in a grisly fashion. It was Asprenas who noticed, just after we passed through the gate, and he happened to look down in the ditch.

"By the *gods*! Centurion! Centurion Pullus!"

His voice was sharp with alarm, and I whirled the horse about, my free hand dropping to my *gladius*, fully expecting that some of the mutineers had decided to come after us, but to my initial puzzlement, Asprenas was not looking back into the camp, but down into the ditch. Since I seriously doubted that there were men hiding there waiting to spring a trap, I was more curious than anything; I was certainly not prepared for the sight that met my eyes when I reached the Tribune's side. Following his gaze, it took a moment for my mind to comprehend what I was seeing; there were easily two dozen men lying or sitting semi-upright in the ditch, all of them bloody. It was not as much the blood as it was the similarity of their wounds, all on the backs of these men that told me the story. Then, one of the men who was sitting upright, hunched over with his bleeding torn back already drawing flies, although the blood had dried, turned dull eyes up at us.

"Pilus Prior Sentius!" I gasped more than said his name, and then I was swinging down off my mount, dropping down into the ditch to hurry over to him.

"*Salve*, Pullus," he croaked. "I'd get on my feet, but I don't think I can."

"What happened?" I asked, without thinking, then before I could stop myself, I went on, "I mean, after…"

Suddenly, I stopped, not even wanting to say it aloud, but it was even worse because his eyes were on my face, searching it for any hint of how I truly felt.

"After they did this?" He lifted a hand listlessly, weakly waving it in the direction of his back. "They dragged me out here and threw me in the ditch. They said," for the first time, he showed some emotion, his eyes filling with tears which, while understandable, did not make me any more comfortable, "if I tried to come back into the camp, they'd kill me." Then, more quickly than I would have imagined possible, a hand shot out and grabbed my arm with a surprising strength, as he whispered, "Where are you going, Pullus? Why did they let you leave?" When I told him why, a look of desperate hope came into his eyes, and he rasped, "Take me with you! I can ride!" He leaned slightly to look past me, although even that caused a groan to escape from his lips, but with his other hand, he pointed up and exclaimed, "You have a spare horse! You can get me out of here!"

"Pilus Prior," I tried to be gentle, "you're in no condition to ride."

"Just try me!" he shot back, a flash of anger that reminded me of the man who, perhaps two full watches before, had been the Secundus Pilus Prior of the 1st Legion. "I'll show you! I can ride!" His voice cracked, and his body seemed to convulse, which turned into a wracking sob, as he begged me, "Please, Pullus! If you leave me here, I'll die!"

"Take me too!"

"Don't leave me!"

Within a heartbeat, the voices of the other wretches who had been dragged out and dumped into the ditch like so much refuse rang out, all of them crying to me for rescue. That was the moment I realized I had made a terrible error, yet there was no way for me to undo my action of dropping down into this ditch.

"I...I can't," I told Sentius. "We're under orders, and we have to find Germanicus as quickly as possible. We can't be slowed..."

"I said I won't slow you down!" Sentius pleaded. "I swear it, Pullus!" I must confess I was tempted, but then Sentius said something that changed everything. Refusing to relinquish his hold on my arm, he lowered his voice and whispered urgently, "Pullus, I can pay you!"

"Pay me?" I had not been expecting this, but he clearly misinterpreted my confusion for interest.

"Yes!" He nodded emphatically. "I can pay you! Fifty thousand *sesterces*! I'll have my plutocrat hand you the money the instant we get back to Ubiorum!"

I was flabbergasted, so much so that I could only dumbly repeat, "Fifty thousand *sesterces*?"

Once more mistaking me, now there was no hesitation as he said, "All right, one hundred thousand!"

"How," I asked, more to give me a moment to think, "could you possibly have that much money?" I got my answer, not verbally; nevertheless, it was in an unmistakable fashion, as the sudden look of guilt flashed across the Pilus Prior's face, and in the span of a breath, everything fell into place. "You've been extorting your men?" I gasped, still not quite believing it. "Your own Cohort?"

Perhaps, just perhaps, if he had maintained his composure, had denied it, I might have at least dragged him out of the ditch and helped him in some way, but instantly. his face changed, his mouth twisting into a sneer as he snapped, "Oh, don't play games with me, Pullus! You," he jabbed a finger up in the direction of my face, "of all people!" My face must have registered my surprise, which he once again mistook, because he went on, "Oh, I know how rich you are! Everyone knows it! And you're trying to tell me that someone with as much money as you didn't earn it the same way I did?"

I could not trust myself to speak immediately, taking a deep breath instead before shaking my head, and telling him, "I didn't do anything like that. I didn't have to," I hurried on before he could offer a retort, "because my Avus earned it, the honest way. And, he passed it on to my father, who passed it on to me."

Now I recoiled at the idea of this man touching me, and I yanked my arm from his grasp, and without another word, I turned to walk away. He made a lunge for my legs, but I had anticipated this and stepped lightly out of his reach, causing him to let out a frustrated half-snarl, half-groan.

"Don't you leave me, Pullus!" he shouted, but I still did not respond, climbing up out of the ditch, where Asprenas, looking more bemused than anything, still sat his horse.

I did not say anything to the Tribune, simply threw myself into the saddle, and without a backward glance, urged my horse forward. We could hear not just Sentius, but several of the men, screaming at us as we departed, cursing us to all manner of torments for deserting them, and I wondered how many of the men in that ditch were actually like Sentius, and to what degree. Their voices faded quickly enough, but I was not in the mood for conversation after that, and thankfully, Asprenas was wise enough not to try. Either that or, more likely, he did not relish the idea of having to speak to a man of my class.

Only once did we run into one of those patrols Sacrovir had warned us about, and just as he had predicted, along with the livestock and sacks of grain, there were a half-dozen women with them, all of them bound and, in our manner, roped together by the neck. Thankfully, the commander of this bunch, wearing a filthy tunic with a white Optio's stripe, was not a man I recognized from our Legion, and he confirmed that he was with the 20th. If I had run across someone from my own Legion, and he had been an Optio or, even worse, a Centurion, I knew myself well enough to know that I would be unable to show the kind of restraint I had with Pusio, especially if it was Structus.

After perusing the tablet with an almost comical slowness, he handed it back, then nodded his head at Asprenas, asking, "I suppose he's the one carrying our demands?"

"I am," the Tribune answered stiffly, though he did not say anything else.

"Maybe," the Optio, who looked like one of those men who always bear the appearance of needing a bath, even after they have just stepped out of one, "I should take a look at that list, and see what's what." He grinned up at me, showing a mouth missing its share of teeth. "Just to make sure that the boys back in camp didn't forget anything."

"You will do no such thing!" Asprenas snapped, and this time, I could not stifle a groan.

"Says who?" the Optio sneered. "You? Apparently, you've forgotten something, *boy*. You being a Tribune isn't worth a mound of *cac* anymore. We," he made an expansive gesture at his comrades, numbering about a half-Century, although I assumed that there were more men about, probably searching a nearby farm, "are the ones in command here. So," he pointed directly at the Tribune, "if I say you get down off that horse and give me that fucking list, you'll do it!"

Sensing that matters were rapidly spinning out of control, I spoke up, but I did not address the Optio.

"What do you boys think?" I called out, trying to be genial. "Do you really think it's a good idea to delay us? We're on our way to Germanicus, just like Regillensus said. And the quicker we get there, the quicker Germanicus comes and gives you what you want." Giving an elaborate shrug, I jerked my thumb at Asprenas, saying, "Now, no doubt the Optio here is right. If you want the Tribune here to give you that scroll, and he doesn't want to, I know you can make him. But," I warned, "I'm going to have to try and stop you." Taking a bit of a gamble, I asked, "Do you all know who I am?" Some men nodded, others muttered something, but I could see that they all recognized me, and I made sure to keep my voice at a conversational level, as if we were just swapping tales around the fire. "Now, how many men do you think I could kill before you got me?" I made a show of looking around, as if counting them, and I was gratified to see some lips being licked and a fair amount of nervous shuffling. "Five? Six? Maybe ten? And," I pressed, "at the end of it all, what will you have to show for it? Germanicus won't get your demands for the gods know how many days before Regillensus figures out that we didn't make it to him. I don't know about you," the chuckle sounded forced, which it was, "but I'd *hate* to be one of those men who let their comrades down, all because this one," I pointed down at the Optio, who was scowling up at me, "needs to show he can make a Tribune do anything he wants."

"He's right, Macrianus," one of the rankers called out. "I say we let them get on their way."

This was instantly echoed by most of the others, and the Optio, knowing he was outmaneuvered, tossed the tablet back up to me, gave a disgusted wave, and walked away, letting us resume our journey. Once we got past this one group of mutineers, our progress was swift, as we only stopped to switch out the horses. We rode through the night, although at a much slower pace, arriving on the opposite bank from Ubiorum shortly after dawn. As we waited for the bridge to be drawn across, which had become a very smooth and relatively quick process, I faced my first challenge with Asprenas.

"We're going to rest here until midday," Asprenas announced.

"That's," I replied carefully, "not what our orders say, Tribune. We," I repeated from memory, "are to make the best time possible to reach Germanicus."

"We must rest," Asprenas insisted. Seeing I was not moved, he said, "We need to rest the horses, at least."

"We're switching out the horses," I replied, thinking of Latobius, waiting in his private stable that I paid the *immune* in charge of the horse pen a fair amount for, "and we'll get something to eat. Then," I turned to look him in the eye, "we keep going."

Asprenas opened his mouth, then shut it, opened it again, before finally breaking his gaze and muttering something that, while I could not hear it clearly, I took for assent. By this point, the bridge had been drawn across, and we guided our horses onto the wooden surface. Once across, we moved up the road from the river at a trot, reaching the camp gates, whereupon we had to undergo the process of recognition when anyone approaches not knowing the watchword. Thankfully, the Centurion of auxiliaries who had the watch immediately recognized me and waved me in, and we headed in the direction of the stables. I wasted no time, telling the *immune* to go bring Latobius to me, along with spare mounts, while Asprenas selected another horse to go along with his own, and while I was tempted to intervene and insist that he leave his personal mount as well, I relented, for two reasons. The first, and most important was that he had been riding the spare for the last part of this leg to Ubiorum, but also, I had observed Asprenas and the manner in which he treated his personal mount, and I understood why it was important to him. After all, here I was drawing my own personal mount, and when he was led around the corner, his ears already up and forward, telling me that he had caught my scent, despite the circumstances, I felt my spirits rise. With a quick toss of his head, he yanked the lead rope out of the *immune's* hand and broke into a trot heading straight for me, beginning what had become a game between us as he appeared to have every intention of running me down, then with a nimbleness that had saved my life more than once, came to a stop as he lowered his head to thrust it into my chest, whereupon he immediately thrust his velvet nose into the folds of my tunic around my *baltea*, since I had doffed my armor once I was certain we were out of danger from the patrolling mutineers.

Laughing in delight, I had to tell my horse, "I'm sorry, boy. I didn't bring an apple. But," I promised him, and my change in tone must have alerted him, because his head jerked up, his ears once more pricking forward in eagerness, "we're going for a ride today."

"You," the *immune* grumbled, "spoil that horse too much, Centurion."

Even as he said this, Latobius had turned, and without being told, obediently trotted over to the spot where all the bits of tack and saddles were stored, waiting to be saddled, although he was impatiently pawing at the ground, and I pointed to him doing that, saying, "He may be spoiled, but look how easy he's making it for you."

Laughingly agreeing, the *immune* turned and walked to where Latobius was waiting, while I walked to the handful of other mounts that would serve as the next spare horse. As I did so, I felt someone's eyes on me, and I turned to see Asprenas regarding me with what appeared to be curiosity.

Seeing me turn, he said, "You must ride that horse quite a bit, Centurion. And," he turned to examine Latobius, and whatever his other faults, I could see he knew horseflesh, "it's a magnificent animal. I'm surprised that it hasn't been claimed by one of the officers."

Realizing what he meant, I felt that stab of anger, but I kept it in check as I simply said, "He has been, Tribune."

"Oh?" Asprenas looked startled, turning back to me. "And yet he allows you to ride him whenever you please?" Sniffing, he said, "You and this officer must be very good friends."

There was something in his tone that caused me to actually look up at him from where I was putting the bridle on the spare horse I had selected, and I saw he was wearing a smirk, or more accurately a lascivious leer, and that initial flare of anger blossomed into a full flame, yet somehow I managed to keep it within myself, mostly anyway. By this time, Latobius was saddled, the spare mount had been bridled, and tossing a coin to the *immune*, I leapt into the saddle, and in the same movement, put him into motion.

It was only as I rode past that I deigned to answer Asprenas, simply because I needed those extra heartbeats to get myself under control, saying, "I suppose you could say that we're good friends." Only when I had gone past did I explain, "Because I'm the officer who owns this horse."

"You?" Asprenas' voice expressed what sounded like a combination of surprise and indignation, but heavier on the latter. "You?" he repeated, but while I did not look back, I could hear he was following behind. "Why would a…" That was when I did turn around, fixing the Tribune with a cold stare, his face coloring as he apparently decided to use a different word than the one he originally intended, "…Centurion need a horse, especially one of this quality?"

"Tribune," I could only shake my head; it was not like I had not heard things like this before, "what you don't know about us…Centurions," I deliberately matched Asprenas' tone when he had used the word, "could fill the Tabularium."

Hearing his gasp of shock at my words took much of the anger away and brought a smile to my lips.

The only other delay in Ubiorum was when we went from the stables to the *Quaestorium*, where I signed for a supply of three days' worth of rations for two men, getting even more satisfaction from the look of dismay when I handed Asprenas his sack containing three round loaves of *Panera Castris*, a hunk of boiled pork, and a smaller sack of lentils and chickpeas, although I did not bother mentioning we would have no time to stop and cook them. Let him figure that out on his own, I thought with grim amusement; he just thinks he's unhappy right now. We made just one other stop, but this time, I did not let Asprenas know where we were headed, since I understood that he would feel compelled to try and assert his authority. While I suspected that it would be inevitable at some point, unless we were fantastically fortunate to run into Germanicus in the next day or so, I thought it better to delay that moment, so I moved Latobius at the trot, then only when we drew abreast of my quarters did I bring him to a stop.

"I'll be back in a moment," I said shortly, already off and striding to the door.

Balio had been left behind, and thankfully for both of us, he was where he was supposed to be, seated at his desk, and not obviously fucking off, although he leapt to his feet with an expression of surprise and a fair amount of guilt.

"Princeps Prior!" he exclaimed. "I wasn't expecting you!" Suddenly anxious, he followed me as I strode past him, heading for my private quarters. "Is there something I can help you with?"

"Grab me two clean tunics," I told him, although this was not my main reason for being here, "and go outside and roll them up in my *sagum*. It's on Latobius."

Naturally, he complied, and I waited just long enough to make sure he left the building, listening for the door slamming, before I turned to my real purpose. Under my desk, there was a floorboard that, to outward appearances, looked like every other one, but under which I had hollowed out a space in the foundation. Pressing on one end of the floorboard, the opposite end tilted up, just enough for me to grab and lift out, followed by the other three. Reaching down, I found what I was looking for only after some rummaging around, moving aside the wooden box in which the copies of my Avus' scrolls were kept for safekeeping and, most importantly, away from prying eyes. I could not even begin to imagine how a man like Tribune Asprenas would react to the information contained therein, particularly the knowledge that I might be even wealthier than he was. So much had happened so quickly after the Princeps' death that I had not even had time to ponder what this might mean for the Pullus family, and I was reminded at this moment as my fingers brushed the box. It was something to think about, and to investigate, whether or not Tiberius, in his role as *Imperator,* would lift the edict that barred my family's name from being entered into the equestrian order, but this was not the time. Retrieving a leather bag, I opened it and quickly examined the contents, feeling the weight of the coins, and judging whether it would be enough. Next to the box of scrolls was another box, this one banded with iron, with a lock, and there was even more money there, but I decided this would have to do, simply because I did not want to make Asprenas suspicious and have him come barging in. Quickly replacing the floorboards, I pulled the carpet back in place, then left my quarters, just as the outer door was opening.

Seeing Asprenas standing there, before he could step inside, I reached him, saying, "I apologize for the delay, Tribune. I'm ready now."

I could tell he wanted to complain, but this stop had lasted perhaps a span of two hundred heartbeats, if that, so he contented himself with giving me what I am sure he thought was a severe look. Balio had finished as well, my *sagum* back in place, though I double checked to make sure it was tied securely; satisfied, I remounted Latobius and began moving again, so rapidly that it forced Asprenas to scramble a bit to get back on his own horse, making him look a bit like a boy following his father and trying to keep up, which was precisely what I intended. We were going to be heading south, but I led us to the Porta Decumana, which was located on the western side of the camp, because I did not want to contend with the people in the town who, seeing two officers of the Legion, would immediately assail us and demand to know about what was going on across the river. Granted, this was now the second full day of the revolt, yet now that we had learned there was a level of coordination, I believed that operating on the assumption that the civilians knew about it was the best course, so I led Asprenas around the outskirts of Ubiorum. If this had been even five years earlier, we could have completely avoided any dwellings, but the town had been steadily growing, except for the period of time immediately after the Varus disaster. Now that enough time had passed and people no longer feared that a horde of Germans would come swarming across the river at any given moment, the growth had resumed. Once clear of the town, we turned south, our first destination, Colonia Augusta Trevorum, the road to which we took ten miles south of Ubiorum. I think it suited us both that neither wanted to engage in conversation with the other, and fairly quickly, I was reminded of the simple pleasures of riding a horse, especially where both animal and man knew each other so well. Although we made good time, it was still almost ninety miles to Trevorum, as we called it, although now we were back on this side of the Rhenus, we were on good, Roman roads. Stopping at midday, and realizing that we had essentially ridden an entire day, since it was around noon when we left the camp, when I unsaddled Latobius, rubbed him down, and strapped his bag of feed over his nose, did the same for the spare mount, then without saying anything, went under a tree and rolled out my *sagum*, I did so confident that Asprenas would not object.

"What are you doing?"

Stifling my impulse to offer some retort, I tried patience. "We've ridden for a full day, Tribune. I think we should probably rest for at least two parts of a watch."

"I didn't agree to that," he said stubbornly, and I lifted myself onto one elbow to regard him, dismounted and holding his horse's reins.

Sighing loudly enough I knew that he would hear, I asked, "So are you saying that we keep going, Tribune?" Struck by a small inspiration, I made a show climbing to my feet as I said, "If you insist..."

"No!" He held up a hand, looking startled. "I'm not saying that at all! I agree that it would be wise to stop, especially since," he glanced up at the sun, "it's the hottest part of the day. I just..." He stopped then, and I thought with a fair amount of amusement that he was at a loss about how to get out what he wanted to say without sounding petulant, then he settled on, "...should have been consulted, that's all that I'm saying."

Frankly, I realized immediately that this was not an unusual demand, especially from a Tribune who technically outranked me, and it was with some chagrin I admitted to myself that I had been so intent on showing Asprenas that I was the one truly in command that I had created this situation.

"You're absolutely right, Tribune," I found myself saying, "and for that I apologize. Now," I lay back down on my *sagum*, "I would respectfully suggest that you find a good spot to get some rest."

I did not look directly at him, but out of the corner of my eye, I could tell that he had expected an argument, so he stood there for a moment, seemingly at a loss before, finally, he tended to his horse in the same manner I had with Latobius. My last memory of this period was hearing both horses in my care munching contentedly on their meal, and it was in this manner that we traveled for the next two days, never stopping for even a full watch, which was incredibly wearing, even on a much younger man like Asprenas. And, despite my resolution to avoid any kind of meaningful interaction with the Tribune, riding mile after mile wears even the strongest will down. The problem was, what to talk about? One by one, I mentally discarded each topic. Politics was, naturally, completely out of the question. Anything about either myself or the Tribune I dismissed almost as quickly, believing that it would inevitably lead us to something like politics. Talking about the mutiny was just as fraught with dangers, and I was despairing of thinking of anything. Finally, more out of desperation than anything, I broached the subject of chariot racing. For a span of time, I smugly congratulated myself for my choice, since Asprenas turned out to be an ardent supporter of the Greens, and he enthusiastically described the strengths and weaknesses of each driver, their teams, to the point that, before we had gone ten miles, I was very unhappy with myself. Still, I tried to keep in mind that it was better than the alternative. When we reached Trevorum, as hopeful as I was, if only to stop learning more about the Greens and chariot racing than I ever wanted to know, I was not all that surprised that Germanicus was not there, but we did learn that he was making his way down to Lugdunum. This, as far as it went, was good news; that Lugdunum was more than five hundred miles from where the mutiny was taking place was not. In one way, Asprenas and I were of a like mind, in that neither of us were willing to part with our personal mounts in Lugdunum, but as a precaution, and keeping in mind my lesson when we stopped that first day, I suggested to Asprenas that we actually obtain two spare horses apiece.

"I'd rather you figure out a way to find a spare rider," the Tribune answered wearily, and just the manner in which he said it made me burst out laughing.

His initial reaction was to glower at me, but then I suppose the impact of his own words caught up with him, and he laughed as well, the two of us sharing a moment of camaraderie, both just weary travelers still with many miles to go.

"Would that I could, Tribune," I replied. "Would that I could."

I was sorely tempted to linger a bit longer in Trevorum, looking longingly at the row of inns that lined both sides of the road on the outskirts of the town, and a glance at Asprenas confirmed he was of a like mind.

"We need to keep going," I said, and he opened his mouth to say something, though before he could, I pressed on, "because I don't know about you, Tribune, but I don't want the deaths of every officer trapped in the *praetorium* haunting my dreams if the mutineers run out of patience."

Snapping his mouth shut, Asprenas only gave a curt nod, then, with our mounts switched out, and with two extra horses apiece now, we did exactly that.

If it were not for a chance meeting with a rider carrying dispatches, we would have continued on to Lugdunum, when Germanicus was actually not there, but north and slightly west in Augustodunum, which had been created by the Princeps as the regional capital of the Aedui, the primary inhabitants of the area. All I really knew of the Aedui was that they were one of the many tribes who were subjugated by Divus Julius, and more importantly to me, my Avus. That, however, had been more than fifty years before, and they had since settled down under Roman rule, enjoying all the benefits that come with it. And, as often happens at momentous times, if we had been only a sixth part of a watch sooner, or later for that matter, we would not have hailed the rider heading north towards us, just as he was turning west, where a secondary road led to Augustodunum, though we did not know that yet. Holding up a hand, I hailed the rider as he approached, thinking that if he was coming from Lugdunum, which was likely since that was the only large population center in the direction we were heading, he would be able to tell us at least how close to Germanicus we were. He ignored me, which I should have understood would happen, but thankfully, young Asprenas had that invisible aura that every person of the lower classes of Rome learns to identify from an early age, along with the fact that we had agreed to resume riding in full uniform, as tiring as that was, for moments such as this, so that when he shouted at the rider to stop, he actually did so. Not, I will confess, that I was particularly happy about it, especially when Asprenas went trotting past me, looking insufferably pleased with himself, and I followed behind, murmuring my thoughts to Latobius, while Asprenas addressed the courier.

"I am Senior Tribune Marcus Nonius Asprenas of the Army of the Rhenus. We're looking for the *Propraetor*, Germanicus Caesar," Asprenas intoned, and since I was behind him, I indulged myself in an eyeroll as he spoke. "We're on official business on behalf of Legate Aulus Caecina Severus, and it's extremely important that we reach the *Propraetor* as quickly as possible. Do you know where he is?"

The courier, who appeared to be perhaps in his mid-twenties, looked at the Tribune first, then to me, clearly surprised.

Pointing down the road in the direction he was about to head, he said, "He's in Augustodunum, Tribune. I'm bringing dispatches for him."

"From who?" Asprenas asked, but I could have saved the Tribune the trouble.

"I can't tell you that, sir," the courier answered, and for a moment, I thought Asprenas would press the issue, then he gave a shrug to show how much it did not matter.

"How far is Augustodunum?" I asked him.

"From here?" He pondered for a moment, then answered, "Thirty miles."

"Pluto's cock," I muttered, and Asprenas did not look very happy either. Looking up at the sun, which was on its downward arc, I guessed, "If we push the horses, we might make it before dark."

The courier coughed, in a manner that told me it was not random, and when I looked over, he shook his head, saying, "Centurion, if it was flat ground, that would be true, but in about ten miles, the road starts going up. Not much," he allowed, "but if you've already been pushing your mounts, and," he indicated our spare mounts, which we had just switched out, "it looks like you have, that might be asking too much. Although," the courier turned his head to examine Asprenas' horse, which he had switched to not long before this meeting, then he looked at Latobius, who I was leading at that point, "if those two horses are as strong as they look, you might just do it."

"When do you plan on arriving?" Asprenas asked, and at this, the courier gave the Tribune a grin.

"Sooner than you, sir," he answered cheerfully, "but that's because," he reached down and patted the neck of his horse, "I'm on Lightning here."

Asprenas turned to look at me with a lifted eyebrow, and for a moment, we were just two men who appreciated horses...and competition.

"Centurion, I suggest you switch to your mount," Asprenas said, but I was already swinging out of the saddle, preparing to switch it to Latobius.

"I'm sorry, Tribune," the rider told Asprenas. "I can't wait. By regulations, I shouldn't have stopped."

Dismissing him with a wave of his hand, the courier wheeled his horse, and before he got too far away, I called out, "Don't worry! We'll catch up."

He looked over his shoulder, grinned, and put his horse to the canter.

"Centurion," Asprenas said, his face serious, "it would have probably been a better idea not to warn him about that."

Glancing up, I recognized what I had learned was his amused expression, which consisted of a slightly different tilt of his head so that his nose was just a shade lower, and I had to laugh.

"Good point, Tribune."

Despite our best effort, the courier, more familiar with the road, along with the advantage of having a fresher mount that was selected by the courier service specifically for its speed and endurance, made it to the walls of Augustodunum very shortly before we did. The only reason we lost sight of him was because it finally got too dark to see, but we had closed to within about three or four furlongs, if that. Latobius was tired, but not to the point I worried about him, while Asprenas' horse was in slightly worse shape. Despite not quite catching him, the courier had done us one slight favor, and that was to inform the guard detachment at the town gate not only that we were just behind him, but who we were, so our delay on arrival was minimal. Since this was a settlement that had been created during the long reign of the Princeps, finding the *Praetorium*, where we knew Germanicus would be, was not difficult; navigating through the people thronged in the streets was another matter. This was slightly unusual since it was after dark, but I honestly did not think much about it since I had never been to Augustodunum, or around the Aedui, and I assumed these were people who liked to congregate even after the sun went down. And, as we quickly learned, many of them did speak Latin, if a heavily accented version of it, but any of us who had been on the frontier were adept at making out what was being said. It was what they were saying that caused both Asprenas and me to draw rein, exchanging a look where, I was certain we bore identical expressions.

"They already know?" He did keep his voice low. "They've already heard about the mutiny?"

I stifled my first response that my ears worked in the same way his did, saying instead, "It sounds that way."

This quickened our pace, but the traffic was heavier the closer we got to the center of the town, and when we made it to the forum, while it was not packed, there was a sizable crowd, all of them facing the *Praetorium*. I quickly lost count of the number of times I heard someone mutter the word "mutiny," yet I assumed that the citizens were all talking about the mutiny of the Rhenus Legions, and as I thought about it, I realized that it was actually reasonable that they would know already.

"They're talking about what's happened in Mogontiacum," I said softly to Asprenas as we crossed the forum at a walk, both because of the people and the fact that, frankly, our horses were too tired.

"That makes sense, I suppose," Asprenas allowed. "It's closer than to our camp."

We had reached the steps, where we dismounted, and in something of a surprise, when I told Asprenas to go ahead while I tended to the horses, which consisted of using my rank to order one of the sentries standing on the porch watching us approach to stand guard over them, the Tribune actually balked.

"I'll wait," he said, but when I glanced over at him, he refused to meet my gaze.

He doesn't want to give Germanicus the news alone, I thought, which was understandable, and once again the delay was minimal. Pointing to one of the four men who were standing there, looking down uncertainly, I snapped the order for him to descend the stairs, having learned long before how important tone is when issuing orders to a strange ranker. Turning to the men next to him, there was a muttered conference, but just before I was about to raise my voice, the man I had selected came down the steps, slowly enough to send the signal of his reluctance.

"Juno's *cunnus*," I muttered to Asprenas. "It looks like disobedience is contagious."

Asprenas gave a curt nod, then began ascending the stairs as I handed the reins to the surly ranker, who I vaguely recognized as being one of the men who were more or less permanently assigned to serve Germanicus, not as a personal bodyguard, but as an adjunct force to provide security like this.

"Is the *Propraetor* present?" I heard Asprenas ask of the three remaining sentries.

"He is," one of them spoke up, "but may I inquire into the nature of your business, Tribune?"

"You may not!" Now, I thought, that sounds like the Tribune I started out with, but I had to intervene, since this was precisely what the sentry should be doing.

"Excuse me, Tribune," I interrupted him, gently, "I seem to have misplaced my copy of our orders. You have yours, I'm sure."

Now there had only been one scroll containing the orders from Caecina to go find Germanicus, but to his credit, Asprenas immediately recognized my purpose.

"Ah, yes." He did sound somewhat embarrassed, pulling both scrolls from his pouch, and using the firelight, opened one of them to scan it. Then, handing the other to the sentry, he said crisply, "Here are our orders, signed by the Legate Aulus Caecina Severus of the Army of the Rhenus, directing the Princeps Prior and me to come to Germanicus in all haste." He emphasized the last word, and I did not think it would hurt for me to add, "The Tribune is correct, of course, and I don't think you want either of us telling the *Propraetor* that, after almost killing our horses, we were held up by you...what did you say your name was? And your rank?"

As I expected, this had the desired effect, the man handing the scroll back to Asprenas without even glancing at it, stepping aside even as he assured us, "That won't be necessary, at all, sirs. You may enter." Following Asprenas, I smiled when the sentry added helpfully, "I believe that he's still up and in the *Praetor*'s office."

I only nodded, mainly because my mouth had suddenly gone dry, and as we strode from the vestibule into the outer office, my mind was racing as I tried to prepare myself for telling Germanicus that at least two-thirds of the Army of the Rhenus was in revolt, since at that moment, I was certain that, while he knew about Mogontiacum, he was ignorant of the situation with the 1st and 20th. That just shows the dangers of assuming anything, because I was as wrong as I could be.

As the sentry had indicated, Germanicus was not only up and working in the office that normally belonged to the man officially in charge of a Roman-controlled town, he was actually pacing back and forth, listening to two of his aides engaged in a vociferous argument. That we were able to actually approach the door without any aide or even a clerk intercepting us I took to be another sign that Germanicus was at least partially aware of what was taking place in Germania. Even through the door, I

315

recognized the muffled command to enter as being issued by Germanicus when Asprenas knocked, and as was proper, I stood aside as Asprenas entered first. The gentle nudge I had to give him when he suddenly froze in the doorway got him moving again, but his nerves were such that he did not even turn to reprimand me for being so impertinent.

Looking at Asprenas, Germanicus' eyes narrowed, although he sounded calm as he said, "*Salve,* Tribune Asprenas. To what do I owe the pleasure of this visit?" Then, when he saw me, his mouth dropped open for an instant, and even by the lamplight, I saw him go pale. "Pullus? What…" He looked back to Asprenas and clearly saw something in the Tribune's face, although I had not yet drawn abreast of him. Germanicus' aides had stopped their bickering, their expressions mirroring each other; concern and curiosity in equal measure. However, Germanicus turned and said, "Leave us. I'll summon you when I need you."

The two men, who might have been cut from the same cloth as the Tribune I was with, clearly did not like being dismissed in such a summary manner, although they both obeyed without a word of protest, and I felt a small smile forming as I thought about how, when Germanicus had been sent to do an impossible task by his adoptive father Tiberius, so many of the young nobles under his command gave him an argument about every order. Much had changed since then, but my reminiscing about days gone by was cut off by the unsubtle slamming of the door.

"Neither of you would be here if it was good news." Germanicus had moved to sit on the edge of his desk, facing us. "So, what is it?" His expression shifted slightly, and he asked, "Is it the Legate? Has he fallen ill?" Standing up, he went on, "Is he dead?"

"No, sir," Asprenas answered quickly, but instead of acknowledging the Tribune, Germanicus looked at me for confirmation, and I shook my head, even as I saw the flash of irritation on Asprenas' face out of the corner of my eye.

Since Germanicus was looking directly at me, I spoke up, "At least, he wasn't when we left, sir. But that might change." I was actually about to continue, then thought better of it, turning instead to Asprenas, saying, "You should tell him, Tribune."

Now, I honestly thought I was doing the right thing, but Asprenas looked anything but pleased, shooting me a look that expressed his feelings quite eloquently, though he did not hesitate, informing Germanicus in what, I had to admit, was a very thorough report of the situation. By the time Asprenas was finished, Germanicus had fallen back to land heavily on the desk, his mouth agape in shock.

"Of course," I added, "judging from what we heard out in the streets, you've already heard about Mogontiacum."

This elicited a completely unexpected response from Germanicus, a loud gasp, which served as our first hint that, in fact, matters were much, much worse.

"Mogontiacum too? Silius' Legions have revolted as well?"

Asprenas and I exchanged an alarmed glance, and I gave a slight nod to him that he should be the one to speak.

"You mean," Asprenas asked, "you didn't know about Mogontiacum? Then, what were the people in the streets talking about?"

Germanicus did not respond immediately; he had put his face in his hands, his head bowed into them as he slumped forward, trying to absorb this, leaving the two of us to wonder for the span of heartbeats before he spoke, very, very long, slow heartbeats. Finally, he lifted his head, and I suddenly realized that his eyes were red-rimmed, making me wonder if they had looked like that when we entered and I had not noticed, or this latest bit of news we brought had been the cause.

Not that it mattered, and Germanicus said dully, "No, Tribune Asprenas, I did not know about Mogontiacum. What the people of the town are excited and worried about, and understandably so, is that the Army of Pannonia," Germanicus paused long enough to look over at me and gave me a smile that held no humor, "has risen in revolt as well."

Now it was our turn to be staggered, but this was doubly true for me, which Germanicus knew and was why he had looked at me when he imparted the news. Indeed, I actually spotted a chair and headed for it, though I was in sufficient possession of my senses to look inquiringly at Germanicus, and he nodded, whereupon I fell into it so heavily that it cracked. I spent the next breath waiting for it to collapse, thinking that this would be oddly appropriate, but thankfully, it held my weight. Meanwhile, Asprenas had removed his helmet and, like me, found a chair, while Germanicus silently watched us. Finally, he spoke.

"We clearly have quite a bit to talk about," he said, in what I still rank as one of the greatest understatements I ever heard in my life. Thankfully, of the three of us, Germanicus possessed enough of his wits to ask, "Have they made any demands?"

With some chagrin, Asprenas rose, withdrew the scroll, and handed it to the *Propraetor*, then settled back on his chair. None of us said anything, waiting for Germanicus to peruse the list, though he did shake his head a couple of times, and once muttered what I assume was a curse.

When he had finished, he looked up and said ruefully, "I have to hand it to whoever was behind this, because..." He suddenly twisted to look for something on his desk, then grabbed up another scroll before he turned back to address us. Holding up the one Asprenas had given him, he waved the other one as he remarked, "These could have been written by the same man. They're almost identical." Turning to me, just as Sacrovir had predicted, Germanicus asked me, "Pullus? What do you think? You know the rankers' thinking better than either of us do. What's behind this?"

I had been preparing myself for this moment for the entire journey, and I did not hesitate, feeling the pressure of the advancing watches and growing worry for my fellow Centurions with every heartbeat. "I think that on that list, there are two things that are non-negotiable, and if the men don't get them," I did not feel particularly happy saying it, but I was determined to get it out, "there will be a lot of bloodshed. And," I felt compelled to add, "I don't think that it would be long before Arminius would hear about it and recognize this was the opportunity he's been waiting for." Germanicus nodded, though I had no way of knowing if he was accepting everything I was saying was true or whether he agreed with it, but I continued, "I think there are a couple more items that might seem unacceptable, but I'd argue that they would actually help strengthen the Legions more than harming them."

Only then did he speak, asking, "And those are?"

I felt confident, just by the manner in which he asked this, that he at least suspected what they were, but I was committed now, and I answered immediately, "Getting rid of the men of the emergency *dilectus*. Send them back to Rome where they belong. From everything I've heard, they weren't told that they would not only be expected to complete sixteen years, but that it was raised to twenty not long after they...volunteered." I will not deny that Pusio's face was prominent in my thoughts as I said this, but there were a lot of Pusios throughout the Army of the Rhenus. "And," I added, "I agree with one of the demands that I think they will not bend on, and that's raising their pay."

Germanicus did not answer me immediately, choosing to stare off in space for a moment. Then, he heaved a deep sigh before his gaze returned to me, and I could see by his expression how doubtful it was that I would like what he was about to say.

I thought he was going to prove me wrong when he began, "On the matter of pay, that *might* be possible," he allowed, but then he shook his head as he went on, "but I'm afraid my father will never agree to letting those men come back to Rome."

This was the one thing I had my heart set on, which is what I blame for my interrupting him.

"But why?" I knew my tone was improper. "Sir, those men are like a tumor!"

Germanicus was not irritated by my outburst, but neither was he willing to indulge me, answering immediately, "You know why, Pullus. There was a reason the Princeps got rid of them in the first place. He made the calculation that they were less of a danger in the Legions than they were in Rome. And," he took a breath, "I must say I agreed with the Princeps then."

This did not make me happy, and I made no attempt to hide that, but as ever, Germanicus did not flinch from looking me in the eye. Also, by doing so, he sent a signal that this subject was closed, and I decided not to press further, at least right then.

Taking a breath, I stood up, sure that I knew what was coming, and when Germanicus looked towards me, I said, "With your permission, sir, I'm going to go make preparations. I need to get our horses taken care of, and we need to find an inn to get some sleep, but we'll be ready to leave with you first thing in the morning."

Asprenas opened his mouth, and judging from his expression, he seemed about to object, but he did not need to, because Germanicus shook his head.

"We can't leave tomorrow, Pullus," he said. "Not unless there's a miracle of some sort, and I hear from my father."

It took a moment for this to work its way through my tired, agitated mind, and as usual, once I comprehended what this meant, there was nothing in between my ears and mouth to stop me from blurting out, "Are you *mad*? We can't wait that long!"

Even Asprenas looked alarmed at this decision, rising to his feet to address Germanicus. "Sir, I know that it's not my place to do so, but I must agree with the Princeps Prior in this. When we left the camp, the Legate and most of the Centurions and Optios were trapped inside the *praetorium*, and we don't know if the ringleaders of this mutiny are men of their word!" As he briefly glanced over at me, I understood why he did so when the Tribune, speaking in a low voice went on, "The mutineers were in the process of flogging a number of Centurions and Optios when we rode out of camp, sir. The gods only know what those…animals have done since we left."

Germanicus turned his head to look at me inquiringly, and I nodded confirmation, though I was not particularly happy about Asprenas' description of the rankers, but this was not the time to quibble.

"That," Germanicus admitted, "is quite troubling." He thought for a moment, then shook his head, saying, "But I can't just go galloping off without hearing from Tiberius. Remember," he reminded us, "there are two rebellions going on, in two different armies. In two different places. For all I know, Tiberius is going to deem the Army of Pannonia to be more important…"

"Than Germania?"

The only real surprise was that I had not been the one to speak, and I could see that Asprenas was just as surprised by his interjection as Germanicus, and certainly me.

His face flushed a deep red, but Asprenas argued, "*Propraetor*, while I know that there was all manner of unrest in Pannonia, and that you," he surprised me when he turned and indicated me, "and Princeps Prior Pullus were a crucial part of quelling it, I would say that it wasn't nearly as dangerous to Rome as what happened in Germania and Varus. And," he finished, "Arminius is still in command of the tribes. What do you think he's going to do when he learns of this? Because we both know he will."

Despite my ambivalent view of Asprenas, I was deeply impressed, and I made a mental note to let him know that;

whether he would appreciate my appreciation was another matter. More importantly, his words had an immediate impact on Germanicus, and he fell back on the edge of the desk, his face a study in conflict. Clearly, he accepted what Asprenas had said as being extremely likely; I would have gone farther and said it was as close to guaranteed as it is possible to be, yet he also had a better grasp on the political situation back in Rome. It should be remembered that, during these days immediately after the death of Augustus, there was an enormous number of questions about what that meant. While most of us in the Legions all assumed that the wishes of the Princeps would be respected, and Tiberius would be recognized as his successor, because of my unique perspective, both from my own observations and experience but also from reading my Avus' account of the last time there was a vacancy at the top of Rome, I was probably one of the few men who had a glimmer that it was likely that what was assumed by most was not the case. Judging from the way Germanicus was behaving at this moment, I felt a small burst of satisfaction that it appeared as if my caution was warranted.

Finally, Germanicus spoke, but all he said was, "Let me sleep on this tonight. Asprenas," he acknowledged the Tribune, "I understand what you're saying, and I think you're absolutely correct in your assessment. However," he hesitated for just a heartbeat, then went on, "there are other factors that I must keep in mind, which make this a difficult decision. So," at this, he stood up from the desk, "let me think about this."

Seeing us out, Germanicus called to one of the men who had been arguing, and I heard him give the man instructions to see to our needs.

The last thing he said to us was, "You'll stay here. There are rooms for visiting dignitaries, and you'll each have one." Turning to me before I could bring it up, he grinned at me and asked, "Pullus, did you ride Latobius?" Both impressed and touched that Germanicus would remember my horse, I could only nod, and he turned to Asprenas. "Does he still spoil that horse?"

The Tribune, who I had come to, if not exactly like, at least tolerate, answered Germanicus with a laugh, although he was looking at me, "Terribly, *Propraetor*."

"Well," Germanicus was still smiling, "I will personally guarantee that he's cared for, Pullus. Does that ease your mind?"

"Yes, sir," I replied, only partially comprehending that I was being teased, something I do not normally like much, since I was still grappling with all that had taken place, and that Germanicus had remembered Latobius. "He'll appreciate it. Although," I did recover slightly, "not as much as I do."

As I hoped, this made Germanicus laugh, and he turned away, leaving us in the care of one of his aides. Honestly, I was tempted to go check on Latobius, but I realized that, if Germanicus heard that I had, he might take it as an insult, or more likely use it to tease me more, so I contented myself with caring for my own needs, which consisted of asking for and getting a large chunk of bread, a couple small cheeses, some boiled pork, and an amphora of water, which were brought up to my room. True to his word, we were led to the opposite wing, where we ascended a staircase and were shown two rooms, side by side. The aide, a nobleman who Asprenas said he did not know, clearly thought it beneath him, but I was too tired to take offense and so was the Tribune, and by rights, he should have been angrier.

Standing there, each of us in front of our rooms, we paused for a moment, though I cannot say why, and Asprenas turned to me to ask, "Pullus, what do you think Germanicus will do?"

I considered for a moment, and when I responded, I was not playing him falsely when I said, "Well, you did a good job of reminding him what's likely to happen. Honestly," I added, "I should have thought about it in those terms as well. Arminius isn't going to hesitate once he finds out what's going on."

323

Again, I was being honest, but I could see that this pleased him, which in turn, seemed to encourage him to compliment me. "I think the *Propraetor* needed to hear what you told him, Pullus."

After an awkward silence, we bade each other a good rest, exchanging a grin at the thought of more than two parts of a watch of sleep. The food I had requested arrived immediately afterward, but I did not finish before, for the first time in days, I doffed my armor, took off my *caligae*, and collapsed on the bed; I cannot say for sure, but I believe I was asleep before a count of ten.

Awaking the next morning, while I could have slept more, I still felt better than I had when we arrived, and I made my way to the office, where not surprisingly, I found Germanicus already awake, though this time, he was seated. I was allowed in immediately, but when he looked up and saw me enter, he gave a weary shake of his head.

"I haven't decided yet, Pullus," he told me.

Naturally, my first urge was to argue, but I caught myself, understanding that, of all the people in Rome, Germanicus was the last man who needed to be reminded of all that was at stake. Instead, I simply requested his leave to see to Latobius, which he granted.

"Don't go far," he warned. "Because once I do decide, we're going to be moving fast."

Assuring him that I was only going to the stable, I chose to ignore the grin he gave me, waving a dismissal to me to proceed. After checking on Latobius, which essentially consisted of bringing him an apple and ensuring that he had been rubbed down the night before and had hay and water, I returned as quickly as I could to the *Praetorium*, not wanting to be the cause of any delay, so certain was I that Germanicus would not tarry in his decision. By the end of that day, my confidence was wavering, I was growing increasingly restless and bored. Unsurprisingly, Asprenas had sought out the company of his fellow nobles, but since there was no Legion with Germanicus, my choices for chatting as we waited were limited. I had not brought anything to read, naturally, so I was essentially consigned to sitting in the outer office, pacing about, or occasionally going to relieve myself and get some fresh air. If I had known that this would be the case for the next three days, I cannot say whether it would have made me appreciate this first day or not. It was not for a lack of trying on not just my part, but that of Asprenas, in urging Germanicus that every day of delay was one that we could not afford, and I will say that the *Propraetor* bore the harassment with a fair amount of grace. Until, finally, on the second full day after our arrival, he indulged in a rare fit of temper, something that I had never seen before, and even being the object of his ire, I have to say that I was a bit impressed in his use of language. I had come into the office for what, as he pointed out, was the fifth time that day, and he finally had had enough, banishing me from his presence in a quite colorful manner, warning me that he did not want to see my face the rest of the day. If this had been Tiberius, I would have been shaking in my *caligae*, certain there was at least a flogging in my future, although if it had been Tiberius, I would have never behaved in that manner. This is not to say that I was not slightly worried, but I suppose I was counting on our previous relationship and my knowledge of Germanicus as a man who did not bear grudges. And, seemingly in answer, not long after I resumed my spot in the chair that I had essentially appropriated as mine, one of Germanicus' clerks came looking for me.

"The *Propraetor* wants to see you," he told me, so I naturally leaped up and followed him back into the office.

Germanicus was still behind his desk, perusing a tablet with a deep frown, but he looked up at the sound of the door. Waving at me to enter, as he did so, he ordered the other occupants out of the room; as normally happened, the clerks, a combination of slaves and freedmen, hopped up and went scurrying out, while the noblemen made a more leisurely exit, all of them expressing their displeasure to varying degrees.

Once we were alone, Germanicus pointed to the chair in front of his desk, which I took to be a good sign, and as I sat down, he said, "I apologize for that display earlier, Pullus. I understand your urgency, I truly do, but you have to understand how much pressure I'm under right now." He paused as if considering something, then gave me a direct gaze and continued, "What I'm about to tell you cannot leave this room, Pullus. Do I have your word that you won't divulge any of what I'm about to tell you?" He surprised me then by suddenly giving me a grin, which I understood when he finished, "Not even to that horse of yours."

"I swear on the black stone," I answered solemnly, then returned his smile. "Not even to my horse."

Nodding, Germanicus pursed his lips as he tried to frame his thoughts, then began, "As I mentioned the first night when you and Asprenas got here, matters are complicated, not just with these two revolts, but particularly back in Rome. Pullus," his tone turned cautious, "I know you recall when we served together, things between my father and I were...tense."

That, I thought, is putting it mildly, but aloud, I agreed, "Yes, sir. I do recall that."

Germanicus sighed, and the look he gave me was tinged with what I believe was a genuine sadness as he continued, "I wish I could say that matters between us have improved, but they haven't. He was against the Princeps giving me *Propraetor* authority, and even more adamant that I not be given overall command of the entire Army of the Rhenus."

I do not know why this surprised me; nonetheless, it did. I suppose I had believed that, by this point, Germanicus had proven beyond any doubt that he was loyal and had no intention of attempting to usurp Tiberius.

As if reading my thoughts, he went on, "With the death of the Princeps, things have only grown more tense." Suddenly, his expression betrayed his anger. "I don't know who's behind it, but I've learned that there are…factions in Rome who are dripping poison in my father's ear that I have pretentions to claim *Imperator* for myself."

Now this did *not* surprise me, and my mind immediately went back to Claudius, the former Tribune, and the role I had played in his downfall at the behest of Augustus. That was when I had learned that, despite appearances of tranquility and peace, the world of Roman politics is anything but; there are always small men who dream of greatness. And, frankly, I considered Germanicus to already be a great man, despite his relative youth, and I understood that there are always men who look at someone like Germanicus and think, "If I was in his position, this is what I would do," never understanding that one reason for his greatness was in his recognition and acceptance of his current role. As far as Tiberius and his suspicions went; well, having served the man in the capacity I had, I am forced to admit that he had good cause to be suspicious of others, given how shamefully the Princeps treated him for so many years. He had endured a succession of humiliations, as Augustus continually pushed forward one potential heir to his title after another, all at the expense of Tiberius, his most loyal and able general.

"So," Germanicus explained, "that's why I'm not doing anything until I hear from Tiberius. Now, I sent a courier to Rome less than a third of a watch after the message from Siscia came, and that was two days before you and Asprenas got here."

While I appreciated his speed of action, I did not see how this helped our situation on the Rhenus, and I said as much.

"No, it doesn't," Germanicus agreed, "but my hope is that my father sends someone from Rome who has been given the authority to make decisions in his name, and that they run into the courier I sent shortly after you got here."

That, I thought, is one of the most forlorn hopes I have ever heard, but I decided not to say as much. However, as matters turned out, that is exactly what happened; that it would impact me so directly and dramatically I had no way of knowing, although I will say that when the agent from Tiberius arrived, I did have at least a modicum of warning that I would probably not like how matters turned out.

It was not until the next day, which both Asprenas and I spent in the same fashion as the previous ones; I alternated between sitting in the outer office, short trips outside, and trying to keep myself from going mad. Only by happenstance was I actually sitting in my spot, shortly before sunset, when the outer door opened, and a lone man strode in, removing a light cloak spattered with mud, under which a courier bag was strapped across his body. My first reaction was only mild curiosity; for the first couple of days, I had leapt to my feet every time one such man arrived, certain that he would be bringing instructions from Rome. And, honestly, in my initial cursory glance, I did not recognize the man, although I should have, but he certainly recognized me.

"Pullus? By the gods, what are you doing here?"

I had already looked away, but it was the combination of hearing my name, and recognizing the voice that drew my attention back, causing me to leap to my feet. Staring at me in open-mouthed astonishment was Tiberius Dolabella, but it was a version of the man I barely recognized. Although it was true that I had not seen him for some time, it was clear that Dolabella had aged far more than one would expect. Part of it was that his face was gray with fatigue, although when I stood to face him, I saw even that color drain from his face, but it was how gray his hair had gotten, the deep seams that now lined his face, and most pronounced, the heavy, dark circles under his eyes, even as one of them looked past me as always.

Motioning to him, I walked into a corner, where he followed me, his eyes searching my face, and I whispered to him, "You'll find out in a moment, but first let me ask you a question. Are you coming from Rome?" He gave a perfunctory nod, and I asked, "Are you bringing Germanicus instructions about what's happening in Pannonia?"

At this, he hesitated, and he asked suspiciously, "Why?"

"Because if you are, there's something you should know before you walk in there," I explained patiently, not surprised at Dolabella's reaction.

I took a breath, then plunged ahead, telling him as briefly as possible about the revolt of the German Legions, and why I was there with Germanicus. Before I was finished, he was staggered to the point where he fell against the wall; this was disturbing, but then when he grabbed his chest, I felt a stab of alarm. Not, I should admit, out of any real concern for this man who had been such a rock in my *caliga* for so many years now, but because if he pitched over dead at my feet, it would require some explanation.

"Are you all right?" I did ask him, but while he was gasping for breath, he nodded his head.

Finally, he seemed recovered, then gave me a look that I had rarely seen on the agent's face, sort of a rueful sadness, telling me, "I've been having these…spells recently. They come and go." When he gave a small laugh, I was certain I heard a note of bitterness as he said, "I suppose things have been so…exciting the last few weeks, I shouldn't be surprised." Taking a deep breath, he seemed to gather himself, asking me, "You said they have a list of demands?"

I nodded, and he asked me what they were, and I saw no reason not to tell him, although the thought did cross my mind that I was stealing Germanicus' thunder, so to speak.

Once I was finished, he said grimly, "Those are almost identical to the ones given by the Pannonian Legions." Sighing, he said, "All right, thank you for warning me, Pullus." His expression changed slightly, and he looked up at me, regarding me thoughtfully, which I did not quite understand, then he said, "Actually, you should come with me to see Germanicus."

Without waiting for an answer, he straightened up, took another deep breath, then strode to the door, clearly expecting me to follow; naturally, I did so, and because I did, I saw, or more accurately, heard the knock that Dolabella gave at the door, consisting of three sharp raps, then a pause, followed by two more but delivered even more quickly, then without waiting for a response, he opened the door. Curious, I made sure to be hard on his heels, certain that Germanicus would be at least irritated at Dolabella not waiting for permission, but instead of being angry, he looked relieved, which told me that this was a signal.

Nevertheless, Dolabella displayed the proper decorum, approaching the desk while saying, "Please forgive this intrusion, *Propraetor*, but I come from…"

"I know where you come from, Dolabella," Germanicus interrupted, then amended, "or I know *who* you come from. Are you here bringing instructions, though? That's the important thing."

"I am, sir," Dolabella answered, but then he turned to indicate me. "However, when I saw Princeps Prior Pullus here, I was quite surprised. Naturally, I asked why. And," Dolabella's voice turned grave, "he explained why, so I know about Germania."

I was slightly surprised that Germanicus looked more relieved than anything, though thinking about it, I decided that I could understand why, if only to save time.

Nodding, Germanicus asked tightly, "So? What does the *Imperator* want me to do?"

"Actually," Dolabella answered, "nothing." Unsurprisingly, Germanicus' expression hardened, and I thought that this was another example of how Tiberius did not trust him, but then Dolabella continued, "Because he's sending Drusus to handle that. And," Dolabella smiled slightly, "the reason he sent Drusus is because he suspected that there might be a similar situation in Germania." This was when Tiberius' agent produced a scroll, and I saw Tiberius' seal on it, and he stepped closer to hand it to Germanicus, saying, "He had two sets of orders. These are what I was supposed to give you if his information was correct."

Germanicus snatched the scroll, unrolled it, and read it quickly. When he looked up, it was to me, and he gave me a smile. "Well, Pullus, it looks like we'll be leaving for Germania at first light."

"Actually, *Propraetor*," Dolabella spoke up, and despite playing it over in my mind, I do not believe that I could have possibly predicted what he was about to say, "I do have a request." Germanicus frowned, but he indicated for Dolabella to continue, and I believe I can be forgiven for not paying close attention, not remotely imagining that I would be involved in any way; I was about to learn differently when Dolabella said, "I'd ask that Pullus come with me. I'm heading to Pannonia to…aid Drusus in his efforts to end this rebellion of the Pannonian Legions. And," he turned to me, his face giving away nothing, "I believe Pullus here could prove to be a very valuable asset in that effort."

Germanicus was clearly skeptical, but I was no less so, and I protested by saying, "I understand that I served in the Army of Pannonia, but it's been years. I don't see how I could possibly be any help." Struck by a thought, I pointed out, "I'm too far removed by now. Atticus was my Primus Pilus, but he hasn't been in that post for some time, ever since he was named Camp Prefect. And," I added, "let's not forget why I was transferred from the 8th to the 1st. I can't imagine the men have forgotten that." Shaking my head, I said, "I'm sorry, sir, but I don't see how me going to Pannonia will help anything."

I could see that Germanicus was amenable to my argument, and I was certain that whatever Dolabella had in mind would be stopped right then, but then, Dolabella made what I thought an extremely odd request.

"Sir, may I speak to Pullus privately?"

This obviously startled Germanicus as much as it did me, but he nodded his permission, and Dolabella motioned to me to follow him out of the office. Although I did so, I was not happy about it; too many times I had found myself in a web of Dolabella's making, so I was preparing myself for telling him that I had no intention of being entangled in this one; that I was completely unprepared for what was coming is an understatement. Following him out of Germanicus' office, we retreated to the same corner we had been not long before, but Dolabella was careful to check for any prying ears before he turned to me.

"There's something you should know, Pullus," he began. "Something about who's involved in what's happening in Pannonia."

This elicited a sudden rush of icy cold that was so overpowering that it made my fingers tingle. It is a funny thing about a man's mind, how it will go to extraordinary lengths to protect itself, and this moment was no exception. Only now, with the distance of some time, as little as it may be, can I see how a part of me instantly understood Dolabella, and about whom he was speaking, yet in the moment, I refused to make that association.

"Who?" I heard myself gasp. "Not Asinius!"

Dolabella physically jerked, staring at me in disbelief, and he assured me, "No, not Asinius." He stared up at me for a long moment, and I got the sense that he was trying not to say the name that, by this point in time, I knew was on the tip of his tongue. Which I refused to acknowledge, prompting him to close his eyes for a brief instant, then say aloud, "Titus Domitius. He's one of the leaders of this rebellion."

Titus Domitius, the man who had befriended me as a fresh-faced *tiro* when I enlisted in my father's old Legion, the 8th, the grandson of my Avus' childhood friend, Vibius Domitius. The man with whom, on one memorable night, I had been forced to flee over extremely rough ground, simply to stay alive during the rebellion of the Colapiani. He had been my close comrade during my time in the 8th, the holder of my will, and I had been a guest in the home he had made with his woman Petrilla more times than I could count. I had also trusted Domitius more times than I could count, but I know he would have said the same. Despite our family history, which I had been worried about from the moment I first learned of his identity, Domitius was, and many ways still is, the closest friend I have ever had, no matter what transpired between us. Although I had been with the 1st for a decade by this point, I had kept up my correspondence with Domitius, but within a matter of heartbeats after Dolabella informed me that Domitius was one of the ringleaders of the Pannonian rebellion, I realized that, while I had continued sending him letters, he had not responded for at least a year. Up until this instant, I had put the lack of return mail down to him being busy – he had a family, after all, and he had been promoted into the Centurionate, currently serving as the Secundus Hastatus Superior – but now I was confronted with an uglier possibility, that he had not written me because he was busy planning this insurrection. Dolabella spared me no detail, describing to an uncomfortable degree the level of Domitius' involvement in the mutiny of the 8th Legion in particular, and the other Pannonian Legions.

"I wouldn't put him at the very top of the men responsible for this," Dolabella told me, "but he's probably in the top three or four men involved."

Despite this being a cold comfort, I confess to a small glimmer of, if not happiness, then at least pride that Domitius had this level of influence among his comrades. I made sure this did not reflect in my expression as I listened to Dolabella continue.

"I think that if anyone can reach Domitius and the men of the 8th, you'd be at top of that list," Dolabella said, yet while I was always suspicious of this man, as I stared into the one eye that was looking into mine, I did not sense any deceit there, and I suppose a part of me responded to this flattery, no matter how true it may have been. Even more unusual was Dolabella reaching out to grasp me by the arm as he finished urgently, "Pullus, I need you to come with me to Pannonia. We're supposed to meet Drusus, but," suddenly, his voice dropped even lower, and he took a quick glance around as he whispered, "Drusus isn't Germanicus. I'm afraid, and," his expression turned even grimmer, "I think Tiberius feels the same way, that Drusus will need...help."

"To do what?" I countered, still unwilling to commit to this, although I confess the idea of seeing Domitius again, no matter the circumstances, was tempting.

"To try and keep Drusus from making matters worse." Dolabella did not hesitate. "If he's left to his own devices and without anyone to control him, there's no telling how bad he'll make things."

"What about Germanicus?" I asked, but again, he did not waver, responding, "Between Germanicus and Drusus, I'd trust Germanicus much more than I trust Drusus to handle a delicate matter in a way that causes the least amount of trouble."

He hesitated, and I understood why when he said, "Pullus, I know you don't trust me, at least under normal circumstances.

But these aren't normal circumstances. I'm asking you. No," he shook his head, "I'm *begging* you to come with me to Pannonia."

Honestly, he had me convinced already, but having Tiberius Dolabella, a man who, over the years, had created so much trouble for me as he worked first for Augustus, then Tiberius, begging me was something that I could not help enjoying.

Regardless of my personal feelings, all I told him was, "If Germanicus allows it, I'll go."

He immediately spun about and reentered the office, but when I moved to follow him in, he turned and motioned me to stay where I was. For some reason, and for one of the only occasions, I did not argue, nor did I try to follow him into the office, choosing instead to sit back down and wait. Asprenas had been off doing something with some of his Tribune friends; by this point, we had begun switching off being present while we waited for the messenger, who had turned out to be Dolabella, and as I waited to hear my fate, Asprenas returned, heading directly for me with an inquiring expression.

"I just heard from one of the guards outside that a courier's arrived," he said, but there was an extra layer of tension, which was explained when he said, "and the guard said that, while he doesn't know the courier's name, he says that he's a man who usually carries messages for Tiberius."

I agreed by saying, "His name's Dolabella, and yes, he does." Asprenas turned, acting as if he intended to go into the office, and I said, "I don't think that's a good idea right now, Tribune."

I was not surprised when he shot me an annoyed look, that air of disdain at being spoken to by an inferior resurfacing, though it was just a glimmer, but I was a bit surprised that he heeded me, muttering to himself as he came to my side and leaned against the wall. Fortunately, at least for Asprenas, we did not have long to wait; the door was opened by Dolabella, and we heard Germanicus call for us. My heart was beating quite a bit more quickly than normal for just sitting down, and I was in a unique state of mind, one where I was equally torn. On the one hand, I felt my duty was to go back to Germania and help Germanicus in restoring order to the Legions there, especially the 1st, but I could not deny that the pull exerted on my heart by the knowledge that I conceivably had an opportunity to reunite with Titus Domitius, Asinius, Galens, and many others was very strong as well. That short walk into the office seemed much longer than it had been every other time I made it, and I scanned Dolabella's face as I entered, trying to get a hint of what lay ahead for me, and for the Army of the Rhenus. Germanicus was still seated behind his desk, but while he was normally expressive and not one for hiding his feelings, this time, his face was a mask. Thankfully, he was not disposed to keep either of us in suspense.

"I've received instructions from my father," he began, "but when he issued them, he was unaware of what was happening in Germania." My heart sank, thinking that I was about to hear that we were in for another wait. Then, he paused for a deep breath and continued, "However, I was just informed that he is sending my brother Drusus to Pannonia, and while his instructions are to join him there, since Drusus has been given *imperium* by our father to act on his behalf, I've decided that I'm going to Germania immediately."

Now, this was not exactly the situation that Dolabella had described; nevertheless, I did not try to hide my relief, nor did Asprenas, who let out an explosive breath that he had obviously been holding in as he listened. Relieved as I was, I also was waiting to see if Dolabella had been successful in his plea for me to go with him to Pannonia.

"Tribune," Germanicus addressed Asprenas, "you need to go get ready. We leave at first light, and we're going to be riding hard." For a moment, Asprenas did not move, and I felt his eyes go towards me, clearly expecting me to go with him, which Germanicus caught and correctly interpreted. "The Princeps Prior and I have some things to discuss. However, you're dismissed."

Asprenas stiffened, coming to *intente*, although I suspect some of his rigidity was an automatic response to what he took as a rebuke, but he rendered a salute, executed an about-turn, and marched out of the office, leaving me alone with Germanicus and Dolabella.

We waited for the door to close, and once I heard the latch engage, only then did Germanicus speak again, saying evenly, "I won't waste time here, either. Pullus, I know that you're aware that Dolabella has asked for your presence down in Pannonia." I simply nodded, which was enough for him, and he leaned back in his chair, eyeing me closely, then asked, "What are your thoughts on that, Pullus? Where do you think you'd be of more use?"

This was completely unexpected, although when I thought about it immediately afterward, I suppose I should not have been surprised, given the capacity under which I had served Germanicus as his Primus Pilus, when he had never been shy about asking for my advice. I suppose I assumed that, after all that he had been through, and the inevitable seasoning brought on by passing years, he would not have been as disposed to ask.

In the moment, I tried to think through the conflicting swirl of thoughts and emotions I was feeling, then before it fully formed in my mind, I said, "I think I should go to Pannonia, sir."

Germanicus did not respond immediately, just kept looking at me for a long moment, his face giving nothing away, to the point where I convinced myself that I had given him an answer that displeased him.

Finally, he said, "I agree." Turning to Dolabella, he added, "You have my permission to bring Pullus with you to Pannonia. But," he warned, "I expect him back as soon as those troubles are over, do you understand?" While I appreciated that he seemed to think I was valuable to him where I was, I did not think this admonition was all that necessary, but then Germanicus said something that chilled my blood. "He's not to be used for any of those…special tasks that my father's used him for in the past, which I know you're involved with as well. Pullus is still in the 1st Legion, which is part of the Army of the Rhenus. I am *Propraetor* of that province, which means that every Roman, citizen or Legionary, is my responsibility, and I will not have him doing any of those things as long as he is under my command. Is that understood?"

By the time he had finished, Germanicus' voice had turned hard, his tone flat and, frankly, for the first time since I knew him, there was a sense of menace in it that I saw was not my imagination, just by the manner in which Dolabella visibly flinched, and what little color had come back into his face since his arrival once more drained away.

"Understood."

Dolabella's meek acceptance of this condition underscored that this man, who had been playing the very dangerous game of serving the interests of the rulers of Rome, recognized that Germanicus was every bit as dangerous and powerful as any of them.

"Well, Pullus," Germanicus stood, then leaned over the desk to offer his arm to me, "you should get some rest. You'll be leaving just as early as we will." He gave me a mischievous grin, and I was certain I knew what was coming, which he affirmed by teasing, "Now go give Latobius an apple." Then the smile vanished and he said soberly, "And may Fortuna bless you and your efforts to help my brother. I suspect," he finished grimly, "he's going to need it."

Saluting, I turned and left the room, leaving Dolabella standing there, my mind once more awash in the emotions unleashed by this twist in fate.

Dolabella looked better the next morning, though not by much, and despite my feelings for the man generally, I did feel a stab of sympathy. He was older than I was by about seven years, and I knew how much longer it took me to recover from a stretch of hard travel now that I was older. It did relieve us of the need to have a conversation, and it was reminiscent of my journey with Asprenas, who was now accompanying Germanicus on a hard ride back to Ubiorum, or perhaps Mogontiacum, where the miles initially passed in silence. It was when we arrived in the town of Cabillonum, another former stronghold of the Aedui, and we did not turn east to take the road to Vesontio that I was moved to speak to Dolabella.

"Why aren't we going that way?" I asked Dolabella. "That's shorter."

"It is," he agreed, "but it's slower. Remember, I've spent the last fifteen years traveling all over this side of Our Sea." He turned and grinned at me, but it was not with his usual sly malice, saying, "You're going to have to start trusting me at some point, Pullus. It might as well be now."

I immediately knew there was no arguing this, so I did not try. When we reached Lugdunum, late the first day, we stopped only long enough to switch out our horses, each of us once more taking two spares, and buy some meat pies from a vendor. As an experienced traveler, this was Dolabella's suggestion, that whenever possible we buy food that was already cooked, and thereby saving the rations we had brought along with us for those times where we could not do so, which we could eat in the saddle. Reaching Vienne after dark, where once more we did not turn east by taking the road to Augusta Praetoria, only then did I begin to have a suspicion about what might be going on.

Turning on Dolabella, I asked suspiciously, "Where exactly are we going?"

"To Siscia, of course!" he answered, but I was not thrown off, and even in the dark, I saw he was refusing to look in my direction.

"By way of where, exactly?" I asked Dolabella.

Sighing, only then did he turn to face me, and he answered evenly, "We're going all the way down to the coast, then we're following the coast on the Via Aurelia."

While I heard him clearly enough, I was not quite believing my ears.

"That means we're heading to Arelate."

"Well," Dolabella answered blandly, "if we plan on taking the Via Aurelia, then yes, we are going through Arelate."

"But that's my home." Even to my ears, I sounded dazed.

"Yes, Pullus, I know that," Dolabella acknowledged, and only then did he turn to look at me as he finished, "and I think we can probably spare a watch for you to visit your family home." With a shrug, he added, "We have to stop to rest at some point, and it might as well be there."

This was too much for me to take in, and on an impulse, I suddenly kicked the horse I was riding in the ribs, forgetting that Latobius was on a lead, so it did not reply immediately, which only served to make me feel a bit more foolish. Finally, I got the beast moving, with Latobius and the other spare mount trailing behind me, working it up to a canter as I fled from Dolabella so that he would not see me cry. It took some time for me to get control of my emotions, but I finally did, and drew up to a halt to wait for Dolabella to reach me. Seeing him coming out of the gloom, I was in a bit of a quandary about how to approach the question that was foremost in my mind.

Which, of course, meant that I immediately blurted out, "Why are you doing this for me? I mean," I added, "given that our relationship has been…"

I trailed off, certain I did not need to expand, and I could see Dolabella understood, which was confirmed as he said lightly, "Troublesome? Is that the word you're looking for?"

He said it in such a way that, despite my continuing distrust of the man, I could not help myself, and I laughed, agreeing, "That's certainly one way to put it. So, yes, let's settle for 'troublesome.'"

He had been smiling, but I saw it vanish in the light of the half-moon, and he did not answer immediately. Indeed, I was just beginning to believe that he had no intention of saying anything when, at last, he resumed speaking.

"I suppose I could give you some *cac* about how it serves the interests of our new *Imperator*, but I suspect you'd see through that fairly quickly." He was looking ahead, not meeting my gaze. "And, as you know very well yourself by now, Tiberius isn't much for taking into consideration the feelings of other people, especially those of us who have served him." This, honestly, made me acutely uncomfortable, and I had known Dolabella long and well enough to hear the undisguised bitterness in his voice, speaking the words of a man who had endured the indifferent treatment from Tiberius more than I had, and perhaps more than just about anyone else. Still, I did not stop him, just continued looking at him until he continued, "But that's only part of it, Titus." This was when he looked over at me, as if gauging my reaction to his use of my *praenomen*, which was the first time he had done so in quite some time, but I did not object, which seemed to please him. "The truth is that, as I've gotten older, I've come to realize all that I've sacrificed to serve others. Not," he allowed, "in the most honorable manner, and certainly not as honorable as you and the men of the Legions."

Now this was one of the more startling conversations I had had with Dolabella, but I did not accept what he was saying, shaking my head as I reminded him, "Don't include me in that, Dolabella. You know more about the things I've done for

Tiberius than anyone, so I'm not even a shade of those men you're talking about."

"The only reason," Dolabella countered, "you did what you did was because you were forced to." There was a distinct pause then, and once more, he turned to look me directly in the eye as he went on, "And while you were forced to by Tiberius, and," he allowed, "the Princeps, they did it with my help. All I can say in my defense was that, at the time, I thought I was doing it for the good of the Republic. Now?" He heaved a huge sigh, one that was more expressive of his turmoil than his actual words, which were, "Now I don't even know why I'm doing what I do. Somewhere along the way, the meaning of it all got lost." As I absorbed this, we rode along in silence, then he shifted in his saddle, shrugging as he said simply, "This is my own way of making amends, as sorry as it may be, for the role I played in corrupting you."

How, I wondered, do I respond to that? The simple truth is that, after all that had transpired between Tiberius Dolabella and me over the years, there was a part of me that still did not trust the man. I will not deny that there was also a part of me that wanted to believe him, but too much had happened for me to be instantly convinced of his sincerity, here on this road south to my home.

However, I was not so ungrateful that I said nothing, choosing to say only, "Thank you…Tiberius. I appreciate that."

Happily, this seemed to be all that he expected, and while I may have still held some doubts about his motives, I chose to believe that the smile he gave me was genuine.

The walls of the city where my childhood home is located are visible from several miles away when approaching from the north, so I had more than enough time to work up a case of nerves. My parents were dead, as were two of my siblings who had survived childhood, Sextus of course, and Valeria, who had died in childbirth. That left Gaius, Septimus and Miriam, with Gaius being the oldest surviving sibling, and it was with a sense of shock when I realized that he would be nearing his thirtieth name day. Part of the cause of my nervousness was based in the fact that I barely knew my younger brothers; I had left when they were still very young, although oddly enough, I knew Miriam better, simply because she was the family favorite. She had married, but she still lived in Arelate, her husband a member of the equestrian order, which may seem odd since we were officially members of the Head Count. However, there are few secrets in small towns, although Arelate had since grown into what can be described as a small city, but the Pullus family was never truly considered a member of the lower classes, despite our name being inscribed in the rolls as such, thanks to the enmity the Princeps held towards my Avus. Speaking of the man himself, much, if not most of this viewpoint came directly from the first and greatest Titus Pullus, a man who I had finally come to accept I would never even hope to match in his renown and fame. A truly remarkable man, he was one of the only men of his class for whom the combination of his fame and the wealth that was built on the strength of his right arm, and advanced even farther than the peerless Diocles, transcended the invisible but very real bonds of the Roman class system.

Speaking of Diocles, I was always mindful that I had left Alex behind in Germania, but such was my faith in Germanicus that I was not that worried that he was in danger. It did not mean that I did not feel a pang of regret he was not with me, since I would be seeing his mother Birgit, and his brothers and sisters. It had been quite a fight to get Birgit to move back to Arelate after Sextus was killed, and I was not all that certain that she had forgiven me for exercising my status as *paterfamilias* of Diocles' family in forcing her to move. Her mother had died by this time, so I could understand why she did not feel any strong pull to the city, but I was certain then, and even with the trepidation I felt as we approached the city, I still was confident I had made the correct decision in sending her back, especially now with yet another rebellion in Pannonia, just five years after the end of the Batonian revolt. Ultimately, none of that mattered; what did was how Birgit viewed my sudden appearance, as well as my brothers. I suppose that, if I had given it more thought, it might have occurred to me that it was likely that one or both of my brothers were absent from Arelate; if only that had been true, perhaps I could have been spared from so much heartache and shock. While it seemed to take forever, we finally reached the gates of the city, immediately given entrance because of the pass imprinted with the seal of the new *Imperator* that Dolabella flashed to the guards, and we rode through the gates. Immediately, I could see the changes wrought by the growth of the city, starting with the fact that the walls had been moved out well more than two hundred paces, probably closer to three hundred. I knew this by the absence of the huge tree that had been just a matter of a dozen paces outside of the northern gate; at first, I assumed that it had been cut down, but it was only after we were inside the walls that I saw that it had not been removed, but now served as the basis of a small park, where a fountain bubbled the waters from the aqueduct that fed the city its fresh water, which we called the Julian Aqueduct, although I do not know if Divus Julius actually ordered its construction. Since he had been responsible for founding the veterans' colony here, I suppose it was natural that his name be applied to the aqueduct, along with a number of other official structures. That the tree was almost a furlong inside the walls was the most potent sign of how much Arelate had grown since the last time I had been there. Still, there was enough familiar that it was not a challenge to navigate my way, while Dolabella rode at my side, but slightly behind me, content to allow me to lead the way. All the sights, sounds, and smells assailed me, plunging me back to what, when all things are considered, was an idyllic childhood. The baker my family used was still in business, and even later in the day, the aromas of freshly baking bread reminded me of how Sextus and I, despite neither of us needing to do so, stole a fresh loaf, simply for the thrill; it was not until I was a grown man that I learned that this was one of a dozen businesses in which my Avus, with Diocles acting as his agent, owned, so we essentially had stolen from ourselves, which probably explains why we were never caught. On the other side of the street, I saw what I assumed to be the son of the man who had sold wine to my family, while next to his shop, there was a butcher shop, the smell of draining blood and fresh meat competing with all the other smells. I did not take the most direct route, choosing instead to take a more circuitous path that brought me to the theater, which had just been completed the last time I had been in Arelate, when I escorted Diocles' remains home to honor his final wish, to be interred next to my Avus. It was impressive, but I was more interested in the business that was located a short distance away, down the same street, with only an *insula* separating it, the *ludus* where Maximus Vulso, the *lanista*, had taught me how to fight like a gladiator. Of course, Vulso had long since retired, dying peacefully not long after my father, but it was still owned by my family. That was what I thought, anyway, until we drew up in front of it, and I sat Latobius, staring up at the unfamiliar sign that was hung above the gateway. My first thought was that, for some reason, my father had decreed the name be changed before he died; then, I recalled the letter I had received from Miriam, informing me that, in my absence and with Sextus' death, my brother Gaius was now running matters concerning the family. That this letter was actually written in my sister's hand, and not dictated, was a source of quiet pride in our family, since my father had decreed that, when Diocles became our tutor, the women of the family be included. To a point, it should be said; they were expected to be literate, but they did not have lessons in Greek, or rhetoric, or mathematics that the Pullus boys received, secretly of course, but I recall at the time being jealous that my sisters' afternoons were free, because I would have much rather been on the back of Ocelus, roaming the countryside and undoubtedly getting into some sort of trouble. Pausing only briefly at the gates of the *ludus*, I shrugged, thinking I would simply ask Gaius when I got to the villa.

"Pullus," Dolabella's voice interrupted my thoughts, and I turned to see him regarding me with a peculiar expression, but I understood why when he said, "delay isn't something we can afford to do. Remember where we're heading and why. We can't spend as much time here as I'm sure you'd like."

I did not answer him verbally, but I knew he was right, although I was still grappling with why this man, who had been an adversary for years and, while most of the time he was relaying orders from above, had placed me in moments of peril, was showing me this kindness. In answer, I turned about, headed back towards the forum, and within a span of perhaps fifty heartbeats, I saw the wall surrounding my home. The gate was closed, but when I tried to open it, I discovered it was barred, and although that was not unusual, especially since I was not expected, I did feel a bit odd standing outside my own house, unable to enter. Using the iron knocker that signaled whoever was inside that there was a visitor, I had to do it twice before the small window in the postern door was opened. The eye that peered out was unfamiliar to me, and it suddenly widened as it took in the sight of me, though I was only dressed in a soldier's tunic and *baltea*, but that was not unusual and was something I had seen happen my entire life.

"M-master Titus?" I did not recognize the voice either. "You *are* Titus Pullus, yes?"

He had spoken enough to place the accent as Gallic, and I tried to remember if we had any of them in our employ the last time I was here, but I could not recall.

346

"Yes," I answered, "it's me."

The eye disappeared, but I immediately heard the locking bar being lifted, then one of the gates swung open.

"I'll be at that tavern on the other corner of the forum," Dolabella told me, already turning away to head in that direction.

I do not know why, but I called out to him, "No. Wait."

Turning back, he looked curious, but he was as unprepared to hear it as I was to say, "Come in. You can get something to eat here. And," I grinned, "we have better wine."

A sudden rush of embarrassment caused me to turn back to lead Latobius and the other horses through the gate, not seeing if he followed, but my ears told me that he did so. Now that I could see the owner of the eye, I knew I had never seen him before; that was not the disturbing part. Around his neck was a bronze placard that signified he was a slave, which is an extremely common sight. That it was inscribed with my family name, however, caused me to stop and stare down at it with a frown, which the slave, a slightly built man around thirty or thereabouts, interpreted as displeasure, and he dropped to his knees immediately, bending over at my feet.

"Have I displeased you, Master Titus?" His voice was slightly muffled because his face was so close to the ground, then he turned his face upward, and while I was as aware of the manner in which slaves try to manipulate their masters' feelings when it is in their interest to do so, I was certain the fear in his eyes was unfeigned. "Please, Master," he begged me, "tell me what I have done to offend you! I apologize profusely, whatever it is!"

A moment ago, I had been embarrassed by my gesture of hospitality to Dolabella; now, I was mortified at this display, and I reached down to grasp the slave by the arm, gently pulling him to his feet as I assured him, "You did no such thing. I'm not displeased in any way. I'm just...surprised, that's all."

347

Naturally, the slave allowed me to do so, yet his face still betrayed a caution that indicated to me he thought I might be playing some sort of cruel trick on him, and now I was deeply disturbed, which led me to do something I normally would not have done to a strange slave.

"The reason I'm surprised is that my family stopped keeping slaves a long time ago," I explained to him, which clearly was news to him.

"I wouldn't know anything about that Master," he told me, keeping his eyes averted. "I've only been here for a little more than a year."

That, I thought, explains it, at least a little bit, since that meant it was after my father had died.

Understanding there was no point in continuing this discussion, at least with a slave, instead I told him, "Please see to these horses, and to my…friend here," even though the word felt strange in my mouth, I made a clear gesture to Dolabella, who had since dismounted. "Now," I asked, "are either of my brothers here?"

"Only Master Septimus is right now," the slave answered readily enough, "but Master Gaius is out in town doing some business. He's expected back shortly."

I suppose my exchange with this slave served as a warning to expect the unexpected, yet even so, when I walked to the entrance to the villa and once more knocked on the door, heard the kind of light footfall that told me it was a female, I was still unprepared to see Birgit answer the door. And, as unexpected as it was for me, it was more so for Birgit, who collapsed in a dead faint at my feet. Such was my homecoming.

Chapter Seven

"Things are...different here, Titus."

Thankfully, Birgit had revived quickly, hugging me fiercely, then completely unsurprisingly immediately began besieging me with questions about Alex, not only asking how he was but demanding to know why he was not with me.

"I didn't know I'd be coming through Arelate! I swear on the black stone!" I was laughing as I said it, but I was serious, remembering that for a small woman, Birgit was someone one did not want to trifle with, especially when she was angry.

Fortunately, she accepted this and led me by the hand past the *triclinium* and into the main room, and I suppose that this was when it finally hit me: my parents were dead. As strange as it might seem to say it, what I understood as I surveyed the room, essentially unchanged since the last time I had been here, was that this was the first moment where I actually thought about and accepted that my parents were dead. According to Roman law and custom, that made me *paterfamilias,* yet I also realized that, when it came to the running of the various enterprises owned or partially owned by my family, the responsibility for which Gaius had been charged by my father, both when he was alive and in his will, I had not received any correspondence from my brother for some time. Perhaps Birgit somehow sensed my thoughts; more likely, it was just a natural moment to bring it up, because she led me to the table, where she made a point of sitting me down in what had been my father's spot.

This was just sinking in as well, that this was my rightful spot, as Birgit sat on the bench to my right, and with a glance in the direction of the doorway that led into the rest of the house, she repeated quietly, "Titus, things have...changed here." While I still thought of her as a beauty, she suddenly looked tired, or more accurately, worried, and she heaved a sigh as she told me, "Gaius has had some…setbacks managing your interests, Titus. And," she placed a hand on my arm, her tone earnest, "he was very young for so much responsibility."

This got my attention, and I felt my first stab of unease, which only mixed in with the other things I was feeling, but before I could question Birgit further, I heard a commotion, and the door opened. Through it walked a man, a young man to be certain, though it was not his age I noticed, and I was suddenly seized by such a powerful feeling of an emotion that I could not readily identify, because my initial impression was that, somehow, Sextus had come back to life.

"Septimus?" I gasped, because in that brief moment, I did recall that, as a child, he had favored my younger brother. "Is that you?"

Although Septimus nodded, when he opened his mouth, nothing came out, while Birgit, watching this, remarked dryly, "Yes, the resemblance is uncanny, isn't it, Titus?"

The mention of my name seemed to yank my youngest brother from his dazed state, one with which I could certainly identify, and I felt my legs shaking when I stood up, as Septimus gasped and essentially repeated my own words, "Titus? Is it really you?"

Despite the awkwardness, I had to laugh, and I answered him, "Do you know anyone else this size who looks like you?"

This seemed to break the dam, and he crossed the room, while I met him halfway, but when he held out his arm, in the manner of Roman men who are just meeting each other for the first time, I ignored it to sweep him into an embrace. I suspect I squeezed the life half out of him, yet he did not seem to mind all that much, as we both laughed and talked at the same time. At some point in this, I glanced over to see Birgit, still seated, but looking up at us with tears streaming down her face, and I wondered how hard it must have been for her as Septimus grew up and looked more like our brother, her love and the father of young Gaius. Finally, I let go of my little brother, and we stepped away from each other, but thinking of Sextus prompted me to turn and ask Birgit where her children were.

"They are here and about," she assured me. "I'll send Nasua to find them."

"Nasua?" I was unfamiliar with the name, while Birgit and Septimus glanced at each other, as if they were silently willing each other to say something, so I solved the problem by guessing, "Is he the slave who met me at the door?"

My guess, as it turned out, was incorrect, as Birgit shook her head, saying, "No, that's Berdic."

"How many slaves do we have?" I asked. "The last time I was here, only Chickpea was left."

Once more, there was a silent exchange between the two, but this time, it was Septimus who admitted, "Honestly, I don't know. Gaius has leased some out to other businesses around town, and then there are some that work for us directly."

Birgit interjected something, correcting a misassumption on my part. "Chickpea wasn't a slave, Titus. Once Gaius brought them in, he was dismissed."

All of this disturbed me; it had been my mother, born a slave, who had insisted that our family divest ourselves of any servant in bondage, and now here I was hearing that Gaius was going against her wishes. In turn, this led to another thought, even more unsettling than the first.

"When did this start?" I had to swallow the lump that formed as I asked, "Was this our father's decision?"

"No." Both Septimus and Birgit answered in unison, but she left it to my brother to tell me, "Gaius started buying slaves not long after Tata died."

What else has he been up to? I wondered, but I kept that to myself.

351

Suddenly, I remembered something, and I turned to Birgit, asking her, "Can you see to the needs of the man who's with me? His name's Dolabella, and I imagine that he's waiting in the *triclinium* by now. I told," I had to recall the name I had just heard, "Berdic to take care of the horses and Dolabella. Just make sure he has whatever he needs."

I do not know why, given all that I had learned, but instead of Birgit hurrying away, she simply walked over to another new addition to our home, a bell, hanging from the wall. After she yanked the cord a couple of times, I do not believe a count of five passed before another person arrived, this one a female. A young, very comely female, who entered the room with her eyes cast demurely down, but it was what she did that shocked me, dropping to her knees in front of Birgit.

"Yes, Mistress?"

As troubling as her demeanor was, her accent rocked me to my core; it had been a few years, but I knew when someone was from one of the Pannonia tribes, the Breuci specifically, and this young woman was definitely speaking with that particular affectation.

This prompted me to ask her, in her tongue, "What's your name, girl?"

Naturally, hearing this huge Roman speaking her own language caused her to gasp in shock, causing her to lift her head and stare up at me with wide, expressive eyes; despite the circumstances, I could not help noticing what a beauty she was, and the corresponding stirring within me at the sight.

"J-Juno, Master," she answered me, but I shook my head, and trying to keep my tone gentle, I admonished, "No, girl. Your real name. Not the one you were given by…us."

It felt awkward to include myself in this, whatever it was, but I knew that she was unlikely to view me as being separate from her owner since we were Roman, and he was presumably my brother.

352

This seemed to ignite a spark in her, and for the first time, she showed a hint of the kind of pride that the Breuci are known for, answering me, "Algaia, Master."

"Well, Algaia," I continued speaking to her in her tongue, "stand up. And please see to my guest in the *triclinium*. Give him anything he asks for."

She did not respond immediately, looking over to Birgit, who gave her a nod, though I have no idea how much Birgit understood. It was true she had spent a fair amount of time in Siscia and had undoubtedly picked up a few words, but dialects vary widely among the tribes. I had to suppress a flash of irritation that the girl looked to Birgit for confirmation, though it made sense. Rising to her feet, there was no hiding the lithe grace with which she moved, and I caught Septimus staring after her hungrily; when he finally tore his eyes away from her retreating figure, he saw me watching him and turned a deep red. I gave him a grin and a lifted eyebrow, but while he smiled back, he said something that seemed odd in the moment.

"Gaius isn't going to be happy," he commented but refused to say anything more when I pressed him.

When I turned to Birgit, her face had suddenly assumed a carefully neutral expression, yet at my silent inquiry, all she said was, "Gaius has certain…standards for the slaves."

The more I was hearing, the more disturbed I was getting; worse, for everyone involved, I was getting angry.

"When is he expected back?" I asked Birgit.

"Soon," was her only answer.

Seeing that I had to be content with that, I said nothing else, though within no more than a handful of heartbeats later, there was another commotion, except this came from deeper within the house, and I heard footsteps descending the stairs that were made by more than one person. As I turned in that direction, yet another beautiful young woman entered the room, but she was no slave, and I recognized her immediately.

Nevertheless, out of reflex, I stood up and gasped, "Gisela?" Looking over at Birgit for confirmation, she nodded, an expression on her face that I had seen my mother wear whenever she looked at Valeria, the pride a mother has for a beautiful daughter. "This can't be Gisela!"

Laughing, she assured me, "It is, Uncle Titus! I just grew up."

That, I thought, was one way of putting it, but she had already crossed the room at a run to throw herself into my arms, and this time, I was the one struggling for breath as she hugged my neck fiercely. Naturally, to do so, she had to leap upward, so her feet were several inches off the ground, which did not help my air supply. Still, if I had to suffocate, being smothered by someone who loved me was not a bad way to go. Putting her down, I looked past her to see Scribonia, who was now almost fifteen, and I realized that the last time I had seen Diocles' other children, Gisela had been Scribonia's age. Now, the only one of Diocles' children missing was Titus, but when I asked Birgit where he was, a shadow flitted across her face reminiscent of when my brother Gaius' name had been mentioned. Before I could ask more, the final, and in some ways, the most painful reminder of all that our family had lost came trailing in, eyeing me with open curiosity, but no real recognition.

"Gaius," Birgit beckoned to him, "come greet your Uncle Titus. Don't you remember him?"

"Not really," he admitted, which did sting a bit, but I could not blame him, given how young he was when I packed his mother and the family off for Arelate.

Still, he did come forward to greet me, but then as he got close and he naturally had to crane his neck to look up at me, suddenly, a light of recognition flickered in his eyes.

"I...I think I *do* remember you." With all eyes on him, he seemed embarrassed, and he shrugged and mumbled, "I just remember a giant who let me ride on his shoulders."

"That," I was smiling, but he was shimmering because of the rush of tears that flooded my vision, "was me." Then, on an inspiration, I reached out, tweaked his nose, then presented him with my fist, except with my thumb protruding from my fingers as I told him, "And I used to steal your nose, just like I did now."

His eyes went wide, but it was the sudden grin that made my heart feel like it would burst.

Laughing in delight, he cried, "I remember that! You're...Uncle Ti."

Now he was joined by all of us, me more than any of them because this was absolutely true; Gaius had been at an age where, apparently, my *praenomen* was too much for him to say, and he had shortened it to just "Ti," something that was quite amusing to all of us. With the exception, perhaps, of his brother, also named Titus, and this memory jerked my thoughts back to where Diocles' youngest son was, and more importantly, what he was up to, but even as young Gaius hugged me around the waist and I was about to turn back to Birgit to ask more, there was yet another commotion. This time, however, it was because of the arrival of my brother Gaius, who burst into the room angrily, his face dark with fury.

"Why isn't Berdic waiting for me?" I heard him yell before he actually entered the room from the direction of the rear entrance, and naturally, we all turned as he stormed into the room in the middle of saying, "By the gods, I'll flog him again for this!"

I did not make a conscious decision; at least, I do not remember it, but I do recall crossing the room. I also remember grabbing my younger brother by the front of his tunic, lifting him off the floor, and hurling him against the wall, his body slamming into it so hard that the plaster cracked, while his head whipped back with only slightly less force, smacking into the wall hard enough that I knocked him senseless. Dropping him in a heap to the floor, unconscious, I became aware of the sudden,

355

shocked silence in the room, and I turned to see all of them, both families of mine, staring at me in wide-eyed horror and fear.

Rather than apologize, I said, "When he comes to, tell him he's to meet me in Avus' library."

Then, without saying another word, I strode past them and stomped up the stairs.

Entering this room, even in my enraged state, which I was pleased to see was essentially unchanged, evoked even more powerful memories, not just of my Avus, but of my father. It was in this room that we discussed my joining the Legions, something that, while he certainly did not forbid it, neither did he encourage, and he gave me the ultimate compliment for me at the time, talking to me as a grown man. He held nothing back, nothing at all, yet I was undeterred, and now, standing there surveying the shelves crammed full of scrolls that make up a library that I knew was superior to even those of some men of the Senatorial class, I had no regrets for the path I chose. Still, seeing what was my Avus' pride and joy, which brought him such comfort in his last years, only served to remind me of how I had fallen short of even matching his deeds, let alone surpassing them as I had vowed to do, back when I was a callow boy who had no idea of what it took. I had turned forty, this the year of the death of the Princeps, and while I was a Centurion of a first line Cohort, I was not Pilus Prior; the first Titus Pullus had already been Primus Pilus of the Equestrians several years by this point. After a few moments just standing there, I found my feet moving, tentatively, towards the chair at the desk in the center of the room, and I sat down in it, somehow feeling as if I did not belong there, which I suppose is understandable. Settling down, I was still looking at all the scrolls, trying to remember which ones I had read and deciding which ones I would take with me when we resumed our journey. The light streaming through the open window was fading fast, reminding me that time was against me; I could only imagine what Dolabella, sitting in the *triclinium* and being treated as an honored guest, was thinking. Getting up, I found a tinder box and lit the lamps that illuminated the room, then sat back down. It was then I noticed a stack of wax tablets on the desk, and I reached out, took the one on top, and opened it. At first, I could not make any sense of it, then I gradually realized that what I was looking at were figures, and more quickly, I understood that these were sums of money. Matters only got worse from there, as I deciphered what I assumed was my brother Gaius' hand and his own unique method of record keeping. It was certainly not anything taught in the Legions, which made sense given that Gaius had never served under the standard, but before I had finished perusing the first tablet, I was wishing that I had not even opened it, as the bile came rushing up into my throat. The second tablet was no better news, but before I could finish it, I heard the sound of footsteps, and I laid the tablet down on the desk. Somewhat oddly, there was a knock on the door, which I had not been expecting, yet it somehow served as a signal to me as to how I would handle this moment.

"Enter!" I said sharply, just as if I was seated at my own desk in my office in Ubiorum.

And, just as often happened back in Ubiorum, the door opened very slowly, as if the person opening it was not eager to do so, which was understandable, and my brother's face peeked around the door.

"Get in here," I snapped.

His face flushed a deep red, and he opened his mouth as if to argue, then he seemed to be propelled into the room by an unseen force, which turned out to be my other brother Septimus, whose expression was almost impossible for me to read. Gaius stood there, staring at me defiantly, his fists balled up, but Pullus he may have been, trying to stand up to me after all the moments

357

like this that I had experienced, on both sides, as it were, meant that he quickly wilted under my hard, cold stare.

Pointing at one of the other chairs, I said curtly, "Sit." Then, I looked at Septimus, trying to decide whether he should stay, deciding at that instant, "You too, Septimus. You might as well be here for this."

He grabbed a chair, but I could not help noticing how he moved it, slightly farther away from his brother, and I wondered what that meant, though I made no comment, just tucking it away as an observation.

Picking up the first tablet I had perused, I opened it and turned it so Gaius could see the interior, where he had incised what, even to my unpracticed eye, I could see was a catastrophe for our family, asking, "Would you care to explain this, Gaius?"

"Explain what?" he replied, and I realized how little I knew about this man, despite him being my brother, yet even so, I was not willing to indulge in any back and forth, always conscious of the time pressure I was under, and I raised my voice just a fraction, countering, "You know exactly what I'm talking about!" Waving the tablet in his direction, I asked, "Are these figures correct?" My throat seemed to constrict as I continued, "Have you really lost our family more than a half million *sesterces*?"

I suspect that hearing it put so baldly served to deflate my brother, because his earlier show of defiance vanished, his shoulders slumping as he closed his eyes to break my stare.

"Yes." He whispered the word, but even knowing this to be the case, hearing it confirmed served as a punch in the gut, prompting me to say, "What? I couldn't hear you, Gaius. What did you say?"

Taking a deep breath, Gaius opened his eyes, yet he would not look at me directly, answering dully, "I said, yes, it's true."

"How?" I asked, truly wanting to know, my bewilderment outweighing my rage. "How could you lose that much money?"

The story came out, in fits and starts, but after perhaps a third of a watch, which I knew I could not afford, I had learned the essentials, and I felt numb. It all began with the drought four years earlier, when the Princeps was still alive, and all of Italia was still struggling to cope with the Varus disaster. My father was still alive at this point, but what I learned from Gaius, and Septimus confirmed, he had become more and more disinterested in the daily running of the family interests, in which he had taken on a more active role upon the death of Diocles. Essentially, he had given Gaius more and more control, but also more latitude to make his own decisions, and my brother was simply not capable of handling so much responsibility. While Gaius was relating how our family fortune, which at its peak could have technically bought the family a seat in the Senate were it not for Augustus, had been cut by more than half, I was reminded of something Sextus had told me when he arrived in Siscia, with Diocles and his family. In effect, he had warned me that both Gaius and Septimus had lived very different lives than Sextus and I had, since they had been born and raised in Arelate, after my father's injury and retirement from the Legion. Naturally, they had heard the stories that are part of every family's lore, although I rather think that it is unlikely other families have events where rebelling Pannonian tribes pursue them, and one of the children of that family kills a man when he is only ten years old. But hearing about them and actually living through them are far different matters, and my two younger brothers, as well as my sister Miriam, who had been born but was a babe in arms during our ordeal, had no experience of our family when we were just part of the faceless mass of the Head Count. Listening to Gaius, I was struck by how much he sounded, both in his mode of speech and his attitude, like Volusenus, especially when he first arrived to take the post his father had purchased for him. There was a haughtiness, as if

359

Gaius was daring me to find fault with him, his tone making it clear he believed that his older brother, by virtue of being nothing but a man of the Legions, could not possibly understand the intricacies of such matters. Despite an almost overwhelming urge to strike him, I forced myself to remain calm and listen. What became clear was that, despite his high opinion of himself, the consortium of merchants that he joined in this venture to profit from the misery brought on by drought saw him for what he was; a callow, arrogant youth whose belief in himself outstripped his actual ability. If I were to take Gaius' version as the accurate account of what had happened, then he was of course blameless, merely a victim of circumstances in the form of a storm that ravaged the fleet of grain ships coming from Egypt, in which my brother had been the major investor, something that only became clear after some pointed questions.

"So let me see if I understand this," I said, once he had finished, not able to resist adding, "in terms my simple mind can understand."

"I didn't say that you were…"

"Shut your mouth," I cut him off. "It's time for the *paterfamilias* to talk."

This was a deliberate use of the term on my part, both because, as I suspected it would, this angered him and also to remind him that, in fact, that was exactly what I was.

"Now," I began, "you put up almost the entire amount of hard cash to buy the grain, while your partners in this endeavor supplied other things, like the fleet of ships and the laborers to load and unload the ships."

"And," Gaius interjected, "the carters. They were an important part of this, because if we didn't have the means to haul the grain on the Via Aurelia to Rome, we would have ended up having to hire men piecemeal and pay a premium to do it. Using Avienus' people cut those costs in half. Also," he pointed out, "we needed storage space in the grain warehouses. I don't know if you're aware of this," his tone turned unbearably earnest, "but the grain warehouses are different from those used to store other goods. They're more tightly built, and they're also under heavier guard."

"Yes, of course, the carters," I agreed, but I could not keep the sarcasm from my voice. "We can't forget the carters or the special warehouses." Pausing for a moment, I went on, "So, everything's in place, and everything goes perfectly, until the storm that sank almost the entire fleet. Which, as you say, was an act of the gods that couldn't possibly be foreseen."

Nodding his head, Gaius agreed, which was not surprising.

"How many ships were lost?" I asked him, as if I was not only interested, but I accepted this version of events.

"Seventeen," he answered cautiously, "or so I believe."

Pouncing, I pretended to be puzzled. "What does that mean, 'so you believe'? Surely you saw the fleet when you inspected it before it sailed."

Now I was certain I knew the answer, yet when his face confirmed my belief before the words came out of his mouth, I still felt a stab of despair. Not, I should add, about the money that I was certain was lost forever, but that my brother could be such a combination of arrogant and stupid.

"Well, no," he admitted, "but what would that matter? I don't know anything about ships."

"No," I agreed, "but you'd at least see that there *was* a fleet. And," I pointed out, "you could have at least laid eyes on the master who was in command of this fleet."

"I *told* you! I told you that you were making a mistake!" Septimus burst out, adding his voice for the first time, rising from his chair.

"Shut your mouth!" Gaius snarled, also coming to his feet, and the pair faced off, fists clenched, faces red.

They, I thought wryly, are definitely brothers, and I was struck by a pang as I thought about the many times Sextus and I had tried to bash each other's brains in; however, this was neither the time nor the place, so I interjected in a conversational tone, "Both of you sit down, shut your mouths, or I'll beat both of you worse than anything you've ever experienced." Looking from one to the other, I asked reasonably, "Do either of you doubt that I can and I will?" As quickly as they had turned on each other, now both of my brothers were united, if their expressions were any guide, in turning their anger on me, which bothered me not at all. "I asked you a question," I put some iron in my tone, "and I expect a fucking answer." Deciding it would be appropriate to do so, I stood as well, although I did not move closer to them, just using the high ground offered by my height, and I saw both of their eyes glance down at my scarred left arm as if trying to determine how much power I was still capable of producing. Apparently, they came to the same decision individually because they both mumbled that they did not doubt my abilities. More sheepishly than with any defiance, they both resumed their seats, as did I, and I resumed my questioning with Gaius.

"So it's clear that you didn't actually meet with the master, nor did you actually see this fleet," I continued, and while he looked sullen, neither did he argue the point. A thought suddenly occurred to me, and I asked him, "Who arranged to contract with this fleet?"

"Avienus," he answered, then realizing the name was meaningless to me, "Decimus Avienus. He's the largest grain merchant in Arelate." Then, before I could respond, he shifted uncomfortably in his chair as he added, "At least, he *was* the largest grain merchant in Arelate."

Nodding that I understood that we were not the only ones who had been impacted, I asked him, "What about these carters you were talking about? Who did you deal with about that?"

"Avienus handled that," Gaius explained, which made sense, then he added, "as well as the warehouses."

"Well," I allowed, "I can see why he's not the biggest grain merchant anymore, since he had to pay for all of that."

Once again, I got my hint from Septimus, although he did not say anything; his expression was enough warning that there was something I was missing. It was from Gaius' lips, however, that suddenly, everything became clear, and much, much worse.

"Actually, Titus," Gaius said in a voice little more than a whisper, as he studied the floor at his feet, "Avienus isn't the biggest grain merchant anymore because he moved."

"He moved?" I echoed, though it was more to gain a moment of time, suddenly suspecting the worst. "Moved to where?"

"We don't know," Septimus spoke up.

"How much money did Avienus put into this joint venture?" I asked, yet I already knew the answer.

"Not much," Gaius answered miserably, but then Septimus made a noise, and I turned to see him glaring at Gaius, forcing his brother to admit with a heavy sigh, "All right. Nothing. He was only providing the services through his contacts and men he'd worked with before." Perhaps it was hearing it aloud, but he was not quite ready to admit defeat, as he offered a last spark of defiance as he defended himself, declaring, "That's why I," he amended, again because of Septimus making a noise, "I mean, we were going to get three-quarters of the profit from it! And Avienus, knowing the business as well as he did, told us that we could expect to get triple the money, and the only limit to how much profit was based in how much grain we could buy!" He paused, his eyes searching my face, and now there was no missing his pleading tone. "Titus, this would have brought more money into the family in one move than Diocles or Tata ever earned before!"

That was when another, and in the way that counted, most important aspect of this sorry tale became clear, dissolving that hard knot of anger that had been building, and I actually saw my brother, as my brother, for the first time. I realized in that moment that, while it was in a completely different manner, Gaius had been trying to live up to what it meant to be a Pullus, attempting to live up to the expectations created by living in the shadow of the giant that was my Avus. *Our* Avus, I reminded myself; no, neither Gaius nor Septimus had known the first Titus Pullus, but I saw in this moment how Gaius at least had been driven, not only by our Avus, but in this manner, at least, more by the example of Diocles and our father.

"That," I spoke slowly, mainly because the thoughts were forming as I said them, "is why you sold the *ludus*?"

His face flushed, but he did not hesitate in affirming this.

"What else did you sell?"

While I thought I had prepared myself, I quickly learned I had not, as he spent the next several moments listing what, as far as I could remember, was almost everything we either owned outright or in which we held a stake.

Suddenly, I was struck by a horrible thought, and I cut him off. "Gaius, please tell me that you didn't borrow some of that money by putting up the villa as security!" My relief when he shook his head was so intense that it made me dizzy, but I was still moved to ask him, "So what exactly do we have left? How much money, not counting the value of our home?"

In answer, he pointed to the tablet that had been at the bottom of the stack, the third one that I had yet to open, saying softly, "It's all in that tablet."

I twisted around and picked it up, my heart starting to hammer in my chest, yet even as I prepared myself for the worst, I still let out a gasp when I read the bald truth contained in those figures.

"Three hundred thousand *sesterces*?" I gasped. "That's all we have left?"

"Not really," Gaius answered immediately. "We have more than that in terms of property."

"I said we're not counting the villa," I snapped, but he surprised me by shaking his head.

"I don't mean the villa," he replied.

"Then what are we talking about? You just told me we'd sold everything."

"In real property and businesses, we did," Gaius answered, but then he seemed to have some sort of thought that prompted his mouth to snap shut, and he returned to his earlier posture, staring at the floor, refusing to say anymore.

I looked at Septimus, wondering if he could interpret Gaius' sudden reticence; he could, and he explained it by telling me, "Gaius invested in slaves, Titus. We have," now, Septimus looked to Gaius, asking him, "how many slaves, Gaius?" Turning to me, he said, "He would never tell me how many."

"Two hundred," Gaius finally spoke, his eyes still on the floor.

"Two hundred?" I repeated, again more to allow my mind to adjust, but the anger that had vanished a few moments earlier came rushing back, and I glared at my brother as I reminded him, "You know how Mama felt about owning slaves! You," I indicated the three of us, "me, Septimus, all of us, come from a mother who was a slave! And you know," I came to my feet, "that Tata agreed with her! The last slave we had was Simeon, and he was given his freedom so he could return to Armenia!"

Without having a thought to do so, I crossed the few feet and found myself once more snatching my brother up out of his chair, and this time, I was angry enough that with my right hand, I lifted him off the floor, while I slapped him across the face with my left hand, once, twice, perhaps three times before Septimus grabbed my arm. I know he did not intend to do so, but when he did, he grabbed the scar tissue of my left arm, which made me roar in pain, even now almost twenty years after I had been wounded, but it served to get me to drop Gaius, who once more collapsed in a heap at my feet. Unfortunately for Septimus, he

365

became the object of my rage, and I hurled him bodily across the room, flinging him much as a dog shakes a rat and tosses it into the air. He hit the far wall, bounced off, and went to his hands and knees, but I was already turning back to Gaius, drawing my fist back as he struggled to his knees. It was when he looked up at me, and I saw the stark terror in his eyes, that expression created by the fear of dying at the hands of his own brother that did more to quell my rage than anything he could have said or done.

Lowering my fist, instead I pointed a shaking finger directly into his face and snarled, "You're selling every one of those slaves, starting tomorrow morning! Do you understand me?" He did not say anything, but he did nod, and I decided that was good enough, but I was not quite through. Dropping into a crouch so that we were at eye level, now that he had drawn himself up onto his knees, I made sure that we were looking each other in the eyes. I did not yell this, but just told him calmly, "And, Gaius, if you don't do as I command, I'll assert my right as *paterfamilias*, and I will come back here. And, Gaius, I *will* beat you to death with my bare hands, brother or not. Losing the money is one thing, but you've brought eternal shame onto our family by going against the wishes of our mother and father, and there won't be a jury in the Empire that would convict me for killing you. Now," I finished by repeating, "do we understand each other?"

He nodded, but this time, I was not accepting that, and I told him as much, and while it took him two tries, he finally stammered, "Y-yes, Titus. I understand you."

Rising from my squat, I walked over to Septimus, who had come to his feet, shaking his head groggily, and I did feel a qualm about what I had done. Not, however, that much of one.

"You should have written me, Septimus," I told him, and he immediately dropped his head, looking away as he admitted in a small voice, "I know, Titus. I know I should have."

Raising my voice so they both could hear, I went on, "From now on, neither of you has any power or authority to make decisions regarding this family. If you have some question, or something comes up, you will write to me, and you'll wait until you get my answer before acting. Is that clear?"

Both of them agreed, though I could tell that Gaius did not like it, but I did not care; all I cared about was that they obeyed.

"Now, I'm going back downstairs to spend time with the rest of the family," I told them. "Both of you are free to join us, but," I warned, "if either of you utter a word about what we just discussed… Well," I gave them a grim smile, "you're not going to like what happens next very much."

Then, without waiting for an answer, I walked to the door. Before I left the room, a thought occurred to me, and I turned to tell them both, "And before you come down and rejoin the family, I want you to write down everything you know about this *cunnus* Avienus. And I mean *everything*. His family, where he came from originally, who his friends were, everything. Then, you're going to come and celebrate your brother coming home." I gave the room one last glance, then shut the door behind me.

Descending into the main room, I was in for another surprise, except this one was quite pleasant, as Miriam, accompanied by her two children, completely forgot about what is expected of a Roman matron, came running at me, squealing with delight and leaping into my arms. She had launched herself with such force it drove me backward, but I was laughing and crying just as hard as she was.

"You hit me harder than any German I've faced," I joked at her, even as I lifted her up, holding her out from me as I had when she was a child, although it took a bit more effort than when she was ten.

"Swing me," she demanded, both of us falling immediately back into our childhood, and I protested, "We're indoors, you silly goose!"

"I don't care!"

She laughed again, and since I had never refused the most adored member of our family anything before, I complied, whirling her about, although I did it only once since my arms were about to give out, and with not nearly as much velocity as I normally did, not wanting to break anything. When I set her down, she was breathless and happy; her children, a boy and a girl, were standing there gazing up at me in a combination of what I believe was astonishment seeing their mother behaving in this manner and envy.

"I'm your Uncle Titus," I told them, then before they could respond in any manner, I thrust out my arms and said, "Who wants me to spin them around like I did your Mama?"

As I hoped, any reserve they may have felt at this large, scarred stranger who they had never seen before but, presumably, had at least heard about, was overpowered by the simple joy of being spun around in the air. Somewhat surprising, it was the girl who stepped forward first, holding her arms up in a gesture that any adult recognizes.

"Where are your manners?" Miriam chided her, looking down at the girl who, to my eyes, was my sister as a child, the pride in my sister's gaze unmistakable.

"Sorry, Mama," she mumbled, then looking up at me, she started, "*Salve*. My name is…"

"Wait," I interrupted her, "don't tell me. Let's see if I can guess."

Clearly intrigued, she regarded me with wide eyes as I pretended to think about it; naturally, I knew her name because my sister had informed me of her birth in a letter written in her own hand, but I was enjoying this too much not to indulge myself.

"Let me think," I mused, then looking into her shining eyes, I asked, "Is it Fulvia?"

"No!" She shook her head, her curls flying around her face in a manner that brought back even more memories, and I guessed again, "Is it Sabina?"

"No!" she howled, giving me a grin that was notable because it displayed that she was in the last stages of losing her baby teeth, and I decided that this had gone on long enough, so I made a great show of thinking, before I finally said, "I know! Your name is Atia!"

As I hoped, this delighted her, and she clapped her hands, squealing much like her mother had moments before. "Yes! That's right! It's Atia!"

"Well, Atia," I scooped her up, and in one motion, began spinning her around, telling her, "I hope you're ready to fly!"

I completed a few revolutions, just enough that I felt the beginning of dizziness, then I realized that I had yet to do the same for her brother, and set her down, breathless and happy.

I turned to the boy, who I knew was seven; he was a bit leerier, though he came willingly enough when I extended my arms to him.

"I know your name as well," I decided to forego the game I had played with his sister, "you're Manius."

He did not speak, his eyes wider than his sister's as he gazed up at me, but he did nod, and that was enough. Picking him up, I spun him around, but unlike his sister, Manius was clearly frightened, beginning to wail before I had finished a complete revolution. His fear was so clearly evident that I immediately put him down, looking at Miriam in apology, but she gave me a look that held no censure, even as she stepped forward to kneel down and comfort the crying boy.

"It's all right, Titus," she assured me. "Manius isn't as...adventurous as Atia."

"He's a big baby," Atia spoke up, looking at her brother scornfully. "He won't even ride Ocelus!"

That name brought me up short, sending an unexpected stab of sorrow into me, and I looked down at Miriam, who was kneeling and hugging her son.

She looked up at me apologetically and answered the unspoken question. "Servius bought me my own horse, and I named him Ocelus. But," she assured me, "this one is a gelding. But, he's gray, and," Miriam's eyes misted a bit, "I always remembered Ocelus. So," she shrugged, "that's what I named him."

"It's a good name," I assured her, not wanting her to feel badly for using the name of my Avus' horse, despite the fact that he had specifically willed him to me, surprised by this feeling of protective jealousy of what, next to my Avus' *gladius* and his scrolls, has been my most prized reminder of Titus Pullus. "I can't think of a better one."

By this time, not only had Gaius and Septimus rejoined us, but Birgit reappeared; frankly, I was not aware she had vanished, but when she came back into the main room, she had Dolabella with her.

"I was concerned that your guest was feeling neglected," she said with a casual tone that, perhaps, only I could tell was forced, and I was reminded that, while she may not have known Dolabella's identity exactly, she was aware of his role in my life. "So I went and got him."

Dolabella looked distinctly uncomfortable, yet I was unwilling to banish him back to the *triclinium*, where he had now spent almost a full watch. It was true that he had been fed, and I was certain he had been offered wine, but never far from my mind was the recognition that the only reason I was standing here was because of this man.

Consequently, before I could actually think about it and talk myself out of it, I said, "Thank you, Birgit." Extending an open hand in his direction, I said, "This is my...friend, Tiberius Dolabella. He's the reason I'm here."

My family, both by blood and extension, turned and greeted him, and I was amused by how flustered it made the otherwise unperturbable spymaster. Still, it obviously pleased him, and he made an awkward bow to the small knot of people who now filled this room, almost all of the people I loved and cherished in the world.

Pointing to a seat at the long table, I told Dolabella, "Sit there," then turned to Birgit and asked, "Would you please pour Tiberius another cup of wine?"

"I don't need another cup of wine," he protested, but I was certain his heart was not in it, and when I pressed him, he shrugged and said with a grin, "Well, if it means that much to you."

This prompted the others to laugh; at least, most of the others were amused, but Gaius was the exception. He opened his mouth, presumably to protest, but I caught his eye, and I did not even shake my head, just looking him directly in the eye, which prompted his mouth to snap shut, just as I expected. Turning away from him, I took a moment to survey this small crowd, and even as angry as I was with Gaius, and to a lesser extent Septimus, I was filled with an almost overpowering feeling of love that it took my breath away. With the exception of Alexandros and his brother Titus, everyone I truly cared about who was related to me by a bond of blood or by decades of service was present, and before I could stop myself, I began to weep. And, before I could have counted to three, I was surrounded by my family, even Gaius, whose eyes were filled with tears as well, and we celebrated this moment, however brief, that the Pullus family was all together.

We spent most of that night celebrating being together again; Dolabella had graciously agreed that we could afford to leave at dawn the next day, giving me about five full watches of time with my family. Despite the contentious nature of our conversation, Gaius, grudgingly at first, also got into the spirit of reunion, and we passed the time sitting around the table. If he resented the fact that I sat at the head of it, where my father had always been, he was wise enough not to make an issue of it, and although I enjoyed myself thoroughly, I was also paying acute attention to not just what my family members were saying, but how they were saying it. Being a Centurion, at least a successful one, means that he learns to pay attention to not just the words coming out of a man's mouth, but the manner in which they behave around others. And, the more I watched, the more certain I became of something, that the wrong brother was handling our interests. Septimus did not talk all that much, but when he did, it was always an extremely astute observation, in which he betrayed a razor-sharp wit, and the kind of sense of humor that I appreciated the most. He was clearly very observant, and I noticed that, when there was some point of contention between Gaius and Miriam about some event from the past, which happened quite often, they both looked to Septimus as the ultimate arbiter of the actual truth. Not, I will say, everything; there was a fair number of stories from their early childhood that had become somehow jumbled or altered in the telling, and for that, they looked to me. It gave me a taste of what it meant to be *paterfamilias*, and I cannot say that it was not pleasing, despite my understanding that it was short-lived.

During this abbreviated period of time, a great deal of the antipathy I felt towards Tiberius Dolabella was washed away by his graciousness and his choice of not reminding me that time was our enemy. Instead, he sat and listened, and much to my initial discomfort, seemed more than happy to regale the others with tales of my deeds that he had claimed to witness personally. At first, I glared at him, certain that this man who had been such a constant irritation and danger to me would gleefully recount some of my darkest, worst moments in which he had been involved. Instead, he restricted himself to more humorous and lighthearted moments he had witnessed, along with my deeds on the battlefield, though sanitized quite a bit, and fairly quickly, I discerned that the anecdotes he was relating also made me out in a flattering light. I confess that, in the back of my mind, there was a suspicion there that he was up to something, except I made a conscious decision when this pushed itself into the forefront to place it firmly back in the recesses where it belonged. Honestly, I was enjoying myself too much to allow any darker motives to impinge on the happiness that I was feeling, one that I could see my family was sharing.

Nevertheless, despite Dolabella not bringing it up, I was aware of the passing time, so finally, well after midnight, I made a show of standing up, yawning, and saying, "Well, as much as I'd love to continue this, Tiberius and I have to leave at first light."

The chorus of protest at my announcement was both gratifying and painful, but I could not allow myself to give in, as much as I wanted to. Young Manius had fallen asleep, so I contented myself with kissing him on the cheek, while Atia, displaying not just the physical similarity to her mother but her stubborn refusal to succumb to the demands of sleep in order not to miss any of the fun, was still awake. I lifted her and gave her one final spin around before her mother took over, but Miriam did something I found slightly disturbing, going to the bell and ringing it. The Breuci girl instantly appeared, making me wonder if she had been awake all this time or was such a light sleeper that she was able to come instantly alert and respond in a manner that would have done no shame to a Legionary answering an alert.

"Take Atia and Manius to my room," she told the girl peremptorily, and while the young woman obeyed, I could not help looking at Miriam for a long moment. Seeing my look, she misinterpreted it, smiling, and assuring me, "Oh, we spend a lot of time here, Titus. Servius travels a lot for his work, and he feels better when he knows we're here instead of being alone."

For the briefest moment, I considered enlightening Miriam that my consternation was not due to the idea of her and her children spending time here at the villa, but I suppose I did not want to ruin the moment, so I forced myself to smile at her, which she seemed to accept. Scribonia and Gisela received a hug from me, and I whispered to them that they needed to find husbands, which seemed to amuse them both a great deal, then they retired as well. Fairly quickly, the only ones left were Dolabella, Birgit, Gaius, Septimus, and me. Whispering to Birgit, I asked her to have someone show Dolabella to a room where he could get what little sleep he could, and she answered that she would do it herself; I believe that she had seen and understood my discomfort with my siblings and their easy command of the slaves. Asking Dolabella to follow her, she left the room, leaving me alone with Gaius and Septimus, which neither of them seemed particularly happy about, but I had said my piece, to Gaius at least. Instead of revisiting a sore subject, I turned to Birgit, who had just returned to the room, motioning to her to follow me, and I led her into the atrium of the villa, although before I did, I demanded that Gaius hand over the tablet I had spotted tucked into his tunic, correctly assuming that it was the information about Avienus.

I was not surprised that my brothers did not follow us, and I wasted no time, asking Birgit, "Where's Titus?"

She answered readily enough, although she looked everywhere but up into my eyes. "I told you, he's out in town somewhere. He's fine, though."

Rather than reply, I just looked at her, and I was rewarded when, suddenly, her shoulders sagged, and she dropped her face into her hands and began weeping.

"Oh, Titus," she was hard to understand between her sobs and her hands muffling her words, "I don't know what to do! Titus is...he's," she looked up at me then, her face streaked with tears, and I saw the agony of a mother whose child is someplace where she has no way of knowing if they are safe, "...he's lost!" Gathering herself slightly, she told me, "He fell in with some bad people here in Arelate, Titus, and I think he's in the *collegia* that runs all the gambling and whoring."

"Do you know which one?"

She shook her head because she was not sure, but then she said a name that brought back memories and caused a stab of alarm.

"I'm not sure, but I heard from a friend that he's running with the Poplicolas."

"The Poplicolas?" At this point, I was more confused than anxious, saying, "I thought that we...," catching myself, I corrected, "...that the Poplicola brothers killed their father, and they were executed for it." Her head came up, and she eyed me with a shrewd expression that I had seen from her before, and she said softly, "So that was what you and Sextus did when we brought Diocles home." I did not answer her, but she gave me a smile that was poignant for its combination of pain and fondness, telling me, "It was the one and only secret Sextus kept from me. I knew that you and he had done something about the situation with Vulso and the *ludus*, but he would never tell me, just that it was taken care of." Clearly taking my silence for confirmation, she confirmed, "Well, yes, the two brothers were executed." She paused for a moment, then added, "The two oldest brothers. But there are, or were five Poplicola sons, and they took over their father's interests. And," she shuddered at this next part, "they've expanded quite a bit. Titus, it was quite bloody around Arelate when they were taking over." Birgit stopped abruptly, and she seemed to consider something before, closing her eyes, she said, "I think Titus was involved in the last

R.W. Peake

bit of what took place, because the Poplicolas didn't drive the last rival *collegia* out until about six months ago." For the first time, Birgit looked every bit her age, but it was the haunted look in her eyes as she looked up at me that was the most painful as she implored me, "Titus, please help me! Can't you stay for a bit longer? He does show up eventually, and I know he'll be coming home sometime tomorrow."

"Birgit," I said as gently as I could manage, "I can't, I just can't do it. We've already stayed longer than we should, and that's only because Dolabella allowed it."

Cutting me off, her face hardened, and she asked bitterly, "So this Dolabella still has some sort of hold over you that you can't help me?"

This was harsh, and despite the sympathy I felt for her plight, this jibe reignited the anger that I had quelled with my brothers. I was about to say something just as harsh in reply, but I just could not do it, yet neither could I afford to delay our departure.

Sighing, I resigned myself to the idea that I would not be getting any sleep that night, since this was the only help I could offer her, saying, "Here's what I will do, Birgit. I'm going to go looking for Titus tonight. But," I hardened my voice, "if I don't find him by sunrise, I'm sorry, but I can't stay any longer." Struck by a sudden inspiration, I decided to at least partially divulge why we were here and why we were heading to Pannonia, telling her, "Something's happened in Pannonia, and it involves Domitius. Dolabella and I have been sent by Germanicus to see what we can do to help."

This, as I hoped, caused a reaction, and her expression softened. "You mean Titus Domitius?" When I nodded, she asked, "What is it? Is he all right? What about Petrilla and the children?"

"That's all I can tell you about it," I replied. "But it's important that we get there as quickly as we can. You understand now why I can't stay?"

She swallowed hard, and I did sympathize with Birgit, imagining the turmoil she must be feeling at this moment; finally, she nodded and said sadly, "Yes, Titus, I understand. Please try to find him and…"

This was the one part I could not really determine from Birgit, what she expected me to do, but I decided that I would just make it up as I went along. After all, I thought wryly, that's what I do most of the time anyway.

"I will," I promised her, then turned to practical matters. "Now where's a good place to start looking for him?"

She mentioned three possibilities – two taverns and one brothel – but I was only familiar with one of the taverns, since it had been the headquarters for the Poplicolas and their gang for as long as I could remember. It had been the spot where Sextus had met with the brothers to set them and the *lanista* up who served as Vulso's second in command at our *ludus,* Gundorix, so I decided that was where I would head first.

"Titus," she took my hand, and the tears made her eyes shimmer, "thank you. And," she warned, "be careful." I laughed at this, but she warned, "I know you can take care of yourself and then some, Titus, but there are a lot of them."

I instantly understood she was right, so before I left the villa, I walked over to where my gear was piled in the corner, strapped on my *gladius*, then on an impulse, picked up the *vitus*, not as much as a weapon, but to send the proper signal to anyone I should encounter that I was a Centurion of Rome.

Just as I was about to leave by the back door, I was struck by a thought and asked Birgit, "How will I recognize him?"

"Because," Septimus, who had clearly been listening from the other room, entered and said, "I'm going with you." He gave me a grin. "It's been a long time since I've seen my big brother thrash anyone, so I don't want to miss it."

Touched, and frankly, happy for the company, I did ask him, "Where's Gaius?"

"He went to bed," Septimus answered shortly, "and I don't think he'd come anyway."

This tempted me to rouse him, but as always, the time constraint was never far from my mind, so I gave Septimus a nod, asking him, "Do you have your *gladius*? The one Tata gave you?"

Suddenly, he did not look quite so eager, but he did answer immediately, "Yes, it's in my room."

"Go get it," I told him, then added, "it's better to have it and not need it than the other way around. Besides," I grinned, "I want to see if you still know what end to hold."

As I hoped, this prompted not only a laugh, but as he left the room to ascend the stairs, he called out, "I hope I remember!"

Birgit and I did not speak for a moment, then I was struck by a thought, telling her, "Wait until we're gone, but someone needs to tell Dolabella in case he wakes up early where we went and that I'll be back in time to leave."

She nodded her assent, then Septimus was back, fumbling with the *baltea* and the scabbard, causing me to shake my head in mock dismay.

"Come here." I sighed. "Let me make sure you're not going to trip over it. And," I added, "let me see if you kept it sharp."

The way he walked over to me, his head hanging, evoked memories of other times, when I had been the one with bowed head as my father admonished me for something, but a quick tug on his *baltea* informed me that he had at least strapped it on correctly. His blade, however, was another matter; it came out smoothly enough, which was a good sign that he had not allowed it to rust into the scabbard, but that was where the good news ended.

"You *might* be able to cut a loaf of bread with this," I scoffed after running my thumb along the edge, then handed it back to him, "but that's about it."

"Hopefully, all we run into are loaves of bread, then," he responded, and I took this as a good sign, that he was able to laugh.

"Let's go," I said simply, then with a nod to Birgit, I led the way out of the villa and into Arelate.

I suppose it would be appropriate to acknowledge the hand of the gods in what took place that night; or, perhaps it was just a probability that the one tavern where I knew the Poplicolas congregated would be the same one as when I was living here as a youngster. Whatever the cause, we made our way quickly through the deserted streets, heading for the tavern, which we could have found just by the noise generated by the men, and women, who frequented these spots, present in every military town or any sizable town or city.

As we walked, I talked with Septimus, asking first, "Anything I should know about young Titus?"

"He's a hothead," Septimus answered instantly, then he hesitated for a moment before he added, "Actually, he reminds me of you in that way."

I looked down at him, amused and somewhat surprised, but I could not dispute the truth in what he said, at least as far as I was concerned.

"Maybe it's the name," I sighed, though it did prompt me to ask, "Can he fight?"

"Oh, yes." Septimus nodded, then turned his face and pointed to a spot above his eye, asking me, "Did you notice that scar? He gave it to me."

I had not noticed, and it was too dark now to see, but I had no reason to think he was not telling the truth, and I asked him, "So do you two get along?"

"Most of the time," Septimus answered, then with what I clearly heard was a tinge of sadness, he added, "In some ways, Titus and I are closer to each other than I am with Gaius."

"What happened with Gaius?" I asked this without thinking it through. "How could he have gotten to a place where he thought buying slaves was the right thing to do? After all that Mama and Tata drilled into us about how this family would never own other people ever again."

My brother did not answer immediately, and I realized that I was putting him in an awkward position, but this was not the cause of his hesitation.

"Gaius," he said slowly, "thinks he is the cleverest person, not just in our family, but in all of Arelate." After another pause, he said, "But that's not what worries me about him, Titus."

"Well," I assured him, "it shouldn't anymore. Not now that I'm involved. Remember," I felt it appropriate to remind him, "neither of you are to make a decision without clearing it with me. Gaius doesn't want me coming back here; I was serious about that, Septimus."

"I know you were, Titus." Septimus sighed, then shook his head, his eyes still straight ahead down the street we were walking down. "But that's not what I'm talking about." Now I was thoroughly confused; a part of me wishes I had remained that way. "Gaius likes to...hurt people, Titus."

Only then did he look back up at me, clearly trying to gauge whether I was accepting this, yet as soon as the words were out of his mouth, I somehow knew they were true.

"Hurt people?" I echoed, then I met his gaze and asked, "Or just slaves?" When he nodded, another thought came to me, and this brought me to an abrupt stop. Grabbing my brother by the arm, I demanded, "Is that Breuci girl one of them? Does he beat her?"

"He does more than beat her, Titus," Septimus answered bitterly. "He hurts Juno in...other ways. And," his face turned hard, and in that moment, I saw my brother Sextus more clearly than ever, "she doesn't deserve that! She's a wonderful girl! And he treats her…" His voice dropped to a hush, and he admitted, "If Gaius wasn't my brother, I'd…I'd…"

I put my hand on his shoulder, which caused him to look up at me, and I assured him, "Trust me in this, Septimus. I know exactly what you mean, and I don't blame you." Taking a deep breath, I said, "All right, enough of that. We need to go find Birgit's wayward son."

We resumed walking, and my mind, which I thought was already overwhelmed with all these new discoveries, was even fuller now as I wondered what to do about my brother Gaius being a cruel man.

Turning the corner, we saw the small crowd of people, and I remembered that this tavern was also used by the Poplicolas to run whores of the lowest kind, the ones that took their customers into the space in between the buildings on the opposite side of the street to finish their transaction.

"All right," I told Septimus, "stand right here," I directed him to a spot slightly behind me and to my right, and I finished sternly, "and don't fucking move from that spot! Do you understand me? Your one and only job is to keep anyone from getting behind us."

"Yes." His voice was hoarse, but I took that as a good sign, not needing any kind of false bravado from him.

"Let's go," I said, and we resumed our approach.

The guttering lamps hanging on the brackets outside of the tavern created pools of light, and it was when we entered that first pool our presence was noticed. That it was noticed by the two heavyset men, both of them wearing tunics that were stretched tight across their chests, their arms heavily muscled, and most importantly, bearing the scars and bent noses of brawlers, that was what meant the most. It began when the man nearest us, leaning against the wall, gave a casual glance in our direction in a reflex motion, then he looked away, back to where a whore and customer were haggling over the price of her services. For an instant, I thought we might be able to get close enough that I had the advantage, but his head whipped back around, and I saw his eyes narrow as he looked me up and down, then straightened up and gave his companion a nudge to get his attention.

"Oy, you're a big one!" he called out with a false geniality that I had heard more times than I could count, knowing that there would be a jibe or taunt coming next, the prelude by a man who thought he was tough provoking a challenge. Then, however, his eyes dropped down to my waist, and he saw both my *gladius* in its scabbard and my *vitus* in my left hand, and whatever he planned on saying was forgotten as he turned to squarely face us. His companion, still unsure of what was going on, but reacting automatically, stepped away from his spot and came to the other man's side. Pointing at my *gladius*, the first man sneered, "I hope you don't think you're coming in here with that, soldier boy!" He smiled, revealing the broken off stumps of his top front and bottom teeth so that he looked like he had fangs. "But you can just hand it to my friend Nerva here," he indicated his companion, "and we'll keep it safe for you. Then," he made a mocking bow towards the entrance, "you're more than welcome to enjoy the delights of this establishment, where we can satisfy every need and taste." His face twisted into a leer as he added, "We even have some tasty young boys, since I know that's what you soldier boys like so much!"

I let him talk without interrupting, but when he stopped then, I said conversationally, "The only way you're getting my *gladius* is if you come and get it, fat man."

Just as I hoped, this got under his skin, since now that I had gotten a closer look, whatever muscle he may have had at some point was now encased in fat, and the light was strong enough I could see his face flush, but it was what he did that was more important. Taking his eyes off me for an instant, he looked to his companion, gave a jerk of his head, which the man clearly understood, because he took a step backward, and then without hurrying, walked over to where a barrel was placed against the wall on the far side of the entrance, and as I expected, reached behind it and produced two *gladii*, which he carried back to his companion, tossing him one. There was more than enough light for me to see that, while they were Spanish *gladii* like the one on my hip, the iron was pitted, with rust spots the length of both blades. More telling, however, was the manner in which these two started waving them in my direction, and I decided there was no need for me to draw my own, at least at first.

Without taking my eyes off the pair, I told Septimus, "Stay right there, don't move."

As I expected, this served to not just freeze Septimus in his spot, it distracted the door guard nearest to me, the man I had taunted for being more fat than muscle, so he never saw my *vitus* sweeping upward in a smooth arc, starting from below my waist, even as I was speaking. The end of the twisted vine hit him, hard, in the pit of his stomach, and I was blasted with the breath that exploded from him, washing me in an invisible blanket of wine, garlic, and rotted teeth. His companion, reacting to my sudden assault, raised his *gladius* above his head, signaling his intention to smash his blade down on my bare head, which I countered simply by executing another thrust with the *vitus,* except this one was aimed in the direction of his face, specifically his right eye, though my aim was slightly off, hitting him squarely between them instead. The result was essentially the same as it had been with the first guard, who had fallen to his knees and was even then in the process of toppling over to his side, his hands clutching his stomach, except that the second guard collapsed straight down to the filthy paving stones as if the bones in his body had simply vanished, this and the sudden crunching sound of the hard cartilage of his nose snapping telling me that I had perhaps hit him a bit too hard. If he ever woke up, I knew that his brains would be too addled for him to be of any use to whatever Poplicola brother was running this *collegia*. Not that this mattered to me a bit, and both men were barely laid out before I was stepping over them, heading for the entrance of the tavern before an alarm could be raised by any of the bystanders, all of whom were standing there, open-mouthed in shock at what had taken perhaps a half-dozen heartbeats. Glancing over my shoulder, I saw that it was not just the onlookers; Septimus was standing there, staring down at the two men, one of them writhing in pain, the other completely still, save for a slight tremor that, when I sensed the movement out of the corner of my eye and glanced at the second guard, told me that I had indeed killed the man.

"Don't just stand there," I snapped, which served to goad Septimus into moving, and I watched him carefully step around the pair of men, his eyes fastened on the second guard, whose body was still jerking spasmodically in his last moment of life.

"Did you...kill him?" Septimus asked, but frankly, I was already focusing on what lay before us, not behind us, and I think I answered carelessly, "Looks that way."

I was just stepping past the entrance into the tavern, and I stopped there to allow my eyes to adjust, but while I saw some faces turn in our general direction, nobody seemed to be alarmed, only curious, which was not unusual. Naturally, I saw some of them do essentially what the first guard outside had done; glance up in a reflexive response, begin to look away, then my size caused them to return their attention to me, their expressions varying from mild concern to acute interest in what my presence might mean for their entertainment; or, more likely given the type of place it was, their health.

"Do you see Titus?" I asked Septimus, keeping my voice low.

He did not answer immediately, and I was beginning to think that he was not in this place when my brother suddenly pointed and said, "Yes! There he is. Next to the man with the eyepatch!"

Following his finger, it did not take more than a heartbeat for me to see him, less time for my eyes to take in the sight, and my mind to realize how much Titus resembled his father Diocles. A bit taller, perhaps, but with hair the color of a crow's wing, the same aquiline nose and olive complexion that was discernible even in the dim lighting of the tavern. This was Diocles in the flesh, although I could see that along with being taller, he was also broader through the chest. He was paying attention to whatever the man in the eyepatch was saying, and while it was not with any certainty, the man looked enough like a Poplicola that I deduced it was probably one of the surviving brothers. The sudden change in the atmosphere, presaged by the muttering of the customers closest to the door, apparently alerted both of them, since they stopped talking to look in our direction. I did not miss that, of the two, it was the man in the eyepatch who reacted first, coming to his feet as he faced me and Septimus, and as we approached, I saw him turn to give a quiet word to Titus. I suspected that he was telling Titus to place himself in between us, in a first line of defense, because when Titus did not move a muscle, it obviously irritated the man, who turned and snarled something at the young man I considered a nephew, who still stood as if rooted to the spot, his eyes wide and staring directly at me.

Again, I did not take my eyes off the man with the eyepatch, knowing he was the most important one in the room, but I told Septimus, "Watch my back. If anyone tries to get behind me, stop them."

"Stop them?" he asked. "How?"

R.W. Peake

He sounded so bewildered that, despite everything, I had to fight a laugh, and I risked a quick glance over my shoulder to catch his eye.

Pointing down at his waist, I said, "You pull that out." He did so, then I grinned and indicated the point of his blade. "Then if someone gets between us, you stick that end right in their guts." Shaking my head in mock exasperation, I asked, "Didn't Tata teach you youngsters anything?"

I did not wait for his reply; my attention had been diverted long enough, but when I turned back, I saw that Titus still had not moved, which clearly enraged the man with the eyepatch.

Snarling a curse, he made as if to grab Titus, but I spoke up, loudly enough for everyone to hear, "If you put a hand on my nephew, I'll gut you."

I suppose it was the sound of my voice that did it, because young Titus gasped so loudly I could hear it from where I was standing.

"U-uncle Titus?" Then, he turned his head, clearly recognizing Septimus. "Septimus? What...what are you doing here?"

"I'm here to get you out of this *cac*hole," I told him calmly, and as I expected, this enraged the eyepatch man even more, who hissed something, then stepped around Titus, careful, I noticed, not to touch him.

"I know who you are!" He pointed a shaking finger at me, but it was easy to see that it was from fury and not fear. "You're Titus Pullus!" Then, he confirmed my suspicion, revealing that the plot Sextus and I had concocted all those years before that resulted in the murder of his father and the execution of his brothers had been uncovered somehow by saying, "You and your fucking *cunnus* of a brother got my Tata and two of my brothers killed!"

Now that I knew the secret was out, I did not see much point in denying it; also, I knew my acknowledgement would further infuriate him, and angry men are more likely to make mistakes, so I gave a shrug that I knew everyone in the tavern could see, replying, "Your brothers were so stupid, I'm surprised they managed to live as long as they did. But," I hardened my voice, "they plotted against my family, so you're fucking right I got them killed. My only regret is that I didn't do it myself."

As I hoped, this scored a telling blow, his face twisting into an expression of utter hatred. Perhaps if he had moved more quickly, he might have gained an advantage, but by the time I was finished speaking and before he could react in an overtly physical manner, I had drawn the *gladius* carried by the first Titus Pullus and was holding it loosely in my hand. However, rather than holding it point down or even in the first position, I deliberately held it in such a way that everyone could see it, away from my body and above my waist, twisting it slightly so that the dark, whirling patterns of the blade caught the light. It was a calculated gamble on my part, because if this Poplicola kept his head, with my blade held away from my body, he could have conceivably crossed the space between us to get inside my guard. Fortunately, as I suspected it would, the appearance of this *gladius* evoked a response far and above that which one might normally expect, because this was Arelate. And, as I heard the sudden buzzing whispers of the people in the tavern, I knew that my ploy had worked.

"I can tell that everyone in here recognizes this." I spoke louder, still holding it high above my waist and outside the plane of my body. "Or," I amended, "they think they do." I turned my head as if I was addressing the crowd, but my eyes never left Poplicola, who was shaking with impotent rage. "Well, they're right. This is the *gladius* of Titus Pullus, Primus Pilus of the Equestrians, one of the first Camp Prefects appointed by our dear departed Augustus, and one of the prominent citizens of Arelate. And," now I stretched out my arm and pointed it directly at Poplicola, "I'm his grandson and namesake. I'm the Quartus

Princeps Prior of the 1st Legion, and I'm here to take my nephew home." Pausing for the span of a couple heartbeats, I asked Poplicola simply, "Do you intend to try stopping me?"

As I expected, the collective attention of the crowd in the tavern turned to Poplicola, who had, quite wisely, not moved a muscle, his arms held out in such a manner that I knew he was signaling he had no intention of doing anything. Nevertheless, I knew that it had to be a bitter draught for him to swallow, here in his own tavern, but as I expected, Poplicola was a cur who needed the strength of numbers, and he had to have deduced by this time that, if the two burly guards outside had not arrived, they would not be coming. There was a table of men who I saw fancied themselves as tough men, but just as I knew they would, suddenly, they had more interest in what was in their cups than standing behind their leader. The silence stretched out, and I was certain that most of the patrons were holding their breath, watching this with the avidity of a mob at the gladiatorial games hoping to see blood, waiting to see how Poplicola responded.

And, just as I expected, he seemed to sag a bit, yet he answered me with empty defiance, "There's no need to try and stop you, Pullus! Young Titus here," he turned and gave him a hearty clap on the back, "will be back soon! Am I right, Titus?"

Titus, whose eyes, I had noticed, had never left either Septimus or me, did not even acknowledge Poplicola's words, nor did he register that he had been touched. Instead, without a word, he stepped out of Poplicola's reach, walking towards my brother and me, though he refused to look either of us in the eye. Once he walked past, I began backing away, but I did not sheathe my *gladius*. Then, Poplicola had to open his mouth.

"Pullus, you need to thank your household gods that I'm in a forgiving mood," he said this louder than necessary, "and letting you walk out of here."

"Pluto's balls," I recognized Septimus' voice, "why did he have to say that?"

Turning to my brother, I ordered, "Give me your *gladius*."

As I said this, I dropped my *vitus* and extended my left hand, which to Septimus' credit, he drew back out and tossed me the blade in one motion, which I deftly caught. Then, in a continuation of the same movement, I tossed the blade in such a manner that it landed with enough force that the point lodged in the floorboards of the tavern, just a pace in front of Poplicola.

"You were saying?" I asked him, but while I did not raise my voice, I did not need to do so. Pointing to the *gladius*, which was still slightly swaying back and forth, I taunted Poplicola, "Something about being in a forgiving mood, wasn't it? Well," I gestured towards the crowd, "I'm not going anywhere after all." My gaze was fixed on Poplicola, so I knew even before I was finished that he was not going to accept the challenge I had offered, but I did allow several heartbeats to pass, in total silence, before I said with a sneer, "I didn't think so."

Then, taking what I suspected the people in the tavern would think was a needlessly foolish risk, I turned around, telling Septimus and Titus, who had been standing there watching, "Let's go."

I was completely expecting that Poplicola would be foolish enough to take advantage of me turning my back, but while I was speaking to my brother and nephew, my eyes never left the people sitting in the tavern, knowing that their reaction would provide me more than enough warning. Somewhat disappointingly, Poplicola was either smarter or more of a coward, because he made no move, either towards the *gladius* or towards me, and we walked out of the tavern. As we exited out onto the street, the body of the second guard was still lying there, but the man I had punched in the stomach with my *vitus* was nowhere to be seen, and I could see that the dead man's purse and shoes had already been taken, with his tunic pulled open, a sign that his body had been thoroughly searched. For a few paces, I kept glancing over my shoulder at the tavern, but nobody emerged from it.

Nothing was said for about a block, then Septimus turned to me and complained, "You left my *gladius* behind!"

"If you want it," I told him with a grin, "you can go back and get it."

"No," he mumbled, "never mind." Laughing, I slapped him on the back, and he regarded me with an expression I could not immediately decipher, but then he said quietly, "Titus, you killed that man. Just with a *vitus*." Shaking his head, he continued, "I've never seen anything like that before."

I chose to make a joke, saying, "I'm just surprised you know what a *vitus* is, little brother."

"Of course I know what a *vitus* is," he shot back. "I'm the son and grandson of a Centurion, just like you!"

I could feel the heat of his words, and however awkward it may have been, I offered him a pat on the back as I assured him, "I know you are, Septimus. And," in this I was being sincere, "I'm proud of you. You didn't hesitate when I told you what to do. I knew you wouldn't let anyone get behind me."

I could tell this pleased him, but he also seemed troubled, then he said, "I've just never seen anyone killed before."

He looked away as he finished, and I was, perhaps surprisingly, sobered by my brother's admission, reminded just how different his life had been from mine, despite our shared blood and name. I was about to open my mouth to say something that I hoped would be comforting, when, finally, young Titus broke his own silence.

"Why did you do that?" he demanded, suddenly rounding on Septimus and me from where he had been leading the way back to the villa. "Why did you humiliate my friend?"

I was more shocked than angry, at least at first. "Your friend?" I echoed, then repeated, "Your *friend*?" This was when the anger started stirring, and I pointed back in the direction of the tavern, my voice cold as I told Titus, "If that man was truly your friend, he'd be chasing us right now. If that man was your friend, he would have never let us leave!" I quickened my pace so that I could stare down at Titus, who suddenly did not look quite so resolute as I continued, "Now, how about you explain to me how you ended up associated with scum like the Poplicolas."

"They're not scum," he retorted, then repeated stubbornly, "they're my friends."

"What about me, Titus?" Septimus broke in. "I'm your friend. We're family."

"No we aren't!" Titus shot back. "Just because my father was your family's slave…"

He got no further, because before I could stop myself, my hand shot out and I grabbed a handful of his tunic to pull him close to me as I roared, "*What are you talking about?*" As I shouted at him, I realized I was violently shaking him. "Who told you these lies?"

"They're not lies!" Titus shouted into my face, and while his struggles were to no avail, I was surprised at how strong he was for his size. "I know the truth!"

"What truth?" Septimus was standing beside me, clearly as bewildered as I was. "What are you talking about? Your father wasn't a slave!"

"Yes, he was!" Titus shot back, and the fury in his voice was unsettling, even impotent. "Don't deny it!" Finally, he shouted, "I read those scrolls that your Avus wrote! I know the truth!" I was so shocked that, with the next spasm of his body, he jerked free of my grasp, staggering backward a step, then standing, feet apart, glaring at the two of us. "Don't lie to me anymore!" He was still shouting, but then his voice cracked with the powerful emotions he was feeling, and he began sobbing, "I know what my father was, and what my mother was! They were *slaves*!" Suddenly, he looked up and pointed a shaking finger, not at me but at Septimus, as he accused, "And now you and Gaius are doing it again! You're buying every slave you can get your hands on! That's not right! That's…"

"That's stopped," I cut in, but in contrast to the throbbing emotion he was displaying, I spoke softly, "as of today, Titus."

Suddenly, he did not seem quite so certain, and he looked from me to Septimus, who nodded, saying simply, "He's telling the truth. He told Gaius to sell every slave, immediately."

I thought this might mollify him, but it only seemed to enrage him further, and he looked to me incredulously, "Sell them?" Shaking his head, he repeated, "*Sell* them? What kind of justice is that? They'll still be slaves!"

Rather than argue, I decided to cut to the heart of the matter, and I answered him by admitting, "It's no justice at all, Titus." Taking a breath, I was forced to confront the thing that I had become aware of just a matter of a bit more than a full watch before. "But the family can't afford to just manumit the slaves we own, Titus."

Somewhat to my surprise, he did not protest this; instead, he looked directly at Septimus, and asked softly, "Because of the grain?"

"Because of the grain," Septimus confirmed, and this caused Birgit's son to heave a great sigh, then shake his head sadly.

"I thought so," he said, but now I rounded on Septimus, the anger that had been bubbling just below the surface now focused on him. "Apparently," I could not keep my voice from expressing my ire, "everyone around Gaius knew that this scheme was a bad idea! So," I pointed, first at Septimus, then at Titus, "why did you two let him go through with it?"

I saw the look the pair exchanged, and in it I saw, or sensed, how much of this sordid episode I would never know, but Septimus replied simply, "Because he was the oldest of us. And," he stared up into my eyes, "you weren't here."

"Or even interested," Titus interjected, but when I glared at him, Septimus took the opportunity to agree, "Absolutely." Feeling as if I was being assaulted from all sides, I turned and stared at Septimus, but he did not flinch as he continued, "Titus, you've never been interested in what's going on here in Arelate, with the family. All you care about is your career and the Legions."

If my brother had punched me in the face, I could not have been staggered any more, and I stared in astonishment, first at my brother, then at my nephew, but neither of them wavered, both still looking me directly in the eye.

"That…" I began, but then, I stood there, my mind racing as I thought through the previous twenty-plus years, and how I had read the letters from my family…then tossed them into the pile of correspondence, so that I ended up saying, "…is true."

Suddenly, I recognized how, in my desire and ambition to first surpass, then match the achievements of my Avus, I had consciously disconnected myself from my family and all its concerns. And yet, I thought, here I am; forty years old, and while I'm a Centurion, it's not even as a Pilus Prior, let alone a Primus Pilus.

"You're right," I said, my voice not quite sounding like my own, "I did everything you said I did. My career in the Legions took precedence over everything." For a brief moment, I considered telling them about Giulia, and how I had never been able to move past that loss in my personal life, so I had turned all of my attention and energies to a career under the standard, but I did not. Shaking my head, I could only say, "And for that, I apologize. I am truly sorry for not being here."

Then, there was nothing else to say, and we stood there for the gods only know how long, then Septimus broke the silence, asking me, "Aren't you leaving at first light?" When I said that I was, he turned and gazed towards the eastern sky, and said,

"It's not long from now." Turning back to me, he smiled, saying, "We should get home."

Understanding he was right, I resumed walking down the street, but I reached out, grabbed young Titus by the collar, and drew him close.

"So," I said lightly, "you were snooping in Avus' library?" He squirmed a little under my grasp, but he admitted as much, and I asked him, "How much did you read?"

"Just one scroll," he answered.

"Well," I laughed, "I can promise you, there's more you don't know than more you do." I looked down at him, and asked, "Would you like to hear the entire story about your father?"

When he nodded eagerly, I grinned at him and said, "That's good, because we'll have plenty of time to talk while we're on the road."

"On the road?" he asked, clearly puzzled, and honestly, I had not really thought matters through, yet somehow, I knew this was the right thing to do. "What do you mean?"

"I mean," I told him, "I'm taking you with me back to Ubiorum." Before he could react, I added, "By way of Pannonia first. But," I finished, "I think you need to spend time with Alex. I think you can learn a lot from your older brother."

I was expecting a fight from Birgit, but when I told her my intentions of bringing Titus with me and reuniting him with Alex, she agreed so quickly that it told me she had been planning on suggesting it herself.

"He needs to get out of Arelate," she said sadly, but then she gave me that look of hers as she added, with a touch of acid, "especially if you handled matters with Poplicola in your usual fashion." Then, she smiled at me, but in a manner that reminded me of the fierce Gaul I saw when she was defending my siblings when we were returning to Siscia, then fighting off bandits to protect her own children, as she asked hopefully, "So, did you kill that snake?"

I felt a bit badly that I had to tell her that I had not, though I did say, "I offered him a chance to stop me, but he thought better of it." The look of disappointment on her face made me laugh, and I assured her, "But if it makes you feel better, I *did* kill one of his men."

"With one blow with his *vitus*," Septimus spoke up, and the note of awe in his voice did make me feel good, something that Birgit did not miss.

"Too bad it was just one of his men," she said tartly, but before I could reply, she turned and said, "Let me go help Titus pack."

She disappeared, and I collapsed more than sat down at the table, thinking that I was in for a hard stretch of watches and wondering if I could afford to snatch even a third of a watch of sleep. But, with everyone gone and only Septimus left, I knew that I could not afford the time, because I had come to another decision. Motioning to my brother, I pointed to one of the benches, and he came, holding two pieces of bread that he had smeared with honey, one of which he handed me. Thanking him, we occupied ourselves with eating them, then I knew I had to begin.

"I've been thinking," I began, "and I've made a decision."

"Oh?" Septimus was not quite through, and he continued munching his bread, regarding me with a raised eyebrow. "What about?"

"About who I'm leaving in charge here," I answered. "And it's not going to be Gaius."

I confess I was a bit disappointed in my brother, because he looked puzzled and confirmed it when he asked, "Not Gaius? Then who's it going to be?"

Rather than answer him verbally, I just stared at him, watching as his expression changed from bewilderment to dawning recognition, but I was surprised when he shook his head.

"Oh, no," he said adamantly, "not me."

"Yes," I replied, "you."

"But what about Gaius?" he protested, then looked down at the table as he mumbled, "He's not going to like that."

I stifled my initial reaction, which was to snap that I did not give a fart in a *testudo* what Gaius did or did not like, realizing that this was not the time to indulge my temper.

Instead, I replied as evenly as I could manage, "Gaius had his opportunity, Septimus. And he wasn't up to the responsibility." I hesitated, then decided to be completely forthcoming. "Besides, what you told me about his...habits and how he treats slaves is proof that he's not fit to be in charge here."

"But we're going to be getting rid of the slaves," Septimus pointed out.

In answer, I gave him a long, level look, but when he did not say anything, I asked, "Are you saying that Gaius only likes to hurt slaves?"

I could see he was torn between being loyal to the one brother he knew well and me, the brother who only appeared once every several years, but finally, the truth won out, and he shook his head, admitting, "No, Titus. No, he likes to hurt...everyone."

"That's why he's no longer in any position to make any kind of decisions," I told him, gently but firmly. "And that's why you're the one I'm depending on." He did not say anything, but after a moment, nodded his understanding, which I took to be his assent as well. Then, I took a breath, not relishing what was coming, but I knew I had to do it immediately. "So go get Gaius and bring him here."

Septimus opened his mouth, but I cut his protest off with a look, prompting a sigh, though he got up and said, "Fine. I'll go get him."

It took long enough that I was beginning to think I would have to rouse myself from the table to go upstairs to get both of them, but I was so tired that I was not sure that I could manage. Then I heard raised voices, loud enough that I could tell it was an argument, though not the words themselves. Muttering a curse, I pushed myself up from the table, then I was saved by the sounds of footsteps descending the stairs, and I sat back down with some relief. Septimus reappeared first, with Gaius following behind him, his very being radiating his sullen anger, which he demonstrated by deliberately choosing the seat at the opposite end of the table, the spot where my mother normally sat. If circumstances had been different, and I had been in a better mood, I would have let it pass, knowing that the message I was about to deliver would be no more or less bitter because of where he sat, but this childish act of defiance was not one I was willing to tolerate.

Pointing to the bench on the opposite side of the table where Septimus was sitting, I ordered him coldly, "Get out of Mama's spot and come sit here where I tell you."

He did not answer, but neither did he move, crossing his arms and staring at me with undisguised hostility.

"Gaius," Septimus spoke up before I could say anything, his voice soft but with an undercurrent to it I had yet to hear from him, "I just saw our brother kill a man with a single blow with his *vitus*. Now," he glanced over at me, and I thought I caught a glimmer of a grim smile, "I don't *think* our brother would kill you. But," he shrugged, "right now, I don't know that I'd wager against it."

Gaius did not respond, nor did he move; at least, until I began to rise from my own chair. Only then did he do the same,

397

and still without speaking, he came and dropped heavily down onto the bench where I had indicated.

"Did you tell him anything?" I asked Septimus, but he shook his head, so I turned to Gaius and began, "I'm leaving shortly, so I'm going to get right to it. After seeing what I've seen, I've decided that you're to have nothing to do with any of the decisions regarding our family and its interests." He stiffened at this, but he turned to glare at Septimus, and I held up a hand, saying sharply, "Don't blame Septimus for this. In fact," I pointed in his face, wondering if he hated this as much as I did and not caring a bit if he did, "he tried to talk me out of this. But I'm the one making the decision, and that decision is final." Turning to Septimus, I reiterated, "But you're still going to have to let me know about anything involving the family and wait for me to decide what to do about it."

"What if it's something that needs to be decided immediately?" Septimus asked, but not in a challenging fashion, and I realized he had an excellent point, which ironically enough, solidified my belief he was the right choice.

I thought for a moment, then said cautiously, "All right, if it's something that can't be delayed, then I'll allow you to make the decision. But," I warned, "two things to keep in mind. First, it better not be something major, like," I turned to look Gaius in the eye, "selling every business we own outright or have a share in, in order to do something like try and make a killing in a business we've never been involved in." As I hoped, this affected Gaius in an almost physical way, and he recoiled as if I had struck him, but he did not say anything, just continued staring at me in disbelief and impotent fury. I could have left it there, but I wanted to hear Gaius acknowledge what I had said. "Is that clear, Gaius? I don't expect you to like it, but this isn't negotiable, and," I thought it wise to remind him, "I have the law on my side." When he only nodded, I snapped, "I want to hear you say that you understand me."

"I…understand." His voice was hoarse, but he was audible, and I contented myself with that.

Then, the sound of the cock crowing from its perch out in the back of the villa signaled that it was time for me to leave. However, I had one last task, so I stood and, turning away from Gaius, I told Septimus to follow me, which he did, avoiding Gaius' glare at him. It was only when I stepped out into the main yard that I realized I had not yet set foot in this part of the villa, but somehow, I instantly understood this had been intentional on my part; there were too many memories here, starting with the stakes that my Avus had put next to the outer wall. This was where he had spent his third of a watch every day, up to and including the last day of his life, and where I had spent even more time, trying to make myself worthy of his name. However, it was what was in essentially the opposite direction from the stakes that I had been avoiding, but there was no helping it now, given that it was time to leave, and I walked towards the stables, thinking of a large gray horse who occupied the last stall on the end. I was still about fifteen paces away when, from the dark recess of the same stall, I heard the unmistakable sound of a horse blowing, followed by the thudding as he pawed the dirt, the same way I had been greeted by Ocelus when he caught my scent. For the briefest moment, a sweetly painful instant, I was no longer a forty-year-old man, but a boy of twelve, hurrying to greet his best friend, who was always as eager for adventure as I was. Then, a nose came thrusting out from the darkness, nostrils distended, but while it was not gray, I instantly saw that it was Latobius. Despite everything, I felt a soft laugh bubble out of me, and I walked to him, letting him search my tunic for his apple.

"I'm sorry, boy," I murmured. "I forgot, but I've got a lot on my mind."

And, as he always did on those occasions where I neglected to bring him something, he reached out with his big, yellow teeth and gave my tunic a sharp tug to signal his displeasure.

Turning to Septimus, who had followed me but was clearly wondering why, I asked him, "How many extra saddles and tack do we have?"

His face cleared, understanding now, or at least thinking he did, answering, "Titus has his own saddle and bridle." He pointed to where they were hanging, and I asked him, "Do you have another one?"

"Another one?" Shrugging, he said he did, then asked me curiously, "But why? Your friend Dolabella already has one, and so do you."

I did not answer him directly, saying only, "You'll see. Now, do you have a saddle and bridle you can spare?"

He nodded, then went into the small tack room, while I saddled Latobius, soaking in memories of all the times I had done this with Ocelus, inhaling the smells of horse and hay. When Septimus returned, I pointed to one of the spare horses, a smaller black mare that only Dolabella could ride, and while he saddled it as I asked, I could hear him mumbling under his breath.

"I told you that you'll find out soon," I assured him.

And, almost as if I had deemed it to be so, I heard the back door open, the sound of voices drifting across the open ground. Leading Latobius out, I tied his reins to the post, then went and led out the spare horses, returning in time to see Dolabella emerge, carrying his saddlebags, followed by Birgit, then a moment later, Titus, also carrying baggage, but in contrast to Dolabella, he was actually struggling to carry what looked like two large sacks. From behind the main house, both Berdic and Nasua came hurrying around the corner, reminding me that the slave quarters were back there, next to the bathhouse, and they both ran towards us, with Berdic offering an apology for their tardiness, in such a fervent manner that I quietly told Septimus to let them know they were not in any trouble, another reminder of how Gaius had obviously treated them. The eastern sky was just turning pink, and the sight of it only served to emphasize how exhausted I already was, and I was struck by the thought that it had been one of the most eventful nights of my life, my adventures with Domitius during the rebellion of the Colapiani notwithstanding, but ironically, it was this memory that served as a spur to keep me moving. By the time the horses were saddled, the spares tied by their halters to Latobius and Dolabella's mount, all of my family, by both blood and oath, were gathered to see us off, and I felt the lump forming in my throat as I looked at them standing there, their eyes on me. Only Gaius was missing, but then I noticed someone else was missing as well, and the anger threatened to return.

Turning to Septimus, I told him, "Go get Gaius. And," I paused, "the Breuci girl."

"The Breuci girl?" my brother echoed, clearly not understanding, then his face cleared, and he asked, "Do you mean Juno?"

"That's not her name," I snapped without thinking, then I relented, saying, "but yes, that's who I'm talking about."

Suddenly, I saw the dawning of understanding on my brother's face, and his eyes went wide.

"Gaius isn't going to like that," he told me, but I was unmoved, and I replied, "I don't care. And," I said grimly, "I want him here to see this."

"Titus," Septimus kept his voice low, but there was a pleading quality to his tone that I chose to ignore, "this will humiliate Gaius! Please," he reached out to touch my arm, "don't do this. I understand that she needs to be sold, but taking her?" He shook his head. "I don't know how Gaius will react."

"Well," I replied, looking into his eyes, knowing that what he saw there was not his brother, but a Centurion of Rome who

401

expected to be obeyed, "there's only one way to find out. Now," I ordered, "go get them."

He did as I directed, while I spent the time walking over to where young Titus was standing there, next to his mother, who had tears in her eyes but was smiling broadly at the same time. Without saying anything, I bent down and began rummaging through his two large bags, pulling out and throwing away one item after another, while Birgit stood there protesting and Titus just looked slightly dazed. Once I was to the point where what was left fit into one of the sacks, only then did I relent, thrusting it into his chest.

"Go tie that to your horse," I told him, and he moved without protest, while Birgit glared at me for a moment.

"Maybe," she admitted, "I packed too much."

Laughing, I agreed, "Yes, maybe you did."

Then, I turned to Gisela and Scribonia, giving each of them a long, hard hug, trying to maintain my composure as they wept, then I squatted down to solemnly offer young Gaius my arm, man to man, which he accepted with equal gravity, causing me to remember what it was like when my father had treated me like a man and not a child. Which, naturally, meant that I ruined it for him by sweeping him into an embrace and a kiss on each cheek, stuffing down the emotion caused by seeing my brother Sextus in his son. Miriam's children were next, but frankly, they were more excited at being roused to participate in what they viewed as this very adult farewell, but young Atia began crying as well, which did not help. Manius, his scare at being swung around apparently forgotten, I hugged as well, then, as I had with young Gaius I offered him my arm, in our manner, being very solemn as I told him to watch out for his mother and sister, something that he promised to do with the same solemnity as his cousin Gaius. By this point, Septimus, Gaius, and the girl had emerged from the house. As I expected, Gaius was still sullen, refusing to look me in the eyes; until, that is, I stepped forward, grasped the Breuci girl by the arm, then pointed to the black mare.

Speaking in her tongue, I told her, "Go get on that horse, girl. I'm taking you home."

Gaius may not have understood the words, but he divined my intent instantly, and this animated him.

"No!" he shouted, then turning to the girl, he pointed back to the house. "Juno, get back in the house!"

The girl was clearly terrified, but it was not lost on me that she looked to me first, not my brother, and I assured her, "You don't have to do what he says, girl." Struck by what I believed was an inspiration, I said, "Unless you want to stay here with my brother. If you love him…"

"I do *not*," she answered instantly and with such vehemence that, whether Gaius understood the words, he at least comprehended that whatever she was saying was not to his benefit.

As I hoped, this prompted her to turn and walk, her back straight, to the mare, where the slave Berdic, who looked slightly dazed, helped her into the saddle.

Finally, Gaius found his voice, and his courage, because he came lunging at me, shrieking at the top of his lungs something that, while unintelligible needed no translation, both his fists bunched as he launched himself at me. He was stopped cold, not by me but by Septimus, who stepped in front of me and timed his punch perfectly so that Gaius' head essentially met his fist, snapping his head back and dropping him, unconscious before he hit the dirt, where he lay in a heap.

Turning to me, my youngest brother gave me a sad smile and said, "I'm sorry how your homecoming went, Titus."

Honestly, I was in such a turmoil of emotions that, while I said something, I cannot recall what it was, but after taking his arm, I embraced Septimus.

"Don't worry about Gaius," he whispered, "he'll be fine." When he broke our embrace, he grinned up at me and added, "When he wakes up." Shaking his hand, he observed, "How can something hurt but feel good at the same time?"

Despite my sadness and the sum of the memories that were crowding in on me, I had to laugh at this, and I clapped my brother on the back, then turned and leapt into the saddle. After one last check to make sure that Titus, the girl, and Dolabella were ready, I lifted a hand to my family and led my party out of the gates; the only people who were not crying were the two slaves, and I remember the thought that they would be joining everyone else once Septimus told them of their fate that they would be going to new masters. Or, I thought grimly, they would be thanking their gods that they were getting away from my other brother.

Nothing was said between our newly enlarged party for the first third of a watch as we rode east on the Via Aurelia, weaving our way through the mixture of traffic; the wagons hauling goods, the poorer people for whom their only method of transport were their two feet, although most of them were pulling loaded carts and were heading in the opposite direction, towards Arelate, reminding me that it was market day. Titus and the girl Algaia were riding behind us, but while I heard some whispering, neither of them spoke up loud enough for me to hear; I guessed that Titus was informing her of the momentous events of what was now the night before. Dolabella looked somewhat refreshed, yet he seemed content to just gaze ahead, examining the road and the variety of people on it. As for myself, simply put, I was in a daze, one created from a combination of exhaustion and all that had transpired in my life and that of the Pullus family in such a short period of time. Trying to make sense of it, I took the approach with which I was most familiar, composing what would be the kind of report after an engagement or notable event that I would write as a Centurion, albeit only in my head and not on a tablet. It was the thought of tablets that prompted me to break the silence, as I suddenly remembered something.

Reaching into my tunic, I withdrew the tablet that Septimus had given me, and I turned to Dolabella, not sure how to start, so I just began by blurting, "Dolabella, I need another favor."

This prompted a slight smile from him, but he turned to look at me and said, "If I can."

I did not hand the tablet over immediately, instead giving a brief account of all that I had learned about the horrendous damage done to my family's fortune, making the decision to leave nothing out, including my judgment of my brother.

For his part, Dolabella simply listened as we rode along, saying nothing until I was finished, when he asked, "What was the man's name again?"

"Avienus," I answered. "Decimus Avienus. At least I think so." Slightly embarrassed by my realization that I had not even opened the tablet, I did so then, reading the contents, precious little that there seemed to be to my eye, but it confirmed the man's name. "It says here," I felt a frown forming, though that was nothing compared to the twisting in my gut, "that, while he was reputed to be the biggest grain merchant in Arelate, he hadn't been there all that long, just three years. Which," I sighed, snapping it shut, "explains why I never heard of him."

"I don't know the man's name, but what you just described sounds familiar," Dolabella said, and I glanced over to see what I assumed to be the same kind of frown that was on my face. Shaking his head, he reached out for the tablet, which I handed to him, then watched as he perused the contents. He did not hand it back; instead, he pulled the bag he always wore slung over his shoulder around in front of him, dropping the tablet into it before swinging it back around behind him. Only then did he resume speaking. "As I said, that name isn't familiar. But," this was

405

when he looked over at me, "the circumstances of what happened to your family are, and while I don't know with any certainty, I wouldn't be surprised if this is the same man."

Dolabella went on to relate another story that, the moment I heard it, I understood why he had said as much, because it did sound strikingly similar. A young, wealthy plebeian had just taken control of his family's fortune; this had been in Massillia, and a relative newcomer to the city had rapidly become reputed to be the most powerful and influential merchant in his business, although this was in wine and not grain. And, just like with Gaius, this young plebeian had been approached with an offer to not just triple, but quadruple his family's fortune by this well-established merchant, and as Dolabella told this version of the tale, I knew this was no coincidence.

"This young pup was shown the vast warehouses capable of holding so many amphorae of wine," Dolabella explained, "and then he was told by an associate of this merchant," he paused for a moment, cocking his head before continuing, "I've been trying to remember this merchant's name. I think it was Servius Nobilior. Anyway, the youngster met with a man the merchant claimed was the owner of the largest vineyard in Hispania, who explained to him that there had been a blight of some sort on the year's grape crop. Naturally, this would drive the prices up. However, the merchant told the boy he had excellent connections in Syria and Judea, and there was no blight there."

"At least he didn't use the drought," I interjected. "Although," I allowed grudgingly, "that was real. What about this...blight?"

Dolabella shrugged, saying, "I don't know if it was real or not. But the boy thought it was, and he scraped up something like a million *sesterces* to hire the merchant's warehouses, contract with a fleet that," now he gave me an amused look, "was provided by the merchant, and of course, all the transportation on both sides of Our Sea."

"Let me guess," I said bitterly, "that plebeian never actually saw either the fleet or met the master."

"Actually," Dolabella replied, "while he didn't see the actual fleet of ships, he did insist on meeting the master of all those ships, which was arranged by the merchant."

I did not know whether to laugh or cry that Gaius had not even taken that precaution, so my only comment was, "That 'merchant' probably went down to the docks, grabbed the first deckhand who looked the part, and paid him to pretend to be the master of a fleet that never existed."

"Probably," Dolabella agreed.

"So where did you hear about this?" I asked him, and he suddenly looked away, warning me that what he was about to say was probably something to which I needed to pay attention.

"As it turns out," he said after a short silence, "the boy's father was known to Tiberius, and had supported Tiberius during the time he was in Rhodes. So," he shrugged, "I was told to look into it. But then, all this," he waved a hand in the air in a manner that communicated his meaning, "happened. I suppose that once this is over, he'll want me to get back to it. Unless," Dolabella's tone turned almost glum, "he deems it necessary to tie up some loose ends with these rebellions."

He looked at me again; there was no need for him to say anything more than this, because the moment the words left his mouth, I understood what he meant. And, given that I had been one of those men that Tiberius had used in the past to tie up those "loose ends," I suddenly felt a stab of alarm and not a little fear. Was that really why I was accompanying Dolabella to Siscia? Had Tiberius given Dolabella orders to have the ringleaders removed? And, most importantly, was Dolabella counting on my relationship with Titus Domitius to enable me to get close enough to him to carry out Tiberius' orders? My mind began running so quickly with all that it meant, I was getting physically dizzy, and I had to reach down and grab the saddle with my free hand.

"Titus. Titus!"

Dolabella's voice finally cut through the noise inside my head, and I turned to stare at him, but I was not expecting the look he was giving me, with an expression that was difficult for me to identify, but seemed to be at least partly composed of sadness. Which, I must add, only served to reinforce this sudden conviction about why I was riding on this road with Tiberius' spymaster.

"No," Dolabella said, quietly but firmly, then nothing else.

"No?" I repeated. "No, what?"

He heaved a sigh, then there was no mistaking the sadness in his voice as he answered, "I know what you're thinking, Titus. And the answer is, no, Tiberius hasn't given me any orders concerning Domitius. And," he actually moved his mount closer to me so he could look me directly in the face, his one good eye fixed on me, "I would never ask you to do something like that. I told you," another sigh came, "I've reached a point where I can't do those things anymore."

This version of Dolabella was one with which I was still struggling, yet something in me told me that he was being sincere.

Still, I felt compelled to point out, "But what if Tiberius does order you to do one of those…things?"

"I don't know," he answered immediately, which convinced me he was being honest about this, at least. "I honestly don't. But," his voice dropped a bit, presumably so that neither Titus nor Algaia could hear, "what I do know is that even if Tiberius doesn't do it, Drusus is likely to, which is why we have to get there as quickly as we can." Nodding that I understood, Dolabella told me, "On this other matter with your brother. As soon as we're done, I'll look into it."

"He's probably run off to Rome," I said glumly, "and we both know he's not going by Avienus, or Nobilior, for that matter."

I was a bit surprised when Dolabella shook his head.

"I don't think he went to Rome," he said without hesitation. "I think he is living across Our Sea by now. My guess would be Alexandria, or maybe Damascus."

"Why?" I asked him, and again, he answered quickly.

"Because the one common theme in both of these things is Africa. The wine was coming from Africa. The grain was coming from Africa. From everything that I've read in what you gave me, and what little I learned about what happened in Massillia, that's the one common thread." Suddenly, he turned and asked me curiously, "Which of your brothers wrote all this down?"

"Septimus," I told him.

"Well, if these observations are from him, and I think they probably are, given what little I saw of your other brother, he's a clever young man. And," he pointed out, "did you read that line about the one time Septimus met with this Avienus? How he had an accent that Septimus couldn't place?"

I had, in fact, missed that, and I told him as much.

"Because of its location on the Via Aurelia," Dolabella explained, "that means that your brothers were likely to hear all manner of accents, but from this side of Our Sea. People from Hispania, Gaul, and Italia would be familiar to him as far as their accents. And," he pointed out, "I know that he was very young, but I'm sure that he heard enough of the Pannonian accent to recognize it again when he heard it."

I digested this, and I confess that I was deeply impressed by Dolabella's reasoning.

When I complimented him, he actually flushed and looked quite pleased, though he warned, "I could be wrong about this."

"You could be," I agreed, then before he could react, I added, "but I don't think you are. Still," I sighed, "we've got other things to worry about."

"Yes, we do," Dolabella replied grimly.

Chapter Eight

Somehow, I survived that first day without toppling from the saddle, although at our first rest stop, I barely got off Latobius, then staggered over to a tree, dropped down at its base, and was asleep before a count of ten. Dolabella took pity on me, and we stayed put for two parts of a watch, but while I felt a little better, I was far from recovered. Nevertheless, we made good progress along the Via Aurelia, heading for Italia, continuing on the Via Julia Augusta, reaching Genua late the second day. By this point in time, I was somewhat better, but the biggest change had come over the girl, Algaia. Understandably, she had been apprehensive about this sudden and dramatic shift in her fortunes, and I learned later that she had actually been suspicious that this was some sort of ploy cooked up by my brother to test her loyalty to him. I knew that it was no such thing, but even if it had been, he would have viewed it as a spectacular failure on her part, because she did not mention either his name or anything remotely resembling concern for him. Indeed, once she accepted that I was not up to something sinister, and then was convinced that I did intend to return her to Pannonia, quite frankly, it proved almost impossible to get her to shut up. Not that most of our party minded, especially young Titus, who hung on every word out of her mouth, causing Dolabella and I to exchange amused glances on more than one occasion. There was one thing that I did, ostensibly to her but more for the girl, and that was when I took notice that she was still wearing the little brass plate around her neck. She had tucked it under her simple shift, which was the entire extent of her belongings, save of a bracelet made of hammered silver that she said Gaius had given her as a gift. When we stopped to acquire different spare horses in Genua, I took a bit of extra time, handing the girl a handful of coins.

"Go get some more things to wear," I said gruffly. Turning to Titus, I told him, "You go with her. Make sure she stays safe." As I expected, this made Titus draw himself up, thrust out his chest, and declare that he would do that very thing, then they both went off, while I watched with a smile and a shake of my head before I remembered what had drawn my attention in the first place. Calling to the girl, when she turned around, I pointed at her neck, ordering, "And when you come back, I don't want to see that thing around your neck. Understand?"

While she nodded, nothing came out of her mouth, and I believe it was this moment she truly accepted that her days as a slave were over, and Titus took her gently by the elbow and led her off.

"Don't be surprised if she's with child by the time we get to Siscia," Dolabella teased me, then with a spark of what I had learned was his sense of mischief when it came to taunting me, he grinned and said, "and who knows? It might be mine."

This did evoke a laugh from me, and I told him, "I have a feeling young Titus might have something to say about that."

It was an offhand remark, one that I offered with little thought; this ranks as one of the few times when I appeared to have the gift of sight like the Oracle of Delphi.

Two days past a week after we left Germanicus, we rode into Emona, the first large town inside the borders of the province of Pannonia, but before we reached it, we saw the first signs of trouble, in the smaller settlement of Nauportus. The place had been thoroughly looted, most of the buildings either seriously damaged or reduced to ruins, but although we attempted to question the few people we saw, the instant they saw us, they fled in terror, something that neither of us understood at the time, although we would be learning why soon enough. As far as Emona was concerned, arriving there about a third of a watch later, I was not sure what to expect; my last time there was during the Batonian Revolt, but that had concluded four years earlier, while my part in it with the *Legio Germanicus* ended a year before the rebellion was finally crushed. Given its location and its importance, Emona was always bustling, and had always been one of the first stops for settlers fleeing from marauding tribes, though that was more the case during my childhood and my early years in the 8th. Regardless, I confess I was surprised to see how much it had grown, the evidence being that there were now a substantial number of buildings, both dwellings and businesses, outside of the town walls, although it was still the same wall, in the same spot it had been the last time I was there. This was the last leg of our journey, Siscia a bit more than a hundred miles away, but even with the urgency, Dolabella and I conferred, and we agreed that tarrying here for an extra third of a watch or two might prove to our profit.

"All we have to do is sit down in The Grotto of Pan, keep our mouths shut, and listen," was how Dolabella put it, naming the spot frequented by the lower classes, which meant people who were most closely associated with the Legions, "we'll learn more that way than we would by asking questions."

Not only did I agree, in this area, even if I did not, I would have deferred to Dolabella's expertise, so we began heading to the establishment Dolabella had mentioned.

"I'm going to show Algaia around the town," Titus informed us. "She's never been here before." He was so earnest that I had to bite the inside of my cheek to stop myself from laughing.

"Well," I answered him genially, "we wouldn't want Algaia to miss all the wonderful things to see in Emona. Would we, Tiberius?"

I turned to Dolabella, who was grinning broadly, and he was no less enthusiastic in agreeing, "No, we wouldn't, Titus. It is a truly wonderful place, Emona, and I wouldn't be able to sleep if I thought that the Mistress Algaia missed any of it."

Titus knew he was being teased, the flush moving all the way up his face to his hair, while the Breuci girl looked off in another direction, but I saw the corners of her mouth twitching as she tried to keep from laughing.

As lighthearted as this was, I still warned Titus, "I expect you back here in a third of a watch. Do you understand? And if we're not out here, you come in."

He opened his mouth as if he intended to argue, but I gave him a look that, like his older brother would, he interpreted correctly, mumbling that he understood. With that, the pair wandered off, and for no real reason, I watched them walking down the street; I was rewarded when, after Titus had clearly decided they had gone a sufficient distance to be out of range of my prying eyes, he reached out his hand. And, completely unsurprisingly, I saw the girl respond to the gesture, her hand falling into his in a manner that told me this was not the first time they had done as much. What *was* surprising was the stab of an emotion that struck me so hard it brought a sudden misting of tears to my eyes, but it took me a moment to recognize it for what it was; a combination of memory, envy, and regret.

"Are you ready?" Dolabella asked, jerking me away from the sight of the pair of young lovers, and when I turned to assure him that I was, I saw him looking at me with an expression that told me he had probably divined my thoughts.

Thankfully, he did not say anything, and I told him that I was, so we entered The Grotto of Pan, a place that any man who has served under the standard for any length of time would immediately recognize. Indeed, I often had the thought that, in some form of magic, every such place I entered, no matter where it was located, was actually the same establishment, just mysteriously transported from one spot to the next.

As always happened, our entry drew scant attention from those patrons nearest the door, until they took in my size, which kept them from turning back to their cups for perhaps a heartbeat or two longer, making a quiet comment to their companions, which prompted Dolabella to mutter, "So much for not being noticed." Before I could respond, he grinned at me and said, "I keep forgetting that just standing next to you draws attention."

Moving to an empty table, we took our seats, which resulted in a small battle about who would sit facing the door, which was a habit that we both had developed, and I was not shy about using my bulk to gently muscle him away from the chair, which he grumbled about, taking the chair next to me and not across the table so that he could at least partially see the door. The woman who served us was just as interchangeable as any of those that worked in Ubiorum, although her eyes did linger on me for a moment, and while I could not be sure, I thought there was a flicker of some form of recognition in her eyes, though she said nothing. I watched her walking away to the counter, behind which the proprietor stood, and my fears seemed to be confirmed as I saw her say something to the man that prompted him to look over her shoulder, directly in our direction.

"So much for that," I muttered to Dolabella, but he had already noticed, although he shrugged it off, saying only, "Maybe they're just talking about how big you are."

This was possible, but I did not believe it to be the case, though there was nothing to be done about it. The woman returned quickly enough, bearing cups containing what I assumed was the normal grade of wine served in such places, except that when I took my first sip, slightly curious as to why the woman seemed to be lingering, I was quite surprised. Pleasantly so, I should say; while not Falernian nor Chian, it was a vintage that was quite good, and Dolabella noticed immediately as well, and we exchanged a glance.

Turning to the woman, who was still standing there, Dolabella said smoothly, "This is an excellent grape, madam. If I had known you served such high quality refreshment, I would have made a special trip to come here long before this."

This amused the woman, who gave a short laugh, "We don't serve that, normally. That's from our special amphora that we only serve certain guests. Besides," she turned away from Dolabella to point directly at me, "this isn't in your honor; it's in his."

I felt the rush of blood to my face, and I stared hard at the woman, trying to recall if we had ever met, and if we had, under what circumstances; my initial guess was that perhaps I had been one of her customers, back when she was young and pretty enough to ply another trade back in Siscia, but she was not familiar to me, not that this meant anything.

Thankfully, she cleared it up as she continued talking, "It's just me and Lucius' way of thanking the Primus Pilus here for what he and young Germanicus did a few years back."

Things fell into place then; although I still did not recognize her, this was not unusual, but more importantly, I understood she was referring to my time serving under Germanicus, and we had indeed spent time in Emona as we hastily assembled a scratch force as part of Rome's attempt to put down the Batonian Revolt.

I did feel compelled to point out, "That was a temporary rank. I'm not a Primus Pilus, just a Princeps Posterior now."

She reacted in the manner of all civilians when confronted with the intricacies of the Legions, with a shrug and a comment, "Whatever you say, Centurion. All I know is that young Germanicus and all you who marched with him helped save us, and we haven't forgotten." I murmured my thanks, which she waved off, but she still lingered, which was only partially explained when she asked, "So, what brings you here to Emona, Centurion?" Before either of us could respond, she added with a casualness that was obviously feigned, "Are you heading to Rome?" Then, she leaned forward slightly, took a quick look around at the other patrons and whispered, "Are you the one the boys from the Legions are sending to talk to Tiberius?"

This changed matters dramatically, at least as far as I was concerned, and this was one time I was happy to defer to Dolabella. I glanced over just in time to see the look of surprise cross his features, but he was far too experienced to allow the woman to see it, and he correctly interpreted my lack of response as the cue to speak for the both of us.

"No, madam," he began, but she made an impatient wave, saying, "My name's Fulvia."

Dolabella corrected himself, "No, Fulvia, we're not heading to Rome. In fact, we're heading in the opposite direction, towards Siscia."

Her eyes narrowed, but it was the expression of what I interpreted as a conspiratorial slyness, and she kept her voice to a whisper, "Are you sent by Tiberius?"

"Now why would you think that?" Dolabella asked lightly, but I could feel his sudden tension.

"Because of him," she nodded at me, but then she surprised me and rocked Dolabella when, only then did she turn to look at Dolabella and inform him calmly, "and because I know you're one of Tiberius' men."

And, just that quickly, I began to worry for this woman Fulvia, who was either too observant, too nosy, or most likely a combination of both, for her own good.

"And," Dolabella's tone was calm enough, but I heard the menace there, "what makes you believe such nonsense? How could you possibly think that I'm, what did you call me," he cocked his head, and he spoke in slightly mocking way, "'one of Tiberius' men'?"

Judging from the manner in which Fulvia suddenly stiffened, then glanced over to where the man I assumed was Lucius was standing there, his eyes fastened on our table, she had realized her misstep.

"Oh," she said casually, "it's just a guess." The laugh she gave was forced, waving a dismissive hand as she babbled,

"Sometimes I just make guesses about things, and I have no idea what I'm saying! It's a bad habit of mine, I know."

"Yes, Fulvia," Dolabella agreed quietly, his good eye never leaving her, which meant that his other eye was looking in my general direction, something I still had not really gotten used to, "it is a bad habit. And," he added, this time not bothering to disguise that there was a warning there, "if I *was* one of Tiberius' men, as you say, I'd be most...upset to know that someone's tongue was wagging and letting other people know that."

Fulvia's face went deadly pale, and she gasped, "Oh, sir! I would *never* do anything like that! You can ask anyone in here. I don't betray anyone's trust! Why," she tried another laugh, but it was even less convincing than the previous one, "if I told half of what I know about the people in this town, there would be so much trouble in every house in Emona! But I don't say a word! I swear it! I..."

Dolabella held up his hand, and I admit I was impressed how it served to cut this woman's words off as if he had stuck a cork in her mouth.

"I believe you, Fulvia," he said, and she sagged in relief for just long enough for Dolabella to add, "but in order for me to *trust* you, I..." He gestured at me. "...we need information."

"Information?" Fulvia repeated, then said eagerly, "Anything you need, good sirs! I wasn't lying when I said that Lucius and I are grateful to the Centurion here, and I'm a good Roman citizen!"

Indicating that she pull up an empty chair, Dolabella watched with quiet amusement at how quickly she moved to do so, picking up a chair and bringing it to our table.

Waiting for her to sit down, only then did Dolabella ask her, "So, what do you know about all the things that are happening in Siscia?"

"Siscia?" Fulvia shook her head. "The Legions aren't in Siscia, Master."

We glanced at each other, and I know that our thoughts were running along the same lines; had we gone out of our way for nothing? Ultimately, we were in The Grotto of Pan for well more than the third part of a watch I had told Titus; indeed, we were there so long that Titus and Algaia came wandering in, and I was so absorbed in what we were hearing from this woman that I barely noticed their respective states, just tossing them another couple coins and telling them to go find something to eat. By the time Fulvia had finished relating all that she knew about the situation with the Legions, which was quite a lot, the sun was hanging low in the sky, my mind was reeling, and I was suddenly certain that we would arrive too late to be of any help, mainly because we learned that the Legions were not in Siscia.

Just as Caecina had done, the Legate in command of the Army of Pannonia, Quintus Junius Blaesus, had marched the army away from Siscia within watches of the word of Augustus' death, choosing a spot I knew very well, near Splonum. I tried to hide my reaction when Fulvia had informed us of this, given how much of a role the seat of the Maezaei kings had played in my life, but I could tell that Dolabella was not fooled. As bad as this was, the other things we had learned from Fulvia were just as disturbing, to put it mildly, although we did learn that what happened at Nauportus had nothing to do with native tribes taking advantage of the unrest with the Legions; indeed, it had been the Legions who had been the cause of it. Specifically, five Cohorts from the 15th, who were now normally quartered in Poetovio since the 13th had been transferred east, had been dispatched to perform some repair work on the roads and bridges in and around Nauportus. They were under command of a Camp Prefect named Avidienus Rufus, it now being the practice that Camp Prefects are assigned more to locations where there is a permanent camp than to a particular army. This was a relatively new development, and I did know that it was not viewed with any favor by those men like my former Primus Pilus, Gaius Sempronius Atticus, who up until this change, had been the sole Camp Prefect of the Army of Pannonia, because in his view, it diluted the prestige of the posting. This was something I had learned in one of Domitius' last letters to me a couple years earlier, before he stopped corresponding, a situation I intended to get to the bottom of as soon as it was possible. Regardless of Atticus' feelings, Camp Prefect Rufus, who was in nominal command of these five Cohorts, had apparently tried to crack down on these men because Blaesus had relaxed the discipline in response to the news of Augustus' death. While it was somewhat understandable – I felt reasonably certain that the men of Pannonia had been as upset and anxious at the news of the Princeps' death as the Army of the Rhenus had been – I also could not imagine that Prefect Atticus had counseled Blaesus to take this step. And, obviously, Rufus had not been in agreement with Blaesus' decision either, because his attempt to instill the normal discipline and habits that are an integral part of life under the standard ended up with him being beaten, put into chains, and made to march as a prisoner all the way back to the camp near Splonum. Not immediately, however; the destruction and looting of Nauportus had to be done first, wagons and carts being appropriated to haul back the loot. Meanwhile, matters in the camp had apparently completely degenerated in much the same manner as they had in the camp near Caedicius', the only difference being that Blaesus was initially allowed to move among the men freely and was not confined to the *praetorium*.

The woman Fulvia had proven to be a true fount of information, which made sense when one considered how effective wine is as a lubricant to tongues, and I have little doubt that her willingness to cooperate was also heavily influenced by Dolabella's quiet but very potent threat. Normally, I would have bridled at how the spymaster had used his status as Tiberius' man to threaten this woman, but given the circumstances and the time constraints, I chose to look the other way in a figurative sense. Honestly, I was every bit as eager to hear whatever news the woman could impart to us about what we were heading into, and in this respect, she did not disappoint. She did mention Domitius' name, but not as one of the men who were causing the most problems, and in fact, he was brought up as one of the cooler heads among the Legionaries who were trying to keep the lid on a simmering pot. All I could hope for was that Tiberius was not willing to be punitive in his punishment of any of the men of Centurionate or Optionate rank who had a role in this uprising, and I confess I was anxious that Dolabella keep this in mind. Unfortunately, my friend's role as a moderate voice was clearly not being heeded, which we learned in more graphic detail from the hundreds of civilians we ran into fleeing in the opposite direction, from Siscia. It was from them we heard what happened after the mutineers from Nauportus returned to Siscia carrying their loot from the town, forcing Rufus to lead the way through the city on their way to the marching camp. If the mutineers persisted in their treatment of the Prefect all the way back into the marching camp, still in chains, it would be a provocation so blatant that Blaesus could not ignore it. Frankly, it was difficult piecing it all together, since not one person we met seemed to know the complete series of events, and that was not even taking into account the normal tendency of people to exaggerate things they may or may not have actually witnessed, or even fabricate things that never happened. The practical consequence of our stopping those fleeing citizens willing to talk was that our progress was slowed even further, but Dolabella and I discussed it, agreeing that it was better to be slightly delayed if it gave us a better idea of what we were heading into.

I briefly considered taking the secondary road that turned southeast at the outpost of Crucium, which served only as a relay point for couriers, but given that it would take us through both Latobici and the heart of Colapiani territory, and given my history with them, chose not to do so. Latobius was beginning to show signs that he was fatigued to the point where I would need to allow him to rest more than a watch, but as much as I hated to do it, we could not afford to tarry. Dolabella brought up the idea of leaving Latobius once we got to the next relay station, then coming back for him on our way back; such was my uncertainty about what lay ahead that I did not take this suggestion. The closer we got to Siscia, the direr the tales; from one fleeing merchant, we heard that the Legions had slaughtered not only Legate Blaesus, but every Tribune, and the majority of the Centurions. He based this on his supposed inside knowledge, which came through being one of the main suppliers to the Army of Pannonia of grain. Only after being pressed did he finally admit that he had no firsthand knowledge, though he insisted that the source for this information was a man he completely trusted. Once we let him go on his way, Dolabella and I quietly discussed it, yet while neither of us thought it likely, we could not completely disregard the possibility that the merchant was telling the truth. Which meant, of course, that we would be too late, and if that *was* true, then the fate of men like Domitius, presuming he was on the side of the mutineers, was already sealed. The only thing we knew with any certainty was that we were closing in on Drusus and his party, although incrementally, since they were essentially doing the same thing that we were, riding horses into the ground to reach the army as quickly as possible, at least so we believed.

Dolabella held out hope that, knowing Drusus as he did, Tiberius' natural son would, after several days of hard travel, be too tempted by the baths and pleasures of Siscia, such as they were, and would stop for at least a night. This was something I found hard to believe, but Dolabella proved that he knew Drusus quite well, because we learned immediately upon our arrival at the camp, still a mile outside of Siscia, that Drusus had done that very thing. This was all well and good, but neither the auxiliary sentry nor the Centurion in command of the auxiliaries left behind by the army could provide anything more substantial than the knowledge that Drusus and his company were staying in the town and not in the camp. This was enough, however, since there were only two possibilities where a man of Drusus' rank would deign to spend a night, and Dolabella seemed certain which of the two he would choose. Although it would not be correct to say that Siscia was deserted, the traffic in the streets was noticeably thinner than was normal for the time of day, late afternoon, but it was the demeanor of the people that was the most telling that something quite unsettling was taking place. Dolabella's guess, if it could be called that, proved correct, and when I asked him how he had been so sure, he laughed.

"Remember, I know Siscia pretty well myself." He pointed to the building next to the inn, which was decorated in a style that was understated yet in such a manner that it left no doubt as to the carnal pleasures that lay within its confines. "I remember Juno's Chamber. And," he added with a grin, "I remember mentioning something of it to Drusus once."

I complimented him on his powers of deduction, but when I began to swing out of the saddle, Dolabella stopped me with a hand on my arm, all traces of his smile from an instant before gone.

"Actually, Pullus," he spoke in a low tone, a habit of his that I had long before supposed he had developed because of his work, "I don't think you should come in." When I opened my mouth, he said quickly, "It has nothing to do with being worried about you being around Drusus. Although," for the merest flash, I saw his mouth twitch, "it might do him some good to be around someone like you before he goes and tries to cow the Legions here. No," he shook his head, "I think it's in our best interest if you get to where the army is camped, ahead of Drusus and whatever message he plans to deliver."

I felt my jaw go slack as I stared at him in astonishment; this was not at all what I had been expecting.

Somehow, I managed to speak loudly enough to be heard. "You expect me to go down there by myself? And to do what?"

He did not look surprised at the question, because he answered readily, "I think you need to find Domitius and talk to him. Let him know why you're there and why you're worried." There was no mistaking the grimness of his tone. "I've told you of my concerns about how Drusus will handle this, but if I'm right about who one of his companions is, I think the chances of him handling this badly are about as close to certain as you can get."

I tried to recall Dolabella's mentioning of whoever this mystery man may have been, but I could not recall, yet when I asked him, he said evasively, "It might be nothing. I just want to be certain. Besides," he pointed out, "it can't hurt to try and contact Domitius before things become really official, because once Drusus shows up, he is Tiberius' representative, and he's been empowered by his father to act as he sees fit, and Tiberius trusts Drusus' judgment. The problem with that is," Dolabella sighed, "Tiberius is blind when it comes to seeing any faults with his natural son, just like he's blind to seeing anything good about Germanicus. At least," he amended, "as far as politics goes." Shaking his head, he finished with, "I'm just trying to do what I can to make sure that this turns out as well for all parties as can be arranged."

Now, I will say that there was a time when, if Tiberius Dolabella had said this, I would have called him a liar and probably would have ended up with my hands around his neck again, something that had become something of a joke between us. But on this journey, I had glimpsed a side to the spymaster I had never seen, and I have wondered on occasion if it had always been there, but my hostility for the man had blinded me to it, or if this was one of the effects of Dolabella aging. The gods knew that, as I grow older, some of the things I viewed as absolute truths no longer seem as absolute, and I doubt I am unique. And, once I shoved the thoughts of my own safety to the back of my mind, I had to acknowledge that Dolabella was correct; if I could get to Domitius somehow, as slim a chance as it might have been, to affect some sort of positive ending to this drama, it was worth taking it.

"What about Titus and Algaia?" I asked him.

"They can stay with me," he replied. "In fact, it might be best if they stay in Siscia when I leave with Drusus."

"I'm going with you, Uncle Titus." Young Titus, who, along with the girl, had been completely forgotten, had nudged his horse forward so that he was beside us.

"No you're not," I answered firmly. "I have no idea what I'm heading into, but the one thing I'm sure of, I'm going to have enough to worry about just keeping my own head on my shoulders. I can't afford to worry about you."

He opened his mouth, but while I could guess it was going to be some sort of objection, the Breuci girl, also moving her horse, reached out and touched Diocles' youngest son on the elbow. When he turned to face her, she said nothing but just gave a slight shake of her head, and I was thankful that Titus was facing the opposite direction, because if he had seen Dolabella and me giving each other a glance and grinning, his young pride would have been pricked, and there is no telling what might have happened.

"Fine," he said sulkily, then twisted his mount's head around to return to the spot he had been a moment before.

The girl did not look triumphant, nor did she look all that pleased, and I suspected she knew that she had embarrassed Titus, but I also knew it was the right thing for her to do, and while I did not say as much, I gave her a grave nod of thanks, which she acknowledged before she also turned to join Titus.

425

"Take care of them," was all I said to Dolabella. "Make sure he doesn't do anything stupid. And," I confess this was something of an afterthought, "try to watch after the girl. I still plan and freeing her once I have the chance."

This clearly surprised Dolabella, and he took a quick glance over his shoulder before turning back and saying softly, "Have you talked to her about this?"

This caught me off guard, so I answered a bit brusquely, "I told her the day we left Arelate. She knows." Suddenly, I felt a glimmer of doubt, which prompted me to ask, "Doesn't she?"

"I think," Dolabella made no attempt to hide his amusement, "things may have changed on that account."

I was about to answer, then realized this was not something that was immediately important, so instead, I turned my horse in preparation to leave Siscia.

"May Fortuna bless you, Titus," Dolabella said solemnly while offering his arm.

"And you, Tiberius," I answered, then grasped it.

"Hopefully I'll still be alive the next time you see me." I tried to sound lighthearted, as if it was a joke, but it did not feel like one, nor did Dolabella take it as such.

"So do I," he answered soberly.

Then, I kicked the spare horse I was riding, and leading Latobius and the other mounts, I went immediately to the trot, leaving Siscia. I had spent the first ten years of my life, then after an interval, another ten years here, but on this occasion, I was inside the town walls less than a third of a watch.

From the moment I left Ubiorum, this journey had proven to be one of the most trying, strangest trips I had ever taken. Between the interval in Arelate, and now, when I was revisiting the countryside where I had seen, experienced and suffered so much, I quickly began to feel the hand of the gods at work, something that I have been unable to shake since. Roads as familiar to me as any I have ever traveled, with memories both pleasant and painful that colored my view of almost every mile, created such an intense sensation that twice I had to stop and catch my breath, despite the fact that I was sitting in a saddle. I was not the only one affected; even Latobius seemed different, his ears pricked forward, blowing through his huge nostrils as he took in scents that were familiar to him, or so I assumed. We gave Splonum a wide berth, but I was not fooled into thinking that I was passing through Colapiani, Breuci, and Maezaei territory unobserved; my hope was that whoever was watching me was at a sufficient distance that I was not recognized, either by my size or by my features. The camp was located almost equidistant between the Maezaei mining town of Clandate, where I had burned the village against the express orders of Primus Pilus Atticus in the immediate aftermath of Sextus' death, and Raetinium, which I had helped subdue with Germanicus, and where one of my oldest comrades Servius Metellus had died. I bring this up as a way to explain my state of mind, and why, despite knowing the dangers of this country better than perhaps anyone, I was caught by surprise by a party of men. The only reason I am alive is because they were fellow Romans, Legionaries from the 9th Legion, who, much like the mutineers back in Germania, had been sent out to forage by their leaders, and they saw me approaching from the north, on the road that served as a secondary artery to the lower half of Pannonia. I only got a bare moment's warning, from Latobius, who came to a sudden stop, his head jerking up, blowing a huge breath out that I knew was his way of warning me that he had picked up the scent of men.

"*Salve*, Centurion!"

The words may have been friendly, but the tone was not, as a half-dozen men suddenly appeared from the underbrush that lined the track, the man who had called out stepping out into the middle of the road, although it was the *gladius* in his hand that gave me a clearer indication of his possible intentions.

"*Salve*, Gregarius," I replied, keeping my voice mild, even as I inched my hand closer to the hilt of my own blade. "Is there a problem?"

As I hoped, this seemed to catch the man by surprise, but he recovered quickly enough, shooting a look over at his comrades, who had arranged themselves in a line across the track. I could have probably cut my way through them, but that was not only not my intention, Latobius gave me a second warning, his ears suddenly twitching and twisting rearward, so without looking, I was certain that there were men behind me as well. And, I thought, if this bunch are even somewhat competent, those men would have javelins, ready to hurl right into my back if I did try to escape.

"I don't know, Centurion," the Legionary I took to be their leader, though he was not an Optio, answered me after his glance back at his friends. "I suppose that depends on why you're here."

This, I knew, was a delicate moment, yet before I could provide an answer, I heard an exclamation from behind me.

"Hold there, Glabius!" While I did not turn, not wanting to move suddenly, the voice seemed somewhat familiar as he said, "This is Titus Pullus!"

I must confess I was slightly disappointed when my name did not seem to make an impression on the leader, who shrugged and answered offhandedly, "If you say so. But," he shook his head, "I don't know who that is or why I should care."

"Because," the location of the voice had moved, and then a figure appeared at the edge of my vision as he walked to stand in such a way that he was facing both me and the other Legionary, "he was in the 8th, and he was Domitius' best friend."

This, I instantly saw, did mean something, but before either of them could speak up, I said, "I'd like to think I still am. And," I added, "that's who I came to see."

That proved to be enough to allow me to pass, although not alone. Despite my protest that being accompanied by men on foot would slow me down, the man identified as Glabius refused to let me continue on alone.

"We're only a couple miles from the camp," he said sourly, and I got the distinct impression that he had been looking forward to some sort of confrontation with me. "It'll only take a little longer."

Given my sense that he wanted me to argue, instead I simply nodded my head, though I did kick Latobius into motion, keeping him at a walk to be sure, but it made the mutineers hurry to catch up with me. As we made our way in the direction this Glabius had indicated, I called to my unidentified savior, who came to walk beside me.

"You're familiar to me," I told him, "but I don't recall your name, Gregarius."

"No reason you should know it," he answered readily enough, "but I was in the Fourth of the Fifth before I transferred to the Ninth." While I instantly understood the deeper meaning, he continued, "I was there the night of the ambush by the Colapiani and Draxo, when you and Domitius guided us into position."

Just the mention of that night brought yet another flood of memories, but it served to make the time pass as the man, his name Gaius Norbanus, and I reminisced about that night, and naturally, Primus Pilus Urso.

"He was a right hard bastard," Norbanus said, though without any rancor, "but I tell you, Pullus, they don't make men like that anymore."

"No," I agreed, "they don't."

Even as I said this, I wondered how much Norbanus knew of my tangled, complicated relationship with the man who had once been my father's second in command, of the Fourth Cohort, how I had been one of the men Urso used for his "off the books" business of selling armor to tribes like the Colapiani, and how, in fact, I had been indirectly responsible for Draxo's rebellion, although it was only because I followed Urso's orders to break a woman's arm. I did not mention any of this, but mainly because I surmised from the sidelong glance upward that Norbanus gave me, sitting on Latobius, that he knew at least part of the story. Besides, I was more occupied by grappling with the realization that, now that two decades had passed, the passionate hatred I had felt for Urso had faded to the point where, when I thought about the man, most of what I felt was positive. He was as crooked as a warped *vitus*, as we like to say, yet despite his greed, when it came to the skills a Primus Pilus needs in order to properly lead a Legion, I recognized that I put him second only to his successor, Gaius Sempronius Atticus, as the best Primi Pili I had served under. I might have considered Sacrovir, but I had not served with him long enough for me to be willing to make that declaration, while I honestly never really warmed to Crescens', nor his style of leadership.

It was the thought of Atticus that prompted me to ask Norbanus, "Where's Prefect Atticus? Is he in camp with the Legate?"

Norbanus gave me a surprised look, searching my face, then he grunted, "Ah. Yes, I suppose there's no reason you'd know about that."

"Know about what?" I asked sharply, suddenly worried that these mutineers had done something even worse than what they had done to Rufus, which he seemed to understand.

Holding up a hand in a placating gesture, Norbanus responded, "No, it's not what you think, Centurion. Prefect Atticus died about six weeks ago." He paused for a moment, I guessed to torment me a bit, before finishing, "Of a bilious fever."

Yet another hammer blow to my mind landed then, and I was assailed by a sudden feeling that my world and all that I had known was collapsing down around my ears. Following immediately behind this came another thought, but this one was something I took great care in expressing to Norbanus, especially when, at that moment, the man Glabius looked over his shoulder to glower at me.

"Six weeks ago?" I asked with a casualness that sounded forced to my ears.

"Two days before Augustus, as it turns out," Norbanus confirmed. He took a step away from Latobius' side, and I saw him glance at Glabius' back now that the man had returned his attention to the front, then he whispered, "I think things might have gone a lot differently if he hadn't died, Centurion." Pausing for a moment, Norbanus kept his eyes glued to Glabius, then continued in the same tone, "Without the Prefect, Blaesus was lost, and it seems like every decision he made was the wrong one." Shaking his head, he sighed, then turned to look up at me and said, "I never wanted this, Centurion. Most of us didn't want this, if the truth be known. But men like him," he nodded his head in Glabius' direction, "they did a good job of swaying those boys who will go whichever way the strongest wind blows. And," he chuckled bitterly, "the gods know there was a lot of wind, if you take my meaning."

"Anyone in particular?" I said this without thinking, and I immediately knew I had erred, Norbanus' expression turning suspicious, and I added hastily, "I'm just worried about Domitius' part in all this, Norbanus. That's really all that concerns me."

This seemed to allay his doubt, and he answered readily, "Oh, Domitius is one of the cool heads in the camp. I don't think he wanted things to go the way they did either, but once it became clear that this was going to happen, he and some of the other Centurions have been doing their best to keep the real hotheads from doing anything so stupid or damaging that it can't be undone."

Even though this confirmed what we had heard, I still had to hide my relief, and despite the circumstances, I felt a jolt of pleasant anticipation at the thought of seeing Domitius again. And, rounding the bend in the road that followed the stream that flowed along a north/south axis, I saw the turf walls of the camp where the mutiny was taking place. From a distance, it looked no different than any other marching camp, but as we drew closer, the signs that something unusual was taking place became more evident with every passing foot. The gates were not only opened, they were unmanned, but it was the sight of men wandering in and out as if it was a festival day that gave the strongest indication of how much discipline had deteriorated.

Almost as if he had read my mind, Norbanus commented, "It wouldn't take a whole lot of effort on the Breuci's part to come down on our heads and wipe us out, would it?" When I agreed, he shook his head disgustedly, saying only, "Not even Domitius or the other Centurions have been able to convince Percennius and his bunch to mount a guard."

"Percennius?" I was not familiar with the name; try as I might, I could not recall of ever hearing of a Centurion or Tribune by that name. "Who's that?"

Norbanus shot me a bitterly amused look, saying only, "Oh, you'll find out soon enough." He seemed to consider for a moment, but I suppose he was encouraged when Glabius, obviously spying a comrade, let out a shout in the man's direction and went trotting ahead. "I suppose he's sort of the leader of this thing, whatever it is." Then, while I know Norbanus was unaware of the import of what he was about to say, he nevertheless identified what I will go into the afterlife convinced was the ultimate cause of the dual rebellions. "He was one of those men the Princeps sent from Rome after the Varus disaster. Supposedly, he was some sort of famous actor in the theaters there. That," Norbanus shrugged, "I don't know about, but I will say that the *cunnus* has a gilded tongue, I'll tell you that."

Although this explained a great deal, there was one part that puzzled me.

"I thought Augustus only sent that scum up to us in Germania."

"He did," Norbanus agreed, "but the Primus Pilus of the 2nd up there somehow managed to get rid of him from his Legion and got him sent to the 9th." Giving me a sardonically amused look, he added, "Supposedly, our Primus Pilus took a hefty bribe to take the bastard; I wonder how he feels about it now."

Before I could reply, we were at the gates, where Glabius had stopped, waiting for us to arrive.

Pointing at me, he spoke in what I sensed was a deliberately provocative manner, saying abruptly, "You need to dismount, then follow me."

Without waiting to see if I complied, he turned about and began stalking into the camp.

Sighing, I swung off Latobius, but when one of the men who seemed to always be at Glabius' side reached out to take the reins, I stopped him with a look.

"You're not touching my horse," I said this quietly enough, since I had no real desire for a confrontation, but he clearly understood I was serious, because he flushed deeply, opened his mouth, then snapped it shut, giving an elaborate shrug as if it did not matter.

"Suit yourself," he said, but I was already moving, stretching my legs to catch up to Glabius before he could sense I was lagging behind.

This man was cowed easily enough, but I had become convinced that Glabius would not only welcome the chance to make an issue of it, he was spoiling for some sort of fight. Fortunately, by the time he did turn around, I had managed to catch up.

"This is where I leave you, Centurion," Norbanus informed me, then under his breath, he said, "May Fortuna bless you."

I made no real reply, giving him a nod instead as he headed down a Cohort street, leaving me alone in what was clearly a largely unfriendly environment, making me glad I was wearing my armor. Not all the looks I received were hostile; some of the men seemed more curious than angry, while I actually heard my name mentioned, and I did recognize some faces. Not many, reminding me how much time had passed since I last served with the 8th, which meant that men like Tiburtinus and Atilius had retired, both of them shortly after the end of the Batonian Rebellion. However, along with Domitius, there were two other men I was almost as anxious to see, but given their respective positions in the 8th, I was expecting to find both of them clapped in irons, and that was the best possibility I could imagine. Even if I had been disposed to ask Glabius about them, there was no time, because we approached the forum from the Porta Praetoria side, where I saw a sight that not only took me a moment to decipher, but was something I had never seen before. Matters were made more difficult because the forum was thronged with men, all of them in their tunics, and with a large number of them not bothering with their *baltea*, yet another sign of the total lack of discipline. As striking as this was, it was the sight of a large rostrum, made not of shields but of squares of turf that I judged to be every bit as high as the turf walls of the camp. Now, a rostrum, even in a marching camp is not all that unusual, except that it is almost always made of stacks of boxes, or sometimes shields, never something as semi-permanent as turf. This was not its only unusual feature; this rostrum was several times larger than a normal one, large enough that it could fit several chairs, one of them curule, with more than enough space left over for several men to stand upon and not be crowded.

As Glabius and his bunch cleared a path, shoving men aside who, from my judgment, were too drunk to take offense at this treatment, I kept my eyes on the large turf structure, the thought suddenly striking me; it looks almost like a stage. The moment it came to me, I recalled what Norbanus had said just a few moments before, about this Percennius character, who I assumed to be the man seated in the curule chair, surveying the scene before him with a satisfied smile. Standing immediately to either side, and I noticed, slightly behind the chair, were a pair of men, one of them carrying a *vitus*, while the other was holding a cudgel, which rested on his shoulder. As if the scene could not be even stranger, it was the combination of the sparkling white toga that the man who I assumed, correctly, to be Percennius was wearing, along with a crudely fashioned garland of ivy that was perched on his head at a jaunty angle that had me almost convinced this was a dream. Since Percennius was absorbed in something that was taking place immediately in front of the rostrum, which I could not make out because of the men thronged around the base of it, all of them equally absorbed in whatever was taking place, it was left to the man with the *vitus* to notice our approach. I saw him lean down and say something to Percennius, whose expression of avid interest instantly changed, and he stood to look in our direction, which in turn alerted the men on the ground with their backs to us that something was happening behind them.

"Wait here." Glabius had to raise his voice to be heard, because now that our presence had drawn attention, the men immediately around us began talking excitedly, their attention torn away from the sight that had captivated them a moment before, which I now could see clearly.

At the base of the rostrum, perhaps a half-dozen men were either on their knees or crouched around a woman, the tattered remnants of her clothing strewn about, where they had clearly been taking turns raping her. And, not surprisingly, they were the only men not paying attention to me.

"Who's that big bastard?"

435

"I bet Tiberius sent him!"

"To do what? He wouldn't send just a Centurion! By the gods, Mummius, you're a thick one!"

"Maybe Tiberius sent him to kill me!"

This came from Percennius himself, who was now standing on the edge of the rostrum, and I noticed the heavy silver cup in his hand, the contents sloshing out as he weaved a bit. In contrast, however, there was no tremor in his voice, and as soon as his words came out, my ears detected the signs of a man trained in the arts of the theater, his voice projecting farther than normal, his speech distinct despite his state of at least mild inebriation, or, the thought came to me, this was all just part of the act. Regardless, his words created an instant effect, as the men around me went from a state of curiosity to hostility in the blink of an eye, and the air of menace surrounding me was so palpable that I had to fight the urge to draw my *gladius*, knowing that it would mean my death.

"However," Percennius continued, after a pause that I was certain was a calculated warning to me, "I do not believe that is why he is here, comrades! Am I correct, Centurion?"

My throat had gone so dry that I was not sure I could answer, yet I surprised myself by responding in what sounded to me like a cool, calm tone of voice. "You are correct..." My voice trailed off in such a way that he correctly interpreted it.

"Aulus Percennius," he said grandly, then made the kind of low, sweeping bow that actors like to give at the end of a performance, "at your service, Centurion." There was no missing the mocking note in his voice, and when he straightened up, any cordiality, however fake it may have been, was gone. "Now, who might you be, and if you're not here to kill me, why are you here?"

Before I could answer, a voice from outside the ring of men called out, "I don't know why he's here, but I can tell you who he is. This is Titus Porcinianus Pullus, grandson of the first

Camp Prefect of the Army of Pannonia, son of Gaius Porcinianus Pullus, Quartus Pilus Prior of the 8th. And," the tone hardened, "he's my best and longest friend."

I did not need to see him to recognize the voice of Titus Domitius, and I turned in time to see men parting, moving out of his way as he made his way towards me. For the moment, I forgot everything else; the peril I was in, the reason I was there, none of it mattered as I first saw just the top of his head approaching through the crowd, a smile forming on my face despite the circumstances. Then, he stepped past the last man between us, and we were there, facing each other, yet while I immediately recognized him, in appearance, it was a very different Titus Domitius from the man I had last seen more than five years earlier, although that did not matter. I felt the stinging of tears threatening to push their way out from behind my eyes, and I could see by his own eye that he was experiencing the same powerful emotions I was. Perhaps, dear reader, you noticed my use of the singular when I describe him, but this is no accident. While his right eye was visible, and to me looked exactly the same, if not for a few extra wrinkles around it, his left was covered with a patch. This in itself would have been bad enough, but the skin around his left eye, extending down his cheek to just above the jawline, was a knot of scar tissue not dissimilar to my left outer forearm, while the top half of his ear was missing altogether. Despite myself, I felt my jaw drop, and the words I had been about to utter vanished as we stood there, just a couple paces apart. If men were talking or even whispering, I did not hear them, such was my concentration on Domitius.

His voice seemed to have suddenly gone hoarse as he said, "And I'm still better looking than you are."

I cannot recall what I said in response, if anything, other than to laugh, and weep at the same time as we embraced, hugging each other tightly about the neck; I was only dimly aware of hearing the men around us cheering.

Finally, I managed to get out, "Pluto's cock, Titus! What have you done to yourself?"

Even with one eye, the look of amusement he gave me stirred so many memories as he replied lightly, "What, do you think? I cut myself shaving? I'm not nearly as clumsy as you are, you big oaf."

My laughter seemed to please him, but before either of us could say anything, Percennius' voice brought us back to the present.

"As touching as this is," he said mockingly, still standing at the edge of the rostrum looking down at us, "I am assuming that your friend…Pullus, was it?" At my nod, he continued, "…Isn't here just to catch up with you, Domitius. Am I correct, Centurion?"

"You are," I confirmed, but I was not disposed to say anything more, which, once it became obvious, clearly irritated Percennius.

"Well," he asked, acidly, and I did not miss that he raised his voice, "are you going to enlighten us as to why you're here?"

I had known when I left Siscia that I would be facing this moment, and I was under no illusions about whether or not Domitius would be able to protect me if the leaders of this mutiny wished to make an example of me, and I had carefully rehearsed in my mind what I was going to say.

"I've been sent by Tiberius' representative to observe for myself the mood of the men, and to determine how seriously the *Imperator* needs to treat your demands."

Percennius smiled, but it was more a baring of his teeth as he replied in the same mocking tone he had used earlier, "So, an emissary sends an emissary? That doesn't seem to me that Tiberius is taking us seriously!" Suddenly, he lifted his face to address the larger crowd, "What do *you* think, my comrades? Does it sound like our new *Imperator* is taking us seriously?"

"*No!*" It was not in unison, exactly, but the roar of hundreds of voices shouting the same word was impossible to misinterpret.

As bad as this was, though not unexpected, I could pick out individual men shouting out their own ideas for what should happen next.

"Flog him! With the scourge! Send him back in bloody bits!"

"Crucify him like a slave! That's what he is!"

"Cut his tongue out!"

This last one caught my attention, mainly because, the part of my mind that is always detached even in moments of danger thought, That would make it hard for me to tell Drusus he needs to take this seriously. Percennius seemed content to let all these ideas for my demise be expressed for the span of a dozen or more heartbeats as he gazed down at me, with what now seemed to be a genuine smile, one of real pleasure, and I wondered if it was because some of these suggestions sounded good to him, or if he simply enjoyed watching me sweat. That was something I was determined not to let him see, and I kept my face a hard mask as I met his gaze, reading the malice in his eyes as plainly as if he was speaking. Finally, he lifted one hand in a simple gesture, and the noise died down; gradually, it should be said, which I saw irritated him, which gave me an insight into the man himself. He likes the power, I thought. He's not drunk from wine, he's drunk from the idea that he's in control of…this.

Once it had quieted some, Percennius said teasingly, "Well, Centurion Pullus. I don't know about you, but I think some of those ideas show some imagination. Perhaps I should consider giving my comrades what they seem to want."

I was not able to respond, because Domitius, taking a single step to interpose himself between me and Percennius, looked up at him and said flatly, "You're not going to do anything, Percennius, except shut your fucking mouth."

Honestly, I could not decide what was more shocking; what my friend had said to the man I had assumed was either the lone leader or the most influential one of this mutiny, or the manner in which Percennius reacted. So certain was I that he would turn and order the two men still standing behind the chair to come and intervene, I actually did drop my hand to my *gladius*, but Percennius seemed to physically shrink back.

"I was only having some fun, Domitius." His voice took on a whining quality to it, transforming from a man in supreme command to a cringing cur so quickly that I was not certain it was not some sort of trick.

"You've had more than enough fun," my friend snapped, then he turned to indicate me, saying, "Pullus and I are going to my tent to talk."

Without waiting for any reply, Domitius turned, and beckoned to me to follow. Still leading Latobius, I watched the men instantly stepping aside as I followed my friend out of the forum, and I was not fooled into thinking that they were moving so hastily for me. Once we were on the street that bordered one side of the forum, the way was relatively clear, although men were still wandering about. More bemused now than I had been shortly before, I followed along behind him.

Turning and glancing over his shoulder, he grinned, and for the first time, I saw the old Domitius, and he asked me, "Are you still spoiling that horse, Titus?"

"Why does everyone think I spoil him?" I complained, though it was done in jest; I was well aware of how much I indulged my horse.

"Because you do," he answered, laughing.

The rest of the way to his tent was spent with us conducting a mock argument about Latobius, who even as we did so, kept shoving his nose into my back, reminding me that he was due for an apple.

"How did you know I was here?" I asked as soon as we were inside his tent.

"Norbanus came and found me," Domitius told me, which confirmed my suspicion this had been the case.

I followed him into the partitioned portion that are the private quarters of a Pilus Prior, which are slightly larger than those of the lower grade Centurions, and this was the first indication I had that he had been promoted.

"When did this happen?" I asked, and I heard the wounded tone in my voice, but honestly, I was quite put out, and Domitius heard it as well, flushing slightly.

"A year ago," he admitted.

"A year?" I was incredulous. "You haven't written a word in that time!"

"I know!" Domitius protested, holding his hands up in a placating gesture. "I was just...busy," he finished lamely.

"No busier than I was," I snapped. "And I found time to write!"

"I know, Titus!" he repeated, then he heaved a sigh, his eye closed, and I saw a tear caught by the lamp he had lit make a glittering trail down his cheek. "I just...couldn't. Not after Petrilla died."

Before he could say anything more, I walked to him, and grasped his shoulders, and told him, "I grieve with you, Titus. Petrilla was a good wife and a good mother. I know you still miss her."

"I do," Domitius replied miserably. "I really do."

"How are the children?" I asked, and he shifted uncomfortably, turning his face away from me.

"Honestly, I don't know," he admitted. "I hired a woman to take care of them, but I don't go into town to check on them as much as I should. I...I just can't."

Since I had no idea what to say, I did not even try, and we stood there, regarding each other awkwardly, then with a self-

441

conscious laugh, Domitius wiped the tear away, pointed to the chair on the other side of his desk, and poured two cups of wine. Handing me one, he dropped into his chair, and I realized that, as much as I was enjoying just spending time with my friend, time was our enemy, as it had been from the moment I began this journey.

"The reason I'm here is because Dolabella sent me ahead to try and talk to you," I began, but Domitius cut me off with a frown.

"Dolabella?" He repeated the name, and his good eye narrowed in suspicion. "Titus, what are you doing having anything to do with Dolabella? That *cunnus* has almost gotten you killed more times than I can count."

This was something I could not deny, so I did not try, agreeing, "That's true. But," I paused for a heartbeat to frame my thoughts for what I was going to say next, understanding that in many ways this would be the most important thing I had to say, "this time is different, Titus. Dolabella doesn't want to see good men suffer because of the misdeeds of a few."

"'Misdeeds'?" Domitius interjected, a frown on his face. "While I agree that men like Percennius aren't helping matters, Titus, surely you see that we have legitimate grievances!"

"I do," I agreed, and I was not being false. "And I think that Tiberius might listen to our grievances, as long as they're presented in the correct manner."

"You mean like Augustus did?" Domitius shot back. "How many petitions did the Army of the Rhenus send to the Princeps the last five years?"

"Quite a few," I sighed.

"And we sent at least a dozen," Domitius argued, "but nothing happened with any of them. So," he sat back and crossed his arms, staring hard at me, "why would Tiberius do anything different?"

442

"Because," this at least I was prepared for, "he's just become *Imperator*, and he doesn't need two of his armies rebelling when he has to solidify his position. You know as well as I do how those patricians are back in Rome. They all think they'd make a better *Imperator* than anyone else. Tiberius has enough on his hands right now making sure they don't form some sort of coalition to bring him down."

"Which is all the more reason for us to strike now," Domitius said flatly.

Again, I could not argue against his logic, not with any conviction, because the truth is that I agreed with him, not only that there were issues that needed to be addressed, but that from a strategic viewpoint, this was the best time to stage some sort of demonstration, although not necessarily for the men who Tiberius determined were the leaders of this revolt. Nevertheless, there was something that stuck in my gut about this business, yet I knew I had to tread carefully.

"While I agree with your reasoning," I began, "there's one thing that's working against you, and I'm afraid is something that's going to be more important to Tiberius in the long run."

"Which is?" Domitius asked, his eye fixed on my face.

"Do you remember me writing you about one of the men in my Century?" I asked, which was an indirect approach that I normally would not have taken. "One of the men sent to us after the Varus disaster?"

Domitius pursed his lips, thinking for a moment, "I remember something about him. What was his name? It started with a P."

"Pusio," I confirmed. "Yes, that's him. He and men like him are behind what's happening up in Germania, and from what I've seen here with this Percennius character, the same thing is true. And," I added, "Norbanus told me that he was originally from the Rome *dilectus* that Augustus held to get rid of all the troublemakers and dump them on us."

"Percennius is scum," Domitius replied instantly. Then, he hesitated for a moment, as if he was considering saying more. "I wouldn't worry about Percennius. He isn't as...influential as he likes to think."

"Well, that's good to know, but is he going to be the man Drusus is going to talk to?" I asked him, and now he looked uncomfortable, which I assumed was because of the nature of the man himself.

"Yes," he admitted, clearly reluctant, then insisted, "but he's just a figurehead, really. He's not going to make any decisions that have to do with what's going on here."

"That's not what it looks like to me," I replied. "Just from what I saw, he looks very much like he's running things, and all the men in the forum seemed fine with it."

Domitius did not respond, not immediately, and I sat watching as he stared down into his cup, as if seeking some sort of answer there.

Finally, he raised his head and said quietly, "Appearances can be deceiving, Titus. Trust me," his voice hardened, "he's not making any decisions."

"Well, who is then?" I asked, puzzled. "Who should we go talk to once we're done here?"

The answer came in the form of the silence that suddenly draped over us, coupled with his unblinking gaze directly into my eyes, and I felt as if I had been punched in the stomach by the recognition of what this meant.

"*You?*" I gasped. "You're the leader of, of...all this?" I waved a hand in a gesture that encompassed everything around us. "By the gods, Titus! Are you mad? Do you know what Tiberius is capable of?"

"No, I'm not mad, and yes, I think I know what Tiberius can and would do to me," Domitius replied calmly.

"I don't think you do," I snapped, still struggling to fully comprehend what this all meant, not just for our personal relationship, but for the mutiny itself. "And believe me when I tell you, I *do* know what Tiberius is capable of.,."

"Because you were the man who did his dirty work?" Domitius challenged, yet despite the flare of anger this caused me, I could neither deny the truth nor did I want to, and I shot right back, "Yes, because of that. No matter what happens, if Tiberius ever discovers that you're the true leader of this, he'll destroy you, Titus. And," I could not keep my thoughts from running in this direction, compelling me to add bitterly, "he'll probably order me to be the one to do whatever it is he decides."

"And?" Domitius asked me quietly. "Would you?"

Despite several attempts to do so, all of which I have scratched out in this account, I cannot summon the words that come close to properly describing the sensations that assailed my mind and body in that moment, as the feeling of reliving a moment struck me with a palpable force. Yet, even as I sat there, I understood that this feeling was not created by anything I had personally experienced, and I confess it took me a moment to realize from where it came.

"Pharsalus." I believed I only thought this, but I must have spoken aloud, because Domitius not only heard, but understood.

"Pharsalus," he agreed. Then, he gave me a smile, the likes of which I had never seen on his face before; a combination of sadness, understanding, and a bit of dark humor at the manner in which the gods choose to amuse themselves. "Just like our grandfathers, neh?"

"Just like our grandfathers," I agreed numbly.

For this was exactly what was happening; because of a cruel whim of the gods, Titus Domitius and I were reliving an event that had had a profound impact on the lives of the first Titus Pullus and his longest and best friend Vibius Domitius, and like the ripples in a pond, extended down to us. Granted, some of the trappings were different; Vibius had been an Optio, while my Avus had been Secundus Pilus Prior, and the mutiny of Caesar's army had occurred at the end of a long, grueling campaign against Pompeius Magnus, after a battle that had sealed Magnus' fate and elevated Caesar to the status of First Man. Also, Vibius had been a minor part of a larger mutiny, but these differences were superficial; the essence was ultimately the same. I was on the side of the man who wielded ultimate power over all men under the standard, while Domitius was representing men who were my comrades in arms, many of whom I knew personally, just like my Avus and Vibius. And, I understood, all I had to do in order to advance my own career would be to do essentially the same thing that my Avus had done, side with the man who had the power. Tiberius is many things, but I had never known him not to reward those men he considered to be faithful to him, and I held little doubt that he would reward me. I had long since given up on the dream of becoming a Primus Pilus like the first Titus Pullus; my aspirations at this point in time was perhaps being a Pilus Prior like my father, but I knew that was as far as I would rise, at least until this moment.

"So?" Domitius asked, quietly. "What are you going to do, Titus?"

I left the camp about a third of a watch later, almost immediately going to the gallop, heading north, knowing that Drusus had in all likelihood set out from Siscia by this time. There was a risk that I would take the wrong road, but I was gambling that, now that Dolabella was with Drusus' party, he would guide them around Splonum and use the same route I had taken to get to the camp. My faith was rewarded about fifteen miles north of the camp, when I saw in the distance a cloud of dust that I knew was too large to be just a few riders. Deciding to slow Latobius but continue moving, it was not long before I caught a glimpse of a standard, one of the polished metal disks catching the rays of the sun, which was my first hint that Drusus had come with a substantial force of his own. Closing the distance quickly, I was able to see a force of at least five hundred horsemen leading the way, but it was the neat, compact groups of men on foot that ignited a sense of unease, although it also explained how we were able to catch Drusus.

"Who are they?" I wondered aloud; Latobius did not seem to know either, though he twitched an ear, his sign that he had heard me at least.

My initial reaction quickly turned into a sense of real dismay as I got close enough to make out the blue tunics of not just the mounted men leading the way, but of the marching men as well, all of whom were wearing their armor. Only Praetorians wear blue tunics, and I spent the remaining time before meeting the oncoming party trying to determine what this meant, although I knew that there was nothing good about it. When I got within a hundred paces, a group of seven riders detached themselves and came at the canter, and I decided the prudent thing to do would be to pull up.

One of the men wore the black feathered crest of a Tribune, and he naturally was leading the small group, yet despite my clear indication that I had no ill intentions, the Tribune snapped an order, and the other half-dozen cavalrymen moved around me, effectively surrounding me.

"Who are you?" the Tribune, who appeared to be in his early thirties, asked abruptly, without any attempt at courtesy or greeting. "State your business!"

"I am Quartus Princeps Prior Titus Pullus, of the 1st Legion," I tried to keep my voice calm, while at the same time conveying that I had no ill intent, "and my business is to talk to Drusus Julius Caesar."

"And why would a Centurion from the Army of the Rhenus be down here in Pannonia?" The Tribune was openly skeptical. Suddenly, something seemed to occur to him. "Unless you're one of the faithless dogs behind this illegal mutiny, and you're

447

down here to confer with the other ringleaders." Before I could respond, or react in any way, the Tribune pointed at me and shouted, "Take this man into custody by my order!"

"Hold! He's with me!"

I had not noticed that Dolabella, seeing me approach, had come from his spot near the rear of the mounted contingent, cantering up to where I sat, already surrounded by a ring of hard-faced, scowling Praetorian cavalrymen.

The Tribune turned at the shout, watching as Dolabella approached, a sneer on his face, and his tone was just as brusque with Dolabella as he taunted, "So one of the spymaster's spies, is that it?"

"I'm not a spy, Tribune." I said this with more heat than I knew was wise, but I was already angry before this slur. "I am exactly who I say I am."

"I sent him ahead to speak with the leaders of the mutiny." Dolabella rode in between the Tribune and one of the cavalrymen to reach my side. "And that's all you need to know, Sejanus." Without waiting for the now-identified Tribune to offer a reply, Dolabella indicated I should follow him with a jerk of his head, leading the way back to where the main party had stopped. This Sejanus character was clearly angry, but I was not all that surprised that he did not make an issue of Dolabella's curt rebuke, and I felt his eyes boring into my back as I followed the spymaster.

Once we were out of earshot, Dolabella slowed long enough for me to pull beside him, and he muttered, "You need to watch yourself around that one, Titus. He's probably one of the most dangerous of Tiberius' clients, and not just because he and his father command the Praetorians. Sejanus has more ambition than a man of his station should, and he's got a cruel streak in him." That, I thought, is probably one reason Tiberius has him around, though I did not articulate that. He had slowed to a walk as we got closer to where I could now see a man who, if I had not known better, I would have sworn was the nobleman for whom I had marched in my first campaign more than twenty years earlier, and for whom this man was named, and his voice dropped lower. "So? Did you talk to whoever is leading the mutiny?"

"Yes," I answered him, but I kept my eyes on Drusus, realizing as we got closer that, while there was certainly a resemblance, there were also distinct differences.

"And?" Dolabella asked irritably, pointing out, "You're going to be standing in front of Drusus in a moment, so if there's anything I should know that you don't want him to hear, this is your only chance."

This was such a decidedly odd thing for him to say that it caused me to look over at him, and I saw that he was regarding me closely. As if, I thought, he's actually waiting for me to confirm something he suspects; the sudden lurch in my stomach made it difficult to maintain my composure.

Somehow, I managed to answer him, without any hesitation or without betraying myself, telling him, "There's nothing unusual. The leader is a *cunnus* named Percennius..."

"Percennius?" Dolabella cut me off, his face registering surprise. "You mean, Percennius the actor?"

"Honestly," I answered, and I was being truthful with this at least, "I didn't know he was an actor until someone told me, but yes, I'm assuming that's the same man."

"I thought we sent him to the Army of the Rhenus," he muttered, and now it was my turn to stare at him in surprise, but before I could press him, we had come close enough to where Drusus, sitting his horse, was waiting.

"Well, Dolabella?" he demanded abruptly, barely giving me a glance. "Is this the man you were talking about?"

"Yes," Dolabella replied, and I noticed that, while his tone was respectful enough, he did not make any other attempt to show Tiberius' natural son deference, which Drusus clearly noticed and equally obviously did not like. "He's just returned from the camp after talking to the leaders."

"Actually," I interjected, "there really only appears to be one man who matters. His name is Aulus Percennius, and he's the man I talked to."

This was certainly true, strictly speaking, that I had spoken to him, but I had no intention of divulging that my conversation with Percennius had been anything but an exchange that held no real bearing on the outcome of this mutiny.

"And?" Drusus demanded. "What does he want?"

In answer, I related the things that Domitius had listed, and while I did not specifically mention Percennius' name, if Drusus made the assumption that they had come from only him, that was perfectly fine with me.

Once I finished, it was not Drusus who spoke, but another nobleman who appeared to be about the same age as Tiberius' son, sitting on a dun stallion slightly behind and to the side of Drusus, exclaiming, "That's exactly the same list of demands that I brought to you from my father, Drusus!"

Drusus looked irritated, but his tone was civil as he answered, "Yes, I understand, Blaesus. But this confirmation is important in itself. Hopefully," he added pointedly, "you can see that."

From where I was sitting, it appeared that Blaesus' son, who I learned later was serving as a Tribune on his father's staff, had been prepared for some sort of argument, so when Drusus agreed, he looked decidedly nonplussed, finally mumbling something that I could not make out, but I assumed to be agreement. Before Drusus could say anything more, I heard horses approaching from behind me and turned to see that the Tribune Sejanus and the other Praetorians were rejoining us; I chose to ignore that Sejanus was still staring at me with a hostility that, frankly, was more puzzling than anything else.

Usually, I thought to myself, people have to at least have met me before they hate me like he apparently did.

"*Proconsul,*" Sejanus addressed Drusus, "what are your orders?"

The title Sejanus used surprised me at first, then I thought about it and realized that it made sense; Tiberius would not have sent anyone of Legate rank, and in our system, a *Proconsul* holds rank over a Legate.

"We're going to continue on to their camp," Drusus told Sejanus, but that was clearly not what Sejanus meant, because in response, he turned and pointed at me.

"I meant what are your orders concerning this...Centurion?" His lips, which were abnormally thin and barely visible under normal conditions twisted into a sneer as he uttered my rank. "Do you want him in chains?"

Drusus appeared startled at this, but not nearly as much as I was, and I nudged Latobius with one knee so that he sidestepped slightly, though not in a manner that suggested I had flight in mind; instead, I got closer to Sejanus, my thought being that he would interpret my doing so as an implicit threat, and I stared, hard, directly at him, which he clearly noticed and was taking correctly if his sudden nervousness was any guide.

My movement seemed to jerk Drusus from his surprise, and he shook his head, answering abruptly, "No, Sejanus. That won't be necessary." The Praetorian Legate opened his mouth, but before he could say anything, Drusus went on, "But I suppose it would be prudent that the Centurion ride with an...escort." He turned to me, and the look he gave me was purely Tiberius in coldness and demeanor, and I imagined that this was how the new *Imperator* looked when he was Drusus' age. His voice matched his expression as he asked me a question that I knew was an order. "I don't believe the Centurion will have a problem with that. Will you?"

Of course I had a problem with it, but I knew better than to argue, so I simply answered in my best Stupid Legionary manner, "No, sir."

With this settled, Drusus led his party past us, which Sejanus rejoined, glaring at me, while his men and I moved aside to allow them by, but when the end of the mounted contingent passed by, and one of the Praetorians reached out to take hold of Latobius' bridle, I said, "You're going to lose your hand if you touch my horse."

Apparently, he believed me, because while his face darkened; he was still a trooper, and Praetorian or no, I was a Centurion, so he gave an abrupt nod, whereupon I nudged my horse forward, falling in at the end of the mounted party. Dolabella remained near Drusus, but I did not hold this against him, and when it became clear that the Praetorians surrounding me were content to either ignore me or only glare at me when they thought I was not looking, I was perfectly content to ride in silence as I retraced my steps back to the camp.

Since we were marching with men on foot, and Drusus was not willing to leave two Cohorts of Praetorians behind given what might lay ahead, our progress back was much slower. One consequence of this was that, while they still did not address me, the Praetorians around me quickly grew bored with the silence and began talking among themselves. Not surprisingly, they did not discuss anything political, instead chattering about the chariot races, their favorite gladiators, and which whore was the best in the brothel that serviced the Praetorians. Frankly, I did not mind, and in truth, I welcomed the distraction of listening to something that was more like what a man under the standard was likely to hear around the fire, and not all the political talk that had dominated our collective conversations for the last few weeks. As I sat on Latobius, pretending not to listen, the thought crossed my mind that, with help from Fortuna, maybe by the time I got back to Ubiorum, Germanicus would have quelled the mutiny there. As far as where things stood between the Army of Pannonia and Drusus, my foremost concern was that Domitius' role never be revealed, although I felt somewhat certain that Dolabella, at the very least, suspected that he was more than just a moderating voice. Secondarily, while I had not marched with the 8th for many years, I still had many friends in the ranks, both in the First and Fourth Cohorts, including the man who had been my first Optio and was now the Primus Pilus of the Legion. Aulus Galens had been Primus Pilus for three years, with Appius Asinius serving as the Primus Pilus Posterior. By this point in time, how these two men came into their respective roles I was sure was known outright by no more than a half-dozen men, although I also felt certain that many more men knew aspects of the story, or had their own suspicions that were close to the truth. Not that it mattered anymore, but I suppose I felt a certain level of ownership in the circumstances that found both my first Optio, and the first Sergeant of the Tenth Section, First of the Fourth rising to the first and second in command of my former Legion, although the true architect was Corvinus, my father's successor as Quartus Pilus Prior and my first Centurion.

Suddenly, as two men were arguing about the outcome of some bout where one of them was convinced it was fixed, I was reminded what might have been the true origin of the sequence of events, that Urso had been selling armor to the Colapiani, and as we learned later, other tribes like the Latobici and Varciani. Using his knowledge about this, Corvinus had approached Urso and essentially extorted the Primus Pilus, an extraordinarily dangerous thing to do, even for Corvinus, demanding that Galens be made a Centurion in the First Cohort, while Urso take on Asinius as his Optio, which of course made him my Optio after my transfer into the First of the First. And, as quickly as I recalled this, I recognized that, ultimately, *I* was the true cause, because in acting as he did, Corvinus was fulfilling a promise

453

made to my deceased father, that he do everything within his power to protect me as long as I marched in the 8th. Not lost on me was the recognition that, most of the time, whenever I had to be saved, it was from myself, in the form of my own actions, going all the way back to my first campaign when I had defied orders to remove myself from the front rank, all in order to slay Vergorix. Yes, it had won me my first accolades, from no less a personage than the man for whom the young *Proconsul* leading our party was named, but only with time can I recognize now that it set a pattern for my future actions. Because of who I was, both as the son of Gaius Porcinus, but more as the grandson of the first Titus Pullus, I had always assumed that the rules and regulations did not truly apply to me, at least to the extent that it did with other men. Strictly speaking, my entire career was a testament to that truth; after all, I had sparked more than one rebellion, although the first time, and the one that resulted in Draxo slaying Urso, only to be in turn slain by me, I was only the instrument when I obeyed Urso's orders to break a Colapiani woman's arm for the "crime" of trying to keep her son from being forcibly impressed into the auxiliaries. The second, however, started by my avenging Sextus' death, I knew fully well would likely end up in the manner in which it did, with yet another rebellion. However, while it resulted in my transfer to the 1st, I knew at the time that it was only because of the intervention of someone else, Atticus in this case, that I did not suffer an even harsher punishment. As the miles slowly rolled by, I alternated between listening to the men continue their bickering and looking more deeply within myself, realizing how, in one way or another, my connection to Titus Pullus was what had sustained my career, far more than it had hampered it, as I once believed. My one hope now, heading towards the camp, was that I could play some small role in protecting my friends and comrades in the same manner they had protected me.

There was perhaps a full watch of daylight left when we rounded the bend and the camp came into view, although the one difference this time was that we had not run into any parties out on the road. Not, I was sure, because they had all returned to camp; it would be a foolhardy bunch of mutineers to allow themselves to be snatched up by a large force of Praetorians. More than once, I was certain that I saw a flash of sun on metal off in the undergrowth near the road, but the Praetorians were oblivious, reminding me how few of them actually had any real experience in the Legions. It is true that most of the rankers are recruited from the ranks of the Legions, but it was an open secret that such men considered perfect for this duty in Rome were more known for their political reliability, their physical stature, and their willingness to obey all orders without any questions or qualms, than for the number of barbarians they had slain. Consequently, I was not surprised a bit when something that would have caused an entire Century or Cohort to become alert went completely unnoticed by the men around me, or the men marching behind us. Once the camp came within view, however, the scene was much the same as it had been on my first arrival, with men milling about just outside the gates, except that it was obvious they were all turned in our direction, watching us approach. This was when Dolabella came trotting back to summon me.

"*Proconsul* Drusus wants you with us to identify Percennius in case he decides to try and blend in," he said louder than he needed to, indicating that perhaps Sejanus had given the Praetorians around me some orders of his own, but they did nothing to impede me as I joined Dolabella.

By the time we were within a couple furlongs, the few men who had been congregated outside clearly communicated our approach, because rankers began pouring out of the gate. None of them were attired for battle, but Drusus still called a halt, obviously nervous at the sudden appearance of so many men,

455

despite their lack of armor or weapons. Not surprisingly, it was Sejanus, who in my short association with him, seemed to have taken it upon himself to serve as some sort of adviser to Drusus, who suggested that the mounted portion stay put while the two Cohorts of Praetorians marched forward.

"Naturally," Sejanus said, "I volunteer to be the representative for you when we move into position. If those mutineers have anything treacherous in mind, you'll be safe."

"They're unarmed and not wearing their armor," Drusus pointed out, but Sejanus was unmoved, rejoining, "Those we can see aren't. But, sir, that's not a full Legion's worth of men, and there are three Legions in that camp. We don't know what they have planned!"

This clearly had an impact on the young *Proconsul*, but as I watched, I could see the emotions play across his stern features, as the pride that is a feature of a young man, particularly a Roman, that bridles at the thought of appearing to be cowed, no matter what the reason, warred with his understanding that what Sejanus was saying was, on its face, the truth. During his moment of indecision, those mutineers outside the gates were in the process of forming up into a rough semblance of the kind of formation that we use to welcome men of high rank. Oh, it was ragged, and I had the distinct impression that this was something that had not been planned beforehand, but this made Drusus' decision for him, because he indicated the two ranks, each arranged on opposing sides of the gate.

"They clearly don't mean me any harm, Sejanus." Drusus sounded confident at least, but I saw his eyes darting between the two bodies of men, giving me the strong impression that he was not certain this was the case. "We'll be fine."

Then he urged his horse forward, and I confess that I was impressed with the young nobleman's courage; his common sense I was not as certain about, although I did not think it was likely the mutineers would assault Drusus. Not, I thought, until they have an idea whether or not he is going to give them what they want.

Dolabella turned to me and said softly, "Let's just wait here for now. When Drusus wants us, he'll let us know."

I had no objection to this, not that it mattered, but when Drusus' personal bodyguards, Germans naturally, began moving with him, as did young Blaesus, the *Proconsul* gave a firm shake of his head, moving forward alone. When he reached the nearest edge of the two lines, I felt myself tense, and I could sense the others around me doing the same, but none of the men on either side, moved from their position. Both ranks were longer than they were wide, extending for more than a hundred paces to the gate, and they were about five men deep, although their alignment and spacing was something one might see with a batch of *tiros*, not men of a veteran Legion. Neither, we immediately saw, did they render a salute to Drusus, and I was close enough to see him stiffen in his saddle when he realized that he would not be afforded the honors due to a man of *Proconsular* rank. This group of mutineers might not have been acting in a physical sense, but before Drusus had passed the first three or four files, the relative quiet evaporated.

"Are you here to give us what we want?"

"You can see for yourself how worn down we are!"

"What is your father going to do to help our suffering?"

Those were just the calls I could make out, as within a heartbeat or two, it sounded as if every man present added his own question or demand. And, very quickly, what began as a plaintive call to a man these mutineers hoped was empowered to help them turned into something darker and more demanding, as the frustration and anger clearly came boiling out of them. We all heard this change, and Dolabella and I exchanged an alarmed glance, while Sejanus began cursing bitterly.

The Praetorian commander turned to snap an order to the Decurion next to him. "Go back and tell Fibulanus to bring up the First Cohort immediately! We're going to teach this scum a lesson they won't forget!"

"That," Blaesus surprised me by being the one to speak up, "isn't what Drusus wants."

"The *Proconsul* is brave," Sejanus shot back, "but he's young, and he doesn't know these lowborn bastards like I do!" Turning back to the Decurion, he reiterated his orders, but before the man could respond, someone else interjected.

"You're not going to do that." For the first time, an older man, who I had barely noticed, spoke up and told the Decurion, calmly and without any real heat to his words, which made the Decurion's response a confirmation of my surmise that this man had to be important in his own right, because he actually complied, not moving his horse.

"This isn't your area of expertise, sir!" Sejanus wheeled on the older man, his thin mouth now offering a smile that was as false as it was obsequious. "The security of the *Proconsul* is my responsibility, not yours! Need I remind you, with all respect, of course, that you have no authority over me and my men!"

"No," the old man agreed, which seemed to surprise Sejanus, then he pointed out, "but the *Proconsul* does, and his orders were clear. Has he given any signal that he needs help?"

This naturally made Sejanus return his attention to Drusus, whose back was to us, but the men still had not moved from their spots and were not making any overtly threatening gestures; mainly, it was the tone of their collective voices that could be described as hostile. Drusus had stopped his horse, roughly midway between our party and the camp gates, and at least from where I sat, appeared to be doing his best to listen to what had to be an absolute cacophony of noise. Frankly, I did not believe it was even possible for him to actually hear a single question or demand these men were hurling his way, yet I also realized that at this moment, the appearance of listening was more important than the actual act of doing so. Finally, he raised both hands in a clear plea for silence, and much to my surprise, the men quieted down more quickly than I would have thought, although it made sense.

"Who speaks for you?" Drusus' voice drifted back to us, but we were a bit too far away for me to hear if there was a tremor in it that betrayed his nerves.

At this, a man down at the farthest end of one of the lines, nearest to the gate, stepped forward, and while he was in just his tunic and *baltea*, he also carried a *vitus*, and for a moment, I felt as if I would topple from the saddle, thinking that it was my friend Domitius. Fortunately, when he turned to face Drusus, I could see that he was not missing an eye, although he was about the same size and stature as my former close comrade.

"I do, sir." The man's voice was a bit easier to hear since he was facing our direction. "My name is Aulus Gabinius Clemens, Sextus Hastatus Prior of the 9th Legion, *Proconsul*." The salute he rendered was proper, but it engendered some angry shouts from the mutineers, which both Drusus and the Centurion wisely ignored. Drusus returned the salute, then Clemens turned slightly and made a gesture in the direction of the gate, which was partially open but not enough to allow any of us an unobstructed view. Nothing happened for a moment, and I did notice the noise level had dropped dramatically, as now everyone's attention was focused in the direction where Drusus was still seated on his mount, Clemens standing facing his direction a few paces away, and the gate behind the Centurion. I, for one, was completely unsure what to expect, but my surprise was nothing compared to that of young Blaesus, when his father came striding out, wearing the regalia of a Legate of Rome, and to my eyes, appearing completely unharmed.

"Father!" the youngster blurted out with such obvious relieved joy that I was struck by an unexpected pang, thinking that this would have been my reaction if it had been my father appearing from such a precarious situation. Oblivious to the rest of us, Blaesus still spoke aloud, "He's lost weight, but otherwise, he looks fine."

"Did they threaten your father?" Dolabella asked.

"At first," the son answered, but he still kept his eyes on his father, "but when he offered himself up to them, telling them to kill him rather than make him endure this shame..." His voice trailed off, and I glanced over to see that there was a glint in his eyes that I knew were unshed tears, making me wonder whether his grief was because his father had been shamed, or from the relief that he had clearly survived. "...they stopped threatening him and gave him the freedom of the camp." His mouth twisted into a bitter grimace. "Under escort, of course. He wasn't even allowed to go the latrines alone!"

As young Blaesus was speaking, I kept my eyes on Drusus, conferring with the Centurion and Legate, trying to get a sense of the tenor of whatever it was they were discussing. I saw Drusus nod his head, then he wheeled his mount and came trotting back in our direction, although he only came within hailing distance.

The mutineers had quieted sufficiently for him to be heard when he called out, "Dolabella, Centurion..." He did seem embarrassed that he had forgotten my name, but he clearly indicated me with a gesture. "...Lentulus, Blaesus and my personal bodyguard and *lictors* will come into the camp with me. The rest of you will remain here..."

I was not particularly surprised that Sejanus cut him off in mid-sentence, nor the fact that Drusus' face darkened, his jaw setting in a manner that reinforced the unfortunate resemblance to a turtle, as the Praetorian Legate said hotly, "That's unwise...sir! *Very* unwise! I insist that I be allowed to bring at least one Cohort of the Praetorians with you."

"This isn't your decision to make, Sejanus!" Drusus snapped. "My orders stand. You'll remain here, outside the camp. The Legate has guaranteed my safety."

Sejanus was not impressed in the slightest, that sneer of his returning as he shot back, "He's been their prisoner for almost two weeks now, but you can see for yourself there's not a bruise on the man! There has to be a reason for that."

"I told you the reason!" Blaesus turned his horse, clearly furious, and while I was not nervous, strictly speaking, I was acutely aware that Dolabella and I were in between Sejanus and the Legate's son.

"That's your version of what happened," Sejanus countered, then in what I could only think was a deliberate insult, ignored Blaesus and returned his attention to Drusus. "Sir, I'm afraid I can't allow you to..."

"*Allow* me?" Drusus did not shout, exactly, but just by the expressions of the mutineers nearest him, they clearly heard him. "You don't allow me to do anything, Sejanus! I'm the one with *Proconsular* authority here, not you! You answer to me, not the other way around."

I was curious as to how Sejanus would respond; from what I had seen, I thought he was likely to respond in the same tone, but instead, he held up a placating hand, and to my ears, his voice had a wheedling, sycophantic quality to it as he replied, "You're right, of course, sir. It's just that your father, the *Imperator* Tiberius..."

"I know who my father is," Drusus cut him off, "and I know that he sent you along to watch out for me. And," the young Roman took a deep breath, "I do appreciate your concern. But I am in command here. You and the rest of the Praetorians will wait here. Now," the manner in which he deliberately turned away from Sejanus could not have been a clearer rebuke, "we've wasted enough time. Come with me."

Without waiting to see if we obeyed, he wheeled his mount and went at the trot to where the Legate and the Centurion from the 9th were waiting.

461

"If you let anything happen to him, Dolabella," Sejanus hissed as we began moving, "I swear by the Furies I'll flay you alive." I glanced over at Dolabella, curious to see how he would respond, but he chose to ignore it, although I noticed his face went a shade pale, but before we got out of earshot, Sejanus called to me, "That goes for you too, Centurion! Don't think I've forgotten about you!"

As far as I remember it, it was Latobius who, of his own volition, spun about on his hindquarters and brought me back to face Sejanus; since I was already there, I suppose I decided that this was as good a time as any to make another enemy for life.

"The only way someone like you could take an inch of my skin is with help," I said, and while my voice was as calm as I could make it, for the second time recently, I felt that beast inside me begin to uncoil itself, a small fire beginning in my belly. "You wouldn't last a dozen heartbeats facing me, Sejanus. Apparently," I added this as I turned my horse, "your spies in the Legions aren't nearly as good as you think they are, or you'd know that already."

When I cantered up and rejoined Dolabella, he gave me a sidelong glance, then with a sigh, simply asked, "What did you do this time, Titus?"

The way he said it made me laugh, and I replied cheerfully, "You know me. I like making friends wherever I go."

This made Dolabella chuckle, but it did not last long, and he reminded me, "Remember what I said about him, Titus. He's a dangerous, dangerous man."

"Well," I shot back, still grinning, "so am I." Seeing that it had been the old man who joined us, I thought I knew his identity, but I asked Dolabella, "Is that Publius Cornelius Lentulus? The former Consul?"

"You're partly right," Dolabella allowed. "He was a Consul, but that's Gnaeus Lentulus; he was co-Consul with the other one."

I thought for a moment as I tried to recall what I could about this lesser known Lentulus, finally asking, "Wasn't he the Legate who conducted a campaign against the Getae? That didn't go so well?"

"The one and the same," Dolabella confirmed, then he looked over and warned, "And I would be careful about saying that where Lentulus can hear you, Titus. He's...sensitive about that. Yes," he allowed, "he's old, but he's still powerful. And," he grinned as he finished, but I knew he was being serious, "you've already made Sejanus your enemy. Try to keep it at that."

And with that, we followed Drusus and the others, right into a trap; it turned out that Sejanus was right after all.

Chapter Nine

We did not realize immediately that we had been lured into what was essentially a trap, as we were allowed to ride all the way to the forum, while the mutineers formed a corridor of sorts similar to what had been waiting outside the camp. And, much like the scene on the other side of the turf wall, these men were shouting at Drusus, listing their grievances, demands, and pleas for his father to heed them. It was disconcerting, even though I was not the real target of this outpouring of anger, frustration, and if I am any judge of things, hope that someone would hear these men. While they managed to maintain a certain amount of distance from our party at first, as we progressed down the Via Praetoria, the men began crowding in on us, until Drusus' bodyguards were forced to place their mounts on either side and behind the *Proconsul* and Lentulus, essentially leaving Dolabella, Blaesus, and me to shift for ourselves immediately behind them, with me on the right side, while the poor *lictors*, the only men of our party afoot, were left to fend for themselves. Not, I will confess, that their plight worried me all that much, if at all. Latobius was getting nervous, so I was more occupied with curbing him than really paying attention to the men, other than making sure no hands reached out to snatch at his bridle, or me for that matter, which meant I was caught completely by surprise when, through the clamor of voices, I heard my name called.

"Oy, Pullus! *Pullus*, you big bastard! What are you doing here?"

It took several heartbeats, and me slowing Latobius to a halt, which he did not like at all, as I scanned the crowd of upturned faces, but even then, it took me a moment to pick out the man calling my name. I believe I can be forgiven, because the last time we had seen each other, he was impossible to miss with a shock of bright orange hair, which was almost completely gone now, while the remaining fringe had faded in color to a more muted bronzish color intermixed with gray.

"Tuditanus?" I pointed, having to almost shout over the men around him who, understandably, did not care about two old comrades seeing each other for the first time in more than a decade. "What happened to your hair?"

Despite the circumstances, my former comrade and fellow *tiro* laughed, revealing several teeth missing from my last memory of his smile, patted his bald pate, and answered cheerfully, "I got old! And thank the gods, because nobody has mentioned my fucking hair for years." He gave me a mock glare as he said, "Until you showed up."

Even as he was saying this, he was pushing his way through the men nearest me to reach my side, and I confess that, while I was happy to see him, I was also a bit nervous as the rest of Drusus' party continued moving and none of the bodyguards, or Dolabella for that matter, seemed to notice I had dropped off. Still, I leaned down and clasped his arm, but when he pulled my arm, hard, my heart leapt as I thought, this is a trap! I should have had more faith in my friend, because he stood on his tiptoes, and pulling me down, kissed me on both cheeks, making me feel foolish for doubting him.

Then, he whispered urgently, "Percennius has something planned, but I don't know what! Clemens doesn't know about it and neither does Domitius!" He released me then and resumed speaking in a normal tone, "If you have a chance, come find me and we'll catch up!"

I think I only managed a nod, but I put Latobius into a trot to return to my party; by the time I did, Drusus was leading us onto the forum, where I could see that, just as I had left him, Percennius was seated on the curule chair, except now there were even more men surrounding him. This was the moment when, even above the continuing noise of the men, the sounds of a *cornu* sounded from behind us, except that it was nothing more than a single note and not a series that denoted a command of some sort. Twisting about, because I was mounted, I could see over the heads of the men, and was greeted by a sight of men, fully armored, carrying their shields and javelins, swarming up the ramp to the rampart on the Porta Praetoria side.

"Pluto's cock! We've been betrayed!"

It was Dolabella's voice I heard a heartbeat before the noise level rose so dramatically that I could not pick out any one individual's voice, but the manner in which the German bodyguards reacted, some of them peeling off to encircle our entire group, including the *lictors*, and facing outward, forming a sort of mounted *orbis*, while drawing their *gladii*, was what mattered. Those men nearest us began scrambling out of the way, since none of them were armed, shoving their comrades out of the way in their haste to get out of the reach of the Germans. I had very little time to observe any of this, because Latobius began reacting to the sudden change in atmosphere, and I had an instant's warning as I felt his muscles suddenly contract underneath me in a manner that told me he was about to rear. It was just enough of a warning that I was not unseated, and it did serve to scatter the men nearest me; it was while I was getting Latobius under control that there came the blast of another horn, but from a different direction, and from the *bucina*, which has a much sharper sound. Latobius had just returned all four hooves to the ground when I turned to see Percennius, standing on the rostrum that he had been perched on, but he was holding his arms up, bellowing something at the top of his lungs. I could not make it out, but apparently Drusus could, because I saw him turn and say something to the German to his immediate right, who clearly did not agree with it, shaking his head vehemently. Only when Drusus pointed a finger directly in his face did the bodyguard relent, reluctantly sheathing his *gladius*, and I realized that the noise level had dropped enough I could hear him bellow the order to his comrades to do the same. Gradually, things died down enough, with the mutineers surrounding us actually backing farther away, in a clear signal to us they meant no immediate harm, so that Drusus felt confident enough to close the distance to the rostrum. By this moment, both Dolabella and Blaesus had reached Drusus, his bodyguards moving their own mounts so that they could flank him, but I was still separated and behind them by a few paces, the distance between us the only clear space within this small formation. My head continued to swivel back and forth, as did those of Drusus' bodyguards, and while our weapons may have been sheathed, our hands were on our hilts, ready to draw them. Fortunately, the men immediately surrounding us seemed almost as confused as we were, and most importantly, not disposed to make any overt, violent action. Instead, their attention was, like ours, on Percennius, still garbed in a toga, who remained standing with his arms extended, palms outward in a peaceful gesture.

"We mean you no harm, *Proconsul!*" I finally managed to hear what Percennius had obviously been repeating as the din gradually subsided, to a point anyway.

Behind us, in the direction of the Porta Praetoria, the power of hundreds of lungs shouting meant that there was still a fair amount of noise, although it was impossible to make anything out from that direction. Before Drusus responded, I saw him turn his head, say something to Dolabella, who in turn twisted in his saddle, searching me out. Meeting his gaze, I interpreted his lifted eyebrow, followed by a jerk of his head in the direction of the figurehead of the mutiny standing on the rostrum as my purpose for being there, and I gave a nod, whereupon he turned back and informed Drusus.

Who wasted no time, speaking at just short of a shout, demanding, "What is the meaning of this, Percennius?"

467

The former actor affected an air of surprise that was clearly exaggerated, and as he had done with me, he bowed with a flourish, answering, "I am both honored and surprised that as powerful a Roman as the *Proconsul* Drusus Julius Caesar would know my name! But, I assure you, sir, you and your party are perfectly safe. As I said, we mean you no harm. This is just a...precaution."

"A precaution against what?" Drusus snapped, while I took advantage of the exchange and nudged Latobius forward, drawing up just behind the *Proconsul*, who indicated our party, saying, "We are here to listen to your demands, and..."

"Listen? *Listen?*" Percennius interrupted him, and a part of me marveled at this man's effrontery. More importantly, both the tone and volume of his voice changed as he straightened up, and made a sweeping gesture as he called out, "Do you hear that, my brothers? Our *Imperator* has sent someone here to 'listen to our demands'!" Suddenly, he pointed a finger down in an accusatory manner, not at Drusus but at Blaesus' son, saying harshly, "If this...*noble* Roman did what he swore on Jupiter's black stone to do, then you would have already known what our demands are and you would be here simply to let us know whether your father is acceding to them or not! Clearly, the Tribune went back on his word!"

As I was certain Percennius knew it would, this elicited a loud roar of anger from the men surrounding us, the noise sufficient that I could feel the vibration caused by their shouting up through Latobius' body. The mention of Blaesus' son also reminded me of the Legate, but my view of him where he, and presumably the Centurion Clemens had been, ahead of our group, was obscured by the bodies of both men and horses of those in front of me.

"He did no such thing!" Drusus had to shout this, and I heard the note of what sounded like desperation as he added, "I misspoke! We know what your demands are! That's why I'm here!"

And, just like that, Percennius' seeming outrage vanished, and once more, he held his arms aloft, making a quieting gesture with both hands, which worked quite quickly.

"That," Percennius smiled, "is good to hear."

My guess is that, in the moment, Drusus felt the need to at least try and reassert some form of control, because he demanded, "Now that that's cleared up, you need to explain the meaning of this...precaution? Is that what you called it?" Only then did the young *Proconsul* twist in his saddle to indicate behind us, and our eyes briefly met, though he gave no sign that he even recognized me. "Why do you have armed Legionaries manning the walls of this camp?"

"Only to ensure that our negotiations take place without any...interruption," Percennius answered smoothly, although I felt certain he understood that we did not believe him. "You came with quite a potent force, after all, *Proconsul*," the former actor continued, "and, given the current mood, it would be far too easy for something to happen that neither of us want." He gave an exaggerated shrug, but what he said next, while it sounded as if it was an afterthought, seemed to carry a deeper meaning, at least judging from the manner in which Drusus reacted. "Given the identity of the man who's commanding those Praetorians, I think it's a sensible precaution."

I could not see his face, but Drusus visibly stiffened in his saddle, and I was sure that the actor's comment would elicit something in the form of a verbal rebuttal or justification; instead, Drusus said only, "Be that as it may, we do have much to discuss." Pausing for a moment, he said pointedly, "In private, preferably."

Even as he said this, I had to stifle a groan, which was drowned out by angry protests from the men, while Percennius opened his eyes wide in such an overblown display of surprise I

469

began to suspect that perhaps the reason he was under the standard now had nothing to do with his politics and everything to do with his lack of ability as an actor.

"In private, *Proconsul*?" Percennius shook his head, also in an exaggerated manner, replying, "I'm afraid that won't do, sir. Why," up went the arms again, "we have no secrets from each other here! We are united, with one cause and one cause only, and that is to right the wrongs that have been done to us, both as men under the standard and as Roman citizens! There is no need for any of what's discussed to be secret, is there, my brothers?"

Naturally, the ground once more shook with the roared agreement of the mutineers gathered in the forum, most of them also thrusting one or both fists into the air in a further sign of their solidarity. For some reason, I was struck with a thought, wondering how it had been decided which men would be here, wearing nothing but their tunics and *baltea*, and which would be armored, manning the walls as they waited for an attempt by Sejanus to storm the camp. Not, I realized, that it mattered at the moment.

It took more than a dozen heartbeats before the tumult died down enough that Drusus could be heard, but he signaled, if not his acceptance then his recognition that, for the time being, he was going to be playing this game the way that Percennius wanted by asking plaintively, "May I and my party at least be allowed to dismount?"

"Of course, sir!" Percennius smiled, his manner expansive as he gestured to the rostrum on which he stood. "As you can see, we have chairs, and we can discuss matters here quite comfortably."

I confess I was a bit surprised when Drusus countered, "What about my men?"

"They have the freedom of the camp." Percennius made another wave of his hand, the same kind of gesture that a man of Drusus' class makes when bestowing some favor on someone

470

lower than him, and I was sure this was a calculated insult. "However," Percennius added, "they will be escorted at all times."

For a moment, it appeared as if Drusus was going to argue, then thought better of it, although he did cast a somewhat apologetic glance in the direction of the commander of his bodyguard, although I could not even imagine that the man, or any of Drusus' bodyguards would go wandering away from the man they were sworn to protect, especially given the identity of his father. Drusus swung down out of the saddle, and somewhat surprisingly, the men who had been in between us and the rostrum meekly stepped aside, without a show of reluctance or hostility, made a path for him; indeed, it seemed to me that some of the men looked somewhat ashamed. For his part, Dolabella swung down as well, as did young Blaesus and old Lentulus, and only then did I see that Blaesus' father, the Legate, had been standing, surrounded by mutineers, a few paces away. From what I could see, it seemed clear that the men standing around the older man were there as guards, but to my surprise, they did not stop father and son from rushing towards each other to embrace. The Germans seemed of two minds; some of them clearly wanted to remain mounted, while others also dismounted. Perhaps this was done on purpose, but I never asked. That left just me, and I was of the same view as the Germans who wanted to remain mounted, but it was as I was sitting there, pondering what to do, I saw one of the main flaps of the *praetorium* be pushed aside, whereupon a face peered out. The instant I recognized the face, my mind was made up for me, and I swung off Latobius, where I led him over to Dolabella.

"Are you going to stay here?" I asked him. When he said that he was, I held out the reins to him and asked, "Will you hold these?"

Even with everything going on, Dolabella retained enough of his wits to look surprised, asking me, "Are you really going to let me watch your horse?" He grinned, adding, "All by myself?"

"You're not alone," I retorted, jerking a thumb over at one of the Germans. "They may not know much, but they know good horseflesh. They won't let you do anything stupid."

He gave a small laugh, but under his breath, he asked me, "Where are you off to? To see anyone in particular?"

"Yes," I answered honestly. "I'll be back shortly." Stepping away from him, I saw there were a pair of men, both rankers, and while they were wearing only tunics, both of them were carrying cudgels, and I asked them, "Are you two going to be the ones following me around?" They exchanged a glance, but then one of them nodded, and I said curtly, "Then let's go. Try to keep up."

With that, I went striding towards the headquarters tent, leaving Drusus just settling, quite reluctantly, into the chair Percennius offered, and I wondered what the next watch held in store.

Not surprisingly, there were men standing in front of the *praetorium* entrance; what was unusual was that there were clearly two different sets of them. Four men who were wearing only their tunics but, like the pair of men who were following me, carrying cudgels were standing a couple paces away from the tent. Directly behind them, with their backs to the canvas, were four fully armed Legionaries, although they were leaning on their shields, and there did not seem to be an inordinate amount of tension or hostility. Nevertheless, when the four mutineers realized that I was actually heading for the tent, they straightened up in what was essentially the position of *intente*, reminding me that the discipline of the Legions is not something that is easily forgotten.

"Yes, Centurion?" The man who spoke wore the white Optio stripe. "Is there something we can do for you?"

"Yes," I replied pleasantly enough, but I was not inclined to do more than that, and I pointed at the flap. "You can step aside. I want to talk to Primus Pilus Galens."

"How do you know he's in there?"

This was not the Optio, but one of the men with him, and unlike the Optio, his tone was belligerent, and I was slightly encouraged to see that the Optio was clearly irritated, and while I was willing to address the Optio with a certain level of respect, that did not go for a ranker.

"Because I've got fucking eyes in my head, Gregarius," I snapped. "I just saw him look out."

At this, the Optio turned and gave one of the Legionaries an inquiring look, to which the man answered, "The Centurion's right. The Primus Pilus wanted to see what all the fucking noise was about this time."

The Optio seemed to consider for a moment, then shrugged and stepped aside, though he actually had to shove the belligerent ranker to move out of my path, but when I began moving towards the flap and the pair of mutineers followed, the Legionary who had spoken raised a hand, while the other three men stood up and hefted their shields.

"You know the rules, Poplicola," the Legionary spoke to the Optio. "None of you lot is allowed inside."

Before Optio Poplicola could speak up, one of the men behind me protested, "But Percennius told us we can't let him out of our sight! We have to go in."

"That's not happening," the Legionary said, but while the mutineers clearly did not like this, it was easy to see they also understood that they were not only unarmored and armed only with cudgels, but were unwilling to do anything to rupture the tenuous peace.

The man identified as Poplicola turned to me, and I read in his eyes a plea that I change my mind and turn around, but while

473

a part of me sympathized with the man, it was simply from my recognition he was in a tough spot.

However, deciding that it would be politic to do so, I did say, "I'm not going to go sneaking out the back; you have my word on it."

One of my escorts snorted, muttering derisively, "Oh, well, his word. That makes a difference."

I turned and pinned the man with my gaze, and while it was cold, I suspect that moving my hand from where I had it hooked in my *baltea* with my thumb and reaching across and tapping my fingers on the hilt of my *gladius* was likely more effective.

"That's all you're going to get," I told him, "but you're welcome to try and stop me instead if it's not enough."

As I expected, he wilted, breaking eye contact and giving a sulky shrug, which I accepted, but when I stepped forward, the Legionary who had spoken held up a hand.

"I'm sorry, Centurion," he was clearly nervous, "but our orders are that nobody be allowed in if we don't know them."

Biting back a curse, I forced myself to sound patient, saying, "Then one of you go tell Primus Pilus Galens that the best *tiro* he ever trained is outside and wants to talk to him."

I confess it was more an impish urge that I phrased it in this manner than any desire to be secretive, but despite looking confused, the Legionary in command of the detachment disappeared inside the tent. Before I could count to ten, the flap was thrust aside, and while he was not smiling, I saw the pleasure in his eyes.

"There's only one bastard who would think something like that," Aulus Galens said, "so I knew it had to be you."

And with that, I was allowed into the *praetorium*.

"What by Cerberus' balls are *you* doing here in this mess?" Galens asked after we had greeted each other properly, which started with me saluting, then ending in an embrace.

My old Optio, then my Centurion as Hastatus Posterior of the First Cohort, who I had known since childhood, was in his late fifties, and every year was etched in his weather-beaten, craggy features, but despite not laying eyes on him for years, I could see that this ordeal had aged him even more. As briefly as I could, I explained how I had come to be here back in Pannonia; when I mentioned Dolabella's name, his mouth twisted into a sneer, and just like Domitius, he had trouble reconciling that Tiberius' man and I were working together, and willingly at that.

"How did that happen?" he asked, as had Domitius.

"It's...complicated," was all I could offer, and like my old close comrade, Galens was clearly unconvinced, though he did not press matters.

There was an awkward silence, so I decided to fill it by asking, "So, how has it been here?" I pointed to the row of cots that lined the walls of the tent, while the desks had all been moved from their normal spots. "How long have you been cooped up in here?"

"Almost three weeks," he answered bitterly. "And it was pretty rough, at least at first. What they did to Rufus was just the beginning of it."

"Did they come after you?" I asked him, and he shot me a savage grin.

"Oh, they tried," he allowed, "but they only tried it once."

"How many men have been killed?"

He shook his head, but I misread him, surprising me instead when he answered, "Believe it or not, nobody has been killed." He paused, then added, "Yet, at least. Oh, there are a fair number of cracked skulls and gods know how many men have something broken, but otherwise, it's been only fists and occasionally cudgels."

"Well," I offered, "now that Drusus is here, it might be that nobody has to die."

Galens shook his head, and his tone was adamant as he said, "That's not going to happen." He pointed around at the other men, all of Centurion rank. "There has to be a reckoning for this, Pullus. Making us hide and cower in here like dogs?" His expression had hardened, but I sensed that, along with the bitterness and shame, there was a real sadness there, which he seemed to confirm when he added, "Unless we get rid of some of the worst offenders, we'll never be able to command these men again."

"Percennius must be at the top of your list," I commented, but at this, he looked directly at me, and my heart skipped a beat, somehow knowing what was coming.

"Percennius," Galens said scornfully, "is a puppet in a toga that he stole from somewhere. He doesn't have the brains for this. And," suddenly, he jabbed a finger in my chest, and I wondered if he had recalled how much I hated when someone did that, "I think you know that. In fact," he added, "I think that's why you're really here, and why Dolabella brought you here."

In this moment, I was reminded that, despite the rough, vulgar exterior, my first Optio had a razor-sharp mind; no man who achieves the rank of Primus Pilus is a simpleton. And, I also realized, that if I was interpreting him correctly, Galens intended to kill Domitius; whether he did it himself or ordered it done did not really matter.

For just an instant, I considered lying but quickly discarded it, choosing to admit instead, "You're probably right. About Dolabella, anyway." I paused for a moment, trying to think of something that might help this situation, my mind racing, then it suddenly came to me, and I asked Galens, "What about this list of demands? Do you think they're unjust? Which ones do you disagree with?"

This clearly caught Galens by surprise, and I saw the warring emotions playing across his features, while the silence drew out for several heartbeats.

Finally, he replied, very grudgingly, "I don't think there's anything that's actually unjust or wrong, Pullus. But," he insisted, "they shouldn't have gone about it the way they did! Here or," he pointed at me again, but this time, I understood why, "in Germania. That's just not the way Roman citizens do things!"

"I agree," I answered, "that this was probably not the best way to go about it."

"'Probably'?" he echoed disbelievingly. "There's no 'probably'! It wasn't right!"

Rather than argue the point directly, I decided on another approach, asking him, "How long have the rankers been asking for these changes?"

For the first time, Galens looked, if not uncertain, then seemingly understanding where I was heading.

"A fair amount of time," he admitted, again grudging every word.

"And," I pressed, "what has the answer been from the *Princeps*?"

"That the time wasn't right," Galens said, sighing as he did so.

Seeing him weaken, I was not about to let up; more than the original reason I had been brought here, once I learned that Galens knew Domitius was one of the true leaders of this mutiny, my most important mission became doing everything I could to protect my friend.

"So," I asked, rhetorically, "when *is* the right time, Galens? If not now, when Tiberius is still not secure as *Imperator*?"

"But that's not right!" Galens protested indignantly. "Hitting the man when he's at his weakest, like this?" Shaking his head, he repeated stubbornly, "It's not right."

"When else would they do it?" I pressed. "Given how many times they've been turned down, really, what choice did they have?"

At this, Galens glared at me, clearly angry that I seemed to be taking the side of the mutineers, and I was prepared for another angry outburst.

But then, without any warning, he let out an explosive breath, waved a hand in disgust, answering, "All right, all right. You made your point." Shaking his head, he insisted, "But I don't like it! And," he lowered his voice, and this time, he made sure to look directly in my eyes as he said, "There are men in this Legion who need to disappear, Pullus. And nothing and nobody is going to stop us," he jerked his head to indicate the loyal Centurions around us, "from setting our Legion to rights."

A lump formed in my throat, and I realized how much of a risk I was going to be running, yet that memory of my Avus' account overpowered any idea of caution, causing me to say as casually as I could, "I understand, and I agree that needs to be done…as long as it's not a Centurion with one eye that you're going to…disappear." Galens' expression hardened, but I did not stop there, finishing quietly, "Because if that happens, Primus Pilus, I'm willing to sacrifice my life and my career to avenge that act."

He said nothing for a long, long moment, and while I returned his stare equally, there was no hostility in my gaze; no, there was just a sense of real sadness that matters had come to this.

Finally, he gave a barely perceptible nod, but I was not satisfied with that, and I said as much. His expression softened, and he said, "Honestly, he's one of the best Centurions in the Legion, and I know that he had more to do with making sure that the bloodshed has been kept to a minimum than anyone, even Clemens." While this was encouraging, I said nothing and continued to stare at him, and he finally muttered, "Fine. This Centurion you're speaking of has nothing to fear. Besides," he shrugged, "he hadn't been himself leading up to this. I suppose you know his woman died?"

I nodded, but I was more curious about something else he had said, and I used the opening to ask him, "What about this Clemens? He's not from the 8th?"

Galens shook his head. "No, he's from the 9th. Honestly, the 9th has been the most half-hearted about all this nonsense, but I put that down to the fact that they haven't been in Pannonia that long."

I knew this, of course; they had been sent to Pannonia by the Princeps after the Pannonian rebellion and the Varus disaster, but I was not sure why Galens thought their relatively short tenure in the province had something to do with it, and I asked him as much.

"You remember what that campaign was like, Pullus," Galens answered, then for the first time, gave me a grin, and I was impressed he still had all of his teeth, minus those on the bottom that had been knocked out in a fight before I joined his Century. "I mean, it's true you were off strutting around with young Germanicus and didn't see any *real* fighting, but I'm sure you heard about how tough it was when you and Germanicus were lying on your couches eating lark's tongues."

"*Gerrae!*" I replied, only part of my indignation feigned. "We had it just as tough as any of you!"

"You did," Galens agreed, which threw me, something at which he was exceedingly good at doing, then after a pause, he added, "as long as you were here. But you weren't here for that last year." This I could not deny, and he correctly interpreted my silence to continue, "I'll cross the river believing that it was the last year of that campaign that's the real cause of what's happening with this army. I don't know about you boys on the Rhenus, but we were treated worse than dogs for the last year of that campaign. Oh," he waved a hand, "I know why Tiberius did what he did. He was angry and frustrated. But he took it out on us just as much as he had us take it out on the natives." His mouth twisted into a bitter grimace as he finished, "Well, this what he gets, I suppose."

I sat there, considering Galens' words, and I did think about pointing out that Galens had essentially offered a defense of the actions of the mutineers, but I kept that to myself, not wanting to inadvertently cause his hostility to turn back onto the men, specifically Domitius.

Instead, I asked carefully, "So, Primus Pilus, I have your word that nothing will happen to Domitius?"

He shot me an irritated look, replying tersely, "I told you nothing would happen to him, didn't I?"

I tried not to let my relief show, but before I could say anything else, we heard a roar of voices from outside, yet the look Galens and I exchanged told me that he interpreted the tone the same way I did, which was one of anger and repudiation, not of celebration that Drusus had given them what they wanted. We both stood, yet before either of us could move, the flap was suddenly thrown open, and I saw by the light that it was almost sundown, but it was the sight of Drusus entering the tent, more stumbling than walking, that caused a thrill of alarm to pass through me. He was followed immediately by Dolabella, Lentulus, then both father and son Blaesus, but I counted the bodyguards, and only four entered the tent as well. Meanwhile, the noise was continuing outside, the anger still clear in their collective voices, and I wondered what Drusus had said, or had not said that had caused this reaction. This was what prompted me to move in the general direction of the *Proconsul*, but he had been given a chair and was completely surrounded by a combination of noblemen and his bodyguards, all of them competing to thrust a cup in his hand while demanding to know what had happened…in respectful terms, of course. Rather than try and shove my way through, I moved around the knot until I saw Dolabella, who at that moment was draining a cup himself, and when I moved to his side, I could smell that it was not water.

"What happened?" I asked him, but before he answered, he jerked his head in an indication to follow him away from the small crowd.

Once we were a safe distance away, the spymaster said miserably, "He delayed as long as he could, but he finally told them that while he had been empowered by his father to make the decision, he didn't feel comfortable doing that, and he'd have to take the demands back to Tiberius."

"Again?" I groaned, and he only nodded. Something came to me, and I asked, "How many times has Tiberius seen this list of demands?"

"At least three times that I know about," Dolabella admitted.

"And have any of the demands changed?"

"No," Dolabella sighed. "They haven't."

Before I could stop myself, I blurted out, "I don't blame them for being angry."

Prior to this, I would have never uttered such a thing in front of Dolabella, certain that he would dangle this over my head as a means to force my cooperation in whatever scheme he was carrying out for Tiberius. And, even in the moment, I acknowledged that I was running a risk, but our time together over the previous days had convinced me that this was a new man, which he seemed to confirm.

"Neither do I," he answered soberly. "But that doesn't do us any good right now."

This was certainly true, and I asked him, "What did Percennius say?"

"I think," Dolabella gave me a grim smile, "that our actor just realized that he's not the puppet master; he's the puppet. But," he added quickly, perhaps because of my clear consternation, "because of that mob outside. They turned on him just as quickly as they turned on Drusus. And," he allowed, "he's the one who told Drusus to get in the tent since this is protected by the agreement."

That, I thought, was a few moments ago. Now I was not so sure that the men I was listening to howling outside, separated by only a thickness of canvas and some words, were of a mind to abide by it. It was this thought that spurred me to do something that, strictly speaking, I had sworn not to do.

"I'm going to go find Domitius," I told Dolabella, "and find out just how much danger we're in."

As soon as I said it, I cursed myself, and completely unsurprisingly, Dolabella did not miss it, turning to stare up at me, his one good eye piercing me, though his tone was neutral as he said, "That's a good idea. Dangerous," he added, "but a good idea. But," he indicated the front flap, "how are you going to get past them?"

"Going out the back," I told him.

"But there's not a back entrance," he protested. "The only opening is to the *quaestorium*, but there's guards on the outer entrance from there too."

In answer, I just tapped the hilt of my *gladius*, saying quietly, "If they can cut their way in here quicker than Pan, then I can do the same to get out."

"I hope," Dolabella sighed, "you know what you're doing."

"So do I," was all I could think to say.

It was not difficult to slice through the thick canvas of the back wall of the *praetorium*, although it did mean I was forced to intrude into the area that are the private quarters of the commander, Blaesus Major in this case, but I did not tarry. What *was* difficult was trying to squeeze my bulk through a single slit without tearing it wider open and leaving a gaping hole that anyone walking by could see. Fortunately, every man that was out and about was in the forum on the opposite side, and I waited just long enough for the sun to finish its descent, then after carefully and slowly stepping through the slit, I stood outside the tent for a moment, examining my makeshift exit. As careful as I had been, I had inevitably torn the canvas horizontally, creating a sagging hole that certainly was not as wide as my body, but was undoubtedly noticeable. Since I had taken the precaution of blowing out the single lamp that had been lit in Blaesus' private quarters, and with the growing darkness, fortunately, the hole was not something that was so obvious that even a drunken ranker would notice. Moving quickly, but not so much so that it would draw attention, I walked down the Via Quintana, the street that runs behind the *praetorium*, and while there were men wandering about, they all appeared to be heading somewhere. Some of them, I noticed, were fully armed; these men were moving at a trot in the direction of the Porta Praetoria, making me wonder if Sejanus, hearing the uproar inside the camp as he undoubtedly had, was even then preparing to send his Praetorians in an assault. That, I was certain, would turn these already angry men in the forum violent, and there was no possible outcome that I could think of that turned out well for anyone, particularly the mutineers. I suppose it should be no surprise that, despite my loathing of men like Percennius here, or Pusio back in my own Century, and my disbelief that their motives were based in anything but self-interest, my heart and sentiment was with the rest of the men of the ranks. Whether or not the method that had been selected by insurrection was a proper way of going about it was the only aspect about which I had reservations, yet I also recognized that the Legions had been formally submitting their list of complaints for more than four years and had been continuously rebuffed, being told it was not the right time. Only once as I made my way to Domitius' tent did I draw attention by a small party of a half-dozen men, wearing just their tunics but carrying cudgels. Feeling their eyes on me, I ignored them as I strode by, and while I saw one man's mouth open, nothing came out that might have created trouble.

At the time, I told myself that they just did not want to tangle with a fully armored Centurion of my size, but when I thought about it later, it was just as likely that they thought I was part of the contingent of men manning the walls. I was slightly concerned that one of the older veterans I conceivably could have run into during my walk might recognize me, but that did not happen, and the growing darkness certainly helped, especially since whoever was running things clearly did not have sufficient organization or control to send out men to light the torches that are placed around camp. Reaching Domitius' tent, I suddenly realized that he might not be inside, and as I thought about it, I believed it more likely than not that he was elsewhere given all that was taking place. The mutineers in the forum were still shouting, but it had lost much of its power, dying to a dull roar that was still unsettling, but had lost the raw edge of anger that had been present moments before. Nevertheless, I rapped the piece of wood, yet when Domitius' clerk opened the flap, I was prepared for him to inform me that my friend was not present. Instead, he did not appear surprised to see me, and, taking a quick glance around to see if we were being observed, waved me inside.

As soon as I did so, the clerk, who I did not recognize, confirmed my sense by saying, "The Centurion told me to expect you at any moment. He's in his quarters," he pointed, "and said you should go right in."

Naturally, I did as he directed, walking to the flap in the partition, thrusting it aside, and getting yet another shock; Domitius was not alone, but more than the presence of two other men, it was the identity of one of them that stopped me in my tracks.

"Titus," Domitius looked calm and completely unruffled, "have you met Primus Princeps Prior Clemens?"

"Not formally," I managed, stepping the rest of the way into Domitius' quarters, "but I know who he is."

Clemens' expression was likely akin to the one I was wearing; a combination of caution and not a little worry, but I suppose that, like me, he also trusted Domitius, and I would like to think that whatever hesitation on my part when he thrust out his arm was so short that he did not notice, or perhaps he was too polite to mention it. Whatever the case, I grasped his arm, and we shared a moment of grim humor as we both opened our mouths, then realized there were really no words or ritual greeting that covered this situation.

"This," Domitius indicated the other man, "is Primus Princeps Prior Quintus Justus Catonius of the 15th."

As I had with Clemens, I offered my arm to Catonius, whose expression mirrored that of the other Centurion, yet also like Clemens, he accepted my hand without any comment other than the muttered niceties we all use when greeting a stranger.

With that done, I turned to Domitius and asked bluntly, "So what now?"

"That," he answered without any overt sign he was irritated by the manner in which I had asked the question, "is what we're talking about now." Domitius then turned to the other two and indicated me, explaining, "This is Quartus Princeps Prior Pullus of the 1st Legion. He…"

"I know who he is," Catonius interrupted, who was of about the same age as Galens. "I was on the Primus campaign with his grandfather my first year. He," he was staring at me, but while it was not overtly hostile, it was far from friendly, "was a great man, your grandfather, the best man I've ever seen with a *gladius*, and that was when he was about my age now. But," now he turned to Domitius, and his tone became challenging, "that doesn't explain why he's here right now."

Domitius opened his mouth to answer, but I beat him to it. "Because I spent my first decade with the 8th, and *Proconsul* Germanicus personally ordered me to come down here to observe and offer what help I could to the situation."

Now, strictly speaking, this was not quite the truth, yet neither was it a lie. Regardless, I was not surprised when Catonius looked doubtful, while Clemens, who had been silent, maintained a neutral expression that I found impossible to interpret.

Seeing Catonius was still suspicious, I suppose that was what prompted Domitius to point out, "He was Germanicus' Primus Pilus six years ago for the *Legio Germanicus* during the revolt here."

This clearly had an impact, and while I had not known the man long, Catonius' expression relayed a sense of chagrin, which he confirmed when he admitted, "That's right, I had forgotten about that." Turning to me, he gave what I suppose was his smile as he offered, "Forgive me, Pullus. It's just hard to know who to trust right now."

"I understand," I answered honestly, but then there was a sudden increase in the noise outside, which caused me to return to the original topic, "but I think you have more important things to worry about right now."

The three of them nodded, then resumed their discussion where they had left it when I interrupted, while I moved slightly towards the corner, determined that I would do nothing but listen. Which, of course, meant that I did no such thing.

It was not until later we learned that the sudden eruption of the noise that had remained at a dull roar before that moment was due to old Gnaeus Lentulus. Depending on who you asked, he was either caught trying to sneak out of the camp to inform Sejanus that Drusus was in dire peril and needed to be rescued, or, as I learned from Dolabella, he was angered by being forced to effectively cower inside the *praetorium*, had stood up and announced to all within earshot that he was too old for such nonsense, and that he was returning to Rome to live out however many days the gods had deemed he had left.

"Apparently," Dolabella had said this with a grin, "he was most concerned that his young wife was in danger of being corrupted. That," he added, "is how he put it anyway. But from everything I've heard, young Lentula doesn't need any help in that department, if you know what I mean."

While this was somewhat humorous, what was taking place while Domitius, Clemens, and Catonius were vociferously arguing about their next course of action, was anything but, because it almost cost Lentulus his life. No matter why he did it, what is inarguable is that he was caught before he could make good his exit from the camp, and was stoned by angry mutineers. Whatever his faults as a Legate may have been, and despite his age, Lentulus was a tough old bird, because he somehow made his way up the rampart, then threw himself over the wall, whereupon some of Sejanus' Praetorians rushed forward, and using javelins to cover their rescue, dragged the badly cut and bleeding old man to safety. This prompted what all who had been present for the entire mutiny agreed was the tensest, most dangerous moment, when some of the mutineers, whipped on by Percennius and his lackeys, threatened to storm the *praetorium,* claiming that Lentulus' escape was proof of bad faith on the part of Drusus and those who had remained loyal, like Galens and Asinius, who I had yet to see but had been resting in the *quaestorium* on our arrival, after standing watch the night before. It was only through the intercession of a handful of men from the 9th, all of whom worked for Clemens, who went among those mutineers clamoring for blood, convincing them that this would remove any chance they had of achieving any of their aims. Thankfully, cooler heads prevailed, but it had been a close-run thing. Meanwhile, I had finally taken a stool to sit and listen for some time as the debate raged back and forth between Catonius, Domitius, and Clemens, as the Centurion from the 15th argued, with some justification, that the fact that Drusus had not been empowered to make any concessions on behalf of his father was proof that the new *Imperator* had no intention of ever dealing fairly with us. His idea was to take Drusus hostage and bargain with the *Imperator* for his son's life, insisting that this would be the only way to achieve their aims. Domitius was just as vociferous in insisting that doing so would spell disaster, not just for their hopes of getting Tiberius to agree to their demands, but to them personally.

"Don't think that he won't find out that Percennius and his bunch aren't the real leaders of this," my friend argued, "and when he does, we're all dead men."

"I'm prepared to sacrifice my life if it means getting the men what they deserve," Catonius shot back, and somewhat to my surprise, Clemens nodded his agreement; he had been almost completely silent during their back and forth, making me wonder if that by common consent, he represented the tiebreaker between the three of them, since it was quickly apparent that Domitius was the moderate, while Catonius was more of a hardliner.

"I know you are," Domitius answered, his tone directly contrasting Catonius' heat, "but what about your family, Catonius? How old is your oldest son?"

This caused the older man to close his eyes, take a breath, then answering with a sigh, "He's twenty, you know that." He opened his eyes, but while he glared at my friend, it was without rancor. "And my oldest daughter just married an Optio in the Third of the Fifth."

Domitius did not respond, at least to Catonius; instead, he shocked all of us, especially me, when he turned to me and asked quietly, "What do you think, Titus? Do you think Tiberius would be content with just getting rid of us if we do as Catonius wants?"

Now it was my turn to glare at him, except there was a great deal of rancor in my gaze, because I knew why Domitius was asking me. No, I had never openly confessed my role as one of

Tiberius' men, those who performed his deeds that he had no wish to become public, when he removed those he considered dangerous to the Princeps when he was still alive, to Rome, or, yes I will admit, to himself personally. But my friend is a clever, clever man, and I had always suspected he had guessed that I provided some form of service to Tiberius, although, as I have mentioned, it had been quite some time since Dolabella had darkened my door with a task.

If he read the anger in my face, he gave neither a sign nor did he relent in meeting my gaze, regarding me steadily until I finally admitted, "No, I don't. I think he would consider you holding Drusus hostage as a personal attack on his *dignitas*. And," I felt compelled to add, "he'd be right. There would be no way that everyone in Rome wouldn't hear about how you took his son hostage to force him to agree to your demands. And the Head Count wouldn't like the idea of their *Imperator* essentially being extorted any more than he would, so they'd have no problem with whatever steps he took to avenge the assault on his family."

Catonius had been listening, but his expression remained hard and implacable, although I noticed that a muscle in his jaw had begun twitching as I continued speaking, not that I knew the man well enough to determine if this was significant. Clemens was every bit as attentive, yet I noticed that his eyes kept darting over to Catonius, clearly trying to gauge what impact my words were having in bolstering Domitius' argument.

I finished speaking, and there was a silence that stretched out for several heartbeats, and I was beginning to think that perhaps this would be enough, and more importantly, Catonius would not ask the obvious.

Naturally, this meant that when he opened his mouth, it was to demand, "And how do you know so much about how Tiberius thinks, Pullus? I mean," he indicated himself and the other two, "more than any man of the ranks who's marched for him."

Misreading my expression, he did hold up a placating hand. "I mean no offense when I say that, Pullus. But this is too important a matter to base our decision on what you think Tiberius will do."

I felt the flush of blood running up my neck, my face turning hot, but I do not know if it was what Catonius said, or that I sensed Domitius' remaining eye fixed on me, waiting for what came out of my mouth next. And, as the gods as my witness, I was not going to say anything that would expose myself to the censure and contempt of these men, especially since I felt certain that one or both of them would have no reason not to spread this around the army. Yes, they were the army of Pannonia, but there is a steady flow of traffic between their army and that of the Rhenus, so it might be a month, perhaps two before who and what Titus Porcinianus Pullus really was became known to my comrades in the 1st. Then, from where I can only surmise, an image flashed through my mind, of words on a scroll, written by my Avus, and I was reminded why I was truly here, to correct the one mistake that I was certain haunted the first Titus Pullus for the rest of his days.

Closing my eyes, not wanting to look them in the face, I opened my mouth, yet it was Domitius who spoke first, saying quickly, "Titus, wait!" Opening my eyes, I looked at him, except he was not returning my gaze but was facing Catonius, and he said, "Before Pullus tells you what I think he's going to tell you. Which," he added forcefully, "should convince you that he knows what he's talking about, I'm demanding that both of you take an oath on your eagles that you won't ever utter a word of what he's going to tell you. To anyone."

For men under the standard, there is only one oath that is more binding than the one that we swear on the black stone of Jupiter, and that is on the eagle standard of our Legion, which told both Catonius and Clemens, in some ways even more than what I was about to say, how important it was to my friend.

Catonius shook his head, his mouth turning down into a frown. "I don't know that I'm willing to swear an oath when I don't know what he's going to say."

"That's the only way I'm letting him tell you," Domitius replied immediately.

Catonius did not seem inclined to agree, then Clemens, for one of the few times, spoke up, "Quintus, has Domitius ever lied to us? Or when he told us something is important, has he ever been wrong?"

"No," Catonius admitted, and I was gratified to see the obvious respect both men held for my former close comrade, with whom I had shared so much. Taking a breath, he nodded and said, "Very well, I swear it." He addressed me, "Nothing you say will leave this tent, ever."

I spoke for the next several moments, and in an odd way, it felt…good, I suppose, to finally say aloud what I had kept to myself for so many years, although I did not go into any real detail for the most part, with one exception. Truly, I cannot say why I did so, but it seemed important that I relate the first time Tiberius, through Dolabella, of course, sent me on one of his "errands," as the spymaster called them, leaving nothing out, including how I felt afterward. Perhaps I just wanted to convince them that it had been against my will, that I took no pleasure in what I had done; more likely, I was trying to convince myself, since I had long before stuck this memory in a compartment of my mind and had not thought about it until this moment. By the time I was finished, I was hoarse, and Catonius and Clemens were regarding me with expressions that I had not seen on either man during our short association, but it was Domitius who I was most concerned with, yet when I glanced over at him, I was not prepared for the look of, if not pride, then a sort of satisfaction, which seemed confirmed when he gave me a nod and a faint smile.

"Well," Catonius broke the silence, "you were right, Domitius. I'm convinced. But," his face turned glum, "that leaves us back where we started. If we can't use Drusus. And," he held up a hand, although none of us objected, "I now agree that's something I'm not willing to do…" He paused, then admitted, "…I'm willing to sacrifice myself to get what we deserve. But my family? That I can't do. But," Catonius continued, "this has all been for nothing if we can't convince Tiberius we're serious in some way."

This compelled me to speak up, and I assured him, "Believe me, he takes it seriously. He showed that by sending his two sons here and to the Rhenus. And," I pointed out, "while I can't say I know Tiberius intimately, I know him well enough to know that he's aware of the possibility we'll do what we've been talking about. He's a hard man to figure out, but I do know he loves his sons. At least," I amended with a grim smile, "he loves the one that's sitting in the *praetorium* here. Germanicus, I'm not so sure about."

The other three men seemed to accept my words, and there was a long silence.

Then, Domitius suddenly turned towards me and asked, "All right, Titus. What do we do?"

This caught me by surprise, although it should not have, but I wanted no part of being involved in a decision that ultimately did not impact me personally, aside from the fate of my friend. And, I freely confess, it was with Domitius in mind that I answered at all.

"I think that you're going to have to allow Drusus to leave the camp and take your demands back to Tiberius."

"We already allowed that with Blaesus' boy," Catonius argued, yet there was no real heat in his words, and I could see that, like the other two men, he was exhausted from this ordeal. "And nothing came of it."

"No," I agreed, "but Blaesus' son isn't Tiberius' son. And," I pointed in the general direction of the *praetorium*, "I suspect that young Drusus is frightened out of his mind right about now."

"He's not the only one," Clemens muttered, and while it was not that funny, just the manner in which he said it, coupled with the fatigue and tension caused uproarious laughter, in which I joined as heartily as the others.

Once our mirth subsided, there was a silence, then Domitius said, "All right, Titus. You can go back to the *praetorium* and let Drusus know that he's going to be allowed to leave to return to his father the *Imperator*, and that we will abide by whatever he decides. And," Domitius indicated Clemens, "we do ask that Clemens here be allowed to accompany Drusus as our representative."

Since this clearly did not surprise Clemens, it told me that they had at least planned for this possibility. When I nodded my agreement, Domitius took that as a signal and stood up, as did I, and we embraced, though I do not really know why, since I was certain I would see him before we departed.

"What about Percennius?" I thought to ask. "What if he's not willing to agree to this?"

Domitius did not answer me, directly at least, turning his only eye to Catonius, who was the one to speak, giving me what might have been a smile but looked more like a grimace. "Percennius has outlived his usefulness." His tone was matter-of-fact, and I also took this as an indication that the matter of the actor had been decided beforehand as well. "He'll be dealt with shortly. By the time the sun rises, Percennius and his bunch won't stop Drusus from leaving the camp."

I was about to ask another question, then thought better of it, deciding that the less I knew the better, not for my own sake but for that of Domitius, and to a lesser extent, Catonius and Clemens, who seemed to be good officers who wanted the best for their men. Without saying anything more, I left the tent and made my way back to the *praetorium*, aided by the now total darkness and the fact that the torches still were not lit. The uproar we had heard, of which I did not yet know the cause, had died down, leaving the steady humming of men talking, but my ears told me that the sound was not coming solely from the forum, but from the surrounding tents, a sign that things were calming down and the mutineers, who, after all, were mortal men like the rest of us, were tired and at least some of them were retiring for the night. I was certain that whoever was commanding the armed men guarding the camp had organized matters more than Percennius had with his segment of mutineers, so that there would be a rotating shift along the walls, making it unlikely that Sejanus would try an assault under the cover of darkness. Or so I hoped, at any rate, but it was the thought of the Praetorian that made me realize I had forgotten to ask about who was in command of the armed Legionaries, and if whoever it was belonged to Percennius, or answered to the triumvirate of my friend and the other two Centurions. It was a troubling thought, and I considered turning around and going back to find out, since I was certain that I would be asked, but then I realized that I needed to trust Titus Domitius, who had clearly been skilled enough to avoid being identified as one of the ringleaders. If that had been a concern, I told myself, he would have warned me; still, it was a nagging thought as I reached the slit in the back of the tent, stopping a few paces away just to observe and listen for any sound that might indicate someone was inside Blaesus' quarters, waiting for whoever might choose to come through the hole. I counted to a hundred, but heard or sensed nothing suspicious; nevertheless, I considered drawing my *gladius* but quickly discarded the notion, thinking that a shadowy figure sneaking into the *praetorium* through a slit someone had made with a *gladius* in their hand would be hard to explain, no matter who I was. Still, I did keep my thumb tucked in my *baltea,* putting my hand near the hilt as I stepped through, then stopped just inside for a moment, halfway expecting the sudden rush of air and sound of feet on the carpeted wooden floor as men came rushing at me. Thankfully, that did not happen, and when I made my way out of Blaesus' private quarters, through his private office, then out into the large room, nobody even bothered to turn and look in my direction, causing my legs to begin shaking from the sudden relief. Of course, the fact that everyone was still occupied chattering about Lentulus leaving the *praetorium* and the speculation of what had happened to him, based just on the sounds the occupants had heard, meant their attention was elsewhere. Circling around close to the wall, I moved until I saw Dolabella, who was engaged in a discussion with Galens and the other two Primi Pili of the 9th and 15th, surrounded by a small number of Centurions, all of them listening intently to whatever Dolabella was saying. I did not want to just walk up, since it would engender questions about my whereabouts from the others that I had no wish to answer, so I had to wait until Dolabella stopped talking, then tried catching his eye. Which, as I had learned many years ago, could be a confusing task, since I always forgot which of his eyes was the good one. This delay turned out to be fortuitous, because I spotted a lean figure on the outer edge of the small crowd, recognizing the man immediately just by the manner in which he carried himself. Maneuvering around the others, I had hoped to catch Appius Asinius by surprise, but as always, that proved to be fruitless.

His expression was essentially the one I remembered him wearing every time he regarded me; a combination of a bit of amusement and a large portion of what I had only learned over time was worry about me, which he confirmed when he spoke first. "Galens told me that you were around here somewhere tripping over your feet." With an exaggerated shake of his head, he said, "I should have known that somehow you'd find yourself right in the middle of all this *cac*."

"I'm not the one trapped in a fucking tent," I shot back, but it was with a smile that I felt certain would split my face. "I can come and go as I please."

"So can I," he retorted, then returned my smile for the first time, "at least if I have someone following me to the latrine."

I was not content with a gripping of arms, although we started out that way, then I pulled him in for a hug, which he returned, and despite his normally laconic demeanor, I could see he was as pleased as I was to be reunited, however briefly.

"Galens told me why you're here," he offered, for which I was thankful, since I had become tired of explaining myself. "And," he lowered his voice, "I know you went to see Domitius."

This I did not even attempt to deny, yet somewhat to my surprise, Asinius did not ask me anything about it.

"Do you still have that horse?" Asinius asked, with a completely straight face, although I suspected that Galens might have put him up to it.

"Yes," I sighed, "I still have Latobius."

"Then you might want to get on him and get out of here," Asinius said quietly, except this time, I did not get the feeling that he was indulging in his normally mordant sense of humor, and when I looked him in the eye, I knew he was serious.

It is difficult to describe what it feels like when someone who you hold in as high a regard as I did Asinius was, even these many years later, trying to look after my best interests, which all began when my father extracted Corvinus' promise to do whatever he could to protect me. Appius Asinius, who I was not altogether surprised to see had not aged, especially compared to Galens, had been given that task by Corvinus, when I was a *Tirone* assigned to his section.

Since I did not know what to say, as always, I made light of it, joking, "And what? Miss all this excitement?"

The look Asinius gave me was one I immediately recalled as one he had given me often, both as my Sergeant, then as my Optio, one of resignation at my determination to take the hardest possible road I could find.

"Well," for the first time he gave me the glimmer of a smile, "if you're going to be stupid, I can't say I'm not happy to see you."

"How bad has it been, really?" I asked him, but like Galens, he insisted, "Not nearly as bad as it could have been. And," he gave me a direct look, "that's thanks in large part to Domitius." He hesitated for a moment, then said cryptically, "I hope you say something to your friend that works for Tiberius and let him know that."

Although my initial reaction was one of surprise, I quickly realized that it should not have been; Appius Asinius was not only one of the most intelligent men I knew, he had a shrewd insight into others that I had long before learned meant that it was next to impossible to hide anything from him.

"I already have," I assured him, once I had recovered myself a bit.

Even as I said this, I saw Dolabella scan the room and look in my direction, though he did not stop talking, just giving me a curt nod as he finished whatever he was saying.

"Speaking of," I told Asinius, "I think he's done talking, and I need to tell him something."

Asinius did not appear surprised, but when he thrust his arm out again, for the first time, he gave me a smile, saying only, "I'd tell you not to do anything stupid, but that's never worked before, so I won't waste my breath now."

As I am sure he hoped, this made me laugh, then after a clap on the shoulder and a promise to talk again before I left, I turned to where Dolabella had extricated himself and was making his way over to where I was standing, his eyebrows raised in a silent question. Before I did so, I asked him about the uproar that was now about a third of a watch earlier, which was when he informed me about Lentulus, and his suspicion that a straying wife was the real cause for the old man to show the fortitude to just try and walk out of the camp.

"So what's the situation?" Dolabella asked, and I briefly explained the outcome of what had been decided. When I was through, he closed his eyes, exhaling a huge sigh of relief, then his expression sharpened, and he asked, "But what about Percennius? Did he agree to this? He left the forum a while ago, so I assumed he was meeting with...others." Dolabella's tone turned careful, and I was certain that it was because he had been about to utter a name that would have complicated matters for me a great deal.

While we never discussed it afterward, I am certain that Dolabella and I were engaging in a very delicate dance with each other, both of us careful not to lay bare a situation that would force me to openly choose sides in a way that would come to the attention of more than just Tiberius' spymaster. It is another reason that I know now that his change of heart and attitude towards serving our new *Imperator* was genuine.

"No," I answered him, "he didn't go meet with anyone...important," I settled on that word, "concerning what's going on." Realizing I had not actually answered his original question, I went on, "But he's not going to stop Drusus from leaving. Provided," I warned, "that we keep the *Proconsul* here until sunrise."

Dolabella, rather than seeming pleased at that, sighed again, but it was not out of dissatisfaction as he glanced over his shoulder where, following his gaze, I saw that Drusus was now standing, still surrounded by a combination of Tribunes, bodyguards, and some Centurions.

"That," Dolabella replied, "is going to be difficult. The moment that ruckus happened after Lentulus left, Drusus decided he wanted to leave. They've been trying to talk him out of it ever since, but," he indicated the knot of men, "they aren't making much progress."

"Then you need to tell him that it's been arranged that he can leave, unharmed, but he just needs to wait a while longer," I told him.

"I'll try," he sounded doubtful, then he looked up at me, the lines of concern making the already deep grooves in his face appear even deeper, "but what if I can't and he decides to go ahead and do it? What do you think happens then?"

"Nothing good," was all I could answer. We stood for a moment, sharing in the concern, and I suppose that it was what prompted me to mutter, "If you think it will do any good, I'll go over there with you."

Dolabella was clearly surprised, and I could see, touched, but then he frowned and shook his head, pointing out, "Pullus, if you do that, he's going to want to know how you can be so certain. And that means you're going to have to..."

He trailed off, though he did not need to finish, because I knew not only what he was going to say, but that he was correct. So I do not know who was more surprised between the two of us when, instead of answering, I just started walking towards Drusus, knowing that Dolabella would follow. And, I was certainly prepared to do whatever was necessary to keep Drusus from making matters worse, even if it would force me to divulge my source of information. Fortunately, it never came to that, because it was at this moment that an event occurred, similar to one that had taken place many years earlier, when I was a new Optio and we executed a night attack on the rebelling Taurisci, along the shores of a lake far to the north of where we were at the moment. Both nights, there were men convinced that this was some sort of act on the part of the gods, expressing their displeasure over our actions; that night on the lake, however, it did not stop us from doing our duty. This night, it averted a catastrophe and, in the process, ended the mutiny of the Pannonian Legions.

The first indication that yet one more thing had gone amiss was a sudden and sharp increase in noise out in the forum, where men who had either chosen not to sleep or could not because of the tension were still gathered. It was not a huge crowd, numbering perhaps a thousand men, but when that many either gasp aloud, make some sort of exclamation, or what I discerned to be the most common, offer up a prayer to the gods, it is impossible not to hear it. The occupants of the tent, which was much brighter than would be normal for this hour because of the extra lamps lit, had more or less the same reaction, although manifested in different ways, a combination of concern and unease. Which, while I had not been there for the actual event, I could easily understand when the affair with Lentulus had occurred just a bit earlier. Before there could be any kind of an organized reaction, however, the tent flap was thrust open, and one of the fully armed Legionaries entered, but while he was an Optio, it was not the same man who had tried to bar my entry earlier, telling me that they had been relieved. Since I was already walking in Drusus' direction, who was immediately surrounded by the four Germans, I continued moving so that the Optio and I arrived at roughly the same time.

The Optio did remember to salute, but that seemed to be all he could think to do, as his mouth opened, then shut, then opened again, while nothing came out, which prompted Drusus to snap, "Well? What is it, Optio? Have you been struck mute?"

This seemed to shake the Optio into speaking, although what he said certainly did not explain anything.

"Yes, sir. I mean, no, sir, I'm not mute. It's just that..." He struggled for words, then finally said only, "I think you should see it for yourself, sir. I can't explain it."

Drusus muttered something under his breath, but he began to move in a manner that suggested he was going to do that very thing, except the German in command of the bodyguard actually stepped in front of him, saying in heavily accented but understandable Latin, "Sir, I beg you not to go outside! Who knows what kind of trap those...men outside are setting?"

This clearly angered the Optio, which in turn seemed to give him stronger powers of elucidation, because he snapped, "If they can do what's happening to the moon right now, then that would mean the gods are on their side!"

It was mention of the moon that did it for me, and before I thought about it, I spoke up.

"*Proconsul*," I addressed Drusus, who turned and regarded me warily, "I actually think I know what the Optio's talking about, and why the men are acting like that," I jerked my thumb in the direction of the forum. "May I have your permission to go out and check and see if my guess is correct?"

I was not surprised at the flash of relief on the face of the German, but I was a bit surprised by an identical expression crossing Drusus', as if his desire to go outside was more for the sake of appearance.

"Yes, Centurion Pullus," Drusus answered immediately, then added, "but don't be long. And," he glanced over at the German commander, "take Sergovax with you in case it's a trap."

It will probably not surprise anyone who reads this, since they will be of my blood, that I bridled at the idea I needed protection, yet somehow, I managed to keep my mouth shut, although I exacted a petty revenge by simply saluting, then turning about without waiting for Drusus to return it.

Sergovax followed me, while I did the same behind the Optio, who looked over his shoulder at me, waiting until we were close to the flap to ask in a whisper, "You know what's happening with the moon, Centurion? Because I don't."

I was about to assure him that I did, then thought better of it, saying instead, "Let me see what's what first."

Then, we were outside, where the remaining Legionaries guarding the entrance had actually stepped a few paces away, out from under the canopy so that they could gaze up at the sky. Technically, the Optio could have written them all up for abandoning their assigned post, and for not remaining alert, but considering that not one man out in the forum was doing anything any differently, this was one of those moments where it made sense for him to ignore it. Of course, he was as fixated on the night sky as everyone else, and it took me a moment to locate the orb that is normally the predominant feature of the night sky, despite there being very few clouds in the sky. Once I did, I felt a sense of, if not satisfaction, then relief that my guess had been correct, and I waited only long enough to discern the movement of the shadow across the face of the moon, then turned about, immediately bumping into the German in the process, who was as transfixed by the sight as everyone else.

Just as I was about to step back into the tent, over the buzzing of talk from the mutineers, I heard the first distinct shout, "The gods are sending us a sign that they're displeased!"

That was the last intelligible thing I heard, but despite the darkness, I was still happy that my back was turned to the mutineers so they could not see me smiling. Entering the tent, Drusus had moved so that he was only a couple paces away from the entrance, his expression betraying the tension, and the strain of the previous watches.

"Well?" he demanded, not bothering with returning my salute. "You said you thought you knew what it is. Were you correct in your guess?"

"I was, sir," I answered immediately, yet while I thought about playing the Stupid Legionary and saying nothing more, I discarded it as not the time, going on to explain, "It's an eclipse of the moon. Although," I allowed, "it doesn't look like it's going to be exactly the same as the one we experienced," I had to think for a moment, and it caught me by surprise to say, "eighteen years ago. Although," I added, "it was in the fall as well."

For an instant, I thought about explaining what I knew of eclipses, which was a bit more at this point in time than I had known the night by the lake, but I immediately realized that this could not only be seen as an insinuation that Drusus was not educated enough to know about such celestial movements, it would in all likelihood bring on questions about how a lowly Centurion, a man from the ranks, knew of matters that only the highly educated would understand.

I am happy I did refrain, because it was Blaesus' son who said, "I've always been told that these kinds of things are signs of displeasure the gods give us."

Drusus turned and gave the Legate's son a look of such searing scorn that the son's face turned red, without the *Proconsul* saying a word; indeed, he did not even dignify Blaesus' comment with a direct rebuttal, other than to say, "Well, it sounds like those mutineers certainly seem to agree."

He was about to say something else when, adding to the sound of voices, suddenly there began a discordant, shattering noise, composed of *cornu, bucina,* drums, and I heard even the shrill sound of flutes that some men play for pleasure. I must be clear; this was not some tune they were playing, but just a series of random notes, blown without any sense of a rhythmic pattern, while whoever was banging on the drums seemed content to just whack the skins at random intervals. Simply put, it was a cacophony of noise with no discernible order; oddly enough, it was young Blaesus who knew what was happening.

"They're trying to drive the darkness away," he explained. "They think that some evil portents can be forced to flee if they make enough noise."

He seemed somewhat embarrassed as he said this, but his mention of this practice jogged my memory, and I suppose I took some pity on him, because I exclaimed, "That's right! I'd forgotten about that!" Turning to Drusus, I said, "The night it happened against the Taurisci, I heard some of the men calling for the *Corniceni* and *Bucinator* to start blowing notes."

"Did they?" Drusus asked, and I shook my head.

"No, sir," I told him, which was true enough, but not because they refused; it was not until the next day, when it was too late to do anything about it, that I overheard some of the men claiming that if we had done so, the moon would never have disappeared completely. "And it didn't help."

"It won't help them here either." he said shortly, then considered for a moment, and when he asked his next question, I do not believe it was aimed at someone specific, but was perhaps meant more rhetorically than anything, "But I wonder if they'll think that the gods are sending them a sign to desist in this nonsense?"

Now, at that moment, if he had asked for my opinion, I would have said that it was unlikely in the extreme, yet it turned out that was exactly what was happening. The more religious men among the mutineers, seeing the face of the moon at least partially obscured, began declaiming that this was indeed the judgment of the gods on their deeds. This was not met with agreement; until, that is, the clouds that had been absent when I had gone outside, now moved in and completely obscured the moon, thereby preventing the men from seeing what I, and apparently Drusus, understood would be a temporary condition, with the silver orb disappearing for only a period of time. When there was no way for any of the mutineers, religious or otherwise, to see that the shadow that covered the face of the moon moved on and allowed it to shine as it normally did, this signaled the end of the mutiny for all intents and purposes. Frankly, it was quite shocking; at first, I, and I was far from alone, did not credit that these men, who had been so adamant for weeks about holding out for what they viewed as the justice due to them, suddenly gave up, simply because the moon disappeared. But, never let it be said that the superstition of men of the Head Count is not powerful, because over the period of the final watch before the sun rose, it became clear that this was exactly what happened, to the point where men came to the *praetorium*, begging Drusus to forgive them, while at the same time, asking that he take their petition back to Tiberius.

Dawn was breaking by the time there was a semblance of formality, when a group of twenty men, which appeared to be equally composed of rankers, Optios, and Centurions, approached the *praetorium* in a manner that made it clear that this was both official and peaceful in nature, the latter signaled by none of the men being armed or armored, save the Centurions their *viti*. The Optio who had alerted Drusus about the eclipse still had the duty, where those of us who were late arrivals and did not have cots along the walls or in the *quaestorium* next door, were sprawled on the floor, trying to catch what little sleep we could. Naturally, Drusus was not with us; he had taken Blaesus Major's quarters, unceremoniously expelling the Legate, which in turn meant that some Tribune was forced to shift for himself, but since it was his son, I suppose he was fine with it.

I was in a light doze, having finally discarded my armor and helmet, using my *sagum* to bolster my head, when I heard someone speaking, coming fully awake when Drusus called loudly, "The mutineers are outside, requesting permission to speak with me."

This understandably created quite a disturbance as men sprang to their feet, none of us wanting to miss this moment, and I include myself in that number, despite only being involved for barely more than a full day. I did not don my armor, but I did strap on my *baltea*, more out of habit than any real belief that there might be trouble. As I moved to the back of the crowd of men as they gathered behind Drusus, there was a slight delay because the *Proconsul* deemed it important that he be properly attired, with the *lictors* due him because of his status as *Proconsul*, who had been relegated to sleeping in the *quaestorium,* attending to him. Finally, he deemed that all was as satisfactory as it was likely to be, and I watched from behind him as the younger man squared his shoulders, took a breath, then, following his *lictors,* stepped out of the tent, the flap held open by the Optio. Once Drusus was outside the tent, there was a somewhat comical scene behind him as all the upper class Romans, always concerned with their status among their fellow nobles, engaged in a mostly silent but spirited jostling match to be the next ones out. If this is a trick, I thought, you're going to regret wanting to be sniffing Drusus' ass. Thankfully, for all of us, it was not, and finally, I brought up the rear, meaning that I had to use my height to scan the party of men facing the *praetorium.* The fact that I immediately spotted Domitius was due less to his standing in front, along with Catonius, Clemens, and a couple other men I did not recognize, but that he was the only one with an eyepatch, and of course, I was looking for him. My concern had been that it would only be the three men who I now understood were the true leaders of the mutiny, but that was assuaged somewhat by the larger number of men who were standing there.

It was actually Catonius who spoke, surprising me a bit since I had thought that Clemens would be the man to accompany Drusus, but there was nothing to fault in both his demeanor nor the salute he offered Drusus as he said, "*Proconsul*, we accept your offer to take our list of grievances back to the *Imperator*," he paused for a moment, and I understood why when he continued, "and we humbly beseech you to advocate to your father, on our behalf, that he grant these…requests to address them."

I never had the opportunity to ask any of them, but I assumed then, and still believe, that the manner in which Catonius characterized their demands as requests had to rub many of the mutineers the wrong way, given how they had been essentially allowed to run rampant for so long. Regardless, I also thought it was an extremely intelligent thing to do, and I was equally positive that my friend Domitius had something to do with it.

Then, Drusus opened his mouth, and just that quickly, I was certain that he would completely rupture this seemingly miraculous change.

"Where is Percennius?" he demanded abruptly without acknowledging anything that Catonius said, his face rigid and his tone cold, which I found quite surprising. "Why isn't he standing there with you?"

This obviously caught Catonius, Clemens, and the others by surprise, while Domitius shot me a look that I took to be a silent inquiry, but I could only shrug, since this was a far cry from the manner in which the *Proconsul* had been behaving inside the tent.

This was when Clemens either chose, or on some unseen signal, spoke up, informing Drusus, "Gregarius Percennius won't be attending this meeting, *Proconsul*."

"Why not?" Drusus demanded. "He needs to be present to see this!"

I cannot say whether Drusus caught Clemens exchanging a quick glance with Catonius first, then Domitius, who I was somewhat relieved to see was standing slightly behind the other two men, but I certainly did, and given the conversation that I had been part of just a watch before, I was certain that Percennius' face would never be seen again.

"Actually, *Proconsul*," Catonius spoke again, "he's…deserted." This sounded hopelessly lame to me, but if it was, Catonius had clearly decided this was the horse he would ride. "Once it became apparent that we," he turned at the waist and indicated the others with a sweep of his arm, "were willing to have you return to Rome, he seems to have decided that his presence was no longer welcome."

Drusus did not appear angry as much as flummoxed at Catonius' claim, making me wonder what the *Proconsul* had had in mind for the actor; I got my answer when he responded, "Well, if you can't produce Percennius, I want the men who were the most militant in this affair."

Thankfully, standing behind the knot of men, none of them saw me wince, followed by an angry glare at my friend when Domitius spoke for the first time, asking in a mild enough tone, "For what purpose, *Proconsul*?"

"To be punished, of course!" Drusus snapped, and I was at the right angle to see the flush of red creep up his neck. "I am a *Proconsul* of Rome, empowered by *Imperator* Tiberius Claudius Nero, and I was *assaulted*! Those men who participated in this crime, and," he pointed a finger at Catonius, which did not please the Centurion in the slightest, "those who either ordered or encouraged those men to behave in this manner must be punished!"

And, as quickly as I believed that the mutiny had ended, any chance of a peaceful conclusion seemed to evaporate in the length of time it took Drusus to utter these words. However, if I had been irritated with Domitius a matter of heartbeats before, there are no words to describe how I felt when he stepped forward, past both Catonius and Clemens, to address Drusus.

"*Proconsul*, I think there are some things we need to discuss in private." His voice was calm, but I knew him well, despite our years apart, and I saw by the slight fluttering of his fingers as he drummed them on his thigh that he was feeling the tension.

"There's nothing more to talk about," Drusus answered, and this time, I could not stifle a groan, which earned me a scathing look from Dolabella, who was standing a couple paces behind Tiberius' son.

With that, Drusus gave every appearance of turning about to reenter the *praetorium*, but to my surprise, it was Blaesus Major who, grasping the younger man by the elbow, whispered something in his ear. Judging from the manner in which he reacted, Drusus did not like what was being said, yet he did not jerk away, and he did listen. Once Blaesus was through, Drusus' face was a study in consternation, while his words belied the irritation he was clearly feeling.

"Very well," he said stiffly, "we'll talk in private."

Then, without another word, he turned and strode to the *praetorium* entrance, forcing me to step aside and the Optio to scramble to pull the flap back. As interesting as that was, my attention was focused solely on Clemens, Catonius, and Domitius, who held a whispered conversation that only took a matter of a couple heartbeats, then much to my alarm, all three of them followed Drusus.

As Domitius passed by me, I hissed, "What are you doing? There's no way to keep your role secret if you go in there!"

"I know," he allowed, yet he did not slow down, "but this is too important."

"What about all that talk in your quarters?" I demanded, but in answer, he only gave me a small, sad smile and a shrug.

Then, they were inside the tent, and the talking began.

Not surprisingly, the discussion between the leaders of the mutiny and Drusus did not take place in the large outer area, but in the Legate's private office, and equally unsurprising was that all but a small number of men were excluded from this crucial meeting. This meant that, like everyone besides Blaesus Major, Dolabella, and Sergovax, the latter who was there simply for security purposes, which caused a bit of hard feelings on the part of the trio of Centurions, the rest of us were left outside, speculating about what was taking place. Normally, it would have been a simple matter for one or more men to linger near the partition that served as the wall to the Legate's office, but just before they disappeared inside, I heard Drusus order the other bodyguards to stand there to discourage this behavior. I smelled the hand of Dolabella in this, since I believe that Drusus was too distracted at the moment to think of this precaution; whoever it was, it meant I did not even bother trying to loiter and eavesdrop, although several Tribunes and, much to my surprise, even Galens tried, with no success. For a brief moment, I thought of going outside the tent, then decided against it, and more to pass the time, as well as distract my old Centurion, I wandered into the *quaestorium*, and requisitioned for myself some bread, cheese, and a jug of wine that was more water, returning and inviting Galens and Asinius to break their fasts with me; to my disappointment, Asinius demurred, but explained that he was going to take advantage of this lull to go check on his Century. Once Galens and I settled down, he wasted no time.

"Those German bastards have forgotten they're fucking barbarians," Galens complained, although he took the hunk of bread I offered, settling down beside me with our backs to the outer wall of the tent.

"You're just angry because they didn't let you listen in." I laughed at him, but while he did not join in, I did see the glint of amusement in his eyes that I recalled from long before.

"Maybe," he admitted grudgingly, then added, "but I'm a fucking Primus Pilus, aren't I? I should be involved in this!"

"Neither of the other Primi Pili are," I pointed out, "so at least Drusus is being fair."

"I don't give a fart in a *testudo* for fair," he growled, but then a corner of his mouth lifted slightly.

Thinking to change the subject and getting his mind off his exclusion, I said, "I was just thinking about something."

"Oh?" he mumbled through a mouthful of bread. "You were thinking? That's unusual."

Ignoring the jibe, I went on, "I was remembering our trip to Rome."

As I hoped, Galens smiled at the memory, admitting, "You know, I'd forgotten all about that."

For the next several moments, we chatted about that trip, when we had accompanied our Primus Pilus Atticus to answer charges that we later learned had been engineered by the Princeps, as a reminder to our former Praetorian Primus Pilus where his loyalties lay, and to send a message to a coalition of powerful men in Rome that their attempts to create an atmosphere whereby Augustus would be forced into naming Tiberius as his heir would not work. Of course, it did happen, just not eighteen years earlier when these men tried to do so. I had a purpose for bringing this up with Galens other than to distract him, because when I lay down the night before, I gradually realized that somewhere in the recesses of my mind, I had been devoting time to thinking about how we had come to this moment, where not one but two armies had risen in revolt.

Finally, I tried out what was still a half-formed idea about our situation, asking Galens, "Do you think that all this," I waved a hand around us, "actually started a long time ago?"

Galens surprised me by not answering immediately, actually thinking about it for a moment. Finally, he sighed and agreed, "I've thought that as well. And, yes, I think this has been building for some time." He shot me a glance, asking curiously, "Are you talking about anything specific?"

"Do you remember Arruntius?" I asked him, not so much to stall but to give Galens an idea where I was headed.

"The Tribune who defended Atticus," Galens answered, nodding.

"Yes, that's him. Do you remember what he told me about how I might be used as a symbol because of my grandfather?"

Galens nodded again, though he said nothing, and I continued, "Well, I think that what led to this actually started even before that, during the first Titus Pullus' time under the standard."

This seemed to lose Galens, which he confirmed by asking, "I'm not sure what you mean."

"I think that once the patricians saw that whoever owned the Legions owned Rome, it opened up this Pandora's Box where we're used as pieces on a board."

"That's not new," Galens scoffed.

"No," I agreed, "but think of the timing. These mutinies happened, in two separate armies, within days after the Princeps' death."

My old Centurion twisted to stare at me, though his expression was unreadable.

"And?" he asked, saying no more.

"And I think that the men who came before us, the veterans of the civil wars, got used to the idea that they were the real power," I explained, speaking slowly because, frankly, this was the first time I was uttering my thoughts aloud. "Which they passed on to men of your era when you were *tiros* and they were ending their careers." Struck by something, I asked Galens, "How many watches do you think are passed sitting around the fire, with younger men sitting and listening to the veterans talking about 'the good days,' and how much money they made just because they were being courted by a rich patrician who wanted to be First Man?"

"That's true," Galens granted, but he shook his head, pointing out, "but that was before the Princeps solidified his power. Now we've had, what, forty-odd years where he's the unquestioned ruler of Rome?"

"That's actually my point," I replied. "This is the first time in forty years where the Legions have the chance to improve their situation because there's instability at the top. There wasn't anything we could do when it was Augustus, but his death just created a chance for men of the later generations to take advantage of the situation. But," I finished, "I honestly don't think it would have occurred to anyone under the standard that this was even possible if it hadn't been for what took place during the time of my grandfather."

I could see this scored with the Primus Pilus, who sat, chewing his bread thoughtfully, before he finally grunted, "Maybe."

Understanding this was all I would get from him, I returned my attention to the other side of the tent, where the guards were still standing, their backs to the flap leading into the Legate's office. After a couple tries, even the Tribunes had gotten the hint that their attempts to listen in would be fruitless, and they had contented themselves with standing in a small knot, glaring at the Germans. Who, I saw with some amusement, were retaliating in the best way a man from the ranks can, completely ignoring the collective ire of the young Roman noblemen. Blaesus Minor, not surprisingly, was the clear leader of this group, but finally, with a great show of disgust, he went and took a seat on one of the vacant stools, whereupon he was quickly joined by the others, all of us settling in to wait and see what happened next.

Over the course of the next watch, on a couple of occasions, we heard a muffled, unintelligible voice, and despite not being able to make out the words, just by the tenor of it, we knew that it was the same man doing the yelling.

"I'll bet you twenty *sesterces* that it's Drusus doing all the yelling," Galens offered at one point, but I just laughed, saying, "I'm not taking that bet. It'd be the same as just handing you the money."

Aside from that exchange, we did not talk much, other than to do some more reminiscing, and by unspoken consent, we restricted our swapping stories to lighthearted moments, neither of us wanting to dwell on those times that end up haunting our dreams. Such is the way of the Legions and Legionaries, at least that I have known. Only once did Galens change the subject; more accurately, he returned to the topic that I had introduced, which informed me that he had been ruminating over what we had been talking about.

Seemingly out of nowhere, he asked me, "So, Pullus, if what you said earlier about how the seeds were planted for what's happening now back in your grandfather's day, why is it only the Pannonian and Rhenus armies mutinying?"

Honestly, I had not considered this question, and I had to pause to collect my thoughts before I answered with what I thought was the likely explanation.

"None of the other armies have done as much fighting as these two," I answered at last. "Syria's quiet, Hispania's quiet, and nothing has happened in Africa in decades." As I talked, I was convincing myself that this was, indeed, the answer, but while I did not need to, I also reminded Galens, "And none of those places lost three Legions at once."

Galens did not take nearly as long to reply this time, and his nod was, while not emphatic, sent the message that he had in all likelihood reached this conclusion already, and I was just confirming what he had worked out for himself. I would also add that, if he was inclined to say something, he never had the chance because, just at that moment, there was a sudden commotion across the tent, as the Germans turned about to face the flap. We looked over just in time to see Drusus emerge first, followed by Blaesus Major, then the three Centurions, with Domitius trailing behind the other two, but then it was Sergovax, with no sign of Dolabella. This meant my attention was torn between the men who had emerged, trying to read from their expressions anything that might hint at what lay ahead, and glancing over at the flap, watching for Dolabella. Just from what I saw, it seemed as if matters were back to an impasse again, judging from the angry expression on Drusus' face, while Clemens, Catonius, and Domitius just looked exhausted.

"So, I suppose you're wondering what happened in there."

Dolabella's voice, coming from a completely unexpected quarter, directly behind Galens and me, elicited a reaction from both of us that was completely unbecoming of two veteran Centurions of Rome.

"You better have a good fucking reason for sneaking up on us, you cross-eyed *cunnus*," Galens growled immediately after the yelp of surprise that he unleashed, although in fairness, it could have been me.

"How did you do that?" I asked, since that was more of a concern for me, and ignoring Galens, he gave me a grin.

"I used the hole you made," Dolabella admitted, but the grin vanished as he gave his real reason, "because I didn't want to be seen walking over directly to you right now."

"Why?" Galens asked, and if Dolabella was angry at Galens' slur a moment before, he hid it.

"Let's just say that our *Proconsul* isn't in a forgiving frame of mind," he answered, glancing past us to where the two parties were still mingled, engaged in some sort of discussion.

"Don't tell me that he's fucked this up and refused their terms!" I exclaimed, experiencing an intense stab of relief when Dolabella shook his head.

"No, he's returning to Rome, along with Catonius, and he's going to advocate for the men. At least," he added grimly, "that's what he says now. Between here and Rome?" He gave a shrug, admitting, "I don't know about that."

"So why's he still acting like they pissed all over his boots?" Galens asked, and Dolabella gave the Primus Pilus a bitterly amused look.

"Funny that you should characterize it like that, because that's almost exactly the way Drusus expressed it." Dolabella sighed. "When you boil it down to its essence, this is about a young man not wanting to appear weak or ineffective to his Tata. What he's angry about is the fact that Catonius and the others have already dealt with Percennius and some of his bunch." This did not make sense to me, and I said as much, while Galens nodded, so Dolabella explained, "Drusus is worried that if word gets out that he wasn't the one to enforce the punishments that he publicly decreed, it will fatally undermine him. That," Dolabella allowed, "is how he puts it. But I think he's more worried about how Tiberius will view it. And," the spymaster admitted, "I think he has good cause to be worried. Tiberius is likely to believe that the Legionaries pulled one over on Drusus and that Percennius and a few others are going to get away free of any punishment."

I considered for a moment, then asked him, "So what did Catonius and the others say about what Drusus said?"

The look Dolabella gave me sent a clear message that he was not fooled by my mention of Catonius and not Domitius, though he said nothing about it, replying, "They offered to show Drusus proof that Percennius and the others have been dealt with. That," he nodded in the direction of the party, and I turned just in time to see them exit the *praetorium*, "is where they're going now."

"Do they have them in chains?" Galens asked; Dolabella shook his head, then gave us both a look that I knew was meaningful.

"No," he replied, "they're not in chains. Apparently," his face did not register any emotion, nor did his voice, "they're out in the ditch." Seeing this was not descriptive enough for us, he added, "At least, their bodies are."

Galens and I exchanged a startled glance, and he let out a low whistle, saying only, "Well they didn't waste any time, did they?"

"No," Dolabella agreed, "they didn't. They want this to be over as much as anyone else. Maybe," he allowed, "more than anyone else."

"We might as well go out and see what's what," Galens said this casually, but neither the spymaster nor I were fooled, though I did not blame him.

He and those Centurions and Optios who remained loyal had been confined to the *praetorium* and *quaestorium* for more than two weeks and had been allowed out only to go to the latrines, and that was after a tense few days where there were negotiations that kept matters from becoming so violent and bloody that neither party could ever go back, so it was no surprise that the tent was already almost completely deserted, most of the officers following Asinius' example. While Domitius had not said anything about this period, from Galens and others, I learned that my friend had been instrumental in keeping a lid on the simmering pot that men like Percennius were determined to make boil over for their own purposes. I will say that I was curious about what the actor and those men of his faction had hoped to gain by making the mutiny a bloody affair, but if Percennius confided in anyone, they either never talked, or more likely, were with him. Which, as we found out quickly enough, was exactly where Dolabella had said they would be, thrown into the ditch on the Porta Praetoria side of the camp, with throats cut to a man. There was no need for Dolabella to explain why they had chosen this side to make their demonstration, sending a clear message not just to Drusus, but to the Praetorians who were still waiting outside that the mutiny was over. Walking out into the forum, I found that the atmosphere was unlike anything I had experienced to that point; there was an air of relief that was palpable, while the expressions of the men who surrounded the forum seemed to be equally divided between men who looked as if a huge weight had been lifted from their shoulders, those who looked somewhat sheepish, and those who seemed determined to take a wait and see attitude. Frankly, if I had been in their boots, I would have been with the latter group, simply because of my belief that Tiberius would do everything within his power to avoid giving in to the demands of the mutineers. Perhaps I was being cynical, but I tried to look at it from his viewpoint, as the newly anointed *Imperator*. If he gave in to the demands of his Legions in Pannonia and on the Rhenus, would he be vulnerable to the other armies if they got it in their heads to do the same? Regardless of my personal feelings, ultimately, my primary concern was that I could return back to my own Legion once matters here with Domitius were sufficiently settled that I felt confident that I had accomplished what had become my most important, and frankly, only goal, ensuring that I at least partially appease the shade of my Avus and his long-time best friend. Honestly, I cannot point to one passage in the account of Titus Pullus where he said outright that he regretted his decision concerning Vibius Domitius at Pharsalus, but I did not then, nor do I now feel that I was making a huge assumptive leap in my belief that he regretted how matters between them turned out. Still, I wanted to return to Ubiorum, but in this I was more confident in the abilities of Germanicus to handle that mutiny than I was with Drusus.

Trailing behind the *Proconsul*, Blaesus, and the trio of Centurions were the Legate's son and other Tribunes, who were clustered together in a manner that informed us that they were not as confident that the mutiny was over as the *Proconsul* seemed to be. Walking with Galens and me were the Primi Pili of the 9th and 15th, Aulus Vetruvius and Gnaeus Mancinas, but we were essentially surrounded in a protective cordon by some of the other Centurions and Optios who had been trapped in the *praetorium*. I did not hear any of the Primi Pili give the command to do so, but it was an understandable precaution; however, there was really not much hostility, overt or otherwise, aimed in their direction by the rankers, although they had formed what I suppose could have been viewed as a gauntlet down the Via Praetoria. My observation was that, just like the men who had been standing in the forum, their comrades were similarly relieved that the ordeal was over; not happy, exactly, just ready for things to return back to normal. I still felt a flicker of unease when, reaching the rampart, I saw that the men who had been standing ready to stop any attempt by Sejanus and his Praetorians to storm the camp were still present, but a quick glance told me that their posture was not indicative that they were expecting trouble, most of them turned inward to watch the procession. Somewhere along this portion of the walk, Dolabella managed to use the small crowd of officers to disappear; I was unaware of his absence until I turned to ask him a question, but when I realized he had vanished, I was not unduly alarmed, given his profession, certain that he had more than one man inside these three Legions who were essentially me in terms of their role. The gates were closed, but they swung open quickly enough just as Drusus and his party reached them, and my body tensed a bit, somewhat expecting a sudden rush by Sejanus' Praetorians. Since my view was blocked by the gaggle of Tribunes and our impromptu guard, I watched the men on the ramparts for any change that might indicate matters would degenerate at this late moment. Fortunately, while most of them turned back to face outward, nothing in their reaction suggested that there was any kind of organized assault now taking place. Our progress halted momentarily while Drusus examined the corpses of Percennius and the couple dozen men who Catonius, Clemens, and Domitius had used as dupes. A short time later, the rest of us were able to resume our own movement, and naturally, we all stopped to survey the pile of bodies lying in the ditch; I was certain it was no accident that Percennius' body, still clad in his toga with its snowy white color now marred by the copious amount of blood from his throat, was positioned in a manner that made his corpse impossible to miss. His mouth was hanging open, not unusual, nor that his eyes were opened widely in that look of surprise worn by those for whom death comes unexpectedly, although my thought when I gazed down on him was, What did you think was going to happen? That you would act your way out of being killed because your hubris was so powerful that you made yourself the symbol of this mutiny? How could you not know there would be a reckoning for that? Or, I acknowledged, maybe he did know that there was death in his future, but he thought he would have a chance to savor this, what I am certain was the largest, most important role he had ever played in his life. Whatever the truth was did not matter now, and I did not linger that long, other than to perform a quick scan of the other bodies, all of whom, like Percennius, were carefully displayed so their faces showed.

Which was what prompted Galens to grunt, then nudge Mancinas with an elbow as he pointed at one of the bodies, asking, "Isn't that your man Vibulenus, who caused us so much trouble the first week?"

Mancinas confirmed that it was, which Galens, seeing my questioning expression, explained, "That *cunnus* almost got us all killed the first couple days of the revolt because he claimed that Blaesus had ordered his brother executed."

"For what?" I asked, and Galens replied, "Well, Vibulenus claimed that his brother was actually one of your bunch up there on the Rhenus." He thought a moment but had to turn to Mancinas, who was the one who said, "Supposedly he was an Optio in the Fourth of the Seventh of the 5th Alaudae." Galens nodded his thanks to his counterpart, continuing, "Right, that was it. And supposedly, he'd been sent down by the men responsible for the trouble up there to confer with the mutineers here to coordinate their efforts, and when the Legate found out, he let the Legate in Mogontiacum know, and had the brother executed."

I shook my head, immediately dismissing this. "I would have known about someone from the Army of the Rhenus coming down here. That never happened."

Galens shot me an amused look, saying dryly, "Yes, we figured that out. Which is why he's there now," he jerked his thumb over his shoulder since we had continued walking, "with Percennius."

By this point, Drusus had stopped about fifty paces beyond the wall, raising an arm to signal where Sejanus and the mounted contingent of both the bodyguards who had remained outside the camp and the Praetorian cavalry were mounted and waiting. The manner in which they began moving, going immediately to the gallop, was sufficiently alarming that Catonius suddenly rounded on the *Proconsul*, and even over the noise of the onrushing horsemen, I could hear him.

"What's happening, *Proconsul*?" he demanded, pointing at where the Praetorian Tribune was leading what looked to my eyes to be a cavalry charge. "I thought we had an agreement!"

"We do!" I heard Drusus, but he said something else, which was now drowned out by the sound of hooves.

"This is bad," Galens muttered, but the only person moving of the group leaving the camp was Drusus, who was walking his mount forward, holding up his arms in a clear command to Sejanus and his men, making a patting gesture with both hands.

This seemed clear enough, but Sejanus did not slow down, at least immediately, and Catonius, Clemens, and Domitius suddenly reversed their progress with Drusus and began walking backward, keeping their attention on the oncoming riders. Before I gave it any thought, I quickened my own pace with the idea to provide protection for Domitius, since I was wearing my armor and was carrying my *gladius*. Fortunately, before I went a half-dozen steps, I saw Sejanus at last raise a fist, the sign to come to a halt, although by the time he drew up, he was close enough that Drusus was actually spattered with dirt from the

Praetorian's horse sliding to a stop. Even before the animal had come to a complete halt, Sejanus was out of the saddle, crossing the few feet to where Drusus had also come to a stop, offering the *Proconsul* a salute that, to my eyes, was almost as theatrical and flowery as one I would have expected from a man like the recently deceased Percennius.

"*Proconsul!*" The Tribune spoke more loudly than was necessary, since I could clearly hear him more than fifty paces away. "I'm happy to see you unharmed! Know that I ordered the sacrifice of a white bull for your safety!"

"Pluto's cock," my old Primus Pilus, who had caught up to me, muttered disgustedly, "can that man's tongue get any farther up Drusus' ass?" He turned to me and asked, "Who is that *cunnus* anyway?" I answered Galens, and the mention of Sejanus' name evoked a reaction that informed me that we were of a like mind, although his only comment was a sour, "I've heard of the bastard."

The glance he gave me, however, told me that he knew more than just the man's name. Now that it did not appear as if Sejanus intended to run us all down, Catonius, Clemens, and Domitius had resumed their course but stopped several paces short of where Drusus and Sejanus were talking. Now the Praetorian's voice was no longer audible, but judging from his demeanor, he was not happy about whatever it was that Drusus was telling him. His entire body seemed to radiate repudiation of Drusus' words, which I assumed was the *Proconsul*'s explanation of the agreement he had struck with the mutineers, and in seeming confirmation, the Praetorian leaned over to look past Drusus where my friend and the other two Centurions were standing. I did not need to be closer, nor did I need to know Sejanus to see the poisonous, hateful glare he aimed towards them, and it made me wonder if Catonius would actually arrive in Rome intact. Regardless of this fear, my main concern was for Domitius, and it was him I kept my eyes on, somehow sensing that he might be inclined to do something that I would object to, like suddenly decide he needed to accompany Catonius. Thankfully for both our sakes, after a short conversation, Sejanus finally came to a rigid *intente*, offering a salute to Drusus, which he returned in a manner that informed those of us watching that it was over at last.

Chapter Ten

I spent only one more night in that camp, and frankly, despite my ambivalence about leaving Domitius behind, I was ready to return to my own Legion, if only to learn whether Germanicus had managed to quell the insurrection there. Given my reasons for this account, I must stress that matters were far from settled with the three Legions, and there was still an air of uncertainty and not a little discontent as a sizable number of rankers were unhappy that, essentially, nothing had changed. Around every fire, there were discussions, some of them minor disagreements among comrades, some of them more spirited, and more than a few where men came to blows. Thankfully, their battles were fought only with fists, but what was highly unusual was that the officers, Centurions and Optios alike, decided to allow these disputes to be settled in this manner. Frankly, I disagreed with the collective decision, made shortly after Drusus returned to the Praetorian camp, which had been constructed during the night before, though I did not say anything to Domitius. From my viewpoint, the chances of matters escalating between comrades was less of a concern than my fear that there would be some clash between men of different Legions, whose passions were already running high. Just from my relatively short time spent with them, it was clear that Galens' assessment was correct that, of the three Legions, the 9th appeared to be the least upset at what so many of their counterparts in the 8th and 15th viewed as simply another tactic of delay with this next embassage to Tiberius. Whether their attitude was attributable to their short tenure in the province I do not know, but the men of the other two Legions, if I am any judge from the tenor of the snatches of conversation I heard as I made my way to Domitius' tent, seemed to take this lack of passion as a personal insult for some reason. From my perspective, looking in from the outside and based on just a matter of two days of observation, the passive manner in which the Centurions from all three Legions were handling the still-roiling tensions of that day seemed to be based in their belief that the eclipse from the previous night was sufficiently fresh so that the rankers' fear of the gods' anger was much more powerful a deterrent to violence than their Centurions' *viti*. And, given how matters turned out, the next morning, I was forced to grudgingly acknowledge that they knew their men better than I did. Truly, I was more concerned that this night would, in all likelihood, be the last I would likely spend with Titus Domitius, and I had decided that I would tell him of my conversation with Galens, although I was unsure about how I would broach the subject. He was clearly exhausted, but I think that he was as cognizant that this would, at the very minimum, be the last night before a period of separation that might last years, or more likely, we would never meet again.

He was still just in his tunic, but when he suggested I shed my armor and I demurred, he laughed, shaking his head, "Don't worry, Titus. There's not going to be trouble tonight. I think," his humor did not vanish as much as it subtly changed, giving me a grim smile as he went on, "without men like Percennius to stir them up, they'll be content to bash each other and not do anything more. Not to mention that if they're as tired as I am, they'll have shot their bolt bashing Publius for not agreeing with them about whether it's Mars who's angry, or if it's Jupiter himself."

This did elicit a chuckle, since I had heard something almost identical to that very argument as I made my way through the camp about which one of the gods they had offended, and what it meant in terms of punishment. We lapsed into a silence then, both of us sipping from our cups of unwatered wine, which Domitius informed me was the last amphora that he had been saving for the end of this ordeal.

Realizing that there was no good way to go about it, as normal, I plunged ahead, telling Domitius, "In case you're worried that Galens is going to harbor some hard feelings for your part in this, don't be."

As soon as the words left my mouth, I braced for any number of reactions, but not for the one I got, because he answered simply, "I'm not. I know you talked to him."

I felt my jaw drop; it had not occurred to me that I would be the one who was surprised.

"How do you know that?" I asked, and he did not reply immediately, but even missing an eye, I caught the amused gleam in his good one that informed me he was having some fun at my expense, then he finally admitted, "Because Galens came and talked to me to tell me that I had nothing to worry about." Then, his manner changed slightly, and I understood why when he added, "Not from the Primus Pilus or anyone connected with the Legion. As far as Tiberius goes?" He shrugged, and he looked away as he finished, "There's nothing I can do about it, so I'm not going to waste time worrying about it."

"No, there's not anything you can do about it," I agreed, and I decided to exact a little revenge of my own, pausing to take a deep swallow of wine, "but there might be something I can do about it. Actually," I was more thinking aloud now, "I may have already done what needs to be done."

Domitius had been moodily staring into his own cup, and his head came up sharply at that, his eye narrowed as he searched my face.

"Titus," he warned, "I don't want you doing something that's going to get you in the *cac* with Tiberius for me."

"I'm not," I assured him. "I know you find it hard to believe, but Dolabella isn't the same man you knew. Something's changed for him, and I think he's just trying to do as little damage to other men now as he can."

I was not surprised that Domitius was skeptical, and being brutally honest with myself in that moment, I had nothing other than a feeling in my gut that the spymaster's change of heart was sincere.

"Well," Domitius said, clearly unconvinced, but equally apparent, unwilling to talk about it anymore, "whatever you can do, I appreciate it."

Understanding his implicit message, I turned to safer topics, and we spent most of the evening reminiscing, until I saw his eyelid drooping to a point that I realized I only had a matter of moments to get out the other thing I had decided to say.

"There's one other thing I wanted to tell you," I began. "Since it's unlikely we're going to see each other for only the gods know how long." This at least served to make his eye open wider, and he leaned forward, studying me intently, clearly sensing this was something important, at least to me. Searching for the words, I finally came up with, "I've been thinking about our grandfathers a lot lately."

"So have I," Domitius answered immediately, but before I could continue, he asked a question of his own. "Why do you think that is, Titus?"

Indeed, I had spent a fair amount of time wondering this myself, and while I could not say I was certain about it, I did feel I had a grasp of the basic reason, so I offered, "I think," I spoke slowly, "that all of this," I waved my hand around, "has something to do with it, but more than that, I think it's because Augustus died." Warming up to it, I went on, "Think of it, Titus. We're in our forties, and we've lived our entire lives with Augustus playing a prominent role, starting with our grandfathers."

Domitius considered this, then pointed out, "But remember, my grandfather fought for The Liberators, not for Augustus."

"True," I granted, "but he did it because Augustus was named Caesar's heir, not Antonius, which started everything that led to the second civil war."

He did not reply verbally, but he nodded in a manner that I knew from experience meant that he agreed with my assessment.

"So," I went on, "that's one reason that the death of Augustus puts us in a place none of us have ever been before. What," I asked, rhetorically, "does Rome look like now that he's gone?" The next part was more personal, but I was still fairly certain about it. "And, let's be honest." I grinned at him, pointing to his missing eye. "Not only are we not getting any younger, we're getting whittled down bit by bit."

As I hoped, this made my friend laugh, and he shot right back, "I didn't get this," he pointed to his eyepatch, "until a couple years ago. You," now he indicated my scarred left arm, though the knotted tissue was now almost completely white, with tinges of pink, "started getting chopped up when you were a ranker! But," the grin on his face remained in place, but there was a melancholy quality to it, "you're right. We're not getting any younger."

I took a deep breath, then before I could stop myself, I went on, "But while those are important reasons, they're not the most important one."

When he did not say anything, just lifting an eyebrow, a habit that persisted to this moment despite the fact that it was the one over his missing eye, I knew he was not going to make matters easy for me. Consequently, I went on to explain my belief about Titus Pullus' one real regret in his life, and from where I had learned it. Domitius was aware of the existence of my Avus' scrolls, but I had never gone into any detail, and honestly, the only time I brought them up was when there was a piece of information in them that I thought relevant to whatever we were experiencing at that moment, whether it was because of circumstances, or we were traversing terrain over which he and his comrades had marched. I do not precisely know how long I talked, but I was gratified to see that Domitius no longer seemed sleepy, perched on the edge of his chair, listening with an intensity that was somewhat unsettling.

When I finished, he sat there, considering for several moments, then he said, "If I'm being honest, I've always wondered how your grandfather felt about what happened at Pharsalus. After all," he pointed out, "I've only heard what my grandfather's side was, through my father, and we never really talked about it. At least, not to this level of detail."

This was certainly true; our conversations about this subject had been deliberately vague on my part, especially in the beginning when I did not know exactly how Domitius viewed matters that, in its own small way, had a profound impact on not just our respective families, but on the entire Republic, as it was known then.

Realizing there was not much more I could say on the matter, I simply answered, "Now we have."

I ended up spending the night on a pallet in Domitius' quarters, grumbling in a good-natured way about the quality of the accommodations, and I slept more easily that night than I would have thought, since I was still partially convinced that all of this effort to keep the peace would come to nothing, as angry men sought an outlet for being thwarted in their aims yet again. My last conscious thought was of how I hoped that my Avus would be proud of me. Perhaps we will find each other in the afterlife, and I can ask him.

There was one last surprise in store, and that was when we rose at the dawn call of the *bucina*, it was immediately followed by the call for all senior Centurions to assemble in the forum. Since I had no official role to play, I decided it was time to go seek out Dolabella and find out what my instructions were now that matters seemed to have been, if not resolved, then successfully delayed once more. Parting with Domitius, we promised to meet back at his quarters once we knew what our respective futures held, and I made my way out of the camp, the gates now open and without more than the standard watch set on the walls. The same could not be said for the hasty camp prepared by Sejanus and his Praetorians, and I could not help feeling a glimmer of satisfaction when I saw just what the Praetorian version of a marching camp looked like. Clearly, these men had not been forced to dig a ditch and build a wall in some time, if they ever had now that there are men who enlist straight into the Praetorian Guard and do not come exclusively from the Legions. The rampart sagged in some places because the ditch was not as deep in that spot, which conversely meant there was not enough dirt to maintain a uniform height. They did have stakes placed, but otherwise, it bore closer resemblance to the kind of camp a Legion of *tiros* might have constructed without supervision, based on what little they knew of such matters. I was briefly detained at the gate there, which was of the earthen variety, as an Optio wearing a blue tunic sent a runner to the *praetorium*, either to ascertain my identity or whether I was to go there. The latter, it turned out, were my instructions, though it was not to attend to Drusus, but on behalf of Dolabella. Walking through the camp, I ignored the openly hostile stares of the Praetorian rankers; their antipathy to the Legions is well-known, and at least in my case, is certainly reciprocated. Inside the camp, I will admit, was another matter in terms of the manner in which it had been constructed, looking in every respect like a Roman marching camp, with its grid of streets and neat rows of tents. Speaking of the tents, while I was not at all surprised that they seemed to be newer and unexposed to the normal treatment by the elements, I did take notice, with some indignation, that their tents were clearly larger than those of the Legions. Not by much, I will grant; perhaps a foot longer and two feet wider, as well as a bit taller, but I personally found it offensive. I suppose my height had something to do with it, given how I had to bow my head in every part of the tent except for the center between the poles. The other thing I noticed was that some of the tasks that are normally performed by rankers as part of the morning routine were being attended to by slaves, and the thought crossed my mind that perhaps that was why the construction of the camp's exterior was so slipshod, not that it mattered. Dolabella was actually standing outside the tent, which was something of a relief, since I had no desire to be inside where Drusus and all of his party were, certain that there would be nothing but a lot of bickering.

Which Dolabella inadvertently confirmed when he said by way of greeting, "I needed to get out of there, and you don't want to be in there."

"That bad?" I asked, and he gave a grim nod, his features almost identical to Domitius' in the reflection of the fatigue he was feeling.

"Sejanus is…suggesting that by the Legions taking care of Percennius on their own, without orders, they're not only demonstrating blatant disrespect, but the fact that they're hiding something."

As he said this, I understood that he was not only correct, but I could easily envision someone like Drusus being swayed by this argument, but this raised a question in my mind.

"Why is Sejanus doing this?" I asked. "What's in it for him?"

"That," Dolabella admitted, his mouth twisting into a frustrated grimace, "is something I wish I knew. I've been thinking about it, and I can't quite see what he's up to. But," he spat into the dirt, one of the most ancient and common methods of cursing a man, "whatever it is, it's for the benefit of Sejanus and nobody else."

"I know that someone summoned all the Centurions to the *praetorium* in their camp," I told him, mainly because I was hoping he had some inside knowledge as to why, but he only commented, "They're probably being told the latest developments, or maybe they're deciding how to conduct their business from this point forward."

As it turned out, this was close to what was actually happening, which I learned when I saw Galens, dressed in his full uniform, stride into the Praetorian camp. We had been walking from the forum, but seeing him approach, we stopped, both of us closely examining his expression as he neared, but while he looked sober, there was no sign of overt concern.

Saluting him, I simply said, "Good morning, Primus Pilus."

Dolabella, however, was more concerned with the meaning of Galens' presence, and after exchanging a brief nod, he asked bluntly, "What are you doing over here? Were you summoned?"

If Galens did not care for the preemptive tone, he hid it well, and more importantly, he answered without hesitation, "I'm coming to let the *Proconsul* know that the 8th is leaving this camp and returning to Siscia to wait to hear from Tiberius."

This, to my mind at least, was welcome news, but Dolabella, being more attuned to what men did not say as much as what they did, instantly understood there was more to Galens' words and asked, "What about the other two?"

This caused Galens' lips to compress into a thin line, which I had learned long before when he was my Optio that he was angry and struggling to remain composed.

"You'll have to ask them," he told Dolabella, but when he began to resume his walk to the *praetorium*, Dolabella said, in a tone that was half-question, half-guess, "They're staying here, aren't they?"

Galens did not stop walking, but he did say over his shoulder, "It looks that way."

Fortunately for all concerned, whatever argument Sejanus used to sway young Drusus that there was a more sinister reason for the handling of Percennius and the others was not sufficient to change the *Proconsul*'s mind. Once Galens informed him that only the 8th was returning to Siscia, a full watch passed as Drusus and his advisors bickered and debated about the best way in which to respond to the fact that the 9th and 15th were staying put. The ultimate result was that we spent another day there, although the official party going to Rome, consisting of Blaesus Minor, Catonius, and a man named Lucius Aponius, who was one of the gaggle of Tribunes and other minor nobles accompanying the *Proconsul*, left that day. There was a brief period where I thought I would finally be allowed to leave and return to Germania, but for reasons I never learned, Drusus ordered me to remain there, through Dolabella of course, despite the fact that my usefulness, such as it was, seemed to have come to an end. It was midday before the 8th finally left the camp, and since Domitius and I had said our goodbyes the night before, I spent more time with Galens and Asinius, along with the few remaining men I had served alongside in one capacity or another, chatting with them as they prepared to depart. The almost unanimous sentiment among these older men was they were just happy that it was over; what was far from unanimous was their outlook on whether this would finally be the time that Tiberius listened. I certainly did not take a vote, but my sense was that it seemed evenly split between men who thought that, now that the Legions had demonstrated their seriousness, Tiberius would recognize that and, while not granting all the concessions, would certainly agree to some of them. The other half viewed matters more pessimistically, yet rather than being angry, they appeared to be resigned to whatever fate awaited them. Ultimately, my sense was that these men were just tired of all the angry tension, with the constant threat of matters turning bloody, and perhaps most importantly, they just wanted to return to their families. Which, by regulation, they were not allowed to have, and I confess that the thought had crossed my mind that

Tiberius might use this flaunting of a regulation that had been in place since Gaius Marius reorganized the Legions as a pretext for denying their demands. Whatever happened, in most ways, I was of a like mind with my former comrades of the 8th in that I just wanted to return to my own Legion, which I had come to think of as my home. Always there, lurking in the back of my mind, was a sort of envy of those comrades who had gone on to have families, which, if I allowed it, would cause me to wonder how different my life might have been if I had ever been able to shake the hold the *numen* of Giulia held over me. Whenever this happened, I would force myself to think of something else, and on this occasion, it was recalling the sadness of my friend Domitius at the loss of Petrilla, and how he could not bring himself to spend time with his children. Not surprisingly, this did not make me feel better, so I went and checked on Latobius, who I had ensured was properly stabled and cared for the first night. Once that was done, the 8th had finished packing up and was standing in the forum, ready to march away. Since I was in uniform, as were the men of the 8th, I saluted the Primus Pilus as I passed him by, and while he returned it, he also threw me a grin.

"Try not to fall off that fucking horse, Pullus," he called out.

Laughing, I assured him that I would do my best, then walked down the column to essentially do the same with Appius Asinius, whose Century was next in the column, exchanging a few quiet words that ended with a clasping of arms. Finally, I got to where Domitius was standing, where we also exchanged a salute, but this time, we also embraced. Awkwardly, I would add, since we were both fully uniformed, and it caused us both to chuckle.

"Try to write this time?" I asked him gently but with a tone that told him I was serious.

He flushed, but he nodded and promised, "I will."

I was not through, however, adding, "And go see Domitilla and Titus as soon as you get back?"

Domitius' head shot up, and I saw a glimmer of anger, except it passed so quickly I might have imagined it, but there was no mistaking the pain in his eye.

Taking a breath, he replied, "And I'll do that as well." After a pause, he looked up at me and asked grumpily, "Anything else you want me to do?"

"Yes," I answered, except this time I grinned. "Don't lose that other eye. I don't want to have to lead you around when we're old men."

As I hoped, this made him laugh heartily, then with one last embrace, I walked away, and so far, I have not seen Titus Domitius again.

I left at dawn the next morning, riding along with Drusus and his party, which naturally included his bodyguards, the Praetorian cavalry, his staff, and not surprisingly Sejanus, who left the Praetorian Cohorts under the command of another Tribune. Now that he no longer felt the need for protection, our party was entirely mounted and made good time, most of which I spent near the back of the rough formation, making myself as inconspicuous as possible. Dolabella alternated between spending time up near Drusus, then falling back to me, whereupon he would grumble about what he had overheard.

"That bastard Sejanus never stops," was one memorable comment he made. "Even when he seems to be just gossiping about everyday things going on in Rome, it's always about certain men."

I considered for a moment, yet I could not honestly find anything objectionable in this; after all, even rankers spent a fair amount of the time on the march chattering about the latest bit of scandal and gossip concerning our social betters.

Nevertheless, I knew Dolabella was not just making a random comment, which prompted me to probe further, "Which 'certain men' are you talking about?" When he did not answer immediately, I amended slightly, "What do these 'certain men' have in common with each other?"

This elicited a reaction, as he turned to look at me with a searching gaze, yet he answered readily enough, albeit with another question, "Are you asking what they appear to have in common with each other? Or what I think is really going on?"

"Let's skip to the second part," I replied.

He returned his attention forward, over his horse's head, and while it was always hard to tell, I felt certain that with his good eye, Dolabella was staring at the back of the Praetorian Tribune.

"I think," he lowered his voice, "that these men have either run afoul of Sejanus in some fashion, or he views them as possible rivals."

"Rival for what?" I asked, curiously.

The spymaster shook his head, hissing in frustration.

"I wish I knew," he answered honestly, and he turned to look at me again, and I could see how troubled he was, reminding me that Dolabella being unable to unravel some knotty mystery probably did not happen very often. "All I'm certain of is that he's determined to get as close to Tiberius as he can and make himself seen as indispensable to the *Imperator*. But," he finished bitterly, "I know it's not because he's loyal to Tiberius."

I made no reply, primarily because I did not know what to say. Frankly, I realized that at least part of Dolabella's concern was for himself, but I could not fault him for that. Of all the things I knew and can say about Tiberius Dolabella is that, although he had certainly switched his allegiance from the aging Augustus to Tiberius, I am convinced that it had been done with, if not the outright consent of Augustus, then at least with a tacit but unmistakable sign to Dolabella to do so. My reasoning is straightforward; if Augustus had viewed Dolabella's switching his allegiance to Tiberius as a betrayal, he would not have been riding next to me. Most importantly, and a reason for his longevity in his capacity as the man who dealt in Roman politics in the back alleys, *tavernae,* and whorehouses of the lower classes, Dolabella was unfailingly loyal to the man he served, which convinced me that not all of his concern about Sejanus was about his own skin. Traveling northeast, when we came to the road that was considered the "back passage" around Splonum, where the village of Clandate still stood, I experienced some trepidation about which route Drusus would take and had decided that if the *Proconsul* took that rougher but more direct route, I would be forced to continue on my own, taking the road that led through Splonum. Not that this route was without its own hazards, but given my history with the Maezaei and my actions in Clandate in the aftermath of Sextus' death, I decided that the route through Splonum posed less risk to me, at least slightly. While it was true I had been in Splonum more recently with the *Legio Germanicus*, I had been part of an army, led by Germanicus, so even with my size, I was just one Roman among many who had partially destroyed their town, but the same could not be said about Clandate. Thanks to Fortuna, I did not have to make this choice, since Drusus continued straight and did not take the road branching off to the north. Being entirely mounted, we made better time than the 8th, so that despite the day's head start, we could see them actually entering the gates of the camp, barely missing catching up with them. Now I had a second decision to make, and that was to entreat Dolabella to extract Drusus' permission to leave this party and return to my Legion. I was determined to not only do this, but to do so immediately, pressing on and staying in Siscia only long enough to collect Titus and the girl Algaia, although I wondered if she had changed her mind about not returning to her people. Naturally, this put a fair amount of pressure on Dolabella to convince Drusus in a very short period of time, but while he was not optimistic, he assured me he would do his best.

"I suppose that's the least he owes you," Dolabella commented as he left me, standing next to my horse and pack animal, and I wholeheartedly agreed.

While Dolabella was busy with this, I went to the inn I had sent Titus and Algaia to stay in, wondering what I would find. It was true that it had only been a matter of three days, but I knew just how volatile and fleeting young love, or lust, could be, so I confess I was quite surprised when the pair emerged from the inn, having been sent for by the innkeeper's slave. That they were holding hands, I was certain, was meant to send a clear signal to me, as if I needed it after seeing their almost identical expressions, a combination of nervousness and defiance.

Rather than directly challenge either of them, I simply turned to the girl, and asked her quietly, "Are you sure about this?"

To her credit, she did not hesitate, nodding her head and saying, "I am, Master."

Sighing, I answered, "First, I'm not your master. Second," I paused, but it was mainly to tease the couple, then I grinned and said to her, "Don't say I didn't give you the chance. Once you get sick of him, you're going to be up in Germania, a long way from here." I was about to add, "Or Arelate," but recalling what she had endured there at the hands of my brother, I felt certain it would be the last place she would want to go.

"I would never get sick of him." Algaia seemed almost angry, turning to look up at Diocles' middle son, who just stood there looking like a moonstruck cow, gazing back at her in adoration.

Sighing, I told them to go make preparations to depart, telling them to wait outside the camp gate for me to return.

Going back into camp, I went straight for the forum, somewhat expecting Dolabella to be waiting, but he was not, nor did he show up for almost another third of a watch. Just when I was at the point where I told myself I would have to enter the *Praetorium* and approach Drusus myself, the door opened, and Dolabella emerged. Immediately studying his face, I suppose I noticed the small satchel he was carrying, but its importance did not become apparent right away. He was not smiling, but there was not an air about him that indicated to me he dreaded giving me bad news; it was as he was descending the steps I saw a tightly rolled scroll in his hand, which he extended to me once he drew near enough.

"Here is your written pass," he said, then turned it so I could see as he continued, "with Drusus' personal seal on it." He paused ever so briefly, but there was a hint of a smile on his face, prompting me to ask what he found humorous, and he answered readily enough, "I wasn't sure I should tell you this, but I suppose it won't do any harm. This," he pointed to the scroll that I had now accepted, "is actually the second copy. The first one had an...error," he finished, and now the grin was clearly visible, and somehow I just knew the cause.

"He forgot my name, didn't he?" I asked, and when he nodded, I was torn between indignation and relief, but when Dolabella burst out laughing, I could not help joining in, seeing the absurd humor of the situation.

"I was so important to what he had to do that he couldn't remember my name." I shook my head, still a bit incredulous.

"Actually, that's not a bad thing," Dolabella pointed out, his smile fading, "but aside from that mistake, he actually wrote something else." He lifted the small satchel, handing it to me as well, explaining as he did so, "It seems that he wrote a rather...glowing report about your actions and behavior during this whole matter. It's," he indicated the leather bag, "in there, also under his seal. And," he warned, somewhat humorously, but

539

I could tell he was serious, "no, you're not going to break the seal and read it."

Something did not make sense to me, and I suppose it was due to my suspicious nature, especially where it concerned the upper classes, that prompted me to ask, "Wait. He didn't know my name for my travel order, but he wrote something good about me in this other scroll?"

I got my answer before Dolabella actually spoke, in the manner in which he suddenly looked away past me towards the forum, mostly deserted by this point.

"Well," he finally admitted, "he might not have actually *written* it. But he did sign it. And," Dolabella pointed to my travel orders, "his seal is on it just like your travel orders."

Once more, I was unsure what to say; this entire episode that I had spent with Dolabella had been with a seemingly different man than the one I almost throttled very early in an association that now stretched almost two decades.

"Why did you do that?" I blurted the question before I could stop myself, and he looked every bit as embarrassed as I felt.

Finally, he gave a shrug and said simply, "Because you deserve to be recognized for what you did, Titus. That's all." Only then did he look up directly at me, then gave a self-conscious chuckle. "But I can see why you'd be suspicious of me, given our history." Then, before I could respond, his tone turned brisk and businesslike, and he indicated the satchel again. "But that's not all you're carrying. Drusus is sending a dispatch to his brother, along with a personal letter."

The dispatch was not that surprising, but a personal letter was, prompting me to comment, "I didn't know they were that close."

"They're not," Dolabella answered, and I sensed there was some worry in his voice, then allowed, "or at least I didn't think they were." He gave me a shrug that signaled he was not going to comment more, finishing with, "Just make sure Germanicus gets both."

The mention of his name reminded me to ask, "Speaking of, was there any word from Germania about what the situation is?"

To this, he could not do anything other than shake his head. "No, nothing."

Then, there was no reason to delay; I still had roughly a half-day of daylight, and I did not want to waste it, yet for some reason, it felt as if my feet were rooted to the spot, and I know now that I was simply stalling for time when I asked Dolabella about his plans.

"I'm going back to Rome with Drusus," he confirmed my guess. "Then?" Another shrug, yet this one seemed more…fatalistic than uncertain. "Only the gods know where I'm going."

"Well," the words came awkwardly, "whenever you get to Ubiorum again, be sure and find me."

"I always do," he answered cheerfully, but then he realized my true meaning. Something flashed across his face, an expression I had not seen often, if at all, then he added, "And, yes, I certainly will."

He offered me his arm, which I took, but I confess I was not ready for him to pull me into an embrace, yet I did not resist.

Thankfully he did not try to kiss me, but his voice was husky as I turned to mount Latobius.

"Travel safely, Titus Pullus."

"You as well," I answered, then added, "and watch your back."

"Always," he assured me.

I turned my mount and immediately went to a trot; this was the last time I saw Tiberius Dolabella, and I suspect that, deep down, I knew this.

Now that it was the middle of October, there was a bite in the air, but at least the passing countryside was more colorful, as the trees shed their leaves in many varieties of color. Using the power of Drusus' seal, which was now presumed to be the symbol of at least the third most powerful man in Rome, I was able to switch out mounts for both myself and the young couple at relay stations, enabling Latobius to have some respite, since I was determined to cover the distance as quickly as possible, something of which I pressed the importance on Titus and Algaia. It was on the second day, north of Emona, that we spotted a single rider approaching from the opposite direction, riding at a steady canter. As he drew nearer, I recognized the cloak that designated he was a member of the courier system established by the Princeps. Knowing that they are under strict instructions not to stop for any purpose, such as being hailed by a stranger on a deserted road, I did not have much time to think of a way in which I could get him to at least inform me from where he was coming. Ordering Titus and Algaia to remain where they were, I trotted a few yards ahead, then perhaps a handful of heartbeats before it would have been too late, I was inspired to extract my travel pass, turning it so that Drusus' seal was facing towards the approaching rider. Once I did, I arranged Latobius, the pack animal, and my spare horse in a manner that blocked the road, holding the scroll up so he could see it. Now he could have easily gone off the road to go around me, and frankly, I was expecting him to do so, but I suppose this was a sufficiently odd sight that he slowed, first to a trot, then a walk, once he was about a hundred paces away.

"*Salve*, brother!" I called out, thinking that using an appellation that Legionaries often use with each other might help my cause. "I'm Titus Pullus, Quartus Princeps Prior of the 1st Legion, returning from a special assignment on behalf of *Proconsul* Drusus Claudius Nero!"

While I had been speaking, he had slowed even more, and there was no mistaking his suspicion, but I did not blame him for his hand on the hilt of his *gladius*.

"So?" he finally spoke. "What's that to me? And why are you trying to stop me?"

"I'm not trying to stop you," I assured him. "It's just that I'm heading back to my camp at Ubiorum, and when I left, things were..." I searched for the correct way to describe the situation without using the word "mutiny," settling on, "...a bit unsettled there."

This prompted a snort from the rider, who looked a bit old to be one of the members of the couriers, but he did reply, "That's certainly one way to put it, Centurion. But," he repeated, "what does that have to do with me?"

"Nothing, other than that I'm looking for information about what happened while I was gone. And," I added, "what I can expect when I get there."

"You know I can't let you know anything about what I'm carrying and who it's for," he countered, yet he did not seem particularly hostile, which I took as a good sign.

"I know," I agreed, "but all I want to know is what's happening there. I don't want any details about it, just whether or not things are settled."

"Settled?" He gave a sharp laugh. "I don't know about that, Centurion. But," he hesitated, staring in my direction, his eyes going from my face to the scroll, which I was still holding up, "if you toss me that scroll so I can see the seal up close, I'll consider telling you what I can."

This was far from ideal; nor, I realized, did I have any choice. Yes, he was well mounted, and between the condition of his horse and my knowledge that a relay station was less than a dozen miles up the road, it was within the realm of possibility that he would immediately try to escape. I suppose, however, I had enough faith in Latobius, who I was sitting on at the moment, along with my own horsemanship so that, somewhat reluctantly, I tossed the scroll to him. He caught it quite deftly, then turned it so he could examine the scroll.

"I've seen enough of his seal to know this is genuine," he said finally, then tossed it back, though while I managed to snatch it, I was not nearly as adept as he had been. "So, what's your question, Centurion?"

Now I would have thought it was obvious, but despite the sharp retort that came to my lips, I managed to ask, "Is the mutiny over?"

"No," he answered immediately, and I do not know whether it was because my distress was so obvious, but he pointed to the leather tube attached to his back. "In fact, what I know is this is a dispatch from the *Proconsul*'s brother, informing him that he's in the process of negotiating with the Legions."

Once the initial stab of alarm ebbed somewhat, I was about to ask more questions, then thought better of it.

Instead, I simply thanked the man, but when he did not move immediately to resume his progress, I realized that he was waiting for a reward more substantial than some words. Without thinking about it, I produced a small handful of coins, then urged Latobius forward, and when I drew abreast of the courier, I dropped them into his hand, which was outstretched.

"It seems like you've done this before." My voice was cold, but while he blanched, he neither denied it nor withdrew his hand.

With a jerk of my head, I signaled that he could resume his journey, while I indicated that Titus and Algaia could join me. I imagine there was a huge difference in our respective hearts; mine was still troubled, and in some ways, was even worse than when I had departed from Pannonia, while he was probably happy to earn a few coins.

We reached Mogontiacum a week after leaving Siscia, and for the entire day before I reached what is now the largest city in this part of Germania, I tried to prepare myself for what I would find. Knowing that the mutiny was not yet over was certainly disturbing, but while the one in Pannonia supposedly was, many of those men were still disgruntled and, if no longer outwardly angry, were sullenly waiting to hear from Tiberius. And, I felt confident, if he refused to accede to any of their demands, matters would return to their former state of open insurrection, which ironically enough, would at least not make the continuing intransigence of the Rhenus Legions be quite so obvious. While I had more faith in Germanicus and his ability to soothe the collective mood of the Army of the Rhenus, I was not sanguine that the result I was sure would happen in Pannonia if Tiberius refused would not be duplicated in Mogontiacum, and Ubiorum. This was why, once the walls of the city came in sight and I could make out enough detail, we pulled up and I simply observed for several moments, watching the outer gate. That it was open I took to be a good sign, but I was most concerned with the flow of traffic, particularly since I had not passed as many other travelers that would be normal for this time of year. After thinking about it, I realized that it made sense that an event like the mutiny would disrupt the flow of commerce and travel for a period of time beyond the end of the insurrection, prompting me to resume my progress. Reaching the gate, I briefly waited while the town watch examined the cargo of the wagon in front of me, giving me a bit more time to observe my surroundings. There were no extra men to be seen, nor was there anything more than the standard lone man standing in the tower, watching the southern road. Once it was our turn, all it took was the flourishing of the pass from Drusus, along with the explanation that my two young companions belonged to me, something I had warned them I would be saying in order to avoid answering awkward questions, and we were allowed into the town. To my eye, everything appeared normal, or at least close to it. Perhaps the people who were going about their business gave us a wider berth than normal, and I caught more than one glare as I passed by, but otherwise, it could have been any other day in the town, another good sign as far as I was concerned. The real proof would be when I crossed the bridge and went to the whole purpose for the very existence of this now-thriving town, and as always, I could not help marveling about how much things had changed in the twenty-two years since I first visited this place, when it was nothing more than a frontier town, with the smell of raw wood, plaster, and *cac*. Ordering Titus and Algaia to dismount and wait on the civilian side of the bridge, I crossed over to the camp. Just as it had worked at the gate, my pass got me in with a minimum of fuss, although I headed not to the *Praetorium* first, but the *Quaestorium*, to arrange passage on the next barge traveling downriver to Ubiorum, where Drusus' pass worked in the same manner. Passing the *Praetorium*, I saw the small pennants hanging outside that informed me that both the 14th and the 2nd were in their permanent camp in Vetera, another good sign as far as I was concerned, although I also knew that these two Legions had not revolted in the first place. For some reason, it was not until this moment that I recalled a similar one, when I had been carrying a pass impressed with the seal of the man who was now our *Imperator*. The result with this pass was the same as the one belonging to Tiberius; there was a barge leaving at dawn the next morning, and I was given space for myself, the two youngsters I claimed were my slaves, and our horses, although I left the spare mounts behind. I could have requisitioned space for myself in the camp; instead, I opted to return to the town and take a room at one of the inns, not particularly wanting the worry of Titus and Algaia in an unfamiliar military town, but while I would have normally paid extra for accommodations that catered to members of the equestrian order, this time, I wanted to hear what the civilians of my class were talking about. My reasoning was straightforward, that the Head Counters of Mogontiacum would have a closer connection to the members of their class under the standard, and thereby I felt confident I could get a better, more accurate sense of the mood of the army, rather than hearing the Tribune who took my orders tell me what he had been instructed to say by the Legate. It is true that I could have prowled around the camp, but given the climate, and the fact that I was from the 1st, and I had already been accused of being an instigator of insurrection, I decided against it.

Returning to find the pair where I had left them, I led them to the inn I had selected, then once I took care of Latobius and the pack horse, while Titus and the girl did the same for their mounts, we retired to the common room of the inn, tucking ourselves into a corner, then ordered some food and drink. Normally, I consume my meals quickly, but while I was certainly hungry, satisfying my appetite was not the most important matter to me at this moment. I was noticed, naturally, and at first it was clear that the other people, an assortment of wagon drivers, merchants of modest means, and, of course, a sprinkling of women who were plying their own trade, were all cautious about what they were saying, their eyes continually darting in our direction. As time passed, and more importantly, wine flowed, and no doubt aided by the presence of two youngsters who were clearly attached to me in some way, gradually I was forgotten, so that by the time we had finished our meal, and I had consumed two cups of wine that I cut with water, my fellow travelers were chattering away, and naturally, the topic was the mutiny. More accurately, they were talking about the actions that Germanicus had taken upon his arrival in Ubiorum, which sounded very much like exactly what Drusus had done, declaring that he could not make a decision of this magnitude on his own, and had sent for guidance from Tiberius. Perhaps most importantly, there had been no word of any real violence, at least of a scale that news of it reached these citizens of Mogontiacum. This piece of information was comforting, but I was also cautious about taking it too seriously, understanding there was only one way to find out, and with that in mind, we retired to our room, which I had paid extra to have just the three of us. My calculation is that no more than a hundred heartbeats had elapsed after I lay down on the filthy, lumpy bed that I began itching from the bites of all the vermin that lived for the moment when a traveler arrived, and both Titus and Algaia confirmed that their pallet, which they were sharing, was no better. Not much longer after that, I was regretting my decision, realizing that we could have taken my meal in this inn but slept in relative comfort somewhere else. Somehow, I must have fallen asleep, despite the discomfort and my mind racing, trying to think of every possible situation I might find myself in when I finally returned to Ubiorum, to home.

The barge docked at the wharf in Ubiorum late on the second day of our departure from Mogontiacum, after the overnight trip down the Rhenus, and I spent the final few miles leaning on the rail, watching the land on the Roman side slide past, mentally preparing myself for whatever was coming. Young Titus must have sensed this, because neither he nor the girl made any attempt to intrude, despite the fact that I was certain they were bursting with questions about what was going to be their new home. So deep in my reverie was I that, when the bow of the barge struck the wharf, it startled me so much that, for a brief instant, I was afraid I would topple over the side. Recovering quickly, while the crew secured the barge, I saddled Latobius and put my baggage on the pack horse while the others did the same, and since we were the only passengers, we were first off the barge. Leading our animals down the plank, I traveled the short street that leads from the wharfs up to the Porta Dextra, while I told Titus and Algaia to go to The Dancing Faun, telling them I would either come for them myself or send a messenger. My heart was beating much harder than warranted from the slight slope up from the riverbank, but when I arrived at the gate, the situation appeared almost identical to the eye to what I had encountered in Mogontiacum. Although there was nothing overtly out of the ordinary, I did notice that the camp was inordinately quiet, the Via Principalis being almost deserted, and the few men out and about were auxiliaries, meaning that I did not stop them to get an idea of the situation. Like at Mogontiacum, there were guards on the door, and I immediately recognized them as belonging to Germanicus' bodyguard, which did aid me in gaining entrance, since one of them recognized me from my time with the *Propraetor* in Pannonia. Then, I was inside the building, whereupon I stopped for a moment, both to let my eyes adjust to the dimmer light and to observe a bit. Unlike outside, there was all manner of activity inside as clerks crisscrossed, each carrying something like a wax tablet or scroll, while a trio of Tribunes were bent over a desk, poring over something that, from my experience, could as easily have been an erotic poem as a dispatch. Fortunately, the duty Tribune was where he was supposed to be, except I realized I did not recognize him, which could have been meaningless…or it could have been significant, and this possibility put me on my guard. My entrance had been noticed, and I recognized some of the clerks, those who were normally left behind when the Legions marched, all of whom acknowledged me with a nod, which I returned, having long become accustomed to the officiousness of *Praetorium* clerks. I had chosen to wear my uniform, but without my *phalarae*, arm rings, or the torq that I had been given by Germanicus in recognition of my service to him in the Batonian revolt, and I strode to the desk, came to *intente,* and saluted. The Tribune at first seemed determined to play the silly game of ignoring me, but I extended the scroll lower than normal so that Drusus' seal was in front of his nose as he stared down at a wax tablet, which from my height I could see were the orders for the day that are posted every morning. Regardless, he seemed determined to ignore the scroll, but in an unconscious reaction, I saw his eyes dart up as it entered his field of vision. The results were both gratifying and amusing, his eyes taking in Drusus' seal, going wide in surprise, followed by a very undignified yelp as he hopped up from his chair.

"Quartus Princeps Prior Pullus, returning to Ubiorum as directed by the *Proconsul* Nero Claudius Drusus." I managed to keep a straight face, but it was made even more difficult because, now that he was standing, the Tribune's gaze alternated between my face and the scroll, which he still had not taken from me. Finally, I lost my patience, although I managed to keep my voice level, "Tribune, until you accept this, I'm not officially reporting."

"Er, yes, I see," he mumbled, his face turning a bright red, but thankfully, he finally took the scroll, whereupon the next problem presented itself. Even as it exchanged hands, his eyes never left it, until he looked up at me, and I suppose this was the first moment I realized just how young he was. Several heartbeats passed, then he swallowed hard and finally stopped his eyes long enough to look up at me and ask in a whisper, "Centurion, am I supposed to open this? I mean," he added, "since it has the seal of a *Proconsul*."

Despite my overall ambivalence about Tribunes as a group, something in the youngster's manner reminded me of young Volusenus, I suppose, so I nodded slightly and kept my voice low as I assured him, "Since these are my travel orders, Tribune, and you're the duty Tribune, you have to open the scroll in order to verify that I am who I say I am, and that I've reported in within the specified time." Then, before he could respond, I thought to tap the satchel that I had slung over my shoulder, saying with a grin, "Now the ones I have in here? If you opened one of those, you and I would both be in the *cac*."

The grin he returned did not seem feigned, and I found myself warming to this Tribune, slightly; only when I saw him performing his duties would I have a better sense of his overall value to the army. As he cracked open the seal, I saw his eyes move rapidly, telling me he was adept at reading, then his eyes, which had returned to their normal size, widened again.

"Wait," he gasped, looking back up at me, "you're Princeps Prior *Pullus*?"

This was such an odd thing to ask, I was not offended that he clearly had not been listening, although I did say, "That's what I told you when I handed you my orders, Tribune. But," I added, "yes, I'm Princeps Prior Pullus."

The color came back into his face, and he admitted, "I suppose I wasn't paying close enough attention, Centurion, and I apologize for that. But," his manner changed slightly as he cocked his head and examined me more closely, "whoever has the duty has been given standing orders that whenever you reported in, you were to be taken to the *Propraetor* immediately."

I had not given it prior thought, but I realized this made sense, given that Germanicus had been the one to send me with Dolabella.

"Please wait here," the Tribune said, moving from behind the desk. "I'm going to let the *Propraetor* know you're here."

He hurried across the room, and now I could sense that the other Tribunes present had taken notice, feeling their eyes on me, which I ignored. Fortunately, the duty Tribune was not gone long, emerging from the door that led to the Praetor's outer office, whereupon he beckoned to me. Crossing the distance, when I reached him, he held the scroll out to me, but I did not accept it.

"Tribune, you need to go enter this into the Army diary," I told him. "Until you do, I'm not officially here."

For the third time, his face glowed, and I wondered if the back and forth of all the blood to his head was making him lightheaded, and he mumbled, "Ah, yes. Of course. I'll do it now."

I made sure to thank him, then stepped past him and entered into what was the outer office of the Praetor, expecting to go through another similar procedure with Germanicus' secretary, whose desk was placed in between the outer door and the inner one. Instead, Germanicus himself was standing in the doorway of his office, and while he gave me a smile, I had served him long enough and been in close enough proximity to see the strain underneath his exterior.

Nevertheless, his tone was cheerful, saying cheerfully, "*Ave,* Pullus! You don't look bad for having traveled across half the Empire!"

"Nor do you, sir," I lied, saluting as I said this, which he returned.

Then he beckoned me to follow him into his private office, not bothering to see if I followed, so that by the time I had entered, he was already dropping wearily into the chair behind his desk, suddenly looking older than I had ever seen him before.

"Shut the door." He waved, but while I thought he meant for me to do it, a slave I had not noticed seated on a stool in the corner leapt up and hurried to do it instead. Gesturing to the chair on the opposite side of the desk, Germanicus, always polite, asked if I cared for some refreshment.

"Just water would be fine," I assured him, and this made him laugh.

"Want to keep a clear head with me, neh?" He said this jovially, and I did not detect anything there that might have struck a false note, but I still assured him this was not my reason. Waiting just long enough for the slave to hand me a cup, once done, Germanicus dismissed him, then even as the door swung shut, he did not hesitate. "Well? What happened in Pannonia?"

Frankly, this shocked me to my core.

"You mean you haven't been informed?" I asked, trying to keep the doubt from my voice. "I'm the first one with any news?"

In answer, Germanicus gave an impatient wave, saying flatly, "No, I know that the mutiny is over; I received a dispatch about that three days ago. But," his handsome features hardened, "that's not what I'm talking about." Suddenly, he looked down on his desk, rummaged through a small pile of scrolls, then extracted one, which he held up, and when he did, I saw that it bore the same seal as the one on my orders, and on those in my satchel. "I know what my brother told me. What I want to know is what *really* happened."

Even as the words came out of his mouth, I felt a stirring of anger, not at Germanicus, but myself, realizing I should have anticipated this. Yes, they were brothers, but by adoption, and now that Augustus was gone, circumstances had drastically changed for both men. Also, I knew that there was no love lost between the pair, although now that I had been in Drusus' company, I felt certain that the impetus for whatever hostility they felt for each other originated more from Drusus than the other way around. Granted, I have no way of knowing this with any certainty, but I knew Germanicus fairly well by this point, and even as he had hardened because of his experience in the Batonian revolt, his was not a naturally suspicious nor disagreeable nature. Drusus I only knew very slightly, but enough to see that he was more like his natural father than his adopted brother, and Tiberius was naturally more taciturn and suspicious, a trait that I had seen only get worse over the period of years I worked for him. Now, sitting in front of Germanicus, I roundly cursed myself for not being prepared, and I suppose this became apparent because of my hesitation.

"Pullus," Germanicus' tone was almost apologetic, "I know I'm putting you in a difficult position. It's just that this," he waved the scroll disgustedly, then tossed it back on the desk, "only tells me what Drusus wants me to know."

In answer, I spent the next several moments giving Germanicus my assessment of not only the mutiny itself, but my opinion of Drusus' handling of the matter.

He listened intently, which was not surprising, only occasionally stopping me to ask a question or pressing me to expand on something, but I could not really discern what he was listening for, until, at least, I finished by saying, "Honestly, sir, I don't know how long this peace is going to last. Many men were angry that Drusus arrived without the authority to do anything about the demands the men had made."

"That," he muttered under his breath, and I am not sure whether I was meant to hear or not, "I understand." More clearly, he said, "I can't lie and say that I'm not happy to hear he had some...difficulties."

"Probably more trouble than you've been having," I countered, thinking that this might help his state of mind.

Instead, his head came up sharply, his eyes narrowed, and there was such a change in his demeanor that I felt a sudden stab of alarm that I had inadvertently said something offensive.

"What makes you say that?" he asked sharply. "Where did you hear that? Who told you that I've been having an easy time of it?"

Thinking I understood, I assured him, "I don't mean to imply it's been easy, sir. Just that, from what I heard in Mogontiacum, there hasn't been any real violence."

"That," to my ears, he sounded rueful, "I'm not so sure about. But," he regarded me thoughtfully, "that's what the people are saying?"

Promising him that this was the case, he was silent for a moment, his eyes going back to his desk, though I had the sense that he was not really looking at it.

"Maybe," he said softly, "that will be enough." Then, he shook his head, returning his attention to me. "So, what do you know of what's happening here?"

"Not that much," I admitted. "I know that the 2nd and 14th were in their camp, but the clerk in Mogontiacum couldn't tell me exactly where the 5th and 21st are, and he knew even less about the 1st and the 20th." His face, while not betraying any real emotion, still unsettled me, and I asked, cautiously, "How are the men, sir? What's the mood of the Legions here?"

It was easy to see this was the question he had been expecting, yet even so, he did not seem disposed to answer me, but he finally spoke.

"They're clearly still unhappy, since they've refused to move from their spot near Caedicius' camp, and as of today, they still refuse to move until I hear back from my father." He sighed, then added, "And the same goes for the 5th and 21st. They're actually not that far from the 1st and 20th."

Understanding I was in potentially dangerous territory, I still felt compelled to delicately press, "Do you have any idea what he'll do, sir?"

"I wish I did," Germanicus answered honestly. "I truly do. But," he sighed, "I don't."

"So," I asked, though I felt certain I knew the answer, "you've actually been to our camp?"

"Twice," he answered. "In fact, I just got back earlier today. But," he sighed again, "now that you're here, I might as well go back with you. The gods know that I'm not getting anything done here."

For some reason, this reminded me, and I opened the satchel, handing him the other correspondence given to me by Dolabella, from Drusus, and I did not miss the grimace when Germanicus saw the seals, although he accepted them from me readily enough.

When he broke the seal and began to unroll the first one, I felt quite uncomfortable, wondering if it was the one that Dolabella had essentially written that sang my praises.

"Do you want me to leave, sir? So you can read what your brother sent?"

He had obviously already begun reading, since this seemed to startle him, as if he had forgotten my presence, and he looked up at me but shook his head.

"No, if you don't mind, go ahead and sit there while I read this," he waved the scroll, "letter from my brother. So far, it's more or less the same *cac* he sent in the dispatch, just with a bit more detail. I might have some questions for you."

Now, he had been courteous by asking if I minded, but I knew it was an order, so I assured him I was perfectly content to sit and sip my water, although I briefly considered asking that it be changed to wine. As he continued reading, I surreptitiously studied his face, thinking that, since I was somewhat familiar with him, I might get an idea about how he was taking whatever it was Drusus had written. Suddenly, his brows plunged down together, which I knew was the sign he was concentrating on what he was reading, then he looked up at me and gave me a sharp look.

"Is this true?" he demanded, but before I could answer, he gave a small laugh and said, "Of course, since you have no idea what I'm reading, how could you possibly know?" Glancing back down at the scroll, he said, "According to Drusus, he ordered the execution of the ringleaders, which was carried out? But," he seemed to be getting more agitated with every word, "without actually promising the Pannonian Legions anything?"

I suspect that I can be forgiven for my sudden wish that the floor would open underneath my chair and swallow me up. Regardless of my desire not to become entangled in whatever was brewing between these two men, now second or third in line to be *Imperator*, I also felt a strong allegiance to Germanicus, and essentially none to Drusus. That I had now observed both men under duress and seen how they handled it also meant that I did not hesitate, at least perceptibly enough for Germanicus to notice.

Before I did, however, I thought to ask, "Did the *Proconsul* mention anything...unusual? About the circumstances, I mean?"

That this puzzled Germanicus gave me the answer, and I went on to explain about the true cause for the collapse of the mutiny. As he sat listening, his expression grew stony, and I noticed that he had one hand under the desk, which told me that he was rhythmically pounding his thigh with his fist, his habit when he was angry that I had first observed during the Batonian revolt. By the time I had finished, only leaving out any mention of Domitius' role, he was as angry as I had ever seen him, even more than when he confronted Scipio outside Raetinium the day after the town burned down.

"That...*viper*," he hissed, waving the scroll in my general direction, "didn't say one word about any eclipse, or that the ringleaders were taken care of by the Centurions who remained loyal!"

Now that was not exactly the way I had related it, but if that was how he took it, I certainly was not inclined to correct him. He sat there, visibly fuming for a moment, then, slowly, his demeanor changed, and he finally said, "But, while he doesn't know it, my brother gave me an idea." Giving me a wan smile, he continued, "I know you're tired, Pullus, but I'm afraid you're only going to get a night's rest. I need you to accompany me back to your Legion."

"It's a fucking mess, Pullus."

Darkness had fallen on the next day, with Germanicus and me arriving perhaps a watch before, and I was now sitting in a quiet corner of the *praetorium* with the Primus Pilus, along with Macer, the three of us all with cups. It had been Sacrovir who uttered this, only after I had told, now for the fourth time, of all that I had witnessed with the Army of Pannonia, this final time for the benefit of the Pili Priores, who Sacrovir had sent for once he was satisfied that I had told him everything. First, of course, had been to Germanicus, but my second retelling had actually been to Alex, as I walked with him back out of camp to the smaller camp that was serving as Germanicus' *ad hoc* headquarters that he had ordered constructed on his first visit to the disaffected Legions, which was manned by a motley combination of Germanicus' personal bodyguards, a Century of auxiliaries, and two Centuries composed of rankers, one from the 1st and one from the 20th, who had remained openly loyal. It was similar in purpose, if constructed better, as the camp Sejanus had ordered outside the Pannonian Legions' camp, and Germanicus had assured me that there had been no attempt on the part of the mutineers to seize control, or to make any threatening overtures. To demonstrate his faith in the Legions, at least as far as his personal security was concerned, he had allowed his wife and youngest child to accompany us from Ubiorum, which was the only reason I had consented to bring not only Titus, but Algaia with me. I know that it was somewhat cruel, but I made no mention as to *why* we were going to Germanicus' camp, aside from mumbling something vague about needing to retrieve something there. Alex was clearly skeptical, but he was more interested in hearing about what I had been through than trying to decipher what I was up to, which I divulged only by entering the *quaestorium* and insisting Alex enter first. It took a moment as, his eyes slowly adjusting to the dim lighting, he glanced around the interior, where some of Germanicus' clerks who worked for him in his role of *Propraetor* had been consigned, along with a half-dozen *immunes* attending to various tasks, and in fact I saw him pass over the young man and woman sitting there on sacks of grain against one wall of the tent, watching us in the doorway. Then, his head swiveled back around to the pair, and perhaps a heartbeat after that, I had to steady my nephew as his mind caught up with his eyes. This was the last coherent moment, as Titus leapt to his feet, ran to his brother, and threw himself into Alex's embrace, both of them openly sobbing with happiness at seeing each other. Only Algaia hung back, but while I would have loved to stay and observe this small reunion that I had created, there was too much waiting back at camp for me to stay. I gave Alex the pass I had gotten from Germanicus that allowed Titus and Algaia spots in the tents belonging to the servants, although Algaia was going to be staying with Agrippina's retinue of female attendants and slaves, and permission for Alex to remain out of the main camp overnight.

Only then did Alex seem to regain at least some of his senses, because he reached out and grabbed my arm as I turned away. "Uncle Titus! Wait! I haven't told you about everything that's happened!"

"Don't worry about that," I assured him. "I'm sure I'll hear all about it from Macer."

"But what about the Century? Don't you want to hear about Structus and what he's been up to?"

I could see that this truly bothered him, reminding me how seriously he took his duties as the chief clerk for the Century, but I also knew that, while Alex could certainly provide some important insight into what had transpired during my absence, his observation was not the one that mattered; ultimately, it was what Macer, my Pilus Prior, and Sacrovir, my Primus Pilus, thought. Naturally, I did not say this. It was plain to see he was torn about whether to return with me, but I gave him a nod of my head, towards his brother and the girl, so he obeyed me; when I left them standing outside the *quaestorium*, it was with the sounds of tearful laughter and excited chatter in my ears. During my return to the camp, which was about two furlongs away from Germanicus', I thought about how Titus was going to explain the presence of the Breuci girl, and more importantly, how Alex would react to the idea of his younger brother having a woman of his own, especially since Alex had been dismissed by the girl he loved when someone with better prospects showed up, which had only occurred because he had heeded my poor advice and not made any kind of commitment to her. When I returned to the *praetorium*, I learned the reason it was not packed full of men, being informed that, unlike the Pannonian camp, an agreement had been reached that allowed men the freedom of the camp until darkness, when those officers who remained loyal were expected to either return to the *praetorium* or, if they chose to stay in their quarters, they agreed not to leave them until daylight. While I did not ask how this came about, I did not need to, at least as to why this liberty extended to only the daylight hour; plotting and conspiring is rarely conducted when the sun is up. Consequently, I made my way to the Legion office, whereupon I spent a third of a watch before the sun went down just with the Primus Pilus, but it was a singularly unsatisfying and unsettling experience, because while he pumped me for information about all that had transpired in Pannonia, he gave me very little detail about what had happened with our own Legion. Then, he said something that, while true, I found a bit odd that he would bring it up.

"Actually," he spoke in a contemplative tone, his eyes narrowed as he examined me sitting across the desk, "you're in a unique position, Pullus. You saw the men down in Pannonia and their mood, and you'll have the chance to observe them here. You," he pointed a blunt finger, "can be very valuable, both to me and to the *Propraetor*."

All I could think to say was that I was happy to do whatever was asked of me, and then I was dismissed. Before either of us could speak again, there was a knock on the door, and the clerk announced that the call to return to the *praetorium* had sounded.

"I'd normally spend the night here, but we still have things to discuss."

We both got up and exited Sacrovir's private quarters, just in time to see my Pilus Prior, who had heard I was back, entering with a broad smile on his face, while he was greeted by the same on my own, and we clasped arms. Sacrovir informed him of his decision to go to the *praetorium* for the night, and while he did not order Macer to accompany us, he immediately turned around and the three of us walked back to the *praetorium*. We were far from alone; Sacrovir told me that about a third of the Centurions and Optios in both Legions did not feel safe staying in their own tents at night, and made the nightly pilgrimage to the *praetorium*, but what struck me was how relatively calm it was. When I remarked on this, however, I saw Macer and Sacrovir exchange a glance, but it was the Primus Pilus who said, "Don't worry. That will change once the sun goes down and the wine starts flowing."

By then, we had reached the *praetorium,* entered and gone to the spot Sacrovir had appropriated as his own whenever he was in the tent, using his status as one of the two Primi Pili to claim a larger space than everyone else. The office and the private quarters for the commander was currently being occupied by the Legate for the 1st and 20th, Gaius Caetronius, who, unlike Blaesus, had not ventured outside of his office for anything other than calls of nature, and only then, with an escort, at least according to what Sacrovir had told me. With Germanicus' arrival, he had essentially been banished to the *Propraetor's* tent in the other camp, which, despite its small dimensions, still sported a headquarters tent even larger than normal, which was natural since Germanicus was both governor and commander. Not, I would add, that I ever heard even a whisper that Caetronius fought being essentially sent out of harm's way. We sat down on stools, and after a brief toast to my return, we all took a sip, then Sacrovir finally uttered the first words about the mutiny here.

"It *is* a fucking mess," Macer immediately echoed Sacrovir, when I instinctively glanced over at my Pilus Prior for confirmation, which I saw did not please the Primus Pilus, though he said nothing about it.

"How so?" I asked, somewhat puzzled, which I explained, telling them what I had heard in Mogontiacum, which prompted Sacrovir and Macer to exchange an amused glance.

"Well, it's good to see that the money the *Propraetor* spent to spread that tale appears to have been well spent," Sacrovir commented. Then, after another sip, he collected his thoughts, and began, "I'm not saying this as a criticism of Germanicus, Pullus, I want to make that clear." I thought this was an odd thing for a Primus Pilus to say to a subordinate, until I thought about it later and recognized that Sacrovir understood I had a relationship with Germanicus. He went on, "I think his reasoning was sound, that the respect the men held for him under normal circumstances would stand him in good stead, but not this time."

Essentially, the tale Sacrovir told of Germanicus' ordeal paralleled what I saw with Drusus, in that just his appearance, as a sign of good faith on the part of our new *Imperator*, was not enough to assuage the mutineers, which also aligned with what Germanicus had told me the day before. What I learned from Sacrovir, that Germanicus had not mentioned, was that he first visited the 5th and 21st, who were in a marching camp a short distance across the river from Mogontiacum, whereupon the mutinying men surrounded him as he entered. And, in a manner similar to what Drusus endured, he was accosted by men who were intent on showing the physical symbols of all that they had endured during their time under the standard. While Drusus had been unable to impose any sense of order on the mutineers, Germanicus was at least able to convince the men to assemble in the forum, in their proper spots in the formation, whereupon he made his plea for the men not to continue with this action. Rather than settling the men down, his words only inflamed them further, and the formation dissolved into an angry mob, surrounding the rostrum from which Germanicus was speaking. Another difference was that, unlike Drusus, who was not physically touched by any of the men, some rankers actually grabbed Germanicus by the hand and thrust it into their mouths so that he could feel their teeth, or more accurately, the absence of them, while others confronted him with their scars, pulling up their tunics to display them. For once, Germanicus' ability to connect with all ranks was used against him, as he was surrounded by men who were demanding that he should declare himself *Imperator*, promising that they would march on Rome if necessary to raise him to the purple. That Germanicus recoiled at this suggestion did not surprise me in the slightest, but men who had only viewed him from afar and had never been directly involved with the *Propraetor*, were certain that his protestations were simply a matter of form and not sincere. Consequently, when Germanicus declared that he would rather end himself than be part of this usurpation of power, not only were the mutineers unmoved, according to Sacrovir, who had been in communication with the Primus Pilus of the 21st, one of them actually produced his own *gladius*, declaring that it was sharper than Germanicus' own, identifying this man as one Calusidius, from the 5th Legion. As I sat there listening, I was assailed by so many different thoughts and emotions that it made my stomach churn, realizing that, in some ways, matters with the Rhenus Legions had been direr than with the Pannonian. Thankfully, the actions of this Calusidius were so startling that it shook enough men from their madness that, forming an impromptu bodyguard that protected the *Propraetor*, they enabled him to escape to the *praetorium* tent, which in an identical manner to Pannonia and to our own camp, had been declared a sanctuary for those who refused to participate in the mutiny.

Hearing this part prompted me to ask, "Where were Germanicus' personal bodyguards?"

Sacrovir gave a snort of disgust, replying, "Outside the camp."

Seeing my face, I suppose, Macer broke in, the first time he spoke. "The *Propraetor* refused to let them accompany him into the camp, Pullus. Apparently," he hesitated, then continued, "he was certain that the men wouldn't do him any harm."

"Well," Sacrovir broke in, "he learned differently." Once more, my face must have betrayed my alarm, because he assured me, "No, in the end, he wasn't hurt. But supposedly it was a close-run thing. And," he added with some grim humor, "I suppose that in one way, he can thank that bastard Calusidius for waking up some of the men that Germanicus was in real danger."

"What happened then?" I asked.

Sacrovir continued, emphasizing that this was all secondhand, but from a source he trusted, the man being a fellow Primus Pilus, and I understood why he would feel that way. According to the Primus Pilus, when Germanicus was relatively safe inside the *praetorium*, therein a debate raged for more than three watches, with one faction insisting that to give any concessions at all would set a dangerous precedent, and would only invite further trouble. This, in essence, was the same argument I had heard in Pannonia, which I mentioned. Finally, Germanicus decided to make what, in hindsight, was a desperate and foolish move, and when Sacrovir described what took place, I was reminded that, of the few flaws that Germanicus possessed, one that I had observed during my time with him, and was a common one among the upper classes of Rome, was his belief that because the vast majority of Head Counters were uneducated, it also meant that they were stupid. That this is not the case Germanicus learned the hard way, when his solution was to forge documents that he claimed to have carried from Tiberius, essentially granting all of the mutineers' demands. Specifically, those men who had already served their twenty years, instead of being extended for another five, would be released immediately and unconditionally, while those men who had at least sixteen years of service would be released as well, with the only condition being they be available to serve in the event the Germans finally did invade across the Rhenus, for a period of four years. Finally, all the donatives that had been promised in the last years of the Princeps' reign and in the aftermath of his death were promised to be paid to the men. If Germanicus had led with this, instead of trying to prevail upon the men's sense of duty, honor, and loyalty to Rome, perhaps this might have worked...for a period of time, until Tiberius became aware of his adopted son's deception. Of course, it was entirely within the realm of possibility that the new *Imperator* would feel he had no choice but to go along with Germanicus' fiction; for the safety of my family and myself, I will not divulge any more than to say that this was certainly a *possibility*. What transpired, and caught Germanicus by surprise, was the mutineers immediately seeing through this fiction, for the simple reason that, if he had been in possession of these documents when he arrived, he would have presented them immediately, instead of prevaricating and trying to essentially shame the men into ending their revolt. Not surprisingly, Germanicus' attempt to deceive the men served to exacerbate the tensions rather than reduce them, creating an atmosphere that was so volatile that the *Propraetor* had asked the mutineers for another chance to address them, and when they assembled in the forum, he promised that, out of his own personal funds, he would pay all of the donatives demanded by the men. As for the issue of the length of enlistment terms, he informed them that, while he did not have the authority to make that concession, he begged the mutineers to be patient, because a delegation from Rome was heading for Germania. While this quelled the worst of the violence, it quickly became clear to Germanicus that the situation was still extremely volatile, so under the cover of night, he left the camp and returned first to Mogontiacum to retrieve his family, then went to Ubiorum. That his wife and youngest child accompanied him into such a potentially dangerous situation requires some explanation, particularly as it pertains to his young son.

Germanicus Julius Caesar is devoted to his family, something that I knew was not exaggerated for effect; the man truly loves both his wife and his children. However, it was his youngest son Gaius who was adored by the hard-bitten men of the Legions. He had been given the nickname Caligula, both because Germanicus' wife Agrippina had had a small but completely accurate Legionary's uniform made for the boy as soon as he could walk, down to his *caliga*, and also to differentiate him from Germanicus' oldest son, who was named Gaius as well, yet another consequence of the peculiarly Roman habit of only having about a dozen names to choose from, and our fixation for using the same names within a family. His wife, Agrippina, was also popular with the men, held up as a model of what a Roman woman, wife, and mother should be, and she was certainly fertile, having several children, although some of them died young. However, while the older children had been left back in Rome, Germanicus had Agrippina and his youngest, the toddling boy Gaius who had been informally adopted by us as something of a good luck charm, remain with him in Germania, although there was a fair amount of gossip that our *Propraetor*'s strong-willed wife made it clear he had no real choice in the matter.

Absorbing everything Sacrovir told me took a few moments, then I asked, "What about here?" Suddenly, the Primus Pilus did not seem disposed to continue, and I saw him glance over at Macer, who shifted uncomfortably in his chair as he peered down into his cup, which prompted me to say, only half-jokingly, "That bad?"

This at least served to elicit a response from the Primus Pilus, who echoed, "Bad?" He considered for a moment, then shook his head, "I wouldn't say that it's bad, exactly. It's just that some things took place that I would have preferred hadn't happened."

He lapsed into silence then, prompting Macer to explain, "Some of the troublemakers managed to slip out of camp and make their way to where the 5th and 21st were camped, and told the leaders of the mutiny there that both the 1st and the 20th had made plans to return to Ubiorum and burn it to the ground, then head for Gaul." He paused for a heartbeat, then finished, "Where we were going to march from one settlement and town to another, burning everything down until Tiberius gave in."

Perhaps the only good thing is that I did not have a mouthful of wine, because I would have spewed it all over my Pilus Prior; instead, I simply felt my jaw drop open as I stared at him incredulously, although I knew from his expression he was not joking.

All I could think to say was, "Germanicus didn't mention any of that to me when I reported to him."

It was Sacrovir who gave a short bark of a laugh, saying with bitter amusement, "If you were him, would you?"

"So," I realized that there was still so much I did not know, and I had grown tired from what was an eventful day, "where do things stand now?"

"The real violence and unrest is over for the most part, although there's certainly still a lot discontent." Sacrovir answered. Then, he added, "Thanks to a handful of men. But as of this moment, we're waiting for that delegation from Rome to arrive."

With that, I asked to be excused, which Sacrovir granted, along with Macer, whereupon we walked into the *quaestorium*, where space had been cleared for the cots belonging to those of us who had chosen to take shelter there, and I asked him about Structus, who had been with the mutineers when I left.

"Actually," Macer informed me, "there's some good news on that front. In fact," he turned and pointed to the section of the large tent where all the Optios were staying, "you can see for yourself."

Following his finger, I saw my Optio, who had not seen me, perhaps because he was involved in a dice game with about a half-dozen other Optios and a couple Centurions, and I looked back at Macer with a raised eyebrow, though I said nothing.

"He showed up outside the *praetorium* the day after you left. He wanted to explain why he seemed to be siding with the mutineers."

"And?" I asked coldly. "He must have convinced you."

"He convinced me, and he convinced the Primus Pilus," Macer said quietly, "and he's the one that matters when all is said and done." This was something I could not argue, but neither did I like it, although I suspect that I am not alone in feeling that it should be the Centurion who is the direct superior of an Optio whose opinion counts the most. Macer continued, "He's like a lot of us, Titus. He agrees that there should be a redress of these grievances, and his goal was to try and keep the men of your Century out of the worst part of all the troublemaking. And," he allowed, "for the most part, he was successful." However, there was something in his voice that caused me to look over at him, which he caught. Giving me an awkward shrug, he added, "I do wish he had been a bit...stricter with a couple of your men. Or," he amended, "one in particular."

"Pusio." I confess it was not as much a guess as a confirmation of what I had assumed, and Macer nodded.

"Pusio," he agreed. "Pullus, he was one of the men who left the camp to go to the 5th and 21st."

This was something I had suspected the moment Macer had informed me of this, but hearing it confirmed was still like a stab in the gut, and I renewed my inner oath to rid my Century, Cohort, and Legion of Pusio. However, despite being somewhat disappointed in Structus, I understood how he felt about the situation, as well as his hesitance in dealing with Pusio, because that would have been a bold move by an Optio, even when acting Centurion, to either handle himself or arrange the removal of a ranker through unofficial means, no matter how justified or needed the act might have been. Otherwise, Macer assured me that the Third Century was in good shape, in a relative sense, and no more or less disaffected and angry than the rest of the Legion.

"I just worry about what happens if Tiberius refuses to agree with Germanicus' concessions," Macer commented, echoing the same concern Domitius and his comrades had voiced.

"When do you think we'll hear?" I asked, since I did not know the specific chronology of events as far as the Rhenus Legions sending their demands to Tiberius.

"The Primus Pilus thinks it will be any day now," Macer replied. "No more than another week anyway."

We parted then, and I went to find something to eat in a thoughtful, pensive mood, wondering why Germanicus had not been more forthcoming about what had taken place here. Not, I acknowledged to myself, that he owed me anything of the kind, but I did find it troubling that matters were far more volatile here than he had led me to believe.

Oddly enough, there was something else going on that helped distract me, but in a good way, and that was watching Alex and Titus getting reacquainted. Once they had spent the night in Germanicus' camp, Alex had returned to spending his nights in the Century office, while Titus was allowed to come and go, though he spent every night in Germanicus' camp. My initial thought with Titus had been to find him a position as a clerk somewhere in the Legion, like Alex, except it quickly became apparent that Titus was not cut out to be a scribe. It was not due to a lack of intelligence as much as it was a paucity of interest in anything that kept him indoors and sitting at a desk, although I will also say that, once I saw his hand at letters, I understood that Titus as a clerk would have been a disaster. For the first days after our arrival, I was content to allow the brothers to spend time together, which meant that Alex was absent from the office probably more than he should have been, then I finally put an end to it by informing Titus that I was giving him a choice.

"If you want to be attached to the Legion, it will have to be as a laborer or handling stock," I explained, but when his face lit up, I held up a hand, cautioning him, "Titus, that means that you'll be working with mostly slaves." When he shrugged and said this did not matter, I realized that he did not fully comprehend the import, and I added, "It also means that you're going to be treated like the slaves are treated, at least to a certain degree."

This seemed to get through to him, but I confess I was a little irritated when Titus looked to Alex for confirmation, which his older brother was quick to do, telling him simply, "You don't want to do that, Titus."

Although he accepted this, it was clear to see he was not happy about it, and he asked, "Then what else can I do?"

"I've thought about that," I assured him, "and personally, I think it's better that you're not attached to the Legion. So…"

"But why?" Titus cut me off, his face reddening, clearly surprised, and if I was any judge, a little hurt. "If it's good enough for Alex, why isn't it good enough for me?"

Before I could reply, Alex spoke up, his voice quiet but also matter of fact, explaining, "Because of Mama, Titus."

"What do you mean 'because of Mama'?" Titus' expression turned suspicious, and he asked accusingly, "Did Mama write you and tell you not to let me work with the Legion?"

"No," Alex countered, rolling his eyes. "How could she have gotten a letter to me before you showed up? I didn't even know you were coming."

I could see that, while he did not like it, Titus recognized this as the truth, but he persisted, "Then why don't you want me working with you, and if Mama didn't write you, what does she have to do with it?"

"Because if she lost both of us," Alex answered calmly, "it would kill her."

Titus looked as if Alex had punched him in the stomach, his mouth dropping open, and it took him a couple of attempts before he managed, "What...what do you mean?"

Instead of answering, Alex looked up at me, which I took as the sign he was asking me to let Titus know the brutal truth, and I did not hesitate.

"What he means is that we're almost certainly going on campaign this coming season," I said. "And we're finally going to be going after Arminius. It's probably going to be the hardest fighting this Legion will ever see."

I hoped this would be enough, but Titus, while he was not slow-witted, was completely inexperienced in the reality of life under the standard, having been too young to remember that much about his life in Siscia when Diocles had been alive and brought his family back with Sextus.

"So? What does that have to do with being a laborer or a clerk like Alex?"

"You remember what happened to Varus and his Legions?" Alex broke in, and when Titus nodded, he said, "How many of the noncombatants attached to the Legion do you think survived?"

There was a look of dawning recognition on Titus' face, yet he still seemed reluctant to give in, which prompted me to add, "And how do you think they died, Titus? Do you think the Germans who slaughtered the men of three Legions in the most horrible manner you could imagine were merciful to the slaves and freedmen?" Before he could respond, I continued, determined to impress on Titus the possible fate that awaited him. "Remember, I was there at Caedicius' camp, Titus. We found what was left of the bodies, and even though they were just bones by then, you could see they had been mutilated and defiled, and that was just a small portion of Varus' army. Now," I nodded to Alex, "your brother has been part of the Legion and he's been on campaign, and he's been through battle. If he's telling you that you don't want any part of this, if you're not going to think about yourself, then think about your mother and your sisters and brother."

Thankfully, this was enough, so that when I informed Titus that I would make arrangements for him to become an apprentice to one of the town's civilian blacksmiths, which I had thought was a good compromise, he did not balk. It is certainly a physically challenging job, but it would keep Titus from being attached to the Legion, which had been Alex's request to me. I will not say he was enthused at first, but he did not reject it outright; the next topic I just hoped went as smoothly.

"What about Algaia?" I asked Titus, and his face, which had returned to normal, became flushed again, except this time, he did not seem to be upset with me, but looked at Alex.

Who, I saw, was similarly flustered, and I got a sinking feeling in my stomach that I was not going to like what I heard next.

"What about her?" Titus responded in what I took as a challenging tone.

"What are her plans?" I asked, but to this, he just gave a shrug, making at least an attempt at indifference.

"How should I know?" he shot back, then in a confirmation of my growing suspicion, he pointed at Alex. "Why don't you ask him? He knows more about her…plans than I do!"

Before I could stop myself, a groan came from my lips, and I glared at Alex, who initially tried to meet my eyes, then turned even redder than he had been a heartbeat before.

"Gods, boy, what did you do? It's only been three days since they showed up!"

"Nothing!" Alex protested, but between his brother's angry stare and my own examination of him, his shoulders slumped, and he mumbled, "I mean, I didn't mean to do anything."

Over the next few moments, the story came out, and by the time I had heard both sides, I was not sure whether I should laugh or cry, but I was certain of one thing; the true architect of this small crisis among the brothers was the Breuci girl. Ultimately, I think that Algaia, while certainly taken with young Titus, as he was with her, upon meeting his older brother, made a calculation that Alex presented the best opportunity for a better life between the two of them. And, initially, once this matter came to my attention, my reaction was one of anger towards the girl; until, that is, I recalled what she had been forced to endure at the hands of my brother. After all, I realized, the whole reason I had removed her from my brother's household had been to offer her a better life, so how could I fault her for doing that very thing, even if it did mean that young Titus had to suffer a broken heart? Not to mention the guilt that his older brother felt, although it was not enough to dissuade him from forming a relationship with Algaia; as I write this, they are essentially man and wife. Of course, Titus did not view matters in this light, but I am happy to report that his broken heart was soon mended, aided in large part by the daughter of the smith to which he is now apprenticed. Perhaps the best part of all this is that it provided a diverting interlude before the final part of the crisis that was the mutiny of the Legions.

The delegation from Rome did not arrive for another four days, making it well into the last week of October, and it is sufficient to say that the tensions that had been dissipated enough to achieve an uneasy peace that allowed those who remained loyal the freedom of the camp during the day began rising again. There had been no overt acts of violence after my return, something for which all of the officers were thankful, but we also all suspected this could not last forever, though I know we all hoped that it would. My Century was no different from any of the others; the men performed their routine duties that are necessary to exist in a marching camp just well enough that I was not forced to take steps to enforce discipline, but it was a far cry from what I had set as the standard. Unfortunately, the arrival of the delegation served to inflame the passions that had been smoldering, when, upon entering our camp from Germanicus' small one to meet with the *Propraetor*, who was now spending his days in the *praetorium* of the larger camp, one of those men sent from Rome was recognized as Lucius Munatius Plancus, who had served as Consul just the year before. Since I was not outside of the headquarters tent at that moment, I cannot say exactly how events unfolded, but the version that was most repeated was that, when Plancus was recognized, one of the troublemakers loudly claimed that the only reason such a lofty personage as a former Consul would be sent from Rome was to revoke all the concessions that had been extracted from Germanicus. This obviously found a receptive audience, because from what I heard, the delegation was quickly surrounded by angry rankers, whereupon matters rapidly escalated from merely angry words to threats of violence against Plancus. Events worsened so quickly that Plancus and the delegation, numbering a dozen men, were forced to flee through the camp, dashing across the forum to the *praetorium*, with an angry mob of men from both Legions chasing them, furiously declaring their intentions to slaughter these men who, thanks to one of the mutineers essentially convincing his comrades this was the case, they were now convinced had come to strip them of all those concessions. Plancus was not a young man – when I saw the rest of the deputation, my guess is the youngest was in his late thirties – but despite his age, Plancus proved fleet of foot, making it into the *praetorium*, which was still mutually agreed to be sacrosanct. However, this time, the chasing mutineers did not stop at the front flap, instead choosing to continue their pursuit of Plancus, who was the focal point of their anger and hatred, bursting into the large outer office.

It was from this point forward that I can attest to what occurred, because I happened to be in the *praetorium*, along with a few dozen other Centurions and Optios from both Legions, to witness everything that happened, something I have never seen before, nor do I hope to ever witness anything like it again, because it shook all of us who were there to our core. We heard a commotion outside, of course, before Plancus came through the flap, which was thrown open for him by a quick-thinking provost standing guard, so our collective attention was turned to the entry. Which meant that we saw the mutineers who, rather than stopping at the spot a half-dozen paces from the entrance where a pair of posts had been driven into the ground that marked the boundary, as they had always done before, instead continued their pursuit, the men in the lead hurling themselves at the pair of provosts to be the first through the entrance, both of whom I was not surprised to see chose to duck out of the way, and honestly, I could not really blame them. Under other circumstances, I suppose it would be considered comical, given how four men tried to jam themselves through an entrance where only three normal-sized men might fit, creating something of a logjam. Equally unsurprising, given their state of what I think was hysterical fury at the thought they were about to lose all that they had gained, none of the four were willing to give way to the others, so for the span of a couple heartbeats, they were jammed together, shoulders pressed tightly against each other, snarling at the nearest man pinned next to them with a hatred that, to my eyes, looked every bit as potent as that which they were aiming towards Plancus. Frankly, I was surprised that the canvas did not rip, so it could not have been that long, because before either that happened or those of us nearest to the doorway could react, one of the men in the middle managed to wriggle free and lurched forward into the office. Speaking of the former Consul, he had taken a staggering step in our general direction, and while I had never seen the man before, the naked fear on his face was plain to see, his hands outstretched in a plea to us to help save him.

"What do we do?" I recognized Macer's voice, not daring to turn my attention away from what was taking place no more than fifteen paces away.

Before anyone could respond, however, more of the mutineers poured into the tent, which spurred Plancus back into action. Panting from the exertion and, no doubt, fear, he resumed moving, and at first I was unsure of his intent, because he did not head directly towards the opposite side, where the flap that served as the door to Germanicus' office was located. His eyes glanced about wildly, and just as the first man through the door was reaching to grab him, he darted to the side, directly for the small altar where, when the Legions are in camp, the standards are placed. There are actually two of these altars, on opposite sides of the outer office, for each Legion, and I do not know if it was by design, or just because he was slightly closer to it, but he lurched towards the standard of the 1st. The leading mutineer, who I recognized as a man of the 1st, although I could not place him any more specifically than that in the moment, managed to snatch the very edge of Plancus' toga, which he had worn into the camp because of the official nature of his visit, giving a good yank on it. This did not stop Plancus; somehow, he managed to wriggle free of the heavy folds of white cloth, which I noticed was now spattered with mud, presumably from his dash across the camp, and in doing so, he went stumbling up to the altar in just his tunic.

Reaching out with both hands, Plancus grabbed the stout pole of the standard, and in a voice that betrayed his abject fear, screeched, "I claim sanctuary! I claim sanctuary under the eagle!"

This had absolutely no effect on his pursuers, the others having caught up to the first man, who had hurled the toga from him in disgust, but thankfully for Plancus, and probably every man in both Legions, Gnaeus Calpurnius, the *Aquilifer* of the 1st, who was both present in the building and happened to be standing next to the altar, literally leapt in between Plancus and the men who were about to tear him to pieces.

"Brothers!" Calpurnius bellowed. *"Stop this madness! Don't shame our Legion like this!"*

Now, if by some act of the gods, all that was going on could have been stopped, with everyone frozen in place, and I had been asked if I thought Calpurnius' words would have any effect, I would have declared absolutely not. And, I will also say that for one of the few times in my life, I would have been happy to be wrong, because this did indeed stop the men in their tracks. Not, it should be said, that it suddenly cooled their ardor for Plancus' blood, but they managed to confine their actions to verbal threats as they surrounded Calpurnius and the visibly trembling former Consul, shaking their fists at the pair, declaring that this was not a cessation, but an interruption of their plans to murder Plancus. It is with a certain amount of shame that I say that I had done nothing other than stand, rooted to my spot, watching in gape-mouthed astonishment; all I can say in my defense is that I was far from alone. In truth, it was only Calpurnius who leapt into action, while everything I have just described took perhaps fifty heartbeats from the moment we heard the commotion to this one, which I suppose can be called an excuse for my inaction. Regardless of the reason, this was where matters stood when the flap to Germanicus' office was thrust aside, and he emerged, clearly alarmed. Dividing my attention between Germanicus, the mutineers, and Calpurnius and Plancus, simply because I did not think this cessation of physical hostility would last, I saw the play of emotions crossing the *Propraetor's* face as his eyes took in the scene. The sudden presence of Germanicus seemed to have almost as much of an impact on the mutineers clustered together around their former quarry as the actions of Calpurnius to stop them from fulfilling their dire promises, but his tone seemed equally helpful to his cause.

"What," he did not have to raise his voice because his appearance had stopped the shouting instantly, "is the meaning of all this?"

Faced as they were by the presence of the man who, despite everything that had taken place, all but a handful of men, proportionally speaking, still admired and respected, none of the mutineers seemed anxious to speak up. Although, I noticed, most of them turned their attention to the mutineer who had managed to divest Plancus of his toga, and finally, after glaring at his comrades, he was the man who responded.

Pointing a finger at Plancus, who was still cowering behind Calpurnius – I was close enough to see the tremor in it, which I found telling – the ranker said, "This man came here to break all the promises *you* made to us!"

The manner in which he said this, and the way he put it, made me think that he hoped that somehow Germanicus would share in the indignation. Despite the tension and gravity of this moment, I had to suppress a snort of disgust that this ranker would actually think this might work.

"Who told you that my promises were broken?" Germanicus asked, reasonably enough given the circumstances.

Now the mutineer did not look quite as certain; apparently, he was bright enough to understand where this might be heading, but he was not ready to capitulate just yet, answering stubbornly, "Nobody did, but we don't need to be told, do we, boys?" He turned to his fellow mutineers for support, and while they gave it, there was a mumbled quality that indicated their hearts might not be in it as much as he might have hoped or needed. Turning back to Germanicus, he finished, "It's obvious!"

Again, Germanicus maintained his calm demeanor, asking reasonably, "Obvious to whom?..." His voice trailed off in a manner that made it clear he wanted the mutineer to give his name, and he confirmed this by adding, "I'd rather not just address you by your rank, Gregarius. This," he pointed in the direction of Plancus, "is too important a matter not to know who is representing you men." Then, without any warning, his voice hardened, "You men who were about to do harm to an *ambassador of ROME!*" Germanicus did not bellow often, which made this even more effective, and he did not relent, continuing in the same tone if not quite the volume. "Men who are considered protected and untouchable by any *civilized* nation! Are you barbarians?" He paused a beat, then his voice softened, and there was what sounded like a plaintive note when he asked, "Is that what you've become? Barbarians? Savages who can't be trusted to honor a convention that has been in place for centuries?"

I cannot say that this was taken well by the mutineers; several of them looked angry, but more of them suddenly looked ashamed, breaking the stare of their general by either looking at the floor or glancing to one another.

The mutineer who had spoken either sensed that Germanicus' words were having an impact on his comrades, or perhaps the words hit home with him personally, but he was still not quite ready to capitulate.

The defiance in his demeanor returned somewhat, which meant I was quite surprised when he answered Germanicus' first question, saying, "My name is *Gregarius Immune* Publius Quintidius, Fourth of the Eighth," then he confirmed my suspicion, "of the 1st Legion. That standard," he nodded in the direction of the eagle, "is as much mine as any man's in the Legion, I don't care who they are!" Pausing for a moment to lick his lips, betraying the true state of his nerves, the now-named Quintidius demanded, "And, if it's as you say, that it's not a given that the *Imperator* is breaking your promise, then when will we know?" Turning and giving a contemptuous look at Plancus, who was still clinging to the standard with one hand, although he had at least pulled himself erect, he demanded, "Will he tell us now?" This seemed to restore some of his equilibrium, because the mutineer finished, "We could end this all right now, sir. All he has to do is tell us a simple 'yes' or 'no.'"

Germanicus did not hesitate, replying coldly, "He will do no such thing. Not right now. We," he indicated Plancus, "must have a chance to confer first."

By this point, I could see that the majority of the men who had come bursting into the *praetorium* had cooled their ardor enough to understand that they had almost committed a crime so serious, so unforgivable, that not one Roman citizen, nor most men under the standard, would have any sympathy for the perpetrators. Some of them were glancing over their shoulders at the door, and had begun taking small but noticeable steps in that direction. One of the men standing immediately behind Quintidius leaned forward and whispered something in his ear; it became clear what it was when he glanced over his shoulder, took in the collective mood of his comrades, then realized that he had been thwarted. He might have taken it upon himself to be the man who spoke for them, but he obviously understood that, without the support of his fellow mutineers, he had no chance of winning this battle.

His face contorted in a fury that was no less vehement because he recognized he had lost, but he managed to answer, "Very well, *Propraetor*. It will be as you say. But," I suspect that he could not stop himself from trying to salvage something of his pride, "we'll be outside." Turning back to Plancus, he finished ominously. "Waiting."

Without exception, every one of the intruders walked backward towards the door, with Quintidius out last. The sight of the flap falling served as a signal, as I believe every single man in the *praetorium* exhaled at the same time. Germanicus' expression of calm resolve vanished in the time it took for the flap to close, his face instantly transforming into the look of grave concern that I had witnessed on a handful of occasions during the Batonian revolt. Those of us who had not moved a step from the spots we had been occupying when this whole episode began only then made any move, and I turned in the direction of Germanicus, though I cannot say why, since I should have conferred with Macer first, given he was my direct superior. I did feel my Pilus Prior's eyes on me, but I chose not to acknowledge him, intent as I was on speaking to Germanicus first, but before I reached him, he beckoned to the commander of his bodyguard, who was closer than I was and reached him first. I was within earshot, so I heard what the *Propraetor* said, and it sent a thrill of alarm through me.

"Go to my camp and find my wife." He sounded calm enough, but there was no mistaking the urgency in his voice. "Tell her that she needs to pack, quickly, taking only what she needs for herself and Gaius. I'm sending them back to Ubiorum as fast as possible."

"You don't think they're in danger, do you?"

I did not think I had spoken, but it was certainly my voice, and Germanicus, turning his attention to me, gave me an inquisitive glance.

"Why wouldn't I, Pullus?" he countered, then gestured towards the door. "You saw what just happened. They were about to kill Plancus just because of what they *thought* he was here for, to tell me that my father denied my request."

"I know," I acknowledged, but I could not accept what he was suggesting, "but they wouldn't do any harm to either Agrippina or little Gaius!" While I was certain he already knew, I thought to remind him, "You know what we call him, don't you?"

"Yes," Germanicus answered, nodding wearily. "I know the men call him Caligula. But," his tone turned firm, "Pullus, you're not a father, or a husband. You don't know what it's like to have a family." Shaking his head, he said flatly, "No, I'm not taking the chance that because the men think of Gaius as some sort of good luck charm, they wouldn't do anything to either him or Agrippina. Not after what I just saw."

I knew that Germanicus did not intend to be cruel, but his reminder to me of my loss did not sting less because of that. And, when I shoved the memory and the feeling that came with it back into the cupboard I keep it in my mind, I had to acknowledge that, given the reality of the situation, this was a sensible precaution.

"Now, if you'll excuse me," Germanicus, as always, was being polite, but it was no less of an order when he continued, "I need to go talk to Plancus."

Without waiting for an acknowledgement on my part, not that he needed one, he turned and walked over to where Calpurnius was standing next to the former Consul, our *Aquilifer* holding Plancus with a steadying arm, which was understandable given how shaken the man was. Taking this as my cue, only then did I return to Macer, who was now surrounded by Vespillo and Volusenus of the Centurions, and Structus, Closus, Sevilla, and Gillo of the Optios.

When I joined the group, Macer asked, "Where are Philus and Cornutus?"

It was Vespillo who answered, but while his tone was neutral, I was certain that his message was understood by our Pilus Prior.

"They're out in the camp. Along with Saloninus," Vespillo named his own Optio, then added with, what to my ears sounded like some satisfaction, "and yours, of course, Pilus Prior."

Macer shook his head, saying, "I sent Fabricius on an errand to go to the Cohort office and check on Lucco." He took a deep breath, then said, "That's probably where Philus and Cornutus are as well, taking care of something, or in their own offices. What about Saloninus? Is he doing something you told him to do?"

I know I was certainly aware that there was more going on in this exchange than what the words implied, but I wondered if Volusenus understood; a glance at his face informed me that he did.

Vespillo stiffened, but he did not try to dissemble, answering flatly, "No, Pilus Prior. He doesn't have my permission to be anywhere other than here."

Macer did not comment, just giving a nod, then he turned to Sevilla and Closus, telling them, "Go find your Centurions and order them to report to my quarters by the beginning of third watch." Turning to us, he said, "I need to go talk to the Primus Pilus. You all heard what time I expect you."

Without waiting for an acknowledgment, he turned and strode off.

Vespillo, as was his duty, was the one who took command, telling us, "We go back to the Cohort area together, in case those bastards out there are still angry enough to try something stupid."

Even if we had been disposed to argue, that it was the ranking Centurion meant we would obey, but I could see that the only other one who was not happy about this was the only other man in the Cohort who was my size. Regardless of the slight to our pride, neither of us said anything, and as we exited the *praetorium*, the other Centurions and Optios were busy organizing themselves in the same manner to return to their respective areas. This is what it's come to? I wondered. Just having a *vitus* or a white stripe isn't enough anymore? With that troubling thought rattling around in my head, I followed the others out.

"Tomorrow is going to be a big day," Macer began the meeting, albeit slightly delayed, "but first, we have to get through tonight. And," his face was grim, "you can hear that it's already not pretty."

This was something of an understatement; there had been no overt acts of violence, but the word of Plancus' arrival had swept through the camp, along with the attack on him, and I shuddered to imagine what the story being told about that sounded like. And, as I well knew, once the sun went down and with every passing watch through the night, that story would change, becoming more lurid, and more crucially, farther from what actually had taken place. Nothing any of us who had been present could say would have made any difference, given how most mutineers viewed Centurions and Optios at this particular moment. Only later would we learn that what had transpired inside the tent would certainly play a role in what was to come, but not in the way I, for one, would have thought. Meanwhile, our missing Centurions and Optios had been located, so Cornutus and Philus were present, but while nothing was said by Macer that might create an awkward situation concerning their whereabouts, I suspected that there would be a reckoning in the future.

"Does the Primus Pilus have any idea when we're going to find out why Plancus is here?" Volusenus asked.

Macer shook his head. "All I've been told is that we're having our normal morning formation as always." Then he added, "I think he wants to conduct business as usual."

"No chance of that," Cornutus muttered, loud enough for Vespillo and me, seated on either side, to hear, prompting us to exchange a look, wondering what he knew that we did not.

Macer either missed it or chose to ignore it, understandable given what came out of his mouth next.

"What we need to talk about now is how each of you are going to handle your troublemakers in the event that the news from Rome is bad."

"I know what we should do," Volusenus burst out, "and I suggested that we do it more than a week ago!"

This was news to me; I had only had one conversation with the young Hastatus Posterior since my return, and most of it had been devoted to me retelling my account of Pannonia.

Macer responded to Volusenus with a weary sigh. "Yes, Volusenus, I'm well aware of your feelings on the matter. But," his voice hardened, and he pointed directly at the young Centurion, who I saw suddenly stiffen out of the corner of my vision, "you're not going to do *anything* along those lines, especially now! Is that clear?"

Since it was appropriate, I swiveled in my chair to look directly at Volusenus, who was visibly fuming, making me wonder if it was Macer's words or the fact that our Pilus Prior had shaken a finger at him, given how much I loathed that myself.

Regardless of how he felt about it, or what the cause of his anger was, Volusenus' tone was controlled as he answered Macer, "Yes, Pilus Prior. I understand and will obey."

This satisfied Macer, and shortly thereafter, we were dismissed; all but Cornutus and Philus, that is, neither of whom looked happy at being held back, which I could understand, being close to positive I knew what questions our Pilus Prior would be asking them. I made sure to walk out with Volusenus, though I waited until the other Centurions had drawn away and were out of earshot to say, "I realize we've only talked once since I've been back, and I haven't heard about whatever it was you suggested to the Pilus Prior."

Volusenus glanced over at me, giving me the impression he was trying to determine my motives, but despite our rocky beginning, we had reached, if not a real friendship, then a mutual regard, at least partially based in our similar size and all that came with it.

Finally, he looked away and shrugged. "I thought we should arrest the men who are the troublemakers in each of our Centuries and separate them from the rest."

I immediately understood the appeal of this approach; it was certainly straightforward, but I think it was because of my experience, both as a Centurion and as one who had been either under the standard or around men who were for so much of my life that it prompted me to try and educate the young Centurion on why this was a bad idea.

Thinking for a moment, I decided to fall back on the manner in which first Scribonius, then Diocles used, so instead of telling, I began by asking, "On what charges would we have done that?"

Volusenus shrugged again, answering in an offhanded manner, "Whatever we could think up in the moment, because that's not important. What is would be getting these bastards away from the good men."

I sensed him glancing over at me, so I gave a thoughtful nod, then asked, "Then what?"

For the first time, Volusenus' face reflected an uncertainty, and he admitted, "Actually, I hadn't thought about what happened after that. Just that getting them away from their Century before the delegation got here would have given us a better chance to control the reaction of the men, in case things don't go well."

That, I was forced to admit to myself, was not a bad idea; at least, Volusenus' intentions were good and his judgment that this would help our cause was sound. What I realized, however, was that he had indeed not thought past the immediate benefit that would come from removing the men like Pusio.

"How do you think the rest of the men would have reacted?" I asked him.

To his credit, he clearly understood that I was not asking idly, so he was silent for a couple paces, then answered, "They probably wouldn't have liked it much. But," he insisted, not quite ready to concede the point, "not to the point where they would have done anything about it."

I did not hesitate, asking him pointedly, "How sure are you about that?" Seeing this had scored, I pressed further, "And, what if they *did* have a problem with it? Not," I allowed, "because they have any love for any of these faithless cocksuckers, but because in their minds, if it happened once, it could happen again. To them."

We had been slowing our pace as we talked, and now Volusenus came to a stop, turning to face me, and I saw the warring emotions playing across his face. He took a breath, let it out slowly, then answered, "I…see your point. But," his tone turned vehement, "I don't like the idea that a Centurion can't enforce discipline on his men! That we're hostages to our Century and have to make sure we don't do anything to displease them!"

Now I completely agreed with Volusenus in terms of his sentiment, but I also wanted to make something clear to him.

"First, I'd be more worried about you if you didn't feel that way. And, I will say that under normal circumstances, I'd never tell you what I just did, but these aren't ordinary circumstances.

In fact," I said truthfully, "I've never seen anything like what's happening now."

He seemed to consider this, then an expression crossed his features that I had not seen before, an awkward hesitance, and he finally asked, "Wasn't your grandfather at Pharsalus?" When I nodded, he asked, "Did you ever hear anything about how he handled it?"

This prompted a sudden stirring of feelings that were both unexpected and powerful, and it was a struggle to maintain my composure, but I did answer him, though I still do not completely understand how and why I did so in the manner that I did, because I divulged something that I had kept a secret from almost everyone but one or two very close, trusted friends, like Titus Domitius.

"Actually," I heard the words coming out of my mouth, and I recognized my voice, but it was as if someone else was saying them, "I know quite a bit about how he dealt with it, because he wrote about it in his account."

This clearly caught Volusenus by surprise; that is the only reason why I believe the first thing he blurted out was, "Your grandfather was literate? He knew his letters?"

My initial reaction was, naturally, one of irritation, then I reminded myself of his own background and that he was only repeating what most members of the equestrian class, along with the higher-ranking plebeians and patricians of course, believe. And, being brutally frank, he was not wrong to make that assumption.

Rather than making a biting retort, I simply answered, "Yes, he was actually quite well-read. Although," I acknowledged, "that was later in his life, once he was in the Centurionate."

Volusenus seemed to accept this and returned to the topic he had broached. "So, how did he deal with it?"

Again, I am not sure why, but Gaius Volusenus became one of the very few people in whom I confided the contents of my

Avus' extraordinary life, and I left nothing out when I described the events that followed Pharsalus and are as famous as the actual battle itself. We had stopped walking as he stood listening to me recounting how Titus Pullus had advanced his career by his display of loyalty, but at the expense of a lifelong friendship with Vibius Domitius. The only thing I left out was what I had just done in Pannonia to repay the debt of honor that I believe the Pullus family owed to the Domitius clan, although at this point in time, I had no way of knowing whether I had been successful or not. As might be expected, Volusenus listened intently, saying nothing as I talked, then once I was finished, he did not reply immediately, and I could see he was deep in thought.

"It sounds like," he finally said, speaking slowly as if the words were not coming easily, "that while it did his career a great deal of good, it wasn't without a heavy cost."

I cannot say how I was expecting Volusenus to respond, but it certainly was not like this, and I confess I was not only surprised, I was also impressed with his insight in discerning the hidden cost of my Avus' actions at Pharsalus.

"That's a good way of putting it," I replied. "That's very astute of you, Volusenus."

I was being completely sincere, which seemed to please him. We remained standing there in silence for a few heartbeats, then he finally said, "I'm just not sure what to do about my Century." He was looking down the street as he spoke, but then he glanced over at me, and I read in his face the uncertainty and the anxiety that, if every man wearing a transverse crest past and present was honest enough to admit, we all experience at some point in our respective careers. Continuing, he made a point to look me in the eye as he stressed, "It's not the whole Century, though. I don't want you to think I'm worried about all of them. There's just three," he stopped, amending himself, "actually, four men who are causing almost all of the trouble, but they've managed to influence a half-dozen more into doing things they've never done before."

"What kind of things?" I asked, more out of habit than anything, since I was certain I knew, and he confirmed it, replying, "Being slow to complete their daily duties, and they're slow to respond to orders, both from me and from Gillo."

"And you've figured out that beating them into a better frame of mind hasn't worked," I finished for him, and now he did not bother hiding his feelings, nodding unhappily. "Well," I assured him, "you're not the first man with a *vitus* to figure that out, and you won't be the last. And," I tried to imbue my voice with the sincerity I felt, "I've had the same issue in my Century."

"You mean Pusio?" Volusenus asked, and something in my expression he must have found amusing because he burst out laughing. At first, I was not happy with his reaction, but despite myself, I joined in, agreeing, "Yes, that bastard."

"He's famous," Volusenus commented, "and not just in the Fourth."

"Thanks for reminding me of that." I heard the sour note in my voice, but I could not help it. Returning to the larger problem, I told Volusenus, "I understand your frustration, Volusenus, I really do. But this isn't the time to try and take care of the problems you're having. Wait until tomorrow, and we'll have a better idea how to proceed."

"I know you're right," Volusenus sighed, "but it's just hard knowing that if I just got rid of a few men, my Century would be better for it."

His words reminded me of something I had heard my Avus say, and I told him, "My grandfather used to say that ninety percent of the problems a Centurion has in his Century are caused by ten percent of the men."

Volusenus absorbed this, nodding his head thoughtfully, agreeing, "That sounds about right."

Clapping him on the shoulder, I said lightly, but I was serious, "We both need to get ready for tomorrow. It's going to be a big day." Just as I said that, we heard a sudden clamor of voices several streets over, and there was no mistaking that whatever had caused the outburst, it was not because men were happy. This prompted me to amend, "But first, we have to get through the night."

Between the disturbance and the setting sun, we turned and headed for the *praetorium*, yet despite this reminder that matters were far from settled and that it was likely to be a long night, for some reason, I felt absurdly pleased about this exchange, thinking that perhaps I had done something that Gaius Volusenus would remember later in his career. And, I thought with some humor, maybe he'll be the old Centurion counseling the young one, and he'll say, "I served with the grandson of Titus Pullus, and he taught me..." Then, I turned my mind towards the immediate future, and suddenly, I did not feel quite so good.

Chapter Eleven

That night proved to be every bit as long as I feared, made even more so because, adhering to the orders of the Primus Pilus, the officers stayed in their respective quarters, their instructions from Sacrovir being that only in the direst emergency were they to leave them, and if at all possible, not go out alone. Although none of the Centurions of the Fourth discussed doing so beforehand, I found out later that we all had essentially the same idea. In my case, it was to have Structus, my *Signifer* Gemellus, who had refused to declare himself with the mutineers, Pictor, the Sergeant of the Fifth Section, and a couple other rankers come to my quarters. Alex, Balio, who I had picked up in Ubiorum and brought with me, and Structus' slave rounded out the company, which made for cramped conditions, but I was confident that any mutineer would think twice about making some sort of trouble outside the Century office, and they certainly would not try to storm it. Once this was done, we settled down to wait, each of us listening intently to the sounds of the night, while I would occasionally send Balio out to take a look around and report back. At least, that was how it started, until Alex realized what I was doing, whereupon he insisted that he and his fellow clerk alternate what, while not particularly hazardous, was not completely without danger. Along with this, every few moments, one of us would get up, open the flap just enough to stick our heads out, both to listen for any noises that would indicate something had occurred that might prove to be the figurative spark that would ignite a conflagration, but more than that, to sniff the air for any sign of a literal one. This, frankly, was my biggest concern, that either through outright malice or, just as likely, drunken exuberance, one of the men who loved to burn things would unleash the beast of fire. Even in a marching camp, especially when it had remained relatively dry for the previous few days, fire was always a concern under normal conditions.

At random intervals throughout the night, we would hear a sudden uproar, over and above the low-pitched but audible sound that occurs when thousands of men are talking loudly. While the Centurions of the Fourth all did essentially the same thing, as did most of the Centurions in the other Cohorts of the 1st, not every officer was so prudent, choosing instead to brazen it out, practically daring their men to incite some sort of violent action against their officers by insisting on walking about their area. In almost every case, this turned out to be a horrible idea, although we would not learn that until later, but it was only through the intervention of the gods that, somehow, none of these foolhardy men were killed. Beaten, some of them severely enough to be put into the hospital, but not killed, and I shudder to think what might have happened in that event. Despite being sure I would not sleep myself, I set watches to allow my fellow defenders to do so if they were able, yet somehow, I managed to doze off for perhaps two parts of a watch, being wakened by Alex shortly before dawn. Somewhat angry at myself for having fallen asleep at all, I tried not to take it out on Alex, asking him if he knew anything about the situation outside.

"I went out not long ago," he informed me.

"And?" I asked.

"And," he replied, "there are a lot of men out and about, but I didn't see or hear any fighting, and there wasn't anything on fire."

I considered for a moment, then all I could think to say was, "I suppose that's the best we can expect."

The others were rousing themselves, and I sent Alex out into the outer office to inform them I would be with them shortly, then I sat on the edge of my cot, thinking about how we had come to a place where the idea that nobody was killed or injured, and nothing burned, would be considered good news. Crowding in on that thought was the recognition that, depending on what happened on this day, how unlikely it was that this would remain the case. I was certain that all of us who had remained loyal, if only outwardly, would be in great danger should the men hear what they were fearing, and as much as Germanicus was admired by most of the men, in their current state, not even he would be safe. This cheery line of thought was interrupted by the sound of the *bucina* signaling the official start of the day, and I got up, went out into the office, where the other men were waiting.

"Let's go see what's what," was all I said, then before anyone could speak, I strode to the door, opened it, and walked out into the street.

Much to our surprise, from appearances it seemed that the sound of the horn blowing had somehow jolted the man from their unruly behavior, because we only caught glimpses of some men just as they were entering their quarters. It was true the Cohort street was littered with debris; pieces of broken camp furniture seemed to be the most common, which I surmised was due to the men breaking off stool legs to use as clubs, but there were other items as well. Aside from this overt sign that the night had not passed in normal fashion, however, there was nothing else to indicate that there had been some sort of disturbance.

It was Structus who actually touched on the reason for this sudden onset of quiet and order, muttering to me, "I suppose even mutinous bastards get hungry. They're probably all in their tents preparing for the morning meal."

Even as he said this, smoke began rising from the fires on the surrounding streets, reminding us that we were hungry as well. Deciding against doing anything that might rupture this normal moment, I returned to my quarters, where Alex had already returned and was stoking the fire to heat up some porridge that was left over from the night before, our usual fare, although we did not have any bread left since none had been made the day before. By the time we were finished eating, the next signal sounded, this time the *cornu*, announcing that it was time for the men to assemble in their streets, forming up to march to the forum to receive the orders for the day. Certain that this would not take place, nevertheless, when I went outside, standing in front of their tents were the men of my Century, waiting for Structus to give them the order to form up, and my Century was far from alone. Glancing down the street in each direction, I could see that the men of the Fourth Cohort, mutineers and those who remained loyal alike, had decided to pretend as if this was a normal day, standing side by side in their usual spots as if nothing out of the ordinary was taking place. I certainly was not going to argue, although I felt as if I was in a dream, moving into my spot as I had done every day for years. Anyone who did not know what was going on would have seen this and thought there was nothing uncommon going on, and fairly quickly, it became apparent that the officers unanimously agreed to play along.

The formation that day was delayed by a third of a watch, which exacerbated the existing tensions, in rankers and officers alike, yet somehow the mutineers managed to behave themselves, although there was more than the normal amount of chatter. Since the camp was home to two Legions, it had naturally been built to accommodate both of them, including the forum, though it was still a bit cramped, requiring us to reduce our normal spacing between Centuries and Cohorts. On any other day, this would not matter all that much, aside from the customary hostility between Legions, which I would liken to having two fighting dogs caged next to each other where they can see, and most importantly, hear each other snarling and snapping. Muttered insults were often exchanged on those occasions, but that was all that it amounted to, at least to this

point. Now, I was not particularly happy about the issue of
proximity, thinking that, depending on which ranker chose to
make an outburst in the event that the news from Rome was bad,
matters could quickly get out of hand, simply because the men
of one Legion saw their comrades in the other Legion were
inclined to refuse accepting Tiberius' decision. Not that any of
the officers could do anything about it, which contributed to the
tension I was feeling, and I was certain I was not alone among
my fellow Centurions and Optios. Compounding matters, just as
in Pannonia, we all knew that there were officers who were
sympathetic to the demands made by the men, some of them
secretly, others openly; I would put my sentiment in the former
category. I suppose it sounds odd, but I had been much more
open about my feelings when I had been in Pannonia, yet when
I returned to my own Legion, I had become more circumspect
about my sentiments. Now that this is in the past, albeit recently,
I can acknowledge that my true motivation for keeping my
feelings about the cause of the mutiny to myself was based on
one simple reason; I did not want to be thought of or seen as
being in any way sympathetic to men like Pusio and all the other
troublemakers who had plagued the Legions for the previous
five years. I must reiterate that, while I understand why he did
so, the decision by the late Princeps to essentially take care of
two of his problems in one action, by forcing the elements in
Rome who were giving him the most trouble to enlist in the
Legions, while it did plump up those Legions, all he did was
transfer the underlying problem to those of us wearing the
transverse crest, and to a lesser degree, the Legates. This, of
course, has been the subject of much discussion among the
officers, and I will concede the possibility of the point that those
few Centurions who defended Augustus in this matter made, that
in the wake of the Varus disaster, the Princeps' actions in
sending a few thousand men was the likely reason that Arminius
and his confederation did not press the advantage and cross the

Rhenus. While I and others, including my Pilus Prior, believed that Arminius' inaction was due more to his own internal problems than the rapid mobilization of the surviving Legions, brought so quickly to full strength by the *dilectus*, neither could we dismiss the possibility that it was not that move by Augustus. After all, Augustus' defenders argued, how could a German chief, hundreds of miles away, have any idea that the men filling the depleted ranks of the Legions were the dregs of Rome? This is certainly true, but neither can it be denied that, although the mutiny likely would have occurred, the presence of men like Pusio, here on the Rhenus, or Percennius in Pannonia, made matters worse by adding a level of contentiousness and volatility that was based in their own discontent and grievances. Now, as we stood at *intente* waiting for the appearance of Germanicus, I am certain the trepidation I felt was shared by all of the men, for one reason or another. The wait was certainly not as long as it seemed, but men were beginning to fidget, while I could hear snatches of whispered speculation between the rankers as the tension grew with every heartbeat.

Finally, the flap to the *praetorium* was thrust aside, and Germanicus strode out of the tent, followed by Caetronius, who I was certain would be playing the role of nothing but a mute witness to whatever it was Germanicus was about to tell us. Because of my familiarity with him, I studied Germanicus' face intently as he walked the short distance to the rostrum, which was not made of turf like the one in Pannonia, nor was it made of crates and shields, but specially built for a marching camp, constructed in such a way that it can be broken down into pieces, thereby allowing for quick assembly should the need arise. He was wearing his battle armor, which I tried not to view as a bad omen; otherwise, I saw nothing in his demeanor that gave me an indication of what he was about to say. Despite the cold, I felt a trickle of sweat make its way down my back, while my heart started beating faster, as if I had just made some sort of sudden movement and was not just standing at *intente*. The tension, which I could literally feel radiating outward from the men of my Century did not help, and I became conscious of how tightly I was clutching my *vitus*, which led me to wonder if just that would be enough to impose order should the news be bad. Not surprisingly, there was none of the normal whispering that is the norm for formations once Germanicus emerged, a certain amount of which Centurions ignore, so he did not need to use his usual volume when addressing two Legions. Before he spoke, however, for some moments, he simply stood there, his *paludamentum* fluttering in the slight breeze that carried with it a promise of real winter, the kind of biting cold that made fingers numb and ears burn, his face impassive as his head moved slowly across the ranks. During this silence, my eyes naturally never left him, and I saw how much this ordeal had weighed on him, in the form of dark circles under his eyes, noticeable creases on what part of his forehead was visible under his helmet, but more than anything, it was the downturned mouth that was most striking to me. Usually, Germanicus' normal expression was much more open and engaging, with a slight upward curve to his mouth that informed those around him that he liked smiling much more than frowning, which was directly the opposite from his adoptive father Tiberius, who always looked dour and as if he had some secret complaint that soured his expression.

Only when he was done with his examination, did Germanicus begin speaking, his tone flat, "Yesterday, a delegation, sent from Rome, led by *lictors* bearing the *fasces* garlanded in ivy that designated their status as official ambassadors, sent by my father, and the father of the Legions, *Imperator* Tiberius Claudius Nero arrived here by way of Ubiorum..." He chose to pause then, and his expression suddenly hardened, which his voice matched as, for the first time, he raised his voice to a bellow. *"And these men were attacked! By fellow Romans!"* Pointing a finger, he swept it across the entirety of the formation of both Legions as he continued, *"By you, the men of the 1ˢᵗ and 20ᵗʰ Legions!"* Germanicus stopped again, letting the words hang in the air, and I knew it was my imagination, but they seemed to echo as if he was standing on the edge of a deep gorge, which I suppose is an appropriate way to think about it. More importantly, I saw the impact his charge, which was nothing but the truth, had on the men in the front ranks of the Centuries that formed the leading edge of the formation surrounding the rostrum. While no man within my range of vision broke from his *intente*, I saw heads turning towards a comrade next to them, and there was a low buzz as men muttered to each other. Wisely ignoring this, Germanicus' voice became even more charged. "And the leader of that delegation, Lucius Munatius Plancus, was set upon by some of the men who are standing here before me, issuing such dire threats to his person that he was forced to flee into the *praetorium*!" He turned to face the First of the 1ˢᵗ, and again pointing a finger, said, "It was only through the heroism of the *Aquilifer* of the 1ˢᵗ, Gnaeus Calpurnius, who placed himself bodily between Plancus and those who violated the agreement that the *praetorium* was sacrosanct and would not be invaded by those of you who are involved in this..." For a moment, I was certain he had made a fatal blunder, yet he managed to stop himself, and instead of "mutiny" or "insurrection" settled on, "...matter! Whether you choose to believe it or not, you owe Gnaeus Calpurnius a debt, because if those men who violated the boundary of the *praetorium*, intent on doing Plancus harm, had actually done so, there would have been nothing I could do to stop our *Imperator* from ordering that justice be done! Ambassadors, from *every* civilized nation, have been recognized as inviolate, even during a war between different nations, so how is it that a Roman ambassador should fear for his safety from fellow Romans?" The rustling of whispers that had begun earlier had only intensified as Germanicus continued, and it was with a sense of grim satisfaction that I saw that, almost universally, the expression borne by the rankers directly across from me was, rightfully, one of shame. And, I was cautiously pleased to see, there seemed to be a growing anger there, but while I had no way of knowing with any certainty, I had the sense that it was not aimed at Germanicus, but at those men who had invaded the *praetorium*, bringing shame to every man in the ranks. Returning my attention to Germanicus, still standing motionless, I watched as he took this in, and I was sure that he detected he was making some sort of headway with most of the men. But, as we were all about to learn, he was far from through.

"Because of the actions of these men," he continued, "I have made the decision to send my wife, who as you all know is bearing another child, and my son Gaius, away from here immediately." Now the quality of the noise changed, from the buzzing of men whispering to what was an unmistakable low-pitched moan.

Before he could continue, a voice from far back in the formation, somewhere in the Third Cohort of my Legion shouted, "Where are you sending them?"

I never asked Germanicus, but even in the moment, I had the suspicion that this was not simply a random question shouted by a distraught ranker, and I recalled from my Avus' account how this was a favored tactic of not only Divus Julius, but the late Princeps. That Germanicus did not hesitate in responding was another sign, although the men themselves did not seem suspicious.

"I am sending them to stay with the Treveri," he answered, and this unleashed a chorus of shouted protests.

"You'd trust barbarians over us?"

"We'd never harm your wife! We love her!"

"How could you send Caligula away from us? He's our luck!"

This is just a sampling of the things that were shouted that I could make out, but it is representative of the sentiments being expressed by the majority of the rankers. At first, Germanicus made no attempt to quell this outburst, while I would say that my state of mind was more of bemusement than anything else, and when I glanced over at Vespillo, standing in his spot to my right, when our eyes met, he gave a small shrug that made me believe he was as mystified as I was. Many, if not most of these men had, just the night before, been ready to explode in rage, and a few of them had already attempted to beat Plancus to death, yet now they were all acting horrified that the *Propraetor* would believe his family was in danger because of them. Such is the nature of men when they are in large groups, I suppose; common sense is in short supply.

Finally, Germanicus raised his arms for silence, and it quieted down fairly quickly, allowing him to continue in what, to my ears, was a plaintive manner, "Why do you act so surprised? I love my family! The only things I love more are my father and Rome! But my father's own *maiestatas* will protect him, and those other Legions who have remained steadfast will protect the Empire, but only I can protect my family! And," his tone altered again, becoming charged with a throbbing intensity, "make no mistake! I would willingly sacrifice my family if it was in the cause of your glory, and in the course of protecting Rome, but I will not sacrifice them because of...this!" He gestured around him with both arms, and again, he avoided using the words that would accurately describe what was taking place, yet anyone with eyes could see that his meaning was not lost on his audience. For the first time, I felt a twinge of cautious optimism as I stood there, intently gauging the reaction of the men, because there was no mistaking the almost universal expression of shame that they were now displaying. Oh, there were still some men within my range of sight who looked sullen, or even angry, and I had to fight the urge to turn around and examine my own men to see who among them was unaffected by Germanicus' words. I was successful, mainly because I saw Gemellus had no such qualms and had turned about to stare at our Century, while I made a mental note to ask him what he had seen.

When Germanicus resumed, only a couple of heartbeats later, his tone once more transformed, conveying a sense of true sadness in his words as he said, "I am no Divus Julius. Yes, I bear his name, but I do not deserve to do so. He stopped a mutiny," I winced at his first use of the word, but by this point the men were spellbound and there was no sign of reaction, "when the men of his Legions refused to renew their oath of loyalty, and he did it with one single word." When he paused then, I knew it was for dramatic effect, and while I was cognizant this was a ploy, I could also see that, even if men were aware of this, they did not care. "*Quirites*! That was all he said." He snapped the fingers of one hand. "And the mutiny was over, just like that. Our beloved, departed Augustus," he continued, "was able to stop another mutiny by the Legions at Actium *with a single glance!*" This time, instead of snapping, he shook his head in an exaggerated fashion, but I believe the sadness on his face was genuine. "But I have been unable to restore you to a state of unity and obedience to Rome, despite my best efforts. So, knowing this, I ask you; why did your comrades of the 5th and 21st stop me from ending myself when I wanted to? Why do they, and you revile me so much that you would force me to endure that shame, that I failed to bring you to order?"

Germanicus' face had been turned from my view for most of this, as he slowly rotated his head while he talked so that he could be seen by all of us, but by the time he was looking in my direction, those of us close enough clearly saw the tears that now made his cheeks glitter in the weak sunlight. However, he was far from alone in those tears, and I confess that I was one of those men so affected by his words that my eyes were stinging, but neither I nor any of those who had remained loyal mattered. Thankfully, even with the distance of the open space of the forum directly in front of the rostrum, I could see the ranks of men across from me were similarly discomposed.

"Better that I would have died then than have to endure this shame!" Germanicus' voice, while not raised any louder than it had been, seemed to cut through the air. "Better that I would have died and none of you punished so that you could have a Legate who would lead you on our sacred campaign to avenge Varus and his Legions!" Then, he confirmed a rumor that had been sweeping through camp. "Once the Belgae heard of all that has transpired here, they offered their warriors to help Rome vanquish the Germans, but gods forbid that they should have the honor and glory that is rightfully ours!" Lifting his arms to the heavens, Germanicus offered, "May the spirit of our divine Augustus, now residing in the heavens with the gods and his father Divus Julius, may the spirit of my own father by blood Drusus, be with these men who have marched for you, and turn their hearts back to the path of honor and glory. May they remove the stain of shame for their actions of these past weeks, and convert all of our discord and disagreements into the force we need to destroy our *true* enemies!" Holding this position for a few heartbeats longer, Germanicus lowered his arms and turned his attention away from the heavens back down to the earth, and to thousands of men who, if I am an example, scarcely dared to breathe as we stood, completely captivated by the words of our *Propraetor*. Scanning the formation, Germanicus nodded his head, saying, "I see before me changed faces and changed hearts. If you will allow the deputation to return unharmed to the Senate; if you will return your obedience to our *Imperator*, and your loyalty to myself and to my wife and family..." He stopped, and I saw his chest expand as he took a breath, which I understood immediately when he continued, "...and if you will set yourself apart from those among you who infected otherwise good men with this disease of disloyalty, *that* I will consider your repentance, and a guarantee of your loyalty!"

And with that, the mutiny of the Army of the Rhenus was finally, truly over; although, for a span of several heartbeats, when there was neither a sound or any movement, I, and I am sure most of the men of both Legions, did not know this as fact.

"*AVE GERMANICUS!*"

That shout was like the first dislodged rock of an avalanche, triggering an eruption of noise, issued by thousands of throats, not in anger and repudiation, but in what I am certain was the shared relief that, not only was the mutiny over, there was forgiveness on the part of Germanicus. And, just that quickly, the fate of men like Pusio was sealed, which most of them understood, because what caused the sudden disintegration of the formation of two Legions, as some men came rushing forward towards the rostrum, not as hostiles but as suppliants, was the actual movement by these ringleaders bolting from their spot in the ranks, understanding that their only hope lay in flight. It was a vain hope, because just as quickly, their former comrades, now understanding that their restoration to good standing with the *Propraetor* and *Imperator* was contingent upon the punishment of the relatively few men who had instigated this madness, were hot on the heels of the fleeing condemned men. What had been an ordered scene, with the Centuries standing in neat rows in their accustomed spots, instantly became chaotic, with men seeming to run in every possible different direction. I was moving just as quickly, spinning around, intent on making sure one of my men in particular did not escape. Unfortunately, I did not have the satisfaction of bringing Pusio to ground myself; that honor went to none other than Gnaeus Clustuminus, who had instantly left his spot in the formation and intercepted Pusio, who had also turned and taken the first step of his planned escape, with Clustuminus slamming into Pusio and knocking him to the ground. I only caught the tail end of this, as Clustuminus fell on top of Pusio, pinning him, and in doing so, Clustuminus restored my faith in him, and he returned to the top of my mental list as being worthy of promotion to Optio once Structus entered the Centurionate. I am not blind, nor was I then, to the thought that this was a calculated move on the part of the Sergeant; while he had not been openly consorting with the mutineers, neither had he disavowed them in any way, nor had he completely dissociated himself from them. And, I had instructed Gemellus on my departure, originally to find Germanicus, to keep an eye on Clustuminus, which on my return, my *Signifer* had reported that he had behaved in the same fashion that I had observed before I left, in the first day of the mutiny. Regardless of this recognition, I made the decision in that moment not to engage in any more suspicious thoughts about the motives of not just Clustuminus, but all of the men of my Century who had not declared themselves openly one way or another. Frankly, I was just tired of all of it and wanted matters to return to at least a semblance of normality as quickly as possible. Seeing that Clustuminus had apprehended Pusio, I turned my attention to the handful of other men who I considered to be actively involved in the mutiny and not just passive followers of men stronger than they were. I was happy to see that, like Clustuminus, other men had acted quickly, although some needed help in subduing their quarry, none of whom were cooperating, which was understandable. Similar scenes were taking place in every Century and Cohort in both Legions, and between this and the men who had rushed towards Germanicus, unanimously begging his forgiveness, it was quite chaotic, and so noisy it was almost impossible to be heard. Although my Century had managed to capture the malefactors without having to pursue them through the camp, that was not the case with everyone else, so there were small parties of men, sprinting after a single, or in one case that I saw, a trio of men who were desperately trying to make it to one of the gates. Meanwhile, Germanicus was still on the rostrum, but now he was bent over at the waist, shaking every upthrust hand men were offering in a sign of their repentance and renewed loyalty. Now that I was assured that Pusio and the others were not going anywhere, I thought of making my own way towards Germanicus, slightly concerned that he was putting himself in jeopardy, but then I caught sight of several of his bodyguards who had shoved their way through the crowd to the rostrum, trying to restore some semblance of order. Instead, I looked for Macer first, but I did not see him, although that could have been because of his height, and since Vespillo was closest to me, I made my way to him instead.

"Have you ever seen anything like this?" I did not shout, but it was close to one, and he shook his head.

"I wouldn't even know where to begin to try and think of something that would compare," he answered, then for a moment, we just surveyed the scene. "But someone needs to take command and get things under control before something bad happens."

Even as he said this, over the riotous sounds, we both heard a short, sharp scream, and we turned to see, where the Second of the Second normally stood, a bloodied figure crawling frantically on all fours, towards the rostrum, followed by a half-dozen men, all of whom were aiming kicks at their prey.

"I guess he thinks Germanicus will show mercy," Vespillo's tone was grimly amused, but just as I was about to open my mouth to assure him that this would not happen, the *Propraetor* proved me wrong.

Because of his vantage point, he saw the injured ranker crawling towards him, and he snapped an order that prompted three of his bodyguards to shove through the crowd, all of whom had their backs turned to this scene, and hurry to surround the ranker. Naturally, our attention was drawn in this direction, so I did not see Germanicus give another order, but suddenly, a *cornu* sounded the call to assemble, the signal that he wanted to restore order. I did not react immediately, more interested in what was happening as the Germans got involved in a brief scuffle with the men surrounding the injured ranker, but the sound of the *cornu,* combined with this return to obedience they had just sworn to Germanicus, ensured that nothing more than a couple of shoves were exchanged. Returning to my spot, I checked to see that Pusio and the other men who their comrades had subdued were still under control, then took my spot. Gradually, order was restored, and Germanicus, remaining on the rostrum, waited patiently until we were in at least a semblance of formation, aside from the men who were now bound with their own *baltea* and forced to sit in the dirt of the forum, but in their accustomed spot, which made for yet another sight my eyes had never seen before.

Finally, he spoke again, but it was only to say, "All Centurions, attend to me in the *praetorium*. Your Optios will take command."

Then, hopping down, he turned to stride into the *praetorium* ahead of us, and as he did, he was at the right angle for me to see the small smile on his lips. This was the moment I realized something; Germanicus had made no mention of the decision by Tiberius the delegation had brought with them from Rome, whatever it was. I confess, I was torn; part of me admired the guile of Germanicus for his brilliant maneuver on the rostrum, distracting the men from the real cause of the attack on Plancus and the unrest of the night before, but I was also greatly troubled by the adroit manner in which he had manipulated the situation to his advantage. Those were thoughts best kept to themselves, I decided during the short walk to the *praetorium*, and I still believe it was the right one.

"This," Germanicus declared to the assembled Centurions, "is going to be done legally and in the proper manner."

607

The "this" to which he was referring was the execution of the ringleaders, all but a handful of whom had been captured immediately. Most of those who managed to make it out of the forum had been rounded up, but there was still a half-dozen men who were hiding in the camp somewhere, the Centurions to which they belonged sending out search parties led by their Optios. Speaking of the Centurions, there should have been one hundred twenty of them in the *praetorium*; by my quick count, there were just a handful under a hundred. The other twenty-odd were absent because they were outside, sitting in the forum as prisoners, and to the eternal shame of the Fourth Cohort, one of them was Philus. He had been denounced by Closus, but while neither Macer nor Primus Pilus Sacrovir were disposed to take only the word of an Optio, his charge had been repeated by more than a dozen men of his Century, including the two men considered ringleaders. Nevertheless, I harbored reservations about whether this was enough to condemn the man, and I could see my Pilus Prior was of the same mind.

"However," Germanicus continued, and he began pacing the floor, his head down in thought, which made it somewhat difficult to hear, "we can't afford the time and expense of holding a formal Tribunal for each and every man." He turned to Caetronius, who was standing slightly behind him, back towards the wall that was the boundary to Germanicus' private office. "Do we have a complete tally yet?"

In turn, Caetronius walked over to the desk in front of the door to the office, where one of the Tribunes, along with two clerks, was consulting a pile of wax tablets, with one clerk incising what I presumed were figures into the tablet. As we watched, there was a brief whispered exchange, and while Caetronius' back was to us, judging from the Tribune's expression, I was certain I knew the answer.

Turning back around, the Legate's mouth was turned down into a frown. "No, sir. Not as of yet."

Germanicus did not seem surprised, nor was he irritated, asking only, "What's the count so far, then?"

Glancing back over his shoulder, Caetronius got the answer and said flatly, "Six hundred and twenty-seven, sir."

There was an audible gasp from all of us, but Germanicus remained impassive, though he did inquire, "How close do you think we are to completing the count?"

Instead of the Legate, who indicated to the Tribune he should answer, the young officer replied, "We only have two tablets left, sir. And," he added, "each tablet is from the Pilus Prior of a Cohort."

Germanicus considered for a moment, then he said in a tone that suggested he was thinking aloud, "That means it should be around seven hundred men altogether," reminding me he had an astonishing head for figures, provided he was correct; as it turned out, the total turned out to be seven hundred and one men. Speaking more loudly, he repeated, "There is no way we can conduct a Tribunal for each and every man. Nor," he added, obviously seeing and correctly interpreting the thought that certainly crossed my mind, "can we even take the time if we hold a Tribunal for each Century, or Cohort." Shaking his head, he settled this question by informing us, "We need to conclude this as quickly as possible, because we need to begin preparing for the campaign that I know you all have assumed is coming."

Frankly, it was another shrewd maneuver; by confirming what we had long suspected, that this next season would finally see us embarking on the campaign for which every Roman had been clamoring, the chastisement of the German tribes and the destruction of Arminius personally, none of us were disposed to quibble about his decision to rush this disciplinary matter through a process that was abbreviated, to put it mildly.

There was one sticking point, however, and it was Primus Pilus Neratius who raised it, asking over the noise as we whispered to each other about the coming campaign, "What about the Centurions and Optios, sir? Surely you don't plan on lumping them together with the rankers."

This stopped our chatter, and we turned our attention to Germanicus, who clearly did not care for this question, but neither did he shrink from it.

He did handle it in a more indirect manner, by turning back to Caetronius and asking, "What's the total on Centurions and Optios?"

"Twenty-four Centurions, thirty-eight Optios."

I suppose we were all aware that it was probable there were more Optios than Centurions, but once the actual number was known, I think this more than anything convinced Neratius not to pursue the matter any further. Sixty-two Tribunals, no matter how quickly they were conducted, would take weeks, and now that we knew about the coming campaign, the brutal truth was that we could not waste the time, especially when in most cases the guilt of these men was already established, and by their own comrades at that. However, I think we were also aware that it was within the realm of possibility that men of a Century would be more than happy to rid themselves of a Centurion or Optio they hated. This was raised by Neratius, and Sacrovir agreed with his counterpart, which engendered some discussion in which Germanicus encouraged the rest of us to participate. The point of contention in this area was the idea that a Centurion or Optio's only crime might have been being excessively harsh, or simply unpopular, although personally I did not believe that even the most vindictive ranker would be willing to condemn their Centurion or Optio to death simply because they did not like the man, if only because his comrades would not allow it. This went on for some time, with Germanicus mostly listening as we bickered back and forth, with one faction being adamant that there should be a formal Tribunal, while another saying that there should a Tribunal for the Centurions, and one for the Optios. While I understood this was offered as a compromise, I was certain that this would prove more trouble than it was worth, simply because we would be in the same spot, where a guilty vote would be applied to all of the defendants, while one or more of them might be a victim of revenge.

Finally, Germanicus raised a hand, and once it fell silent, said, "I think I might have a solution."

He proceeded to explain his idea, and by the time he was finished, I saw that most heads were nodding up and down, and mine was one of them. Once this was settled, the final count was tallied, and the method for how we would go about determining the guilt was settled, while the punishment would be carried out immediately. Despite agreeing that this was the proper course of action, I certainly did not relish the idea of carrying it out; when Germanicus pulled me aside, while I was not surprised, I was in an even grimmer frame of mind.

"You've done this before," he reminded me, "with Dodonis. Can I count on you now, Pullus?"

"For all of them?" I gasped, but he shook his head, saying firmly, "No. Not all of them. But for your Cohort."

Understanding there was no real way to refuse, I agreed, then it was time to return to the forum and finally finish this horrible episode in our history.

What Germanicus had come up with was to have the men of every Cohort judge their comrades, each of whom were dragged up onto the rostrum by Germanicus' bodyguards, whereupon their guilt would be judged. For reasons that needed no explanation, Germanicus himself did not officiate, serving only as a witness; that was left to Caetronius as Legate, who stood at the front of the rostrum, flanked by the Primi Pili and with several German bodyguards. It was quite chaotic at first, then something of a system developed, where the Century to which the man belonged stood directly in front of the rostrum, but were flanked by the other Centuries of the Cohort, and there would be a brief debate about each Legionary by the men of the Century, while the other five Centuries then either agreed or disagreed with the decision. By the time a couple dozen men had been dispatched, it was decided that the respective Centurion would be the representative who relayed the decision, with the Centurions for the other five Centuries relaying the agreement, or disagreement, of his own Century. At first, without exception, there was no dissension about the fate of the accused ranker, some of whom stumbled numbly onto the rostrum under their own power, others being dragged, kicking, screaming, and struggling in front of their collective and combined prosecutor, judges, and jury. There might be a brief discussion, then the Centurion of the offender's Century would utter a single word.

"*Condemno!*"

Whereupon the newly condemned man would be forced to kneel, and the man selected from that Cohort would use a *spatha*, supplied from the *quaestorium*, to behead the man. This, at least, was how it started; after one particularly gruesome execution, where the selected man, either through nerves or incompetence, took no less than four strokes to finish the job, while the ranker writhed in agony, his gurgling screams serving to silence the otherwise raucous crowd, it was then decided to have only men who had experience in such matters serve as executioners. Which, of course, meant that I participated earlier than Germanicus had indicated, since he had informed me that I would only be executing the men of the Fourth Cohort, and while it was not something I looked forward to for most of the condemned men, I believe the gods will understand there was one exception. Another issue had to be resolved, and that was the disposal of the bodies. For the first few executions, both the head and corpse of the executed man would be shoved off the rostrum, to land with a sodden, heavy thud on the hard-packed dirt of the forum directly in front of it. Naturally, after a few bodies, it began to create a problem, both because it pushed the judging Century farther away from the rostrum, and the stench of *cac* and piss that is always present at a scene of mass slaughter became overwhelming. After yet another halt for a discussion, the bodies were hauled away by slaves summoned for the purpose, while the heads were left, which still created quite a spectacle as they grew into a mound that threatened to reach the height of the rostrum. We had gone in reverse order, starting with the Tenth Cohort, which, surprising none of us, held a much higher proportion of the malcontents who were deemed worthy of execution, although only one Optio from the Cohort was among the accused. Before we left the *praetorium* to begin this final expiation of the sin of mutiny, we prevailed on Germanicus to make one other concession; while the guilt or innocence would be judged publicly, those Centurions and Optios who received a vote of *condemno* would not endure the final humiliation of having their heads joining the pile in front of the rostrum. None of us were surprised that this was not a popular decision, especially since some rankers were convinced that the condemned officers would not be executed, but Sacrovir and Neratius, in their role as Primus Pilus of each Legion, offered a solution that, if not pleasing to the men, at least appeased them, and most importantly convinced them that there was no plot to allow their officers to escape. Each Century who had a condemned Centurion or Optio would send their *Signifer*, *Tesseraurius*, and the Sergeants of each section to witness the execution in the *praetorium*, after the business in the forum was finished.

While Germanicus had originally selected me to serve as executioner of the men of the Fourth Cohort, because of the bungling done early on, I ended up beheading men from the Sixth and Fifth before the men of my Cohort marched from their normal spot in the forum to array themselves in front of the rostrum, and my arm was already tired. Even with my daily work at the stakes and my status as Cohort weapons instructor, swinging a *gladius* with enough force to cleanly part a man's head from the rest of his body takes a toll, even with the extra weight provided by the *spatha*. My fatigue notwithstanding, as the moment approached that I would be executing men who, while I may not have known personally, I at least knew by sight, my heart began beating at a rate much higher than the exertion of the task required. I will confess that part of it was from the anticipation of seeing one Publius Atilius Pusio kneeling at my feet, but there was also a sense of shame that Philus was one of the accused, although I suspect Macer felt this more keenly as Pilus Prior. It was immediately after I had executed the condemned men of the Sixth Century, with Volusenus looking on with an impassive demeanor that did not betray his thoughts one way or another, when I was forced to ask for another *spatha*, the edge of the one in my hand having gone, that I had an idea. Catching the eye of Structus, who was standing in my place in front of my Century off to the side of the rostrum, waiting our turn, I beckoned to him during the period someone was hustling off to the *quaestorium* to retrieve another *spatha*.

He came, albeit with a reluctance that was understandable, but all I told him was, "Send someone to find Alex, quickly."

Clearly surprised, he nonetheless obeyed immediately, so that by the time I had finished dispatching the men of the Fifth and Philus was being dragged up onto the rostrum for judgment, my nephew was standing at the base of the rostrum, off to the side. Using the disturbance caused by the presence of a Centurion being judged, I crouched down and told him what I needed, his reaction mirroring that of Structus, but like my Optio, he turned and ran off immediately. Returning my attention to the scene, I saw Philus, flanked on either side by a German, stood before the men of his Century, dressed only in his tunic, his *baltea* having been appropriated for the binding of his hands. Without any symbol of his office, Philus could have been any ranker, and like most of the condemned men I had witnessed, he was visibly shaking; otherwise, his face was set in an impassive mask, while he refused to look down at the men he had commanded. The debate, such as it was, lasted a bit longer than what had become usual, but not by that much; his *Signifer* spoke of overhearing Philus conferring with one of the troublemakers in his Century, where he promised to speak for the man should things go badly, which they had. By itself, this was not enough, but then Closus held up a wax tablet that had been discovered in a search of Philus' quarters, which he presented to Macer. Scanning it quickly, I saw my Pilus Prior's lips thin down into two bloodless lines, which I knew was a sign of his anger, but without a word, he walked up to the rostrum, handing the tablet upward to the Legate, who took it.

Caetronius performed the same act as Macer, scanning the incised lines, but I was somewhat surprised when the Legate did not seem convinced, which was explained when he said, "Yes, the words are damning, but since I've never seen this man's writing before, I can't say one way or another if this is worthy of being condemned."

This, on its face, was certainly true, but I was still surprised, if only because we had already judged several Centurions and he had never intervened, although as I thought about it, I realized that this was the first Centurion whose guilt rested on a piece of correspondence. There was a further delay as a man was sent to summon the Century clerks, Macer ordering that both be brought since one of them belonged to Philus personally. Frankly, I did not think this was necessary, but this was based on my observation of Philus, who, on seeing Closus hold up the tablet, I saw close his eyes and his lips began moving in what I felt certain was a prayer. Whether it be for a miracle in the form of a reprieve, or him setting his books right with his household gods, I never asked, and he never said, but I apparently had been the only one watching Philus and not his Optio. The clerks arrived, and it was easy to tell which one belonged to Philus; it also betrayed what kind of master Philus had been to the man, because while I would not call it gleeful, his demeanor certainly did not communicate any hesitance or sorrow as he glanced down at the tablet, then confirmed it was in his master's hand, which was corroborated by the other clerk. Perhaps if Philus had not resigned himself to his fate, he might have pointed out that his slave barely even glanced at the tablet, but he did not, and while Legate Caetronius lifted an eyebrow at this, he did not say anything about it. This was enough for the men of his Century, through Closus, to vote *condemno*, and Philus was summarily dragged off to be held with those other officers waiting their more private execution. Only Cornutus seemed disposed to argue the point, but he had barely escaped being accused himself, since he had been missing the night before, and I saw him open his mouth, then quickly shut it. Fortunately for him, Macer had accepted his explanation that he had been visiting a friend in one of the *ad hoc* guard Centuries in Germanicus' camp, and once the uproar began, deemed it too dangerous to try and return to the main one. Vespillo, Volusenus, and I held a different view of the matter, but in this, we were not given a vote, so Cornutus is still with the Fourth Cohort as I write this.

Finally, it was the turn of the Third Century, but Alex had not returned from his errand, and I resigned myself that I would be unable to carry out my intention. My Century had four men accused of being the chief instigators and agitators among their comrades; as far as I was concerned, there was one and only one man who was truly responsible for the misdeeds of the other three, and it was not just my hatred of Pusio that led me to believe this. These three men were veterans and had been members of the Century long before Pusio arrived, and none of them had given me any trouble, at least over and above the norm for rankers. Additionally, since I knew these men and their characters, I knew they were the kind who tended to follow the lead of other men, whether it be in their choice of wineshop, or how much complaining they should do about their time spent mucking out the stables. Nevertheless, I also understood that, while I held the nominal authority over my Century, in this moment, I was merely the instrument of the punishment as defined by my men, and I confess this did not set well in my gut. It was during the deliberation about the first accused man that I heard Alex call my name, and I turned to see that he had returned with the item I had requested. Bending down, I took it from him, and as I turned back to face the Century, the Legate saw what I held in my hand.

The frown he wore warned me, and he said, "Centurion Pullus, what are you doing with that?"

He was pointing to my *gladius*, and my mind raced, trying to come up with an explanation of why I was determined to use it and not the heavier *spatha*.

What came out of my mouth was, "Because it holds an edge better than any of the blades I've used so far. And," I thought to add, "I've been carrying this blade since I was a Gregarius, so I'm more comfortable using it." Lowering my voice, I finished with, "I know these men must die, sir, but I don't want them to suffer like some of the others did. My arm is getting tired, and I want to send them on their way across the river with as little pain as possible."

Caetronius studied my face for a long moment, then gave a curt nod, saying only, "Very well."

By the time our exchange was finished, the first of my men had been dragged onto the rostrum, and Vibius Galeo of the Tenth Section was quickly condemned. Galeo was one of those men I did not believe had been an active participant as much as he was swept along the current of mutiny created by men like Pusio, who I had quietly instructed Structus to put last. Although he had walked under his own power, it was only because he was being firmly held by the pair of Germans, and he was shaking uncontrollably, his eyes rolling back in his head from the fear of what was coming. It took an effort on my part to remain impassive as the Germans shoved him down onto the spot that was now covered with a combination of congealed blood and piss, giving off an odor that, while not overpowering, was certainly unpleasant.

Before I could stop myself, I leaned down and placed a hand on Galeo's shoulder, whispering in his ear, "I promise it'll be quick, Galeo. It'll be over before you know it, and then you can go find Fidenas and Rutilus across the river. You'll be whoring and drinking for eternity!"

I had hoped the mention of two of his comrades who had died, one in battle and one from disease, and the prospect of being reunited with them in the afterlife would provide some comfort, but the look he gave me of pathetic gratitude was almost too much for me to bear.

"R-really, Princeps Prior? You believe that? You believe they're over there, across the river, waiting for me?"

"No, I don't believe that. I *know* that," I answered firmly and without hesitation.

He said nothing more, but he gave me a slight nod, then turned and bowed his head, both in prayer and to give me a better target, or so I suppose. And, thank the gods, I was good to my word, even with my *gladius* and not a *spatha*. The next two men, Gnaeus Falto of the Fourth Section and Trigeminus of the Fifth Section, I dispatched in a similar manner, although only with Falto did I behave as I had with Galeo, their heads added to the pile at the base of the rostrum that was now spread out a distance of about ten feet in every direction, with a height close to mine. Then it was Pusio's turn, and if his was not the quickest *condemno* of all that I witnessed, it was among them, during which he showed none of his usual arrogance. Not lost on me, certainly, and judging from the reaction of the entire Cohort, was that he was the only man of the Fourth who could not walk up the steps under his own power, and in fact struggled mightily as he was dragged towards the rostrum. Finally, in exasperation, one of the Germans cuffed him on the head with enough force to daze him sufficiently that he at least stopped struggling, whereupon he was more or less carried onto the rostrum. Seeing that he was still groggy, I deliberately delayed, taking my time wiping my blade down with a rag that had been provided, to the point I could hear the men growing impatient. Reluctantly, I turned back to where Pusio was now kneeling, and at first, I thought he would refuse to look up at me, his head already bowed, his lips moving, which I bent down to hear, not believing that he would be praying.

He was not; instead, he was simply saying, "No, no, no, no…" over and over, and I felt not the slightest flicker of pity.

Instead, deep inside me, that beast that I think of as the dark twin of the divine fury that I inherited from my Avus, the one that unleashes a level of cruelty in me that enabled me to essentially torture Caecina the last few moments of his life, roused itself sufficiently that I bent down to speak in Pusio's ear, just as I had with Galeo, except my message and my intent were quite different.

"Oh, yes," I said, just loudly enough so that only he could hear. "You're about to have your head chopped off. And," I risked a glance over at Caetronius to ensure he was still out of earshot, "my arm is *very* tired. It may take me three, oh, maybe four tries before you're actually dead."

As soon as the words were out of my mouth, I saw a dark stain blossom on Pusio's tunic, the smell just a heartbeat behind, and he unleashed what can only be described as a howl of such an inhuman quality that the men nearest the rostrum either recoiled or made the sign against evil spirits.

"Centurion! What did you say to that man?"

Caetronius had to raise his voice to be heard, because Pusio continued his wailing, shaking his head wildly as I saw his arms suddenly bulge as he tried to break the bonds of his *baltea*.

"Only that I was going to be quick, and it would be over soon. Just like I told the other two of my men, sir," I lied, not feeling the slightest twinge of guilt.

Caetronius grimaced, then simply said, "Well, get on with it! This man's screeching is giving me a headache!"

Without knowing it, so gone with fear was he, Pusio actually aided me in my effort to make his death as painful as possible, because he would simply not stay still, and there was no way for the Germans to subdue him without putting themselves in the path of my *gladius*. Consequently, my first blow, which I made a show of using my entire strength but was really with only about half of it, struck him at the base of his neck, except at such an angle that it cut deeply into his body, aided by how much Pusio was leaning. My aim turned out to be true, because there was no spurt of blood from a severed vessel, and not surprisingly, his scream of terror and pain became even louder, making even me wince, not from any sense of pity but because of the volume, making it feel like someone was shoving an awl into both ears. In an unconscious reaction to the blow, he recoiled away from the direction in which it had come, placing him at an even more awkward angle, which suited my private purposes perfectly. Once more, I slashed down, but between his jerking movement, and the fact that I had deliberately aimed high, my blade sliced through the very top of his skull, sending his scalp and part of the bone flying in a spray of blood and what I assume was some brain matter. There was a roar of mingled alarm and disgust as the men in the front ranks were spattered with his gore, while the scalp and part of the skull struck one of the rankers on the shoulder; it would have hit him in the face if he had not dodged aside. Naturally, I followed the arc of the tumbling bit of scalp with my eyes, and Pusio was fortunate, because in doing so, my gaze met that of my Pilus Prior, who was staring directly at me, his mouth once more a bloodless slit. He was not spattered, for which I was thankful, but I saw he was not fooled in the slightest, and while he made no overt sign, I did not need one to understand that I had to finish Pusio earlier than I intended.

He had inadvertently helped himself because the force of the second blow had knocked him onto his side, and I suspect he was no longer really conscious, although I saw his eyes were open; more importantly, he was no longer moving, and I muttered under my breath, "You have no idea how lucky you are, you *cunnus*."

My blade came down, and it was over, at least for Pusio. The Legate suddenly appeared in my vision, and I tore my attention away from Pusio's face, his eyes still open, hoping that somehow, he still had a spark of life in him so that he could see me staring down at him.

"By the *gods*, Centurion!" Caetronius bellowed this, just inches from my face. "I thought you knew what you were doing!" He pointed down at my *gladius*, still shouting, "I thought you said that using your own blade would keep this from happening!"

Snapping to *intente*, I immediately fell back on the Stupid Legionary, saying, "Yes, sir. I have no excuse. I," even as I said the words, I felt a twinge of reluctance at admitting weakness, even if it was a lie, "suppose my arm just gave out."

He said nothing, just glared up at me for a moment, then turned away, dismissing me with a wave as he addressed one of the Germans. "Get another man up here. The Centurion here is done."

Summarily dismissed, I did not hesitate in obeying, turning and striding across the rostrum, descending the stairs and walking to take my place with my Century. Ignoring the reaction of the men, I joined Structus, the only man whose eyes I met, and as I suspected, he gave an almost imperceptible nod, the only communication we have ever had about what I did to Pusio. My Pilus Prior, however, was another story, but while I felt his eyes on me, I avoided looking in his direction, even as we switched places with the Second Century, temporarily placing us next to the First. The rest of the executions of the men of the Fourth were conducted by one of the Germans, then finally, we were through. As the other Cohorts had done, we then marched away from the forum, returning to our area, where we were dismissed by the Pilus Prior. Despite somewhat expecting it, when I heard Macer call my name, I felt a pang of anxiety, wondering how much of an issue he was going to make, and how far I was willing to go to deny that I had intended to do as I did. Following him, we went to his quarters, but when I tried to speak, he held up a hand, shaking his head, though he did not say anything. Only when we were in his private quarters and the flap was closed, did he say anything, after taking his seat behind his desk, not at the table where we normally sat, telling me this was not a personal exchange, so in recognition of that, I chose to stand in front of his desk.

Sitting silently, he gazed down at it, seeming to frame his thoughts, before he finally looked up at me and said, "Pullus, while I know why you did what you did to Pusio, I won't lie and say that it doesn't give me some…concerns."

When he did not continue, I took that as a sign I was expected to reply, but all I could think to ask was, "About what, exactly?"

"About whether you belong in my Cohort," he answered, and while he spoke quietly, the words rocked me as much as if he had bellowed this at the top of his lungs.

"What?" I gasped, and it took an effort for me to remain immobile. "Why?"

"Why?" he echoed, not in an unbelieving manner, but as if he was asking himself the same question. After a moment, he said, "I've never seen you behave that way, not even towards the Germans, Pullus." He gave me a look that seemed more sad than angry. "I thought I knew you, but apparently I don't."

How, I thought, am I supposed to respond to that? Macer and I had become friends, and close ones, but the only man who knew or suspected most of my secrets was Titus Domitius. Although we had never spoken openly about it, I was certain that, while he did not know the specifics, he was at least aware that I had been the one who had removed Caecina and Mela from our Century. Consequently, I was forced to realize in this moment that, no, Marcus Macer did not know me, at least the side of me that was capable of crippling Maxentius my first year, and slaughtering both Caecina and Mela in a manner that, if I am honest, was done with the same malevolent spirit as what I had just done to Pusio. In that instant, I had to decide how forthcoming to be with Macer, and if I was, whether it would help keep me in the Cohort, or whether it would harm my chances.

"I understand what you're saying," I spoke slowly, trying to form my thoughts as I went, "and I'll confess that I do have a...side of me," I settled on this way of putting it, "that you've never seen. I'm capable of doing things like what I did to Pusio, I won't deny that. But," I pointed out, "it takes something extraordinary for it to come out."

"Well," he nodded, "this certainly qualifies. And, hopefully, it's over." Taking a deep breath, I had to respect the fact that he met my gaze without flinching; nevertheless, his next words were like a dagger. "But I have some things to think about. I'll let you know my decision in the morning."

And with that, I was dismissed to walk, or perhaps stagger out of his quarters, my mind whirling with all the thoughts and worries that I had, finally, irreparably damaged my career. Somewhere along the way, perhaps starting at the very beginning with Vergorix, I had become accustomed to the idea that either my deeds, my name, or a combination of the two would shield me from my own actions as they pertained to my career. Needless to say, I was in a somber mood when I returned to my own quarters, and while I had every intention of informing Alex of what had taken place with Macer, I could not bring myself to do it, not wanting to ruin his state of mind. He was not happy, exactly, but he was clearly relieved, believing that the mutiny was finally over. Instead, I pretended that my conversation with Macer was inconsequential, although I could tell he did not fully believe me. Now that order had been restored, I felt safe sending both Alex and Balio out to run some errands that had been neglected, one of them going to Germanicus' camp and checking on Latobius, while the other went to retrieve rations for the evening meal. The punishment was not over; the 20th Legion had yet to undergo this ordeal, which meant that, every few moments, there would be some sort of noise from the direction of the forum, especially in the beginning, before the toll of seeing men put to death, despite the justification, began to wear on the men, and I include the officers. The execution of the Centurions and Optios came last, which included Philus, Poplicola of the Sixth of the First, and Regillensus of the 20th, but for this, only the Pili Priores were present, along with the group from each Century mentioned earlier, and of course, there was no liberty of the camp that night. Even if there had been, I suspect that only the most foolhardy or, perhaps, desperate to learn of the fate of a friend or relative, would have left their tent. If I had been asked to describe the collective mood of at least my Century that night, I would probably have said that it matched what I saw in Alex, and in Pannonia; a sense of relief that it was over, tempered with caution that there might still be repercussions that reverberated for some time to come.

After a desultory meal, which I shared with my nephew, I retired for the night, deciding that it was a good time to read one of my Avus' scrolls, and I do not believe it is surprising that I selected the scroll about Pharsalus. Despite my fatigue from not only the day but the night before spent in tense anticipation of trouble, sleep was long in coming, yet I must have dropped off because I awoke to the *bucina* call with the scroll, partially open, on my chest. Alex rose from behind the partition in his corner of my quarters, and we began the ritual of another day in the Legions, while I pretended that there was nothing hanging over my head. More than once I caught my nephew, his mouth open, clearly about to ask a question, and I was certain I knew what it would be about, yet something in my face must have quelled his impulse. This meant there was not our usual morning banter, and I think we both pretended our mutual reticence was due to the events from the day before. Then, the *cornu* sounded the initial assembly, and there was no postponing facing my Pilus Prior any longer. Donning my *sagum*, the mornings being cold now that it was almost November, I left my quarters, stepping out into the street, and only after I did so, then saw the neat rows of men of my Century, did I realize I had been holding my breath, anticipating that order had not been restored. And, perhaps most fittingly, there was a fresh blanket of snow, the first of the year, obscuring the churned mud of the street and the roofs of the tents. Calling the Century to assembly, we marched the short distance to the intersection of the Cohort street, where we were joined by the rest of the Cohort, the formation creating a fog that hovered just in front and above the men as they inhaled the cold air and expelled it, either in their breath or in their muttered conversations. Macer was in his normal spot, and he did not do anything out of the ordinary, which meant I was kept in suspense for the march to the forum. Naturally, the forum was also covered in a coating of snow, which I thought was oddly appropriate, masking as it did the scene of the violent end of more than seven hundred men. Their bodies had been hauled off by the camp slaves, then burned in a mass cremation the night of the executions, but while we did not know it at this moment, there had been a disagreement between *Propraetor* and Legate that, depending on which version one heard, either almost came to blows or at the very least resulted in voices raised to the point that the clerks, Tribunes, and both Primi Pili could hear through the canvas walls of Germanicus' office. Whatever the truth of the matter was, what was known with any certainty was that Caetronius had insisted the heads of the mutineers should be displayed in the forum, as a reminder to the rest of the men the cost of mutiny. Germanicus, wisely in my view, refused to do so, insisting that the executions themselves had been enough of a warning to those disposed to incite another insurrection, also pointing out that they had removed the ringleaders of the mutiny, thereby eliminating the possibility of future trouble. Although I would not have gone quite that far in my certainty there was no likelihood of further trouble, I believe his logic was sound as far as it went. The end result was that, between the snow and Germanicus' decision, there was no sign of anything that would indicate the day before had ended so violently, and I believe this pristine coat of snow did more to reduce the chances of further trouble than anything else Germanicus could have done. The only unusual note was that it was not Caetronius who made the morning appearance before handing matters over to the Primi Pili, but Germanicus himself. In another sign, he was not wearing armor, and had foregone his *paludamentum* for a *sagum*, although its quality was superior to mine and other Centurions, both in the cloth of the cloak and the fur that lined it. Additionally, he made no mention of the day before, simply reciting the words that are essentially a ritual for Legions in the winter, that the duties for the day would be decided by the Primi Pili.

However, he did surprise us by adding at the end, "I am ordering a meeting of all Centurions at the beginning of the second watch today, in the *praetorium*." Then, turning to where

Sacrovir and Neratius were standing, he told them, "Primi Pili, carry out your orders for the day."

Waiting until Germanicus had returned to the relative warmth of the *praetorium*, first Neratius, then Sacrovir, mouthed the same words they always did for a day like this, then we were dismissed to begin the day. While some Pili Priores insisted that the men of their Cohort be marched off the forum back to their area, most simply dismissed their men and allowed them to make their way back on their own. Macer was of the latter sort, and once he gave the order, the Cohort, rankers and officers alike, broke up into smaller groups, walking across the forum, which had already lost that pristine, clean look from all the hobnailed soles of the men. I was walking, alone, towards our area when, from behind me, I heard Macer call my name, instantly sending my heart to a galloping rhythm that was more appropriate to breaking into an all-out sprint.

Of course, I slowed to allow him to reach my side, but rather than stop, he continued walking, and we did so side by side, both of us looking straight ahead, although I certainly kept glancing over out of the corner of my eye, but for several paces, Macer said nothing, until he broke the silence by saying, "I've thought about it, and I need you in this Cohort. You're not going anywhere. And," I sensed that he turned to look up at me, so I did the same, meeting his gaze, "we're never going to speak about this again, nor will I have anything entered into your record. Do you agree to this?"

I assured him that I did, then he turned back to the scene ahead of us of men hurrying to their quarters to prepare for the day. For a moment, I did not think it was wise to say anything, given the circumstances.

So, of course, I said, "Thank you. I appreciate it and I won't let you down."

"You better not," Macer said lightly, but I took him seriously.

"I won't," I assured him, then I changed the subject, asking him, "Any idea what Germanicus wants to tell us?"

I was encouraged by the manner in which Macer again turned to look at me with a grin, replying, "I was hoping you'd know, since you and Germanicus are so close."

This made me laugh, and if it was heartier than perhaps it should have been, I would simply say it was as much from relief as the humor.

"Now that we've put this…unpleasantness behind us, it's time to settle our business with Arminius once and for all."

Germanicus was standing on the desk outside his office, with the remaining Centurions of both Legions standing around him, the Pili Priores arrayed in front, while those of us who were taller moved to the back. Which, of course, meant Volusenus and I were standing side by side on the last row, yet despite the distance, and the relatively dim lighting, it was easy for all to see how haggard Germanicus was, but I believe that I was one of the few who knew him well enough to see how forced his hearty tone sounded.

"Before I begin," he said, "I wanted to let you know of the steps I've taken to bring the 5th and 21st back under the standard. I sent a message to Caecina, telling him what we did here, and ordering him to read my message to the Primi Pili and *Aquiliferi* of both Legions. I'm…" he paused as he thought of the correct word, which he uttered with a small smile on his lips that informed us it was anything but, "…suggesting that the Legate and Primi Pili take the same approach that stopped the mutiny here. I haven't heard back yet, but I'm optimistic that the situation will be resolved in a similar manner as it was here." When one reads the words, it does not properly express Germanicus' mood, because he said this in a manner that, knowing him better than any of the other Centurions present, informed me that he was certain of the outcome; only later did we learn that he actually ordered Caecina to read Germanicus' letter word for word, which essentially was a transcript of his speech to us. He stopped speaking for a moment, presumably to allow us to digest this, before he resumed. "We're going to be busy this winter," he continued, "both because there's much to do to bring the men back to rights, but also because, and I think you will agree, an important factor in what occurred is that we didn't keep the men busy enough. And," his mouth turned down into a grimace, "I bear the responsibility for that."

"We all do, sir."

I could not see him, but I recognized Sacrovir's voice, which was quickly joined by others, all of them adding their assent to the Primus Pilus. While I would not say he was pleased, Germanicus was clearly relieved that his Centurions were not willing for him to bear the responsibility for the mutiny of the Army of the Rhenus alone.

Once things were quiet again, Germanicus continued, "Whatever the cause, I'm determined that we put this behind us, and I know all of you will do the same with your Centuries. Now," for the first time, he smiled, although it was a grim one, "that's not to say we're not going to work the men harder than they've ever been worked before, but since it's for a good cause, I think they'll turn to their tasks without more than the normal amount of complaint." He paused for a moment, then asked a question that I do not believe he would have asked under normal circumstances, and again, I suspect I heard a note in his voice that few of the others present did. "Do you agree with that assessment?"

We assured him that we did, and thus assured, Germanicus began outlining his plan for the coming campaign in broad strokes, and the first surprise was that he was not going to wait until next spring. Instead, he was launching a limited punitive campaign against the Marsi, which he intended to begin as quickly as possible. As we all listened intently, I realized that this was clearly something he had been thinking about for some time, certain that he could not have come up with the level of detail this quickly. He spoke for perhaps a third of a watch, and by the time he was through and asked for questions, he had been so thorough that there were very, very few.

"Naturally, we're going to be adding more details as we get closer to marching, but you should know that, now that I've finished the census in Gaul, I'm going to be with the army for the duration of not just this campaign, but the one coming up this spring. And," he said, "if you have any ideas or concerns that I and my staff are missing something, please don't hesitate to have your superior bring it up with me. Now," he finished, "I also know I don't need to tell you that our first order of business is filling the posts of the Centurions and Optios who…" his voice trailed off, but he clearly saw he had no need to remind us of their collective fate, and he continued, making a slight gesture with his hands, "…and I'd like those spots filled within the next two days. The sooner we can do that, the quicker we can get things back to normal and get to work."

With that, we were dismissed, and as was customary, we returned to our respective areas with the Centurions from our Cohort. It was during our walk back that Macer pulled me aside, which was not unusual in itself, but clearly, Vespillo, Cornutus, and Volusenus sensed that this was about something out of the ordinary. If they had asked, I would have agreed with them, certain that, despite his claim that what had taken place with Pusio would never be mentioned again, he was having second thoughts, not that I could blame him. Happily, in more ways than one, I was completely wrong, although it did explain why the other three Centurions were clearly unhappy about being excluded, since they had a better idea of what was really going on than I did.

"Do you think Structus is ready for promotion?" Macer asked without preamble, catching me completely by surprise, which might have been his intent, because without thinking about it, I answered, "Absolutely."

"So do I," he agreed, then he hesitated for a moment, and I understood why when he went on, "which is why I'm putting him forward to the Primus Pilus to take over Philus' Century."

This brought me to an abrupt halt, not because I thought it was a bad idea, but that it was not the customary method, and my first thought was that it might actually hamper Structus' chances of entering the Centurionate.

"Are you sure?" I asked, but then before he could respond, I felt it important to add, "It's not because I don't think he can handle it. I do, very strongly. But it's just..."

"Unusual," Macer finished for me, and I nodded. "Yes, it is," he agreed, "but this is an unusual time, and Sacrovir has already let it be known he's open to the idea of promoting eligible Optios into the Centurionate in their own Cohorts and not just shifting men who are already Centurions up and filling the third line Cohorts with new Centurions. He thinks that having men who may be inexperienced as Centurions but are familiar with the men of the Cohort is more important, especially after all that's happened." This made complete sense to me, and I said as much. "Good." Macer sounded relieved, making me wonder whether he thought I might have objected, or if it was just one of many details that he had to attend to, which seemed to be confirmed as he asked, "And who do you have in mind for your Optio?"

"Clustuminus." Again, I answered immediately, but this time, Macer did not nod, nor did he say anything. We had resumed walking, and the next several paces were covered in silence, until I could not take it anymore, asking, "Is there a problem with Clustuminus?"

Macer pursed his lips, not answering immediately, then he said, "I just recall wondering how involved he was with the mutiny." He turned to look up at me and asked, "What do you think?"

There was no way I could deny that this had not been a concern for me, and I admitted, "I wondered the same thing. But," I confess I was making this up as I went, since I had not had the time to sit down and gather my thoughts on the subject, "I think that he was like a lot of the men who agreed that we were owed these concessions by Tiberius. And," I took a breath before I said, "I agree with the men who feel that way."

This caused Macer to look up at me in surprise, exclaiming, "*Gerrae*! Really?"

"Yes, really," I answered.

"But you never gave any indication that you felt that way," Macer did not seem to actually be aiming that at me, speaking in more of a musing tone.

I did not know how to respond to that, so I did not try, and we both remained silent the rest of the way to our area.

Stopping at the Cohort tent, Macer started to enter, then turned and asked me, "Are you sure about Clustuminus?"

"Yes," I answered without hesitation.

He did not say anything, just gave a nod, and I resumed walking to my own quarters, wondering what he would do about my Optio. I got my answer less than a third of a watch later, when Alex came to tell me that Lucco had just taken the warrant for Structus' promotion to Quartus Hastatus Prior to the Legion office. And, before the end of the day, his promotion had been approved, prompting me to send the warrant for Clustuminus to Macer, which he did approve, but not until the next day. Just as Germanicus had decreed, all the empty spots for both Legions had been filled by the second day after the end of the mutiny, and the preparation for this short campaign against the Marsi began in earnest.

I do not know if the complete story of what happened with the 5th and 21st as it pertains to Germanicus' letter to Caecina will ever be known, but ultimately, it is the result that matters, not the method. And, as with my Legion and the 20th, the ringleaders of the mutiny were turned on and executed by their own comrades, which was apparently a bit less organized and much bloodier than what had occurred with the 1st and 20th. All that mattered, at least to the Centurions, was that things had returned to a semblance of normality, and fairly quickly, the work of preparing for yet another winter campaign, like the one early in my time with the 1st under Tiberius, occupied every waking watch of men of all ranks, which served to keep the chatter about recent events to a minimum. And, with that, gentle reader, I must close, because I have much to do as the time to march rapidly approaches.

Chapter Twelve

Normally, I do not spend any time on this account while on campaign, but because of something that happened shortly before we left Ubiorum that has completely upended my world, I am compelled to spend what little off-duty time a Centurion has in recording what occurred. Simply put, I am incapable of sleeping as it is, so I might as well put this time to use, if only to attempt to make sense of it in my own mind, although it might be impossible.

It began innocuously enough, after our return to Ubiorum, when I happened to be in the Cohort office delivering the daily report, and Volusenus entered.

Lucco and I were chatting about nothing important, so when the Hastatus Posterior walked in, Lucco excused himself from the conversation, calling to Volusenus, "Centurion, you must have gotten my message." Without waiting for a reply, the clerk looked down at a small pile of scrolls, frowning as he picked through them, then finding the correct one, held it out. "Here it is. This came for you a few moments ago. From Ubiorum," he informed Volusenus.

"Ubiorum?" Volusenus' frown mirrored that of Lucco, but he took the scroll, saying as he opened it, "I don't know why anyone from Ubiorum would want to send me anything."

In fact, I did, or at least thought I did, because Volusenus had confided something to me, which was what prompted me to grin and guess, "Maybe it's from your…friend. You know the one; her husband might be out of town again."

I was rewarded by a sudden flushing of Volusenus' face even as he returned my grin, although it was somewhat guilty, but it vanished as soon as he began reading the contents.

Between his height and the way he was standing, I could not see what was written on the parchment; I have spent a fair amount of the intervening time wondering, if I had managed to catch a glimpse of the hand in which the words were written, would I have been better prepared for what was about to happen to my life?

In the moment, I was just mildly concerned at the sudden change in Volusenus' expression, and I asked, "What is it? Bad news?"

This seemed to yank him from his reading of the scroll, and he looked up at me, more bemused than anything else.

Shaking his head, he said, "What? No, it's not...*bad* news, exactly." He hesitated, then said with what sounded to me like a forced casualness, "It's just that my mother is coming to Ubiorum and is asking to see me."

"Your mother?" I echoed, then before I could stop myself, I teased him, "Is she coming to make sure you're being treated well by all of us other Centurions?"

This irritated Volusenus, and he shot me a scowl, but it was nothing like the look he would have given me early in his tenure as Hastatus Posterior; indeed, I suspect that my jibe would have caused us to come to blows.

"No, Pullus," he sighed with an air of exaggerated patience, "she just loves her son. And," suddenly, he grinned back at me, "she stopped worrying about me when I was ten years old because I was as big as my father, and she said she felt silly thinking that some other boy could thrash me."

As I suspect he hoped, this did make me laugh, because this was something we had in common, and over the years as we became closer, we had often talked about some of the little things that men of our size experience.

Volusenus turned serious, waving the scroll, explaining, "She was visiting my aunt in Mogontiacum when the mutiny happened, and now that it's over, she decided to come see me before she returned home to Mediolanum. She sent a courier ahead to let me know she should be in Ubiorum just before dark."

I recalled that, while we had never talked that much about our respective families, I was aware that, before he died, the *paterfamilias* and his son had not been particularly close, but I knew this was not the case with his mother. It was not that he mentioned her all that often, but when he did, anyone with eyes could see by his expression how he felt about her, and I suppose this was another way in which we were similar, since I felt much the same way about my departed mother, Iras.

It was Lucco who interjected, informing us both, "The Pilus Prior is planning on giving the Cohort the liberty of the town tonight."

"Well," I said cheerfully, "it looks like Volusenus doesn't have any excuse not to see his mother."

Sighing, Volusenus asked, "You're never going to let me forget this, are you?"

"No, I'm not." I informed him with a broad smile that almost hurt my cheeks.

"Well, I *was* going to honor you by introducing you to her," he grumbled, heading for the door as he did, "but you can forget that now."

"Why, Volusenus," I tried to appear upset, "that hurts my feelings!"

"Yes, I can tell," he answered dryly, but he was closing the door as he did so, leaving Lucco and me chuckling.

I actually had no plans to go into town that night, but Macer talked me into it.

"We haven't had a night off since the mutiny began," he reminded me, "and the gods know when we'll have another chance."

This was certainly true, and honestly, I did not have to be pressed that hard, knowing that all I was going to do was stay in my quarters and read. Alex had been spending his nights in town with Algaia, but my worries about friction between the brothers were unfounded, since before a week was out, Titus had taken up with the daughter of the smith for whom he was now an apprentice.

"Oh well," I sighed. "The Dancing Faun it is."

The rest of the day passed quickly, aided by the fact that by this time of year, there are barely more than two full watches of daylight. This is a boon for those men who love to debauch, since the traditional time to allow men to leave camp is shortly before it gets dark, and this night was no exception. As was normal, we left camp in a group of all but one Centurion, and most of the Optios, talking about the normal things officers discuss among themselves. The missing Centurion was not Volusenus; he was walking with us into town before splitting off to meet his mother, for which he took a fair amount of teasing. Not from me, I would add; I felt I had already had my fun, and it was easy to see that, while he bore it with a certain amount of good humor, just like me, Volusenus did not particularly care for being the object of fun. That it was Cornutus who was missing was neither an accident nor was he missed; he was viewed by the rest of us with a fair amount of suspicion, although not as much because he probably sympathized with the mutineers. So did I, but it was his behavior in trying to avoid being forced to take sides by hiding in his quarters every available moment that did not set well with any of us, for that was what we had heard was the truth behind his actions. Not that we spoke of any of this during our walk into town, since, once the others had their fun with Volusenus, it was time for the Centurions to turn on the newest member of the Centurionate, my old Optio, and in this, I freely confess I was the most vocal, reminding Structus and the other listeners of some of his more embarrassing moments as my

Optio. Putting it simply, it was a normal walk into town, on a normal end of the day, albeit emerging from a period of time that was anything but, and I think that is why we were in such high spirits, reveling in this return to the mundane routine that comprises so much of the life of men under the standard. Reaching the edge of the town forum, which had recently been enlarged, Volusenus suddenly pointed across it to where an enclosed carriage was standing motionless.

"That must be her," he told us, and I gave him a playful shove, saying, "Go on then. Go see Mama." I was joined by the others, which made Volusenus flush even more deeply than when he had read her message in the office.

Macer was the only one who acted with any sense of decorum, telling Volusenus, "Please give your mother regards from your Pilus Prior, Volusenus. I don't want her thinking that we're all low-class brutes, after all."

"But we *are* low-class brutes," Vespillo reminded Macer, then added, "Unlike you and Volusenus; we're not equestrians, after all."

Although the Pilus Posterior said it in a jesting manner, I knew that there was a barb in his words, and I saw Macer did not miss it either, yet another reminder of Vespillo's unhappiness. It must be said, however, in defense of Vespillo, his displeasure at his status was confined to the odd comment like this, which I believe was more from a sense of taking an opportunity to make some remark, and never impacted his actions or the quality of his obedience to Macer in any way. Which, I believe, is why Macer chose to ignore Vespillo, although I suspect it was also because he knew that by not responding, that would get under Vespillo's skin just as much as his jibe had gotten to Macer, a tactic that our Pilus Prior had learned was effective over the years.

Volusenus was too distracted to notice any of this and merely answered, "I'll give her your regards, Pilus Prior."

Then, walking across the forum, he ignored our calls about not staying up too late or essentially anything that one of us considered witty, while we resumed our own progress. Within a few paces, I had forgotten about Volusenus and was absorbed in talking to Structus, commiserating with him about the challenges of having an inordinately stupid ranker in one's Century. We were skirting the forum, walking along the row of small temples, one of which was in the process of being refurbished, prior to its consecration as the temple to Divus Augustus, when Macer's sudden whistle, followed by his exclamation, caught our attention.

"By the gods," he gasped, "that's Volusenus' *mother*?"

I suspect that everyone, when they look back on their lives, have moments that not only seem as if they happened just yesterday, but in the recollection of it, seem to last for much, much longer than they actually did when they happened. Although this one happened recently, I am certain that it will remain every bit as vivid and powerful years from now as it does at this instant; if, of course, I should live that long. Naturally drawn, first to Macer's low whistle, then his words, I turned my head in his direction, since he was standing on the side of our small group closer to where Volusenus was helping a woman out of the carriage. The light of the day had almost gone, but the slaves who work for the town watch had already begun lighting the torches that ring the forum; regardless of this, I do not think I would have needed any of it, because it was not her face that I noticed first. No, it was something in the manner in which she moved, accepting Volusenus' hand as he helped her down, that I recognized immediately, not with my eyes as much as with something deep inside me. The closest feeling with which I have any familiarity that I can liken it to is that it felt as if I had been stabbed, directly into my chest and penetrating my heart with such force that I actually staggered back a step. By the time I did so, my mind had caught up, and I saw her face for the first time, just as her foot touched the ground, but it was only a glimpse because, turning slightly, she lifted her face to accept the kiss from Volusenus just before she was swept into his embrace. Perhaps the most powerful image was how, without any effort whatsoever, Volusenus swept his mother off her feet, lifting her up to his level, something I had done with my mother as soon as I was larger than she was; and, with one other woman in my life. Fortunately for me, none of my companions noticed, since all eyes were rightfully on the scene of mother and son reunited.

"Well," I barely registered Vespillo's voice, or his words, "at least I know why he doesn't want to introduce any of us to her."

Despite their attention being elsewhere, I suppose my staggering must have been noticed, because Structus suddenly turned to look up at me, and I could tell that he was alarmed at whatever he saw.

"Pullus? Are you all right?"

It took a huge effort to tear my eyes away from Volusenus and his mother, yet I managed somehow, and I forced myself to say, "I'm all right. I just got this headache, suddenly."

"Headache?" Structus frowned, but I was further discomposed when our exchange caused Macer to turn away from the pair, and I felt his eyes studying me.

"What's this?" He actually asked Structus, but before my former Optio could answer, I spoke up, "I was just telling Structus I suddenly got a headache." This, I knew, was so unusual that I felt compelled to wince, then press my fingers against both temples. "I don't know why, but it feels like someone has my head in between two stones and is standing on them."

I felt slightly guilty at the look of alarm on my friend's face, but when he said, "Then I'll go back to camp with you," I protested that it was not necessary.

"I'm sure it's nothing serious," I assured him, then tried to give him a grin, "and I'm perfectly capable of making it back to my quarters on my own. Besides," in this, I was honest, "I don't want to be the one to tear any of you from a night's entertainment."

"Well," Macer answered doubtfully, "if you're sure…"

"I am," I assured him. "I'll be fine."

Then, without waiting for an answer, I turned and began walking; stumbling is probably more accurate, away from my fellow Centurions, although it was only to get away from Volusenus and his mother, Giulia, the love of my life who, until a matter of mere heartbeats before, I had thought was dead.

I do not recall anything of my walk back to camp; my first recollection was sitting on my cot in my quarters, trying to make sense of what I had seen, and more importantly, what it all meant. However, while there is one aspect of this that I know is clearly obvious now, I am completely sincere when I say that, in that moment back in my quarters, it still did not occur to me there was a connection between Gnaeus Volusenus and myself. All that mattered was trying to cope with the fact that, for more than twenty years now, I had believed that the woman I loved to the point where I never seriously considered entering into any kind of permanent relationship, simply because I did not want to face the kind of devastating loss I suffered the first time, was actually still alive. It was while I was sitting there that I heard someone entering the Legion office, but I assumed that Balio, who had already been retired behind his partition in the outer office, had gone to the latrines and I had not noticed. The quick knock, repeated twice on the door, informed me that it was not, yet I did not even bother looking up when Alex entered the room, not wanting to interrupt my study of the floor.

"Uncle Titus?"

Realizing that ignoring him was not a viable method of dealing with my nephew, I nevertheless still did not look up, and I asked without any real interest, "What are you doing here? Why aren't you with Algaia?"

He did not answer, which finally induced me to tear my eyes away from the spot on the floor, which I believe was his ploy for getting me to look up at him.

As I had suspected, and feared, he clearly knew something, which he partially explained when he said, "I ran into Optio Clustuminus, and he told me that you were ailing." Hesitating, he added, "He said that you looked as if you'd seen a *numen*. He was worried about you. And," his eyes searched my face, "now that I've seen you, I am too." The mention of a *numen* elicited a short bark of a laugh from me, but not because I found any humor in it, just that it was an appropriate way to put it, and I mentally saluted my new Optio for his insight. "Uncle Titus," Alex had moved from the door to stand in front of me, and there was no way I could miss the real concern in his expression, "what happened? Do you really have a headache? Or did you see something…or," I saw the bony knot in his throat bob up and down, "…someone?"

How, I wondered, can I explain this? How can I possibly communicate to my nephew what this is about?

What I settled on was, "I saw someone I haven't seen in a long time, nephew, and it caught me by surprise. That's all."

He stood there, not responding in any way, though his eyes were eloquent enough in their disbelief, but I think he also sensed that I was not going to divulge anything more.

"Well then," he broke the awkward silence, "I'm going to retire for the night."

When he moved in the direction of his pallet, I protested, "You don't need to stay here, Alex! You can go back into town." I even tried to give him a smile, though it felt as if my face was frozen. "I don't want Algaia upset with me that I'm keeping you away from her when you're going to be leaving so soon."

"She'll be fine," he answered shortly in a way that suggested to me that she was anything but fine about his leaving her bed in town.

Nevertheless, seeing that he was not going to be swayed, I realized there was no point in trying to argue, so instead, I made a show of getting ready to retire myself. And, I would add, I did lay down on my cot and waited for Alex to blow out the lamps in our shared quarters, but not only did I know I would not be sleeping, I did not have any intention of doing so.

Lying in my bunk, I stared up into the darkness, waiting for the sound of the *bucina* that signaled the beginning of the midnight watch, and as soon as it came, I arose. Moving as quietly as I could, I made my way to the hook where my *sagum*, the fur-lined one, was hanging, and grabbing it, I went to the door, where I stopped to listen for a moment.

"Don't try and follow me, Alex," was all I said quietly, yet I was certain that he heard me, and more importantly, understood, then I left my private quarters.

Slipping out into the Cohort street, I did think to reach down and feel my *baltea*, checking that my purse was there, knowing that I might be forced to pay a hefty bribe to the Centurion commanding the guard Cohort to look the other way if he was not of the 1st Legion. The gods were with me in that sense; it was the Fifth Cohort of my Legion who had the guard that night, and I had a good relationship with Pilus Prior Clepsina, so leaving the camp was not a problem. Walking into town in complete darkness, I cannot really recall what I was thinking, but when I reached the town gates, this was the first moment I had to drop some coins into the hands of the town watch. However, this happened on a nightly basis, just not with me, but I knew more men than I could easily count who paid for the privilege of staying in Ubiorum overnight, relying on whoever they were sleeping with to ensure they were roused in time to get back to camp in time for the morning call. Volusenus had not said where his mother was staying, but he did not need to in order for me to know where to go. Despite the fact that Ubiorum was almost unrecognizable from the time I had transferred into the 1st, which was the first winter my Legion spent on the site of what is now a good-sized town, there is still really only one inn that caters to the upper classes, and this was where I headed. Just as I reached the entrance, I was struck by something, and it was powerful enough that I stopped and seriously considered turning around. What if, I thought, Volusenus asked Macer permission to spend the night in town, and he's sharing the room with his mother? I am not known for indecisiveness, but that night, I was in a quandary that caused me to stand, motionless, for a lengthy span of time, before I reached for the latch and opened the door. Because of the hour, the proprietor was not awake, but as was customary, there was a burly slave who served as a night watchman sitting on a stool, and seeing me enter, he leapt to his feet, his eyes wide with alarm; whether or not it was because it was unusual, it was my size, or a combination of the two, I did not know.

It did serve to cause me to hold out both hands and say, "*Pax*. I mean no harm, to you or to any guest."

This seemed to soothe him somewhat, but I noticed his hand was still within an inch of the cudgel leaning against the wall. As befitting a slave addressing a man of the Legions, which I obviously was because of both my *baltea* and my *gladius*, his tone was deferential, but it was also cautious.

"Is there something I can do for you, Master?"

This was when I realized I had not given any thought to how I was going to talk my way past this man to get to Giulia, and without thinking about it, what came out of my mouth was the truth, or a version of it at least.

"I just found out that the mother of one of my fellow Centurions is an old acquaintance of mine from when I was with the 8th Legion in Siscia," I explained, and I was heartened to see him relax slightly but noticeably.

Nevertheless, he was not sufficiently swayed to simply let me pass, and while his tone was polite, there was a note of skepticism that I understood, when he asked me, "And why would you want to see this lady at this hour, Master?" Speaking the words seemed to firm his spine, because he shook his head and added. "Master Aulus would have me flayed if I let you past."

Feeling a sudden surge of desperation, I reached for my coin purse, holding it up and shaking it gently so that the slave could hear the solid sound of the coins clinking together, but while he was clearly tempted, he remained steadfast.

"I'm sorry, Master," his head continued to shake back and forth, and I was running out of ideas about how to make it nod up and down, "but there's no amount of coin you can offer that would be worth the price of my skin." I think he must have realized something, because he added, "I was not jesting about being flayed, Master. Master Aulus would do it, and," a shadow of what I suppose was a combination of fear and hatred crossed his face, "he *has* done it before, to the slave who held this job before me."

My heart sank, realizing that my choices were rapidly dwindling, and a growing sense of desperation caused me to begin thinking about how I would force my way past this guard. I wish I could say that part of my calculations included a desire to avoid causing this slave, who was only doing his duty, any harm, but the only aspect I considered was how I could subdue him, as quickly and quietly as possible. As always, I had my *vitus*, and my *pugio* as well, although I will say that the latter I only considered as a last resort. The silence dragged out between us, and I suppose my face must have betrayed my intentions because his hand went to the cudgel, though his eyes never left me, while I shifted my grip on my *vitus,* with the intention of using it as a quasi-stabbing weapon. Before matters could disintegrate into an action that I know neither the slave nor I, for that matter, wanted, we were both saved by a voice, literally from above us. Not from the heavens, but from the top of the stairs where the rooms for the guests were located, and it was a voice I had not heard in more than twenty years, yet it still made my knees go weak.

"I will see the Centurion, Mandalonius," Giulia spoke from the top of the stairs, but while I could hear her, I could not see her, although the way the stool was placed at the bottom of the stairs allowed the slave to look up the stairway at her. "There's no need for any trouble. He's…" I heard the hesitation, and the quaver in her voice matched the feelings that were rushing through me, "…a friend, just as he said. We've known each other many years, and I am perfectly safe."

It was clear to see that the slave Mandalonius was torn between his standing orders from his master, who sounded like a right bastard to me, and obeying the orders of a guest who, while clearly belonging to the upper class, was a woman, and I was also reminded that learning the name of a slave she would only meet once in her life was something Giulia had always done even when she was young, and it likely had an effect on his thinking as well. For several heartbeats, his gaze kept alternating between looking up the stairs, then back at me, his eyes going to the *vitus* in my hand, and I began thinking that I would have to resort to the tactic that had come to my mind before Giulia appeared.

Then, Giulia said, "Please, Mandalonius? I assure you I'm in no danger from the Centurion, and I won't be alone in my room with him."

This caused the slave to take a deep breath, then he nodded his head; more importantly to me, his hand left the cudgel, and he stepped aside to allow me to pass him and ascend the stairs. I was in a state that I have never experienced before, where I wanted to bound up the stairs, yet was terrified of doing so, because I had no idea what to expect, not just from Giulia, but from me. Regardless of my agitation, I was sufficiently possessed of myself to hand over all but a couple coins from my purse, although Mandalonius seemed discomfited by the gesture.

"This," I said quietly, "is for you and you alone. And," I added, "if your master does *anything* to you about this, you send a message to Quartus Princeps Prior Pullus of the 1st, and I'll come and explain."

Frankly, he seemed more grateful about this than the money, although he took the coins when I held them out. Then, I could delay no longer, and I turned to look up the stairs, where Giulia, wearing a gown of a deep green, a color that always suited her, was standing with a lamp in one hand. Ascending the stairs, I could not tear my eyes away from her face, the dancing flame of the lamp playing on her features, which should have made those lines that come to all of us with age stand out in deeper relief, but were almost completely absent. Naturally, I was still two steps from the top when our eyes were level with each other, and we stood there for a moment, neither speaking, until she finally broke the silence.

"*Salve*, Titus. I suppose you have a lot of questions."

Giulia had not been lying when she said that she would not be alone in her room, but despite my fear that it would be Volusenus, instead it was her body slave, a woman of about my age whose eyes went wide at the sight of me entering the room.

"*Blessed Juno!*" she gasped, then began, "He looks exactly like..."

"*Silete!* What have I told you about your mouth?" Giulia's tone was sharp, and I was reminded how imperious she could be

647

when she chose. This clearly chastened the woman, but Giulia was not through. "That will be all, Carissa," she commanded. "You can wait downstairs with Mandalonius while I speak with the Centurion."

"But," Carissa protested, with a horror that I could not tell whether or not was feigned, "it's not proper, Mistress!"

"*Gerrae!*" Giulia answered scornfully. "I'm a widow, not a wife. Besides," there was a subtle change to her voice, "I saw the way you were making eyes at that German down there."

That this must have been true was betrayed by Carissa's response, as she turned a deep red, breaking eye contact, and she only mumbled, "Very well, Mistress."

Giulia and I waited for her to leave the room, but then she spoke in a voice slightly louder than necessary, which I understood when she said, "And, Carissa, you're not going to be listening at the door, or I'll have you whipped."

While I appreciated the idea, I confess that my first thought was about another servant of Giulia's household, Plotina, who Giulia's mother had personally flogged to death, and I felt a stab of worry that perhaps Giulia was more like her mother than I had thought.

Whether she read my mind or understood how this could be taken, once she waited to hear Carissa's footsteps descend the stairs, only then did she turn to me and admit, "She knows I'd never do it, but I don't want her listening in either, and she knows when I say that, I'm serious." Then, for the first time, I sensed how nervous she was, seeing her hand shaking as she indicated a chair, asking, "Would you care to sit down, Titus?"

This was such an incongruous, needless thing to say that, for an instant, I thought she might have gone mad, but I suppose the habits of courtesy still held sway, not only with her but with me, because before I gave it any thought, I had actually moved towards the chair she indicated, while she sat on the small couch at the end of the bed. Because this room was reserved for the upper-class guests who found themselves in Ubiorum, it was lushly appointed, and was much larger than a normal room at an inn. There was a partition between the back of the couch and the bed, so it was not visible, but I barely noticed, suddenly realizing how ludicrous this was, a mummer's play where Giulia was playing the role of proper Roman matron hostess, and I was simply her guest. I suspect that this was what caused me to stop in my tracks, and suddenly, I could contain myself no longer.

"How could you let me believe you were dead all these years?" I cannot express what an effort of will it took for me to keep my voice at a reasonable level, but I suppose I was in possession of myself enough to know that bellowing at the top of my lungs would destroy any chance of me learning the truth. To my utter horror, I felt the pricking of tears as I stared down at her, deciding to remain on my feet and in possession of the high ground, so to speak, as I repeated, "How could you?"

This seemed to unleash something in Giulia as well, because she was unable to stop herself from bursting into tears, and she buried her face in her hands, whereupon she began sobbing uncontrollably. Despite my anger with her, before I had any conscious thought, I had crossed over to her, dropping to my knees in front of her, yet when I reached out to touch her, she recoiled.

"Don't!" She dropped her hands from her face, and I saw the telltale sign of anger in the dilation of her nostrils, which I thought was aimed at me, but she said, "Don't try to comfort me, Titus! I don't deserve it! I...I..."

While I recall every moment of that night, I will not speak of much of it, taking the memory with me across the river; all I will relate is the story of why Giulia hid the birth of my son from me, and how she did it.

"My mother told me that if I did anything to try and contact you, she would spend as much money as necessary to have you killed," Giulia's voice was flat and matter-of-fact, if slightly muffled because her head was resting on my chest. "And," there was a slight change then, as she showed a flash of bitter hatred, "after what she did to Plotina, I knew she was perfectly capable of doing it."

While this made sense, and I completely understood and agreed with her assessment of her mother's ability for hatred, I cannot lie; the idea she would be able to find someone with enough skill to kill me was something I did not accept easily.

However, there was one thing I did not understand, and I said as much. "But what about your father? I know he liked me; he told me as much."

I felt her chest expand, and the sigh she let out was one of true melancholy, although she answered readily enough. "As much as I loved my Tata, Titus, I'm not blind now and I wasn't then. He was a good man, but he was a weak one, and he loved my mother more than she deserved to be loved." She lifted her head to look me directly in the eye, and in the guttering light of the small lamp on the table next to the bed, I saw those golden flecks that had so captivated me early on, yet her tone was level as she acknowledged the one thing we had never discussed. "That was why he forgave my mother after she had an affair with that Legate." Before I could reply or react in any way, she turned away and dropped her head back on my chest, and finished, "Besides that, he was as scared of her as I was."

Now that, I thought, I *could* understand, and I recalled the short conversation I had had with Lucius Livinius, after my confrontation with his wife Livinia, when he had admitted as much.

Despite my acceptance of her explanation of the early days of her pregnancy and the birth of our son, I was not ready to capitulate on my anger, and more than that, the hurt I felt, prompting me to ask, "That explains early on, but your mother died, what, three years after you left?"

"Four," she corrected, but I was certain she was stalling, and I brushed this aside, hearing the impatience in my voice. "Three, four, five, it doesn't matter. Why didn't you let me know that you weren't dead? That you had borne a son?" Somehow, I managed to get this past the sudden lump in my throat. "*My son?*"

Despite my best intentions to avoid it, I could feel the anger growing in me, which caused me to remove myself from our position, sitting up against the wall so that I could look her directly in the eye. In a move that I remembered loving every time she did it, Giulia sat up as well, and did not draw the sheet around her to cover her nakedness, while she looked me directly in the eye, which, even as angry as I was, I respected.

"Because it would have destroyed Gnaeus' life," she answered quietly. At first, I was confused, since I rarely called Volusenus by his *praenomen*, if I ever had. "And he would have been cast out of my husband's home, been branded as a bastard, and never would have had a chance."

This, I knew perfectly well, was inarguable, but I was not yet ready to be reasonable; however, her mention of the man who had been my love's husband took control of my mind, and I asked her, "Did he know that he wasn't...Gnaeus' father?"

"Yes, he knew," Giulia answered but then did not seem disposed to say anything more, except I was not about to let this be all she said on the subject.

"And?" I demanded; for a long moment, she did not answer, and this time, she did look away from me.

Finally, she heaved a sigh and said, "And he was in so much debt that my father was willing to pay him out of that he convinced us both that he wouldn't ever hold it against me, and that he'd raise Gnaeus as his own son."

The lump reappeared in my throat, but I forced myself to ask, "And did he?"

"Yes," Giulia answered immediately, but then added, "and no."

I listened as she went on to describe what her life had been like, and as I sat there, I realized that, despite myself, I could sympathize with Quintus Claudius Volusenus. What Giulia told me aligned with what little Volusenus had told me about his father, that, while he had not been mistreated by the man he thought was his father, neither had they been close. Now that I knew the truth, I could understand why the older man treated the boy he knew was not his with some reserve, but neither could I suppress a twinge of sorrow for the young Volusenus, not knowing why his father did not seem to love him.

Suddenly, I was struck by another thought and I interrupted Giulia, "How did he treat *you*? Did he…mistreat you?"

I confess I was not only surprised, but a little put out when she answered immediately, "No, he didn't. Oh," she allowed, "sometimes when he'd had too much wine, Quintus Claudius would say something, but he did it in such a way that only I knew what he was talking about and not our son."

I felt a sharp stab of envy at the fact that she had referred to Volusenus as "our" son, assuming that she meant herself and Volusenus, but I was reminded how well she knew me, despite the years that had passed, because she read my face correctly, and said softly, "No, Titus, I'm not talking about Quintus Claudius and me; I'm talking about *you* and me. He's our son, and I've never forgotten that."

"Did you love him?" I blurted this out before I could stop myself, yet once more, Giulia did not look surprised, although I was certain I saw a flash of irritation, which she confirmed when she sighed, replying, "You men all think alike. That was the one thing that Quintus Claudius asked, especially in the beginning, if I still loved you." She tilted her head slightly, a shadow of a smile as she continued, "Now, here you are, asking me the same thing about him."

"That didn't answer the question," I pointed out.

"No, it didn't," she agreed readily enough, but then she broke my gaze, looking away as she sat silently for a moment. Then, as if asking herself, she echoed, "Did I love Quintus?" I realized I was holding my breath as she considered this, before she said, "I was...fond of him. Aside from the fact that he was horrible at business, he was essentially a good man, and he provided well for me and for Gnaeus. With," she added, "my father's help, since he left us quite a bit of money." Suddenly, she turned back to regard me with a raised eyebrow, and there was something in her eyes that gave me a moment's warning, asking me, "What about you? Who have you been in love with since we were together?"

"Nobody," I answered immediately, and truthfully, looking her directly in the eye.

I saw she was torn – I assumed between being doubtful and being pleased – but she countered, "So, you're saying that you've been celibate all these years?"

That, I admit, caused the blood to rush to my face, but I also had to laugh, admitting, "I didn't say anything about celibacy." My smile vanished, because I wanted her to understand I was being sincere. "But, no, I've never loved anyone since you, Giulia."

Her eyes filled with tears, which caused a similar welling in my own, but this time, I was not ashamed that she saw them, and without saying anything, she reached out and placed her tiny hand on the scar on my left arm. We sat there, silent and motionless for a long moment, both of us absorbed in our own regrets, I suppose.

She was looking down at my arm as she stroked it softly, and she murmured, "I remember the first time I touched this; it made me so sad for you."

"Sad?" I smiled, mainly trying to make light of it and not betray how touched I was. "Why should it make you sad? You told me you found it quite attractive!"

"I did," she agreed, a smile coming to her own face, but it only was there for a heartbeat, "but then I would think about how much pain it must have caused you, and it would make me sad." She lifted her head to examine my face, and she reached out to touch the scar on my cheek, then glanced down at my knees, which were visible now that I was sitting with my legs crossed. "And you have even more now."

I took her hand from my face, not as a rebuke but because I did not want her to dwell on what is essentially a hazard that comes with the occupation of being a Centurion, but I suppose my thoughts were running in the same direction since I was struck by something, and I realized that I had forgotten to ask, "So, how did you know I would show up? In fact," I added, "how did you know that I was here in Ubiorum and not still back in Siscia?"

Once more, I sensed by her hesitation that there might be something I would not like, although she admitted readily enough, "I've known you were in Gnaeus' Century ever since not long after he showed up." She frowned at me then and said severely, "He told me of another Centurion his size who was making his life miserable because he didn't think Gnaeus belonged in a first line Cohort."

The blood that had left my face came rushing back, but I was not about to try to defend myself, and I replied flatly, "Because he didn't." It was her turn to become angry, signaled once more by the dilating nostrils, but she surprised me by replying, "He admitted as much. And," she added, "he gave you the credit for making him worthy of being in the Centurionate. Not," she allowed, "at first. It was probably a year after he showed up when he said that."

I was awash in a number of emotions, but the one that was strongest was a sense of pride that I had never experienced before. During my career, I had certainly helped other men under the standard, like Marcus Macer, yet this was profoundly different, and I think this was the first moment where I had the slightest idea what it might have felt like for my father.

Setting this aside, I returned to something else that puzzled me, asking her, "That explains you knew I was in the Cohort, but how did you know I'd come here tonight?"

"Because Gnaeus told me he had walked into town to meet me with all the Centurions of his Cohort but one. I thought that you might be the missing one, but I suppose somehow I just knew that you were one of them. And, he wanted to introduce me to all of you."

I suppressed a gasp, silently thanking the gods for averting what would have been an utter catastrophe, and I was honest enough with myself to know that, if this introduction had occurred, the beast that resides in me could have easily been unleashed.

Giulia must have either sensed this, or simply understood how badly things would go, and she told me, "That's why I pleaded that the journey had tired me out, and we only spent a short time together before I retired to my room." She hesitated, and I understood why when she said, "I told him that we'd spend time together tomorrow evening, once he was secured from his duties. But," she shook her head sadly, and there was no missing the pain in her voice, "we both know that I can't stay here, so Carissa and I are leaving at dawn tomorrow. Or," she gave a laugh that held no joy, "dawn today."

Then, without saying anything more, she suddenly threw herself into my arms, and we held each other for a long, long moment, both absorbed in our own thoughts, our tears mingling together for all that we had lost.

After we made love again, Giulia's demeanor changed, becoming, if not distant, then somewhat agitated and hesitant.

"Titus," she had put her dressing gown back on and was sitting on the edge of the bed, and I noticed the distance between us, "I have a request to make."

"You want me to keep my mouth shut and not let our son know that I'm his father." I was certain that this was her request, yet even so, I felt another stab of anger when she simply nodded, and that probably contributed to my response. "I don't know if I can do that, Giulia."

She surprised me then, because she did not get angry or even impatient at my intransigence, countering instead by asking, "And what would be accomplished, Titus? Yes, he'd know the truth, but," now her lower lip quivered, and I heard the mother in her, "he'd also hate me. And think horribly of me. Please, Titus, at least don't tell him now, not before you both go out on this campaign he told me about!" Tears reappeared, yet despite my anger and conviction that Volusenus had a right to know the truth, I felt a deep twinge of guilt, and I was forced to ask myself, was telling him the truth for Volusenus or for me? A part of me reminded myself that I was the wronged party in this, at least as much as Volusenus, but while I wanted to be angry at her, I simply could not bring myself to feel that way towards her. And, I thought, being brutally honest, what *would* be accomplished?

Nevertheless, I was still surprised to hear my voice saying, "All right, Giulia. I won't tell him." Then, I added, "Now, anyway. But he needs to know at some point in time."

Only after this came out of my mouth did I get a sense of how tense she was, because she literally collapsed forward on the bed, holding her head in both hands, once more weeping uncontrollably, which of course prompted me to move to her and take her in my arms again, cursing the gods who had placed me in this impossible position.

"I swear I'll tell him, Titus," Giulia whispered, "but in my own way, and in my own time."

Honestly, I was not happy about this, especially the part about doing it in her own time, acutely aware that it was extremely likely that my idea about the length of the appropriate time and hers was probably quite different. However, the end of our time together was signaled by the call of the slave whose only function is to keep the time, announcing that the morning hour was just moments from occurring.

"Will you come back to Ubiorum sometime?" I asked, hating myself for the note of hopefulness in my voice.

In answer, Giulia reached up to touch my cheek and smiled at me, her eyes shining as she answered, "One reason I came was to tell Gnaeus that I'm thinking of relocating. Not," she warned, "to Ubiorum. That would be too close for his comfort. But to Mogontiacum. It's become quite habitable, actually, and Quintus' sister lives there now. We grew quite close over the years, and she's a widow like me. Although," she made a face, "the weather is wretched."

"That's not so far away," I answered, trying to match her light tone, but neither of us were fooled. I could not restrain myself from reminding her, "And it's all the more reason to tell Gnaeus the truth, since he's going to wonder why I'm suddenly visiting his mother."

She did not say anything, but that was because I kissed her, one more time, then opened the door and left her standing there. I felt her eyes on me as I descended the stairs, but I managed to refrain from looking back. Judging by the way Giulia's slave Carissa suddenly darted across my line of sight, and the manner in which the slave Mandalonius was shifting uncomfortably on his stool while tugging at his tunic, it appeared that Giulia's judgment about Carissa's interest in the slave had been sound. Winking at the German, who gave me a self-conscious grin, I exited the inn, breaking into a run almost immediately. Even for a Centurion, being absent for the morning call without permission was an offense, but honestly, I remember even less about my return to camp than I do about my journey into town. So many thoughts, many of them in conflict with each other, were competing with the equal tug of warring emotions, but overpowering it all was a sense of hope that, perhaps, just perhaps, Giulia and I could be together again. And, I had a son.

The moment I laid eyes on Gnaeus Volusenus, when we marched to the forum for the morning orders, was even more difficult than I thought it would be, yet despite being certain he would sense something was amiss, he gave no sign that he did. There was one moment that threatened my composure, when, as we were walking back to our area, Macer asked Volusenus how the visit with his mother had gone.

"It wasn't much of a visit," Volusenus answered, and I actually slowed a bit so that I was out of his line of sight, just as a precaution, "because she was so tired from the ride. We're going to see each other tonight."

"You better make it a good one," Vespillo interjected, "since we're leaving tomorrow."

This had been the word given to us by Germanicus, that he deemed the Legions ready to march against the Marsi, which was true enough; the only task left to the men of our Cohort was to grease their *sagum*, which we always do last because the waterproofing wears off fairly quickly.

I said nothing, but it was difficult, fighting an almost overwhelming urge to let Volusenus know that when he went to the inn that night, Giulia would be gone; however, I could not think of any way to bring it up in a manner that would not raise all the questions I had promised Giulia I would not mention. It was surprisingly agonizing, frankly, as for the first time I looked at Gnaeus Volusenus, who was completely oblivious to the fact that his father was just a pace behind him, not as a comrade or as a young Centurion who I had seen promise in, but as flesh of my flesh. I suppose this was what prompted me to call Alex into my quarters as soon as we returned.

"I need you to bring me some of the best vellum you can find," I instructed him, then added, "and at least four sheets."

When he returned, I did something quite unusual for me; instead of dictating to Alex, whose hand is better than mine, I sent him to find Clustuminus and inform my Optio that he would be overseeing the Century for a time, then I sat down and, very carefully, began writing. It took me more than a third of a watch, but I was oddly proud of myself that I did not need to use the spare sheet, perhaps the most potent sign of the care I was taking with this document, along with the copy I made that would be sent to Rome and the one I would give to Macer, which may be the most important I ever write. Even more significant than this account, but I confess that I rejoice in my heart knowing there is now someone to whom this will go, along with those scrolls already dictated to Diocles by my Avus. Once I was done, I rose from my desk, and walked to the Cohort office, asking Lucco if Macer was in his office. When he nodded, I knocked on his door, then once he bade entry, I crossed to his desk, holding out one of the scrolls, which I had attached to the spools myself.

"What's that?" Macer asked curiously.

"It's my new will," I told him, which clearly surprised him.

Macer had been the holder of my will since my second year with the 1st, and while he reached out to accept it, I saw a mixture of amusement and concern on his face.

"Did you finally find a whore you can't live without?" he joked, then, completely by accident, actually guessed the truth, though I managed to avoid letting on that he had done so. "Or did you find your long-lost son or something?"

The smile I gave him felt completely false, and he knew me well enough that I was certain he would pick up on it, yet somehow, I managed to respond in the same joking manner,

"Something like that." Then, making it up on the fly, I added, "Now that Alex's brother is with us, I wanted to make sure he was included. I don't want him to feel left out."

He shrugged, accepting this easily enough, taking the will and placing it in his strongbox, and I only breathed easier when I saw him lock it.

Turning back to me, he asked, "So? Are your men ready?"

This had become something of a running joke, because I always answered the same way, snorting and countering, "Readier than yours, Pilus Prior."

And, as he always did, he responded with a grin, saying only, "We'll see."

Saluting, which was a bit unusual for an exchange like this, Macer returned it nevertheless, and I turned to leave.

"Pullus," his voice stopped me, and I looked back to see that, while he was smiling, there was a look of concern, "are you sure everything's all right?"

"Better than they've been in a long time," I assured him, then exited his quarters.

And now, this is where I must end. We are on campaign, and Gaesorix and his Batavians have reported that contact with the Marsi is imminent, probably happening tomorrow. As always, I will be at the head of my Century, but this time, I will be fighting with the knowledge that my son is nearby, and while it is a new sensation, it is also a truly wonderful, terrible, and awesome feeling, rolled into one.

Epilogue

"Is it true?"

Giulia Livinius Volusenus stood, having risen from her favorite couch, frozen in place, staring at her son Gnaeus, who, without any advance warning whatsoever, had somehow managed to obtain leave from his posting in Ubiorum to come to Mogontiacum, where she now lived. Despite her shock at his sudden appearance in the villa that she had purchased recently, along with the abrupt and seemingly elliptical manner in which he was addressing her, somehow, Giulia knew exactly what her son was asking.

Nevertheless, she did not reply, looking up at him with an outward calm she did not feel, which prompted him to repeat, this time more distinctly, "Is. It. True?"

There was a long silence, while mother and son regarded each other, the latter with an expression on his face that she had never seen before and could not readily identify.

"Yes," Giulia finally replied, hearing the quaver in her voice, but far more concerned with her son's reaction to her confirmation; the gods knew as well as she did that Gnaeus had a volcanic temper, something that she knew he got from his father.

However, his reaction not only surprised her, she found it quite worrisome, because he suddenly staggered to the nearest couch and collapsed so heavily onto it that she could hear the wood cracking, although it bore his considerable weight. For the rest of her days, Giulia Livinius Volusenus would remember the stricken expression on her son's face as he regarded her with a look of such sadness that, before he uttered the words, although she did not know exactly how Gnaeus had learned the truth, she suddenly understood why he was there, confronting her.

"He's..." she began, then could not form the words, but there had always been a bond between mother and son that meant he instantly understood her question.

"Yes, Mother," she could tell he was trying to imbue his words with a cold anger, but she heard the pain there, "Titus Pullus is dead."

Despite being certain this was the case, Giulia could not keep the sob from bursting from her, and, like Gnaeus, she dropped back onto the couch, burying her face in her hands and leaning her elbows on her knees as she began to weep. She was unable to see it, but her son's rigid expression underwent a similar transformation, his own eyes filling with tears, both at the sight of his mother's grief and for the sense of a loss that he could never have described, mainly because he barely understood it himself. Nevertheless, he did not rise from his seat to go to Giulia's side to comfort her; there was still a healthy dose of anger in the swirling emotions he was feeling in the moment, and he did not trust himself to contain his temper. How could she have lied to him all these years? he wondered as he stared at her heaving shoulders. She had not shown this much grief when Quintus Claudius Volusenus, the man he had been told all of his life was his father, had died unexpectedly, and it was this display of raw pain on her part that unsettled him, although that was not all of it. No, what had shaken him to his core, even before he had ridden like the Furies from Ubiorum to Mogontiacum to confront his mother, was the recognition that, when the truth had been revealed to him, in the form of the will of Titus Porcinianus Pullus, somewhere deep inside him, he had been fairly certain that Pullus was his real father for some time. Giulia would have been shocked to know that, as angry as Gnaeus was with her, a fair proportion was aimed at himself for being too cowardly to confront Pullus with his suspicions, which he knew now had been with him almost from the first moment he had first met the Quartus Princeps Prior, although he was the

Quartus Pilus Prior at the time of his death. And, along with the anger was a massive sense of guilt, because Pullus had sacrificed himself to save Gnaeus' life during the recently concluded campaign to finally avenge the Varus disaster, against Arminius and his confederation of German tribes. What would have surprised Volusenus a great deal, at least until he gave it some thought, was that in this moment, the mix of emotions he was experiencing mirrored those his mother was dealing with, just a matter of a few feet away. Slowly, her sobs subsided, and so did Gnaeus' anger, until she finally lifted her face from her hands, her eyes red and already puffy, her cheeks wet with her tears.

Regarding her son for a span of heartbeats, she finally said, in a voice made hoarse by grief, "I suppose we have a lot to talk about."

This was such a massive understatement that, to his horror, Gnaeus' first reaction was to burst out in laughter, but it was the kind that just as quickly transformed itself into tears, and then it was his turn to begin sobbing as his mother had, mimicking her posture to bury his face in his hands. In his case, it was to hide his shame at what he thought of as a display of weakness; Roman men, especially Roman Centurions, were not supposed to show this side of themselves, even in front of their mothers. Regardless of this, when he felt her gentle touch on his shoulder, without any thought about how it would appear to the servants, he buried his head in her breast, pouring out his grief for all that he had lost, before he ever had a chance to fully understand what it meant that Titus Pullus was his father.